W9-AMX-504

BRIGHT STARRY
BANNER

ALSO BY ALDEN R. CARTER

FICTION

Brother's Keeper
Crescent Moon
Bull Catcher
Between a Rock and a Hard Place
RoboDad
Up Country
Sheila's Dying
Wart, Son of Toad
Growing Season

NONFICTION

China Past—China Future

NONFICTION FOR CHILDREN

Battle of the Ironclads: The Monitor and the Merrimack
The Colonial Wars: Clashes in the Wilderness
The American Revolution: War for Independence
The War of 1812: Second Fight for Independence
The Mexican War: Manifest Destiny
The Civil War: American Tragedy
The Spanish-American War: Imperial Ambitions
Last Stand at the Alamo
The Battle of Gettysburg
The Shoshoni
Radio: From Marconi to the Space Age

The American Revolution Series
Colonies in Revolt
Darkest Hours
At the Forge of Liberty
Birth of the Republic

Illinois
Modern China
Modern Electronics and *Supercomputers* (with Wayne J. LeBlanc)

BRIGHT STARRY BANNER

A NOVEL OF THE CIVIL WAR

ALDEN R. CARTER

Jefferson-Madison
Regional Library
Charlottesville, Virginia

SOHO

18274819

The map on page 120 is used by permission of the
Nautical and Aviation Publishing Company of America, © copyright 1983

Copyright © 2003 by Alden R. Carter

All rights reserved.

Published by
Soho Press Inc.
853 Broadway
New York, NY 10003

Library of Congress Cataloging-in-Publication Data

Carter, Alden R.
Bright starry banner : a novel of the Civil War / Alden R. Carter
p. cm.
ISBN 1-56947-355-2 (alk. paper)
1. Stones River, Battle of, Murfreesboro, Tenn., 1862–1863.
2. Tennessee—History—Civil War, 1861–1865—Fiction.
3. United States—History—Civil War, 1861–1865—Fiction.
I. Title.
PS3553.A7695B75 2004
813'.54—dc21   2003053006

Design by Kathleen Lake, Neuwirth & Associates, Inc.

10 9 8 7 6 5 4 3 2 1

FOR THE WONDERFUL women of my family.
My wife, Carol Shadis Carter
My mother, Hilda Carter Fletcher
My sister, Cynthia Carter LeBlanc
&
My daughter, Siri Morgan Shadis Carter

ACKNOWLEDGMENTS

MANY THANKS TO all who helped with *Bright Starry Banner*, particularly my agent, Bill Reiss; my editors Juris Jurjevics and Bryan Devendorf; the staff of Stones River National Battlefield; my cousin Charles Paradise; and my friends Don Beyer and Leigh and Linda Aschbrenner. As always, my daughter, Siri; my son, Brian; and my wife, Carol, were an inspiration in countless ways.

For source material, I am indebted to the fine historians who have written about the battle of Stones River, especially Peter Cozzens, author of *No Better Place to Die* (University of Illinois Press, 1991); James Lee McDonough, author of *Stones River: Bloody Winter in Tennessee* (University of Tennessee Press, 1980); and David R. Logsdon, compiler of *Eyewitnesses at the Battle of Stones River* (Kettle Mills Press, Nashville, 1989).

This was the last of my books that my mother, Hilda Carter Fletcher, had an opportunity to read and critique before her death in May 2002. She was an exacting editor, a great creative support, and a wonderful mother to the end.

THE IMAGINATION WORKS best amid scenes half known and half forgotten. When time shall have thrown its shadows over the events of [this] century, and the real and unreal become so intermingled in the minds of men as to become indistinguishable . . . here the blue and the gray will meet to fight—and to be reconciled.

—Brigadier General John Beatty
The Citizen Soldier
December 1863

PROLOGUE

December 23, 1862
West Point, New York

H E HAS KNOWN all the soldiers and not a few of the politicians now gracing or disgracing the rank of general. But personalities no longer concern Brevet Lieutenant General Winfield Scott, former general in chief of the United States Army. In his great age and detachment, only the problem of strategy holds his interest. The late afternoons are his best time, the winter light fading beyond the windows of his study overlooking the Hudson, the ache in his gouty foot warmed away by the fire, Spanish sherry, and the anticipation of dinner. He no longer cares to entertain, is content to sit alone, gazing at the wall map where his aide has marked the latest positions of the Confederate and Federal armies.

The daily reports from the War Department arrive courtesy of his onetime subordinate, Major General Henry W. Halleck, who commands all the Northern armies in this second Christmas season of the rebellion against the national authority. Scott acknowledges the courtesy every so often with a note but rarely offers advice. After fifty-three years in the service of his country, forty-eight of them as a general, he has given all he has to give. In his last months as general in chief, he offered a strategy to win the war. The press derided it as too cautious, labeled it "Scott's Anaconda" after the lethargic South American constrictor. But the plan was sound: fix the Southern armies in place in the East, split the rebellious states along the line of the Mississippi, blockade the coast, and squeeze. But the people and the politicians demanded battles, rushed ahead to fight tooth and claw.

Scott shifts his gouty foot, focuses more closely on the map. Burnside is back across the Rappahannock after butchering thirteen thousand of his own men in a frontal assault against Lee's army on the heights behind Fredericksburg: a result so predictable as to be uninteresting. In the West, Grant has attempted to march overland from Grand Junction, Tennessee, to Jackson, Mississippi, and thence to the Confederate stronghold at Vicksburg. But the distance is too great. Confederate cavalry rips up his supply lines, burns his base at Holly Springs, and forces him into an ignominious retreat. Again an outcome as predictable as it is dreary.

Only the third major Federal effort offers promise for a pleasant hour's contemplation before dinner. The recovery of unionist east Tennessee and the opening of Georgia to invasion are goals dear to President Lincoln's heart. Scott sees it as a bloody undertaking, yet the campaign offers intriguing problems of supply, maneuver, and battle. The army designated for the invasion is at Nashville, exactly where it had been ten months before when Brigadier General Don Carlos Buell originally took the city. Not that it has been idle. Since first occupying Nashville, the army has fought at Shiloh, in the siege of Corinth, and along the railroad line east toward Chattanooga in a first attempt to invade east Tennessee. But Buell was forced to abandon that effort when General Braxton Bragg invaded Kentucky with his Army of Tennessee. Buell rushed north, intercepting Bragg at Perryville on October 8. Despite a three-to-one advantage in numbers, Buell failed to crush Bragg, who drubbed one wing of the Northern army and then skillfully extricated his force and retreated over the Cumberlands. A disgusted Lincoln relieved Buell three weeks later, replacing him with Major General William Starke Rosecrans. Scott knows Rosecrans more by reputation than personal contact: a brilliant engineer, a gifted tactician, a querulous, impolitic subordinate. But all in all, not a bad choice.

Rosecrans moved the Army of the Cumberland from Louisville back to Nashville where it could better prepare for an invasion of east Tennessee. Bragg responded by taking a defensive position around Murfreesboro, thirty miles to the southeast. As it always does, the Lincoln administration demanded immediate action. The War Department repeatedly ordered Rosecrans to move against Bragg, but the big, sandy-haired general demurred. He must have more cavalry, horses, repeating carbines, and supplies before he can march. Lincoln and Secretary of War Stanton considered relieving him, but that would have meant elevating the army's second in command, Major General George H. Thomas, a Virginian with a reputation for excessive deliberateness.

After the debacle at Fredericksburg on December 13, the need for action by the Army of the Cumberland became imperative. Only today Scott has another missive from Halleck complaining of Rosecrans's recalcitrance:

Rosecrans doesn't understand. We must have a victory before the turn of the year. The British parliament meets in January, and our friends in that august body will be hard put to stall southern recognition longer if they have no evidence that we may yet win this war. If the Gladstone government concludes that our defeat at Fredericksburg indicates the utter futility of our efforts to suppress the rebellion, it will urge a vote in favor of recognition. The French will follow without a scruple since Napoleon III wants to go adventuring in Mexico and South America. By spring we can expect to see the combined British and French navies cruising our waters, challenging the blockade, and thus presenting us with the impossible choice of making war on both Europe and our own South or letting the rebels have their independence.

For a time we thought the president's Emancipation Proclamation might dissuade the British from intervening in our affairs, but I fear that the general opinion among the diplomats is the same as expressed by our opposition press: the Proclamation is nothing more than a cheap fraud intended to prejudice elements of parliament—the prime minister especially—against granting recognition. That is far too cynical a view, for the Proclamation is a great moral statement as well as an act of military expediency. But for it to have practical benefits in that latter regard, we must have victories to demonstrate to both our friends and foes that it is not merely the desperate act of a desperate government.

I know, dear General, that nothing I have said here is more than you already know, but if you can offer me any counsel in this exceedingly difficult time I would be even more your debtor than I am at present.

—Most respectfully, H. W. Halleck, maj. gen.

Scott reads the note again, returns it to its envelope. He has no counsel for Halleck. Burnside is defeated, the Army of the Potomac in shambles. Grant is stymied, his army falling back in disgrace. Only Rosecrans and the Army of the Cumberland can win the victory critical to the survival of the Union into 1863 and beyond. There is no secret solution to the problem. *Rosecrans must move.*

Book One

CHAPTER 1

Christmas Night, 1862
Nashville, Tennessee

*F*OR A MOMENT, Lieutenant Colonel Julius Garesché, chief of staff of the Army of the Cumberland, fears that the window will not open. Patiently, he presses slender fingers along the stile, testing for the point where the damp of early winter in Tennessee has swollen the frame within the jamb. He finds the spot and gives it a firm but not immoderate rap with his knuckles and the sash slides up with only the mildest of squawks. He tests the tension of the counterweight, then dusts his hands absently as he turns to inspect the table where the generals sit with their toddies, cigars, and maps. Reassured that all is satisfactory for the moment, Garesché folds his arms, leans back against the wall, and closes his eyes against the sting of smoke and fatigue.

If he were a self-conscious man, Garesché might notice the two young lieutenants on either side of the door exchange glances of fond amusement at his expense. No other senior officer in the room would rise from his chair to wrestle with a stubborn window. Not with a dozen lieutenants and captains standing about, any of whom could be ordered to the chore and then blamed if the window proved recalcitrant, made too shrill a protest, or—overcome at last—were left standing too wide or too narrow for the comfort of the generals and colonels. No doubt there are even those among the senior officers who would blame an aide for the coolness and dampness of the evening itself, for the finding of fault is ever the right—even the duty—

of superior rank. Or so it seems to the lieutenants who find in Garesché the bemusing exception to the rule.

But Garesché is not a self-conscious man and he worries not at all about the opinion of the aides standing duty on this Christmas night. The room needed fresh air, and what matter if he or some junior opened the window so long as the service was done? In his twenty-one years in the army, Garesché has opened many windows and doors. He has escorted his generals' wives on shopping trips and home from parties. He has given his opinion on flower arrangements and ball gowns, tutored the younger children in arithmetic and drawing, and listened to the older sons and daughters complain of how impossible it is to be the child of a general. He has frequently been persuaded to attempt mediation between wife and general or child and general, efforts in which he has a remarkably high ratio of success. He is known throughout the army as the perfect gentleman and the perfect staff officer, and even if it still rankles on occasion to be so labeled and dismissed, by now he is accustomed and largely content to serve greater men.

Garesché opens his eyes for a moment to study his new general: voluble now, drink in one hand, gesticulating with his cigar to make some point of military history. Yes, this is the man, Garesché thinks: the one who will win for us here in the West and then in Virginia. And I will help him do it. Help him though my poor spirit trembles at what we must do to win this war.

He rests chin on chest and meditates on the suffering to come and how each hurt, each death, must wound God. He wishes for a moment that he could take some of the suffering upon himself, but he recognizes the sin in that desire and says a small prayer asking forgiveness for his pride. Tonight he will sleep on the floor, let the cold, hard planks remind him of God's goodness in allowing him to serve in the nation's ordeal by fire. In the end, the fire may consume them all, every soldier of every army North and South, but no matter if the nation come pure and tempered from the fire.

Garesché wonders if old John Brown, with so much blood already on his head, prayed to God or to the cleansing flame itself when he stood with his hand on the furnace at Harpers Ferry in the moment before he threw wide the door and let loose the fire. Garesché imagines the old man but a hollow thing by then, a figure of cornstalk and straw with dry, crackling fingers so weak that they could barely lift the latch. Then the bursting fire, setting old John Brown alight, making of him a tower of flame with veins and sinews of blue molten steel. It is then that he rises up, mighty, burning, blazing arm outswept, voice like the voice from the Pit: "Let this nation be purged with fire!"

Yes, Garesché thinks. Yes. And in the imagining of the fire, he is cooled, refreshed. He opens his eyes to check the table where the generals sit.

Except for George Thomas, who dozes by the hearth, the generals are a convivial lot. Alex McCook is being encouraged to sing and after a few moments of feigned protest, consents. Why, Gareské wonders, must these Irish always protest when all the world knows they love the stage? He tightens his lips, reminds himself of the charity he owes all made in the image of God—owes particularly on this night of the Redeemer's birth. But he does not trust Major General Alexander McDowell McCook, despite the man's reputation as a fighter. But the Ohio clan of "Fighting McCooks" has powerful connections, and its only West Point graduate, modest though his abilities, now wears two stars and commands the right wing of the army.

McCook sings a song just arrived from the East in that mysterious way songs, jokes, slang, and rumors fly unerringly between armies while critical orders go wildly astray and routine reports disappear altogether. *Honest Pat Murphy of the Irish Brigade* is suitably mournful for McCook's fine tenor, and Gareské is moved by the obvious emotion in McCook's performance. Maybe it is only his youth I distrust, he thinks. Perhaps he is a better man, a deeper man, than I give him credit for.

If he is honest with himself—and in this Gareské is rigidly consistent—he must admit that he envies McCook both his youth and his combat experience. In spite of himself, Gareské sighs. If he had only been a little less comfortable in the shadow of generals, a little less inclined by temperament and manners to life in the East, perhaps he would not have become the perfect staff officer. Perhaps he, too, would have been a fighting soldier.

He had missed the fighting in Mexico where many of his contemporaries had won one, two, or even three brevet promotions. Some even won fame, among them Braxton Bragg, who now commands the Confederate Army of Tennessee at Murfreesboro. Bragg, elected ugliest man in the corps by his classmates at West Point—and not entirely for his scarecrow looks, for even then Bragg was a disagreeable man—became a hero at Buena Vista, when old General Taylor gave the famous order: "A little more grape, if you please, Captain Bragg." That the actual wording of the order required considerable expurgation before appearing in the press made little difference. Bragg became the public's ideal of the dashing and hugely competent West Point professional: the new soldier of a nation stretching out to embrace a continent. Gareské and those who know Bragg can only shake their heads, remembering the pallid, petulant martinet that is the true Bragg.

Gareské smiles to himself, wondering how his old friend Bill Hardee is getting along with Bragg. How much better for Hardee if he had stayed loyal to the Union and served in this army and for this general, who is the opposite of Bragg in almost every regard. Gareské's general is a soldiers'

general: informal, humorous, and immensely popular with the men. He is
an imposing figure, particularly on horseback: tall, muscular, and handsome.
The livid fire-scars that disfigure one side of his face seem only to confirm
an indestructible constitution to match an indefatigable energy. He has been
in the saddle constantly in his two months in command—inspecting,
encouraging, cajoling, berating. No harness, no belt buckle is too small a
matter for his attention. He preaches that the accomplishment of great plans
depends on the execution of the smallest details, and the men believe, take
pride. Thus he transforms the Army of the Cumberland into one of the
world's great armies.

Garesché knows that his general has weaknesses: that the reddish nose
indicates too great a fondness for whiskey, that he sleeps too little, talks
too much, and can be both excitable and profane. Yet Garesché believes,
with the absolute faith that he has in nothing else besides the Trinity and
Great Mother Church, that Major General William Starke Rosecrans is the
military genius of his age. Moreover, that he is a truly great man—a man
destined to command all the Union armies and, when the war is won, to
rise to the presidency itself. To these ends, Garesché will serve him, if
needs be, to the death.

Fresh cigar in hand, Rosecrans is again talking of the order of march
toward Murfreesboro. When and where Bragg will choose to fight—if he
chooses to fight at all—is the unknown, so the army will move in three
columns, always close enough for rapid concentration. Major General
Thomas Crittenden, who commands the left wing of the army, as McCook
does the right, unfolds a map and peers nearsightedly at the route.
Garesché steps forward. "If you will permit me, General." He slides a better map from lower in the pile and positions it before Crittenden, who
smiles a quick thanks.

Garesché likes Crittenden, finds his manner gentle despite the shoulder-
length hair and the staring face that lend him a somewhat wild appearance.
Son of old Senator John J. Crittenden of Kentucky, Crittenden owes his general's appointment to the Lincoln administration's desperate efforts to keep
the Bluegrass State in the Union. But Thomas Leonidas Crittenden is a man
of achievement in his own right: lawyer, businessman, volunteer aide on
Taylor's staff in Mexico, and American consul to Liverpool in the Fillmore
administration. True, he lacks military training, but he seems sensible to his
staff's advice. Perhaps he will do well enough, Garesché thinks.

Like the McCooks, the Crittendens are a fighting clan. Half a dozen
brothers and cousins donned uniforms within weeks of Fort Sumter. Brother
George, West Point graduate and career soldier, accepted a Confederate

major general's commission, while cousin Thomas Turpin Crittenden became a Union brigadier. To the family's mortification, both were soon disgraced. George's small army was crushed by Brigadier General George H. Thomas at Mill Springs, Kentucky, on January 19, 1862. Seven months later, cousin Thomas Turpin and his entire garrison were rousted from bed and captured at Murfreesboro by the Confederate raider Nathan Bedford Forrest in an exploit that won Forrest his first star.

Forrest's success was both shocking and dishearteningly familiar. The ability of Confederate cavalry to outride, outfight, outthink, and altogether overmatch their Federal adversaries is a continuing crisis in all the Union armies—threatens to be so in this campaign. As if prompted by Garesché's recollection, Rosecrans chooses this moment to turn to him. "Garesché, is that damned Forrest still out west giving old Useless fits?" There are chuckles about the table where most agree that anything that will give Major General Ulysses S. Grant difficulty in Mississippi cannot be without humor and benefit to the Army of the Cumberland. Garesché smiles slightly, prays that Rosecrans will forbear in revealing the full extent of his loathing for Grant to these officers still unused to so forthright a commander. "Our reports are that General Forrest is tearing up track and burning bridges north toward Trenton, General."

"Tough on old Useless. Drive him right to the popskull, I expect, if the Mississippi swamps and the snakes haven't already."

There is laughter this time and a resounding hoot from McCook. Only George Thomas, commander of the center corps of the army, fails to join in. He opens an eye to gaze balefully at McCook, then shifts in his chair, lacing fingers over belly, prepared to return to his dozing.

Two years ahead of Garesché and Rosecrans at West Point, Thomas seems somehow much older, beard grown gray and mouth gone hard. He is "Pap" to his men, "Old Slow Trot" to his brother officers from the Old Army. Both his nerve under fire and his deliberateness in all things are legendary. "What of Morgan?" Thomas rumbles, eyes still closed.

"Yes, what is the latest of our friend Morgan?" Rosecrans asks. "Didn't you tell me that he's abandoned his nuptial couch for the rigors of a different saddle?" There is more laughter.

Garesché tries not to wince, though Rosecrans's raw humor is one of the few things he does not admire about his general. "Yes, General. We have reports that Colonel Morgan has left his bride and gone raiding in Kentucky, which will put him well out of our way for the present."

Rosecrans looks the length of the table to where his cavalry chief, Brigadier General David Stanley, has turned to say something to an aide.

"Well, Stanley, that will make your task easier. Keep young Wheeler off our trains until we find and beat Bragg. After that, Wheeler, Forrest, and Morgan put together won't matter a damn."

Stanley, who has little head for hot punch, has to speak carefully to avoid slurring. "Yes, General. My men will do their part."

Let us hope so, Garesché thinks. I give us a week to make this movement before the Reb cavalry are on our trains like wolves. If we haven't destroyed Bragg by then, we won't manage the job at all. The War Department is already out of patience with us. If we don't provide a victory soon, we will pay for it with our careers.

He pictures the unholy trinity bent over the telegraph, waiting for word that the Army of the Cumberland is on the march: Lincoln, gaunt, saturnine, apish, president by a fluke; Stanton, the ferocious little lawyer trying to run the biggest army in the world; and elbow-scratching, pop-eyed General Henry Halleck, more chief clerk than general in chief. That men such as these should threaten a man such as Rosecrans is almost beyond bearing!

Garesché is surprised at the choler of his thoughts. I am tired, he thinks. Already tired and the march not even begun. I must remember Charity, even for those who plague us. He senses a subtle change in the atmosphere of the room. Rosecrans is staring into a far corner, mouth set, quiet for once as the talk goes on around him. It is up to him, now, Garesché thinks. We have gathered the supplies, reorganized the army, brought the men to a fighting edge, laid out the movement, and issued the orders. Lincoln, Stanton, and Halleck have given us all the time they are going to. Now he must take this army and use it.

Rosecrans slaps a large, fire-scarred hand on the table. "Gentlemen, to our duty! We move tomorrow. We shall begin to skirmish as soon as we pass the outposts. Press them hard! Drive them out of their nests! Make them fight or run! Strike hard and fast! Give them no rest! Fight them! Fight them! Fight, I say!"

There is a brief silence as Rosecrans sweeps a blazing glance around the room, then men are cheering. Garesché is surprised to hear his own voice among them. Like a cadet, he thinks. My God, I do not believe that I have given a shout for anything in twenty years. He feels George Thomas watching him and blushes. Thomas rises, alone silent among all the others, nods for his aides to follow, and leaves the room where now McCook is proposing a toast: "To Victory and the Army of the Cumberland. And God damn Braxton Bragg and Jeff Davis!"

Typically, Rosecrans does not sleep. He scans through a stack of reports, orders, and requisitions arranged on his desk by Gareschè, signs most, setting aside two or three to read closely. He rises. "I'm going to have a stroll about camp before turning in. Care to join me, Julius?"

"It would be pleasant, General, but I have work I should attend to."

Rosecrans accepts his cape from Magee, the ubiquitous headquarters orderly, takes his sword from a corner, and steps into the night, trailed by a lieutenant who will record all that the commanding general finds amiss around camp. Gareschè parses the stack of paperwork that Rosecrans has signed and hands the items that will not wait to his deputy, Major Charlie Goddard. "Get these on their way, Major, and then get some rest."

Like Gareschè, Goddard has been up most of the last few nights, preparing the army to move, and his face is haggard with fatigue. "Thank you, Colonel. You should sleep, too."

"I will as soon as the general gets back." When Goddard is gone, Gareschè rubs his eyes and begins sorting the next stack of reports from farther down the staff chain. Tomorrow morning this will change, he thinks. Tomorrow morning we will all have less time for reports and more for action.

The night is still, the air sweet with the smell of mist and autumn leaves. Rosecrans selects a direction and sets off along an avenue lined with Sibley tents. After tonight, these big tents with their stoves and straw bedding will seem an incredible luxury, as all but the most senior officers will sleep in two-man shelter tents or lie exposed to the elements.

For a week now, Rosecrans has occupied the plain house on the edge of camp rather than his comfortable quarters in the Cunningham house on High Street. But he wants to be close to the soldiers as the army limbers its muscles for the march south. He knows that rumors are flying and that some of them have made their way to Bragg in Murfreesboro. But this does not worry him. Let Bragg worry, doubt, lose sleep. The Army of the Cumberland will move when and how Rosecrans wills it. The worries of Bragg, Halleck, Stanton, and Lincoln concern Rosy Rosecrans not in the least.

Near a battery of artillery, a sentry braces, presents arms, manages a quavering "Good evening, General."

"Good evening, son. Where are you from?"

"Findlay, Ohio, General."

"Your battery?"

"Battery E, First Ohio, General."

"That would be Captain Edgarton, would it not?"

The sentry stands a little straighter, though he is already braced almost to the breaking point. "Yes, sir!"

"Well, I hear you're good men. I'll look forward to seeing you on the march." He smiles. "Good night, son."

He continues down the avenue, knowing that Battery E, 1st Ohio, is now his to the man. In the morning, every man will swell with pride at the news that the commanding general has heard of them, even knows their captain by name. They will write home, bragging, proud in turn of their general. The remembering of a few names is a trick so easy for Rosecrans that it amazes him that others find it impressive. He has always been able to memorize lists, tables, and charts on a single reading. Scanning the daily transfer reports, his mind subtracts and adds units and names without effort while poor Garesché must squint at his lists, laboriously scratching out old entries and writing in new ones. Rosecrans accepts his brilliance casually. It amuses him to do several things at once. He will read and sign reports while alternately dictating different letters to a pair of scribbling clerks. It is rather like juggling balls in a parlor for the entertainment of children. He knows Garesché finds the practice distressing, but fond as he is of his old classmate, he cannot resist showing off.

He spots a dim light glowing through canvas. He strides to the tent, unsheathes his sword, and swings the flat of the blade smartly against the taut canvas. The effect is an ear-splitting crack something like that made by a sail snapping to catch the wind on a fresh tack. There are cries of consternation and a chorus of curses from the cardplayers inside. Rosecrans steps to the front of the tent, hides his smile, and sweeps back the flap with the tip of his sword. This produces an even more marvelous effect as the soldiers leap to their feet, scattering cards, spilling mugs, and overturning boxes and stools.

"I hope," Rosecrans says, "that you don't similarly curse the provost marshal or any of the others I have duly appointed over you." This is, of course, an impossible question to answer with either an affirmative or a negative. The men stand to attention without speaking. Rosecrans lets himself smile. "Stand easy, soldiers." They do so with exhalations of relief. "What regiment are you?" Rosecrans asks.

"Forty-ninth Ohio, General," a sergeant replies in a brogue thick with the old country.

"Ah, Colonel Gibson's regiment. I have heard good things about you. Now, men, we will shortly be fighting the Rebels. For that, I need soldiers who have rested and gained strength in their time in camp. I set the curfew for your benefit and for the benefit of this army's success. Please keep that in mind the next time you hear tattoo, no matter how absorbing you find your game of cards."

There are murmurs of assent. The Irish sergeant says, "We'll remember, General. We're proud to serve under you."

"And I am glad that I have so many Buckeyes with me. It will make the task ahead easier."

He bids them good night and steps again into the chill darkness. Forty-ninth Ohio is his as well, although Colonel Gibson will not escape a sharp note in the morning about the lax curfew in his regiment, for it is always Rosecrans's policy to hold his officers responsible for the derelictions of their men, no matter how trivial.

He hesitates a moment, and the aide says, "General?"

"It's nothing. For a moment I could not remember Colonel Gibson's middle name. Unlike me."

"Yes, sir," the aide says, awed as always.

Although Rosecrans has a brilliant mind, it is not a reflective one, and he rarely analyzes the personal and serendipitous circumstances that have brought him, at the age of forty-three, to the command of one of the Union's three great armies. He is the eldest son of one Crandall Rosecrans, a dour Dutchman and former army captain who owns a general store and tavern in Homer, Ohio. As a boy, William attended only four terms of formal schooling, but his father taught him bookkeeping and mathematics, and his gentle mother exposed him to literature and taught him a fair hand. But he was not content with stocking shelves and waiting tables in his free hours. He wheedled the overnight loan of books and newspapers from travelers staying in the rooms over the tavern. At breakfast, the guests would find the boy bleary-eyed but exploding with questions, suppositions, and theories on all that he'd read while the rest of the village slept.

With no other way to afford college, William badgered the district congressman into an appointment to West Point. He excelled at the Academy, consistently ranking fifth or sixth in his class. As a second-year man and a corporal, he met Grant for the first time. The slender, almost diminutive plebe was standing at a relaxed parade rest beside a hand pump in a rear courtyard when Rosecrans made his final inspection of the grounds as officer of the day.

"What are you doing here, Plebe?"

Grant drew himself up, taking just a shade longer than necessary. "Sir, I'm standing guard over the pump, sir. I have been told to do so until after the next call when I shall be duly relieved."

Rosecrans shook his head. Plebes. "Look, somebody's having you on. It's after tattoo. Go turn in."

Grant's slow eyes studied him. "How am I to know that it is not you who are having me on? That in leaving this post I will not be abandoning my duty?"

"Sir." Rosecrans added, not unkindly.

"Sir."

"See my chevrons? I'm officer of the day. You can believe me."

Grant considered and then saluted. "Thank you, sir."

Rosecrans returned the salute. "You're welcome, Plebe." He extended a hand. "I'm Rosecrans. People call me Will sometimes. Mostly William. Never Bill."

"Sam Grant."

They shook and that should have been the start of a friendship. But somehow it wasn't and the two never warmed to each other during the three years they were at West Point together. Like Grant, most of the cadets were ambivalent in their feelings about Rosecrans. He was respected for his brilliance and his easy mastery of the military life. But in a group of cock-sure young men, Rosecrans was just a little too sure of himself. At least in his own mind, he was never mistaken.

Rosecrans graduated fifth in the class of 1842, forty-nine places ahead of his roommate Pete Longstreet. He joined the elite Army Engineer Corps. Very able, he was soon back at West Point as an assistant professor. He was passionately in love with his young wife and likewise devoted to his new faith as a member of the Holy Roman Catholic Church—a conversion made after a long talk with his former classmate Julius Garesché. When the country went to war with Mexico in 1846, Rosecrans made little effort to obtain a transfer to the field. This uncharacteristic lapse of the Rosecrans ambition proved to be a terrible mistake. While his contemporaries won brevet promotions by the bushelful, he remained a lowly first lieutenant. He was posted to Newport, Rhode Island, in 1847 and spent the next six years overhauling the naval facilities at Newport and Washington. His performance was consistently brilliant, but he remained a first lieutenant.

Entering their second decade of service, Rosecrans's contemporaries began receiving regular appointments to the brevet ranks they'd won in Mexico. Even Sam Grant, lonely and drunk in far-off California, received his promotion to captain. But in his drive to solve engineering problems, Rosecrans had suffered few fools among the numerous members of that species in the higher ranks of both army and navy. Unlike the quarrelsome Braxton Bragg, Rosecrans had no war record to compensate for his tactlessness. Frustrated beyond endurance, he resigned his commission in the spring of 1853. In eleven years of service, he had never heard a shot fired in anger, having missed all the army's confrontations with Seminoles, Mexicans, Plains Indians, and Mormons.

He became superintendent of the Canal River Coal Company in Kanawha County, Virginia. Once he had the company running smoothly, he resigned to build a refinery in Cincinnati to turn the company's coal into coal oil. But the refinery was an indifferent success, its product too cloudy to sell as lamp kerosene. In 1857, Rosecrans was working late in his laboratory on a process to remove the impurities when a retort exploded, spraying him with glass slivers and burning kerosene. He managed to beat out the flames on his body and then calmly extinguished the fire in the laboratory. He walked home, his clothes still smoking. His wife summoned a doctor to treat the terrible burns. When the bandages were removed months later, Rosecrans's face bore livid scars across his forehead and one cheek, the latter giving his mouth a perpetual smirk. His voice, previously a clear tenor, rasped because of the scar tissue in the back of his throat.

It took Rosecrans eighteen months to recover. In his absence, the refinery languished. He returned to the laboratory to work at a furious pace. He invented a new chlorine soap, patented two new lamp designs, and perfected his process for removing impurities from coal oil. Yet none of his work generated an income to satisfy both creditors and domestic wants, and William Starke Rosecrans—by character an optimist—was on the point of despair when war lifted him out of the mundane with a promise of the exaltation he had always expected from life.

It is past two in the morning when Rosecrans returns to his headquarters. He has spoken to nineteen sentries, noted two dozen irregularities, rousted three more tents of cardplayers, and created the impression of ubiquity. A good night's work.

Garesché is still bent over his paperwork. Rosecrans sends him to bed and then makes himself comfortable in a chair before the fire with a tumbler of whiskey and a fresh cigar. Since boyhood he has needed but a few hours sleep a night, and he wants to relish his wakefulness this night of all nights. He has beaten them: Halleck and Stanton and the longshank Illinois lawyer who is president by an accident of history. They have cajoled, begged, pleaded, and threatened, but he has faced them down, forced them to acknowledge that they cannot do without him. Now, and in his own time, he has given the orders to advance.

It has not been easy reaching this point. He started the war as George

McClellan's colonel of engineers in the Ohio militia. Within a month, they transferred to United States service, Mac as a major general and Rosecrans as a brigadier. Lincoln sent them across the Ohio into the unionist counties of western Virginia in June 1861. They fought the decisive battle of the campaign at Rich Mountain on July 11. Rosecrans devised the strategy and led the difficult enveloping movement over a narrow mountain track to hit the Confederate rear. But at the moment when McClellan should have attacked to annihilate the enemy, he delayed and most of the Rebels escaped. Disappointed, Rosecrans contented himself with the belief that he and McClellan were off on a successful partnership.

With Rosecrans doing much of the work, they drove the remaining Rebels over the mountains and set about establishing a civilian assembly to debate statehood. But in his bombastic report on the campaign, McClellan gave Rosecrans scant credit. Rosecrans, with characteristic impolitesse, spoke openly of his chagrin to a reporter. Reading his deputy's comments, McClellan was much displeased. When he was ordered east to take command of the Army of the Potomac after Bull Run, he left Rosecrans behind in western Virginia. Rosecrans imagined that McClellan would soon call on him to strike at the Rebel capital by way of the Shenandoah Valley in a repeat, on a vastly larger scale, of their tactics at Rich Mountain. Instead, McClellan stripped his army, leaving him with barely a brigade. That, too, was soon lost when Major General John C. Frémont was ordered to take command of the newly created Mountain Department.

Rosecrans was ordered to Washington to await orders. He briefly considered resigning his commission but then had a cordial interview with Stanton. The new secretary of war sent him to find a division mysteriously gone astray on its way to Frémont. Rosecrans assumed far more authority than granted by his simple orders, attempting to coordinate several small armies operating in and around the Shenandoah Valley. Enraged, Stanton banished him to the West.

Rosecrans joined Halleck in the ponderous advance on Corinth after Shiloh. When Halleck was ordered east, Rosecrans worked for Grant. At the battle of Iuka on September 19, 1862, he failed to close the trap Grant had laid for General Sterling Price. Grant was furious. When Rosecrans again talked too openly to the press, Grant resolved to get rid of him. But events intervened. Price and Major General Earl Van Dorn struck at Corinth. Rosecrans drew in his army, skillfully prepared his defenses, and defeated the Rebels in two days of vicious fighting on October 3–4. The battle demonstrated his considerable tactical skill and immense personal courage. Reporters noted that unlike most of the Union's senior generals,

Rosecrans had never suffered a defeat. Why wasn't he commanding one of the major armies?

Why, indeed? Lincoln read the reports of Perryville and Corinth and decided to replace Buell with Rosecrans. Stanton snapped "Rosecrans is a contumacious, obstreperous, unbiddable ass, Mr. President!"

"But is he a witless ass, Mars? I think not. And if he has been an obdurate subordinate at times, perhaps that defect will become a virtue if he is made commander of our army in Kentucky and Tennessee. I would like to see General Bragg treated to some obduracy on the part of one of our generals."

"Mr. President—"

"Tut, Mars. I think we shall go with Rosecrans."

And so it is that ten weeks later Rosecrans sits before the fire at his Nashville headquarters, enjoying the last of his strong, sweet cigar. The orders are given, the campaign begun. With dawn the army will move, rising like Medusa over Tennessee, its columns uncoiling, rippling down the roads, blue on red clay, blue steel against winter sky, brown fields, and the dark green of the cedar barrens between Nashville and Murfreesboro. Or so he imagines it.

He tosses his cigar into the grate and settles himself to doze a while. Garesché will disapprove when he finds him sleeping in the chair, cluck at him about minding his health. But Rosecrans needs to sleep close to a fire, has needed to ever since the night when the retort exploded in his laboratory and he stood momentarily transfixed by the cloud of burning kerosene reaching out to embrace him. How beautiful it had been, and when he breathed it in, he became of the fire. The same.

But that is a secret.

★ ★ ★

Bierce is dreaming, limbs twitching like a hunting dog's, as the nightmare takes him back into the rain and horror of that first night at Shiloh. In his waking hours, Lieutenant Ambrose Bierce is the most rational of young men. It is a cast of mind that makes him a superb topographical engineer. He records exactly what he sees, never letting imagination add anything to the preparation of his maps. That his maps are also the most detailed in the corps is due to Bierce's stone courage. Time and again, he has scouted far forward to determine the lay of the ground between his brigade and the enemy. Under fire, he is able to make exact observations, complete lengthy calculations, and then sketch land and positions with a clear, steady hand. In a war where accurate field maps are at once essential and almost impossible to obtain, Bierce's talents are quickly noted. And so, at twenty, the army makes him an officer.

Bierce enjoys the rank and—in his waking hours—the war. Perhaps because it is so foreign to his character, Bierce is fascinated by irrationality; and war brings it out in men like no other cataclysm of spirit, body, or society. He puts it about that he wants to hear every unusual story, to see every bizarre case of injury and death. He records all in a weathered journal, as he might bearings, angles, and distances of topography.

Perhaps because he is determined to banish emotion from his mapping of war's realities, Bierce's dreams have taken on an unremitting savagery. Night after night, he wakes sweating and shaken. It is in these moments that his courage fails him, that the horror becomes insupportable. Then even his famously steady hand falters as he records the dreams in his journal. But no one sees the trembling in the darkness, and the writing restores his equilibrium—for dreams, even his own, are simply measurements.

Dreaming now, he groans, flails an arm, and then rears up with a suddenness that almost stops his heart. Around him, rain beats, soaks, runs in streams down sodden canvas. The army is asleep in the rain. He sits shaking, the dream still more real than the waking. Since Shiloh, he has come to believe that dream is to the mind more camera obscura than camera lucida; that the light of images is sucked by dream through the pinhole of recollection to be blasted on the dark screen of the unconscious mind, colors intensified like blood intensifies red, yet the image all the clearer for that, its sharpness unsoftened by the sanity-preserving deception of memory. It is a realization that might have driven Poe mad. Perhaps did, though first he was driven to write, as now Bierce must.

Bierce finds his journal and writes without seeing from long practice in the dark. There is nothing new in this repetition of the dream, and he writes mainly to calm himself. With daylight the army will march, and he is determined to rest while he can, though he hopes not to dream. A page filled, he lies back and closes his eyes, listening to the rain. Cannot sleep.

The army wakes to mist, cooks and eats, then moves, 43,000 strong, as a harsh westerly wind brings a cold rain pelting on the red clay roads of Tennessee.

CHAPTER 2

Friday Morning
December 26, 1862
Murfreesboro, Tennessee

General Braxton Bragg's Army of Tennessee is dispersed along a front from Franklin, thirty miles west of army headquarters at Murfreesboro, to Readyville, twelve miles to the east. When reports of the Federal advance first reach him, Bragg considers falling back to the Cumberland Plateau between Murfreesboro and Chattanooga. In many ways, this is the logical choice since Murfreesboro has little strategic importance. But retreat goes against Bragg's every inclination. He is already blamed (unfairly) for losing Kentucky and much of Tennessee. The weather is terrible, and a retreat may weaken the army to the point it can't fight at all. Here, at least, he can make a stand while his army is fed and rested. Above all, there is lure of the great victory that will so devastate Yankee morale that the people of the North will demand an end to this unjust persecution of their Southern cousins.

THE CRAMP SEIZES his bowels, bending him double in the chair and turning his gray skin ashen. General Braxton Bragg jams both fists against his swollen abdomen, his face below the famous eyebrows contorted like a gut-shot corpse. He breaks wind tremendously, gasps with the effort, presses hard again, and lets loose a second thunderous delivery. He straightens slowly, forehead beaded with sweat, and glares at the bedraggled corporal of cavalry standing in the cluster of staff officers before his desk. "How many days' rations?" he croaks.

For a moment the corporal seems confused, his report forgotten in the wonder of Bragg's stupendous flatulence. "Uh, we was only able to grab one Yank, Gen'rl. And he didn't have no rucksack on him. Probably left it by the road when he went to answer a call of nature." The corporal gulps, hurries on, omitting details of the Yank's humiliation on being captured with trousers around his ankles. "But he said they'd been told to cook three days' rations."

"Did he know the destination of the march?"

"No, sir. He was just a private. Green as a persim' and shakin' and cryin', all the time thinkin' we was gonna cut his throat like Billy Wrench said we would if he made a peep. Anyhow, the lootenant couldn't get much out of him. Me, I just don't think he knew a lot."

Bragg glowers, waves a dismissive hand. A boyish lieutenant hustles the corporal from the room. Outside, he says in a low voice: "There'll be something hot in the kitchen from breakfast. Get a plateful and then get on back to your troop."

"Lootenant, is the gen'rl all right? I mean, he sure made a powerful . . ."

"Yes, yes. He's fine. Just a small complaint of the digestion. Now go on back to the kitchen. Tell your lieutenant he did good work."

The corporal moves off, grateful at the prospect of hot food and early escape. The lieutenant gazes wistfully at the rain-chilled morning beyond the hall windows. He straightens his shoulders, reminds himself of honor and duty, and with a deep breath slips back into the vaporous closeness of Bragg's office.

When he has sent the last of his staff scurrying, Bragg leans back, welcoming the solitude. He checks his body's various complaints and then concentrates on the map of middle Tennessee tacked to the opposite wall. Why is it so damnably difficult to get decent maps in this war? Had he known the lay of the land better in the fall, he would not have chosen his present base at Murfreesboro, which is easily flanked by roads north and south of the town. But in the making of maps, as in all things, he has been poorly served.

Bragg grimaces, feels his stomach skirl at the recollection of his error in sending Forrest and Morgan raiding. John Pemberton, commanding at Vicksburg, had, as usual, been wailing for someone to do something to disrupt Grant's advance. And, as usual, Bragg had been expected to make the sacrifice. To make matters even worse, President Davis had personally detached an entire 7,500-man division of infantry from the Army of Tennessee and sent it to Pemberton. Bragg would have called another man a damned fool for such folly, but Davis is a friend—more really, considering

how much they owe each other for the events of that day in Mexico—and
so he blames that loss, too, on Pemberton.

He wonders sometimes at how little his life has changed since his boyhood in Warrenton, North Carolina. Even then he had enemies and humiliation in abundance. Rich boys (and poor boys, too, though they did not
matter so much) mocked him with calls of "Jailbird" because of the absurd
story that he had been born during his mother's brief and unjust incarcera-
tion in the county lockup for the fully justifiable shooting to death of an
impertinent nigger (free though that particular nigger had been).

As a stripling, he grew tall and thought himself not unattractive. But the
girls giggled at him, called him "Gloomy Brax," when all he attempted was
a small measure of dignity. He knew better than to seek parental sympathy—certainly not from his mother, whose outraged dignity was demon-
strably murderous, nor from his father, a morose plodder who built the
outbuildings and occasionally the homes of the well-to-do. At sixteen and
already grim of spirit and mien, Braxton Bragg departed for West Point to
learn the craft of war. Then, as now, he was secretive, implacable, raging.

Bragg occasionally allows himself the bileful luxury of ruminating on his
time at West Point. Many of his classmates were two, three, even four years
older, and this made him a target for the hazing of not only upperclassmen
but the boorish within his own class. He survived, became in his turn an
upperclassman. The experience might have inclined another boy to go easy,
to make friends and allies among the underclassmen. But he was harder on
them than any of his classmates. He recalls with pleasure bracing a rumpled
Henry Halleck. How Halleck's eyes had popped that day, how desperately
he'd tried to find enough chin to tuck into the requisite number of folds.
Bragg had hissed in his ear: "If you showed up in my company looking so
slovenly, I'd have you flogged, Plebe. And the second time, I'd have
you shot!" Yes, a good memory among the many bad from those years.

Now Halleck commands all the Federal armies and has sent Rosecrans
south in force. But with what objective in mind? Until he knows, Bragg can't
bring in his scattered divisions. He has no huge reserve of food depoted in
the rear for the army to live on while it waits. He must depend on Wheeler
and his cavalry to scout out the Federal intentions first.

Bragg has no doubt of the wisdom of young Wheeler's appointment.
Forrest is a bayou-bred killer: a vicious, wily ruffian without a trace of the
gentleman about him. John Hunt Morgan is a gentleman but equally
untrained and undisciplined: a dandy making a sport of war. But Joe
Wheeler is a professional. Moreover—and unlike most of Bragg's other generals—Wheeler is a man of honor and loyalty.

With three or four exceptions, Bragg despises all his generals. First among them in rank and mutual antipathy is Bishop Leonidas Polk, who resigned his West Point commission with its ink barely dry to study for the Episcopal clergy. Now, these three and a half decades later, he is a lieutenant general and commander of the right wing of the army. It is absurd: Polk knows little of war, less of obeying orders. Yet he is untouchable, twice consecrated by church and government.

Lieutenant General William J. Hardee commands the army's left wing. Former commandant and professor at West Point, Hardee is incapable of making a report without including a pedantry on the craft of maneuver and battle. The soldiers call Hardee "Old Reliable," but the only utter reliability about Hardee is his penchant for sniping at his superiors. That and a thoroughly reliable lust. During the army's foray into Kentucky, the widower Hardee insisted on kissing every comely farmwife and farmgirl he met. Then, if the response was sweet, he would detail a staff officer to arrange a more private encounter once the army camped for the night. Bragg, devoted both to his wife and to the concept of womanly virtue, is appalled and would have Hardee relieved for conduct unbecoming his rank and station. Yet, like Polk, Hardee is unassailable because of his connections among the powerful in Richmond.

Among his division commanders, Bragg reserves a particular loathing for Major General John C. Breckinridge, former United States senator, vice president, and presidential candidate in the election of 1860. Stationed in Louisiana in the summer of 1862, Breckinridge wrote to Bragg, suggesting that the army march north to free Kentucky from Union occupation: *Thousands of Kentuckians will enlist under your banner to drive the hated Yankees north of the Ohio. No result is more certain.*

Bragg planned accordingly. Breckinridge would lead the advance into Kentucky: the heroic native son returning home. Bragg would follow with the main army and a long train of wagons bearing thousands of muskets to equip the enlisting Kentuckians. They would install a civilian governor who would call a convention to vote a bill of secession. By the time Buell could bring his army north, Kentucky would be securely bound to the Confederacy.

It all came apart. Breckinridge spent two critical weeks getting his small division across the rickety rails from Louisiana to Tennessee—a task he might have left to one of his brigadiers. By the time the division reached Tennessee, he was too late to join the expedition. Without Breckinridge, Bragg was forced to issue his own proclamation to the men of Kentucky, but the Kentuckians were not in a suasible mood. Only a few hundred recruits joined the ranks, leaving the Army of Tennessee badly outnumbered when it collided with the Army of the Ohio under Major General Don Carlos Buell at Perryville. Polk was in field command of the army while Bragg installed a secessionist governor at nearby Frankfort. On October 7, Polk sent Bragg a message, suggesting that the approaching Federal force was not large and that he and Hardee should attack. Bragg approved the plan. Meanwhile, Polk and Hardee changed their opinion of the strength of the Federal force, deciding that they faced not a fraction but the main part of Buell's army—a reality best addressed, in the opinion and experience of the Bishop and the Professor, by calling a leisurely staff meeting.

Arriving on the scene, Bragg was horrified to find his sixteen thousand infantry facing three or four times their number. Before he could order a withdrawal, Buell attacked. Or rather, his ever-aggressive brigadier Philip H. Sheridan attacked, crossing Doctor's Creek at the Union center and seizing the high ground beyond for his artillery. Then there was no hope of retreat unless the Yankees were first stunned into immobility, or at least caution. Bragg hurled Major General Ben Cheatham's and Major General Simon B. Buckner's divisions against Buell's left while holding off the Federal center with a scant two brigades of infantry and the entire Federal right with a single brigade of cavalry. Amazingly, his tactics worked. Cheatham and Buckner crashed through the Federal left, routing McCook's corps. Buell's center, under the command of Charles C. Gilbert, an Old Army captain temporarily elevated to brigadier general, hunkered down to wait for developments. On the Union right, Major General Thomas L. Crittenden did precisely nothing with his nine brigades.

The fighting on the Union left became chaotic. Sheridan's artillery ripped into the flank of Buckner's division, slowing the Rebel charge. Reinforced from center and rear, McCook's brigades rallied and soon units from both armies overlapped and mixed, uniforms difficult to distinguish in the smoke. Polk mistook a hotly engaged Union regiment for one of his own and shouted to its colonel: "For the love of God, cease fire! You are mistaken! Those are your friends!"

The bearded colonel turned. "I don't think there can be any mistake about it. I am sure they are the enemy."

"Enemy?" Polk roared. "Why, I have only just left them myself. Cease firing, sir! What is your name?"

"Colonel Shryock of the 87th Indiana. And pray, sir, who are you?"

Polk stared at the begrimed faces of the Hoosier infantrymen turning to look on—eyes red-rimmed, hard, suspicious. But a certain flair for theater is necessary for a bishop of the Episcopal church, and Polk's pulpit confidence did not desert him. He leaned down from his horse, shook a huge fist in the colonel's face. "Who am I? I'll soon show you who I am, sir! Cease firing, sir. At once!" Then whirling his horse about, he rode off into the smoke, spine itching as he imagined a hundred rifle barrels coming to bear on his broad back. He crossed into the Confederate line and without turning his head growled to the colonel in command, "They are the enemy. Kill them." A volley ripped from the Confederate line, tearing the 87th Indiana to shreds.

The fighting continued into the night, when finally the difficulty of distinguishing friend from foe brought it to a halt. At midnight, Bragg began withdrawing. By daylight, the army was clear. Bragg had saved it, yet he knew that Polk and Hardee would pen letters to their friends in Richmond, calling his brilliant escape yet another disgrace, another blot on the reputation of Southern arms.

The two-hundred-mile retreat into Tennessee was an unspeakable ordeal for the army. The country was desolate, stripped of food and forage. An October snow fell, the first in anyone's memory, and the men marched hungry, many of them barefoot, through the freezing mud. Typhoid, dysentery, scurvy, and pneumonia swept the ranks, dropping hundreds by the roadside. Bragg thought of Napoleon in Russia, of Washington at Valley Forge, of Raglan in the Crimea. He concentrated his will, drove the army south toward safety. In east Tennessee, Confederate storehouses were bulging with the fall harvest, but he was forbidden to draw rations. No, the flour, bacon, and beef were reserved for Lee's Army of Northern Virginia. He pushed his army on, knowing that he was hated by his soldiers but determined to save them. And all the time he brooded, weighed and portioned out the blame, this much for Polk, that much for Hardee, and the largest serving of all for Breckinridge. He, before all others, would pay.

An aide knocks hesitantly on the door, snapping Bragg's attention back to the present. "General Breckinridge to see you, sir. He is most—" But before the aide can finish, John Cabell Breckinridge, former vice president of the United States, brushes by him to beseech his commanding officer for the life of Private Asa Lewis, 9th Kentucky Infantry, condemned to be shot to death by musketry at noon on the day after Christmas 1862, as a deserter.

☆ ☆ ☆

If there were a millet seed of humor in Braxton Bragg's temperament, he might in this moment find an occasion for amused irony. But it is difficult for a man whose guts have plagued him all the fifteen years since he drank the dysenteric water of Mexico to maintain a sense of the ironic, a humor that requires at least a small separation of intellect from self and event.

Bragg listens to Breckinridge, but his attention remains fixed on his gurgling innards. He kneads his stomach with a hand hidden below his desk while Breckinridge tells once again of Lewis's courage at Shiloh, his soldierly conduct in camp, and how he took the unauthorized leave only to visit his recently widowed mother.

"Attempted to take it twice, I believe," Bragg growls.

"True, General, but he is a good man. If his superiors had understood— if I had understood—the real circumstances, we would have granted him a furlough. But his request was mishandled. The man shouldn't have to die for our error."

Bragg feels like telling Breckinridge that if he wants to confess error, he should talk to Leonidas Polk in his sacerdotal capacity while leaving the interpretation of military justice to the commanding general. He attempts to control his anger, succeeds little. "So you suggest that I should pardon every Kentucky man who, disagreeing with the decision of his officers, gives himself the right to issue his own furlough papers? Is that what you are suggesting, sir? For then I will have to give the same right to every Tennessee man, every Georgia man, every Mississippi, Alabama, Louisiana, and Texas man in this army. Do you think then that I shall have any army left?"

"General, I am only asking that in this particular case—"

"Are you aware, sir, that during our advance into Kentucky, desertion from Kentucky regiments exceeded those of all other states combined? That when Kentucky men should have been leading the march against the Federal occupiers of their home state, they were instead deserting by the hundred?"

"But they were close to home, General. They came back in a few days. They were there for the fighting, and I understand Kentucky boys fought well at Perryville."

"So you would grant Kentucky men the right to decide when and where this army should fight? That while they are home, feeding themselves up and making more brats, that the army should mark time, waiting for their return?"

A flush spreads across Breckinridge's handsome features. "I am suggesting no such thing, General. Nor do I think it fair to criticize Kentucky men who have come south to fight for this Confederacy when they might have stayed at home and accepted an easier lot under the yoke of Yankee occupation."

Bragg notes the flush, knows that his own face has grown paler with his anger. "Well, sir, I found in my time in Kentucky that the majority of Kentucky men were quite content laboring under that yoke! That when we offered them arms and a chance to fight for their liberty, that they possessed no more fighting spirit than so many oxen."

Breckinridge's flush has become a deep red. "Sir, I must protest—"

Bragg's fist hits the desktop. "No, sir! You must not protest! I have had protestations enough from Kentucky men. If the blood of your men is too feverish for this army, if they require too often the company of their slatterns, then they shall pay the price for that libidinous weakness before the firing squad!"

"General! Private Lewis only wished to see his *mother*!"

"Then so much the worse for her as well as for him. Your man *shall* be shot at noon. Now I bid you good day, sir. I have matters of greater consequence to concern me than the fate of your corn-cracker!"

For a moment, it seems that Breckinridge will strike him. Bragg is unafraid, hoping almost, for then he will have Breckinridge summarily shot. Instead, Breckinridge exerts a stupendous effort to maintain control. "Sir, Kentucky men will never be slaves under this or any government. What you order is murder and will be so recalled!" He spins on his heel and slams out the door.

Bragg stares after him, feels a fresh stab in his guts—downward this time, through the bowels to his sphincter. He grits his teeth, rises carefully, makes for the latrine behind the house.

At noon, Lewis is shot. Bragg hears the volley from his office, does not look up from his letter to his wife.

CHAPTER 3

Midmorning Friday
December 26, 1862
South of Nashville

*The Army of the Cumberland marches in three columns of roughly fifteen
thousand men each, the length of each column extending some fourteen
miles from advance scouts and skirmishers to the last wagon, ambulance,
and camp follower. On the left, Crittenden's corps advances toward Lavergne
on the Murfreesboro Pike. In the center, McCook's corps takes the Nolensville
Pike toward Nolensville and the village of Triune beyond. Thomas's corps,
temporarily on the right wing, follows the Franklin and Wilson pikes south to
Old Liberty Road, where it will turn east, crossing McCook's rear to take up
its accustomed position at the army's center.*

HE ARMY TRUDGES south in the rain, the roads turning
quickly to mud beneath the thousands of feet, wheels, and
hooves. The roads cut across low ridges and streamy bottoms, a
land of patchy woodlands, untilled fields, and thick cedar brakes. Eighteen
months of war have stripped the land of human habitation, leaving only
blackened chimneys sentinel against gray skies. This is bitter country, and
the army moves warily, expecting trouble.

Stanley's cavalry is supposed to screen the advance, but none are in
position at daylight as the infantry files onto the roads. So the army plunges
ahead with little idea of what is in front of it. Leading McCook's march,
Brigadier General Jefferson C. Davis, namesake but unrelated to the

Confederate president, deploys his headquarters escort, a single company of Illinois cavalry, to scout the roads ahead. Five miles north of Nolensville, they drive in a Confederate outpost, pursuing the Rebel troopers to the edge of town before drawing rein in the face of a strong line of dismounted cavalry.

Davis hurries his division forward, intent on the honor of winning the first battle of the campaign. At thirty-three, Davis is a hard-eyed professional, his handsome features elongated by aggressive chin whiskers. He is not West Point but up through the ranks of the Old Army on hard work and ambition. He is resentful, quarrelsome, touchy: a disposition that puts him almost constantly at odds with his superiors. Those who cross Davis should beware. Before Perryville, Davis argued with his superior, Major General William "Bull" Nelson. Nelson made the error of cuffing Davis, who promptly borrowed a pistol, chased the bigger man, and shot him to death. Only the army's desperate need for experienced brigadiers keeps Davis in the field pending a court-martial that Rosecrans has postponed indefinitely.

Davis deploys a battle line left and right of the road and sends it forward at the double-quick. The Rebels immediately fall back, mount, and retreat. Davis gives his men a short rest at Nolensville and then pushes on toward Triune in the early afternoon.

☆   ☆   ☆

A half dozen miles to the east, Rosecrans's staff tops a brown rise, the general in the lead, Garesché next, the rest fanning out behind in approximate order of seniority. Garesché cannot remember being so happy, his fatigue of the night before replaced at dawn by an immense elation as the army clattered into action. It will take time for the multitude of pieces to synchronize, to steady into rhythm, for this is not an oiled and steaming machine but an agglomeration of men, flags, rifle-muskets, mule teams, wagons, cannons, cavalry mounts, sabers, and on and on in a cacophonous profusion of the animate and inanimate. Sometimes, though it is his job to understand its every organizational nuance, he cannot comprehend the whole of it. Yet here it is, sloshing south in the rain, with each mile finding its gigantic internal rhythm, becoming like unto. . . . Garesché pauses, meditates. Certainly not a machine, for its purposefulness, its very animation in existing, must argue against likening it to anything of mere wheels, belts, pulleys, and gears. No, it is far more than a machine, far more than anything of the physical world. Like unto Faith, he thinks, and the thought pleases him. Faith, the most militant of the virtues. The virtue in armor, sword uplifted, reflecting the Light.

Ahead Rosecrans draws rein, lifts his field glasses. I must share the simile with him, Garesché thinks. But not now. Now he needs no distraction from what he must do. He halts beside Rosecrans, leans forward, hands on the saddle pommel to ease his back, watches the blue column coiling along the valley floor, its head lost to sight in the low clouds and mist lying on the ridge beyond.

Rosecrans shifts the cold butt of the cigar in his teeth. "It's an awesome sight, an army on the move, isn't it, Garesché?"

"Yes, General. It is indeed."

"Ah, here's Crittenden." He points to a party of horsemen cutting through a break in the column and cantering toward the rise.

Garesché cranes, can barely make out the guidon of a major general and must lift his field glasses to pick out the lean form of Crittenden. Rosecrans, whose sight and hearing seem to become preternaturally sharp when he is in action, does not bother with his field glasses. "Tom looks satisfied. Things must be going well up ahead. We'll listen to his report and then ride over to see McCook."

"I believe, General, that we agreed that you should establish a new headquarters before it is much later in the day. As it is, we have messages chasing us all over the field."

Rosecrans grimaces. "You know, Julius, I sometimes think I would have lived a happier life in the time of the crusades. No wig-wag, no telegraph. Armies small enough for a general to command with a battle cry and an uplifted sword. A damned sight more convenient, eh?"

Garesché smiles. "Yes, General. I can easily imagine you in armor."

Rosecrans looks at him sharply and then laughs. "Yes, that would be a picture. Well, better me than all the runty generals we have in this war. Beauregard, Joe Johnston, old Useless. I could smite them all a pretty good lick."

Coming within hailing distance, Crittenden calls "Good afternoon, General."

"Good afternoon, Tom. How do you see it?"

"We scared off some Reb cavalry up the road a ways. Wheeler's boys, according to a prisoner. They've fallen back toward Lavergne."

"Good. Very good. Now listen, Tom. I want you to push across that little creek north of Lavergne by dark. For some reason it's called Hurricane Creek, though God knows why this far from the sea. Come first light, we'll advance on the village itself."

Rosecrans begins explaining his plan for the morrow. Garesché half listens, watching as two officers break away from the column below and come trotting toward the rise. He recognizes Colonel William B. Hazen, commander of one of Crittenden's brigades. Garesché smiles: Bill Hazen no doubt needs an opportunity to vent the latest of his sulfurous complaints. He gestures Goddard to take his place near the generals and rides down to meet Hazen.

Hazen is indeed angry, but Garesché can hardly remember a time when Hazen was not angry about something. "Julius, that damned cavalry of ours was out of position half the morning! They just now broke up that Reb outpost up ahead, and they should have done that hours ago. And they are doing better than McCook's! I haven't seen a one of his yet, and they should have been in touch with our right flank all day. Which means we don't know where the hell his left flank is and whether we're covering it, or he's covering ours, or if half the damn Reb army is in between. Now, just what in the hell is—"

Garesché holds up a hand. "Now, Bill. Remember your manners."

Hazen looks confused, then glances at the young lieutenant sitting a small sorrel a pace behind him. "Oh, yes. You insist on knowing everyone, don't you? This is Bierce, my topographical officer."

Garesché touches his horse's flank, moves forward to extend a hand. "Julius Garesché, your colonel's devoted and very patient friend."

The young officer looks surprised by the familiarity, hides it well. He salutes quickly, takes the hand. "Ambrose Bierce, Colonel."

Garesché turns back to Hazen. "Bill, I hope someday you command an army, but I doubt if your stomach will last so long. We know about the cavalry situation, and General Rosecrans had me speak to General Stanley. I'm sure that tomorrow morning the cavalry will be mounted and moving while your men are still boiling coffee. As far as McCook's flank goes, I'm sure he has that well in mind and well in hand. By tomorrow, General Thomas's corps will be back in the center, certainly in time to present a solid front to any Confederate attack."

Hazen seems mollified at the mention of Thomas, attempts a more reasonable tone. "Julius, I wish I didn't have to go on complaining, but this Pioneer Brigade General Rosecrans has devised. . . . My God, I don't have a man left who knows how to swing an ax or lay a corduroy because they're all in the damned Pioneer Brigade, wherever it is. And in this mud, we've got to have men who know how to do those things. Otherwise, we're going to have a hell of a time getting all the guns and wagons up."

"Oh, certainly it isn't as bad as all that. Two thirds of your men are farmers, and you've got bright young men like Bierce to engineer your road work."

Hazen snorts. "He's a good map-maker, but I've never seen him particularly energetic in anything else except inspecting the dead."

Garesché lifts his eyebrows. "Really? An interesting hobby. Do you plan to become a doctor, Lieutenant?"

"No, Colonel. But I would know war," Bierce says.

"Ah. Well, it seems we are all learning something of it these days. . . . Come, ride with me for a few minutes, Colonel Hazen."

Bierce sits his horse, watching as the two colonels ride off a few dozen paces. "Bill," he hears Garesché begin, "as we have discussed in the past, you must curb your temper. It does you no good. It does the army no good. . . ." The voices drift off. Bierce looks toward the top of the rise where Rosecrans and Crittenden are talking. He wonders again what manner of men these are. Yes, he would know war and those who make it.

★　★　★

Brigadier General Joe Wheeler, who abhors surprises, has been surprised. Since early morning his pickets have been forwarding reports of Federal columns on the Nolensville, Franklin, and Wilson pikes to the west. Yet somehow they have failed to get word to him of Crittenden's advance down the Murfreesboro Pike until the Yankees are within a few miles of his headquarters in Lavergne. How the devil could this happen? He mounts, rides hell for leather to have a look for himself.

Wheeler is very young for a general, only twenty-six, and would look even younger without his thick, black beard. But no one denies that he is a fighter. In the retreat from Kentucky, Wheeler and his men fought thirty engagements covering the retreat of the infantry across the Cumberlands. But to Wheeler's frustration, his men seem endemically unsuited to the routine of soldiering. In slack times, they are prodigious sleepers, foragers, rakes, and lollygaggers. Hence the fumbled scouting, the incomplete reports, the unpardonable surprises!

Wheeler and his staff thunder across the bridge over Hurricane Creek a mile north of Lavergne. His chief of staff shouts something about caution. Wheeler ignores him. Perhaps the report is wrong. Perhaps there is no Federal infantry column, just a little cavalry or nothing at all. He has seen it happen before: entire armies, entire hordes, made corporeal by nothing more than the imaginings of overwrought vedettes. He swings sharply off the road, fights through brush, kicking his mare hard as they emerge and begin climbing a rocky hill. He feels a brush of wind, hears a minié ball buzz, then another. Damn it! His staff dodges behind trees and bushes, opens fire, trying to make the Yankee snipers show themselves or at least duck and shoot high. Powder smoke hangs in puffs in the cedars, the pop and crack of pistols and carbines deadened by the sodden air.

He is nearly there, spurs digging, quirt flailing. He hears the *thwack* of a ball striking flesh, feels the shiver of the impact through his thighs as the mare plunges. He pulls her head up hard, slashes at her flanks. The mare leaps forward, rocks clattering under her hooves, and they are suddenly atop the hill, horse shivering as the blood streams down her chest, man cursing in a steady vocative hiss at the sight of the long blue column of infantry on the turnpike.

Wheeler guesses there are four thousand men within his view and more coming. He steadies the horse with one hand, fumbles field glasses from their case with the other, and focuses on the blue soldiers. More minié balls buzz around him. He ignores them, ignores the shouts of his chief of staff. How much more blue infantry? Another division? A full corps? Damn! Almost halfway to Murfreesboro by the shortest route, and he hasn't done a thing to slow them. He whirls the mare, sends her careening down the steep slope, blood flying from the pumping chest wound.

"Get the troops up!" he shouts at his chief of staff. "We'll hold them behind the creek. Stop 'em for tonight." They pound onto the road again, picking up the fragments of the staff from behind the bushes and trees. Wheeler's mare stumbles, and he jerks her head up. An aide presses up close. Wheeler shouts: "Around the next bend. She'll last that long."

They hurtle around the bend. Wheeler's mare is stumbling every third or fourth stride. He waits, judges the moment, and then jumps free as her legs go rubber. The aide is off his horse, holding out the reins as Wheeler runs up. He grabs them, swings aboard. He kicks the horse savagely, bends low over the neck, catching up to the others. The aide swings up behind another junior staffer. Wheeler passes the mare, who, relieved of her burden, has kept her legs. She stands now, head drooping almost to the ground, confused—as he imagines all things with sudden mortal wounds must be confused—by the rapid imminence of non-being. Damn good horse, he thinks, but without sentiment or gratitude. He has no time for either. Never will.

✯ ✯ ✯

Colonel William Hazen's second brigade, Palmer's second division, Crittenden's left wing, is still on the turnpike when Federal artillery opens fire on Wheeler's troopers on the east bank of Hurricane Creek. Bierce watches

Hazen, knows that he wants to order the men forward at the double-quick. But it is late in the day, and the men have marched a long way in the rain carrying heavy packs. Grimly, Hazen lets them continue forward at route step.

Bierce finds the pack loads of the infantrymen endlessly fascinating: what men imagine needing, will carry, suffer for; what in the first fatigue they will throw away; what they will cling to as long as life. In nothing else except the examination of the dead has he found so much of the character of humanity revealed. Though this is only the first day of the march, a stream of items leaches from the column into the ditches by the road: pistols, bowie knives, canteens, pots, frying pans, packets of letters, books, religious tracts, extra shoes, shirts, pants, and so on. With each day, the army will travel lighter, sorer, angrier, wearier. But first before all the other firsts, seconds, and thirds that will cadence the hardening of the army, there is the skirmish up ahead to fight: the first scraping away of the forgetfulness between campaigns. A reminder of how men die.

A staff officer gallops down the column, showering the men in the ranks with mud. They curse, shake their fists. A hoof kicks a testament from the ditch, sending pages scattering as if in forlorn reminder of the fragility of the Third Commandment. Bierce laughs, feels the glare of a few men nearby. *Officers.*

The staff officer pulls up in front of Hazen. "Colonel, General Palmer directs that you hurry your men forward at the double-quick. You are to form to the right of the pike while General Cruft's brigade forms to the left. Cruft will advance to turn the Rebels' right flank while you hold onto their left."

"Am I just to hold their flank, or may I cross the creek?"

"Cross if you can, Colonel, but the major effort will be General Cruft's downstream."

"All right," Hazen says, turns to shout the order for the double quick.

After a jog of a quarter mile, Hazen's brigade dumps packs by the road and forms in a marshy field on the west side. Hazen gives the men a few minutes to catch their breath. "Bierce," he shouts. "Go see how Cruft is coming along."

Bierce gallops up and over the road, passing behind two Napoleons and a howitzer shelling the far side of the creek. Cruft's brigade is half formed. Palmer and Cruft, both civilian generals but competent and well-liked, sit their horses a few dozen yards to the rear. Bierce turns his horse, trots back to Hazen. "I'd say ten minutes, Colonel."

"Good. We'll push forward to the creek and hope the Rebs mistake us for the main effort."

Joe Wheeler is perched in a tree, trying to make out the Yankee preparations on the north side of Hurricane Creek. He curses the rain, wipes the lenses of his field glasses on a uniform sleeve, and peers again through the gray drizzle. He knows his line is spread thin, its flanks hanging; but if he can guess right, perhaps he can hold the Yankees until dusk. He leans forward, squinting. Yes, here they are at last, coming through the brush west of the pike. A feint? Possibly, but the ranks are heavy—a brigade at least— and the Yankees are rarely subtle.

He swings down from the tree, feeling a moment of remembered joy from a boyhood not so long past though it is an eon ago. He lands like a cat, sprints to his horse, already giving orders to pull in the right to reinforce the left.

The Yankees pause twenty yards from the creek and the two sides blaze away. Powder smoke hangs in the drizzle, thickening until neither side can make out anything but the blurred shapes of swamp oaks and cedar. Wheeler paces, waiting for the assault. An orderly reports to his chief of staff, who turns to Wheeler. "General, the Yanks are coming across downstream. At least two brigades."

Wheeler curses. "All right, let's get the boys out. We'll fall back on the town and wait for dark."

There is no panic in the Rebel skedaddle. The men fall back from the stream in small groups, each pausing to lay down covering fire as the next squad follows. In less than ten minutes, the brigade is mounted and riding hard for Lavergne, where three of Wheeler's staff are already laying out new lines.

Bierce walks among the dead. There are not many, perhaps a dozen Confederate, a like number of Federal. As always, he finds a variety of expressions on the faces: the instantly dead seem peaceful, while those who have had a moment or two to recognize death seem startled. The expressions of the lingering dead are more varied, more interesting: agony, horror, disgust; and about the eyes of each, a squint of loneliness, a resentment toward all who have left them behind to die. Or so it seems to Bierce as he inspects the dead in the cold drizzle as dusk falls along Hurricane Creek.

☆   ☆   ☆

At the end of the first day's march, Davis's division, leading McCook's corps, camps two miles south of Nolensville at Knob Gap and four miles north of Hardee's positions at Triune. Sheridan's and Johnson's divisions of McCook's corps and Negley's division of Thomas's corps halt at

Nolensville. Rousseau's division of Thomas's corps bivouacs at Owen's Store on the Wilson Pike. Leading Crittenden's corps, Palmer's division camps astride Hurricane Creek, a mile north of Lavergne and sixteen miles from Murfreesboro.

Rosecrans's headquarters is in a large stone building at the tiny hamlet of Hamilton's Church on the Murfreesboro Pike. The staff processes a steady stream of incoming dispatches and outgoing orders. When a pause finally comes, Garesché leans back in his chair to ease his back and rest his eyes. At the adjoining table, Rosecrans signs a final order with a flourish and bounds to his feet to pace the room. Two newspaper reporters hurry forward to join him. Garesché sighs, wishing his general had the sense to rest now while he has a chance. But no, he must pace, talk, speculate on the battle to come.

"Bragg will concentrate northwest of Murfreesboro," Rosecrans tells the scribbling reporters. "He's an artilleryman and he appreciates ground. He's too easily flanked where he sits in Murfreesboro, and that's why he'll probably fight along Stewart's Creek. He'll set up with his forward units west of the creek and try to hit us a quick pop or two before we can come into line of battle. But we'll come down on Stewart's Creek well closed up. Crittenden, Thomas, and McCook, left to right. Bragg will probe, find that out, and drop back to fight on the defensive. Artillerymen are always more comfortable on the defensive. That's why I expect. . . ." He stops, hesitates, covers the sudden thought by lighting a cigar. "That's why I expect to give Braxton Bragg a round, good thumping. Thank you, gentlemen. I'll see you in the morning."

When they are gone, Rosecrans says, "I need to talk to McCook. Tomorrow morning, he's going to run into Hardee at Triune and I want him to be ready. Before, I wasn't certain, but while I was talking to those reporters I suddenly saw it all clearly. Bragg won't pull in Hardee until he's bloodied us once."

Garesché sets down his pen carefully. "General McCook has received your instructions, General. I copied them out myself. I think you would do better to stay out of the damp and get some rest. The army will depend on you very heavily over the next few days."

Rosecrans glares at him. "Colonel, sometimes I swear you forgot how to be a soldier in all the time you spent in Washington. Well, let me remind you what soldiering is: it's about besting the other man every chance you get. And that means I've got to best Braxton Bragg not tomorrow, not the next day, but right here, right now on this cold, godforsaken, rainy night. Is he going to go see Hardee tonight? I doubt it. But if I go talk to McCook and give him one suggestion that will help him beat Hardee, then it matters not if I sleep a wink!"

Garesché stands, stiffly formal. "Very good, General. I will assemble a party."

It takes fifteen minutes for Garesché to gather staff and escort. He briefs Goddard, who will remain behind to run the headquarters staff. The major shakes his head. "Colonel, I think this is unwise. You could all get snapped up by a Reb patrol, and then where would we be?"

"I know, Major. I know. But the general has his reasons for taking the risk. If we're not back by three in the morning, contact General Thomas. Tell him that he is to act in General Rosecrans's absence."

"Yes, sir. And, Colonel, have you recharged your revolver in all this damp weather?"

Garesché is embarrassed. "No, Major. I'm afraid I neglected that."

"Let me do it for you quickly."

"Thank you, Major. That is very kind." Garesché fumbles with his holster, withdraws the unfamiliar Colt.

Rosecrans comes out the door, pulling on gauntlets and puffing on a fresh cigar. He slaps Garesché on the shoulder. "Don't mind me, Julius. You're the best damned chief of staff any general ever had, and I know part of your job is looking after me. But Hardee's a wily old dog, about as wily as Alex McCook is thick. I don't want Alex handled too roughly in the morning."

"Yes, General, of course."

They mount. Goddard hands up the reloaded revolver and two extra cylinders to Garesché. "Be careful, Colonel."

Trailing an escort of a dozen cavalry troopers led by a young lieutenant, they trot into the gloom.

It is preposterous. They are lost somewhere in the rainy dark between Crittenden's and McCook's corps with Union and Confederate cavalry creeping about, nervous, fingers on carbine and pistol triggers. Rosecrans has already upbraided the miserable cavalry lieutenant leading the escort and has, over Garesché's protests, taken it on himself to find their way. He knocks on the door of a cabin, quizzes the woman who comes to the door with four children clutching at her skirt. Rosecrans is courtly, calls her "Madam," charms her into giving them directions though her husband is probably fighting in Rebel uniform. They continue, stopping at several more cabins, Rosecrans seeming to enjoy the interviews. At last they come out on a hill overlooking Nolensville and see the fires of McCook's camp spread out below.

They make their way through the artillery park and the long jumbled lines of supply wagons to where McCook has his headquarters in a pair of roadmaster wagons. McCook is delighted to see Rosecrans and Garesché. He summons his chief of staff, and the four of them sit about on the floor of one of the wagons, peering at maps by the light of a candle burning in a bayonet socket. McCook offers whiskey. Rosecrans accepts, Garesché refuses.

McCook laughs. "You know, Hardee was commandant when I taught at the Point. We didn't exactly see eye to eye on some of the details in his precious book of tactics. In fact, we had quite the go-arounds on the subject. I had to give in then, but I've got a few of my own ideas to try on him tomorrow."

Rosecrans frowns. "Pitch into him, General, but watch your flanks. Hardee is no fool; he'll bait a trap."

"Don't worry, General. I got jumped that day at Perryville, but this time we'll be on the offensive. I'll pay old Bill Hardee back."

Rosecrans continues to frown. "Gentlemen, if you would be so kind."

Garesché and McCook's chief of staff exit, stand in the drizzle without speaking. Rosecrans and McCook emerge a few minutes later. McCook is still cheerful but perhaps a shade less ebullient.

When they have said their goodnights and are riding again, Garesché asks, "Are you in agreement on tactics?"

"Yes, I think he'll be fine as long as he doesn't give Hardee a chance to turn a flank."

Garesché wishes he were as confident in Alex McCook, but says nothing.

☆　☆　☆

Braxton Bragg glowers at the map tacked to the wall of his office. Fourteen hours since the bedraggled cavalry corporal stood before his desk, and still there is no certainty about Rosecrans's intentions. His diseased gut tells him that the Yankees are moving in force on Stewart's Creek, but he must be certain before he concentrates the army. Polk and Hardee will seize any mistake, any sign of panic, as another excuse to assault his reputation. Oh, he knows all they have done, have tried to do. He knows of their secret meetings, of the secret letters they've sent Davis. Knows and will someday be revenged. But that is for someday. Now he must know what Rosecrans is doing, must be certain before he acts.

He glances impatiently at the clock. Where is Wheeler? Two hours since he sent for him and still not here. He feels a momentary thrill of concern for the young man, is surprised by the unaccustomed sentiment. He opens a desk drawer for pen and stationery. He will begin a letter to his wife, use that to pass the time. Patience, he tells himself. Rashness is what kills generals and their armies. Wait for Wheeler and then decide.

But instead of writing, he stares again at the map and the twisting course of Stewart's Creek. That would be fine ground to defend, far better than the ground at Murfreesboro. But Rosecrans will have seen that, too, will have devised a way to flank the position. Better to draw him south toward Murfreesboro, stretch his supply lines, tire his army. And while the Yankees march in this wretched weather, Bragg will plan a way to use the ground around Murfreesboro to advantage. A snare baited with the apparent weakness of his position. A trap. Yes.

The two Confederate officers press themselves into the wet earth, trying to escape trampling by the horses of a party of Federal officers. The horses sense the men concealed in the brush, but the horsemen are not sufficiently conversant with the ways of their mounts to translate the skittishness. Finally, the big gray bearing the party's commander distends its belly in disgust and urinates a thick stream on the nearest of the Confederate officers. The gray's rider waits patiently and then kicks his steed into a trot down the slope toward the fires of the Federal camp in the valley above Nolensville.

When the riders are out of earshot, Major W. D. Pickett of Hardee's staff, the victim of the urination, indulges in a string of erudite curses, the concluding one delivered in Greek. Colonel Tom Harrison of the 8th Texas Cavalry is amused. "Son, I thought you were going to draw and start shooting. That horse gave you one prodigious pissing."

"God, I was tempted. Who the hell do you suppose they were?"

Harrison shrugs. "Could have been Rosecrans and his staff for all I know."

"It wasn't Rosecrans. Maybe some brigadier, but you'd never catch an army commander wandering around in this weather. That's what they've got staffs for: to get good and wet and goddamned miserable in this goddamned miserable country."

Harrison grins. "Well, son, maybe you should get done with your spying so we can find a fire."

Pickett grumbles, lifts his field glasses again. "I figure two divisions, maybe three. This isn't a foraging expedition; they're looking for a fight."

"That's what we've been telling you people most of the day."

"We believed you, but Bragg's staff kept asking. They're starting to let the fires burn down. We can go."

Together, they begin the slow crawl off the ridge and then the scuttle through the brush to where an orderly, frightened almost to tears, waits with their horses.

Lieutenant General William J. Hardee pushes his chair back to gain some distance from the young staff officer. Hardee has been a soldier twenty-eight of his forty-seven years and knows well the odors of camp and barracks, sweating horses and unbathed men. But this young major is more than ordinarily malodorous, and Hardee wonders what accounts for the sharp smell of horse urine. He clears his throat. "Good work, Major. Get some refreshment and a change of uniform. I'll send your information on to General Bragg's headquarters."

The major leaves, face burning. Hardee sighs, wishing he had said less. He studies the map on his desk. So, Rosy Rosecrans is coming in force, he thinks. I thought he would wait until spring, but perhaps Lincoln and Stanton have forced him to move. Probably the debacle at Fredericksburg has them worried about the French and British again. He leans back, stares at the rain-streaked window. Is there, he wonders, any hope that France and Britain may yet recognize our independence? He doubts it. Oh, he supposes *ce grand bouffon* Napoleon III may yet dream of an alliance with the Confederacy. But the French won't move without the British, and the Gladstone government is caught between its lust for cotton and its revulsion for slavery. And we, Hardee thinks, are too stiff-necked to make even the most innocuous promise about improving the lot of the black man.

Damn slavery. We can tell the world ten thousand times that this war is not about slavery, but the world will choose to believe otherwise as long as we keep slaves. And the world may even be right. But ordinary logic cannot explain our society, cannot explain how delicately things are balanced here. Pat Cleburne told me once that he thought we should enlist the niggers and let them earn their freedom by serving in the army. I warned him never to speak of the subject again. A good man, but odd. Not born of us.

He meditates on Rosecrans, wishes he knew the man better. Where are you going, Rosy? Shelbyville is my guess, with that boy McCook leading the way and Thomas on his right flank. Odd. I would have led with Old Slow Trot and had McCook protecting the flank.

He ponders a while longer, then picks up his pen. He writes a long message to Bragg, carefully qualifying every point as a lawyer might the provisions of a complicated contract. With a reminder about the importance of maintaining interior lines, he concludes, *Very respectfully, W. T. Hardee, Lt. Gen.* The message is a masterpiece, covering all eventualities and avoiding most responsibilities. He gives the message to an aide and then lies down on the day bed. Let Bragg make the decisions, take the risks. Bill Hardee has a clear conscience, is a good if not a loyal follower. He falls asleep to dream of silks and petticoats rustling across a polished dance floor, of the young women at Morgan's wedding. So pretty, so graceful, so . . . *ripe*. Yes, that is the word. His hand finds his genitals, rests there, warm, anticipatory.

☆   ☆   ☆

Bierce rises before midnight to take his watch as staff duty officer. He is writing in his journal under the fly of the headquarters tent when the rain stops and a heavy fog envelops the camp. He feels the chill brush of it against his cheek and looks up from his journal to see it rolling in. And though he is the most rational of young men, the sight startles him, for in its thickness, its weight, the fog is prodigious: a fog out of Poe or Mary Shelley or one of the haunted tragedies of Shakespeare. He watches as it enfolds the lanterns and campfires, turns them to yellow and red splotches in its grayness. Bierce takes a lantern from the pole above the table and walks into the fog, lets it embrace him.

He is standing still, breathing it in, feeling it seep into his every pore, when a figure materializes, trips over one of Bierce's feet, and sprawls. The little man bounces up, fists squared. "Where are you, you bum? I'll fix you." He jabs, follows with a looping cross, striking only air. Bierce steps back, starts laughing. "Is that you, Ransom?" the man snarls. "God damn you. What are you doing sneaking around out here?"

"I'm Bierce."

"Pierce? I don't know no Pierce. You sure you ain't Ransom?"

"I'm not Ransom. I'm Lieutenant Bierce, Second Brigade. What or whom are you looking for, soldier?"

The man drops his fists. "Officer, are ya?"

"Yes."

"Doesn't give you no right to go about tripping men."

"You tripped over me."

"Well, you got a lantern. Why don't you hold it up so a man can see? And you shouldn't laugh. I coulda broken my neck."

Bierce shakes his head, smiles. "All right, I'm sorry. All fault is mine. Now what are you doing here?"

"I'm from General Palmer's headquarters. Got a message for Colonel Hazen."

"That would be my colonel. I'll take it."

The man holds the message uncertainly. "You sure you know where to find him?"

"Absolutely."

"You sure you're really with Hazen?"

"Come with me, and I'll let you wake him yourself."

"All right, damn it, I will. I don't trust nobody out here sneaking around in the fog tripping up honest men."

Bierce leads the man toward the headquarters tents by the gauzy light of the lantern. The orderly is old for his trade, a small wizened man of forty or more, wearing the stripes of a corporal. Bierce holds out a hand for the message. "I need to log it in."

The man squints at Bierce's shoulder straps, grudgingly hands the sheet over. Bierce records the date and time, casts a quick glance down the message itself, and frowns at the implication of the order attaching the brigade to Wood's division. He holds out the message to the man. "Colonel Hazen is on the left-hand side, his adjutant on the right. Personally, I'd wake his adjutant first, but. . . ."

The orderly steps back. "That's all right, Lootenant. Now I'm sure you're who you says, I'll be getting back." He tosses a half salute and is gone. Bierce shakes his head. A fool out of Shakespeare with only the look, not the wit. A pity to waste such a fog on him. He goes to wake the adjutant and the colonel.

Hazen reads the message by the light of the lantern Bierce holds. "We're going to try to force a crossing of Stewart's Creek in the morning. We're assigned to Tom Wood's division. We're to go see him immediately."

Bierce senses Hazen's excitement on the ride to First Division headquarters. Brigadier General Thomas J. Wood is considered one of the army's thorough professionals. By rights he should command the corps, but the job is Crittenden's because of politics. At least Crittenden has the sense to listen to Wood, who is generally considered the real brains of the command.

Wood rises from behind his field desk when they enter the headquarters tent, shakes Hazen's hand, acknowledges Bierce with a nod. "Is there any sign the fog's lifting, Bill?"

"None, General."

"Well, I suppose it may work to our advantage if it lulls the Rebs into thinking we'll hold position. Come and look at what we need to do." Bierce edges in to study the map over Hazen's shoulder as Wood explains. "I'm going to hit the creek with a flying column of three regiments and a battery straight ahead, hoping we catch the Johnnies napping before they can fire the bridge. If that doesn't work—and it almost certainly won't—then I'll feint with one brigade left of the turnpike and make the main assault with the other two on the right."

"Bloody work," Hazen says. "I thought Rosy would use the full corps. Maybe wait until Thomas is up."

"It seems we're here faster than Bragg anticipated. So far we don't have any indication that he's in great strength on the other side of the creek. If we can force a crossing before he's ready, we'll save ourselves a lot of work."

"So where do you want my brigade?"

"Ah, now that's my little surprise. Look here." He traces the creek downstream toward Stones River to the point where the Jefferson Pike crosses it a mile south of the hamlet of Smyrna. "We don't think they've burned the bridge here, which is one hell of an oversight. I want you to grab it and create a diversion. If you can draw off enough of the Rebs, it'll make our job up here a lot easier."

Hazen nods. "Do I have discretion in tactics?"

"Of course, Bill."

CHAPTER 4

Saturday Morning
December 27, 1862
Hamilton's Church, Tennessee

Rosecrans has issued orders for the day: McCook is to push south on the Nolensville Pike, driving Hardee from Triune. Crittenden is to advance through Lavergne and force a crossing of Stewart's Creek. Thomas is to cross the rear of McCook's corps on the Old Liberty Road to assume the center, thus restoring the army to its proper alignment.

ROSECRANS LIGHTS HIS first cigar of the day from the lantern hanging beside the door of his headquarters. "Not much progress this morning, I fear. I suppose you'll have me signing reports until this damned fog lifts."

"There are some details that need your attention, General," Garesché replies. "In the meantime, should we caution General McCook against an advance?"

"No, McCook is not that great a fool. He'll wait until he can see." Rosecrans considers. "I imagine we shall have to march on the Sabbath to make up for lost time. I will talk to Father Treacy."

Garesché glances quickly behind them to see if anyone has overheard. As a devout Catholic, he appreciates Treacy's presence on the staff. Yet it is exceedingly unwise for Rosecrans to speak of consulting the priest about a tactical decision. Other generals have been destroyed for less in this political

war. Fortunately, Treacy is worldly enough to absent himself from the councils of war. Still, there are rumors of Papist influence in the army.

Rosecrans swings his arms against the chill, seems to recover his accustomed enthusiasm. "Perhaps we'll have some clearing by noon. Then we'll
find out how much fuss Hardee is going to make over Triune and if Bragg
is going to fight us along Stewart's Creek. Let's go in and hear mass and then
we'll get at your infernal reports."

★   ★   ★

South of Nolensville, Alex McCook can barely suppress his disappointment.
It is as if William J. Hardee, erstwhile commandant of the United States
Military Academy at West Point, has arranged the fog as yet another humiliation for his one-time subordinate. How McCook had loathed Hardee's
seminars for junior instructors. He can picture Hardee even now, shaking
his head in that sad, seemingly sympathetic way: "I'm sorry, Lieutenant
McCook, but it seems that you haven't quite mastered the concept. Report
to my quarters after parade tonight, and I'll try to present the principles in
a more elementary fashion. This is, after all, a skill you will need in the
field." Oh, he made it sound sympathetic. Made it seem like he was trying
to remove some of McCook's embarrassment. But you could tell the son of
a bitch was enjoying every second. All right, McCook thinks. You had your
chance then, and a long time later you got lucky at Perryville. Now it's my
turn. Fog or no fog, I'm coming for you this morning.

The thought invigorates him. Hardee will not expect this. No, his precious *Rifle and Light Infantry Tactics* warns against advancing in thick fog
over unscouted ground. But don't generals become great generals when they
dare great risks? McCook shall be Wolfe taking the twisting path up the cliff
to the Plains of Abraham. He shall be Washington crossing the ice-choked
Delaware to attack at Trenton. He shall be. . . . Well, there are many exam-
ples, but he needs to think of other things now. He turns smiling to his chief
of staff. "Order the skirmishers forward. Once we have some firing, we'll be
able to read the Reb positions. Don't worry about the fog. We'll be all right."

The skirmishers edge forward in fog so thick that men a dozen feet apart are
mere shadows in the whiteness. Droplets of mist cling to hair, eyebrows, and
beards. Men sweat cold fear, pant huge puffs of it in the wet air. Will they see
the muzzle flashes if the Rebs fire? Will their own rifles work in this damp?
Perhaps they should fix bayonets. But no one stops now, the thought of
falling behind more frightening than advancing. Ahead, the sudden loom of

a tree, grotesque, monstrous. Then another and another. They push forward into the woods with a rustle of undergrowth against brogans and pant legs. A stick snaps under an unwary foot, heart-stopping as thumbs jerk back rifle hammers in a long ragged clatter. A panting pause. Nothing. The word is passed down the line to ease up on the hammers. Then forward again, edging through the fog, feeling for Johnny Reb, knowing he is there.

The neigh of the horse is unearthly, something out of dream, myth, an ancient collective terror. The skirmishers hesitate in midstride, then dive for trees and bushes as the earth reverberates. The horsemen hurtle out of the fog in a roar of hooves and yells. They are huge, should wear winged helmets, wield battle-axes in their immensity. It is Forrest. Must be. Forrest the unkillable, swinging his gigantic saber, snatching blue-coated soldiers from the ground, using them as shields, and then hurling them aside.

The skirmishers fire wildly, desperately. Horses scream, horsemen throw out their arms, tumble. A bullet in the shoulder spins a youth from his saddle. He hits the ground hard, rolls over, tries to sit up. A sergeant runs forward to dispatch him with a rifle butt, stops at the sight of a blue jacket. My God! Oh, Christ, no! He screams: "Stop, stop, they're friends, they're friends! For Chrissakes, stop shooting!" The yell is taken up as others find blue bodies, make prisoners of men in blue. The firing dies, is replaced by curses and cries. The youth with the shattered shoulder whimpers to the sergeant: "Somebody's horse spooked. And then mine did and some others, too. We wasn't charging you boys. Didn't even know you was coming. Oh, God, I hurt, Sarge. And they're going to take my arm. Oh, God." The sergeant, who has seen many such wounds, knows better. No, this will take your life, son. He hides his face.

The skirmishers stand about staring at the wounded and the dead, all thought of advance forgotten. Oh, damn. Oh, goddamn. Oh, goddamn it to hell.

The casualties are carried back to camp. McCook cancels the advance, goes to his headquarters in the roadmaster wagon, where he sits, head in hands, weeping. His chief of staff stands apart, unspeaking, unsympathetic. If only damned fools serve fools, he thinks, then I am truly damned.

☆ ☆ ☆

Irish Pat Cleburne stands beside Hardee on a small rise above the road into Triune. They stare into the fog as the muffled sound of musketry fades. "Ours?" Hardee asks.

"I don't think so. We're pulled well back from there. They must be shooting at each other."

Hardee shakes his head. "Young McCook probably pushed a skirmish line forward and collided with his own vedettes. Predictable. He should have learned better at the Academy, but I guess he's the same fool he always was."

Cleburne, the one-time corporal, rarely comments when other generals mention the hallowed halls of West Point. But Hardee is a friend, and he chances it. "I thought McCook taught tactics at West Point."

Hardee scoffs. "McCook taught drill. He was good at that. I'll venture to say almost as good as you are, though I'm sure no British veteran would admit it."

"With all respect to American methods, it is difficult to imagine."

"No doubt. Well, my young Irish friend, I think it's time you put your division on the road. The fog will break eventually, and you'll want to be well clear of this place by then."

"The order is already given, General, though I still wonder why we shouldn't fight a little here. McCook is anxious, Thomas is still a long way behind. We can bloody McCook and then fall back. Or—"

"Or we can attack with everything at hand and crush McCook before Thomas arrives. I agree entirely, Patrick. But General Bragg prefers to fight before Murfreesboro on poor ground."

"But certainly if General Bragg understood the advantages we have here—"

"No, Patrick, he is set on his own plan. And I will tell you exactly how he will attack. He will send the men forward shoulder to shoulder in an immense wheel to crush Rosy's flank. It's all right out of Napoleon and half a century old. But Braxton Bragg never forgot an old tactic and never learned a new one. And unless we are very lucky, the Yankee artillery will butcher us before we are in rifle range."

On the road to their left, wagons are moving south toward Triune in the fog. Cleburne listens closely, hears the first tread of marching infantry coming behind. Good. The schedule is holding. "Surely this will be General Bragg's last battle. I am told that he looks terrible. And they say his stomach complaint is very active."

Hardee laughs. "It's beyond active. It's a small wonder that his headquarters doesn't explode from the concentration of foul gases. But Bragg will continue in command until he is utterly prostrated. He is a man of the worst kind of arrogance; he believes himself irreplaceable."

"General, if he's unfit—"

"Of course he is unfit, Patrick! He's physically unfit and he's temperamentally unfit. He was unfit at the beginning of this war and he's unfit now. He is *unfit*. But not God himself is going to convince his excellency Jefferson Davis that his best friend from the Old Army is unfit to command one of the two great armies of this, our new and glorious Confederacy!"

Cleburne looks away, mutters, "I don't know President Davis."

"I know you don't. But I do and very well. People think Jeff Davis is a cold man. They think he is pure, grim, unemotional purpose. But people are wrong. Jeff Davis is a man of great passions, plethoric prejudices, and extraordinary, if nonsensical, loyalties. He feels he owes Bragg his life, and he will never abandon him. I tried to talk to him at Morgan's wedding, but when I wanted to discuss Perryville, the president brought up Buena Vista. When I tried to talk to him about the starvation of the army on our retreat from Kentucky, he lectured me about the hardships of the march to Agua Nueva. He will not hear reason where Bragg is concerned. And so we are hitched to Bragg's fortune and will be as long as his excellency remembers what Bragg did for him in Mexico."

Cleburne has heard the story of Buena Vista from Hardee, has seen him draw the lines of Davis's famous V on a sketch of the battlefield. Yet he cannot quite imagine the battle, cannot picture Davis and Bragg young, fighting the charging hordes of Mexicans in the high desert of so long ago. To Cleburne, who is thirty-three, these are old men, the glory of their past unimaginable and irrelevant in this war where his division alone would outnumber old Taylor's entire army.

An orderly brings coffee. Hardee is gracious to the boy, inquires where this bounty of good dark coffee comes from. "Yankee prisoners, General. They've got rucksacks full of the stuff."

"Ah. Well, we should thank them for carrying it all the way from Nashville for us."

"Yes, sir, General. Next time I see one of them bluebellies, I'll be sure to do that." He catches Cleburne's cold stare, retreats quickly.

Cleburne concentrates on the fog-shrouded road again, listening to the tramp of marching feet. The pace is a little slow but not bad. Good enough.

Hardee sips from his cup, smacks his lips in appreciation. "You don't approve of my bantering with the men, do you, Patrick?"

"I was a common soldier, General. I've never seen any good come of familiarity."

"Oh, I was hardly familiar with him. You're a hard man, Patrick. Still, I can't argue with your results. Well, I should be getting on to Murfreesboro. I need to talk to Breckinridge before I see the commanding general. That's if Bragg hasn't shot him since yesterday."

"General, I would like to stay with the rear guard. Neither of my brigadiers is much used to their new responsibilities, and—"

"No, Patrick. You're a major general now and command a division. That means you must delegate and trust. I would like to stay, too. Alex McCook exhausted my considerable patience at the Academy, and I would love to give him a difficult time this morning. But I must look to my entire corps, and you must do the same for your division. Difficult as it is, we must leave the brigadiers to fight the brigade battles."

After Hardee and his staff have disappeared into the fog, Cleburne stands for another hour on the hill. He drinks more of the good coffee, takes reports, signs orders. It amazes him that he commands a division. In truth, his entire life since he set foot in this country amazes him. Cleburne is a native of County Cork, the son of a Protestant physician with a large and largely uncompensated practice among the Catholic poor. After the good doctor died and Patrick failed admission for apothecary school, he joined the army in order to help the family. He served three years, buying out his enlistment when his stepmother embarked the family for America.

He stepped off the boat in New Orleans on Christmas day, 1849. He soon left the city and the family for the Arkansas frontier and a job managing a drug store for two young doctors. He worked from dawn until late at night, returning to his Spartan rooms to study law into the wee hours. It is an archetypal American story, not unlike that of a certain Illinois rail-splitter turned lawyer and politician. In two years, Cleburne was a partner. A year later, the three partners sold the store for a healthy profit, and Cleburne took up the practice of law. He enjoyed Helena's best society, joined the Masons, and made common cause with Thomas Hindman, a future Confederate general, in battling the anti-immigrant Know-Nothings. Frontier politics was a rough business, and he and Hindman carried revolvers. When the two were attacked on a public street, Cleburne killed a man and took a bullet through a lung. He recovered but wheezed ever after. By 1860 Pat Cleburne was both well-to-do and respected in his adopted land of Arkansas, sovereign state in the union of sovereign states. Although he is a liberal and opposes slavery, he knows exactly where his loyalties lie; Arkansas is his nation and he will stand by it to the death.

Like Ulysses Grant, he bartered his skill as a drillmaster into a colonel's commission and command of a regiment. Professionalism and aggressiveness won him a star and command of a brigade at Shiloh. At Richmond, Kentucky, he commanded two brigades and designed the battle plan that destroyed Bull Nelson's army. Early in the battle, a minié ball pierced

Cleburne's cheek, shattering most of the teeth on one side of his lower jaw before exiting through his mouth, which was fortunately open to shout an order. But he was back in the saddle at Perryville, five weeks later, helping Hardee smash McCook's corps. That time a piece of shrapnel disemboweled his horse and sliced open Cleburne's leg. Swearing loudly, he was carried protesting to the field hospital. Assured that he would recover, his men joked that "Old Pat" might dodge a few missiles if he rode anything but the slowest, most docile plowhorse available. But in all but his choice of steeds, Cleburne is ferociously brave. And though he is remote, he is also fair and humane. His men adore him.

Cleburne calls for his horse. His mount is a thickset gelding of considerable age and great resignation. He clambers into the saddle, his personal orderly giving him a discreet leg up. He jogs down the hillside and then walks the plug beside the column. The men lift their hats, smile, keep the order to be silent on this march. Cleburne responds in his quiet voice: "Hurry on, boys. We want to get well clear before the fog lifts. General Bragg is preparing a surprise for the Yankees, and we want to be in Murfreesboro to help." They grin, nod. This is a remarkably democratic war, even in Cleburne's division, and they appreciate being included in the plan.

★ ★ ★

Time and the fog hang heavily on the four Federal brigades waiting on the northern outskirts of Lavergne. Brigadier General Tom Wood reads a military text in French. Hazen paces. Bierce writes in his journal. By the roadside, the soldiers brew coffee, try to nap on the soaking grass, bitch about the weather, officers, the war. Cold rain begins falling, but the fog persists until nearly noon, when the visibility finally improves enough for the division to advance down the Murfreesboro Pike. The division slogs through Lavergne. Only a few houses remain intact. The rest of the village has been reduced to blackened chimneys standing in beds of ashes puddled with rain.

Hazen's brigade splits off onto the Jefferson Pike. Wood returns Hazen's salute, rides ahead to push the pace of his column toward Stewart's Creek. The men see Wood's intensity, catch it. Something is about to happen. They bend to the weight of their packs and rifle-muskets, tighten their ranks.

Wood has given Hazen ninety troopers of the 4th Michigan Cavalry. This is an almost unheard-of luxury for the commander of an infantry brigade. Even more amazing, these troopers are a well-trained and scrappy lot with a sturdy young captain, James Mix, in command. Hazen decides to gamble. "Mix, stay a quarter mile ahead of us in screen. The minute you hit anything, pull in to the pike and go like hell. I don't want you to fight, to scout, or to do so much as spit. Just go like hell down that road and don't stop until you're across the bridge. Then dig in and hold on. We'll be coming after you at a run. Do you understand?"

"Yes, Colonel. I'm not to stop until I'm across the bridge."

"Exactly. I'm sending Lieutenant Bierce with you to scout the ground south and west of the bridge. Give him a man if you can spare one. Otherwise, let him take care of himself."

"Yes, sir. Come on, Bierce."

Bierce rides with Mix and his first sergeant behind the screen of troopers. Mix is watchful, untalkative. They splash through muddy pools along the narrow road which only some civic booster in Jefferson would dignify with the name "pike," though Bierce supposes that once there might have been an actual tollgate. Then suddenly, improbably, it is there. An old man stands before it, frowning furiously at the approaching horsemen. Mix's troopers draw rein in confusion. Mix, the sergeant, and Bierce ride forward. "How many men you got here?" the gatekeeper demands. "Can't sneak around through the fields. That there is private property. Everybody's got to stay on the pike and go through the gate. It's five cents apiece, no exceptions 'ceptin' doctors and preachers."

Mix scratches his beard. "We're United States cavalry on duty in suppression of rebellion."

"I don't give a hoot in hell who you are. I'm paid by the township to collect the tolls, and you're gonna pay or you ain't gonna pass."

"And I suppose the Johnnies have been paying," the sergeant says.

"Damned right they have."

"Horseshit," the sergeant says, and kicks his horse forward to push through the gate.

"Hold it right there, you blue-bellied bastard!" From under his coat, the old man drags an ancient horse pistol. It catches in his pants and he wrestles furiously with it. The sergeant unstirrups a boot and kicks him in the chest. The old man sits down with a thud, starts to cry.

Bierce dismounts, takes the horse pistol from him. "Should hang the old bastard," the sergeant says.

Mix sighs. "Grandpa, you got another gun around?"

"No, I ain't got no gun, you blue-bellied bastard!" the old man sobs. "Why you all come down here? Why you doing this to us?"

Mix turns to one of his troopers. "Look around. Make sure he doesn't have a shotgun hidden in the bushes. Turn him over to the first chaplain who comes by. Then catch us up if you can."

Down the road, Bierce hands the horse pistol to Mix. Mix glances at it without interest. "Want it?" he asks.

"No," Bierce says.

Mix pops the cap off with a thumbnail and tosses the pistol into a gully. Bierce will regret for the rest of his life that he did not say yes.

Three miles short of the creek, there is a sudden smattering of pistol fire ahead and to their left. Mix gives a whoop, digs spurs to his horse. Gray troopers and blue troopers explode from a copse of trees. The Rebels cut across an open field, but the Federal horsemen swing in for the road, falling in behind Mix. They are yelling like Indians, blazing away at the gray troopers, who fire back wildly, leap ditches, tumble, try to work in toward the pike, break off to try the fields again, falling behind as the Yankee troopers hurtle down the road.

Bierce cannot believe the glorious irrationality of it all. He is swallowed up in the noise, the smoke, the smell, the wild ferocity of the ride. He hears his own voice yelling, fires his revolver at a gray rider, though he knows he has no chance of hitting man or horse and that he would be far wiser to concentrate on staying aboard his careening mount. Yet he cocks and fires until his revolver clicks empty.

Then ahead, butternut infantry scrambling up from campfires this side of a narrow bridge. They are the real danger, for if they stay cool, they can shoot down the Yankee troopers easily with their long-barreled Enfields. But the Yankees are on top of them, horse-borne, screaming, revolvers blazing, sabers swinging, ten feet tall and growing. It is too much; the Rebel infantrymen break and run for cover. Two make the mistake of trying to get across the bridge ahead of the cavalry, are ridden down, trampled screaming beneath iron-shod hooves.

Mix is off his horse on the far side of the bridge, carbine in hand, shouting orders. "You, Bierce! Get down before they shoot your damned fool head off." The troopers are sprinting to cover the crossing. Bierce wishes that he had thought to borrow a carbine, fumbles another cylinder into his revolver.

A weasel-faced private plucks at his sleeve. "Captain says if you want to go on your scout, now's the time. In a few minutes, the Rebs is gonna figure out there ain't many of us. Then it'll get hot until our infantry shows up."

"All right. Let's go."

They run along the road past a dozen troopers spreading out to form a perimeter. The private grabs a burly corporal. "Benny, don't you let the boys shoot my ass when I'm comin' back. Or the lieutenant here either. I'll wave my hat, call out your name. That's our password."

"Right, Jims. Stay low."

Bierce and the private called Jims dodge down through the trees to the stream bottom. They hear hoofbeats and shouts across the way, then a crackle of carbine fire from Mix's men. "The Reb cavalry's caught up," Jims says. "Where we going, Lieutenant? I should be back there."

"Don't talk. Just watch behind us." Bierce leads them another hundred yards along the bottom and then chances the higher ground to the left. The brush gives way to thick second growth, then to a spongy field. Bierce pulls out his dispatch book, sketches rapidly.

Downstream, the firing increases. "How long do you think till the infantry gets here?" Jims asks.

Bierce looks at his watch, tries to calculate. "Three-quarters of an hour. Maybe a little less."

"That's a long damn time. We goin' back or goin' on, Lieutenant?"

"I've got to see what's on the other side of that rise."

"Lieutenant, there ain't nothing more than this low sort of ground. We oughta—"

Bierce glares at him and the private falls silent. They skirt the field, mount the rise on the far side, crawling the last dozen yards to keep below the skyline. Lying on his belly, Bierce studies the ground ahead through his field glasses. There is not a Reb in sight, no sign of an army preparing to dispute the crossing of Stewart's Creek. "Lieutenant, we got to get back," Jims pleads.

Bierce rolls on his back, stares at the man. "Why are you in such a hurry to get killed? You're a lot safer here."

Jims wets his lips. "They're my people, Lieutenant. They're fightin'. I gotta be there even if I do catch one."

Bierce shakes his head. "All right. Just a minute and we'll head back." He sketches.

They return to the creek bottom, work along it toward the firing. They are perhaps three hundred yards from the bridge when they nearly collide with three Rebel infantrymen wading the stream. The stream bed is treacherous, and the Rebs, intent on their footing, do not see Bierce and Jims. Bierce raises his revolver, points it at the chest of the blond-bearded sergeant in the lead. He is suddenly very aware that he has never shot a man at close range. In truth, he is not sure he has ever shot a man at any range. He has fired many times into a throng of Rebel infantry, never knowing if any of his bullets found flesh. But here there will be no question. Behind him Jims cocks his carbine.

"Sarge," the Reb following the sergeant says. "Better stop."

The sergeant looks up, freezes. He and Bierce stare at each other. "Uh, what now, friend?" the sergeant asks.

Bierce is about to reply when the third Reb slips on a wet stone. Trying to get his balance, he swings his Enfield toward Jims, who shoots him through the head. The other two Rebs, not understanding quite what has happened but suspecting the worst of the Yankees, try to defend themselves. Bierce fires, the revolver jumping in his hand. His first shot hits the sergeant in the chest just to the right of the heart with a sound like an overripe piece of fruit hitting a wall. His second shot sings over the shoulder of the falling sergeant to bury itself in the mud bank of the far shore. The third hits the remaining Reb in the neck, tearing through the jugular vein in a spray of blood. The man falls to his knees in the stream, hands clutching at his throat. He stumbles up, falls, tries again to stand, then topples backward into the deep water below the ford. His hands slip from his throat, and he floats still for a moment before rolling over like an otter to slide downstream with the current.

Bierce steps to the sergeant, begins to say "I'm sorry," stops himself. It is pointless. The sergeant is dead and this is war. Accident within accident within accident of human frailty. All pointless.

There is a cheer from the bridge, the sound of a heavy infantry volley. "Our infantry," Jims says.

"Yes," Bierce says. "They made very good time."

Three miles upstream on the Murfreesboro Pike, the Confederate troopers guarding the bridge over Stewart's Creek are enjoying the restful hour after the midday meal when the 3rd Kentucky Union Volunteers come around the bend at the head of Wood's flying column. Brigadier General Milo Hascall screams at the regiment's colonel: "Don't deploy. Go for 'em in column!" The 3rd Kentucky, its colors still furled, bayonets unfixed, breaks into a run.

The Rebels have a 12-pounder Napoleon loaded with canister on the near side of the creek. The troopers scramble clear, and the gunner jerks the lanyard, sending a blast of canister straight into the face of the charging column. The 3rd Kentucky recoils, recovers, storms past the Napoleon, clubbing and shooting the fleeing cannoneers. Ahead, coal oil blazes up on a stack of railroad ties in the middle of the bridge. The Rebs rally on the far shore, shooting steadily as the blaze takes hold. But the Kentucky blood is up and the Third roars onto the bridge. Men tear apart the burning pile with their bare hands, heave the ties over the rail into the creek. They charge on, break onto the far shore, send the Rebel troopers fleeing.

Fifteen minutes later, General Tom Wood rides onto the bridge. Wood, who is not easily surprised, who has trained himself to react logically to the wild vagaries of his profession, is amazed. Bragg's army has ceded the best defensive ground west of Stones River with hardly a fight. He pauses at midstream, smoothes his mustache absently, wonders what Braxton Bragg has in mind.

Hascall rides onto the bridge from the far side. He shakes a fist in the air, ecstatic. "It's a splendid bridge, General. Every bit as fine as the one our Pioneers could build if we ever found the lazy bastards again."

Wood grins, which—like surprise—is a rarity for him. "Well done, Milo. You're right; it is a splendid bridge. Now if General Crittenden will give us permission, we'll go see what's over in that next line of trees."

☆ ☆ ☆

North of Triune, the rain finally washes away the fog in the early afternoon. McCook gives the order to advance and the skirmishers go forward again. But just as they are pushing Cleburne's rear guard across Nelson's Creek, a freezing wind shrieks out of the west, turning the rain to sleet. Visibility drops to a few feet in a matter of moments. Under the cover of the storm, the remaining Confederate infantry and artillery withdraw south. About 4:00 P.M., the wind and sleet abate enough for the blue skirmishers to resume the advance. The Reb cavalry fires a few shots, makes a mock dash at them, and then retreats. The day is gone, and McCook orders the corps into camp. It is very cold.

Rosecrans glares at the dark line of trees overlooking the fields on the far side of Stewart's Creek. "My God, Crittenden! Why didn't you get a brigade into those woods? We could have developed the Reb position, but you've squandered the light! Tomorrow it may take two divisions to cross that field. Daylight is precious, sir, as precious as blood! I told you that we must press them and press them and press them! And you have not. Learn to be a general, sir, because there can be no place for missed opportunities in this campaign or in this army."

Crittenden stares up at Rosecrans, mouth open in shock and hurt. "I'm sorry, General. I thought we'd done well and accomplished all that you assigned."

"Your men did superbly. You, sir, did not. Now they may pay with their blood for your failure. See that you make no error tomorrow! Garesché will send you orders." He spins his horse, dragging so hard on the reins that his gelding snorts with pain.

Crittenden watches him go, then walks, head down, to his mount. His staff looks away, embarrassed, for Tom Crittenden is liked if not respected.

Braxton Bragg climbs to the widow's walk two floors above his office to watch the columns marching into Murfreesboro through the winter dusk. Bragg should like to feel pride, perhaps even love for these cold, muddy, exhausted thousands. But he cannot, dare not, for only discipline keeps this army from becoming a mob. So he steels himself, watches critically. When a particularly bedraggled regiment passes, he orders his adjutant to send a sharp note to its colonel.

Of all the troops that pass, Cleburne's men hold ranks best, seem in the best spirits. Bragg does not entirely trust Cleburne. Oh, he is a good soldier, utterly reliable, but he is Hardee's creature. He should separate the two. After this battle is won, he will be able to do many things. Free himself of Hardee and Polk, at least. Breckinridge he will keep, discipline, force to submit.

He climbs down and returns to his office. Another courier from Wheeler waits. The Yankees have carried the bridges over Stewart's Creek. Bragg scowls. Once again Wheeler has let them win through too easily. Forrest, goddamn him, would have made the Yankees pay. Well, no great matter. Bragg's infantry has moved quickly, leaving him plenty of time to deploy. He reaches for a sheet of paper, dips pen in ink, and begins:

Memoranda for General and Staff officers:
1st. The line of battle will be in front of Murfreesboro, left wing, in front of Stones River, right wing in rear of the river.
2d. Polk's corps will form left wing, Hardee's corps, right wing.
3d. Withers's division will form first line in Polk's corps, Cheatham's the second. . . .

He writes on, his hand fluid, a picture of the dispositions clear in his mind. His guts gurgle steadily. He eructs, farts, plans death.

✮　✮　✮

Headquarters of the Army of the Cumberland has shifted again, this time to one of the few houses still standing in Lavergne.

Lieutenant Colonel Julius Gareschém pushes his spectacles up on his forehead, then takes them off and folds them carefully, remembering his wife's admonition to treat them gently. They are bottle-thick, so strong that at first they made him queasy, but Mariquitta has insisted that he must use them to save his sight. Garesché sighs. He has yet to write to her this week. And he must write, for she will know from the newspapers that the army is on the move. He must reassure her that chiefs of staff seldom see the enemy and are even more rarely in danger from them. Thirteen years an army wife and still a girl in so many ways. God, how he loves her, loves her with an intensity that still shakes him, for he had always thought himself meant to love only God.

"Colonel, would you like some coffee?"

Garesché looks up at the hovering orderly. "Thank you, Magee." He accepts the mug, gauges the amount of paperwork remaining, and decides he can afford a minute to rest. He leans back, closes his eyes, and sips from the hot mug.

To love only God. Had the family not fallen on hard times, he would have become a Jesuit. But the family already had one priest and could not afford two. So Julius Garesché went to West Point to become a soldier. He relished the spartan life at the Point, felt his spirit expand as his body hardened to the discipline. For a time, he was the only Catholic in the school. Yet he never pitied himself for the bigotry of his classmates, but welcomed it as a mortification granted by God for the good of his soul.

He graduated in 1842, receiving orders to the 4th Artillery at Sacket's Harbor on Lake Ontario. There he was visited by another recent graduate of West Point, First Lieutenant William S. Rosecrans. After some fumbling, the normally self-assured Rosecrans said, "Look, Garesché, I wanted to talk to you about your church."

Garesché felt his heart sink. To think that he'd supposed friendship when Rosecrans—obviously a new convert to some militant Protestantism—came only to try to turn him from the Faith. He sighed. "I am at peace with my course. I have no desire to attempt justifying—"

"No, no! I'm not trying to talk you out of anything. I'm thinking of . . . well, converting. It's going to play hell with my family back in Ohio, but I've been studying. Back at the Point, I always admired how you seemed so . . . well, so certain."

Forgive me, Father, Garesché prayed. I had forgotten how wonderful is Your grace. He smiled at Rosecrans. "I know very little, but you are welcome to whatever I can tell you."

Rosecrans was baptized in the Faith, and they began to correspond, eventually forming the Association in Honor of the Devotion to the Sacred

Heart among the Catholic officers of the army. When Rosecrans resigned from the army in 1854, they lost contact for a few years but not for want of affection.

From his first posting, Garesché was drawn by temperament and skill into staff work. He longed to test himself in action, but the closest he came to war was the dismal supply depot at Point Isabel, Texas, in the waning days of the war with Mexico. Home in St. Louis on leave in 1848, he considered resigning to enter the Church. Instead, at his mother's urging, he agreed to marry. The marriage was arranged according to the custom of French émigré families. Garesché again took leave and, feeling old at twenty-eight, returned to St. Louis to undertake the burdens of married life. To his surprise, he was enthralled by the teenage beauty his mother had found for him. And Mariquitta de Coudroy de Lauréal was equally taken with him.

The wedding was a blur, the wedding night a terror. In the bridal chamber, he stood hands behind his back, starched in his dress uniform, and confessed to a complete absence of experience and knowledge of the ways of married men and women. He had to this point in his life devoted himself to a quest for purity in soul and—

Standing near the bed, Mariquitta was seized by a paroxysm of laughter. He was concerned, then frightened as she sank to the floor, leaning back against the coverlet, clutching her stomach, hoop skirts ballooning about her. He knelt next to her, tried to calm her hysteria with apologies for his bluntness. She seized one of his hands, shook her head, finally managed to choke out that her sisters had prepared her in such exhaustive detail that she had been left more confused than ever by the entire subject. She has counted on him in his goodness, his gentleness, his wisdom. And now to find that he knows nothing? Oh, God, it is too ridiculous. They will have to call in her sisters, his brothers. Perhaps visit the stables to observe the animals.

They sat side by side, laughing until the tears came. Later, after a bottle of wine and much giggling over the advice received before the wedding, Julius and Mariquitta made love. And though they lacked the experience, they lacked nothing of the verve accorded begrudgingly by all the world to the French.

Mariquitta found army life hard. Point Isabel was desolate, the other army wives well-meaning but not of her breeding. Her first pregnancy threatened her physical and emotional stability. Reluctantly, Garesché sent her back to St. Louis. In 1850 she gave birth to their son, Julio, at her mother's house. When Garesché received news that both his wife and child were recovered and strong, he begged Mariquitta to join him at his new posting in Brownsville on the Rio Grande. She consented, but the child became ill on the journey and died within weeks of her arrival. Garesché blamed himself and, despite the counsel of the priest and the comforting of his wife, searched his soul for the sin for which God had exacted such terrible retribution.

As the years passed, Mariquitta spent more and more time at her mother's home, usually expecting another child. In all, they have four sons and four daughters. Three of the daughters live past infancy, only one of the sons. Garesché, although formally posted to Texas, served mostly on temporary duty in Washington. He wrote long, tender letters to Mariquitta, translated military texts from the French, wrote religious meditations, and took daily cold baths. During the long illness of his daughter Marie, he made a religious vow to read a chapter a day from St. Thomas à Kempis's *The Imitation of Christ*.

Finally, in 1855, he received a permanent transfer to Washington, where he was assigned to the assistant adjutant general's office. He brought Mariquitta and the children east and they settled into a blissful family life. Among the wives of staff officers, Mariquitta found convivial friends. Garesché rapidly became an all-but-indispensable part of the adjutant general's staff—so much so that when war came in 1861, his superiors would not hear of his transfer to the field. Garesché's workload doubled and then doubled again until he was weighed down to the point of collapse. The vow to read daily from *The Imitation of Christ* became a terrible burden. The print was minuscule and his eyesight failing. Yet he never missed a day. Rather, he drove himself even harder in matters of religious devotion. He skipped meals to attend mass, rose in the night to pray, visited the military hospitals nearly every evening, often staying until dawn to comfort a dying man. Mariquitta and the children do what they can for him, but Papa is a saint and, hence, beyond real comfort in his anguish.

Late one afternoon, beneath the sunlit window of a café near the War Department, he confessed to his brother Frederick, the priest, his presentiments of death.

Father Frederick smiled. "That hardly seems odd for a soldier. Why, I should think—"

"I am very serious, Frederick. Last week, when I was kneeling in St. Catherine's, a very old woman sat down in the pew behind me and spoke to me of death. I have seen her often at St. Catherine's and several other churches as well."

"Many of the old and destitute spend their days in our churches. It is a very hot summer and the stone churches are cool. The reverse happens in the first cold days of autumn when the stones are yet warm from the summer."

"Yes, yes, I know. But I don't think she comes for physical comfort. I think she is a very holy person."

"Well, I have no doubt seen her, too. Describe her."

"She has a short leg and a heavy shoe. She is always in black with a floriated crucifix pinned over her heart."

"Ah, yes. Rosamunde, we call her, although I'm not sure that is anything like her real name. She may be holy, but she is also more than a little simple."

Garesché studied the flute of red his nearly untouched wine glass cast on the white tablecloth between them. "But are not the simple more often than not chosen by God to speak for Him?"

"Julius—"

"She whispered: 'Beautiful soldier, you will die in your first battle. But fear not. You are but the lamb destined all your life for this.'"

Father Frederick blanched at Garesché's words. "Julius! Beware the sin of pride for your soul's sake! The Lamb of God is one and one only. Many men may be called on to sacrifice their lives in a great struggle such as this, but we dare not compare our paltry sacrifices to our Lord's."

"I make no comparisons, Frederick. I only repeat what she said. But if I am destined to die in this war, if that is God's will, am I not cheating God by remaining here in safety?"

"We all owe God a death, Julius. But if God means to have your life in this war, the time and the manner should be, *must* be, His. It is wrong for you to attempt to predict or to arrange or even to wonder on the circumstances. For He may choose *not* to take you in this war."

"But if—"

"No, Julius. Listen. It is prideful for you to interpret the superstitious babblings of a half-crazed old woman as the revealed word of God. You have been working very hard and perhaps you dozed for a moment and only imagined her words. It may be that all your so-called presentiments are but the imaginings of a fatigued mind, mere fumes of an overwrought fancy. Now finish your wine and then go home to Mariquitta and the children without stopping at St. Catherine's or at any of the hospitals. I want you to eat well, to spend a little time appreciating the many blessings God has given you in your home, and then I want you to go to bed for a full night's sleep. Tomorrow, if you care to, you can come by and we will talk further of presentiments, but no more today. I order you to do this both as your older brother and as your priest."

Garesché did not reply but sat staring at the reflection of the wine on the white tablecloth, the flute of red turned to an amorphous splash by some trick of the late afternoon light.

CHAPTER 5

Sunday
December 28, 1862
Nolensville, Tennessee

Rosecrans decides against sending Crittenden across Stewart's Creek in force until the army has had a day to rest. McCook has orders to send a brigade to determine Hardee's location. Otherwise, the Army of the Cumberland will rest on the Sabbath. At Murfreesboro, Bragg continues to draw his army together, posting its elements along Stones River northwest of town.

EORGE THOMAS SOMETIMES wonders if he is fated to for-ever follow roads broken and rutted by other men. For two days, his corps has struggled south and then east along roads ground to a clinging paste by the passage of McCook's corps. The mud has mired cannons and wagons to their hubs and killed many a good army mule with exhaustion. Yet the men have managed. Negley's division has reached Stewartsboro behind Crittenden's right flank, while Rousseau's division has labored into Nolensville behind McCook's left.

He would not have hesitated to advance on the Sabbath. But Rosecrans commands, and Thomas will not gainsay him. In the fierce competition among generals, Thomas is one of the few who will not conspire against his superiors, manipulate congressmen, or spread rumors in the press. Not that he is without ambition. He was bitterly disappointed not to receive com-mand of the army when Buell was dismissed. But at least the job went to Rosecrans, whom he likes and respects.

Thomas remembers Rosecrans from West Point: an ebullient, confident boy with an easy charm and a casual irreverence toward the protocol of the institution. Thomas, older by several years than most of the cadets, felt no particular reverence for protocol either, and was frequently the confidant and advisor of younger boys. (It was they who gave him the nickname "Pap.") Yet he was taken aback on first overhearing Rosecrans call him "General Washington." He called Rosecrans into the hall.

Rosecrans, still a plebe, came to an easy attention. "Yes, sir?"

"Am I mistaken, Mr. Rosecrans, or did I hear you call me 'General Washington'?"

"No, sir. You were not mistaken."

Thomas ponders. "Why, may I ask?"

"It is your dignity, sir. Your *gravitas*."

"Ah. You find me ponderous."

"Not at all, sir. I spoke in respect."

Thomas studied Rosecrans. "Very well, then. I acknowledge the compliment, however undeserved. I would suggest, though, that other upperclassmen might take less kindly to nicknames."

"I understand, sir. Thank you, sir."

Thomas kept an amused eye on Rosecrans in the next year, grew to like him when he saw that Rosecrans, though sometimes thoughtless, was never malicious. They became friendly, even friends, though Thomas permitted few of these in his life. In the spring of 1840, Thomas's last year, Rosecrans and three other cadets came to the door of the cramped private room granted to Thomas as a cadet officer. Thomas looked up from the artillery text he was reading. "Pap," Rosecrans said, "we want to know the story."

Thomas guessed, of course, what Rosecrans meant, but evaded anyway. "What story is that?"

"About Nat Turner, Pap."

"That was almost ten years ago. Why should you want to know about a dead darky?"

"Because you'll be gone next month, and no one will ever know the truth about you and him."

"Rumors are always more exciting than facts. Enjoy them."

"Come on, Pap. You've got to tell sometime."

He did not have to tell, cared not at all what stories were told about him. He remembered too well Nat Turner's rebellion, sometimes woke sweating with the memories. Yet Rosecrans was not easy to refuse. Thomas hesitated, then closed the text and gestured for the boys to find places. Rosecrans perched on a corner of the desk. Harvey Hill, dark, brilliant, impatient, took the foot of the cot. Earl Van Dorn, cocksure, romantic, leaned elaborately against the doorjamb. But try as he might, Thomas cannot, twenty years later, summon the face of the fourth boy, who slipped into the corner farthest from the light. Yet Thomas has the disturbing sense that it was Grant—quiet, watchful, gauging.

Thomas told the story methodically, without emotion or circumlocution. He was fourteen when Turner's men came over the hill drunk, wild, waving muskets, machetes, and a flag hacked from the bloody dress of a white woman. The house slaves, Miriam and Tobias, rushed Thomas, his mother, and sisters out the back of the big house and across the fields to the woods. From there they watched as Turner's hellions surrounded the house, smashing the windows, taunting, cursing, yelling for the white folk to come out to meet Judgment. "Miz Thomas, we's got to go," Tobias pleaded. "Ain't no good stayin'."

Thomas's mother said nothing, her face set with the quiet fierceness Thomas had seen as a little boy when she'd set off for the barn, fowling piece in the crook of her arm, to chase off a peddler who had abused one of the slave girls. He feared that she might decide to confront Nat Turner, demand that he and his riffraff drop their weapons and sit quietly by the well to wait for the sheriff. "All right," she said. "Miriam, you take one of the girls, I'll take the other. Tobias, you lead the way. George, go warn as many of the neighbors as you can. We'll be all right."

On the backtrack of Turner's march, Thomas found terrible things: people disemboweled, decapitated, hacked limb from limb. A young matron he had seen at church with her husband and infant daughter lay naked in a furrowed field, her torso ripped from pubic bone to throat, her guts spilling on the ground—the first naked woman he had ever seen. He went to investigate the house, heart hammering, bowels loose so that he had to stop to empty them before climbing the porch.

It was still inside, save for the lazy buzzing of flies and the rustle of a breeze in the curtains of the smashed parlor windows. A long gash of blood ran down the hall to the back porch where the headless body of the young husband lay jackknifed over the steps. Thomas searched for the baby, moving deliberately from room to room, though his fear screamed at him to run, to hide. Upstairs, he looked in closets, chests, and under the beds. No baby, and the rest of his life he will periodically dream of making the search, of pursuing down long corridors of nightmare the cries of an abandoned, invisible child.

Night found him hunkered in a swamp. He had warned a dozen farms and plantations by that time and had been lent a horse—a spavined, disconsolate creature that stood, head drooping, hooves slowly sinking into the muck, as if it would accept with equanimity being swallowed entirely. Thomas squatted, clutching the blacksmith's hammer he had carried since leaving the plantation where the baby is forever missing. The sky of Southampton County glowed orange with the flames of burning houses and barns. About him, insects of all the innumerable species of the South buzzed, sang, chirruped, chittered, rasped, and bit. He listened for snakes feeding on the insects and frogs, knowing that they were there and that they were likewise aware of him, of the man-heat, of the squatting mammalian reality of him. Thomas pondered his fear, pondered the ways of serpents and insects, men and societies.

He continued his circuit of the neighborhood through the next day. By then, most of the holdings were abandoned or strongly defended. He refused offers of shelter and kept moving. In midafternoon, he found his mother and sisters safe at a cousin's plantation. That night, he camped with a party of enraged town and country men hunting Turner's gang. To his surprise, he found himself a hero: the stalwart youngster who, refusing all offers of safe haven, had spread the alarm through a countryside crawling with murderous niggers. Thomas tried to tell them that the few slaves he had come across all begged him to say that they were good and true niggers who knew nothing of Nat's craziness. But this was interpreted as modesty, only further increasing his reputation for courage beyond his years.

He took no part in the hunting of the rebels over the next few days, nor the eventual capture of Nat Turner six weeks later. He did not attend the trial, nor did he go to the execution of Turner and his principal lieutenant. Instead, he returned to his studies and his responsibilities about the plantation. The story that Andrew Jackson personally presented him with an appointment to West Point is utter nonsense.

Rosecrans looked crestfallen. "I thought you just held onto it until you were older."

Thomas shook his head. "No, I received my appointment from my congressman, same as most."

Rosecrans mused on this disappointment. "But you did know old Nat Turner?"

"Yes, everyone in the neighborhood did. He wasn't very old, only about thirty."

"How did you know him?"

"He delivered things, he preached to the darkies, he was a fine carpenter. His owner used to rent him out to build things. He was about as free as a darky could be who didn't have his papers."

"Did you ever speak to him?"

"Of course."

"What did he say?"

Thomas shrugged. "He said 'good morning' when I said 'good morning.' Or 'good afternoon' when I said 'good afternoon.' He was always friendly, polite."

"Well, what made him do it then?"

"I wouldn't know. Perhaps he was crazy, though he never seemed so to me. Hill probably has a better explanation."

Harvey Hill sucked at his unlit pipe. "I imagine he felt wronged. He had some education I understand, could read and write. A slave with those talents is likely to feel himself wronged."

There was a silence, for they all knew that they were treading close to a subject taboo at West Point. Thomas considered telling them what he learned that night in the swamp with the insects, snakes, and the old disconsolate horse: that constancy must come before courage. Must, indeed, come before all virtues. For without it, all men, all systems, all nations fall into chaos. He has seen the sky turned red with fire, and he dreads revolt, rebellion, revolution. That is why he holds to constancy before all else, knows that it will carry him through, will carry his nation through if people choose aright.

But he did not tell them for fear that he would not find the words, that he would make constancy sound as ponderous as he sometimes felt among those as quick and facile as Rosecrans, Hill, and Van Dorn.

He graduated that spring, twelfth in his class, and took his constancy and his *gravitas* to the artillery. He fought Seminoles in Florida and Mexicans at Monterey and Buena Vista, where he served under Braxton Bragg. Except for a pleasant tour as an instructor of artillery at West Point, where Sheridan, McCook, and Stanley were among his students, he spent the next decade in a succession of dismal posts in Florida and on the frontier. He alleviated the boredom by becoming a skilled botanist and geologist, frequently sending samples to the Smithsonian. For the last few years before the war, he was a major with the 2nd Cavalry, where he became close friends with Lieutenant Colonel Robert E. Lee. They fought Comanches. In one skirmish, Thomas was struck in the face by an arrow. To cover the disfiguring scar, he grew a beard, which came in peppered with iron.

In 1861, though his family pleaded, threatened, and eventually declared him pariah, Major George Henry Thomas remained faithful to the Union. His sisters turned his portrait to the wall, vowing that they would never speak of him again. They will keep the promise the rest of their long lives.

Many West Pointers chose to go South: Bragg, both Johnstons, Lee, Beauregard, both Hills, Hardee, Longstreet, and so many more. Thomas claimed no moral superiority, felt only the great tragedy of inconstancy.

He won one of the first battles of the war at Mill Springs, turning back a Rebel attempt to invade Kentucky, fought in the second day at Shiloh and during the siege of Corinth. Before Perryville, he was offered command of the Army of the Ohio by an administration tired of Buell's delays. He refused, unwilling to disgrace a general he respected on the eve of battle. But at Perryville, Thomas had an unaccustomed lapse, misreading the situation and failing to urge Buell into the timely attack that might have destroyed Bragg's army. When Bragg escaped across the Cumberlands, Buell was relieved by the administration, Rosecrans appointed in his place instead of Thomas. Briefly, Thomas considered resigning, but Rosecrans was quick to placate him, consulting him on all important decisions. Altogether, Thomas wishes Rosecrans talked less and listened more. Yet Rosecrans is a good man. Should he falter, Thomas will brace him. Should he tumble, Thomas will lift him up. Thomas will be constant. And if, in the end, this means he must always follow behind other men, so be it. He will do his part in the march.

At Nolensville on this Sunday at the butt end of 1862, Thomas eats his breakfast alone before the parlor fire in the house commandeered for his headquarters. Two of the stray dogs he has rescued lie at his feet, wondering at the warmth of the fire. Thomas's menagerie includes several dogs, half a dozen cats, a donkey, a trio of motley ducks, and a large, ill-tempered goose.

Finished with his meal, Thomas smokes half a cigar and then goes out to check the weather. The goose greets him at the door, honking at the dogs, who make a quick detour around it. Thomas produces a dozen kernels of corn from a pocket and scatters them for the goose, who efficiently scoops them up before waddling after Thomas.

A pair of orderlies watch the goose with open malevolence. They were among the half dozen soldiers who originally liberated the goose from a farm a week after Perryville. They carried it by the feet to camp where one of them made the mistake of setting the goose upright. With two snake-quick strikes of its bill, it was free, flapping away on clipped wings and churning feet. In moments the camp was a furor as a hundred men took up the chase, all intent on a goose dinner. Thomas was in his tent, writing a report on the recent battle—a task that had already put him in a savage mood—when the uproar disturbed him. He threw down his pen and stormed out of the door. He was greeted by a white bombshell of feathers and beating wings coming straight for his chest. But a man who withstood Mexican cavalry charges on the windy desert plateau of Buena Vista meets such challenges with stern courage. Thomas braced himself and received the flapping bird with both arms. The goose dealt Thomas two or three stout blows with its wings then, sensing a friend, settled into his arms and honked at its pursuers. Thomas glowered at the circle of soldiers struck motionless, clubs and frying pans brandished. He has never been a man of facility with words, can produce no ready witticism that might make the moment into a folk story forever endearing to soldiers, press, and civilians. "You heard the beast. Dismissed!" he thundered, turned on his heel, and marched back into his tent, new pet in his arms.

So, these two months later, the orderlies can only watch, mourning the feast never enjoyed, as goose and general stand together, inspecting the weather.

✯ ✯ ✯

Captain Horace Fisher of McCook's staff steadies his horse and surveys the row of downcast farmers. They are mostly old men and adolescent boys, though two seem of an age and fitness to be soldiers. Fisher suspects that these two are deserters, perhaps even spies. He points them out to his burly first sergeant, who pulls them out of line and hustles them away to be questioned—beaten if necessary—for whatever they know of the Rebs.

Fisher clears his throat, introduces himself. He keeps his voice civilized, unbullying. "You men have been brought here to serve as guides for the advance of this brigade. Two of you will go with the cavalry escort, the rest will march in the front rank. If any of you attempts to flee, he will be shot and his farm burned. If any of you fails to warn a Federal officer of trouble ahead, he and another man will be shot and their farms burned. If any of you directs this command down a wrong road or in any other way gives false information, he and another man will be shot and their farms burned. If this command suffers casualties that in my judgment could have been averted by any of you, I will have you all shot and your bodies left by the road for your families to collect. And, of course, I will also order all your farms burned."

He swings his horse away, trots to where Brigadier General August Willich has his brigade drawn up. Willich regards him with disgust. "Vell, have you frightened the bejabbers out of those men?"

Fisher salutes casually. "Yes, General. In this part of Tennessee, the natives aren't likely to be well disposed toward us."

Willich snorts. "They are poor farmers. And like poor farmers everywhere, they are most disposed to stay out of the way of all armies. Come.
We must be about General McCook's orders."

The brigade moves out, the cavalry pushing ahead through the corridor
of dripping cedars. The infantry follows, cursing the mud and the easy-liv-
ing troopers. Fisher rides near Willich, studying the old man who was a
Prussian officer before Fisher was born. Willich's appearance belies his legendary reputation in the Army of the Cumberland. He might, Fisher thinks,
be a grocer or a butcher except for the eyes. The eyes are dark, piercing, the
eyes of a dangerous man, a true believer.

August von Willich was born a *Junker.* A lieutenant at eighteen, a captain at twenty-one, he seemed destined to wear a general's epaulets. But at
thirty, Willich quit the army, dropped the "von" from his name, and became
a communist. The rebellions of 1848 gave Willich a sudden, heady vision of
the future. But the uprisings were mere street bombs, scattering a few cob-
bles and killing a few passers-by while hardly shivering the foundations of
the old order. The armies dispersed the rebels, posted the guards, and drew
up the firing squads.

Willich fled Germany for the New World, settling in the German enclave
in Cincinnati, where he opened a German-language paper for the workers.
For Willich and the other Forty-Eighters, the South's secession was simply
another attempt by a ruling class to maintain its power. They enlisted in
droves. Willich trained a regiment that fought with ferocious discipline at
Shiloh and Perryville. The regiment's performance won its commander a star
and command of First Brigade, Second Division, McCook's corps. Yet to
Fisher, Willich looks old and gray riding in the cold winter rain. Soon, Fisher
thinks, these old men must give way to younger men—men of Fisher's age.
Such is history. And what communist can argue with history?

Through the morning, the infantry plods along in the mud. The cavalry
sends back a trickle of Rebel stragglers. Fisher questions them, alert that
some may be spies. Those he particularly suspects he dispatches with Sergeant Wilson for further, less polite interrogation. Meanwhile, he inspects
captured haversacks for evidence of the number of days' rations carried by
Hardee's men, quizzes the cavalry on the condition of the roads ahead, and
presses the close-lipped farmers for more information on the country. By
noon, he is satisfied: Hardee has turned east on the Salem Turnpike for
Murfreesboro. He communicates this to Willich, who nods and gives the
order for the brigade to halt. He will let the soldiers boil coffee to go with
their noon rations and then move on to Eagleville.

Fisher glances at the bedraggled farmers, who have slumped in a knot by the road. "What do you plan to do with our guides?" he asks Willich.

"Your hostages, you mean," Willich replies.

Fisher shrugs. "They're yours now, General. I'm off to report to General McCook. Wilson! Mount up."

Willich watches Fisher ride off, shakes his head. He knows the type. Prussian, Hanoverian, Austrian, Italian, French, American, it makes no difference. The educated thug. He turns to an aide. "Find those men some rations and something hot to drink. There is no sense in making them our enemies forever." He rides over, dismounts, goes among them, shaking hands, inquiring of their health. They are unwilling to talk at first, but because Willich is emphatically who he is and nothing else, they inevitably warm to him, answer his questions, even smile.

✷ ✷ ✷

Hardee is livid when he storms into Polk's headquarters. He slams a copy of Bragg's order of battle on the table, making plates and silverware jump and nearly overturning the Bishop's glass of wine. But Polk, with the grace not unusual in fat men comfortable with their bulk, sweeps the glass up a heartbeat before Hardee's fist lands to rattle the rest of the Bishop's Sunday dinner.

"Have you seen this—this abortion of a plan?" Hardee snarls. "He is going to split the army in two at the river! Hasn't the man read a single text? Rosecrans will gobble us down in pieces. It will be Cannae. Jena. Austerlitz! Bragg is a fool, an absolute goddamned fool!"

The Bishop shakes a finger, eyes smiling over the rim of his wine glass. "Now, Bill, remember your language and my position. Take a chair. Calm yourself. Have some wine."

"I beg your pardon, Bishop. I forget myself. But have you seen this. . . ." He snatches up the order of battle, shakes it, words failing.

"Of course I've seen it. And though I have never written a book on tactics, I have read a few. Even yours. I recognize the errors."

"But what are we going to do?"

"Do? What can we do but fight according to the order of battle? He is the commanding general."

Hardee slumps in his chair. "Better that you were."

"Or you. We are agreed on that, but his excellency President Davis is not."

"This time we may not get away. Rosecrans is smarter and more dangerous than Buell. And he has Thomas commanding the center. Old Slow Trot won't allow another Perryville."

"Oh, I don't worry about Thomas. Thomas is a plodder."

"Can we wire the president? Tell him that the army faces annihilation because of this insane plan?"

Polk purses his lips. "The president is a dear friend of mine. And I know he has warm feelings for you. But General Bragg is no stranger to the president's affections, either."

"But this plan—"

"Bill, I think you are making too much of the splitting of the army. The river is not deep. We will be able to support each other."

"It's a terrible plan. It violates all the rules."

"I agree, Bill, I agree. Yet armies have survived worse. Usually, though, generals do not."

Hardee frowns. "Are you suggesting that Bragg will not?"

Polk shrugs. "Well, as you said, it is a mad plan. And since General Bragg seems to have the constitution of a horse for all his complaints, I think that evidence of madness may be what we need if you or I—and God forbid the latter—are ever to command this army."

Hardee studies Polk. "I am always amazed, Bishop, at exactly how devious you are."

Polk lifts his palms in mock modesty. "You are too kind, Bill. It is, of course, a pity that the army may suffer from General Bragg's disadvantageous positioning of its elements, but what can we do? We are soldiers involved in two battles, and we must take opportunities as they come."

"Still, if the president saw the order of battle—"

"He would do nothing."

Hardee sighs. "I suppose you're right."

"I am, Bill. I fear that I am. Now let us do our duty by following the commanding general's orders insofar as we are able. We'll leave the rest to God and then draw off the army when the battle's over."

"Yes, we retreat exceedingly well."

"Do we? I always thought we did it rather ill-temperedly. But be patient, Bill. Our day will come. Trust in God. Now have some refreshment."

Hardee looks at the laden table. "Well, if there is enough for two."

"If there isn't, we shall send for more."

Hardee would go on talking of Bragg, but Polk—always mindful of his digestion—insists on talking of other generals. Fortunately, Hardee is a wonderful gossip and, once distracted from his beloved tactics, can produce almost endless anecdotes, rumors, and slanders.

The afternoon is well advanced when Hardee, complexion reddened by a bottle of burgundy and three glasses of port, goes to check on his corps. Polk calls for brandy and coffee, settles back to contemplate. Trust in God, he thinks. Well, he supposes he believes in God occasionally, though the question has not troubled him much in many years. He is, after all, a bishop, and princes of the Church must serve the Church first, God as an afterthought. Hardee says he is devious. But is not God devious? Witness the death and destruction of war. Are the faithful to believe that it is part of the Divine Plan that young men should die in the most ugly, fantastic, painful ways: disemboweled, castrated, decapitated, impaled, blown to bits? Yes, for God is most devious. And so must his ministers be.

Along Stewart's Creek, Union and Confederate skirmishers exchange occasional shots in the last of the afternoon's light. The firing is mostly out of boredom, and when the sun goes down, they cease by common consent and begin calling back and forth. A Union officer records one exchange:

> Rebel: "What command does you-ens belong to?"
> Federal: "Fifteenth Indiana."
> Rebel: "Who commands yer brigade?"
> Federal: "Colonel Wagner. What is your command?"
> Rebel: "We ar Wheeler's; an' I believe you-ens are the fellers we fit at Dobbins' Ferry."
> Federal: "You bet we are! What did you think of us?"
> Rebel: "Darned good marksmen; but whar yer fellers tryin' to go ter?"
> Federal: "To Murfreesboro."
> Rebel: "Well, you-ens 'll find that ar a mighty bloody job, sho."

CHAPTER 6

Monday
December 29, 1862
Stewart's Creek, Tennessee

Bragg has decided to fight close to Murfreesboro, deploying his army on either side of a bend in Stones River. But Rosecrans worries that the Rebel army may be lying under the cover of the woods below Stewart's Creek. He orders a crossing in heavy force by Crittenden's three divisions and Negley's division of Thomas's corps. Thomas's other division, under Major General Lovell Rousseau, is designated as the army reserve.

MAJOR GENERAL THOMAS LEONIDAS CRITTENDEN has his corps awake at two in the morning and under arms by four, in lines by division: Palmer, Wood, and Van Cleve. In all, nearly thirteen thousand men stand poised along the west side of Stewart's Creek for an assault at first light. But as every common soldier in every century knows, hasty mustering is almost always followed by interminable waiting.

The day dawns clear and cold. The fields on the far side of the creek lie white with hoarfrost and empty of Reb skirmishers. Crittenden feels his gut tighten as he imagines the thousands of butternut infantry hidden in the woods. He gulps coffee laced with whiskey. It does no good, and despite his fear that Rosecrans will arrive any minute demanding to know why the assault is not underway, Crittenden loses his nerve. He orders a battery brought forward to shell the woods while the shivering infantrymen wait, stomachs growling.

The order to the battery is fumbled and, when finally received, executed with dismaying clumsiness. The guns finally open at nine-thirty with a mix of solid shot and shrapnel. Everyone along the Union line waits for counter-battery fire. Finally, a puff of smoke plumes from the woods. Three more Rebel guns fire in ragged succession along the tree line. Their shots are well short. Three of the cannonballs bounce a time or two before burying themselves in the wet field. The fourth hits a rock, rebounding absurdly high—an iron-black point traveling a steep parabola against the blue—before becoming suddenly large in its plunge earthward. It hits the creek, throwing up a freezing geyser that douses two dozen men and sets off a wave of jeers and laughter from the rest of the front rank.

Generals Palmer and Wood ignore the scene, concentrate instead on the line of woods. Wood snorts. "That's just horse artillery. There's hardly anything there except some cavalry."

John Palmer, big, gray-bearded, a Kentucky politician turned solid soldier, growls, "Then, for God's sake, let's get across before they change their minds and bring up infantry."

Wood hurries to Crittenden and advises him to order an immediate advance. But Crittenden hesitates, torn between his fear of Rosecrans and his dread of the gray multitude he still imagines in the woods. "A few more minutes, General Wood. Just to be sure."

"I'll tell General Palmer he's to advance in ten minutes."

Crittenden gulps coffee and whiskey. "Yes, ten minutes."

Palmer's men plunge into the freezing, testicle-clenching cold of the creek, wade across, Springfields and cartridge boxes held high, and scramble up the far bank. The line rolls across the fields toward the woods. Fighting Joe Wheeler stands, arms folded, watching them come. He has promised Bragg that he will delay the Yankee descent on Murfreesboro, but there is no way he can stop this blue wave. Not when Bragg won't give him infantry to back up his troopers. Not when his artillery is a pathetic collection of ancient smoothbores that the Yankees can pulverize with their rifled Parrott guns. Not when his own goddamn men keep falling asleep and letting the Yankees steal the march. Those bridges! Both of them should have been fired. Simplest thing in the world, and it would have taken the Yankees the better part of a day to rebuild them for their wagons and guns. Goddamn it, anyway!

"General, they're pretty close to killin' range. Want that we give 'em a little bit of a welcome?"

Wheeler ignores the bearded major by his side. Waits. Thirty more yards. Make it count. "All right, Major. One volley, and then pull back to the position I showed you this morning."

"Yes, sir."

Wheeler takes his own carbine, rests it in the fork of a small tree, and picks out a color bearer at the center of the leftmost brigade. The sound of his shot is lost amid the volley as the major screams: "Fire." The color bearer lurches forward, but the flag hardly falters as another member of the color guard grabs the staff. One less of the bastards, Wheeler thinks. He has killed many, doesn't bother to count.

A volley from a Yankee brigade rips into the woods, but already Wheeler's troopers are scuttling back through the underbrush toward their mounts. Wheeler follows, the anger making him stiff-legged so that he appears more the banty cock than ever.

Crittenden watches his lines sweep into the trees, blue uniforms blending into the shadows so that definition is lost and the forward ranks fuse into a blue-black undulation against the dark green of the cedars. And still there is no blast of hidden cannons, no sudden sparkle of ten thousand rifle-muskets speaking at once to break the beautiful wave. He sweeps his hat in the air, shouts "Hurrah!" His staff is caught off guard, looks at him curiously. A few attempt to cheer but the sound is self-conscious. Crittenden hastily claps hat to head and spurs across the bridge onto the field.

After the long delay, Crittenden's corps advances rapidly, crossing a second creek in early afternoon. General Palmer gestures to a young staff lieutenant. "Take a dispatch for the general commanding: 'We are across. . . .'"

Palmer pauses, waits impatiently while the young man fumbles a dispatch book open and scribbles: *To the Commanding General. We are across.* . . . Up ahead, a Rebel cannon fires from a copse of trees, the shell flying long so that it lands harmlessly between the last rank of Palmer's division and the first rank of Wood's. But the lieutenant has never been under fire before this morning, and when the shell explodes with a *whump* a hundred feet behind him, the pencil point snaps in his shaking fingers.

Palmer doesn't notice, continues dictating: ". . . Overall Creek in good order, the Rebel cavalry retreating before us." (The lieutenant concentrates, swearing that he will remember every word.) "We have the river on our left and will push ahead within sight of the town if possible. Palmer. Got that?"

"Yes, sir."

"Good. And, son, be ready next time."

"Yes, sir."

Palmer rides ahead. The lieutenant finds another pencil in his dispatch pouch, writes quickly: *The creek in good order. We are within sight of the town and pushing ahead.* He hesitates. There seemed to be more, but he cannot quite remember what. Oh, yes. He adds: *The enemy is retreating.* There, that was the gist of it at least. He signs Palmer's name and then digs out his watch. He labels the message precisely 3:00 P.M. and then sets off for General Rosecrans's headquarters. En route, he passes General Crittenden and his staff and wonders why Palmer has not sent the message to the general commanding the corps instead of the commanding general, which would seem to be, in the lieutenant's very limited experience in the intricacies of the chain of command, the proper manner of doing things. But the lieutenant is but a month away from his father's law office in Indianapolis, and he is not about to second-guess a general.

Rosecrans has established temporary headquarters at the hamlet of Stewartsboro. Sunshine has made the afternoon pleasant and he sits in a rocker on the porch, watching Rousseau's division of Thomas's corps marching down the Old Liberty Road. He reads Palmer's puzzling message a second time. "Let's see the map."

A pair of aides unroll a large field map and stand holding its edges as the general and the chief of staff study it. "What time did you say Crittenden got off?" Rosecrans asks Garesché.

"Not until about ten-thirty, General. He decided to prepare his advance with artillery fire. He sent an apologetic note for the late start."

Rosecrans snorts. "Well, I will have to address General Crittenden's tardiness at a later date. But Palmer says he already has the town in sight. That's a long way to advance in four and a half hours. They must not be meeting any resistance."

"So it would appear."

"And he says 'The enemy is retreating.' Does he really mean that Bragg is abandoning Murfreesboro?"

"I can imagine no other interpretation, General."

"Where's the man who brought the dispatch?"

They look about. A staff captain clears his throat. "He rode off the way he came, sir. Must not have known to stay until released."

Rosecrans shakes his head. For a moment he ponders, chewing on his cigar. "All right, then. Tell Crittenden to push a division into town. Then

send word to Stanley that his cavalry is going to have fat pickings south of
Murfreesboro. For once we'll have a chance to tear up the Reb trains instead
of defending our own."

"Yes, General," Garesché says. He glances at Major Goddard, who is
already scribbling notes.

Rosecrans cups a lucifer, gets the cigar going again. "I really thought old
Bragg would fight. Why else would he bring Hardee in from Triune? Well,
we'll follow along and see what he's got in mind." He rises, working the fingers of his fire-scarred hands to stretch the skin; a habit Garesché has
observed often when Rosecrans is deep in thought. "All right, Julius, I'll give
you an hour to badger me with paperwork. Then I'll ride to the front to see
how Crittenden is getting on."

★ ★ ★

Major General Alexander McDowell McCook is feeling poorly. Not physically, of course, since he is and always has been healthy as a horse. Rather,
his confidence is out of fettle. Try as he might, he cannot stop brooding over
the accidental casualties in the fog north of Triune. All his life, his ambitions
have fallen victim to his impetuosity, his thoughtlessness, his downright stupidity. He can still hear his father raging over the broken windows, overturned buckets, bumped and bleeding brothers and cousins. "By Old
Thunder, Alex, can you never learn? All the gods of the Pantheon must be
struck dumb by the incessant obtuseness of my son!" Here he rapped Alex
on the forehead. "There must be some semblance of a brain here, since you
manage to move, breathe, consume nourishment, belch, and defecate. But
I will be goddamned if I can detect thought of more than bestial complex-
ity. Go cut a switch, boy. Cut two. It seems we have work to do in the
woodshed."

Alex never resented the switchings, knowing how certainly they were
deserved. Besides, Old Dan McCook never laid on heavily, for he was more
bluster than bully. Alex vowed each time that he would learn judgment. But
then at fifteen he killed Hannah, Old Dan's favorite horse.

He'd led her down the lane at dawn past the sleeping edge of the village and then, as the sun crested the green Ohio hills, mounted and run her
across fields shining with dew and the webs of night-spinning spiders until
the breaths of horse and boy streamed back in clouds of jubilation. And
though he knew Hannah was a wonderful horse, knew that she was proud
and loyal, he also knew that she was no great jumper, never had been,
and was even less so in these years on the far side of her prime. Knew all

this, but launched her anyway at the ditch. Ever so politely she shied, tried to tell him that it was too wide, but he kept her head straight, dug his heels into her flanks, bent low over her neck, told her that they could make it for they were in this hour unconquerable. And they leaped, horse and boy, soaring against dawn sky and summer hillside.

He heard no snap when they landed. He stood in the stirrups, pumped his fist in the air, and shouted his triumph. And he thought that Hannah tossed her head in like victory over fear, age, and the simple width of a ditch. Then she was stumbling, barely able to keep her legs. He dismounted, felt along her right foreleg, up the cannon to the knee. He could not feel the break but his fingers sensed something askew beneath the quivering muscles. Perhaps she has only twisted the joint, he thought. But even at fifteen some deep discouragement with his luck overcame Alex McCook in this moment, told him that her injury must inevitably be serious. He led her home over the green hills to the farm to tell his father.

Old Dan McCook, the patriarch who would go to war fifteen years later as a paymaster colonel while his son Alexander commanded a corps, came from his breakfast in shirtsleeves. He knelt in the road and grimly examined the mare's foreleg. In a moment, he stood, spoke quietly. "Get my pistol, Alex."

"Papa, it can't be so bad. We should send for Doc Evans. Ask—"

"Alex, get my pistol. Do it now."

By the time he came back, the family had assembled on the porch. The McCooks, male and female, were rarely a silent lot, for they brimmed, each and all, with a eupeptic confidence in the good fortune each day must bring the clan. But they were silent now. Alex tried again. "Papa, can't we—"

"Shoot her, Alex. Get it over with and then we'll talk."

"I can't."

"Then I shall. But if you are ever to be a man worthy of the name McCook, you must do it."

So Alex McCook placed the barrel of the pistol beneath Hannah's ear and, sobbing his apologies, shot her through the brain. Afterward, Old Dan locked himself in his study for the rest of the morning. He came out in early afternoon to eat his lunch and to hand Alex the letter he had composed to the district congressman, requesting an appointment to West Point for his son.

Because of the McCooks' formidable political power, there was never a doubt that Alex would receive the appointment. His going was not a punishment, but an admission by Old Dan that he could not teach this son the judgment the others had demonstrated almost from the cradle. No, in Alex's case, it would take the discipline of the military life. It took Alex McCook five years and the considerable forbearance of his instructors to graduate from West Point. But once commissioned he proved a reliable enough officer. He was popular with his enlisted men, even more popular with his cadets when he returned to West Point as a tactics instructor. He winked at their petty violations of the rules of conduct, never managed to catch anyone sneaking off for a drink at Benny Haven's tavern. War came, and he was quickly a brigade colonel, which was fine, a post he felt well suited to fill. But then, because Old Dan is who Old Dan is, Alex McCook was made a general. And he wishes he wasn't. It terrifies him to command so many men, their lives like water cupped in his shaking hands. But he is a McCook and must not falter.

McCook's corps leaves the Nolensville Turnpike to advance east along Bole Jack Road toward Murfreesboro. Ahead a few miles, the narrow, muddy road will widen into the Wilkinson Pike, but for the moment, it is slow going for the men and particularly for the artillery and wagons. Colonel Lewis Zahm's three regiments of Ohio cavalry screen the advance. The skirmishing begins almost at once, Zahm's brigade breaking through the Rebel vedettes and then fending off probes by Brigadier General John Wharton's gray troopers.

The skirmishing continues into the afternoon along a two-mile front. It is discouraging, this leaking away of lives. The sun seems to hang in the sky, the afternoon interminable. Finally, when the shadows begin to lengthen, the firing eases, and Zahm sends back word that the Rebs have withdrawn to the east side of Overall Creek. McCook turns to Brigadier General Jefferson C. Davis. "We'll bivouac on this side of the creek."

Davis, the slayer of Bull Nelson, argues. "We should push across so they can't—"

"No, Jeff. We have done well enough for today. Let the men have an hour of daylight to start their fires and cook their suppers."

At 4:30 P.M., Davis's division makes camp to the right of the turnpike on the west bank of Overall Creek. An hour later, McCook receives a message signed by Garesché: He is to advance until his left flank comes in contact with Negley's right so that the army will present a continuous front from the Franklin Pike to Stones River. McCook studies the map. It is too far; he has not the courage. He will send Zahm to feel for Negley and call that good.

★   ★   ★

Crittenden's corps approaches Stones River from the northwest along the line of the Nashville Pike, Palmer's and Wood's divisions abreast and Van Cleve's division close behind. It is past midafternoon, the winter sun already low, when the skirmishers spot a heavy line of butternut infantry at the foot of Wayne's Hill just beyond the river's sharp bend to the northeast. To storm across the river at this point will require considerable force and entail heavy losses. But to advance along the pike to the river crossing a mile ahead will leave the Rebels on Wood's left flank. Palmer and Wood halt the advance and consult, deciding that neither wants the responsibility for opening a battle so late in the day.

Just as the weary soldiers are dropping out of ranks to make camp, Crittenden and his staff come galloping up to Wood with Rosecrans's order to push a division into Murfreesboro. Wood is shocked. "General," he attempts, "the Rebels are in heavy force on the other side of the river, and it is far too late in the day to develop their positions and launch an assault. If—"

Crittenden, braced by the day's success and a steady accumulation of alcohol in his bloodstream, for once interrupts Wood. "General Rosecrans has intelligence that Bragg is withdrawing from Murfreesboro. We are to occupy the town and press on in pursuit at first light. Here is General Palmer. He sent the message that the Rebels are retreating."

When the situation is explained to him, Palmer scowls. "I sent no such message. I sent several messages to you telling of our progress but nothing to General Rosecrans and certainly nothing about the Rebels evacuating Murfreesboro."

It takes a few minutes of puzzling and the rapid examination of the flimsy copies from couriers' dispatch books before the green lieutenant confesses that he may have delivered a message somewhat in error and to the wrong general. Wood looks heavenward, wonders what principle the theorists of St-Cyr, Sandhurst, and West Point would devise to explain something so farcical. He is pulled abruptly from his musing by Crittenden. "Nevertheless, we must advance as the commanding general directs. General Wood, prepare your division to take that hill on our flank. General Palmer, you will advance straight ahead into Murfreesboro. Quickly now before we lose the light. I must go to General Van Cleve."

"Please remain here, General," Wood says. "It will be dark soon, and we will need to know where to find you."

Palmer glances sharply at Wood, wondering why Wood should give a damn where Crittenden is once the fighting starts.

Crittenden hesitates. "Very well. I will send for General Van Cleve to come to me."

"Thank you, General," Wood says, and swings his horse away. Palmer salutes and follows. Out of earshot of Crittenden, Wood turns to Palmer. "General Crittenden is badly mistaken in this plan. But I think if we move slowly, he may reconsider in time."

Palmer nods. "Meaning he will lose his nerve."

"Yes, General, meaning he will lose his nerve. Let's put our commands in motion and then return to petition him to wait until morning."

★　★　★

Bragg's army has been in position since early in the day. The Confederate line is bent almost ninety degrees with Polk's corps deployed in a north-south line west of the river, and Hardee's corps at right angles on the east side of the river. The awkward angle is the result of Bragg's paranoia about his right flank. Wheeler's cavalry has identified Rosecrans's three corps, but Thomas's corps seems to be missing two of its four divisions. In reality, those divisions have been left behind to defend Nashville and the railroad line to Louisville, but Bragg continues to worry that Rosecrans has dispatched them on a wide loop that will bring them down on Murfreesboro from the northeast along the Lebanon Turnpike.

The Confederate outpost on Wayne's Hill stands outside the line, half a mile from any support. In his anxiety to cover the five roads into Murfreesboro, Bragg has ignored the hill, but its potential as a site for artillery troubles Major General John C. Breckinridge. Late in the morning, he orders Brigadier General Roger Hanson to take Kentucky Brigade forward to occupy it.

From the west side of the river, Bishop Leonidas Polk watches through his field glasses as Hanson's men advance. Someone has finally spotted the crying weakness in Bragg's dispositions. Too bad. Had the Yankees taken the hill, the Confederate line would have become immediately untenable. The inevitable retreat would have finished Bragg and given the army to Polk. The Bishop shrugs. Well, the same result will take a little more blood now, that's all. He lowers his field glasses and removes his watch to see if it is time to dine.

With a battery in place atop the hill, Hanson watches the approach of Crittenden's corps. The Yankee power appalls him. He cannot possibly hold against such numbers. His only hope lies in a bluff. He sends several regiments marching in and out of the woods at the foot of the hill while officers shout commands to imaginary formations and the soldiers make as much businesslike uproar as possible. The Yankees seem to hesitate, trying to decide whether to attack the hill on their left or push straight ahead toward town. After a few minutes, the Union ranks fall out and begin going into camp. But just as Hanson begins to relax, he spots a meeting of senior officers and their staffs. In ten minutes, the Yankees are falling back into ranks, the sight setting Hanson to vigorous cursing.

★ ★ ★

Assigned to lead Wood's assault on Wayne's Hill, Colonel Charles Garrison Harker considers himself the luckiest man alive. The early dark is crisp with the smells of frost, river, and woods. He remembers how as a boy he loved this time when all the other children—those with parents—had to stay inside, doing schoolwork or reading some improving book while he ran through the empty streets and alleys, playing tag with the shadows and his dreams. Orphaned at nine, he grew up the town pet of Swedesboro, New Jersey, a lithe, bright boy apparently untouched by the loss of his drunken, brutal parents. He slept in the back of the schoolhouse, fed the coal stove in place of tuition, ran errands for the housewives who fed and clothed him. At seventeen, the district congressman sent him to West Point. He studied just hard enough to get by, charmed his way through recitations and inspections. Everybody liked Charlie, always gave him the benefit of the doubt. He graduated and put in three good years of service on the frontier. The war brought colonel's eagles and command of a regiment and, after Shiloh, a brigade. Oh, it is a wonderful life, and Charlie Harker is lucky.

Thank God, Tom Wood thinks when he sees Rosecrans and his staff coming down the turnpike. Silhouetted against the last of the light, Rosecrans is impossible to mistake. He rides firmly upright, reins held in left hand, the right poised as if about to make some sweeping gesture of command. His big head is thrown slightly forward, his Roman nose suggesting the aggressiveness of his intent. And Tom Wood, who does not like Rosecrans, has the sudden feeling that he is staring at a man posing for an equestrian statue.

Rosecrans draws rein before Crittenden, looms over the smaller man. Crittenden, whose nerve is failing with the light, fumbles through a hasty explanation of the situation. Finally, he takes a deep breath. "At the request of General Palmer and General Wood, I have just ordered a one-hour delay so that I could consult with you."

"Absolutely correct, General," Rosecrans booms. "Night attacks are rarely worth the cost or the risk, and almost no plan succeeds when based on faulty information. We will postpone any further advance until morning."

Wood speaks up. "General, do I take it that, under your command, subordinates have the right to disregard orders if, in their judgment, army headquarters has based them on faulty information?"

Rosecrans hesitates momentarily. Of all the officers in this army, Wood is closest to being his intellectual equal, and Rosecrans does not trust very intelligent men. "You may ta-take it so, General Wood." Rosecrans feels himself blush and is glad of the darkness. The stutter has been missing for months except for the occasional lapse when he is very tired. He speaks with care. "We are not fighting in the time of Frederick of Prussia. Modern armies are too large and modern battlefields too vast for a commanding general to survey either at a glance. Absolute obedience is a luxury he cannot demand or afford. He must depend on his subordinates to exercise their best judgment in interpreting his orders. But beware, General. The errors of subordinates must under this system result in even heavier consequences than suffered of old."

"Thank you, General. Please excuse me; I should order Colonel Harker's brigade to withdraw now."

But it is too late, for at that moment Charlie Harker's skirmishers rush the ford. From the other side of the river, there are shouts and a crackle of fire. But Harker's skirmishers—six companies spread out in front of the main line—splash through the icy water in moments. They hurl themselves up the far bank, firing at the winking muzzle flashes. The force of the charge breaks the Rebel picket line, sending the butternut soldiers fleeing across a pasture toward Wayne's Hill.

The Yankee skirmishers pursue through the dark. Men run headlong into waist-high fences that jackknife them head over heels; step in holes and trip over rocks, wrenching knees and ankles; smash into each other and land in heaps of two, three and four, already swinging fists and shouting: "What is your regiment, goddamn it? You Reb or Yank?" Although the pasture is mostly cleared, one private has the misfortune of colliding with a sapling which gives nearly to the ground and then whips him backward with the force of a catapult, dislocating his shoulder. The man lets out a howl of pain and terror that is somehow misinterpreted by his fellows, who take it up like hunting wolves until the riverside echoes with howls and yips as the Yankee skirmishers go plunging and leaping into a field of unpicked corn.

Behind his main line, Charlie Harker can hardly contain himself. Oh, this is wonderful. Silence and stealth might have been wiser, but this is better, grander. It is all he can do to keep himself from galloping forward to join his skirmishers, to ride beside them, better yet to leap from his horse to run with them through the frosty dark. . . . "Steady, boys," he says to the shadow of the battle line moving in front of him. "You'll have your chance soon."

Lying on the far edge of the cornfield with Wayne's Hill a dark convexity against the starry sky behind them, the soldiers of the Confederate 4th Kentucky listen to the pursuit. The officers pass down the rear of the line, murmuring: "Wait for the colonel's command, wait for the colonel's command."

The Rebel skirmishers start coming through the line, panting: "Don't shoot! For God's sake, don't shoot! We're Secesh."

The Yankees are coming now, howling, shouting, the dry cornstalks snapping under their rush, the leaves rattling. A leather-lunged Yank shouts: "Slow down, Johnny. Slow down. Give 'er up like good lads. We won't hurt you none if you come easy."

Colonel R. P. Trabue, commanding 4th Kentucky, waits, fingernails digging into his palms. Now. "Rise up, Fourth! Present! Fire!" The volley rips through the dry corn. A few of the Yankee soldiers are almost within bayonet thrust, their shocked faces illuminated by the sudden flash. They are punched, spun, dropped by the blast except for one tall private who stands petrified, impossibly unwounded within two yards of the line. "Lie down and stay down, you damned fool!" an irritated Reb snaps. "We ain't got no time fer formal surrenders."

All along the line, cartridge ends tear in teeth, ramrods rasp in barrels, hammers cock. Out in the corn, there are cries, whimpers, and moans. The leather-lunged Yank calls out: "Goddamn, Johnny. Why'd you have to go and do that?" A few of the butternut infantry laugh, but the voice goes on, pained, genuinely puzzled. "You could've come back with us. We coulda had a good time. Made a little hash. Maybe played a little chuck-a-luck—"

"Hey, Yank!" the irritated Reb calls. "We don't want to go back with you. If you boys'd stayed home, none of this trouble would've happened."

"Spike it, Cochrane," an officer hisses. "You'll tell 'em where we are."

The soldier snorts. "Already know where the hell we are. We just shot a bunch of 'em." He sticks a bare foot out and nudges the tall Yankee, prostrate now in the corn. "How you doin', coz?"

"Uh, fine. Except I shit my pants."

Again there is a ripple of laughter. "That ain't nothin' to be ashamed of, coz. We all have."

The officer is insistent this time. "Shut up, Cochrane! Or I'll stretch you out myself."

"Yeah, sure," Cochrane says, but is quiet. He massages the back of the prostrate Yank with his bare foot. Comforting.

Harker has seen the volley, knows that those of his skirmishers still alive have given over their howling and lie doggo now, still as death, in the corn. The long tramp of his line, in rhythm despite the darkness, reaches out to his left and right. He can see only the vague outline of the hill and a few treetops against the sky. Must do this all by sound now. He hears the crackle of the first stalks under the tread of his men, shouts: "At the double-quick!" The men let out a roar. Ahead, the cornfield blazes with a volley while above on the hillside a battery opens fire, half a dozen six-pounders lined hub to hub, shooting over the heads of the Rebel infantry and into Harker's men as they charge into the cornfield.

After that, Charlie Harker can do very little as commanding officer. His battle line will take the hill or it will not. Vision comes in sudden illuminations of red, orange, and yellow. Men are hit, scream, bleed, writhe on the ground, die underfoot as the line surges forward. Charlie Harker trusts in luck, swings down from the saddle, slaps his horse toward the rear, and charges forward with his men, pistol in hand, saber drawn.

On the hill, Brigadier General Roger Hanson stands by Kentucky Battery, arms folded, willing each shot home as the shells explode among the charging Yanks in red bursts and the near side of the cornfield ripples with musketry. His infantry line is beginning to give way, but that is the plan. If his infantry can make it back to the guns, he can start firing canister, sweep the Yankees right off the hillside. All right, here they come. He turns to the captain in charge of the battery. "They're coming back, Cobb." Cobb lifts a hand, passes the signal to shift to canister after another round of shell. Hanson swings up on his horse and jogs down the path around the summit to see if he is about to get any reinforcement from Colonel Robert Hunt's 9th Kentucky and Kentucky Brigade's adopted sons, the 41st Alabama.

Leading Harker's brigade, Colonel Abel Streight of the 51st Indiana sees the Rebels break for the cover of their guns and realizes in an instant that

chance has given him the better angle. His regiment rolls up the hill, sweeping the fleeing Rebels away on either side. The silhouette of the battery
looms up in front, silent as it waits for the Reb infantry to get clear before
opening on the Yankees with canister. The Hoosiers fire from a dozen
paces, shattering the gun crews, then go in with bayonets and clubbed muskets to finish the job.

For a few moments, the Yankee boys have angle, numbers, and
momentum, but then 9th Kentucky and 41st Alabama come screaming out
of the dark. Suddenly the Yankees have none of the advantages. Cobb and
enough of his gunners are still alive to wrestle three of the six-pounders into
position, and blasts of canister do the rest. Streight and his men throw themselves down the hill, sliding, bumping, rolling into the cornfield.

The fusillade pouring off the hill stops Harker's other two regiments
cold. They hold their ground to let Streight's men through and then pull
back across the cornfield to the pasture. At 10:00 P.M., Wood's order to withdraw reaches them where they lie waiting for reinforcements. They trudge
to the ford and cross the river in a mutinous silence. Some grand chance has
been lost. The enlisted men know it, even if the generals do not.

✴   ✴   ✴

Brigadier General James Scott Negley, Mexican War veteran and peacetime
militia general, commands Second Division, Thomas's Corps. A good-
natured bear of a man, Negley enjoys a reputation as one of the nation's
leading horticulturists, an attainment that has led to many pleasant hours
discussing botany with George Thomas.

By temperament, Negley is not inclined to worry, but he finds himself increasingly agitated as the evening wears on. His left is snugged nicely
against one of Palmer's brigades, but beyond the Wilkinson Turnpike on his
right there is only a dark void where McCook should be. Finally, he halts
his pacing, calls for an aide, and dictates messages to Thomas and Rosecrans:
McCook has not arrived. Should he reorient his line against a possible flank
attack?

At McCook's headquarters on Overall Creek, Colonel Lewis Zahm slumps
exhausted into a camp chair at McCook's invitation. "I'm sorry, General, we
haven't found Negley's right yet. It's darker than the Pit out there and the Reb
cavalry knows the ground better than we do. We'll keep trying, but. . . ."

McCook moistens his lips, recalling Yankee boys killing Yankee boys in the fog north of Triune. "No matter, Colonel. Get your men some food and rest. We'll connect with Negley in the morning."

Brigadier General John Wharton, commanding a brigade of Joe Wheeler's cavalry, watches McCook's camp until the fires are burning high against the night chill and he is sure that the Yankees are not going to move again before morning. They have blundered. He is sure of it. There is a mile and a half gap between McCook on Overall Creek and the flank of the blue line halted short of Stones River. Wharton is a Brazoria lawyer turned Texas Ranger and soldier. He claims no command of grand strategy, yet he senses an opportunity, a chance for something stupendous. He rides to find Wheeler.

Braxton Bragg takes the report of the successful defense of Wayne's Hill without comment. Breckinridge did well to send Kentucky Brigade forward to defend the hill, but he does not bother to send congratulations. A subordinate's successful exercise of initiative needs no praise, should be reward enough in itself. Besides, he has more important matters to attend to.

He scowls at the map for the hundredth time that day. The dispositions are good, the complaint about splitting his army on either side of the river picayune. He has strengthened the line at all points and extended it to the south of the Franklin Pike with McCown's reserve division of three brigades from Hardee's corps. Come the morrow, if Rosecrans is fool enough to attack, Bragg will be ready.

He knew Rosecrans only slightly in the Old Army, does not know Crittenden or McCook at all. He knew Thomas very well, of course—once liked him. But all the memories of that time have grown hazy in his recollection. I am getting old, he thinks, and well before my time. I imagine this war will kill me, but I should like to see my wife one more time before I die.

Wharton is almost to Murfreesboro when he is intercepted by Wheeler in person: "General Wharton, I have the commanding general's permission to go raiding. The roads are filled with Yankee trains. I'll sweep up through Jefferson and then cut back to the Nashville Pike. We are going reap the devil's own harvest. That's what I told him. The devil's harvest!"

Wharton is nonplussed, for Wheeler is not usually given to metaphor. "General, there is a gap in the Yankee line. I think we have a chance to—"

"I've already told General Bragg the Yankee dispositions, and he agreed that now's the time to cut up the Yankee trains, force Rosecrans to fight hungry and short of ammunition. Cover our left flank while I'm gone, John. Pegram has the right." He starts off, remembers his manners. "The next time, it'll be your turn, John. I promise."

Two and a half miles up the Nashville Pike from Murfreesboro, Rosecrans's staff is ensconced in a dilapidated log cabin. Rosecrans reads the message from Negley, balls it in a fist, and hurls it at a wall. The paper lacks the weight to reach its target and the act does little to alleviate the general's anger. He vents his frustration in half a dozen pungent curses. Garesché winces. Father Treacy makes the sign of the cross and stares heavenward before smiling and winking at Garesché. Rosecrans stands for a moment, hands on hips. He turns to Treacy. "I'm sorry, Father."

"You don't offend me, William. However, you might concern yourself—"

Rosecrans brushes this away. "I'll confess it tomorrow, Father. Or the next day. Whenever there is time, but I don't have any now. Garesché, get an escort together. It seems we have to go see McCook."

"No, General. You belong here. I will go. Or better, summon him here."

Rosecrans glares at Garesché, who does not quail. Rosecrans laughs. "All right. All right. I have a father here and it appears a mother, too. Send for McCook. In the meantime, tell Negley to step his right back to guard his flank. I hate to move men this late at night, but we've got to be careful. Bragg always thinks first of the open flank."

As any good general does, Garesché thinks.

"Just like any decent general," Rosecrans says. "Now what are you smiling at, Garesché?"

The night deepens as a cold north wind shrouds the stars with clouds. Standing picket on the lower slope of Wayne's Hill, Corporal Johnny Green and Private Everett Parker of the 9th Kentucky hear the muffled withdrawal of Harker's regiments across McFadden's Ford. Christ, it's cold. They huddle together. When the rain begins, Parker whimpers. Green puts an arm around him, and Parker buries his face in Green's shoulder. "Hush," Green croons. "We'll be all right."

Atop the hill, General Hanson refuses permission to build a fire. No, the Yankee guns would find it too tempting a target.

Elsewhere along the Union and Confederate lines, few officers even attempt such discipline. The men prowl through the woods and fields, gathering brush, cedar boughs, and fence rails. Great bonfires leap up. By unspoken consent, neither army opens with its guns. The green cedar boughs produce immense gouts of crackling sparks. Green can see the silhouettes of Yankee soldiers against the firelight. He tries to concoct a suitable simile of demons around a forge of hellfire. But the boys across the river are just boys: cold, shivering, miserable, and very afraid of dying.

CHAPTER 7

Tuesday
December 30, 1862
Murfreesboro, Tennessee

Crittenden's corps and Negley's division of Thomas's corps hold a strong line from McFadden's Ford on Stones River to the Wilkinson Pike. But McCook's corps is still some two miles to the west, leaving Negley's right flank dangerously exposed. Preparing to meet the Federal advance, Bragg has positioned Breckinridge's and Cleburne's divisions of Hardee's corps on the east side of the river; Polk's corps (Cheatham's and Wither's divisions) west of the river. McCown's division of Hardee's corps protects the Confederate left flank—an awkward command arrangement, leaving Hardee with divisions on either end of the line.

HEELER'S COLUMN OF two thousand troopers stretches more than a mile along the Lebanon Pike running north toward the junction at Waterhill with the road west to Jefferson, Lavergne, and the rear of the Yankee army. Beyond the glow of the campfires, darkness envelops the column utterly. The men are helpless, the horses keeping pace by the sound and mostly the smell of the horses ahead. They plunge on through the dark, following the age-old edict of equine domestication to serve, to serve, to die if asked, but always to serve the master of stirrup, crop, and bit. The ground falls away beneath, heart-stopping, then hooves strike water, splash through the ford across Sinking Creek, and climb the opposite bank spattering mud, all the time the rain falling.

Even the mud, rain, and cedar cannot entirely cloak the sound of hoof-beats. In the Union camp on the far side of Stones River, men pause to listen to a percussive shuffling like distant thunder in the night. Recruits stand puzzled. Knowing veterans exchange glances, knock out pipes, settle themselves by the fires. Better save your hardtack, boys. The Johnnies have gone raidin' and that means lean rations tomorrow.

West of Waterhill, Wheeler's horsemen cross the east fork of Stones River. They have ridden hard since midnight and Wheeler halts the men to rest while his scouts probe toward Jefferson at the confluence of the east and west forks of the river. He is mildly surprised to have encountered no outposts, flushed no Yankee vedettes in all the ride. If the Yankees are at Jefferson in force, they are well drawn in—overconfident, lazy, or stupid.

Creeping through the outskirts of the silent hamlet, the scouts watch campfires rekindled with the first predawn stirrings in the Yankee camp south of the pike—enough fires to indicate at least a full brigade of infantry, maybe more.

Wheeler receives the report in a dripping copse of trees, the staff gathered around him in the dim light of a pair of cloaked lanterns. "We'll swing to the right, ford downstream, and keep going," he tells them. "We're interested in their trains, not a fight with infantry."

"General," quavers a voice from the back of the little crowd. "Beg pardon, General. But I've got a report." The circle opens, lets through a dripping boy, face sallow even in the dim light. He coughs, hacks, breath fetid. "Sorry, General."

Wheeler tries not to show his distaste. "What's your report, trooper?"

"A couple of the boys went down to the river to look for an easy place to cross, and they came back sayin' they heard a wagon train comin' on toward the bridge from the west. Must be a big one too, because it were makin' a parful lot of noise. Captain Beeson said to tell you right quick."

A buzz ripples through the staff. Fighting Joe Wheeler thinks fast. He wants the train but not the fight with the infantry. He will send Colonel William Allen's 1st Alabama and two batteries of horse artillery around to the camp's south side to give it a glancing blow: Good morning, you abolitionist pig-fuckers. Then, while the Yankees are distracted, Wheeler will send the rest of his brigade down the pike to sweep up the wagon train before it crosses the bridge. Without preamble, he starts dictating the orders, forcing his adjutant to fumble quickly for a dispatch book.

Six miles to the south, patchy fog drifts over the fields along Overall Creek. It is not much fog but enough to make Alex McCook hesitate. Rosecrans has ordered him to send Sheridan's infantry forward as soon as they can see their feet, but doesn't common sense dictate that he wait? Surely an hour or two will make little difference. "We'll wait until the fog thins and then send out Zahm," he says.

"General, the Rebs can't see any better than we can—" Sheridan begins.

McCook shakes his head vehemently. "No, we wait!"

Sheridan watches McCook striding toward his tent. The man is afraid, Sheridan thinks. And though almost nothing frightens Little Phil Sheridan—and how he hates the sobriquet—this realization does.

☆ ☆ ☆

Outside the cabin that is headquarters to the Army of the Cumberland, Julius Garesché swallows from the scalding cup, then closes his eyes, waiting for the coffee to jolt him into wakefulness.

Beside him, Rosecrans puffs on a cigar. "Not much fog this morning. McCook should be well underway by—"

The screech of plunging cannonballs drowns him out. The first ball plows into the soaked earth a dozen yards short of the cabin, the second decapitates an orderly, the third howls overhead to thud into the detritus-littered mud beside the turnpike. Garesché's brain locks images: the young orderly rising from beside the fire, cup of coffee in hand, his mouth oh'd in wonder at the sound of iron splitting air, and then the sudden explosion of blood as the cannonball tears through his thorax, severing head from torso. The boy's head whirls into the air above the cabin—rather like a ball kicked in a front yard by a departing schoolboy who has found it abandoned from Sunday's play. It strikes the uneven cedar shingles, rebounds to a surprising height, and sails beyond the sagging roof line. This happens far too fast for the eye to focus on details. Yet for Garesché, the head seems to pause a moment just above the roof peak, the boy's face exhibiting yet a terrified consciousness, as if he would speak some reproach or utter at least some surprise in farewell. And for a moment it is Garesché who sees through the boy's eyes the small crowd in the yard below—soldiers who in another age might have stood beneath the crosses on Golgotha—and in that moment of floating above them, Garesché knows that he is supposed to tell them something. But he cannot summon cogent thought, can only stare in horrified amazement at what has happened to grant him flight.

"They've got the range and the right idea, Garesché," Rosecrans says, voice even though tightened at the edges. "Get the maps. We'll need them today. Quickly, we must be away from here."

The staff is already scrambling, and Garesché is ashamed of his momentary immobility. Has anyone noticed besides Rosecrans? He doubts it. But it cannot happen again. He is a soldier and can spare no time for shock or visions.

More cannonballs scream down on them from the Rebel battery on the low hill beyond the northern loop of the river. Harker's hill, Garesché thinks. What is its actual name? He cannot for the moment recall as he jams unfinished reports into a satchel. Magee, the headquarters orderly, yells at him "Colonel, I'll get that! Here's your horse. Come on, for Chrissake!"

Garesché takes the reins, smiles at the boy. "Don't use any language that your mother would find offensive, son."

"You don't know Ma, Colonel. Now go!"

From Wayne's Hill, Brigadier General Roger Hanson can make out the distant blue figures streaming away from the cabin to climb the rise behind. Captain Cobb, Kentucky Brigade's artillery chief, calls, "That's about it, General. Can't reach 'em now." Hanson lowers his field glasses and waves a hand. Cobb signals the guns to cease fire.

Cobb ambles over, a loose-jointed young man who reminds Hanson of a good-natured coon hound. Hell of an artilleryman, though. "So, who do you suppose we woke up?" Cobb asks.

Hanson shrugs. "Might have been old Rosy himself for all I know."

"There were a pile of 'em. Didn't think that old shack could hold so many. Wonder if we killed any of 'em."

Hanson grunts, uninterested.

Cobb, who is a talker, goes on. "Should be getting some counter-battery by now. Not like the Yanks to waste a chance."

A moment later, guns flash along a brigade front on the far side of the river. "Ask and ye shall receive," Hanson growls as the first shells freight-train overhead.

☆ ☆ ☆

Military plans, even those as simple as Wheeler's this winter morning, are subject to variables limitless in number and absurdity. Wheeler's plan goes awry because of the eternal perversity of army mules. The lead hitch of the lead wagon of the Yankee train plodding toward Jefferson is made up of a pair of young and alert mules who have not eaten since the middle of the previous afternoon. On the morning breeze, itself a perversity for eddying briefly out of the east, they smell campfire smoke: a smell they accurately identify with rest and fodder. Lifting their heads and hooves, they break into a trot, bringing the rest of the team out of its somnambulant plodding and nearly knocking the dozing driver off his seat. He regains his perch and hauls back on the reins, but the team is now united in its gait and ignores him. The driver, who is Irish and hence rather more in sympathy with his thick-headed charges than many of his colleagues, eases off. Well, why not? He could use a cup of coffee and an early breakfast.

He looks behind him, sees the next three or four teams beginning to toss and strain. He whistles to his team, snaps the whip for good measure. "Go, ye flop-eared bastards," he yells. The drivers behind are cursing, squawking, and then giving in as they begin to understand that this is no runaway, but a more sedate demonstration of muleful independence. A jog-away, that's what we've got, the Irish driver concludes. "You, lads!" he shouts to the cavalry escort ahead. "Best bestir yourselves a mite. We're a-comin' through, and the rest ain't far behind."

As a result of the jogaway, nearly the entire train is across the bridge and moving briskly toward breakfast when the Rebel horse artillery opens fire on the camp's south side, setting Wheeler's plan in motion. The encamped Union infantry is a brigade of four regiments of Pennsylvania, Illinois, and Wisconsin veterans under the command of Colonel John Starkweather. A Milwaukee lawyer in civilian life, Starkweather is accustomed to mendacity, and Wheeler's misdirection fools him not a bit. "Look to the train," he shouts.

While Starkweather marshals an Illinois regiment to protect the train, the soldiers of the 1st Wisconsin, many of them swearing in German at being disturbed at an hour when every man should be given an opportunity to drink his coffee, chew his breakfast, and move his bowels, form line of battle to repel the attack on the south side of the camp.

By the time the rest of Wheeler's brigade comes bowling down the pike a few minutes later, fully half of the train is under cover of the camp. The sight of sixteen hundred gray cavalry whooping and firing at the gallop is more than most of the remaining teamsters can view with equanimity. They either flog their teams into a frenzy or leap from their seats and bolt for the trees. Wagons collide, creating an instant chaos of rearing teams and splintering order, which—oddly—also brings an end to most of the shooting.

More accustomed to calming animals than trying to kill their fellow men, farmboys on both sides wade into the confusion to untangle teams and wagons. Left to themselves, the privates might have forgotten the war altogether to make common cause in restoring order. But this is, of course, impossible with so many officers shrieking instructions. The Yankees manage to drag a few wagons into camp while the Rebels give up trying to save anything and fire the remaining twenty or so with coal oil. With more jeers than shots, the two forces disengage.

Across the river and pushing west, Wheeler's officers count casualties. As usual in affairs like this, there aren't many: a handful of wounded, a few missing who will probably show up soon, no dead.

Union losses are heavier. Nearly a hundred troopers in the train escort have been cut off and captured by Wheeler's troopers, while the attack on the south side of the camp has inflicted a score of Federal wounded. Still, there are no deaths except for a pair of German brothers killed by one of the artillery shells. In the old country they had both received something of a musical education and sang beautiful duets at the campfire. They will be mourned longer than is customary among veterans.

At 9:30 A.M., long after Sheridan's men have been able to make out their feet in the thinning fog, McCook finally orders the advance. Fuming at the delay, Sheridan pushes his men down the Wilkinson Turnpike toward a juncture with Negley's right.

Philip Henry Sheridan has risen from second lieutenant to brigadier general in a year and a half, a spectacular rise even in this war. He is a short, barrel-chested man with long simian arms and a bullet head topped with coarse black hair. His pugnacity is legendary, his star bright if he can avoid getting killed. His advance along the Wilkinson Pike soon turns into a nasty business. A mile east of Overall Creek, the division's skirmish line breaks into the wide fields of a prosperous farm family named Gresham. The fields are better maintained than any they have seen in several days, and the farmers among the men begin arguing acreage and yield for various crops. The town and city boys are less impressed, griping as the soaked red clay clings to their brogans in ever-thickening layers.

The skirmish line bogs down halfway across the fields, even the farmers cursing now, as man after man has to stop to scrape the clay off his boots with bayonet or barlow knife while the regiments in column back on the turnpike jeer at their discomfort. At this moment, the Rebels in the woods on the southeast side of the field open fire. Men pitch forward, a few hit, most simply reacting naturally to the surprise as minié balls whiz about them. Fortunately for the blue infantry, the Rebels number only an understrength regiment backed by a single six-pounder smoothbore. Rather than firing case shot to explode over the heads of the Yankees, the Rebel gunners select common shell, which buries itself in the mud, throwing up geysers of red clay on detonation but doing little execution. As the skirmishers rally, three regiments from the turnpike come slipping and skidding into the field. They form into line of battle and push ahead.

The battle line routs the Rebels from the trees, sending them fleeing across the pasture south of the Gresham house. But beyond the farmhouse, the line comes under almost continuous fire. Sheridan deploys fresh regiments as fast as they come down the pike. The battle line flanks a rise southeast of the Gresham house, driving another Rebel regiment and two guns from its slope. By now his division is nearly entirely deployed. An aide brings word that the division's left is in touch with Negley's right, but the hold is weak and Sheridan must send to McCook for support before he can advance farther.

Sheridan waits with his adjutant. "We took a few prisoners, General. They say they're from the Fourth Arkansas of McNair's Brigade, McCown's Division."

Sheridan, who is far more cerebral than his reputation usually allows, considers this information. McCown is an undistinguished West Pointer of Rosecrans's generation. Promoted to major general early in the war, he has held a half dozen positions, each of successively less responsibility. Sheridan frowns, wondering why McCown of all Bragg's division officers should be assigned to hold a critical flank. Very odd.

☆ ☆ ☆

At the Smyrna bridge over Stewart's Creek, taken three days before by Mix's troopers and Hazen's infantry, Wheeler's cavalry runs into a Yankee lieutenant who imagines himself Leonidas at Thermopylae or Horatio at the Tiberian Bridge. A few rounds of horse artillery and the threats of several of his own men change his mind. The Yankees surrender and are quickly paroled. Only the glory-bereft lieutenant objects to the terms. The Confederate sergeant in charge of recording the roll shakes his head, looks at a weathered Yankee corporal. "What do you think, friend? Want to take this dumb bastard along back to Nashville, or should I just shoot him for you?"

The corporal shrugs. "He's got a ma, Sarge. She's been good to some of the boys when they was home on furlough. I'd kinda hate to have to tell her he was dead, though you're right: he don't have shit for brains."

"All right. Get him outta here. First, what's his name? And yours."

Two miles east of the Nashville pike, Wheeler again splits his force, taking three regiments galloping up the roadbed of the Nashville–Chattanooga while Colonel Allen takes the rest of the brigade along the road.

At noon, Wheeler's horsemen explode into Lavergne from two sides. The Yankee infantry protecting a train of three hundred wagons immediately surrenders. Wheeler's men tear through the wagons like feral dogs ripping through a flock of sheep. A Forrest or a Morgan might have controlled them, but Wheeler cannot. In search of plunder, they litter the street with caved-in boxes and barrels, ruptured valises and trunks. They rob their prisoners down to the underwear, leaving the Yankee boys barefoot and shivering. Then the real work of destruction begins. The wagons are pushed together and set alight while the mules are butchered in their braying, screaming multitude. It takes a strong arm to saber a mule, and after a few minutes, the men begin relying on their pistols.

One of Wheeler's artillery lieutenants is sent to deal with a herd of nearly five hundred mules corralled on the north edge of town. Confronted by the jittery, wheeling mass, the lieutenant has an inspiration. "Wilke," he shouts to a sergeant. "Unlimber number two and load double canister."

"Ain't a good idea, Lootenant."

"Just do it. Else we'll be here all day shooting mules with one hand and fighting off Yankee cavalry with the other."

The sergeant shrugs, gives the appropriate orders. Mounting to get the best possible view, the lieutenant gives the command to fire. The gun flashes, the plume of leaden balls slaughtering two dozen mules at a swipe and throwing the rest into panic. They charge every side of the corral simultaneously. The fence shatters. The gun crew abandons its field piece and flees. The lieutenant is swept away by the mules, laying to either side with his saber until it is torn from his hand. He is last seen hugging his horse's neck for dear life as together they ride the crest of the stampede out of town.

The crew returns to its overturned gun. The sergeant looks after the disappearing cloud of mules, spits tobacco juice. "Told him it weren't a good idea."

On a rise beyond the range of the Rebel guns on Wayne's Hill, Rosecrans's cavalry escort has constructed an awning of gutta-percha blankets for the staff. The officers stand about a smoky fire, waiting for orders. Rosecrans paces while the sound of Sheridan's skirmishing swells and fades. It is one of those times when the commanding general can do little. Sheridan's contact with Negley's right is as yet tenuous, and McCook must deploy his other two divisions before he can drive forward to straighten and seal the line. Until that is done, Rosecrans can only pace and worry.

Garesché stands to one side, greatcoat hunched around his shoulders against the raw wind, reading his daily chapter of *The Imitation of Christ*. Major Goddard approaches. "Would you like coffee, Colonel? There's a fresh pot."

"What was his name?"

"Pardon me, Colonel?"

"The orderly. The one who was hit by the cannonball. What was his name?"

"I'm not sure I ever heard. He was new."

"Yes. I'd meant to ask his name. He seemed rather lost."

"He was very young, sir. And new to the army. I think he was a nephew to one of the surgeons."

"Yes. . . . Well, see to finding his uncle. He should be told."

"Yes, sir."

"And, Major, did you happen to see where the boy's head landed?"

"Uh, no, sir. I was concerned with other things at that moment."

"Of course. Well, I suppose it doesn't matter. . . . Yes, a cup of coffee would be comforting. Thank you."

At 2:00 P.M., McCook resumes his advance with seven brigades in line and two in reserve. With the artillery shelling the woods ahead, the Yankee infantry pushes into the fields surrounding the Harding house.

✯　✯　✯

Lieutenant General Bill Hardee has found temporary headquarters in a small frame house not far from the Wilkinson Pike bridge over Stones River. The house is spare, the family without a young widow or a shapely daughter to fondle. Not like the farmhouse closer to town the night before, where Hardee had managed to corner the hired girl in the back hall long enough to feel her young breasts through the cotton dress. She had pushed his hands away, but he had felt the nipples rise. *Aha.* This one might try to act the innocent but she had known a man's hands before. He would find out how much more she knew later on. He had murmured in her ear, let drop a gold dollar between her breasts. (They always so much preferred gold to silver. From the lowest to the highest, scullery wench to plantation matron, they could all be bought with gold.) But when he again had time for diversion, he could not find her, found only the hard-faced old farmer sitting in the kitchen, eyes bleak and resentful.

Hardee smiles to himself now. Perhaps it was the old man who had been showing the girl the ways of sin. His wife was a sucked-out, dried-up hag; why shouldn't the old boy have a little fun swivving the hired girl?

An aide taps on the door, shows in Lieutenant Colonel George Brent, Bragg's chief of staff. Hardee likes the broad-beamed young man who seems to accept all Bragg's petulance with remarkable good humor. He rises, extends a hand. "Good afternoon, Colonel. To what do I owe the pleasure?"

"Orders from General Bragg." The colonel looks vaguely discomforted. "He wants you to shift Cleburne's division to the left to support General McCown's line."

Hardee is startled. "Why? I've just come from General McCown's line. Our flank is secure, and the Yankees appear to have halted for the day."

"General Bragg says he will explain this evening. You're to deploy Cleburne and then come to headquarters."

Bragg is doing it again, Hardee thinks. He's laid out a bad plan and now he's going to make it worse. Next he'll start reorganizing the command structure so that no one will know who commands what. Still, maybe he has information on the Yankee plans. God, I wish Rosy *would* attack our left with McCook. Pat Cleburne, my splendid Irish wolfhound, would eat him alive.

At this moment Bill Hardee knows that he won't go along with Bishop Polk's ridiculous plan to undermine Bragg. No, he will fight this battle as hard as he can. He'll lame Rosecrans and demolish that young buffoon McCook. If Bragg loses the battle, it won't be because of Hardee. Let Polk have the command when Bragg is relieved. Hardee will manage to keep the Bishop from doing anything stupid. Then, when finally they are winning, he will take command of the Army of Tennessee. Let Polk go to Richmond then. That is where the Bishop wants to be, of course: sitting at the right hand of his old friend Davis where he can conveniently drop poison in his excellency's ear.

★   ★   ★

They took too long in Lavergne. Wheeler knows it, they all know it, and ride hard, pushed by the fear of time slipping irretrievably away. The Yankee cavalry, slow and stupid as it is, will ride them down if given enough time. Or in the next hamlet or around the next cedar-constricted bend, they may come up against Yankee infantry, cool veterans this time, who will hold against a charge, gun it down with a battery of Napoleons and rank on rank of Springfields. Time. How have they wasted so much goddamn time?

Wheeler's raiders hit tiny Rock Springs on the road to Nolensville, tear it apart, burn everything. It is sloppy work, no care spent saving anything. They mount, push on, the fear nipping at their heels. In this mood, the men are more inclined to pay heed to their officers. Later, if things go badly, they will become a mob. But for now, they will listen.

The gray horsemen explode into Nolensville out of the rainy light of midafternoon. A long train of wagons stands in the village square, its head pointed east toward Stewart's Creek, the Nashville Pike, and the rear of McCook's corps. The escort puts up no fight, and Wheeler's officers go from wagon to wagon, tearing back the tarpaulins to inspect the loads beneath. Some twenty wagons are laden with ammunition. They cull these and half a dozen new ambulances and send them rolling west. "Burn the rest," Wheeler yells, and the men go crazy in their anxiety to destroy and be gone. One detail begins shooting and hacking at the mules while another dashes buckets of coal oil on the wagons. Inevitably, someone touches a torch to a wagon before its mule team is dispatched. The terrified mules bolt, the wagon gouting smoke and fire, the flames sweeping back to ignite another wagon in passing, then another and another until in moments the street is pandemonium. The mules trample men, overset barrels of coal oil, scream as the incendiary splashes on their coats. One of the Alabamans apparently forgets that his bucket is filled with coal oil, not water, and casts it on a burning wagon. The explosion drenches him with flaming oil and he staggers about the crossroads, screeching until the flames beat him to earth.

Wheeler rides into the chaos, screaming, "Shoot the mules! Shoot the mules, you damned fools!" He empties a revolver into the leaders of one team and they go down, the second hitch crashing over them, the wagon upsetting. A dozen other officers and noncoms are firing now, bringing down hitch after hitch. One team, the mules aflame so that they seem creatures out of some Persian myth of fire, plunges down the road to the southwest toward Franklin after the departed ammunition wagons. Wheeler and two of his staff officers chase them, firing their pistols. Bullets puncture the flames, crash through the brain of the right-hand leader, dropping him in his traces. The remaining three mules pivot right, dragging their dead comrade, and in a final desperate lunge to escape the flames slew the wagon beneath the portico of the Presbyterian church. Wheeler and his officers rein up, momentarily stupefied, watch as the flames shoot up, engulfing the overhang and setting alight the steep roof of the church. "Christ," Wheeler mutters in disgust, spins his horse, kicks it back toward the town square. They must move.

By the time the modest rose window over the west front of the church explodes, showering the brown grass of the lawn with stained glass, Wheeler has his column pointed southwest toward escape.

Braxton Bragg has guessed wrong. Rosecrans has no plan to attack the Rebel left with McCook's corps, intends rather to smash Bragg's right and center with Crittenden's and Thomas's corps.

Beneath the awning of gutta-percha blankets Rosecrans sits in close conversation with Crittenden. Van Cleve's three brigades will cross Stones River at McFadden's Ford as early as practicable to strike Bragg's right flank. Fording upstream of Van Cleve, Wood's three brigades will come in on his right, taking Wayne's Hill as Bragg's right gives way and retreats into Murfreesboro. Once in possession of the hill, Wood will open a bombardment of the Confederate center as Palmer's division and Thomas's two divisions attack along the axis of the Nashville and Wilkinson Pikes. Meanwhile, McCook will put pressure on Bragg's left to prevent any shift of troops to reinforce the center and right.

Garesché thinks Crittenden looks a bit dazed by the effort of following Rosecrans's plan, but his chief of staff is taking detailed notes. "So, do you have any questions, Tom?" Rosecrans asks.

Crittenden glances quickly at his chief of staff. "I don't believe so, General. We will have written orders, won't we?"

"Of course. Garesché will send them to you shortly. I have called a meeting for six o'clock with Generals Thomas and McCook. Come back then and we'll go over everything again. Bring Wood, Palmer, and Van Cleve with you. And, Tom, I will be with you in the morning to see that you get off well."

"We will be honored by your presence, General."

Rosecrans smiles, rises, claps Crittenden on the shoulder. "Let's just worry about honoring Braxton Bragg with our presence come the morning."

When Crittenden and his staff have departed, Rosecrans stretches. "Well, I suppose it's about time we got back."

"General?"

"Back to our cozy log cabin, Julius. We can't spend the night out here in the open."

"I've already arranged to have tents erected. They should arrive any—"

"Oh, I prefer a solid roof over my head. Come, get the staff started. The Johnnies aren't likely to give us any trouble now that it's nearly dusk."

"But, General—"

"Colonel, I would prefer not to argue small matters right now! Call for my horse."

"Yes, sir."

They ride down the slope toward the cabin, the rest of the staff nervously trailing. Rosecrans, who seems to have genuinely discounted the Rebel cannon on Wayne's Hill, rides lost in thought. This is not braggadocio, Garesché thinks. He simply does not worry about cannonballs, though aides may be killed around him by the score. "McCook must hold the right," Rosecrans says. "Bragg may not wait for our attack but make one of his own."

"But didn't you say he would follow Jomini, taking a blow and then counterattacking?"

"I thought so. I think so now. But he may become anxious. If I recall his reputation aright, patience is not Bragg's greatest virtue."

"Nor yours, General."

Rosecrans smiles. "No, hardly a virtue of mine either. . . . It sounds as if McCook has finished his day's fighting. Find out if he has a firm hold on Negley's right and if he's got a brigade across the Franklin Pike. Remind him to come see me this evening."

Hazen and Bierce ride a few paces behind the two generals toward the meeting at army headquarters. Bierce hears Palmer snort when Wood says that Crittenden is "indisposed."

"How quickly did he become indisposed this time?" Palmer asks.

"I gather he left General Rosecrans about three."

"Well, at least you and Van Cleve had a chance to talk to him while he was comparatively sober." He gestures Hazen forward. "Join us, Bill. You'll have your star soon and you might as well get in the habit of scheming with generals."

Hazen warns Bierce back with a look and urges his horse forward. Bierce drops back among the trailing staff officers. Let the generals have their secrets. Few secrets will last till morning, none long past. The cold rain weighs down the smoke of the campfires so that an acrid fog hangs about the army's bivouacs. They pass medical orderlies and a detail from Scribner's brigade of Rousseau's division erecting a field hospital. The infantrymen complain about the duty after the long day's march and make black jokes about visiting the tents on the morrow to donate a leg or an arm to the surgeon. The medical orderlies, bored with all the tired jokes about their trade, go about setting up operating tables and laying out row on row of bandages. A detail of bandsmen arrives. They place their instruments in the comparative dryness of a field tent and begin unloading litters from a line of nearby ambulances. The infantrymen give up trying to make jokes.

The staff dismounts in a clutch of tents and awnings erected under the cover of a grove of cedars a little distance from Rosecrans's headquarters. A lieutenant from Palmer's staff joins Bierce by a campfire. "I heard the Johnnies almost got old Rosy this morning with some cannon on that hill over there," the lieutenant says. "But Rosy insisted on coming back here anyway. They say the chief of staff had a fit."

"I met Colonel Garesché a few days ago. He's an interesting man," Bierce says.

"He's got to be a goddamned saint to spend so much time around generals. Palmer's all right as they go, but I can't wait to get orders to the line. How's Hazen to work for?"

"He's a good man," Bierce says. "The best I've met in the army."

"Kind, is he?"

"No, not that. Hardly that. But he knows his job." Bierce moves off, finds coffee in the cook tent, and then goes out into the rain again.

As the light fades on the road southwest of Nolensville, Wheeler's cavalrymen run into an unexpected bounty: a train of wagons bearing foodstuffs requisitioned by Yankee foragers from the farms around Franklin. Nothing works like food to distract Confederate troopers from other concerns. Fear forgotten, they gorge themselves. As cooking fires spring up on either side of the road, Wheeler orders out vedettes and sends scouts to examine the roads ahead. If the way is clear, he will turn southeast on the Wilson Pike and, once south of Triune, circle through Eagleville to make a dash for Murfreesboro. With luck, he will have his column within the safety of the Rebel lines by early morning. He wishes he could give Triune a going-over, but the risks have grown too great. Besides, Bragg may need him close to hand by dawn.

He accepts a heaping plate from a member of his staff and eats, thinking about Bragg. He supposes he should be grateful to the old man, reciprocate his fondness; but Bragg seems almost impossible to like. Wheeler wonders if he has always been so, wonders if the striking Mrs. Bragg married a man much different than the man Bragg has become.

Wheeler had met Elise Bragg at a reception in Murfreesboro two weeks before Christmas. Wheeler is a shy man, and he arrived as late as he dared, hoping to make an early escape. He expected to meet either a mousy, much-put-upon woman, or a hard, sedate matron. Instead, he found Mrs. Bragg to be a smiling, self-assured, and altogether charming woman. In her presence, Bragg seemed utterly transformed, eyes merry and pale skin glowing.

Thomas Benton Smith, colonel of the 20th Tennessee and at twenty-four even younger than Wheeler, sidled tipsily to his side. "By God, Wheeler, they actually seem to like each other. I never would have guessed. And she sure is one hell of a lot handsomer than I'd imagined. How do you suppose old Braggsy got her to marry him?"

Wheeler was discomforted by Smith's familiarity but knew that he should practice at this, try to be the hail fellow. "Oh, I understand the general was quite the charmer in his day."

Smith snorted. "First I ever heard of that. I did hear she advises him on strategy. One of the staff boys said he saw a letter that gave the old man holy hell for quitting Kentucky without bagging Buell."

Wheeler was shocked. "My God, Smith, you're not telling me that they read the general's personal correspondence."

Smith laughed. "Oh, come on, Wheeler. Unlimber that load of propriety just a little."

And he longed to, but the rough camaraderie of soldiers has always been utterly foreign to Joe Wheeler. He set his half-empty glass on a table. "I should check on my patrols."

Smith ignored this, locked a grip on Wheeler's elbow. "Now look, Wheeler, everyone knows ol' Bragg confides in you like a son. What's he tell you of his plans? Are we going to take a crack at Nashville? Are we going go back to Kentucky? Or what?"

"If the general has intimates, I am not one of them. I am not privy to his plans."

"Come now, Wheeler. You can—"

"Colonel, release my arm or I shall be forced to strike you."

Smith released his grip, stepped back surprised, and then with the exaggerated dignity of the drunk, bowed formally. "I beg your pardon, General."

For a minute they held each other's gaze. Among Southern men, less has often led to the dueling field. At length, Wheeler replied, "And I yours if I spoke in heat, Colonel. Now if you will excuse me." He turned, made his way through the crowd, aware suddenly of being both very young and very short—shorter even than many of the women. He reached General and Mrs. Bragg, waited patiently for his chance, and then thanked them for their hospitality. "Why, General Wheeler," Elise said, "the night has barely begun. Can you not stay a while so that we can talk of horsy matters? All these infantrymen and artillerists make such dull conversation."

Wheeler knew that here a witty rejoinder was required, but he had none to offer. He fumbled, reddened, finally managed: "I'm afraid that I must check some patrols. I would not want your party interrupted by unexpected guests."

"Yankees?" She put hand to bosom in mock alarm.

"Well, yes. There's always a chance that—"

Elise was suddenly resolute. "Oh, certainly the Yankees won't be so insolent as to invade a party endowed with so many gallant Southern officers. I fear, General, that you are making an excuse to abandon our company. Come, you can tell us what gentle attraction draws you away. Our lips, both mine and my husband's, will remain forever sealed."

Her tone and eyes insinuated of that which Wheeler, devoutly though he has wished otherwise, knows nothing save for the counterfeit experience paid for in brothels. Wheeler looked helplessly to Bragg, who was smiling indulgently. "Let him go, Elise. General Wheeler is a young man with a very strict sense of duty. Return to us later if you can, General."

Wheeler bowed, mumbled another apology, did the best he could in kissing Elise's gloved hand, and—face burning—fled.

★   ★   ★

In the dusk, Garesché goes looking for the orderly's head amid the ferns on the shady side of the cabin. Exactly what he will do if he finds it, he is not sure. Perhaps it has already been found, reunited with the shattered corpse by the burial party ordered to clean the site in the long, rainy afternoon.

Ahead in the dimness, a stooping figure straightens from the bracken, and Garesché stifles a cry of preternatural fright, for the figure's face, half hidden in the folds of its greatcoat, is flattened nearly featureless like the skull of Death itself. The figure laughs softly, raises on high the head it holds by the hair. "And what should we quote at such times? The *Bhagavad Gita*? 'I have become Death, the destroyer of worlds,' said Lord Krishna to Arjuna on the morn of battle. Or *Romans*? 'Who shall deliver me from the body of this death?' Or perhaps the Bard. 'Alas! poor Yorick, I knew him, Horatio; a fellow of infinite jest, of most excellent fancy; he hath—'"

"For the love of God, sir!" Garesché croaks. "That was a man."

The figure lowers the head slowly. "I'm sorry, Colonel. I did not recognize you."

Garesché squints. Hazen's topographical officer, the boy fascinated by the carnage of war. Bierce. Yes, that was the name. He walks to him and without a word takes the head, cradles it, touches the cold cheek.

Bierce, who is not wont to apologize often, tries again. "Colonel, I meant no disrespect for the dead, only irony for the condition of the living. It is the only means I know of . . . of finding a way to go on."

Gareschè raises his anguished face. "I did not even know his name. He was assigned to headquarters for a week or more and I never asked him his name. Did you know it?"

"No, Colonel. I did not know the man."

Gareschè looks down again at the face. Gently, he attempts to shut the staring eyes but they refuse to remain closed.

Bierce hesitates. "It is the rigor, Colonel. The eyelids would have to be sealed with wax."

"Yes, of course," Gareschè murmurs. He digs in a pocket, finds a folded handkerchief, shakes it open, and lays it over the boy's features. Bierce stands by, awkward, powerless. "I saw him killed," Gareschè says. "Saw the cannonball tear through his throat and saw his head thrown over the roof of the cabin. It seemed for a moment that he looked back, as if his eyes could still see. Do you think that is possible? That he might have looked back at us for a moment in wonder at his own death?"

"No, Colonel. I think his death must have been instantaneous. One moment life, the next only darkness."

"I hope you're right. Otherwise, it would be too horrible." Gareschè looks at Bierce again, face more controlled now. "His head should be buried with his body. Can you find the burial party that cleaned the site? Find out where they laid his body?"

Bierce is about to protest, but cannot under the pleading gaze. "I can try, Colonel."

"Thank you, Lieutenant. Thank you. I will tell Colonel Hazen that you may be delayed." He looks down at the head, seems about to say something to it, does not. He hands it to Bierce, who cradles it as Gareschè has.

"Now just how the hell am I supposed to do that, Lieutenant?" The sergeant waves a hand at the long trench, which even now is being lengthened by a dozen men with picks and shovels. "Your man wasn't the only poor devil to get his head blown off today. When armies start trading cannonballs, that's what happens. But maybe you ain't seen enough combat to know that."

"I've seen enough."

"Well, good for you, laddy. Now, there must be half a dozen men without heads down there and another thirty or so that got blown apart some other way today. If you want to climb down there and start looking, go ahead. Otherwise, you can just chuck that head in with the arms and the

legs sent over from the hospital after the hack-and-slash boys got done making cripples out of a few dozen good men. We bury everything equally here.
Let God sort it out if there's a Resurrection Day. Otherwise, let everything
rot in peace."

"What's your guess? Is there or isn't there?"

The sergeant stares at him for a moment and then laughs, shaking his
head. "God, you college boys. Make you officers so you can go around trou-
bling the rankers with questions of philosophy. How the fuck should I
know what happens when we're dead? My guess is we're just goddamned
dead. But I don't *know*. And neither do you or anybody else I ever knew.
They say there's a colonel at the general's headquarters who's some kind of
saint. Why don't you go ask him? Me, I'm gonna get some supper and some
sleep. I've got a hunch me and my boys are going to have one hell of a busy
day tomorrow."

"He doesn't know," Bierce says to the sergeant's back. "He might have
before, but he doesn't anymore." If the sergeant hears, he makes no
acknowledgment.

Bierce steps to the edge of the trench and stares down. He can make
out the line of corpses, a few wrapped in blankets, the rest in only trousers
and shirts. All are coatless and shoeless beneath the thin layer of soil strewn
over them. No one has bothered to sprinkle any dirt on the pile of arms and
legs in a corner of the trench. Bierce is reminded of the clot of maggots he
saw in the abdominal cavity of an eviscerated man who had lain unburied
and rotting for a week after Shiloh. He holds the head at arms' length over
the pile, feeling its surprising weight for a final time, and lets it fall. The
handkerchief wafts away, and the head lands face up in the embrace of
arms and legs, mouth screaming.

★ ★ ★

Captain Drury C. Spurlock, 16th Tennessee Confederate Infantry, is sitting
against a tree near the Stones River bridge, half a mile west of the junction
of the Wilkinson and Nashville pikes. In the dusk one of his privates
approaches him. "Cap'n, Colonel Savage just got a message for you. Seems
your folks are at the Miles Hotel in town."

Spurlock leans his head back against the trunk, closes his eyes. James,
he thinks. It must be about James.

Spurlock finds his horse, saddles it himself, and rides the mile and a half
into Murfreesboro. His father greets him at the door to the narrow hotel
room, shakes his hand solemnly. The old man does not spare words: "James

died three days ago. We buried him next to our little girl. The one that didn't live long enough to get a name." He turns away, goes to sit in a chair by the window.

Spurlock looks to his mother, sees her smaller, more birdlike than he remembered. "It was the pneumonia, Drury. Shot through the lung like he were, it took him real fast."

"Shouldn't have gone," his father says from his chair by the window. "Weren't no good for a bunch of Tennessee boys to go up to Kentucky. Damned Kentucks don't care nothin' for us, why should we care about them?"

His mother is about to break down, and Spurlock steps to her, enfolds her in his arms. She is tiny, her words whispering against his breast. "Can't you come home now? We don't have nobody else left."

"I can't, Mother. The boys elected me captain. I'm responsible for them. Please don't ask me again." He blinks back tears, stares at the darkening window beyond his father's shadowy face.

"At least here you fight for Tennessee, not no damned Kentucky," the old man says, voice gruff with unshed tears.

"You have to get away from here," Spurlock says. "There's going to be trouble like you can't imagine. The Yanks—"

"Can't. The horses need rest," his father says.

Spurlock tries to argue, but it is pointless. He rides back to camp, wondering at his father's stubbornness. Perhaps it isn't stubbornness at all, but only an old farmer's immutable sense of limits: that we can ask only so much of our animals, though they in their inexplicable love for us are always prepared to give more. In this, he supposes, our animals are like our parents, perhaps even our God.

On his way to the conference with Rosecrans, Major General George Thomas pauses on the rise behind army headquarters to study the sky. In the twilight, gray fields and gray sky blend, obscuring the horizon and making the glades of cedar float like islands upon a gray sea. He detects a faint glow over Nolensville and a tall smudge of smoke. Wheeler's cavalry at work. He compresses his lips, wonders if the Army of the Cumberland will ever have horsemen to match.

Rosecrans is smoking on the porch of his cabin headquarters. Thomas swings down, gritting his teeth against the inevitable jar to his injured back. Rosecrans watches with interest. All know how Thomas, bound from Texas for New York on his first visit to his wife in two years, stepped from a smoky car only to discover an instant too late that it had stopped short of the dark platform. The fall wrenched Thomas's spine at an impossible angle and, a year later, there are days he can barely walk. Rosecrans, whose accident in the laboratory left scars that still burn and itch, is sympathetic. He extends an unlit cigar. "A smoke, George?"

Under the cover of the porch, Thomas lets an aide take his greatcoat. He accepts the cigar, rolls it between palms, and then smells it—as deliberate about his pleasures as he is in everything else. "Thank you, General."

Rosecrans lights a lucifer on the porch rail and extends it to Thomas, who bends slightly to get the cigar lit. "Garesché thinks I ought to move back under the trees out of range of the Rebel batteries on that hill," Rosecrans says. "He's right, of course, but I begrudge the loss of a dry night's sleep."

Thomas blows out smoke, studies the cigar. "This is a good cigar."

"I had them sent from a tobacconist in Cincinnati a few weeks ago. I was told he provides old Useless with his cigars, so I ordered a half dozen boxes of the same brand out of curiosity."

"Grant has good taste in cigars."

"Now that he's got a job and can afford them. I've heard that he used to pick butts off the street." Thomas is silent. He does not care for Grant, but finds Rosecrans's overt hatred somehow unmanly. Rosecrans seems to sense the disapproval, says, "But I imagine even he never fell quite that low. Anyway, I'll give you a box before you leave tonight."

Thomas bows slightly, very Virginian all at once. "Thank you, General."

"Did you have an opportunity to read the battle order Garesché sent over?"

"Yes. It's an excellent plan. My only reservation is the security of our right."

"I'm going to instruct McCook carefully. He should manage."

They talk for an hour, eventually moving inside to study the maps. Finally, Thomas again dons his greatcoat and trudges through the mud to mount his big patient black with the smooth gait. Watching him go, Rosecrans says a prayer of thanks for such a second-in-command. On the morrow, they will do great things.

✯   ✯   ✯

McCook is preparing to leave for Rosecrans's headquarters when Captain Horace Fisher brings him an odd report. An old farmer has a tale of a massive movement of troops toward the Rebel left.

"Why would he risk passing through the skirmish lines?" McCook asks. "Is he a John Brown sort?"

"No, just an old farmer, but he claims that a Reb general fondled his daughter. He's mad as hell about that and wants revenge."

"Did he say what general?"

"He said Hardee."

McCook considers. The Hardee he remembers had been a family man with a passel of undisciplined children forever throwing dirt clods at the cadets on parade. "I don't know if I can credit that, but I'll mention it to General Rosecrans."

Trailed by his silent chief of staff, McCook rides the three miles over muddy roads from his headquarters near the Gresham house to Rosecrans's headquarters near the Nashville Pike. He is hours late, as he has been in nearly everything during the last four days. He tells himself that no one has faced so hard a fight on the approach. Yet he has managed to get his corps in position. Surely the general cannot find too much fault tonight.

Ambulances, supply wagons, and caissons jam the roads, and McCook and his staff must ride most of the distance through the fields. The night is cold, the rain turning intermittently to sleet. At least the men have fires, the informal truce between the armies reestablished with nightfall. The piles of burning fence rails and cedar logs trace the facing curves of the two lines. At the top of a rise, McCook stares anxiously at the far end of his line. Rosecrans has ordered fires built for the width of two brigades beyond the actual termination of McCook's line on the Franklin Pike—an old but effective ruse to confuse a potential attacker. Yes, the fires are there. Good, he has done all that he was asked to do.

McCook's staff draws rein under the shadow of the grove of cedars where Gareské has the staff tents pitched. McCook is delighted to see Stanley, who is both classmate and friend, coming to greet him. The cavalry commander looks exhausted. "So, McCook, do you suppose I will be the shortest-serving commander of cavalry in the history of this or any army?"

McCook blinks. "Why? What's happened?"

"What's happened? Nothing except that Joe Wheeler's ripped through our supply trains all the way from Jefferson to Nolensville and beyond. Christ, half of the wagons were yours. You must have known."

"Well, yes. Of course. But—"

"So somebody's got to take the blame. And it seems likely to fall directly on the Army of the Cumberland's chief of cavalry, which I have been for something less than two months."

McCook accepts a cup of coffee, sips gingerly from the metal lip. "It can't be that bad."

"It's worse. We lost at least five hundred wagons and a thousand men, most of them captured, paroled, and already waltzing back to Nashville." He drains the last of his cup. "And after I've told Rosy all that, I'll have to confess that I don't have a goddamn idea where Wheeler is. He headed southwest out of Nolensville but that's all I know. Right now he may be riding around our right flank to get back to Bragg or doubling back to hit more of our trains."

McCook feels a huge relief. Rosecrans may give him a measure of hell for being slow to close the gap with Negley, but he will save the better part of his wrath for Stanley. "I'll go with you. Which tent is he in?"

"He's in that log shack out in the field. Garesché is having a fit about it, but Rosy won't budge from a dry cabin, Rebel cannon or no Rebel cannon."

They follow a path to the cabin, knock, and are admitted by Major Goddard. Rosecrans looks up from his field desk. Surprisingly, he seems in an expansive mood. He waves the two young men to crates turned on end. "Well, General Stanley, how big a hunk did Wheeler take out of us?"

Stanley takes a breath. "A considerable one, General. I estimate. . . ."

At the end of Stanley's report, Rosecrans takes a minute getting a fresh cigar lit. "Well, Stanley, we're going to have to do better. I plan to win tomorrow and then chase Bragg down to Chattanooga. It would be helpful if I had efficient cavalry to do a lot of that chasing, but I don't know that I do."

"Some of the units did very well, sir. Zahm's brigade chased the Rebs out of Franklin on our first day out of Nashville, and those Michigan boys took that bridge on the Jefferson Pike in grand style."

"Yes, we've had a few good moments. But we have to find a way to keep the Rebs off our trains. We'll be all right this time, but that's mostly because Bragg was fool enough to send Morgan and Forrest raiding when he could better have used them here."

"Yes, sir."

"Well, today's past. Now, General McCook, do I understand correctly that you have a solid line from Negley's left on the Wilkinson Pike to the Franklin Pike?"

"Yes, General. Sheridan's holding on to Negley, then comes Davis, then Johnson. Willich's brigade is on the Franklin Pike."

"With the extended line of fires I told you to build?"

"Yes, sir. I checked on them before coming over."

"Good. You've both seen the battle order for tomorrow. It will take time to get Crittenden across the river and in position to strike at Bragg's right. General McCook, can you guarantee me that you'll hold the right long enough for me to execute that maneuver?"

"Yes, sir. I think I can."

"I'm talking if Bragg hits you with three maybe four divisions."

McCook swallows. So many? "We'll hold."

"How long?"

"As long as we have to."

Rosecrans leans back, face in shadow, studying McCook. Damn it, he should have relieved him despite the political power of the McCook tribe. Put Davis, murdering bastard though he is, in this boy's place. "This is absolutely critical, General. You *must* hold until Crittenden and Thomas are able to put everything into their attack."

"I understand, General."

"All right then. Now, General Stanley. . . ." Rosecrans begins going over the cavalry's deployment for the morrow: a straggler line behind the action, strong outposts on the flanks and to the rear. McCook relaxes, stares at the wafting cigar smoke in the rafters, listens to the rain. When this is over, he thinks, I am going to sleep for a week. Then I'll ask for a transfer. Ask for a garrison command somewhere. Or a mustering rendezvous. He no longer wants to be a general with great responsibilities. Sleep, he thinks. I want a posting where I can sleep nights. In his musing, he forgets to mention to Rosecrans the odd story brought by the old farmer whose daughter had been fondled by a Confederate general, supposedly Bill Hardee.

✯ ✯ ✯

Corporal Johnny Green and Private Everett Parker of Kentucky Brigade are again standing picket duty on the slopes of Wayne's Hill. Below them, the fires of the two armies stretch in facing arcs some four miles long. A cold wind has risen with evening, clearing off the smoke so that the fires burn brightly, clouds of sparks billowing skyward whenever someone tosses a green cedar bough on the flames.

An hour before tattoo, bands on both sides strike up. The Rebels roll through *Dixie,* which brings the response of *Yankee Doodle* from the Federal side. Echoes of the last measure of *The Bonnie Blue Flag* are drowned by *Hail Columbia.* And so it goes, sometimes cacophonous as three or four different songs are played simultaneously, sometimes melodious as all the bands join on *Tenting Tonight* or *Annie Laurie.*

Parker and Green smoke their pipes, laugh, hum along, occasionally sing a line or two of a favorite song. A band somewhere out beyond the Yankee center is the first to begin *Home Sweet Home*. Nearby Yankee and Rebel bands join in, the tune spreading along both lines until perhaps a hundred bands are playing in concert. The singing follows the music, sweeping in a gradual swell until seventy or eighty thousand voices join in. Parker whispers, "Oh, God, Johnny." Green nods, tries to clear his throat. He must sing or weep, decides to sing.

> *Mid pleasures and palaces though we may roam,*
> *Be it ever so humble, there's no place like home.*
> *A charm from the skies seems to hallow us there,*
> *Which, seek through the world, is not met with elsewhere.*
> *Home, home, sweet, sweet home!*
> *There's no place like home.*
> *There's no place like home.*

Hardee is with Cleburne, helping him move his four brigades into position behind McCown's three on the south side of the Franklin Pike. Hardee laughs. "What do you really think of this country, Patrick? Here we all are, about to start killing each other but singing together like old friends."

"I think we're about to be the first armies in history to reveal their dispositions with a song."

"Have I ever mentioned that you are altogether too serious? Enjoy this moment, my young friend. It is one that may become part of the folklore of this war. And you are here to witness its truth. You can tell your children and grandchildren about it some day."

Cleburne, who has never married, feels a sudden lump in his throat, angrily swallows it down. This is no time to become a sentimental Mick, he thinks. He feels Hardee's hand squeeze his shoulder. "I'm sorry, Patrick. I sometimes forget how far you are from home."

"Arkansas is my home, General. Not Ireland."

"Yes, of course. But there is more to having a home than a room above a drug store."

Cleburne is both moved and discomforted by Hardee's words. "I am already a fortunate man, General. If this war doesn't kill me, I would hope to find a woman who will put up with me. I should like a family. But if I do not survive this war, I will die grateful for the hospitality I found in this land." He knows this sounds formal, almost a rebuff to the older man's concern, but he can do no better.

Hardee makes a wordless noise of comfort, pats Cleburne on the shoulder, and lets his hand drop. As the chorus swells again, Hardee sighs. "I suppose I should remarry. I have been a widower too many years. When the war is over, perhaps I shall. For the present, my children are well cared for by their aunt. . . . Well, I should go assure General Bragg that we are in position to repel a Yankee attack in the morning."

"I'm not convinced it will fall here, General."

"No, neither am I. That is something I must discuss with him."

About them the song continues, repeated once again:

> *How sweet 'tis to sit 'neath a fond father's smile,*
> *And the cares of a mother to soothe and beguile;*
> *Let others delight 'mid new pleasures to roam,*
> *But give me, oh, give me the pleasures of home.*
> *Home, home, sweet, sweet home!*
> *There's no place like home.*
> *There's no place like home.*

Rosecrans, Garesché, and Father Treacy stand on the porch of the cabin, listening. "Now isn't war a hugely strange thing," Treacy says, the emotion in his voice making his brogue more pronounced.

Rosecrans laughs. "It is when both sides share the same language. A lot of these boys are cousins, brothers-in-law, even brothers. Hell, half the damned bunch is probably related one way or another."

They are all related, Garesché thinks, and I cannot even count the ways.

"Come on, men," Rosecrans says. "We can't let the rest of the army sing without us. Wouldn't be at all fitting." He gestures to the orderlies and aides standing about the porch. "Here we go. On the start of the chorus."

> *Home, home, sweet, sweet home!*
> *There's no place like home.*
> *There's no place like home.*

Braxton Bragg rises from his desk, stalks to the window, and slams it shut. My God, he thinks. Tomorrow morning when they're supposed to be fighting they'll be cooking breakfast together. Then what am I supposed to do? Invite Rosecrans and that traitor Thomas to take lunch with me?

He returns to his desk, picks up his pen to continue the letter to his wife. He reads over quickly what he has written, decides that he should write something other than complaints, and begins a new paragraph:

Something quite remarkable just happened. It seems that our bands were competing with those of the Yankees when one took up the tune Home Sweet Home. *Within a few moments, nearly all the men on both sides were singing as all the bands played the doleful tune. I did not sing, for you know what an appalling voice I have, particularly since my throat condition last winter, and how much even the normal stress of carrying on daily business discomforts me. But though I do not approve of the fraternization of soldiers one side with the other, even in song, I suppose no great harm is done, and it was truly an astounding thing to hear. The largest chorus in history, I would imagine, for I cannot think what would rival it.*

On the morrow, I expect to see much of the future of our cause decided. Generals Hardee and Polk are to visit me shortly, and I will explain my plan to them. Actually, I will suggest one plan and then let them suggest another closer to what I really intend. In that way, though I sacrifice some credit in authorship, I will make them bear more responsibility for the plan's success. The way our troops are disposed tonight, there is really only one reasonable way of utilizing them in the morning, a plan that will occur even to the doltish Bishop and the foppish Professor. Oh, if I had the subordinates Lee has, I should long since have taken Nashville. But I must do what I can with the poor material I have. . . .

When at last, after a half dozen repetitions, the song fades away into the dripping night, men have different reactions. Thomas, Sheridan, Wood, Hazen, and most of the professional officers in both armies file the matter away for analysis when they have time for intellectual idling. For the moment, they have work to do. There are a few exceptions: General Jefferson C. Davis upbraids his chief bandsman—an old sergeant whose service began as a boy in the years following the War of 1812—for playing the song to the possible detriment of the soldiers' aggressive spirit. Charlie Harker, who has sung himself hoarse, is elated, his heart stirred with love for all men. Alex McCook, only thirty-one but feeling immeasurably older, weeps.

Among the commanders who were recently civilians, Negley, Palmer, and Breckinridge are moved by the pathos of the moment to reflect on the grandness of the American character, while Bishop Polk laughs silently at the imbecility of human hopes. Face-down on his cot, breathing heavily through his mouth, Tom Crittenden sleeps through the concert.

On the extreme right of the Union line, Brigadier General August Willich, who is somewhat deaf, must inquire as to the cause when he sees so many of his men weeping. Told the circumstances, he goes among them, giving little pats on shoulders and backs. "Thar now, thar now, my boys. Ve do our duty, and soon ve go home."

With most of the men asleep in their saddles, Wheeler's cavalry plods along the Salem Pike toward Murfreesboro. Wheeler hears the bands playing but cannot make out the tune. The singing is like waves on a distant shore, the forlorn notes of the instruments tinkling flotsam on the roll of the breakers.

When the bands fall silent at last, Ambrose Bierce, the most rational of young men, stands in the dark, listening to the wind and the rain blowing through the cedars along Stones River.

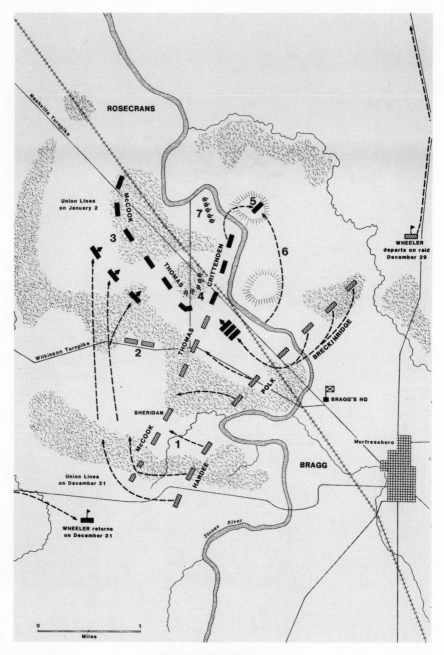

The Battle of Stones River
December 31, 1862–January 2, 1863

CHAPTER 1

Wednesday, Midnight–6:00 A.M.
December 31, 1862
Murfreesboro, Tennessee

The Army of the Cumberland is in position to execute Rosecrans's plan: McCook's corps holds the right flank on the Franklin Pike; Negley's division of Thomas's corps the center at the junction of the Wilkinson Pike and McFadden's Lane; and Crittenden's corps the left flank to McFadden's Ford. Rousseau's division of Thomas's corps is in reserve on the Nashville Pike. In the morning, Crittenden will open the Federal attack by crossing the river at McFadden's Ford, driving in the Confederate pickets, and wheeling to strike the right flank of Bragg's army.

Bragg has decided on an almost identical plan: he will strike Rosecrans's right flank with the divisions of McCown and Cleburne, break through, and wheel clockwise to roll up the Federal line, Polk's divisions joining in as the attack gains momentum. With the exception of Cleburne's division, which is crossing to the west side of Stones River en route to its new position behind McCown's division, the Army of Tennessee is in position by midnight.

BRAGG SENSES THE malignity of their approach. Polk and Hardee will come in from the rainy darkness together, smiling and obsequious but united in their contempt for him. Well, so be it. Their disdain is nothing to the revenge he will take once he has wrecked the Yankee army.

He turns a final time to his letter to Elise:

> *Beyond the unfairness, east and west, of the distribution of supplies,*
> *men, and able officers, I find myself most outraged at the absence in our*
> *army of one who should have been with us from the beginning. I cannot*
> *comprehend how George Thomas can live without honor. In Mexico, I*
> *reposed more trust in him than in any of my other subalterns. He was, I be-*
> *lieved, an officer of both ability and manly character. In the latter I was mis-*
> *taken. Now, as we face each other, I hope I was also mistaken in the former.*
> *But no matter. My dispositions are sound, my plan impeccable. If the army*
> *executes my orders with determination, victory will be mine.*
>
> *But I grow both weary and wearisome. I will, therefore, bid you good*
> *night, Dear Wife, trusting that now, as always, your prayers are with me, as*
> *mine are with you.*
>
> *Your devoted husband,*
> *Braxton Bragg, Gen'l CSA*

He folds the letter, seals it, and places it carefully in a drawer. He hears voices in the hall and gathers himself to greet his enemies.

Rosecrans glowers at the map tacked to the wall. The damage to the trains has been worse than they thought, and Rosecrans's good mood of the early evening has darkened. "We must have *some* trains left. Wheeler can't have burned them all in a single day."

Garesché points. "There is a concentration here on the Wilkinson Pike beyond Stewart's Creek."

"Where was Wheeler's cavalry the last we heard of them?"

"They waylaid a foraging train here in the valley southwest of Nolensville about dusk, and then paused long enough to cook a meal."

"Insolent bastards. Give me a decent brigade of horse, and I'd give them no rest for picnics. Hell, give me a regiment."

"Yes, General." Please, no bluster now, Garesché thinks. It is late and we are on the brink of something so terrible that I cannot look upon it even in my imagination.

"Well, the little bastard's aggressive, I'll give him that. Wants to be Bragg's Stuart, which makes me think he's not satisfied yet." Rosecrans traces a road with a thick finger. "Suppose instead of going south to Eagleville, he circles back through Triune, tears through those trains at Stewart's Creek, and hits our right flank just when McCook's trying to fend off an attack on his front. That could be a very unpleasant turn of events. Better tell Stanley to go up the Wilkinson Pike to the creek. He's to get those ordnance wagons through to us and keep Wheeler off our rear."

"But shouldn't General Stanley be close at hand in the morning? Perhaps if you sent Kennett or Zahm—"

"No, send Stanley. It's about time he proved he can handle at least one assignment. Besides, he's spoiling for a fight with Wheeler."

Garesché scribbles the note to Stanley and sends it off with one of the orderlies waiting outside the door. Rosecrans lights one of the Cincinnati cigars from Grant's tobacconist, studies the glowing end. "Did you know," he says, "that old Useless never issues a proclamation to his army before battle? I don't understand that. It seems unfair to ask men of little education and less understanding to risk their lives without some encouragement from their general." He withdraws a folded sheet from a pocket. "Shine this up a little and then send copies to all divisions. Let the men hear it at assembly."

Garesché unfolds the sheet, mind already busy with the logistics of making and distributing so many copies this late at night. He scans the message. It is quite good, more restrained than he would have expected. A word or two here and there. . . . "I would suggest, General, that where you say—"

"Whatever you think, Julius. Whatever you think."

Bragg, Hardee, and Polk study the map in the yellow light of the coal-oil chandelier. Bragg has proposed attacking along the axis of the Nashville Pike to pierce the Yankee center.

Polk and Hardee object strenuously. Overbalanced to the left, the army is improperly aligned for an attack on the Yankee center. Readjustments cannot possibly be made before midmorning, and by then Thomas's lines will be thick with infantry and batteries. (Leave it to Old Slow Trot to make sure of that.) Better by far to hit the right flank with McCown's and Cleburne's divisions.

Bragg could chortle at his success. The Professor and the Bishop have conceded the question of whether to attack or to defend. And in so doing, they have fallen in with his tactical plan, which—to anyone save this pair of cretins—should have been obvious once he ordered Cleburne positioned behind McCown.

"Very well then, gentlemen, we will attack the enemy's right flank at dawn. You will have written orders within the hour. Until then, please enjoy the comforts of this house."

When they have left the room, he writes out the orders he has been considering all day. McCown's and Cleburne's divisions of Hardee's corps will open the attack, the successive lines rolling over the Yankee flank and then wheeling to the right. Cheatham's and then Withers's divisions of Polk's corps will advance in echelon by brigade to Cleburne's right, the regiments of the Yankee right and center giving way as they are struck successively in front and flank by the pivoting wheel. Like a gigantic swinging door hinged on the Nashville Pike, the maneuver will sweep Rosecrans's fleeing multitudes before it until it slams against Stones River and Breckinridge's line on the far side. And this time Breckinridge will be exactly where he is ordered to be, or Bragg will have him shot.

★ ★ ★

Brigadier General Joshua Woodrow Sill is not by temperament a soldier. Many people know this, including his classmate, friend, and commanding officer, Phil Sheridan. In Kentucky, they both commanded divisions, but Sill has since been demoted to command of one of Sheridan's brigades.

The two friends sit together in the midnight hour under the cover of a rain fly, their backs to the fallen trunk of an oak. They have stripped off their wet uniform jackets and sit with blankets about their shoulders, blowing on cups of coffee. Sheridan, taciturn even in the best of peaceful moments, is glum over the prospect of little action in the morning.

"May I see the order?" Sill asks.

Sheridan reaches into a pocket and hands Sill a single sheet.

Sill unfolds it and leans close to the fire to read. He frowns. "This is General Rosecrans's order to General McCook. Didn't McCook amplify it?"

Sheridan shakes his head. "No, he just gave us copies and told us to exercise our best judgment as division commanders."

Sill reads: "'Take a strong position; if the enemy attacks, fall back slowly, refusing your right, contesting the ground inch by inch. If the enemy does not attack you, you will attack him, not vigorously, but warmly.'" Sill reads the order through a second time to himself. "'Not vigorously, but warmly.' That's an odd sort of phrase. I believe I detect the Jesuitical hand of Julius Garesché."

Sheridan grunts. "Yes, it sounds like him. What do you think McCook will do with the order?"

"I suppose he will do nothing. Alex hasn't seemed aggressively inclined of late."

"So unless we're attacked, we'll sit here all day trying to stay warm."

"So it would appear."

Sheridan shakes his head. "No matter how many times I consider it, I can't comprehend how a chucklehead like Alex McCook can be a major general commanding an entire army wing."

"Politics. His family—"

"Yes, politics. I know. But Rosy could have demoted him when he took command. McCook was utterly disgraced at Perryville."

"But Rosecrans wants to be governor of Ohio and then president. He'll need the McCooks behind him."

"Well, when the war ends, all this volunteer rank will be just so much paper. Alex, you, and I will be a trio of lowly captains again."

"Not me, Phil. I'll be back in my university while you two are chasing Indians on the prairies. You'll have many a long evening around the campfire to argue seniority. I plan to be at the Metropolitan Opera, a beautiful young thing on my arm."

Sheridan gives him a quick glance, receives a beatific smile in return: they both know it is as likely to be a beautiful boy as a beautiful girl.

To the rear, a horse approaches at a trot, hooves splashing through puddles. A sentry barks a challenge. "God, don't shoot him," Sheridan mutters. "No one's going to be coming at this hour except a courier." There is a muffled exchange of sign and countersign.

A moment later, the duty officer approaches. He is a robust young lieutenant, bursting with excitement and self-importance despite the chill drizzle. "A message from army headquarters, General," the lieutenant announces to Sheridan, snapping off a salute that showers water from his raincoat onto Sill's back and neck.

Sheridan acknowledges the salute. "Thank you, Lieutenant."

"You're welcome, sir." The lieutenant stands smiling, as if expecting to be included in the conversation of generals.

"That will be all, Lieutenant. You may look to your pickets."

"Oh. Yes, sir." The lieutenant bounds away.

Sheridan shakes his head, and Sill laughs gently. "And tomorrow he will fight like a lion and win the new medal Congress is giving out."

"But he'll never be so young again," Sheridan says.

"No. Never so young."

Sheridan unfolds the waxed cover, scans the message, and then passes it to Sill. "The commanding general has issued his proclamation for the morning."

Sill reads aloud: "'Soldiers, the eyes of the whole nation are upon you; the very fate of the nation may be said to hang on the issue of this day's battle. Be true, then, to yourselves, true to your own manly character and soldierly reputation, true to the love of your dear ones at home, whose prayers ascend to God this day for your success. Be cool! I need not ask you to be brave. Keep ranks. Do not throw away your fire. Fire slowly, deliberately; above all, fire low, and be always sure of your aim. Close steadily in upon the enemy, and, when you get within charging distance, rush on him with the bayonet. Do this, and the victory will certainly be yours. W. S. Rosecrans, Major Gen., U.S. Volunteers.'"

Sill looks up. "This is all well and good, Phil. But I don't want to assemble my brigade to hear this. I want my men in line, ready to repel anything the Rebs throw at us."

Sheridan nods. "Of course, although I doubt we have much to worry about. Send it down to the regiments and let the colonels read it to the men when they have a chance." He draws in lips, whistles a short, sharp note.

The duty officer is there in a moment, dripping face eager. "Yes, General."

"Have one of the clerks copy this. Give the first copy to General Sill, then send copies to Colonel Schaefer and Colonel Roberts."

"Yes, sir."

Sill and Sheridan sit in silence for a few minutes, staring into the rainy darkness. Sill asks: "Do you remember when you were assigned to my room after your suspension? It was an odd match."

Sheridan snorts. "It was a perfect match. They knew you had the integrity to report me if I broke the code of conduct. Colonel Robert E. Lee never intended for me to graduate. After all, I'd damned near bayoneted one of his fellow Virginians."

"Yes, one who died fighting for the Union. But do you remember what I told you?"

"That none of us could change the nature given us, but that we could learn to control our inclinations."

Sill smiles. "There was rather more to it at the time, but that was the sum of it. Well, I have learned to control my fear. I am still terrified, but I'll retreat only if forced. But can you retreat at all, Phil? Or are you going to refuse to give so much as an inch of ground, even if it means killing your entire command?"

Sheridan looks at him sharply. "You only asked me to master my temper. I have done that."

Sill smiles, knowing that he has gained the upper hand, as he always could over this Irish mucker's son. "I know you better now. It's more than temper."

"Then the answer is: I don't know what I would do."

"Well, I think your choice may determine whether you become a great general or die a foolish one."

"You are saying that I should learn to retreat?"

"A coward can't advise a warrior. He can only pose the questions."

"You are no coward."

Sill smiles, does not reply. A moment later the young lieutenant is back with Sill's copy of the proclamation. Sill rises. "Good night, Phil. Sleep if you can." He bundles his uniform jacket under his rain coat and steps into the drizzle.

Sheridan arranges his bed, folding the remaining uniform jacket for a pillow. He notices then that it is Sill's jacket, not his own. Well, no matter. In the morning, they will trade.

★ ★ ★

Brigadier General David Stanley is lying under a lean-to of canvas and cedar bows when he is awakened by the courier from Garesché. He reads the orders directing him to take charge of the army's trains between Wilkinson Crossroads and Stewart's Creek, forwarding the ordnance wagons and protecting McCook's rear.

The assignment seems better fitted to a junior colonel than to the commander of the Army of the Cumberland's cavalry, but Stanley is not disposed to argue in the aftermath of Wheeler's depredations. Besides, the cavalry is so wildly dispersed in chasing after Wheeler and protecting the remaining trains that he no longer has all that much to command anyway.

He steps from under the lean-to and turns his face up into the cold drizzle. He feels the first throb of what he supposes will be a hangover by first light. After leaving Rosecrans's headquarters, he and McCook had paused to drink a flask of brandy before parting. McCook will be, as always, unaffected. But Stanley is prone to hangovers—some weakness of the brain, he supposes—and should know better than to match Alex McCook drink for drink.

He calls his staff together and begins issuing orders. It will take at least an hour for the two regiments in the cavalry reserve to get on the road. In the meantime, he will ride ahead to look over the situation at the crossroads. He steps close to the fire, takes coffee from an aide, and drinks. Should he ask if anyone has a flask? No, a bad example, though no doubt many are staying warm tonight with the occasional snort of brandy or whiskey. Colonel John Kennett appears out of the darkness, growls, "What's all this foolishness I hear about Wheeler coming down our backs?"

"Have some coffee, Judge," Stanley says. "It'll improve your temper."

Kennett grumbles, looks about for coffee, accepts a cup and swallows. "God, Jesus! What kind of piss is this? Can't a man of you make a pot of coffee?" There are chuckles among the staff. Kennett glares. "If you came before my court I'd have you all whipped. Revive flogging, I say! Solve half the problems of the younger generation. That and decent coffee." Kennett swallows again, holds out his cup for a refill, still grumbling, though his eyes are merry.

Kennett is an old man for cavalry service—for any field service, really—hair turned iron gray and face furrowed by years of frowning down at petitioners and petty offenders from the bench in his Dayton courtroom. A volunteer officer in Mexico and a militia colonel afterward, he is technically in command of the cavalry division. Yet he is largely supernumerary in this army where Stanley, as chief of cavalry, has only the single division to direct. Kennett has accepted his role gracefully, relays Stanley's orders while daily dreading a discharge that will send him home to old age.

When Stanley has finished explaining Rosecrans's concerns, Kennett scowls. "I should go, you should stay. Come morning, we're going to have a hell of a fight here. I feel it."

"Perhaps, but I think it's more likely that we'll find Bragg withdrawing his left to the far side of the river come morning. That will cause a revision of our plans and another day of waiting. Besides, I'll only be a few miles off if I'm needed."

"Still, General. I think—"

"Judge, I want you to represent me at army headquarters. Colonel Zahm can manage the straggler line and watch the army's flanks."

The judge harrumphs. "Can I issue an order to young Zahm, or do I just pass on your orders?"

"Of course you can issue him orders, Judge. As circumstances dictate or the commanding general directs, issue all the orders you want to. Just keep me apprised of developments."

Kennett turns to demand yet a third cup of "this micturition you call coffee." (By the end of an ordinary day, he will have consumed two or three gallons, causing some on the staff to speculate that the old man actually died years before and is vivified only by the steady affluxion of coffee.) Stanley excuses himself, goes behind the lean-to to empty his bladder. He nearly trips over two orderly sergeants passing a half-gallon jug. They jump to their feet, attempting to hide the jug, then grin sheepishly. "It's a cold night, General," the older one says.

"Yes, it is, Sergeant. Very cold."

The sergeant glances down at the jug. "Would the general care for a bit of warmth?"

Why not? Stanley thinks. A democratic war, after all. "Thank you, Sergeant." He takes the jug, tilts it back, the corn liquor cold as ice water in his mouth, then turning raw fire in his gullet. He coughs, smiles at the grinning sergeants, and takes another, longer swallow, already feeling better.

He hands the jug back and waits for it to pass around to him again. Another swallow or two and he will be ready to go see to the supply trains. Perhaps Wheeler *will* come with the dawn. Perhaps Stanley will have his revenge early, recover all the reputation the last day has cost him. He notices that the sergeants' faces have taken on a rosy glow in the firelight. Damn good fellows. Should learn their names.

Wheeler can push his brigade no farther. A dozen miles short of Murfreesboro, he lets them fall out to bivouac in a field beside the Salem Pike. The men are exhausted, will be useless for anything until late in the day. They fall asleep in clumps, pressed to each other to preserve what body heat they can on the freezing earth. Wheeler rides on toward Bragg's headquarters to report. He knows that captured wagons have been rolling into the Confederate lines all afternoon and evening, and with them reports of all the destruction he and his men have wreaked on the Yankee army. Yet he has a sensation of opportunities overlooked, of greatness missed by an eyelash, of still being "Little Joe"—not "Fighting Joe"—Wheeler.

☆ ☆ ☆

When Garesché lies down, he cannot imagine sleeping. Yet he does sleep. He dreams of sitting over glasses of wine with his brother Frederick, the priest, in the Washington café near the War Department. It is summer again, the afternoon light flooding across the tablecloth so that the glasses are elongated in reflection, the wine as red as the blood running from Christ's side in the crucifixion window of St. Catherine's. He is telling again of sitting beneath the window, the crazy old woman behind him, whispering of death in his first battle, of Julius Garesché rendered no more. He wants very much to hear Frederick tell him again that such presentiments are "fumes of an overwrought fancy." But his brother does not speak, sits rather with face immobile, grim, accepting. Garesché reaches out a hand in appeal: *Tell me that I will see them again. My wife, my children. Tell me—*

But his brother rises, turns without farewell, walks toward the door. As if tipped by some invisible hand, the wine glasses overturn, spilling across the tablecloth. He tries to staunch the spreading stain, blots desperately at it with his napkin, then his coat sleeve, but it overspreads the table, floods onto the floor, no longer wine but blood in an unremitting torrent. He cries out to his brother for help, but Frederick is gone, the open door swinging lazily on silent hinges. Garesché runs after him, his shoes splashing ankle-deep in the gore that flows unnoticed among the crowded tables. No one looks up or pays him the least mind. He steps not onto a Washington street or a Tennessee lane but into a place he has never seen: a blasted landscape of lava-scorched bushes and black ash slopes under a sky so blue that it might have been painted by Donatello or Fra Lippo Lippi except that there is no pity in it.

Bragg dreams of the perfection of flying artillery, of the beauty of his guns, shining bronze in the Mexican sun. This wasn't clumsy horse artillery, no motley collection of nags and men supporting the infantry. A flying battery was a weapon unlike anything the world had ever seen: every man mounted, every gun, limber, and caisson moving with the choreography of ballet. From now on, it would be the decisive factor in battle. Bragg and a half dozen young artillery officers, among them George Thomas, had come to Mexico to prove it so.

It fell to Bragg at Buena Vista to show the world. He wheeled his guns from crisis to crisis, always one step ahead of disaster. He can picture Colonel Jefferson Davis: tall, gaunt, unmistakable in his manliness as his red-shirted Mississippians formed their famous V to repel a Mexican charge. The maneuver was doomed, the last desperate tactic before the Mexicans wrecked Taylor's army. Then Bragg and his guns hurtled out of a deep draw like demons summoned from the underworld. In the brief three minutes before the charging Mexicans could cross the plateau, Bragg's guns swung round, unlimbered, and loosed a blast of grapeshot that eviscerated the Mexican formations. The Mississippians fired their volley and charged, Davis in the forefront, to drive the Mexicans off the plateau. By the time the Mississippians fell to butchering the wounded with their bowie knives, Bragg's battery was limbered and dashing off to another crisis.

What he would not give to be twenty-nine again, flogging his battery through the dust, smoke, fire, and glory of that day. But all is lost now: youth, health, fame, and the flying artillery itself. There are a few recon-stituted batteries—none in this army nor Rosecrans's either—but they are little more than showpieces floating on the immense vulgarity of this war. Bragg opens his eyes, unsure if he has slept. It is the last day of 1862, and even now his troops are moving into position for the assault at dawn. He feels no fear of failure, only a despondency that he cannot win. Not finally. Not ever.

Rosecrans smokes a cigar in the dark cabin, listening to Garesché's deep, steady breathing. He has tried to sleep, but each time he has begun to fall into unconsciousness there have come images of fire—the retort of coal oil exploding, setting him alight: his shirt, his hands, his face, his hair. And as he breathes in the fire, he jerks out of the dream before it can take him utterly.

He thinks back, watches himself turn up the flame under the retort and then grab a pencil to record in his notebook the latest results of his experiment. He was hurrying, skipping steps, taking chances, his mind rushing ahead through the complexities of the problem, forgetting to watch the temperature. Then the moment he turned again to the burner and the retort, saw the oil boiling and knew an instant too late that he had blundered. Then the flash and the fire. All because of haste.

He blows smoke toward the low ceiling, shifts his weight on the narrow bed. He knows that haste is his flaw, that he must guard against it above all else. That is why he refused to march this army from Nashville before all was ready, refused when Halleck and Stanton threatened to relieve him, refused even when that pathetic oaf Lincoln entreated him to move for the sake of the Republic. He has advanced on his own schedule and it has worked. Even the damage to the trains will prove without consequence in a day or two. He reviews his plan for the morning, picturing it step by step, though he is already sure of its every detail. As long as McCook holds, we will be all right, he thinks. A pity that we do not have better cavalry. Unless Bragg is incredibly maladroit, we can only drub him, not destroy him. In the end, he will be able to rescue his army and retreat. But I will never let him come north again.

Lieutenant General Leonidas Polk, Bishop of Louisiana and former Missionary Bishop to the Southwest, lies on his back, hands folded over ample belly, snoring softly. He dreams of Shiloh and the moment when it was first granted to him to see the souls of the dead. He had always imagined fluttering, gossamer things, rising on the breath of God. But they were not so at all, but pathetic dark moths, flapping among the corpses, vainly seeking readmission to their corporeal homes. In that moment he knew that the Resurrection was a falsehood, that the soul of the would-be Christ tumbled from his body into the rubble at the foot of the Cross, ignored by Roman soldiers and praying disciples alike.

Yet with this realization came a new certainty: that the souls of those who expect nothing from God have power and grace, live on as predators in an eternity as savage as carnal existence. Certainly it is so. Polk has proof; for with each minute at Shiloh, he felt his soul changing, transforming, becoming huge and terrible and magnificent.

That evening Polk wandered behind the lines until he found a lonely cabin with a wisp of smoke from the chimney. He pushed through the door without knocking. A woman turned from the fireplace and her stew pot. Polk did not say a word but dropped a silver dollar on the table and unbuckled his sword. The woman understood, swung the pot so that it would hang simmering at the back of the fire, and went to the pallet in the corner, where she lay back, pulling up her faded dress. And though she was a crone, teeth gone, shrunken teats hanging, Polk entered her with a passion he had never felt before, rode her until she wailed, and when he had climaxed and climaxed again, he left her. He would have killed her with his cock if he could have, nearly did with hands about her throat, but left her alive in the last act of mercy in his life.

That night and every night since, Polk dreams he is a great, gray wolf prowling among the piles of corpses on the field at Shiloh, feeding on the souls of the dead.

$$\star \quad \star \quad \star$$

In the darkness beyond the Yankee right, Hardee has McCown's and Cleburne's divisions sidestepping to strike the far end of McCook's line. Hardee sits his horse by the Franklin Pike, watching the troops trudge by in the dark. It is amazing to him that even on a rainy night there always seems enough light for men to march. "Move along, boys," he murmurs. "Keep ranks."

"Why don't you shut up?" a voice hisses back. "General Cleburne said no talkin', an' you ain't him."

Hardee smiles, says nothing.

"My apologies for that, General." Cleburne at his side, out of the darkness.

Even in the gloom, Hardee can read the ungainly proportions of Cleburne's latest plowhorse. But though the beast has been selected for its placidity and lack of imagination, it shifts uneasily under Cleburne. It must be the man's intensity, Hardee thinks. My God, the boy shimmers like a panther tonight. He is my creation, my killer, yet he frightens me. Hardee reaches out, squeezes Cleburne's shoulder, feels the muscles flinch. "No apology necessary, Patrick. You gave them the proper instructions. I was the one who erred in speaking."

"Still, you are horseback and an officer. The man—"

"This is not the British army. Here men are more inclined to speak their minds. Free men fighting for the independence of their country. From such men, I can stand the occasional backtalk."

Cleburne is silent a moment. Sighs. "Yes, of course. And for such men, we need do our best. It is not my place to say it, General, but I am concerned. . . ." He hesitates.

"Go ahead, Pat."

"I am concerned about the control General McCown has of his division. He does not seem to me sufficiently . . . decisive."

"I know. I am concerned, and so is the commanding general. But I have given General McCown thorough instructions. He is to strike the enemy flank at the oblique and then begin the wheel, his brigades moving in echelon. He cannot misunderstand."

Cleburne is silent, the horse shifting under him. Finally, he says, "Yes, General. I should go now and see that my artillery is moving expeditiously."

"Certainly, Pat. I will see you in the morning." And a bloody one it will be, Hardee thinks. God protect you, boy.

Cleburne focuses on minutiae, prodding his division into better order despite the darkness. The division color guard passes, flags furled, and he permits himself a momentary picture of the division on attack. His is the only division in the army granted the right to carry its own unique flag. It is a privilege bought with blood. But, God, it is a glorious banner. Cleburne can picture it unfurling amid the cedars in the dawn, a breeze catching its folds to outspread a silver moon on a night-blue background. And because Cleburne is at heart a romantic—something that not even Hardee understands—he whispers the ancient battle cry of the Irish: "Faugh a ballagh!" *Clear the way!*

Brigadier General Joshua Sill prowls his line, listening to the darkness. It is there, he is sure: a low, steady shuffle, men moving, many men. He goes forward to investigate. At 2:00 A.M., he sends word to Sheridan, who shortly joins him on the picket line. At first skeptical, Sheridan is soon alarmed, and together they ride to see McCook at right wing headquarters near the Gresham house.

The roadmaster wagons haven't arrived, and McCook is asleep on a bale of straw under a rain fly in the angle of a worm fence. He listens bleary-eyed to Sheridan and Sill. Their mouths move in the lantern light, but he cannot at first fathom what they are saying. The Rebs are on the defensive; he is sure of it. Any sound of movement must come from Bragg rear-ranging his line, nothing more.

He yawns, tries to concentrate. Why is it that Sheridan and Sill, usually so calm, seem so exercised? It is he who feels on the edge of panic most of the time these days, he who worries that he may reveal his fear to the likes of these two. He raises a hand to quiet them. "Everything has been antici-pated. Crittenden will advance against the Rebel right in the morning. Our duty is to hold while he opens the battle. By late morning, we may be called on to participate in an envelopment. Until then, I suggest that we stand easy." For another fifteen minutes, Sheridan and Sill try to impress on McCook the danger in their front. But McCook is spookily calm in his refusal to find anything amiss in the right wing's preparedness.

Sheridan sends Sill back to his line while he stops to alert Colonel Frederick Schaefer, commander of his reserve brigade. Schaefer jackknifes to his feet, listens intently to Sheridan. A former sergeant in the army of one of the minor German states, Schaefer is another of this army's many veter-ans of the 1848 uprisings. "Send Sill two regiments as soon as you have your men mustered," Sheridan says.

Schaefer almost clicks his heels, catches himself. "Yes, General."

Sheridan mounts, rides on, knowing that Schaefer will be thoroughly prepared and as calm as stone when the battle begins. He feels equally for-tunate in his third brigade commander, Colonel George W. Roberts, a strik-ingly handsome Illinois lawyer and pre-war militia officer. Roberts bounds from his bed of cedar boughs, all confidence and high spirits. Together they visit each of the regimental commanders. In minutes, the soldiers are rolling out of their blankets to muster under arms, breath steaming in the frosty drizzle turning now and then to snow. Sheridan rides on to Sill's brigade, where with his friend he again walks the line, speaking to each regimental colonel. Whatever happens with the rest of McCook's wing, Sheridan's divi-sion will be ready for the dawn.

Sill and his pickets are not alone in hearing the sound of troops moving in the dark. Pickets in front of Davis's and Johnson's divisions likewise send back reports. But the forest is tricky, letting sound carry in some places while blotting it out in others. Staff officers riding forward to confirm reports hear nothing, berate pickets for panicking.

On the extreme right of McCook's corps, where Willich's brigade straddles the Franklin Pike, Colonel William Gibson of the 49th Ohio sends a combat patrol forward into the gloom. It returns an hour later having found nothing.

At nearly the same time, Chief Surgeon Solon Marks of Johnson's division steps from a hospital tent near Overall Creek, a full mile to the rear of Willich's line, to listen to the rumble of moving artillery. He returns to his bed atop an operating table to rest in the little time before the cataclysm. He doesn't think to report what he has heard. Surely the right wing must already be under arms, waiting for the Rebel attack.

At 4:00 A.M., the sodden wind that has blown all night drops away and the rain eases to a mist. The cedars beyond McCook's line are quiet, the pickets no longer firing the occasional nervous shot. Sheridan wonders if he, Sill, and the pickets have all been mistaken. Perhaps there is no great Rebel force out in front. But he feels the iron weight in his gut, the cannonball of certainty that always tells him when something is about to happen. No, they are there. He can feel the bastards waiting for the light.

★   ★   ★

Brigadier General David Stanley arrives at the wagon park near Stewart's Creek an hour before daylight, where he is greeted warmly by red-faced Colonel Joe Burke of the 10th Ohio. Patrols have been out on the roads all night and report no sign of Wheeler's cavalry. Would the general like a bit of good Irish whiskey to chase the chill? The general would.

They join the regimental chaplain, who is supervising the preparation of a milk punch. Stanley gulps straight whiskey from Burke's flask and then tries the punch. The colonel orders breakfast and the three settle down, in the chaplain's recollection, "to a delightful hot punch and a delicate breakfast."

McCook has not slept since Sheridan and Sill left. He rises now, calls for his chief of staff. "Send word to Generals Sheridan, Davis, and Johnson that they might be advised to have their men under arms at daybreak."

The chief of staff stirs from his usual reticence. "Should I make that a peremptory order, General?"

McCook hesitates. "No. Just advisory. They know better the situation in front of their lines."

In the predawn stillness, Braxton Bragg leaves the comfort of the house in Murfreesboro for his field headquarters behind the Confederate left center, west of Stones River. Joe Wheeler rides with him, delivering his report on the damage to the Federal trains.

"Well done, General," Bragg says. "When will your brigade be ready for further duty?"

Wheeler hesitates. "They're pretty well used up, General. Not so much the men as the mounts. If I'd known we were going to fight so soon. . . ." His voice trails off.

The boy is exhausted, Bragg thinks, has probably not slept more than a few hours in all the time since the Yankees marched from Nashville. He feels a sudden welling of sympathy. He would like to touch the boy, let his hand rest on Wheeler's arm for a moment. But he cannot reach across the distance. He will call him Joe, let drop for a moment the formality of military etiquette. No, not Joe. That is entirely too familiar. He will call him Joseph in a fatherly tone.

But he cannot. Instead he hears his voice using the cool tone of senior to subordinate. "Don't concern yourself overmuch, General. Your men did good work yesterday."

Julius Garesché wakes to a touch on his shoulder, opens his eyes to see Rosecrans's large smiling face. "Time to get ready, Julius. 'Dawn speeds a man on his journey, and speeds him too in his work.'"

Garesché swings his feet off his cot. He feels remarkably fresh, as if he had slept round the clock rather than a few hours. Magee brings him a cup of coffee, and he sits for a few moments savoring it. "I confess I don't recognize the quote, General."

"It's Hesiod. *Works and Days.*"

"Your erudition never fails to amaze me."

"Thank you, Julius." Rosecrans swings a sky-blue cloak over his shoulders. Garesché stands hurriedly but Rosecrans holds up a palm. "It's all right. I'm just going outside to look at the weather and smoke a cigar."

"General, the Rebel guns on the hill—"

"Pah. Let them shoot. I'll watch the fall of shot and dodge as needs be." He steps outside.

A moment later, Goddard comes in with messages. "Nothing very significant, Colonel. General Stanley reports everything quiet out on the Wilkinson Pike. The same seems to be true all along our line. No reports to the contrary, at least."

"Very good, Major. Coffee?"

"No, thank you, sir. I've had mine."

Goddard begins busily arranging the messages on the table. Garesché reads leisurely through the first pile. Why am I so languorous this morning? he wonders. As if nothing could possibly bother me. This is the dawn of my first battle, and I think I could easily go back to sleep. How strange.

He hears Father Treacy's tenor brogue outside the cabin and

Rosecrans's deeper reply. After a moment, the two go to the far side of the cabin. Garesché steps to a narrow, dusty window. Rosecrans is on his knees, making confession amid the ferns where the head of the decapitated orderly had lain the afternoon before. The memory squeezes Garesché's heart, wrings the languor from his thoughts. He returns to the table, flips rapidly through the remaining messages, and reaches for his coat. He, too, must confess, prepare for the day and all its eventualities.

Everyone save Rosecrans, who seems truly oblivious to the danger of the place, is relieved to abandon the cabin. Goddard returns to the tents in the woods to direct the remainder of the staff while Garesché, Treacy, and the usual train of aides and escorts ride with Rosecrans to mass. Van Cleve's division of Crittenden's left wing is camped along McFadden's Lane, its closest brigade a half mile from the ford across Stones River. The men are making coffee and roasting salt pork over small fires in the early light. Like Napoleon, Rosecrans believes in sending men into battle with something on their stomachs besides fear.

The staff stops to hear mass at the camp of the Thirty-fifth Indiana. Father Peter Coone, a smiling, elfin man, greets them in his fluting voice. Treacy steps inside to assist Coone with the sacrament while Rosecrans and Garesché remove their hats and kneel under an awning forming a presbytery before the open door of the tent. Three of the enlisted order-lies join the hundred or so soldiers who move forward to kneel in a rough semicircle about the tent. The rest of the staff stands off at a distance. Some of the men are noticeably uncomfortable, for most of them are Protestant Midwesterners and this is Papism, the stuff of mystery, conspiracy, and corruption.

Coone moves rapidly through the liturgy of the mass. Rosecrans and Garesché receive the sacrament, and then Coone, Treacy, and two younger priests move quickly through the semicircle of enlisted men. When Coone stands again before the congregation, he smiles, raises his arms: "Go, my sons, in the armor of righteousness to restore peace and Union to this land."

Rosecrans shakes hands with Coone, pausing to talk for a few minutes. Garesché spots Hazen astride his bay gelding beyond the edge of the dispersing crowd. He excuses himself and makes his way through to him. Hazen swings down, handing reins to the ubiquitous topographical engineer, Bierce, who avoids meeting Garesché's eyes.

Garesché reads his friend's face and smiles: Bill Hazen is angry again. When was it ever otherwise? "And how is it with you this morning, Bill?"

"I'm fine, Julius. Fine. My men are ready. Have been for an hour."

"Then why do you look like you're about to throw a tantrum?"

"Because this army is moving too slowly, Julius. Van Cleve's men should be on the road and they're still cooking breakfast! He has half a mile to go to the ford and then nearly two more on the far side of the river before he'll be in position to strike the Rebel flank. With the time he'll need to deploy, it will be three hours before he can attack. Meanwhile, our right is vulnerable to whatever Bragg chooses to do. If *he* moved early, there could be hell to pay very shortly."

Garesché shakes his head. "Bill, I am going to recommend to the commanding general that he secure you an independent command. Your talents are lost leading a mere brigade."

"Don't mock me, Julius."

"I am not mocking you. I am completely serious. Or you and I could swap places, since your advice would no doubt be much better than mine. Except, of course, that you lack some of the diplomacy required of a chief of staff."

"Now you are mocking me."

"No, I swear, Bill. But listen. General Rosecrans has anticipated these things and has chosen to sacrifice time for the additional strength that a hot breakfast will give the men. It is not sloth that determines our hour of advance."

"And our right flank?"

"Our right flank is commanded by General McCook, a man in whom I know you have less than full confidence. But General McCook has specific instructions on how he and his wing are to conduct themselves. And whatever you may think of him, remember that he has excellent division commanders." Garesché waits. "Does he not?"

Hazen shrugs. "I suppose they are acceptable. Davis and Sheridan are fighters."

"And General Johnson?"

"Bandbox Johnson? He of the saber-swinging charges? I am not sure the army is the better for regaining his services. I might have delayed exchanging him until we had fought this campaign."

Garesché laughs. "My God, you are a hard man, Bill! General Johnson is a fine officer. Not as well suited to the cavalry as perhaps he might have been, but I'm sure he will do admirably in his present position." Garesché glances over his shoulder, sees Rosecrans preparing to mount Boney, his big gray gelding. "Now I must be off to join the general. He wants to get Van Cleve across the ford, then he'll return to this portion of the field. You take care today, Bill. Let us meet this evening and you can review the performance of the army for me and the reasons your fears proved illusory."

"Happily they will be, Julius."

An orderly hurries forward with Garesché's mount. Garesché takes the reins and swings up. He looks at Bierce. "Have you prepared your arsenal of literary quotes for the day, Lieutenant?"

Bierce smiles, almost shyly. "I have tried, Colonel."

"Good. When all is done, perhaps you will find something more than irony in them. Gentlemen. . . ."

The hour is approaching six. Major General George Thomas steps from his tent resplendent in a new dress uniform. Although he has been entitled to the two-starred shoulder straps since the previous spring, this is the first time he has worn them. The omission represents his only superstition: that an officer should never assume a new rank until he is prepared to prove himself worthy of it on a day of battle. At Perryville he had been caught unprepared, wearing his brigadier's stars. And like the army, he had made a botch of things. Today will be better.

His aides and orderlies stand to attention. Thomas surveys them, growls, "Well?" There are grins, polite applause. Thomas permits himself a grim smile. "Thank you, gentlemen. Let us be about our work." He goes to his horse, sets his jaw, and swings up.

Dawn has chased the fears of Major General Alexander McDowell McCook, and he leans back comfortably in a chair salvaged from the Gresham house. An orderly finishes stropping a razor and begins applying lather to the general's stubbly jaw.

At his headquarters west of the Gresham house, Brigadier General Richard W. Johnson, commanding Second Division on the far right of McCook's wing, washes down griddle cakes with a tumbler of brandy. He accepts a cup of coffee, adds a deliberate lacing of brandy, and stares gloomily at the gray dawn, wondering if his older brother, a Confederate surgeon, is with Bragg's army this day.

At 6:00 A.M., Captain Warren Edgarton, commanding Battery E, 1st Ohio Artillery, attached to Kirk's brigade of Johnson's division, studies the quiet woods beyond the narrow valley to his front. Behind him, the artillery horses stamp impatiently. He decides not to wait any longer and gives orders for watering half the horses at the slender, unnamed brook five hundred yards to the rear.

Down the line from Kirk's brigade, Brigadier General August Willich and his senior regimental commander, Colonel William Gibson of the 49th Ohio, are likewise staring at the fog-shrouded cedars. Willich scratches his beard, shakes his big head. "They are so quiet out there that I guess they are no more here."

"So it would seem," Gibson says.

"Then I go see General Johnson a few minutes. You keep the boys from going larking."

Gibson smiles. "By all means, General."

Corporal Matthew O'Leary, one of Kirk's pickets, opens the heavy watch given him by his father on the day the old man sent him off to war: 6:22 A.M. and the relief is late again. Snapping the case shut, O'Leary looks up to see a long line of butternut soldiers rising up out of the valley mist as if from the ground itself. Silent. Coming at the run.

CHAPTER 2

Wednesday, 5:00 A.M.–8:30 A.M.
December 31, 1862
The Confederate Left South of the Franklin Pike

Hardee has McCown's and Cleburne's divisions in position for the assault on Rosecrans's right. McCown's line will go first, the brigades of Brigadier Generals James Rains, Matthew Ector, and Evander McNair left to right. Cleburne's division will follow five hundred yards behind McCown's, the brigades of Brigadier Generals St. John Liddell, Bushrod Johnson, and Lucius Polk, left to right, with Brigadier General S.A.M. Wood's brigade in reserve to Polk's rear. Cleburne's line will add weight to McCown's attack and fill in any developing gaps, but its real purpose will come later when the great wheel to the right begins rolling up the Federal line. Sweeping around McCown's left flank, Brigadier General John Wharton's cavalry will spread havoc among the retreating Yankees, capturing those who surrender and pushing the rest north toward the Nashville Pike.

There is, however, a flaw in the Confederate dispositions. Hardee has been misled by the fires built beyond McCook's right flank to disguise the terminal point of the Federal line. As a result, Rains's brigade will strike only thin air, its forward progress unabated as it pulls McCown's line to the west (left), throwing off Bragg's great wheel and uncovering Cleburne's unsuspecting line.

Brigadier General Richard Johnson's division holds the right end of McCook's line: Brigadier General August Willich's brigade on the Franklin Pike; Brigadier General Edward Kirk's brigade to his left; and Colonel Philemon Baldwin's brigade in reserve a mile to the right rear. Next in line is the division of Brigadier General Jefferson C. Davis, the brigades of Colonels P. Sidney Post, William Carlin, and William Woodruff, right to left. Sheridan's division holds onto Davis's left, the brigades of Brigadier General Joshua Sill and Colonel George Roberts in the front line and Colonel Frederick Schaefer's brigade in reserve near the Harding house.

*J*T IS COLD, the men shivering in the damp wind as they wait for the dawn. A few of them have thought to secret a piece of hardtack or cornbread on their persons to chew in the long wait, but most are hungry. General Bill Hardee wishes he could give them a hot breakfast, hot coffee at least. The best he can provide is a jot of whiskey for each man.

Cleburne objects: the men have nothing on their stomachs and some of them—particularly the young ones—may become nauseous, even inebriated. Hardee chuckles. "You are a strange Irishman, Patrick. I thought your race habitually went into battle with a glaive in one hand and a flagon in the other."

Cleburne grimaces. "And lost many a battle through drunken stupidity. And this army risks the same disgrace in adopting the practice."

"Come, General. We are giving the men a single small drink to warm them before battle. It is my decision and I take full responsibility."

"Very well, sir. I shall give the order." Cleburne jerks the head of his plowhorse to the right, causing the animal to toss its head in protest.

Hardee calls after him. "Patrick, did you ever hear it said that God made whiskey to keep the Irish from ruling the world?"

Cleburne turns, his face expressionless in the gloom. "No, General, but I expect it is so."

Hardee smiles, shakes his head. For all his virtues, Major General Patrick Ronayne Cleburne is a young man utterly without a sense of humor. If we survive this day, Hardee thinks, I shall have to teach him something of the grace of laughter.

As the sky begins to lighten, Hardee rides forward to a vantage where he can watch the lines advance. A few minutes before 6:00 A.M., he dispatches an aide to tell McCown to advance. The order should not be necessary, but Hardee knows McCown's timidity too well to trust a prompt execution of earlier instructions. He waits. My God, it is quiet, he thinks. How can so many men and horses occupy so small an area and yet make so little noise? He feels more than hears the first reverberation, a palpitation of the earth as of some dread thing coming awake from a long sleep. It is a sound like no other, this first tramp of an army advancing in cadence. And General William J. Hardee, like no other man alive, can claim the exact rhythm as his own, for it is the cadence he prescribed in *Rifle and Light Infantry Tactics* that will take so many into battle, so many to their deaths, this army to victory.

The reverberation deepens, Cleburne's 6,000 stepping out to follow McCown's 4,400 into the mist. Hardee counts the paces without thinking, hears McCown's line go to the double-quick, then to the charge. Still no yelling, no cheering, no noise at all save the sound of all the thousands and thousands of feet pulsating the earth. He cranes, squints, can make them out: the long butternut lines rising out of the valley, the first winking of muzzle flashes ahead in the mist as the Yankee pickets open fire. Bill Hardee, who long ago gave up smoking at his daughters' insistence, wishes he had a cigar to clamp in his teeth to arrest the quivering of his chin.

☆   ☆   ☆

A stag comes first, trailed by two does, one a yearling, the other larger: perhaps its mother. They bound through the camp of the 34th Illinois, dodging among the cooking fires and the sleepy men still waiting for their coffee to boil. Men laugh. One soldier dives for the yearling, nearly catches it. Another grabs for his musket. A sergeant shouts: "Miller, you damned fool, you'll shoot somebody!"

The rabbits come next, skittering this way and that among the men, who try to hit them with sticks and frying pans, all the while laughing. "Watch out!" a burly farm boy shouts. "There's rattlers chasing 'em!" He takes a swing with a musket butt at one of a dozen snakes whiplashing in terror through the camp. Men scatter, then as suddenly forget the snakes at the first popping of musket fire from the picket line.

Captain Warren Edgarton, Battery E, 1st Ohio Artillery, who only moments before sent half the battery's horses off to be watered, leaps atop a gun carriage, peers into the mist. The pickets are running, behind them a long butternut line of Rebel infantry. "Assemble!" he shouts. "Load canister! Get the horses up, for Christ's sake!"

Battery E is an excellent battery, well trained, proud of its six tenpounder Parrott rifles. The gunners sprint to their tasks. Cut fuse, load, ram, prime . . . wait, wait. The pickets coming, running all-out. Infantry assembling behind the guns, the snick of ramrods in barrels, the cocking of hammers, the shouts of sergeants and officers. Men praying almost without knowing, sobbing, growling, panting as though they'd already fought hand-to-hand a thousand demons. And they have, fight them still, the demons that make any sane man want to run, to give way before this awful vision coming out of the dark valley and across the cornfield to the brigade's front. As far as the eye can see in both directions, a thick line of butternut infantry—God, there must be ten thousand, twenty thousand, a hundred thousand—the rising surge of their footfalls sounding to one officer like a ramping surf. These Midwestern farmboys in blue know nothing of surf, nothing of the ocean, but they know of tornadoes, of the coming freight-train roar of cyclonic doom, and hear it in the onrush of the butternut line while above and above it again and again, tearing at the nerves, at the very heart of even the bravest among the blue soldiers, the first quavering, ghastly wail of the Rebel yell. "Fire!" Edgarton screams as the pickets duck between the guns.

The canister makes the Parrotts into giant shotguns, each round spraying two dozen inch-and-a-half iron balls. Yet the butternut ranks seem to absorb the blasts without effect. The Yankee gunners swab, ram canister, fire. Men start dropping in the Rebel ranks. A round of canister strikes a bulge in the charging line where the 10th Texas has pushed out ahead a few yards, bursts it like an immense boil, showering disembodied limbs, heads, and shredded uniforms. From the Rebel line there comes a moaning grunt, as if from a single voice: a fighter struck hard in the midriff but still coming, boring in.

Brigadier General Edward Kirk, Edgarton's brigade commander, shouts at Colonel Joseph Dodge of the 34th Illinois. "Hit that regiment on the flank, or they'll take the guns and we're finished!" Ashen, Dodge waves an acknowledgment, gives orders. Kirk pushes out in front—handsome, still boyish at thirty-four. The 34th is his old regiment and he will lead it now. He turns in his saddle, looks back at the ranks he recruited himself, at the soldiers who elected him colonel, shouts: "Illini! For your state and your flag, forward at the double-quick!"

Seventy-five yards into the cornfield, the 34th Illinois takes a blistering volley from the 10th Texas. Kirk is knocked from his horse, down with a mortal wound in the thigh that will take seven months to kill him. His horse bolts the field, streaming blood from chest, neck, and flank. Dodge takes command of the regiment, leads its survivors back to the guns. They hold there, firing and firing. The color sergeant drops, another man lifts the banner. Then he is down and another man grabs for the staff, waves the banner until he too is shot.

Edgarton is bringing in the horses now, trying to get the guns off. But four Rebel regiments are converging, and a tremendous volley sweeps the battery. Seventy horses are down in an instant, kicking, screaming, dying. The fourth color bearer has fallen, his place taken by a corporal with a shattered left hand and blood streaming from a ragged ear. Edgarton feels a leg go out from under him, knows he is hit, catches himself on the wheel of a limber. The Rebels are in among the guns, gaunt men, eyes flaming, slashing at the gunners with bayonets and rifle butts. The wounded corporal falls, the banner grabbed by a man in butternut. Edgarton tries to draw his revolver, but a Rebel hits him in the chest with a rifle butt and he goes down beside his smoking cannons.

Hundreds of men have fallen in the fight for the guns: half of the 34th Illinois, score upon score from the 11th and 10th Texas, the 4th and 30th Arkansas. Seven of ten company commanders in the 30th Arkansas are dead or wounded. Colonel J. C. Burks of the 11th Texas rides among his men. "Keep going, boys. Keep going," he wheezes. "We've got them now."

One of the Texans notes that Burks is riding hunched forward, coat hugged tight to his right side, his uniform soaked red from chest to knee. "Colonel, are you all right?"

The colonel smiles wistfully, shakes his head, and tumbles dead from his horse. A second soldier pulls the coat away from the wound. A canister ball has ripped through the colonel's chest, shattering ribs and tearing away the lower half of a lung. "My God," says the soldier. "How did he last so long?"

Out in the cornfield, among the dead and wounded, Private John Gorgas, Company A, 34th Illinois, lies staring at the rainy sky. He'd been on picket, had seen the first Rebs rising out of the mist. And he'd run. God, how he'd run. He hadn't bothered to fire his rifle, just dropped it and ran. I'm running to tell someone, he told himself. But that was a lie; he was just running. The first ball struck him in the hip, spun him around, and dropped him in the cornstalks. He staggered up, still managed to run. The second hit him in the left side of the neck, threw him forward into the stubble again. And again he staggered up, ran. "Whoa there, Yank! Halt!" a voice shouted behind him. He ignored it, and the third ball hit him in the side. After that, he couldn't run but only lie and bleed and stare at the rainy sky. He closes his eyes, lets the darkness come, wondering if he will wake again. He will, and survives to marry and tell the story to children, grandchildren, and finally great-grandchildren born in a new century.

Ector's brigade pours into the hole left by the 34th Illinois. Coming in on the right, McNair's brigade strikes the 30th and 29th Indiana. The colonel of the 30th panics, orders his regiment to retreat. The 29th tries to hold, but its fire is blocked by fleeing pickets. It looses a single volley when McNair's line is twenty yards away, gaining just enough time to turn tail and run. A Rebel private captured in the skirmishing the day before shouts: "What you runnin' fer? Why don't you stand an' fight like men?"

A fellow prisoner snaps at him: "For God's sake, Joe! Don't rally the sons o' bitches!"

As luck would have it, their own company comes trotting through the smoking Yankee camp. The sergeant shouts: "Well, I see you boys are still alive. Grab a rifle and come along. Like it or not, you're back in Braxton Bragg's army."

☆   ☆   ☆

The old man amuses Brigadier General Richard Johnson. August Willich seems a man absurdly out of time and place: a kindly German grandfather who should at this hour be lumbering into a warm kitchen, pausing to tousle the heads of grandchildren before accepting a steaming mug from his plump, gray Frau—a mug chipped and cracked and that she would throw out, save that it gives them both pleasure for her to tease him about it in the fondly irritable way of old couples. Settled at the head of the table, he would several times rebuff the pleadings of the grandchildren, finally giving in and telling them a tale out of the Brothers Grimm, something of wolves and winter woods to enliven their foggy walk to school with phantasmal shadows and delightful alarms.

The warmth, the very poetry of the conjured scene rather thrills Johnson, gives him a better regard for the dripping morning. He extends his flask to Willich. "A small eye-opener in your coffee, General?" Willich hesitates, Johnson smiles. "It's all right, General. We're in for a quiet morning on this part of the line."

Willich shrugs his massive shoulders, accepts the flask. Off to the south there is a crackle of picket fire—nothing particularly unusual, since pickets are always finding excuses to discharge their weapons. Willich pours a tablespoon of the brandy into his coffee. The concussive roar of a battery of guns echoes from the south, then the crash of a volley of musketry. Willich leaps to his feet, old eyes squinting toward his distant line. Another crash of musketry reverberates over the distance. Heavy, many hundreds of rifle-muskets. "Mein Gott! Ve attacked be!" Willich shouts. He drops his cup, stumbles over a camp stool, runs on creaking joints toward his horse.

Johnson stares at the place vacated by the old man, at the overturned flask leaking amber liquor onto the soft ground. No, there must be some other explanation. Not an attack, but. . . . He tries to summon a shout to call Willich back, but the sound of artillery and musketry robs him of voice.

His chief of staff comes running. "General! What are your orders?"

Johnson stares blankly at the man. Orders? He has no orders. Has received none since last night, when McCook forwarded Rosecrans's order to hold the line if attacked, falling back inch by inch, defending not vigorously but warmly. No, there is something wrong here, something he is not remembering correctly. Not warmly but vigorously? Attack, not defend?

"General, what do you want us to do?"

Johnson reaches for the flask, shakes it—a modest drink left—puts on the cap, noting that his fingers do not shake but seem, rather, to have lost much of their tactile sense. "I have sent General Willich back to his brigade. I am sure General Kirk is doing his duty. Let us join Colonel Baldwin and the reserve."

"Yes, sir!" The chief of staff runs toward the headquarters tent, shouting commands.

Johnson stands, feels surprisingly steady. That was not badly done, he thinks. I chose my words well and maintained a sense of calm. Calm, I must communicate that. He deposits the flask in a coat pocket, walks with only the slightest sway toward the line of horses where an orderly is hastily tightening the girth about the belly of the general's horse.

The survivors of Kirk's brigade stream west through the woods into Willich's position. The 39th and 32nd Indiana, hastily trying to muster, are swept up in the stampede as Ector's Texans come howling through the woods, firing on the run. A big bearded man riding a lathered horse appears out of the smoke, shouts at a company of Texans. "Gott im Himmel, lads! Turn aboot. Turn aboot. It es not so bad. Ve can stop dem. But you must turn aboot." A Texan officer sticks a pistol between the horse's eyes and fires. The horse goes down, heaving the big man from the saddle. The Texan steps to Brigadier General August Willich, kneels to see how badly the old man is hurt. "You will note, General," he says acidly, "that we wear different uniforms."

The 49th Ohio collapses next, its muskets still stacked and breakfast cooking. A Rebel infantryman noticing one Buckeye sitting by a breakfast fire, coffeepot still in hand, supposes the man frozen in fear. "Let me have a cup of that blackjack, son. I ain't had nothin' all morning." The Yankee does not reply. Leaning close, the Rebel makes out a single red hole all but hidden in the lank hair falling over the man's forehead. "Lookee here," he says to a companion. "The boy's shot through the brain just clean as you please. Went up yonder still trying to pour a cup of coffee."

Willich's last two regiments try vainly to stem the Rebel onrush. Lieutenant Colonel Charles Hotchkiss, commanding the 89th Illinois, orders his men to lie down while the survivors of the shattered regiments flood through his ranks. He waits until the pursuing Rebels are within fifty yards and then shouts: "Stand, Eighty-ninth! Present! Fire!" The Rebel ranks recoil from the blow and the 89th gets off two more volleys. But Hotchkiss knows he cannot hold. Already Rebel regiments are enveloping both his flanks. He gives the order to fall back, hoping to join the 15th Ohio to his rear. But the 15th Ohio is belatedly trying to execute a parade-ground change of fronts. The onrushing Rebels catch it in the middle of the complicated maneuver and the regiment falls back, its lines hopelessly disordered. Yet it hangs together for a quarter mile, firing ragged volleys, until it hits a fence at the Smith farm.

Many of the men had wondered about the fence when they'd come along the Franklin Pike the day before. The seven-foot picket fence stretches, apparently without purpose, nearly two-hundred yards along the southern edge of the Smith home site. In actuality, it is an expression of farmer Smith's loathing for his neighbors, who have failed to buy the boards coming out of his small sawmill. And though the farmer and his fish-eyed wife have long ago left the area, the fence remains.

The better part of the 15th Ohio piles up against the fence. A few soldiers manage to scramble over while others pry frantically at boards with bayonets and rifle barrels. An oncoming Rebel regiment halts, swings Enfields up for a volley. The Yankees throw down their Springfields or hold them up by the barrels in sign of surrender, all the while screaming: "Hold your fire. Hold your fire! For God's sake, hold your fire." But the volley rips through them, dropping dozens. A hundred pleading men manage to surrender.

The survivors of Kirk's and Willich's brigades flee west toward Overall Creek through the fields and woods north of the Franklin Pike. Wharton's cavalry is supposed to head them off, but there are too many Yankees and too few gray horsemen. Moreover, many of the Yankees are not panicked but angry. As they did at Perryville, they shout derisively at fleeing officers: "Sold again! We're sold again!"

A rheumatoid captain of the 32nd Indiana, so crippled that he has applied for a discharge, throws aside his cane and makes for the rear at an impressive speed. The stubborn remnant of his company hoots and jeers. "Come on, boys!" a sergeant yells. "Let's give the Rebs a volley so the cap'n can get a head start." At groves, fences, and farm buildings, knots of men turn to fire at the Rebels. Colonel William Gibson of the 49th Ohio rallies a few hundred men. Lieutenant Colonel Hotchkiss, who has managed to hold together four of the 89th Illinois's ten companies, turns them repeatedly, their volleys slowing the Rebel pursuit. Other officers manage to gather companies of fifty or a hundred men too stubborn, enraged, or slow to run pell-mell.

Sergeant Albert Sims of the 10th Texas is startled to see a Yankee color sergeant turn abruptly and start waving his banner furiously. "Rally, boys! Rally to the flag! We'll hold the sons o' bitches yet."

Sims dashes forward, plants his own battle flag at the Yank's feet and grabs for the staff. "Surrender, Yank! Give me your colors!"

The Yank pushes him away. "Not a chance, Johnny! I'll kill you first!"

They grapple. Minié balls hiss about them, pulling at the colored silk of the flags, almost giving the impression of a breeze. Much of the fire is unaimed and it is impossible to say whether Rebel or Yankee bullets—or both—strike the sergeants. They go down on their knees, desperately holding up their respective banners. Their grappling gives way to an embrace as they sway like drunken men. Then they fall in each other's arms, the flags draping about them in bloody, garish folds.

★   ★   ★

Cleburne's line pushes toward the Franklin Pike, the hour approaching seven, the sun up but the mist still heavy, twilight hanging on in the woods and gullies. Despite—or perhaps because of—his years in Her Majesty's 41st Regiment of Foot, Cleburne dislikes military pomp. No bands play as the division advances, and there is only the steady tramp of the ranks to be heard beneath the cacophony of the battle to the front.

About him, Cleburne's staff is quiet, knowing from the general's scowl that he is listening. In the smoke, fog, woods, ravines, and bedlam of most of the battlefields in this war, more often than not generals must make their decisions on the evidence of sound, and Cleburne has learned to listen.

Irish Pat Cleburne is always amazed by how much of this land is still wilderness—almost all of it, by the standards of his homeland. At Shiloh, his brigade came to a swamp, the ranks dividing without orders to go around it. But he had countermanded the country wisdom of his men, ordered them to maintain the line. He had ridden his horse forward to show them that the bog could be crossed. But the horse sank to its knees, stumbling and snorting. He jammed in his spurs, bellowed at the horse, demanded obedience. And the damned horse, a temperate mare that had given him little trouble, reared, threw him into the muck. The men laughed, because in this army no one, no matter what rank, is spared ridicule. He labored up, summoned dignity, tried to march out of the bog. But dignity was impossible, and he clung to the mare's tail as she wallowed to dry ground.

That night, while Bishop Polk rode a shrieking crone, and Beauregard clutched his pet bird, crooning to its tiny fragility, and Bragg wrote to his wife, complaining of myriad ills and injustices, Cleburne sat apart from his staff, eyeing the mare. He considered shooting her for disobedience, but decided that course would smack of Irish superstition. He gave her to one of his staff and found a new horse ignorant of his small competence in the handling of horses and men.

Cleburne learned to command men and himself far more readily than he learned to manage horses. At Richmond, Kentucky, he fought the Yankees of Bull Nelson in the dusk graveyard, a small part of himself fearing that ghosts might rise from graves and tombs, disturbed by the obscenity, the sacrilege, of battle on holy ground. But by then Cleburne understood that a general fights himself in battle as much as he fights the enemy. Where he had been hot before, he became cold, calculating. The battles at Richmond and Perryville won him promotion over two senior brigadiers, Bushrod Johnson and St. John Liddell. He knows they are bitter, but they are both highly competent soldiers, and he can weather their dislike.

As Cleburne's line begins the clockwise wheel to strike the Franklin Pike at a narrow oblique, he is most concerned about what he does not hear. The sound of heavy fighting ahead has dwindled away in the direction of Overall Creek. Is McCown no longer encountering significant resistance? Can victory have been so easy?

Crossing the road, Liddell's Arkansas brigade passes through Willich's desolate camp. The Ohio soldier shot through the brain still sits by the smoking embers of his fire, the coffeepot still clutched in his hand. The line parts around him, the men commenting in wonder as they pass. One soldier sticks out a boot and rocks the man, then tips him over. The coffeepot clanks, spills, remains clutched. "Why'd you go and do that, Fowler?" another asks.

"'Tweren't decent. Man should have enough sense to fall over when he's dead. Even a Yank."

Bushrod Johnson's brigade advances across the field to the front of Kirk's camp, stepping over the bodies of the dead and wounded. There are many of both, mostly butternut at first but then more and more in blue. The wounded cry out not to be trampled, beg for water. A few of Johnson's men pause to lend canteens, are told to move on by the file closers.

Infantrymen can take little time for pity. There are litter-bearers and hospital orderlies to look after the wounded, burial parties to inter the dead. The infantry must push on.

Cleburne's line clears the camps, moves on through the woods on either side of Gresham Lane. The wheel has put Liddell's brigade west of the lane, Bushrod Johnson's astride it, Lucius Polk's brigade of Tennessee and Arkansas regiments to the east of it. Cleburne is handed a note from Hardee: *Cheatham is slow getting started. I have ordered Wood to fall in to the right of Lucius Polk to close the gap with Loomis.*

Forty feet ahead of Cleburne, a man stumbles and goes down. Half a dozen men to the left, a soldier clutches at his groin, cries out, falls writhing. Quickly, three or four more men are down in the ranks. My God, Cleburne thinks, we are under fire! Where the devil is McCown? He shouts to Johnson. "Halt the line. Shake out skirmishers. It appears that we have become the front line."

He jogs his plowhorse down the line to the right to Lucius Polk's brigade. The Bishop's nephew has been a general for only two weeks, having succeeded to command of First Brigade when Cleburne took charge of the division. Polk has taken half a dozen casualties and his men are kneeling now, peering into the thickets ahead. "McCown must have missed a pocket of Yankees, General," Polk calls to Cleburne. "They're quiet now, but we took heavy fire for a few minutes."

"I don't think General McCown came through here at all, Lucius. It looks like he aimed too far to the west and then neglected to wheel to the right to stay in front of us."

"What should we do?"

"Push forward skirmishers. Be cautious until you're sure what's ahead and then go in hard. Sam Wood is coming up on your right?"

"Yes, sir. We just saw him."

"Good. I'll go talk to him. You should go in together."

☆ ☆ ☆

Brigadier General Jefferson C. Davis, commanding First Division, McCook's right wing, would far rather attack than defend, as those who witnessed his slaughter of Bull Nelson can certainly attest. As Richard Johnson's division dissolves under McCown's assault, Davis dashes down his line in a raging fury. Why must the Rebs always get in the first lick? Shiloh, Corinth, Perryville. . . . Christ! Don't we ever learn? Goddamn Rosecrans! Goddamn McCook! Goddamn Johnson! Goddamn idiots, every one!

He draws up hard behind the brigade of Colonel P. Sidney Post at the far end of his division line. "Post, could you see anything of the fight?"

"No, sir. But it sounded like all hell was coming through. Colonel Housum brought the 77th Pennsylvania in on our right. He says he's all that's left of Kirk's brigade and that Willich's is gone too."

"Then you're the right flank of the army. Pull your men back and get astride Gresham Lane, find a good field of fire, and set up your guns. Then hope like hell we get some reinforcements before the Johnnies envelop our flank."

"But won't General Johnson send in his reserve to cover the flank?"

"God knows what the stupid bastard will do! You're the flank, Colonel. Do your best and hold on for your very life." Davis spins his horse, gallops back to the center of the division, ferocious beard whipping over his shoulder.

Like much of his brigade, Post is inexperienced, but he has about him a reassuring calmness. In twenty years of practice before the Illinois bar, he has seen that most errors in and out of court are made in haste or panic. Already this morning he has stopped the 5th Wisconsin Battery from firing on Lieutenant Colonel Peter Housum's 77th Pennsylvania, left behind by Kirk's brigade and hurrying through the woods to join Post's brigade.

As his staff shifts nervously about him, Post takes a long minute to gaze into the woods to the brigade's front. "All right," he says to his chief of staff, "we'll pull back in echelon, Colonel Housum's regiment first. Maintain a continuous line." He looks to Captain Oscar F. Pinney, commanding the Wisconsin battery. "Captain, put your guns west of the lane. Beyond that I leave it to you to select our new position with your field of fire in mind." He shakes a finger at Pinney. "But, Captain, remember what happened a while ago when your boys nearly fired on Colonel Housum's men. When the fight begins, I want you to be sure of your target. The Rebs will kill enough of us without our helping them."

Blushing, Pinney snaps a salute and hurries to his battery. Within minutes, the guns are limbered and trundling north along Gresham Lane. Post mounts, gazes into the woods to the south once more, wondering how much time he has, and then canters over for a word with Colonel Housum.

Brigadier General Bushrod Rust Johnson waits for Cleburne's order to resume the advance. Ohio-born but long a resident of the South, Johnson became a college professor and militia officer following his resignation from the regular army after Mexico. In this war, Johnson has fought with distinction in nearly every major battle in the West. So he was deeply stung when Cleburne, who is more than a decade his junior, was promoted over his head to command the division. Johnson blamed Bill Hardee's desire to advance a disciple. Oh, he agrees that Cleburne is a fine soldier: cool, precise, indefatigable, implacable. Yet shouldn't there be more to a Confederate major general? Some cultivation, some politeness in the old sense? Cleburne has none of this; is a dreary, taciturn companion. Johnson suspects that there simply isn't much for Pat Cleburne to reveal; that the man is without true intellect or culture but is only Hardee's grotesque, an Irish man-wolf who will do what Hardee commands without fail or misgiving.

A staff lieutenant comes cantering down the line. "General, you can advance. General Cleburne reminds you to keep contact on left and right with Generals Liddell and Polk."

Johnson nods, gives the order to advance. The brigade pushes into the woods beyond Post's abandoned camp. An occasional minié ball hisses overhead, but whoever was shooting at them before has apparently slipped away. Johnson rides behind the center, wondering who he knows among the officers on the other side this day. Thomas and Rosecrans, of course, and he has heard Garesché is chief of staff. Tom Wood is commanding a division, trying to keep old Senator Crittenden's son out of trouble. Olly Shepherd has a brigade of regulars. . . .

He pulls himself back to the present. I should concentrate on my work, he thinks. Perhaps that is why they chose Cleburne, for he never thinks of anything else. How can he? He has no friendships, no ideas, and only a small past of no significance. Hardee's werewolf.

The brigade breaks out of the woods. Ahead, Johnson can see a blue line, brigade length. He feels his gut rumble and wonders if Cleburne reacts this way, if he too worries about controlling his sphincter every time he comes upon the enemy. No, he wouldn't, would only salivate at the prospect of the slaughter to come. He recalls something in Marcus Aurelius that Garesché once quoted to him: *Life is a battle and a sojourning in a strange land; but the fame that comes after is oblivion.* True, no doubt, but easier for an emperor or a saint to accept than a simple college professor who would enjoy a small fame, however insignificant, within the ultimate scheme contemplated by holy men.

Falling back with the last of his regiments to the new line, Colonel Post is delighted to see another Federal brigade establishing a position a quarter mile in rear of his right. It must be Baldwin of Richard Johnson's division. If another two or three brigades come forward, maybe we can hold them, he thinks.

Captain Pinney has placed the guns of the 5th Wisconsin Battery just

west of Gresham Lane and a quarter mile north of the Franklin Pike. Post
disposes the 22nd Indiana and Housum's 77th Pennsylvania to the right of
the guns, the 59th Illinois to the left. On the east side of the lane, he places
the 74th and 75th Illinois across the top of a narrow, swampy field.

Pinney strides uneasily behind his guns. He is a Milwaukee judge's son,
himself a law clerk, but he has always dreamed of a soldier's life. He is fascinated by ordnance, has memorized entire tables of ballistics. He loves his
ten-pounder Parrott rifles, takes pride in the devastating accuracy of the
solid bolts and exploding shells he can fire at long range. But at short
range, the Parrotts lose much of their punch, their rifling imparting a tight
spiral to canister, reducing its spread and effectiveness. At Perryville, he
had fired round after round of canister into the charging Rebel line with little effect. Meanwhile, the twelve-pounder Napoleons that make up the
majority of the Rebel artillery had ripped gaping holes in the Union lines
with their wide blasts of canister and grape. That's why he loves rifled case
shot, which can reach out 800 yards, more than twice the distance of canister, to spray shrapnel over attacking formations. But the manual says that
case shot shouldn't be fired inside of 500 yards because of the danger of
premature detonation. Most Parrott gunners will risk cutting fuse to a
slightly shorter range, but only warily.

Pinney has his field glasses on the first skirmishers coming out of the
woods, watches until the main line appears. No doubt that they are Rebels
this time, although their uniforms vary wildly in makeup, design, and
shade of butternut. Why are the newspapers always talking about the *gray
ranks of the Secessionist legions?* Except for a few of the officers and a little of the artillery, he hasn't seen a Reb in gray in the entire war. He looks
at Post, who is sitting calmly on his roan gelding a few dozen feet away.
Post nods gravely, and Pinney shouts: "Fifth Wisconsin Battery, by number. Rifled case. Fire!"

The battery begins working in steady rotation, a gun firing every six seconds. Pinney clambers atop a caisson for a better view. Two more Rebel
regiments have emerged from the woods east of the lane. Pinney does not
worry about them. The footing is bad east of the lane, the field of hay
untended and the ground sodden, sure to slow the Reb infantry.

A couple of his cannoneers are down, hit by sharpshooters, one dead
apparently, the other rolling on the ground clutching a knee. But the battery
is at its full strength of 110 men and can absorb casualties. The range is
down to 400 yards, the Rebels pushing forward, filling in the holes left by
the case shot. Come on, give way a little, Johnny. "Wisconsin battery!" he
shouts. "Fire canister!"

Suddenly there is a crash that nearly throws him from the caisson. For a moment Pinney thinks one of his limbers has exploded, but then realizes that the 59th Illinois has opened fire. It is uncommon to hear such uniform musketry. Usually a volley has more the sound of tearing canvas, but the soldiers of the 59th Illinois, edgy with the wait, have discharged their 350 rifle-muskets almost as one. Beyond the battery, the 22nd Indiana looses a volley. Seconds later, the 59th fires again.

Out in the field, the Rebel line stumbles to a halt. The 25th Tennessee retreats across the lane. The other two regiments go to earth 150 yards short of the Yankee line, the soldiers firing prone. Pinney stalks behind his guns. Perhaps he should mix in some common shell, scare the bejesus out of the Rebs though it will be less effective than the canister.

"Captain, you've got some competition."

Post, beside him, the roan soft-footed in its approach. Pinney frowns. "Sir?"

"A Reb battery coming round the wood. They look a polished lot."

Pinney swears, hurries again to the caisson, clambers up amid a buzz of minié balls, spots the four-gun Rebel battery coming fast, looking very polished indeed as they swing about to drop their limbers. "First section, shift to common shell!" he shouts at the lieutenant commanding his left section. "Lay into that battery before they unlimber!" He is off the caisson, sprinting for the middle two-gun section. Stay with canister or go to shell? No, stick with the canister. Less tricky setting the range. Go to shell in the third section, see how it works, maybe try a solid bolt or two for effect. Nothing like a rifled bolt howling through a position to make men crap their pants.

The first Rebel shell explodes thirty yards beyond the guns. God in heaven, they're quick. He gives orders to Lieutenant Humphrey, senior of his lieutenants and commander of the center section. Another Rebel shell, short this time, but closer, showering more mud than iron but still killing two men of the 59th Illinois. Pinney runs on. The third section has shifted aim already. He pushes in between the guns, tries to make out the Rebel cannons through the smoke. All their guns off their limbers and firing. Unusual efficiency for Rebel gun crews, which are often undermanned and underequipped, and almost always short of horses. Maybe it's those rich New Orleans pricks. Worse luck. He jumps back out of the way at a warning from the gunner, covers his ears as the gun fires, wills the shot to fly true.

Captain Putnam Darden of the Jefferson Flying Artillery of Mississippi has his first Napoleon unlimbered, common shell rammed. He orders a second ranging shot for 150 yards. A round of canister rips through the battery, the iron balls whirring about the gun crews. Darden ignores it, watches his shell explode short of the Yankee guns.

"One seventy should do it, Jones," he tells the gunner.

"Yes, sir. One-seven-oh."

The second gun is off its limber and rammed. He walks to it. "One-seven-oh, Smith," he tells the gunner.

"Yes, sir. One-seven-oh. Here we go, boys. Let's make 'em jump."

Darden smiles to himself. Smith and Jones. Easy to get them confused. A blast of canister splatters the field to their front, pocking into the damp hay stubble. I'd like to send a little canister their way, he thinks, but I'm afraid it'd hit our boys out in the field. I'd pull them back if I were the general, though I guess it's never wise to pull back infantry unless you absolutely have to. Gives them too much leisure to think.

Darden strolls down his line. His second section is unlimbered, the Napoleons going into action. More Yankee canister, longer this time, better aimed. He pauses to shoot a horse down with half its belly torn away. Must have taken the full load of canister from one of those Parrott rifles.

One of the teamsters is sitting nearby, cradling a broken arm. Darden hesitates theatrically, revolver in hand. "And how are you doing, Partridge?"

"Never felt better in my life, Captain. Not at all like that horse."

Darden grins, holsters the revolver. "Take cover behind Old Nelly, then, and we'll be out of here in a little while." He strolls on, watching the effectiveness of his fire. Odd how little there is for a commander to do if his men are well trained. He is taking casualties, but not many. He pauses to shoot another wounded horse. Only two horses dead. Not bad for unlimbering under fire.

The Yankee line is all but obscured in smoke, and he knows his own is as well. The Yankee guns have gone to shell but are consistently shooting long. Darden wonders if their trails have begun to dig into the wet earth, raising the elevation of the barrels. Have to watch that always, and usually the Yanks do. Can't criticize much about the Yankee gunners. Better than ours on average. He glances at his watch. Fifteen minutes since his first round, both batteries firing with a will. His confidence is growing with each minute. Soon, he thinks, we'll get in the telling shot.

Bushrod Johnson has ridden down the line to watch the battle east of the lane. His regiments are taking and giving a beating: a thousand men blazing away at the Yankee line in the shadow of the cedars not more than 150 yards ahead. Johnson would like to pull the infantry back, wait for the artillery to decide the battle, but he cannot: it is a stand-up fight, a test of courage and, in a larger sense, of the justice of causes. Or so he would like to believe as he watches men fall.

Suddenly there is the *whump* of an exploding caisson in the Yankee line west of the lane. Johnson stares at the rising pillar of smoke, feels all pondering wash from his mind, replaced by the sudden incisiveness of knowing exactly what to do.

Darden, too, has seen the explosion. He grabs his orderly by the arm. "Max, get out there to that regiment lying flat in the field. Tell the colonel that the Yankee battery will probably start limbering up any minute."

"Do I tell him to charge?"

"No! I'm only a captain, for God's sakes. But he'll see the chance."

Darden jogs to his horse, swings up, waves to his senior lieutenant to take command, and goes in search of Johnson. The battle is about to go their way. He can feel it. A minié ball clips a chunk from the mane of his horse, bare inches in front of Darden's hands. He ignores it, focuses on what to advise Johnson. A small part of his mind wanders onto the inconsequential. He has known the same sensation every time in battle, suspects it is the mind's relief valve, easing the pressure lest consciousness explode like an overheated boiler. Smith and Jones, he thinks. Why did I never notice before? I wonder if they find it amusing.

Out in the wet field, Privates John Berry and Dick Janes of the 17th Tennessee roll on their backs to reload their Enfields, ramming fresh cartridges while the Yankee minié and canister balls sing over them. Looking upward, it seems to Berry that his spectacles are dancing with flyspecks, not so much beyond as within the lenses themselves. He doubts the reality of any of this, screws his eyes shut for a moment, but the buzzing and hissing of the balls is too terrifying to listen to in the dark. He rolls back on his belly, is about to rise up the three inches necessary to fire at the Yankee line when a musket cracks directly over his head, the muzzle blast hot against his scalp.

Momentarily deafened, Berry snaps off his shot and rolls on his back, digging for a cartridge. "Goddamn it, Janes! You goddamned near shot me!"

"Na, ah didn't. Keep yer fool head down and you'll be fine."

"Like hell. You parted my hair with that last shot."

"Mus' not 've kept yer head down." Janes pulls his ramrod free, draws the hammer, and sticks a cap on the cone beneath. "Now pardon me, son. Ah got fightin' to do." He rolls over on his stomach, takes aim, and fires before Berry can even turn his face. The blast pocks Berry's spectacles and cheeks with powder and wadding fragments. With a snarl, he whips his ramrod across Janes's head and springs on him. The two roll in the corn stubble, pounding, kicking, and biting. Their sergeant crawls close, grabs fistfuls of long hair, jerks hard. "You damned fools! We're about to charge. The Yankees is gonna kill you in a minute anyways. Now get your muskets!"

Pinney's 5th Wisconsin Battery is a shambles, a gun smashed, at least thirty men down, twenty others with walking wounds. "Colonel," Pinney yells to Post. "We've got to get the guns off. We need some time to reorganize."

Reorganize, Post thinks. If it were only that. "All right, Captain. Take them back."

The horses are brought in, teams of six for each surviving gun and caisson. There is a sudden shout, the 59th Illinois rising up, firing into the smoke. Then the Tennesseans coming, specter shapes resolving into men, a volley sweeping the battery, men and horses going down, pitching, screaming. The 22nd Indiana on the far side of the battery is up and firing, but the Rebels keep coming. Another blast of musketry, and horses and men drop by the score.

A tall, ramrod-stiff officer marches to Pinney: Captain Hendrick Paine, the only regimental commander in the army who has turned down a colonelcy, for he was a captain in Prussia and refuses to be more in this land where colonels' and generals' commissions are granted to lawyers, judges, political hacks, and fakers of every description. "Come, Captain. Ve get the guns off by man hand. My men take three, yours take two." He does not wait for a reply from Pinney, but about-faces and begins giving orders.

The fire of the 59th Illinois and the 22nd Indiana holds back the Tennesseans long enough for Pinney and Paine to get the guns off to the rear. Pinney himself is pushing at a wheel when he feels a stinging slap against the back of his thigh. He sprawls forward in the mud, watches in dumb surprise as his men wheel the gun away into the smoke. He manages to sit up and find the wound, sees that a minié ball has severed the femoral artery in his leg. He tries to stem the gushing blood, cannot. Oh, hell, he thinks. And I was going to ask Fanny Preston to marry me when next I was home on furlough. He tries to summon her face—round, dimpled, a wisp of blond hair falling across a plump cheek. He is unaccountably tired, lies back, the earth soft beneath him.

Post's brigade comes apart in the wake of the battery's withdrawal. The 22nd Indiana misunderstands the withdrawal of the guns and falls back in confusion. The 77th Pennsylvania, already unnerved from watching the destruction of its sister regiments in Kirk's brigade, takes fright and breaks for the rear. The 59th Illinois, like its stern Captain Paine, maintains its composure, covering the guns until they reach the cedars. On the east side of

the lane, the 74th and 75th Illinois, the newest and greenest of Post's regiments, deliver a final volley before falling back into the woods in good
order. But instead of inspiring a sense of safety, the dark cedars frighten the
raw soldiers. Order breaks down and most of the men are soon fleeing
through the dripping trees toward the rear, pursued by fears more terrifying than the actual, which are certainly terrifying enough to unnerve even
veteran troops. Post sends his staff to rally what men they can for a stand
farther up the lane, and then rides calmly after the guns, tears streaming
down his cheeks.

Out of sight of the Rebel battery, Lieutenant Humphrey manages to get
the remaining guns of the 5th Wisconsin Battery under harness. Captain
Paine and four companies of the 59th Illinois bring up the rear, turning
every sixty paces to deliver a volley at the Rebels. A gun lost and too many
men, Paine thinks. And that boy Pinney. Too bad, for he would have made
a soldier, given time. These Americans. All this savagery, all this rush to kill
each other with so little discipline. Shocking somehow, though understandable given the violence of their emotions. That boy Pinney. . . . Too bad.

★ ★ ★

Colonel Philemon Baldwin, commanding Second Division's small reserve
brigade, stares in disbelief at Brigadier General Richard Johnson. My God,
it's just gone seven, we're about to fight the battle of our lives, and the man
is drunk as a fiddler's bitch! Lord, save us from all West Pointers.

Baldwin clears his throat, speaks respectfully but firmly, as he might to
an aged client come to write a son or a daughter out of his will over some
imagined or minor slight. "I think we should move forward, General. Kirk
and Willich are under heavy attack and we should relieve what pressure we
can." (Heavy attack? Christ, they're being absolutely thrashed from the
sound of things.)

Johnson gazes at him, belches. "Very good, Colonel. Advance and
choose a position. But don't go too far."

Baldwin leads his four regiments in column along a narrow alley
hacked through a thick belt of cedars by the Pioneer Brigade the previous
afternoon. The sound of the fighting is shifting steadily to the west, not
artillery or volley firing now, but rather the constant crackle of skirmishing.
A pursuit, Baldwin thinks. Kirk and Willich have broken.

They come out of the cedars into a cornfield, start across. Beyond it lies
a half mile of cleared, uncultivated ground stretching to the Franklin Pike.
Johnson's chief of staff comes cantering up. "The general says to go no

farther than the edge of the cornfield. Halt your trailing regiment back in the trees as a reserve."

Baldwin holds his temper. "Is that where he'll be?"

"That's where we'll set up division headquarters, yes."

"So one of my regiments is to serve as the general's personal bodyguard."

"It will serve as the brigade reserve, Colonel."

Baldwin turns away, sweeps the scene deliberately with his field glasses. Hundreds of men in blue are pouring out of the trees and across the fields to the west, some running in terror, others trudging along sullenly, weapons on their shoulders. A few units still maintain a semblance of formation, their colors flying in desperate pride. We are not whipped, Baldwin thinks. Driven, yes. Not whipped. Not yet. "The general should go rally those men," he says.

"Some of the staff are attempting to do that, Colonel. Now, if you will establish your line—"

"There's a brigade forming four or five hundred yards to our front left. You can't see it from here but the captain in charge of my skirmishers sent back word. He thinks it's one of Davis's. My guess would be Post. We should advance to form at an oblique on its right."

"No, Colonel. The general was emphatic that you go no farther than the edge of the cornfield."

Baldwin spins on him. "And the general is drunk and incapable of making a rational decision! Do you recognize that, or are you drunk, too, sir?"

The chief of staff sighs. "No, I am not drunk, Colonel. And I know the general is. But he is the general and we must follow his orders."

"And what gives him the right to command when he's drunk?"

"The star on his shoulder straps and an appointment from the president."

"And a West Point education," Baldwin sneers.

"Perhaps. I will communicate your desire to push forward, Colonel. But for the moment, set about positioning your regiments in the best manner you can for the ground at hand." He touches spurs to his horse, leaves Baldwin glaring at his back.

Baldwin calls the regimental colonels and his chief of artillery together. He assigns 1st Ohio to form behind a rail fence on the south side of the field. The 6th Indiana will move through the woods to the east of the field, forming under cover of the trees some fifty yards in advance of the left flank of the 1st Ohio. Seventy-five yards to the rear of the 1st Ohio, the Union 5th Kentucky will form a second line. The 93rd Ohio will remain in the woods fifty yards to the rear of the 5th Kentucky.

Baldwin divides the six guns of the 5th Indiana Artillery, ordering the section of twelve-pounder field howitzers into the angle between the 1st Ohio and the 6th Indiana and placing the two sections of ten-pounder Parrott rifles to the right of the Union 5th Kentucky. He is just finishing his dispositions when a fresh regiment comes around the edge of the woods to the west, colors flying and apparently unscathed. He rides over, recognizes Colonel Sheridan Read of the 79th Illinois, one of Kirk's regiments. "Good morning, Read. Where were you?"

"Guarding the trains. Our turn last night. So we've got a hell of mess on our hands, I see."

"More than that. It's Perryville and Shiloh all over."

Read shakes his head. "Christ, we never learn."

"We do, the men with stars don't." Baldwin hesitates. Even now, the etiquette must be maintained. "I don't know that I can advise you to advance any farther. As far as I can tell, Kirk's brigade is entirely smashed up. Willich's, too."

"Then tell me where to form, Colonel. I submit my command to your authority."

"Thank you, Read. Form to the right of the 1st Ohio along the fence, please."

"Yes, sir." Read rides a few yards and then turns. "What of General Johnson?"

"He's back in the trees, libidinously indisposed."

Read grimaces, goes off to put his men in line.

Baldwin waits, occasionally sweeping the fields with his glasses. He is pleased to see men turning aside from their retreat in twos, threes, sixes, and tens, and trudging toward his line. A few larger groups are coming in as well. A sore-footed colonel without a hat, carrying a rifle-musket and cartridge box like an ordinary soldier, limps toward him. He smiles, teeth white in a face blackened by powder smoke. "Hello, Baldwin. It's Dodge, Thirty-fourth Illinois."

"Why, Dodge. I'm glad to see you alive. Where's Kirk?"

"Wounded. I sent him back on a litter. Willich's either dead or captured. I don't know for sure. Where's Bandbox Johnson?"

Baldwin repeats the reply he gave to Read. Dodge scowls. "Then I suppose we'll have to avoid this particular bandbox with a minimum of his advice. I've got a few of my boys and some tagalongs from other regiments. Major Collins kept some of the 29th Indiana together after Colonel Dunn went down. He's putting them to the rear of my boys at the end of your line."

"I appreciate your help, Colonel. Who's firing that gun over by the creek?"

"Gibson of Willich's brigade, I think. He's got a couple of hundred men. All the rest are dead, captured, or headed for the barn from what I could tell." He hesitates. "Don't expect too much of my boys. They got knocked around pretty badly in the last hour. They're shaky."

When Dodge is gone, Baldwin consults his watch. Only fifteen minutes since we took position. Impossible. I wonder if I will be alive in half an hour.

★   ★   ★

Brigadier General St. John Liddell, commanding Second Brigade, Cleburne's Division, does not much like Braxton Bragg. For that matter, he does not know anyone, save Mrs. Bragg and perhaps that boy Wheeler, who does like Bragg. Yet Liddell can at least stomach the company of the man. Very occasionally, he will share a drink with the general and listen to his complaints. Liddell assures him that he overestimates the number and strength of his enemies within the army: Let the general command and his generals will submit. If they do not, cause one or two to be shot, and the rest will certainly obey.

Liddell does not consider himself a West Pointer, though many others do. He had attended the Academy for a year, but had been expelled for wounding another cadet in a duel in 1834. The incident entered the folklore of the Academy, with Liddell cast in the hero's role by his fellow Southerners. His opponent was a burly Michigan bully named Perry, who—unacquainted with dueling pistols—had discharged his accidentally in the air, leaving Liddell to take careful aim at his groin. Perry held his stance as long as he could, then turned to flee. At that point, Liddell fired, putting a ball neatly into Perry's left buttock. Score one for Dixie. Liddell might have returned to the Academy the next fall, but he was a poor student and chose instead to become a sugar planter in Catahoula Parish, Louisiana.

Building a plantation from a swampy tract was neither an easy life nor a gentle one. Slave, overseer, and master alike fought snakes, gators, and clouds of insects to drain the land for sugarcane. The slaves were frequently mutinous and required a hard hand. White neighbors were avaricious for land—however sodden—and testy on the subject of property lines. Liddell feuded with several, fought duels or, discarding formalities, settled differences in the street with his fists.

In the late summer of 1855, five slaves on a neighboring plantation killed their overseer and escaped into the swamps. Liddell joined his neighbors in hunting the murderers. On the second day, he was paired with a stranger: a tall, grim man of military bearing with ferocious eyebrows. He introduced himself as Brevet Lieutenant Colonel Bragg. Liddell recognized the name, of course, since Bragg was famous for his exploits in Mexico. Following on horseback behind the dogs and trackers, the two became acquainted in the cool, formal way of Southern gentlemen. Liddell recounted his short career at West Point. Bragg talked of army politics, of his recent marriage, of his desire to make his fortune after all the years of impecunious living in the army.

It took the Cherokee trackers four more days to discover the escaped slaves hiding in a rude dugout on an island in the swamps. The hunters shot three of them to death and wounded two, then the Indians piled dry cane atop the dugout and set it aflame as the two wounded niggers screamed and begged to be hanged or shot. Bragg stood apart, hands clenched behind his back, face expressionless.

The death of five fieldhands was a costly loss for their owner, but it was justice that had to be done, a necessity they all understood if they were to survive amid the multitude of hard-muscled, murderous black men. That night, Bragg and Liddell talked over whiskey on the porch of Liddell's plantation. They were bathed, well fed, and relaxed, the night beyond the mosquito netting buzzing pleasantly after the canicular heat of the day.

"Do you find our methods harsh, Colonel?" Liddell asked.

Bragg took a moment to reply. "Harsh but imperative. You are an army here, waging a bitter war against nature and the incipient chaos that always threatens a proprietary relationship involving human property. You invoked a necessary cruelty to maintain discipline. And now that it is restored, you may wage your war with greater prospects of success."

"Then you are likewise acquainted with the necessity for harsh discipline?"

"Of course. Most recruits to our army require a good deal of it. I fancy myself not inexpert in the training of soldiers, although some among them have resented my methods."

"Violent resentment?"

"Twice. In Mexico, a private discharged a musket through my tent and then attempted to bayonet me through the canvas. I shot him with a pistol. Unfortunately, I only had his shadow to aim at and I did him only moderate harm. He was captured the next morning a mile from camp with my pistol ball in his upper arm. The surgeon removed it, and General Wool ordered the soldier hanged."

"Without trial?"

"With a minimum of formalities. We were on the march."

"And the other time?"

"The other time, a disgruntled private in my battery placed an 8-inch mortar shell beneath my cot, ran a train of gunpowder off some twenty feet, and ignited it."

"My God, man! Did the shell fail to explode?"

"No, it exploded, but the conoid shape of the blast saved me." Bragg pointed to the candle burning on the table between them. "Above an explosion there is a conic section of vacuum, as there is above the wick of a candle. I survived in that vacuum and walked out of the shambles of my tent temporarily deafened but otherwise unhurt."

"And the man who did it?"

"He deserted. Some two or three years later he was captured on other charges and hanged."

A few months later, Bragg bought a plantation north of Thibodaux, a hundred miles from Liddell's. With the distance and the disinclination of both men to mix in society, they saw little of each other until the war, and it worries Liddell that Bragg has aged badly. The stern professional has become a crabbed and uncertain old man, and St. John Liddell fears that Bragg may equivocate under fire.

Coming out of the trees a half mile from Baldwin's line, Liddell is relieved to find McNair's brigade on his left. He halts his brigade and rides over to find the Arkansas merchant. McNair is a seasoned soldier with combat experience dating from Buena Vista, and an excellent record in command of troops at Wilson's Creek, Elkhorn Tavern, and Richmond. But McNair seems shaken by the bloody fight with Kirk, starts talking too fast, too vehemently. "I'm very glad to see you, General. Rains and Ector angled west toward Overall Creek, and I lost contact with them. I tried to stay to your front, but I must have wandered off course, too."

"And I'm glad to see you, McNair. We were confused when you disappeared from our front. But no matter now. Bushrod's just attacked on my right, and the Yankees are fighting like hell. Let's go break up that Yankee brigade in front, then we'll wheel and give Bushrod a hand."

McNair hesitates. "Better that you go in first, John. We'll come behind in support."

Liddell disagrees, and they argue in increasing heat as the Yankee Parrotts behind Baldwin's line crack every forty seconds, the case shot exploding over the ranks of butternut soldiers waiting for their generals to agree. McCown dashes out of the woods at the head of his staff, anxiety twisting his pale features. "Good morning, Liddell. McNair, where are Rains and Ector?"

"Over west, General. My left lost touch when we broke through the Yankee line. It was hard business, General, and we have many casualties. Liddell proposes attacking the Yankee brigade to our front. I think we should be in support this time."

"By all means. Excuse me, I must find Rains and Ector, get them wheeling according to General Bragg's plan."

Liddell attempts to control his temper. Damn it, hit them with everything! "General McCown, I beg you to reconsider! If we all go in at once, eight Arkansas regiments in line, nothing can stand in our way. We will make quick work of that Yankee brigade to our front and then be able to move to General Johnson's relief with all dispatch."

McCown stares at him, mouth working fishlike. Hadn't he made the right decision? He wanted to be agreeable, wanted both these men to be satisfied. But somehow he's blundered. "Uh, certainly, General. If that is your tactical judgment, then by all means let the regiments go in together."

McNair begins to protest, but McCown has spun his horse and, riding bent forward as if to protect his back, gallops west in search of Rains and Ector. "Very well, General," McNair says stiffly, "I will conform to your left."

Watching McNair and Liddell's line, Colonel Baldwin is mystified by the delay. Finally, the Rebel line moves, its left lagging a little. Baldwin rides to the center of his line where four guns fill the gap between the 1st Ohio and the 6th Indiana. When the Rebs are 150 yards away, Baldwin gives the signal. The guns and the infantry open fire simultaneously. The combined weight of canister and minié balls staggers the Rebel brigade on Baldwin's left, but still it comes on, an officer out in front waving his hat wildly. How can he live? Baldwin wonders, as he has wondered many times before at the seeming invulnerability of some men in battle.

Lieutenant Colonel Hagerman Tripp, commanding 6th Indiana hidden in the woods fifty yards to the left front of the 1st Ohio, tastes blood, releases his lower lip from between his teeth. Steady, he tells himself. The Rebels are pushing forward slowly now, as if fighting through knee-deep snow. Tripp waits, running his tongue over his bleeding lip, until at last the Rebs come abreast. "Sixth Hoosiers," he screams, "aim low. Commence fire!"

The sudden whirlwind from the right flank tears Liddell's hat from his hand. He feels his horse struck by half a dozen bullets in quick succession. The animal grunts, stumbles forward. Liddell pulls his right foot out of the stirrup, swings his leg over the pommel, and jumps free, landing nimbly for all his forty-seven years as the horse rolls on its side, snorting blood.

All around him, Liddell can hear bullets striking flesh, men falling, some silent, some yelling, a few screaming, though usually the screaming comes later when a man has absorbed the fact of being shot. The ranks go to ground without orders, men firing as well as they can on their stomachs. From Liddell's right flank all the way across his front, the Yankee line is delivering sheet on sheet of musket fire while the howitzers thump and farther away there is the bang-crack of the Parrotts. "Come on, boys, we can't stay here!" Liddell shouts. "With me, on three, charge!"

Only the company nearest can hear his command, but when they rise up, so do the other companies and then the regiments left and right. They charge forward, colors waving, are dashed to earth by another hail of Yankee musketry. Liddell stalks among them. "Good, boys. Good. We've made a start. This time we'll keep going. Right over the top of them. Get some use out of those bayonets."

To the rear of McNair's line, Lieutenant Henry Shannon, commanding the Warren Mississippi Light Artillery, deploys his four Napoleons against the Yankee Parrotts and howitzers. His crews must fire over the heads of the infantry down in the grass. Shannon and his men are careful, risk their lives taking extra care in cutting the fuses on the shells and sighting and resighting the guns. But accident is inevasible in battle and one of the Napoleons fires short, the powder charge, perhaps damp from the rain, igniting with a *foommp* instead of a *bang*. The shell lands in the midst of the 6th-7th Arkansas, a combined regiment made up of veterans from two regiments decimated at Shiloh and Perryville. Men scramble away from the hissing shell, one man makes a grab for it, perhaps with some wild intention of trying to extinguish the fuse. The explosion kills half a dozen, maims a dozen more, body parts and torn clothing thrown up with the shrapnel.

McNair knows that he must charge, that Liddell's brigade will be slaughtered if he does not. He gives the order to rise up and, like Liddell, positions himself forward of the front rank. Dear God, he prays, let me see my home again. I shall forever be thy servant thereafter. He waves his sword and the brigade surges forward.

Colonel Dodge, commanding the 30th Indiana and what's left of Kirk's brigade, watches McNair's line come. "Take careful aim, boys," he shouts. "We've got some catching up to do." But the survivors of the last hour's fighting are, as Dodge predicted, unsteady. They fire, reload, fire again, all the while watching the Rebel charge coming faster, crashing through a fence of rails as if it were made of jackstraws. They begin to waver.

To Dodge's immediate left, Colonel Read is walking calmly behind the as-yet unbloodied ranks of the 79th Illinois. He raises his sword to leash the first volley, then, for a reason he cannot for a moment quite understand, stumbles backward. He stares down at his chest, sees the hole in his blouse below the left side of his rib cage. Why, I'm shot, he thinks. I wonder if I can darn the hole in my blouse or if I'll have to buy a new one. Might as well get the pants, too. These are nearly worn through in the seat.

Read falls backward, sword flying from his hand. His regiment immediately begins to panic. Officers call on them to steady, their own voices tinged with hysteria. The regiment holds, fires, fires again, and then breaks as Dodge's survivors give way on their right before the onrush of McNair's Arkansans.

Baldwin watches his flank tearing away, calls to Major Stafford, commanding the 1st Ohio: "Fall back on the 5th Kentucky, Major. I'll meet you there."

Stafford waves a salute, gives the command to fall back. But the Buckeye blood is up: they have held against three charges in twenty minutes and they'll be goddamned if they are going to give in now. Stafford glances hastily to his right, sees the 79th Illinois come completely apart. "Fall back, First!" he shouts as loud as he can over the roar of fire. Again he is ignored, and Stafford, who is a parson's son and among the most pious men in the army, lets fly with a tirade so graphically profane that it shocks even the Buckeye veterans and becomes a legendary event in the history of the regiment. Stafford concludes with the comparatively mild: "And I'll hang as high as Jesus fucking Christ crucified any goddamned man who ever ignores another goddamned order from me!"

Casting awed looks at their young major, the Buckeyes fall back on the 5th Kentucky.

Coming into the woods in the wake of the Federal retreat, Private John Berry of the 6th-7th Arkansas finds a wounded Yankee propped against a tree, a knee shattered by a minié ball. The Yank has looped a belt around his thigh above the wound, his right hand pulling the tourniquet tight to staunch the bleeding. He holds up the palm of his free hand. "I ain't got no gun, John. Don't shoot."

For a second Berry wonders how the man knows his name, then realizes that the Yank has only shortened the sobriquet by which all Southern soldiers are known. "You look in a bad way, Yank."

"Reckon so. But as long as I can keep this here belt tight, I won't bleed t'death. Maybe I can wait it out until the hospital boys find me."

"Help some if you had that leg up in the air. Here, let me find you something to put under it."

Berry finds a short section of dry-rotted cedar, lifts the Yank's leg carefully, and slides the log under the ankle. The Yank's face contorts with the pain, but he does not cry out. He draws a ragged breath. "Thanks, John. I'm obliged."

Berry nods. "Sure, Yank. Good luck to you."

For a moment, neither of them speaks, embarrassed in their brief familiarity. "Lord, I'm almost dead for water," Berry says to break the silence.

"Here," the Yank says. "I filled my canteen half an hour before you boys came." He holds out his canteen.

"No, you're gonna need that water, son. You got a long wait ahead of you."

"Go on. I'll feel bad if you don't."

Berry unscrews the cap from the canteen, takes a swallow. The water is brackish, bitter, no doubt crawling with tiny creatures, yet it is sweeter to him than anything he has ever tasted. He laughs, grins at the Yank, who grins back. Berry takes another swallow, eyes closed, wanting to remember always.

☆ ☆ ☆

East of Gresham Lane, the brigades of Lucius Polk and S.A.M. Wood push into thick cedars. They are still unsure about the location of McCown's line, worry about firing into the backs of their countrymen. The cedars are quiet, the branches dripping with cold mist, the ground spongy beneath, cushioning the footfalls of the men. The silence shatters when the 101st Ohio rises up from the bracken to deliver a fearsome volley directly into the face of the 33rd Alabama and the 46th Mississippi of Wood's brigade. The Confederates try to hold their ground, but a second volley sends the entire brigade tumbling back into the open beyond the cedars. His flank gone, Polk halts his brigade and shakes out skirmishers.

The Yankee ambushers belong to Second Brigade, Jefferson C. Davis's division, commanded by Colonel William Passmore Carlin, who is at this moment standing in a sylvan glade, calmly smoking his pipe. He has scraped a patch of earth clear with the toe of his boot and drawn a quick sketch of the battlefield with a stick. He listens, marking the shifting concentrations of fire. All is quiet to his immediate front again, the Rebs apparently re-forming; but to his right, Post is under mounting pressure. If he goes, what then?

His concentration is upset when Davis comes charging into the glade, slewing his horse to a stop. "Have you seen McCook?" he shouts. "Post is getting shot to hell out there!"

"Haven't seen him, General."

Davis tugs furiously at his beard. "Someone's fighting beyond Post's flank. Johnson's reserve, I suppose. That would be Baldwin. Know him?"

"Not well, but I understand he's a good man."

"Where the hell is that goddamned fool McCook? Christ, Sheridan's got a reserve brigade. McCook should send it over here."

The timbre of the firing to the right has changed. I've got to pull in my flank, Carlin thinks. Post's cannons aren't firing and that means he's about finished. He taps out his pipe on the heel of a boot. "I should pull back my right flank into a crochet, General. From the sound of things we're about to become the army's flank."

At the suggestion of even this small withdrawal, Davis glares at Carlin, the chewed ends of his mustache wet with spittle. Carlin stares back calmly. The only way to deal with this madman is to stay calm, he tells himself. Davis seems to realize the logic of the move. "Yes, do it. Goddamn it, I hate to pull back!" He dismounts, stalks off to stand glaring at the smoke rising from beyond the cedars where Post and Baldwin are giving way.

Carlin gives rapid orders, sending staff officers to pull back the 21st Illinois and 101st Ohio. Done, he refills his pipe, concentrating on the process. Discretion, he thinks. Davis has none, which makes his valor dangerous. Bull Nelson was just like him, which I suppose is part of the reason Davis shot him.

Brigadier General S.A.M. Wood has his brigade re-formed. The men are angry, straining to go back into the cedars to get at the Yankees. The soldiers of Cleburne's division are not in the habit of giving way, and the last quarter hour has been a humiliation. They look about for their Irish general, are for once glad not to see him. Let them regain their honor first. Wood is nearly satisfied with his dispositions, sends word to Lucius Polk that he is advancing.

Carlin is on horseback when he hears the Rebs coming in hard on his front and flank. He guesses immediately where the greatest danger lies and dashes for the flank. But he is too late: a company of the 13th Arkansas penetrates thick scrub between the 101st Ohio and the 21st Illinois just as Carlin and his staff arrive. Carlin feels a sudden blow to his chest above the heart and stares disbelievingly as he rises off his saddle, his horse galloping from under him. He hits the ground flat on his back, head snapping back against a stone. Around him his staff is gunned down by the Arkansans.

With the 13th and 1st Arkansas pouring in between them, the 21st Illinois and the 101st Ohio fight desperately to keep from being surrounded. The 21st loses its colonel and gives way. The colonel, lieutenant colonel, and major of the 101st fall in rapid succession, and a captain leads the regiment back through the thickets. On the left, the 38th Illinois falls back under heavy pressure from Wood's brigade.

The 15th Wisconsin, whose ranks are filled with a stalwart, unimpressionable bunch of Norwegians and Swedes, holds the center of the brigade line. Colonel Hans Heg can see that he must fall back, but he'll be damned if he'll let his men turn their backs to the Rebels. It is a sentiment shared by his men, who give way stubbornly, loading their Springfields as they go, then pausing to fire again into the cedars.

Heg resists the impulse to pick up a rifle and join the ranks. Tall, heavily bearded, fierce, he strides behind his men—shouting commands and encouragement in accented but grammatical English. He could speak his native tongue and be understood, but he will not. No, he is an American now, speaks America's language and fights her enemies. Fights these damned Rebels who would destroy the republic Heg and most of his men crossed the ocean to find. They have sacrificed more than these damned hillbillies can ever imagine. And they will die before they surrender the flag, the honor, or the Constitution of their adopted land. Heg reaches out a great hand, steadies a boy who has stumbled back. "Stand tall, boy! Fifteen Wisconsin does not give way before no damned Rebels!"

The boy looks up into his face, grins. "Ya, Colonel. I stand with you against the damned Rebel bastards."

Private William Matthews, who has volunteered to carry the colors of the 1st Arkansas, is enjoying his first battle. "Boys, this is fun!" he shouts. "Better 'n chasin' coons."

A veteran growls, "Don't be so quick, son. You may get your ninety-day furlough yet. Or worse."

Matthews laughs, goes on bawling, "Boys, this is fun!" He is about to yell again when a minié ball nearly tears off his left arm at the elbow. He yowls, lets fall the flag. The veteran snatches at the staff, misses, and lets another man gather up the colors. I'm already too close to the damned flag, he thinks. Let that fool get himself shot. He glances back at Matthews, sees the boy sitting on the ground, staring at the meaty inside of his arm.

* * *

Colonel William Carlin lies staring at the tops of the dripping cedars, sees a hawk circling high against the gray clouds. Somewhere in the back of his mind, he hears his brother shouting: "Bill! Get up, Bill! The Shimeks' house is on fire!" No, it's not the Shimeks' house, he thinks. Something else, something much bigger. He shakes his head, finds that his neck still works, tries to remember where he is and why he must get up. I wonder how badly I am wounded, he thinks. He feels across his chest, expecting to find blood oozing from a hole that will be only the beginning of the damage: the pit mouth of an expanding tunnel through his chest. He finds only a painful bruise left by the impact of a spent bullet. He pushes himself to a sitting position. Christ, he hurts, but his memory is coming back fast now. He grabs at the hanging bough of a cedar, gets it on the second try, and drags himself up. He stumbles toward the sound of fighting, stepping over the body of an aide he shared a plate of beans with two hours before. The boy's stomach is ripped open, the partially digested breakfast strewn across his uniform. Carlin vomits, almost faints from the pain it causes his head, and stumbles on.

☆ ☆ ☆

Crittenden's left wing begins crossing Stones River at 7:00 A.M. Brigadier General Sam Beatty's brigade of Van Cleve's Division hits McFadden's Ford at a rush, four regiments splashing across, expecting any second to take a volley from the brush along the opposite shore. But nothing happens, and they deploy quickly to hold the crossing, soaked but immensely relieved. Beatty stares at Wayne's Hill, where he knows there are least two Rebel batteries, and wonders why even they are silent. Beatty has the uneasy feeling he might have in the wind-quiet, bird-quiet hour before a storm. It's almost like the Rebs don't give a damn what we're doing, he thinks.

Rosecrans and Garesché watch Beatty's crossing from a low hill overlooking the ford. Rosecrans slaps the pommel of his saddle. "Well done, by God. Old Bragg thinks we're coming at him from the other direction. Didn't even guard the ford. No imagination. That's why we're going to skin him, Julius."

"Yes, General," Garesché says absently, his attention fixed on the sound of firing to the southwest.

Rosecrans glances at him. "Don't worry, it's picket firing, not much more. McCook fought his way into position yesterday and things are still a bit unsettled over on that wing. I would be more concerned to hear no firing at all. Now that would be inexplicable."

Colonel Samuel Price's brigade wades into the stream. The men go in barefoot, holding Springfields, cartridge boxes, and brogans aloft. They curse the slippery stones, make jokes about crawfish, eels, watersnakes, and quicksand. The sound of the fighting to the southwest swells, the shape of musket volleys and cannon fire emerging distinct from the underlying rumble.

Rosecrans turns his head, a slight frown creasing his scarred features. "McCook must have decided to pitch into them a little earlier and a little harder than I expected. Probably hoping he can catch Hardee napping. Well, I hope he doesn't get carried away. I don't give a damn if he likes Hardee or not; this war isn't about personal feelings."

"Should I send a message for him to be careful?"

"No, I'm glad to see McCook's being aggressive. He didn't seem quite himself when we were coming down. More hesitant."

"I think a little hesitancy might be in order for General McCook. It might demonstrate a greater maturity of judgment."

"True, but I don't want the man to lose his fighting spirit, either. By the way, I've been meaning to ask you what you've heard recently of the family. I know Old Dan is now a colonel. A paymaster, I believe."

Gartesché restrains the desire to raise his eyebrows. Why, General? Do your thoughts run to the political future? "Yes, I'd heard that."

They talk as Price's brigade completes the crossing and Colonel James Fyffe's brigade struggles down the muddy bank. Fyffe's brigade is halfway through its crossing, Hascall's brigade of Wood's division waiting on the near side of the river, when the firing to the southwest swells again. Rosecrans scowls. "No, McCook isn't attacking; he's being attacked."

"Perhaps I should go back to headquarters," Gartesché says. "I wouldn't want Major Goddard to be overwhelmed."

"No, it's all right. If Hardee's attacking, he's playing into our hands. . . . You were quite close to him before the war, weren't you?"

"Yes, I'm very fond of Bill Hardee."

"I never really knew him, although I saw him around Washington a few times. He seemed a bit of a fop to me."

Gartesché smiles. "Well, let us say Bill Hardee has his own sense of style."

"Yes, let us say," Rosecrans says absently, his attention fixed on the sound of firing.

Crittenden trots his brown mare up the hill. Gartesché notes that his color has improved considerably in the hour since they rode with him to the ford. Gartesché frowns, wondering how much whiskey the man needed to feel better.

Rosecrans does not acknowledge Crittenden but continues to listen to the firing. "I don't like how the fighting seems to be moving around to the north, though I suppose it's just a cavalry tangle out beyond McCook's flank.

Well, no matter. Just about everything's working as we planned." He turns to Crittenden, smiles expansively. "We're off to a good start, Tom. By noon, we'll sweep through Murfreesboro and cut Bragg off. If he's stubborn enough, we might even bag the whole lot, eh?"

Before Crittenden can reply, the firing swells. To Garesché it is a roar like the coming of a great wind. He shudders, recalling a dream forgotten in the night. He'd wandered through a garden overgrown with ferns until he'd come face to face with a pale, indistinct figure, though surely it must have been Bierce since the orderly's head dangled from his hand. "Colonel, do you know *The Wisdom of Solomon?* Know the warning of the wisest of kings? *For the hope of the ungodly is like dust that is blown away with the wind.*"

And though Garesché's soul would answer humbly, his simulacrum laughed, mouth opening gigantically, unimaginably wide—the Fenris Wolf, one jaw touching earth and the other heaven, gobbling down the stars, swallowing down God, and from the maw that had become Julius Garesché the voice of the mad Scot, the regicide, the child-killer: *Then blow, wind! come, wrack! At least we'll die with harness on our back.*

At the roar of the firing, generals, officers, and soldiers have momentarily frozen, staring in wonder to the southwest. Rosecrans is the first to break from the trance. "Goddamn it! Bragg's hitting McCook with a full corps!" He turns to Crittenden. "General, you'd better tell Van Cleve not to advance beyond the ford for the time being. Tell General Wood to remain on this side of the river. Julius, we'd better get back to headquarters." He pauses, stares at Crittenden. "Now, Tom, we're going to make this right. Be prepared to resume your advance as soon as I send word."

Alex McCook drifts on the waves. The fighting seems too deep to fathom, too towering to breast. He would sink if he could, find a regiment, take a musket, and simply wait for the storm to swallow him. But instead he drifts from fight to fight, trying to comprehend. His usually silent chief of staff has become a nag, badgering him constantly for orders. He has none save those easy to give: "We must hold, refuse our right."

"What should I tell the commanding general?"

"Tell him that we are heavily pressed and request assistance."

"General, I think we are more than heavily pressed—"

"General Rosecrans will understand my meaning."

The chief of staff scowls, scribbles in a dispatch book, hands the message to a staff officer. He begins again to entreat McCook for orders, but

McCook rides off, swaying in the saddle as his horse plods at its own pace to the east toward Davis's rapidly disintegrating line.

Rosecrans and Garesché are halfway back to army headquarters when a cavalry officer comes dashing down McFadden's Lane, splattering mud on the infantrymen waiting in column to cross at the ford. The soldiers curse, shake their fists.

Garesché recognizes the lieutenant as one of Captain Otis's headquarters guard from the 4th Cavalry. Baker, that was it. A good boy.

The lieutenant pulls his horse up hard. "General Rosecrans, sir. The right is broken. Johnson's division is destroyed, Davis's division under extreme pressure."

Rosecrans speaks sharply. "How do you know this, Lieutenant? Who sent you?"

"I saw it, sir. Major Goddard sent Captain Otis, me, and a dozen of the boys to have a look, and we saw what was happening. It's terrible, sir. There's a regular stampede to—"

Rosecrans holds up a palm as another rider comes galloping up, this time a captain. "General Rosecrans. Captain Wegner, McCook's staff. I have a message from the general." He holds out a sheet.

Rosecrans takes the message, reads, his brow lightening. "Well, that's not quite so bad. 'We are heavily pressed and request assistance.'" He looks up at the captain. "Tell General McCook to dispose his troops to best advantage and to hold his ground obstinately. I will send him reinforcements when I can."

"Yes, sir!" The captain slaps his dispatch book shut, spins his horse, and jabs spurs into its flanks.

Rosecrans turns in his saddle to face his staff officers. "Our plan is working. The Rebels have struck hard, but McCook will hold."

The staff rides on, following Rosecrans and Garesché. Lieutenant Baker is left by the road. He says plaintively to no one in particular: "But I saw—"

Major General George Thomas listens to the fighting on the army's right flank, the cold butt of one of Rosecrans's sweet cigars clamped in his teeth. The goose has settled itself on the toe of one of Thomas's boots and fallen into a doze, but the dogs are nervous, listening to the swell and fall of firing. It's happening again, Thomas thinks. That boy McCook. My God, what has he left undone this time? I'd better tell Rousseau to be ready to move.

He turns abruptly, stalks off toward his horse. Rudely disturbed, the goose gazes after him with anserine annoyance.

Rosecrans and Garesché have just climbed the railroad embankment over-looking the Nashville Pike when another staff officer, this time a major, arrives from McCook on a lathered mount. "General, our flank is broken! Johnson's and Davis's divisions are wrecked and driven!"

Rosecrans's face turns pale. "My God. So soon?"

CHAPTER 3

Wednesday, 7:00 A.M.–10:30 A.M.
December 31, 1862
Overall Creek beyond the Federal Right

Broken by Hardee's assault, two Federal divisions flee east toward the
Nashville Pike.

HE CAVALRY COMES first, a shattered regiment of blue troopers
fleeing across the brown fields east of Overall Creek. Chief
Surgeon Solon Marks watches from the veranda of the big house
on the Smith plantation, which has become in the last twenty-four hours the
hospital for Richard Johnson's division. My God, what has happened? Marks
wonders. The blue troopers do not pause to enlighten him, but gallop by,
bent low in their saddles, quirts and spurs flailing and gouging until the
horses bleed. A half dozen wounded, riderless horses try to keep up. A tall
but otherwise nondescript brown nag trails thirty feet of intestines, another
three feet pulling out each time the beast treads on its own guts. "Jesus," one
of the surgeons mutters. "Somebody get a gun and shoot that poor fellow."

"No time!" Marks snaps. "Here comes our work."

Wounded troopers are coming into the yard, the belly- and chest-shot
bent double over their saddles, barely holding on, but still managing a compact grace, while the arm- and leg-shot men dangle their appendages, ride
awkwardly as if barely jointed. There is something pathetically comical
about these latter that reminds Marks of Ichabodian scarecrows "eloped
from a field" and riding negligently toward a meeting with Irving's headless

horseman. He bites his lip, thinks: And I may be an even darker horseman for many of these boys.

Orderlies rush to help the wounded troopers down, laying them in a lengthening row on the veranda. Marks performs triage while his heart quails at playing God. I am a man of science, he tells himself. There is a taxonomy here, an order from highest to lowest of who can live and who will likely die. I must practice my science and pray that my soul will be forgiven for my errors.

The heavy, low-velocity minié balls have inflicted terrible damage, shattering bones and tattering flesh. Many of these men will lose arms, feet, hands, and legs, but these wounds are at least treatable. Most of the wounds to the torso, abdomen, neck, and head are not, though Marks and his surgeons will try to save all but the most hopeless cases as long as there is time. Later the surgeons will have to concentrate on those they know they can save while the orderlies put more and more men down at the end of the porch and out beyond in the rain, a long recumbent line of boys waiting to die.

There is a thunder, the gray cavalry coming hard after the blue, sweeping past, yipping and yelling. A half dozen wounded men split off, come into the yard, a doctor leading them. He gazes down at Marks, reads his rank of lieutenant colonel. "Are you chief surgeon here?" he asks in a deep Georgia accent.

"Yes. My name's Marks." Marks thinks of extending a hand, but the Confederate surgeon's eyes are cold, hostile.

"Trulen, Second Georgia Cavalry. Will you treat these men?"

"Of course."

"Then I will ride on with my brigade. I think you may assume that this hospital now lies within the lines of the Army of Tennessee."

Marks evaluates the Georgia boys' wounds, assigns them a place to wait their turns. Out in the wide field to the southeast he can see the wounded coming: limping, staggering, shuffling, crawling, moving in a widening seepage of humanity toward his hospital while beyond in the cedars the noise and the smoke of battle rise up. God, make me cold, he prays, make my skill glitter hard and sharp as a knife that I may help these men without screaming at the sight of every wound.

★　★　★

Captain Gates Thruston, McCook's chief ordnance officer, has the right wing's ammunition train marshaled in the yard of the Gresham house which, like the Smith plantation, has become a hospital. Altogether, he has eighty wagons containing some two million cartridges and seven thousand artillery rounds. And for the moment he has nothing to do. An hour ago, all hell had broken loose on Kirk's and Willich's line a mile to the south. Half an hour ago, he'd watched Baldwin's brigade march into the cedars to reinforce the line. But from the sound of things, Baldwin is now heavily engaged far short of that goal.

Thruston and his orderly ride down Gresham Lane, breasting a stream of stragglers and wounded men. Around a corner, he has his first clear look to the south. Perhaps a thousand yards ahead, a brigade is hotly engaged, its line nearly hidden in the rolling powder smoke. "Captain?" He looks down, sees a soldier barely more than a boy supporting another wounded private even younger. "Can you tell us where the doctors set up? Charlie here is in a bad way and I ain't much better."

"Keep going up the road. You'll see a white house to your right. It's not far."

"Thanks, Captain."

"Certainly. What brigade is that up ahead? Kirk's?"

The private snorts. "Kirk is long gone. So's Willich. That's Post's brigade. We're from the 59th Illinois and part of it. Best goddamn brigade in the army. But, Captain, there's a hell of a lot of Rebs up there."

Thruston turns to his orderly. "Tom, get back and tell Sergeant Barnes to send two wagons of cartridges and one of artillery rounds forward at the double to Colonel Post. We may be able to do some good."

He wishes the wounded privates luck and then sits for another minute watching the fight ahead. He has a queasy feeling that he is already too late. He turns his mare, takes to the field beside the road. Baldwin, he thinks, I should send him some wagons, too.

The three ammunition wagons for Post are just clearing the yard when he rides in. "Barnes," he shouts to his first sergeant. "I'm taking a couple of wagons to Colonel Baldwin."

"I'll do it, sir."

"No, you stay here. Keep the men in line." He casts a baleful look at the civilian teamsters and his company of infantry. The infantry isn't bad, mostly men on light duty recovering from illness or slight wounds, but there is hardly a man among the civilians—white or black—he would trust with a wagon load of flour. Well, Barnes can handle them for the time it will take to get the ammunition to Baldwin.

He selects two wagons with their teamsters and a four-man guard. The teamsters start to object, but a lanky corporal spins on them. "You shut your holes! I'm sick and fucking tired of all your croaking! You're paid to drive where the captain says. And you'll do it or I'll bloody well shoot you myself."

Thruston raises his eyebrows at the English accent, unusual even in this polyglot army. "His name's Andrews, sir," Barnes says. "Was a British soldier. Has a way with words, don't he?"

"Enviable," Thruston says.

With Thruston leading the way on his mare, the two wagons bump across a cornfield and turn south along one of the narrow, muddy alleys hacked through the cedars the day before by the Pioneer Brigade. Thruston knows by the time they are a hundred yards into the cedars that he has made a mistake. The alley is clogged with walking wounded and the woods to either side crawl with skulkers. He urges his mare into a trot, rides forward as fast as he can. Ahead, the sounds of battle rise toward a crescendo. He hears shouts. "Make way, make way! General Johnson coming through. Make way!" He pulls to the side, stops. The general and his staff come galloping up the alley, scattering mud and wounded men. Thruston waves an arm, expects one of the staff to stop. Perhaps the general himself, who should, after all, care about the resupply of ammunition to his men. But they go by him in a rush, not even acknowledging his presence. My God, we're truly beaten if the generals are running out, Thruston thinks. For a moment he almost turns back, but he must see for himself. He sets spurs to the mare.

He comes out of the forest as McNair's brigade smashes through Baldwin's first line. One blue regiment is falling back in good order, but Thruston can see that the second line is far too skimpy to hold for long. He makes a hasty survey of the fields to the west, can see a mass of gray infantry advancing along the fringe of trees marking the course of Overall Creek. If there is Reb infantry that far on our right, then there is cavalry well to our rear, he thinks. And though Thruston is not a topographical engineer, he has a good feel for land and contour, knows immediately that he has left his ammunition train at the worst possible time. He spins his horse, kicks her, screams at the men on the road to clear the way, knowing that many will think him the worst sort of coward, but knowing that minutes may cost the wing its reserve ammunition.

Andrews sees his captain coming, tells the teamster to pull up. Thruston reins in hard. "We're too late. Things have gone to hell up ahead and I've got to get the train off. Get the wagons back if you can. If you can't, burn them. Nothing falls to the Rebs!"

★ ★ ★

Brigadier General John Wharton has seen routs before but nothing like this. His twenty-five hundred gray cavalry have to ride two and a half miles to find the rear of the splintered right wing of the Union army. The brigade punches through a chaos of fleeing infantry, cavalry, teamsters, Negro work gangs, mules, horses, cattle, ambulances, batteries, and a dozen different sorts of wagons. Except for the cannons, which Wharton dispatches to the rear, he ignores all of it. Once he hits the Wilkinson Pike, he'll set up a line and start gathering prisoners and matériel. Until then, he will keep his brigade together and going hard.

Almost as amazing as the foot speed of the fleeing Yankee infantry is the lack of Yankee cavalry protecting the flank of the right wing. Wharton had expected a fight, but he has seen nothing of the Yankee cavalry except for a single small regiment easily broken up. God, he wishes Joe Wheeler were here. Together they would have five thousand horse, enough to smash in the entire Yankee rear, maybe even force a wholesale surrender.

Ahead he hears a crackle of carbine fire from the cedars along the near side of the Wilkinson Pike. Yankee cavalry. He can tell by the sharp crack of their light, short-barreled carbines. His lead regiment splits with practiced ease, two squadrons going to the right, two to the left, the fifth hanging back in reserve. The men dismount, advance as a skirmish line, the horse-handlers bringing the mounts to the rear. The Yankee fire stiffens: a small force, no more than a regiment.

The skirmish line falls back, having probed the strength of the Yankee position. White's Tennessee Battery has unlimbered to the right. Wharton gives the nod and the guns open, hurling shell and solid shot into the cedars. The Yankee fire dies away. Through his field glasses, Wharton can make out blue horsemen galloping away.

He moves the brigade through the cedars to the Wilkinson Pike. He will send a regiment down the road to the east and another west to see what pickings they can find. The rest he will put in line to gather up prisoners, wagons, guns, and supplies. Then he will send a courier to Hardee for instructions, beg him to send infantry to strike the Yankee rear.

☆ ☆ ☆

Corporal Jeremy Andrews, late of the Queen's 19th Regiment of Foot, supposes he should have found another profession by this time in life. He is forty-two, too old for the rigors of an infantryman's life. But it is all he knows. For twenty-three years, he served his sovereign in Afghanistan, China, India, Burma, the Crimea, South Africa, and India again. And alto-gether, except for the Crimea, it was an agreeable life. Oh, hard marches certainly, the occasional scrap-up with the natives. But always beer and tobacco and dark girls at the end of the difficult times. Above all else, the regiment, the knowing in every fight of having good men to left and right, men who knew their trade and would stand with him, as he with them, to the last. But then the regiment was ordered to Ireland, and he could not bear the gray skies, the cold rain. The girls were not the same either: made demands, expected more of a tired man than he could give. So he'd fallen prey to dreams, to the nonsense of those who sold passages to America.

A year later he was flat on his back with an attack of malaria in a rough St. Louis rooming house, penniless and desperate. But then there was war and he'd gone soldiering again. It is not the same, of course. There are some good men in this army, men he likes and trusts, but not even the few regular battalions can come close to matching the Queen's 19th Regiment of Foot. But it is soldiering, and Jeremy Andrews knows the trade.

He gets the ammunition wagons turned around and headed back for the train, the trail wagon now leading. In the process, he has to cuff the teamster repeatedly. The man is hysterical, begs to be let go to join the refugees streaming past them. Andrews holds the man by the belt, strikes him again. In the wagon ahead, one of the privates rides with a firm hand on the neck of the other teamster. The mules strain as the wheels bump over tree roots and rocks, slew through ruts. Behind there is a sudden uproar: men shouting, swearing, diving off the road as a battery of guns comes hell for leather down the alley. "Get to the side, get to the side, you fucking clot!" Andrews yells. The teamster hauls on the reins but it is too late. The left wheel of the lead gun carriage catches the right rear wheel of the wagon, rides up and over the axle, all fourteen hundred pounds of gun and carriage becoming airborne, smashing down on the young private in the box behind Andrews, shattering his skull, neck, spine, and rib cage, then missing the teamster and Andrews by inches, and landing on the right rear mule, killing it as certainly though less spectacularly than the private, before skidding back onto the muddy road behind its limber and team.

The teamster is screaming, the mules pitching against the weight of their dead companion and the tilting wagon. The limber on the second gun strikes the right lead mule a glancing blow and the team reels left, goes down in a frenzy of kicking, braying muledom. The wagon tips and Andrews leaps. He lands in soft needles and moss, rolls to get clear, and looks back. The wagon has come to rest on its side, the shells and cartridges spilling in a mound of smashed boxes. Thrown clear, the teamster bounds away down the road.

Andrews climbs to his feet, briefly amazed that he has come through uninjured. The other wagon has paused. He waves it on and goes to deal with the mules. His Springfield is somewhere in the wreckage but there are plenty more around. He picks one up and dispatches the mules with cool efficiency. "Cartridges, lads! Fill your boxes and pockets!" he yells. Many of the men are already pausing to scoop up handfuls. Andrews is impressed: These men are not as badly cobbed as I thought.

The dead private is lying like a crushed doll atop a heap of cartridges. It's a gaudy funeral for you, lad, Andrews thinks. He rolls a couple hundred cartridges and three fixed-charge twelve-pounder shells in the wagon canvas, draping it like a lumpy, gray snake over the heap. The last of the retreating blue infantry is almost past. Andrews soaks the rolled canvas with the contents of the wagon's kerosene lantern. Down the road, he can make out butternut figures against the gray light through the cedars. Time to be off. He strikes a lucifer, lights a corner of the canvas, and runs. He supposes a hero might have waited until the Rebs were nearly atop the wagon, sacrificing his own life to send a few dozen of the blighters to Glory and winning the Victoria Cross in the bargain—or whatever it is they give in this benighted country. But Andrews is no hero, is satisfied to be a good soldier. He senses that he has run out of time, ducks into the trees and drops behind a boulder as the first popping confirms his judgment. He covers his head, for what is about to go up must come down.

Captain Thruston and the infantry guarding the train are fighting a score of Rebel cavalrymen when the grove of cedars to the southwest plumes with exploding artillery shells and the burning-grease rattle of ten or fifteen thousand .58-caliber musket cartridges. For a moment everyone stops shooting and stares in amazement. Thruston recovers first. "Come on, boys," he shouts, and dashes for the half dozen wagons captured by the Rebels. The gray cavalrymen don't wait to fight it out hand to hand. They run for their mounts and gallop off west, following a Rebel squadron that is busily wheeling away McCook's supply train.

Thruston wastes no time. He still has his guards and most of his teamsters, though a few have slipped away during the fight. He will take the train overland, cutting through the cedars and fields toward army headquarters. He gives orders rapidly. Whips crack and the mules lean into their harnesses with the usual protests and ill grace of their kind. Thruston looks back toward the grove where the smoke from the eruption still drifts in the treetops. In the foreground, one of his wagons is bouncing over the cornfield. At least they'd saved one. Seventy-six to get away.

An hour later, as the train is laboring along another of the alleys cut by the Pioneers through the cedars, Corporal Andrews rejoins the guard. "We lost one man and one wagon, Captain," he tells Thruston. "Didn't get much good of the loss of either, I'm afraid."

Thruston claps him on the shoulder, is surprised when the man flinches at the familiarity. "Never mind. You did what you could. Go give Barnes a hand clearing the way."

★   ★   ★

Brigadier General Edward Kirk of Richard Johnson's division has bitten nearly through the collar of his wool blouse to keep from crying out with every jounce of the ambulance. When it finally halts, he lets his head fall back, breathing hard. God, he hurts. He feels the blood warm on his thigh, cold where it has puddled underneath him. I shouldn't have ridden out in front of my old regiment, he thinks. Pointless bravado. Now I will pay with a leg certainly, perhaps with my life.

He can hear the two soldiers on the seat whispering. "What's going on?" he asks the private squatted beside him.

"Reb cavalry, General. Lots of it. They've got a line along the pike, taking prisoners."

"Have they seen us?"

"Probably, sir. It'd be pretty hard not to."

"Then you boys better get going. You don't want to end up in a prison camp."

The man hesitates. "Yes, sir. I reckon maybe we will. Sorry, General. I wish we could stick with you."

"Thank you for bringing me this far. Now go on before it's too late."

When they are gone, it is very lonely in the wagon. Kirk blinks back tears. God, he hurts. But it's not so much the pain or the loneliness but the mistakes that hurt. All of them, all his life, but particularly today.

Brigadier General John Wharton sees the three soldiers scramble down from the ambulance and run for the cedars to the east. Curious, he rides over, half a dozen troopers and Surgeon Trulen with him. He pulls back the flap at the rear of the ambulance, sees a Union general with a mangled thigh lying in a pool of blood. "Are you awake, General?" he asks.

The man opens his eyes. "Yes. Whom do I have the honor of addressing?"

"John Wharton, commanding a brigade of C.S.A. cavalry."

The man extends a hand. "Ed Kirk. I wish I could say I commanded anything at this point, but that would be *suggestio falsi*."

Wharton smiles. "You are a lawyer?"

"Yes. And you?"

"The same, though Latin does not come so easily to me. Here, let my surgeon have a look at your leg."

Trulen climbs in, makes a brusque examination. Well, if it's Latin they want. . . . "The bullet penetrated the *adductor longus,* fractured the femur and must be lodged in the *gluteus medius.*"

Kirk takes a breath. "Is it mortal?"

Trulen tries to soften his tone. "Not necessarily, but quite possibly."

"General," Wharton says, "I have things I must attend to. We'll try to find a private house willing to take you in."

"Thank you, but never mind. The same treatment the men get will suffice."

"Of course," Wharton says, knowing that no man would truly turn down better. But a gentleman, even a Yankee, must play the role.

Colonel William Gibson and the stubborn survivors of Willich's brigade come out of the cedars near the Wilkinson Pike with cartridge boxes empty. Gibson stops, stares at the waiting line of gray cavalry. He sighs. "Reverse your muskets, boys. Nothing much we can do but go over and surrender."

No one disagrees; they have done what they could. They reverse their Springfields, roll their colors, form ranks, and set out across the field. The Reb cavalry is good-natured, gives them a brief cheer, tosses a few jibes about "pretty boys marching," though Gibson's men are far from pretty in their torn, bloody, powder-stained ranks.

Gibson is about to present his sword to a young lieutenant when there is a sudden outbreak of firing and yelling up the pike to the west. The officer spins his horse. "Wait here, Colonel! We'll be back," he shouts. The Rebels disappear in a cloud of flying hooves, mud, and manure.

Gibson looks to his major. "I don't know of anything in military etiquette that requires us to wait."

"No, sir."

Gibson turns to the men. "Come on, boys. Let's go find some cartridges."

Up the pike a regiment of blue cavalry is skirmishing with the Rebels as Gibson's men march across the pike, over a strip of field, and into the cedars again. Despite their fatigue and the horrors of the morning, they are laughing. *Wait here!* For the love of Mike, just how stupid do you think we are?

As far as Colonel Lewis Zahm knows, his three regiments of Ohio cavalry make up the only intact force of Union cavalry on the field. General Stanley has Minty's brigade somewhere up the Wilkinson Pike guarding the supply trains, while the dozen miscellaneous companies scattered among the infantry divisions seem to have disappeared entirely. Still, he will do what he can to keep the Reb cavalry from getting too cocksure.

He waits first in the cedars to the south of the Wilkinson Pike, hoping to ambush the Rebs as they approach. But someone is too eager, starts firing, and the surprise is lost. The Rebs bring up a battery and he has nothing to answer it, must fall back.

He waits next in the creek bottom north of the pike, hoping to hear the sound of Minty's brigade coming from the west to join him. After an hour, he sends the 1st and 4th Ohio to the next belt of cedars, a mile to the north, and then leads the 3rd Ohio charging down a country lane toward the pike. It is just a quick slap at the Rebs: dash in, create a little noise and upset, and then get out. Pistols and carbines, no sabers, for God's sake.

The Rebs recoil in surprise, roll up their line to strike back, but by then Zahm has sounded the retreat and the 3rd Ohio is falling back while several hundred Union prisoners bolt for the cedars. A half mile down the pike, Zahm sees a tattered regiment of blue infantry marching defiantly across the pike and into the cedars. Zahm laughs. We've got a little spunk yet, he thinks.

Wharton stares at the captain who has brought him McCook's supply train. The man obviously expects accolades, but Wharton is angry. "What was in that other train?"

"Well, I'm not sure, General. There was a pretty good-sized escort and we couldn't get a look."

"Flat-loaded?"

"Yes, sir."

"Damn it, man! That was the ammunition train. A dozen of those wagons are worth more than a whole damned supply train!"

The captain gulps. "But we grabbed General McCook's personal wagons, sir. One of the boys found his dress uniform."

"What the hell do I care about McCook's dress uniform? Are the Yankees throwing a ball for us?" Wharton stands glaring at the man and then sighs. No point in this. "All right, get back to your squadron. Wait. You said that ammunition train went north?"

"Yes, sir. I mean, I think so. They seemed to be headed that way."

When the man is gone, Wharton stares morosely at the cedars to the southeast where the roar of artillery and muskets has become continuous. Polk attacking and running into heavy going. If only Wheeler were here. . . . Suddenly, his patience with the professionals snaps. To hell with them, he thinks. I'm going after that ammunition train.

✯ ✯ ✯

Rosecrans is issuing orders one atop another. Sheridan is to hold his position at all hazards. Thomas is to send Rousseau in on Sheridan's right. Van Cleve is to withdraw to this side of the river, leave Price's brigade to guard McFadden's Ford, and march Fyffe's and Sam Beatty's brigades up the pike to man a line beyond Rousseau. McCook is to re-form Johnson's and Davis's north of the Nashville Pike.

Garesché scribbles, squinting low over the paper, tears page after page from his dispatch book, handing them to orderlies and aides who dash off into the battle. A shell howls overhead, explodes above the Nashville Pike two hundred yards to the south. Eyes still on the dispatch book, Garesché says, "General, perhaps we should—"

"Where's Burke?" Rosecrans snaps.

Garesché looks up in surprise at Rosecrans's demand for the commander of the provost guard. "You ordered Colonel Burke and his regiment to guard the supply train at Stewart's Creek, General."

Rosecrans frowns. "Yes, yes. Of course. I sent Stanley up there too. Shouldn't have done either. Send for them. No, leave Burke there. Too late for him to do much good. But I need Stanley and that brigade of cavalry."

"But certainly General Stanley has heard the battle and will be coming on his own accord."

"You have more faith in the hearing and initiative of General Stanley than I do, Colonel. Send the order."

"Yes, sir." And how is it to get through? Garesché wonders. He scribbles in his dispatch book: *General Stanley. The commanding general directs that you*. . . .

Rosecrans is already giving another order. "Ask General Thomas to send his provost guard up the pike to form a straggler line. Every man in this army needs to get into a regiment and fight like hell."

"Yes, General," Garesché says, flipping a page and starting the message to Thomas. His hand still moving, he looks about, spots the orderly he wants. Hodges of the shifty, vulpine look. Just the man. He beckons him over, hands him the order to Stanley. "Get to General Stanley. He's up the

Wilkinson Pike this side of Stewart's Creek. You will have to dodge a lot of Reb cavalry. Walk if you have to. Pretend you're a deserter if you need to. But get there."

"I'll find him, Colonel."

"Good man."

Rosecrans has stopped speaking, is concentrating on the sound of battle swelling to the south. A staff captain sent earlier to Sheridan gallops up on a lathered horse. "Report," Rosecrans snaps.

"General Sheridan has established a new line near the Harding house south of the Wilkinson Pike, General. Some of Davis's division are holding on his right. The whole line's bent back pretty far, General. Almost parallel with the pike."

Like a barlow knife closing, Garesché thinks, and we're between blade and strike plate.

The captain takes a breath, trying to control his voice. "The casualties are terrible at all ranks, sir. General Sill's dead."

Rosecrans sucks in a breath. "I'm sorry to hear it. But we cannot help it. Brave men must be killed." He turns to the rest of his staff. "Never mind, we will make everything right. This battle must be won." He wheels Boney, rides along beside the river-soaked, shivering ranks of Van Cleve's men, who are trudging along McFadden's Lane toward the Nashville Pike. He calls encouragement to the men, his tone jocular. "March hard, boys. Whipping the Johnnies will warm you up. Mind your officers. Fire low. Always fire low. Then go in with the bayonet."

The men like Old Rosy, give a cheer as he passes. He pauses briefly to speak to white-bearded Van Cleve, the old farmer who graduated from West Point, served his time, and resigned from the army years before most of these soldiers were born. Van Cleve nods solemnly. Rosecrans kicks Boney into a canter, climbing up the rise to where Tom Crittenden and Tom Wood have established headquarters for the left wing. He ignores Crittenden, speaks directly to Wood. "General Wood, leave one of your brigades with General Palmer to hold this part of the line. Take the rest of your division up the pike as soon as Van Cleve is clear."

"Yes, sir. How far am I to go?"

"Far enough to support Van Cleve's right and to protect our flank."

"Am I to form a crochet or—"

Rosecrans needs to move, loses patience with Wood's obtuseness. The orders are clear enough already. "Don't worry about that, General! I will be there to help you get your men in line. Just get them up the pike for now."

He descends to the railroad embankment, rides on west toward his headquarters, the staff stretching out behind. Wood, who stepped on a nail the night before, adjusts the crutch he has slung like a carbine from his saddle, speaks casually to Crittenden: "Did you see that another of your generals is also gimpy this morning?"

Crittenden is staring distractedly at Rosecrans's retreating staff. "I'm sorry, General. What did you say?"

"I said that another of your generals has a bad hoof today. Van Cleve has a boil on his heel. Quite painful, I'm told. It seems you'll have to depend on a pair of lame division commanders in this fight."

"Yes. Yes, I see." Crittenden manages a smile. God, he needs a drink. Oh, he feels steady enough, but . . . chilled. Yes, that's it. A whiskey to warm the blood.

"I should be about obeying General Rosecrans's orders," Wood says. "Altogether, he seems to be taking the reversal of our plans well. But, in your place, I would stay close to him today. I think he may need your counsel and something of your optimism, your élan."

Crittenden stares at Wood, so grateful that he could almost cry. "Yes, you're right. I think my place is near to his hand. But I will keep in close contact with you, Palmer, and Van Cleve. I'll come see you when you're in position."

"We will welcome that, General." Wood salutes and rides down the hill. Passing Crittenden's chief of staff, an old friend, he growls: "Well, Frank, as one coon said to the other when the dogs were after them, 'We'll all meet at the hatter's.'"

Phil Sheridan stalks behind his line, a sword in one hand, his soft black hat crushed in the other, the butt of a tar-black cigar clamped in his teeth. The Rebel attack is incessant, the sheer weight of it bending in the division's flanks for all the furious stubbornness of his men. A courier hands him a sheet torn from Garesché's dispatch book: *The general exhorts you to hold your position at all hazards. The day depends on it.*

Sheridan crumples the sheet in a fist. Then it is we who are to be sacrificed to make up for the errors of our commanders, he thinks. Goddamn McCook! Rosy should have known better than to leave him in command.

He thinks of Sill, dead in front of First Brigade's line. Can I follow poor Sill's advice? Can I give ground gradually and still obey my orders? He reaches out a hand for a dispatch book, jots quickly: *We are giving ground slowly at great cost to the Rebels. This part of the line will hold together at all hazards.*

He hands the dispatch to an aide, digs in a pocket for a fresh cigar. Sill's uniform blouse is tight across his back and too short in the sleeves, though Sill was a taller man. Odd that Sill, usually so fastidious, had picked up the wrong blouse on leaving their campfire the night before. Now he has died wearing my blouse while I fight wearing his, Sheridan thinks. Did he take a bullet intended for me?

It is a natural enough thought for a man with the blood of Hibernia flowing in his veins. But Sheridan dismisses it with a snort. No, he is not meant to be killed in battle. Somehow he knows this, has known it ever since the Yakima bullet clipped the bridge of his nose and killed the orderly beside him. Private John McGrew. Sheridan has always remembered the name, though he bore the man no particular regard. It is simply something filed in a mind that, for all Sheridan's pugnacity, is orderly, calculating, gauging of men and situations. "Hold there, goddamn it!" he yells at a squad of men giving back a few feet. "Don't give the bastards an inch until I tell you to!"

Phil Sheridan stalks on down the line, fresh cigar puffing furious clouds. He shouts, swears, berates, but all the time he is calculating. Yes, he will give ground but only in exchange for a barrel of blood for every inch. He will not be driven by a bunch of goat-screwing, scratch-ass rednecks. That is for goddamn sure.

Garesché cannot believe the pandemonium on the Nashville Pike. The army that had set out from Nashville, the army that had seemed a mighty engine of Faith in his imagination, is broken now, smashed, become an immense flotsam of men, beasts, and vehicles washing across the pike. From every elevation along the river, Rebel batteries fire into the heaving mass as fast as they can load; the shells and solid shot ripping holes and rents that are closed almost instantly, filled by the rush of human, animal, and vehicular panic. Beneath it all, Garesché imagines a thickening mire of mud, flesh, blood, and despair, a primordial slime infested with slithering, terrible things: great eyeless worms trodden up and sliding among the men, stinging blindly to either side. My God, he thinks, we are done, finished. We can do nothing but flee, hoping to save enough of the army to defend Nashville.

Rosecrans turns to him, eyes seeming to glow in an ashen face. "We must win this battle, Julius. We are going to win it! I will not permit any other result!"

A round of spherical case shot, fired, Garesché would guess, at maximum range, explodes over the pike, spraying a squad of cavalry with shrapnel. The squad itself seems to explode, its fragile order tearing apart in screaming fragments. "General," Garesché begs, "you must not expose yourself in a place like this. If you are lost, we are all—"

"Pah! The only safety is in destroying the enemy! Just make the sign of the cross and go in." Rosecrans brings a gloved hand from forehead to sternum, then shoulder to shoulder, urges Boney forward. Horse and general plunge from the embankment into the mob of refugees, Rosecrans waving his hat. "Take courage, soldiers! Take courage! We will make it right. Reform on the far side of the road. We'll go back in together."

Garesché rides after, his own shaking fingers making a hasty sign of the cross while somewhere in the back of his mind, unbidden, an old woman croons of battle, death, and beauty, of light coming down golden as an aureole, red as a heart pierced in stained glass.

☆ ☆ ☆

Judge John Kennett, commander in name but not in reality of Rosecrans's cavalry division, is not used to being supernumerary. All his adult life he has filled a role of importance in his community, his county, and—in recent years—his state. Hundreds have appeared in his court seeking judgment. Many more have come to his chambers or to his home seeking advice, political support, a few dollars to help them over a rough patch: any of the many kinds of help that Judge Kennett can, and is usually disposed to, give.

When war came, he'd raised a regiment, continuing in field service long after most of the duffers his age went home. He enjoys the camaraderie of army life, the masculinity of it, all those things of youth he had supposed gone from his life. Stanley has been kind to him, and he has tried to be of service, though in truth he has become little more than a hanger-on with little to do but drink coffee, read his Homer, and chivvy the young men of the staff. But, goddamn it, he had not expected to miss the battle entirely!

He accepts another cup of coffee from Magee, the ubiquitous headquarters orderly. Major Goddard, the assistant chief of staff, is seated at his field desk at the far end of the tent, scanning the messages coming in and then sending them down the constantly shifting courier line to Rosecrans and Garesché. Kennett stares again into the rainy morning, listens carefully with his better ear to the sounds of battle. The firing is by far the heaviest to the southeast on the far side of the Wilkinson Pike. But that is infantrymen's business. Kennett is more interested in the scattered but often intense fire to the west. Our cavalry against their cavalry, or perhaps their cavalry against some stubborn clumps of our infantry. Either way, it is a cavalry-man's business. His business.

Judge John Kennett glares into his coffee cup. Christ, the coffee gets worse every day! Two hundred and fifty years of English-speaking civilization on this continent, and we still can't make decent coffee. Appalling. He begins to toss the remaining half cup into the weeds, drinks it instead, then steps around behind the tent to empty his bladder. Done, he buttons up, takes a deep breath of the frosty morning with its dank smell of fallen leaves and wet cedar. In one of the trees a flash of red and a cardinal bobs on a branch. Kennett watches it. Oh, hell, he thinks. I've lived long enough.

Inside the tent, he calls to Goddard. "Major, I'm going for a look over west. I'll send back word."

"Yes, Colonel. I'll tell General Rosecrans."

If he ever shows up and if he gives a damn, Kennett thinks. "Thank you, Major."

Out in the yard he waves to the remnant of his staff: a half dozen youngsters led by a particularly callow lieutenant who is the son of a business acquaintance. "Come on, boys, let's go join the fun."

Captain Thruston, his infantry guards, and his unwilling teamsters have worked the train of ammunition wagons across a half mile of what must be the worst road ever dignified with a name. Not that it is an official name, but by this time Thruston's men have provided so many choice descriptions of the alley hacked through the cedars that Thruston concludes that it must have gained a certain patronymity.

Thruston has scouted ahead as far as the harvested cornfields between the woods and the belt of cedars bordering the Nashville Pike. There are stragglers by the hundred crossing the open but he has seen no Reb cavalry nor any Federal either. If he can get the wagons across the fields, he will have done all he can. If there is no safety in proximity to army headquarters, then there is no safety anywhere.

A dozen shots crackle at the rear of the train. Thruston kicks his mare into a canter, rides back. The corporal in charge of the dozen troopers assigned to guard the rear whips the ramrod out of his musket, slides it in place under the barrel. "There was four of 'em horseback, Cap'n. We seen 'em a few minutes ago but weren't sure if they was Yank or Reb. This time we was sure."

Scouts, Thruston thinks and curses silently. "Get any of them?"

"Couldn't tell, sir. One of 'em hit Jimmy Blackwell with a lucky shot. Blew his kneecap off."

Thruston looks at a private down beside a tree, rocking in agony, two of his friends with him. "Get him atop one of the wagons. Look sharp for the Rebs. If I get any men to spare, I'll send them back to you."

He is nearly to the front of the train when he sees a mounted figure in a black rain cape coming down the road. Thruston's hand reaches involuntarily for the Navy Colt at his side. He stops it, hesitates. No, a courier. Must be. "Don't shoot," the man shouts to the guards ahead of the train. "I'm from Colonel Zahm. Who's in charge?"

"Show me a uniform," Sergeant Barnes yells.

The man looks down, confused for a moment, and then pulls back his cape to reveal a blue uniform. "Lord, son," Barnes growls. "Riding around with one of those things on is a sure way to get yourself shot. Captain Thruston's back there."

The orderly rides up to Thruston. "Captain, Colonel Zahm wants you to push ahead as fast as you can. He's got his brigade up ahead and will give you cover crossing to the pike. But there's a lot of Reb cavalry around and you've got to move fast."

"We're moving as fast as we can. Tell Colonel Zahm we appreciate all the cover he can give us."

Despite Garesché's protests about the danger, Rosecrans has returned to the elevation of the railroad embankment. Watching George Thomas riding up the slope at his usual slow trot, Rosecrans feels a swell of confidence. Thomas is an archetype, he thinks. They have all had someone like him, all the great soldiers: Agamemnon his Ajax, Alexander his Ptolemy, Augustus his Agrippa. Given leisure, he could pair them all down through history: the generals and the grim, inflexible lieutenants who rode with them through victories and defeats, always fixed and fell of purpose. Rosecrans lifts a hand. "Good morning, George."

Thomas salutes. "General Rosecrans."

"Is Rousseau in position on Sheridan's right?"

"Just going in. I sent Colonel Parkhurst and my provost guard up the pike to form a straggler line."

"Good. Given a little time, we can make things all right."

"Of course. But General McCook—"

Rosecrans is suddenly impatient. "Forget McCook, George. I will deal with him later. For the moment I've ordered him to re-form Johnson's and Davis's divisions north of the pike."

"Yes, but it seems that General McCook has not taken up those duties. He came into Sheridan's rear and ordered the 36th Illinois to fall back all the way to the Nashville Pike. Never told Sheridan a thing. Sheridan's adjutant came looking for them and told me about it."

Rosecrans's face goes taut with anger. "Well, if you see General McCook, tell him to take up the new duties I gave him or retire altogether from the battlefield."

Thomas nods and then points at the chaos on the Nashville Pike. "That brigade isn't going to get through."

"Whose is it?"

"One of Van Cleve's. Hascall's, I believe."

"Hascall is supposed to be on the right beyond Rousseau and Harker. I will send word for them to fix bayonets and force their way through. To fire if necessary."

"I think it would be preferable to post Hascall south of the pike in support of General Palmer's line. Bragg is executing a right wheel by echelon. It won't be long before the strength of his attack lands on Negley and Palmer."

Rosecrans frowns. "Bragg should reinforce his left, try to push across the pikes to the river. He'd have us surrounded."

"Yes, but he won't. Once in motion, Bragg does not change direction. He will press the attack on our center next."

Rosecrans chews his lip. For an hour he has been stripping the center to send aid to the right flank. Has he blundered? He turns abruptly to Garesché. "Julius, send a message to Hascall. Tell him to stand in reserve south of the pike. General Thomas, I am going to look to the flanks. Hold the center. Keep Sheridan fighting."

Thomas almost smiles. "Sheridan will fight. There is no need for anyone to keep him at it. I will support him as well as I can."

The impatience has come on Rosecrans again. "Good. I'm going to check on the security of the ford." He spins Boney to the east, forcing the staff to part.

Passing Thomas, Garesché manages to smile. "Good luck, General. God protect you."

Thomas nods. He does not much believe in luck or in Garesché's God. In his experience, constancy is an agency infinitely more reliable.

Colonel John G. Parkhurst commands the 9th Michigan infantry, assigned as provost guard for Thomas's corps. He has managed to maneuver the regiment through the woods and fields north of the Nashville Pike to the bridge crossing Overall Creek. It is a good position for a straggler line and he expects little difficulty in funneling refugees into the fields short of the bridge, where McCook is to reorganize his wing. Parkhurst settles down under a tree to browse through a slender volume of Descartes.

The book is an old friend from the four months Parkhurst spent as a prisoner of war after Nathan Bedford Forrest's capture of Murfreesboro and General Thomas Turpin Crittenden's garrison. During his captivity, Parkhurst attempted to develop a philosophical patience regarding the tragical frailties, as he calls them, of mankind. He excepts from his charity only the Crittenden clan, for whom he nurses an eternal loathing.

At midmorning, Parkhurst is confronted with a truly excessive test of his philosophy when a supply train comes thundering up the road toward the straggler line. Even at a distance, Parkhurst can see the panic on faces human and mule. Good Lord, he thinks, I'd need a cannon to stop them. "Fix bayonets," he yells. "Companies A and B, prepare to fire a volley over their heads."

The soldiers of the 9th Michigan are a veteran bunch, unimpressed by the usual disorder surrounding battles won and lost. But the prospect of being run down by a train of mule-drawn wagons in full flight brings a pallor even to their weathered faces. "Jesus Christ, Colonel," one of the men says. "Let 'em pass. We'll build a barricade, stop the next bunch." There are murmurs of assent.

Parkhurst does not answer, though it is probably good advice. I never understood before how terrifying a chariot charge must have been, he thinks. Well, we shall see if these steeds and charioteers have the stuff of epic in them. He steps to the side of the bridge, nods to the captain commanding Company A. "Present!" the captain yells. "Fire!" The volley rips over the head of the train, apparently without effect.

Company B steps forward, combing through the ranks of Company A. "Just over their heads, Captain," Parkhurst shouts. The volley rips out, and it must be low indeed because there is an instant screaming of "whoa" from the lead wagons, accompanied by a screeching of wooden brakes against iron rims. But not everyone has gotten the point or at least been convinced of it. A wagon in the pack swings out of line, makes a sprint for the front, its driver slashing at his mules. Seeing him coming, the driver of the lead wagon, whether motivated by fear of capture or an overwhelming competitive desire, releases his brake and applies the whip again.

The wagons meet at the narrow entrance to the bridge, colliding with such force that four of the mules and one of the drivers suffer fatal broken necks and some of the infantrymen of Company B, falling back across the bridge in near rout, are thrown from their feet. Two more wagons pile into the mess, killing more mules and another driver. Staring at the wreckage, Parkhurst abandons philosophy. Tragical frailties? More like farcical tragedies. Or perhaps frail farcities. Who the hell knows?

He looks at his men, who are staring in disbelief at the scene, and then at the mob on the road, who are likewise rendered silent for the moment. "All right," he says to his lieutenant colonel. "Let's get it cleaned up. Take half the boys and start gathering up that pack of miscreants."

Rosecrans, Garesché, and the staff pull up at McFadden's Ford in a clatter of hooves. Colonel Sam Price, whose brigade guards the ford, comes hurrying up. Rosecrans leans forward, hands on the pommel of Boney's saddle, fixes Price with a stare. "Will you hold this ford?"

"I will try, sir."

"Will you hold this ford, Colonel?"

Price looks confused. "I will die right here, General!"

"Will you *hold* this ford, Colonel?"

Price snaps to attention. "Yes, sir!"

"That will do," Rosecrans growls, wheels Boney, sets spurs to the gray's flanks.

★ ★ ★

Brigadier General John Wharton's brigade of gray cavalry tears across the Yankee rear, trying to get ahead of Thruston's ammunition train. Coming out of the cedars bordering Overall Creek, the brigade swings hard to the east over fallow cornfields. Wharton can feel his flank coming open, cringes at the thought of Yankee batteries on the pike a mile to the north. As if cued, a gun fires from the trees along the pike, its discharge a white plume against the dark background. The shell roars overhead, explodes amid some Yankee stragglers near the cedars, killing two and scattering the rest.

Wharton's lead squadron breasts a small hill, its captain turning to gesture to Wharton, shouting something over the din of hoofbeats. He sees it! Wharton thinks. We're going to catch the bastards, after all. He comes up and over the hill, feels a sudden relief as it screens out the battery on the pike. Below he sees a farm and, beyond it, the wagon train stretched across the foot of the field, a regiment of blue cavalry on its near flank, two more regiments drawn up near the farm's outbuildings.

Altogether the Yankee force must number nine hundred men, and Wharton—even with numerous detachments on other errands—still has half again as many. For a moment he is tempted to pitch into the Yankees, but experience tells him better. His boys are not French lancers or British dragoons, but country boys equipped with immense enthusiasm but little training in the complex maneuvers called for in a charge. They fight best on foot with their carbines and infantry rifles, rarely resorting to pistols or blades.

Wharton deploys the brigade in line of battle along the base of the hill with White's Tennessee Battery in the center. He rides to White's side. "For God's sake, don't hit the wagons. Just drive off the guard."

A moment later the first gun fires, sending a round howling over the creaking wagons.

From the shadow of the Widow Burris farm, Colonel Lewis Zahm watches Wharton deploy. Like Wharton, Zahm knows that this war's cavalry fights best afoot. He is about to shake out a skirmish line when Colonel Minor Milliken, commanding the 1st Ohio cavalry, goes romantically mad. Milliken has adopted *Morte d'Arthur, Mocedades del Cid,* and the *Chanson de Roland* as his texts, believes absolutely that battle on horseback should be fought with the blade and a strong arm. He would be Lancelot, the Cid, most of all Roland. He has even christened his saber after Roland's great sword, *Durandal.* He draws it now, sweeps it forward.

Zahm is startled by the shout behind him, turns to see the entire 1st Ohio charging into the field behind Milliken. "Stop!" Zahm yells, for it is a simple word inviting no interpretation and also the first to come to his tongue. No one in the 1st Ohio so much as turns a head.

Lieutenant Colonel Douglas Murray, commanding the 3rd Ohio, shouts to Zahm: "Colonel, shouldn't we hit the Reb flank?"

Zahm stares at Murray. "Are you mad?" he splutters. "Milliken's about to be butchered! Get your men down and under cover of the farm buildings. We'll try to hold here until Thruston can get the wagons to the trees."

"But, Colonel, those wagons are full of ammunition. If the Rebs start shelling them—"

"I know what's in them, goddamn it! Jesus Christ, man! Have you a better idea? Now follow orders or I'll have you court-martialed along with Milliken!"

Murray delivers a stiff salute and an icy "Yes, sir."

Zahm watches as Milliken's men hurtle down on the Rebel left. I cannot believe this, he thinks. What a bungle.

* * *

Milliken would have preferred sunshine on snow, the high mountain air of the Pyrenees, the cliff faces echoing with the shrill and thump of Saracen horn and drum. But *Durandal* shines, shimmers in his hand, and behind him there is the thunder of the regiment, three hundred horse, three hundred Union cavalrymen—paladins all—and for a moment Minor Milliken is truly there, riding wings of glory into the pass at Roncesvalles.

Surprise is an incredible thing. In Texas, Wharton has seen the results of a Comanche raid, knows what a mere handful of fanatical and intrepid men can do against many times their number. But the Yankees face odds far too long, have to cross a distance far too wide. Colonel Tom Harrison dismounts his 8th Texas regiment. The Texans kneel, take cool aim, and slaughter half a hundred Yankees like they were so many buffalo. But the Yankee colonel out front seems impervious to the fire, comes on brandishing a polished saber. The Texans fire faster, drop twenty, thirty, fifty more, and still the Yankee troopers come on behind their colonel. Wharton whistles softly through his teeth. Get out of the way, Tom. These Yankees are truly loco.

Harrison pulls his men in so they can fight back to back if they have to, but the 2nd and 4th Tennessee make that unnecessary. The Tennessee boys mount and sweep around the Texans to take the Yankee charge head on.

In his imagination, Milliken has heard the collision of charging horsemen many times: the clatter of armor, the clanging of sword and ax on shield and helm, the rearing scream of battle chargers, the awful hollow chunk of blades bursting skulls. But it doesn't sound this way on the last day of 1862, though there is noise enough. Cavalry horses are not armored battle chargers; and they do not crash into each other, but shy away from collision. The fight becomes a melee of bumping, twisting, terrified horses, their riders trying to aim pistols and sabers while being spun in dizzying circles. Some of the troopers carry three or four revolvers and the wide variety of calibers and constructions produces a rattling cacophony like a snare drum hit from every possible angle. Not until *Durandal* happens to strike the barrel of a Rebel cavalryman's pistol does Milliken hear the long anticipated clang of metal on metal. The Tennessee cavalryman rips a second pistol from his belt, shoots Milliken through the biceps of his sword arm. The shock tears the saber from Milliken's hand. His horse turns two rapid circles before Milliken spots *Durandal* lying in a furrow. He swings down, catches it up with his left hand, his nearly dead right grasping his mount's reins. He examines his arm, sees the blood pumping from the wound. The words come unbidden, perhaps from the *Chanson,* perhaps from some ballad very like it: *I am a little wounded but I am not slain. I will lay me down for to bleed a while, then rise to fight again.* He smiles, would say the words aloud, but at that moment Private Darwin Friemoth, 4th Tennessee Cavalry, leans down from his horse and puts three rounds from a .44-caliber double-action Kerr revolver into Milliken's chest.

So long as they can see their colonel, the troopers of the 1st Ohio fight. But once they lose sight of him, they lose enthusiasm. A few dozen break free to gallop back across the field to the Burris farm. A hundred are swallowed up by the Tennessee regiments and forced to surrender.

The gunners of White's Tennessee Battery have ignored the fight to their left. The first few rounds from the company's Napoleons scatter the troopers of the raw 4th Ohio, dispatched by Zahm to escort Thruston's wagons. The teamsters bolt for the woods, ignoring the shouts, threats, and warning shots of the infantry guards. Thruston tries to form the infantry, but they cannot hold under cannon fire. They fire a single, pointless volley at extreme range, then join the flight for the woods. At the Burris farm, Zahm can do nothing. When White's battery shifts its fire onto the out-buildings, he orders the 3rd Ohio to mount and fall back toward the Nashville Pike.

Wharton sends three of his small regiments to take charge of the train. Hardly a man lost and he has taken a great prize. It strikes him that he has an exploit to match those of Morgan, Forrest, and Wheeler, that perhaps he may at last claim admission to their ranks.

Riding northwest on the Nashville Pike, Colonel John Kennett's luck is running well. He encounters Colonel Parkhurst, the former disciple of Descartes, coming east from the straggler line with two re-formed regiments of infantry and a squadron of cavalry. "What cavalry have you got there, Parkhurst?" Kennett shouts.

"A squadron of the 3rd Kentucky. They were lost more than beaten. As a matter of fact, they're mad as snakes in a bag."

"Well, if I can borrow them, I'll take them where they can bite something."

Shortly after, Kennett meets Captain Elmer Otis and his six companies of the 4th U.S. Cavalry returning from their scout. Otis halts his column, rides forward. "Colonel, I'm very glad to see you. Johnson and Davis are broken, Sheridan's hanging on by his fingertips."

"Any sign of General Stanley or Minty's brigade?"

"None, Colonel."

"How about Zahm?"

"I think he's just to the southeast. A few minutes ago there was a lot of carbine and pistol firing from that direction. Napoleons, too."

Kennett curses his poor hearing. "All right, let's go have a look."

They find Zahm and the 3rd Ohio in the belt of trees south of the Nashville Pike, watching disconsolately as Wharton's men work to turn the ammunition train around. "Hello, Lewis," Kennett says. "I don't suppose we should let them do that."

"I'm not sure we can prevent it, Colonel. Milliken made an unauthorized charge and cost me a third of my command. Another third ran away."

"Well, the third you have left must be the best then. Come, let's talk this over." Kennett calls Otis and the captain of the 3rd Kentucky and quickly sketches a plan. They will rush the wagons, drive off the Rebs, then dismount and fight afoot. Two entire companies of the regulars will concentrate on the gunners if the Rebs deploy their battery again. He glances about. "Where'd the teamsters go?"

Zahm points to the cedars to the east. "They skedaddled for those trees along with maybe a hundred infantry from the guard."

"Send someone to see if they're still there. If they're not, we'll have to drive the wagons ourselves. Tell the infantry to come fight with us." He looks at the three officers. How young they are, how quick to follow a man old enough to be their father. When Stanley shows up, perhaps I should have a fatherly word with him about our arrangement. Over coffee.

Wharton has dispatched half his brigade on a sweep to the west to gather up more prisoners when the Yankee cavalry charges out of the woods along the pike. Wharton is amazed, curses himself for assuming that there was no more fight in them. The gray troopers trying to get the wagon train turned are equally surprised, mount and run. Wharton yells to his adjutant, tells him to recall the rest of the brigade. He turns his field glasses on the scene below, watches a big, gray-bearded officer calmly posting blue troopers along a ditch and a worm fence as the wagon guard of infantry reappears from the woods, driving several dozen teamsters ahead of them.

Captain Thruston stares at his rescuer. By God, it's old Judge Kennett! What the hell did they put in his coffee this morning?

"Good morning, Captain," Kennett growls. "Have you any decent coffee in those wagons?"

"No, sir. Just ammunition."

Kennett scowls. "Very disappointing. This army needs decent coffee a damned sight more than it needs ammunition. Well, I suppose I should help you save your train anyway. I'll lend you a rider for every lead hitch. Grab anyone you like if you're short of drivers."

Wharton watches in frustration as the wagon train again begins creaking north toward the pike. In desperation, he launches a charge, but the dismounted blue cavalry break it up with a cool, steady fire from the cover of the fence and ditch. By the time White's battery comes hurtling over the hill to set up again, the head of the train is already under cover of the woods. "Hit the wagons!" Wharton snaps.

But it is too late. The battery is worn and short of ammunition. The blue regulars pepper the gunners with their repeating carbines. At the edge of the belt of trees along the turnpike, the big gray-bearded officer waits until the last of the wagons and cavalry take cover.

With an anger that he thought he had long outgrown, Wharton grabs a Colt Revolving Rifle captured by one of his troopers and presented to him. He empties it at the distant officer on horseback, but the range is long, the weapon unfamiliar. The officer lifts his hat in ironic salute and rides into the cedars.

✯　✯　✯

Captain Thruston, Sergeant Barnes, and Corporal Andrews are squatting around a small fire, boiling coffee, when Rosecrans comes down off the pike, his staff trailing. "Are you the officer who says McCook's ammunition train is saved?" Rosecrans demands.

"Yes, sir," Thruston replies, standing to attention.

"How do you know?"

"I had charge of it."

"Where is it?"

"On the other side of the trees, General, under as much cover as we could find."

Rosecrans stares at him and then suddenly roars with laughter. "Well, great God, man! That's splendid. How did you get it away?"

"Well, General, we did some sharp fighting and a great deal more running."

"Captain, consider yourself a major from today! And on my staff. I won't let General McCook have you any longer." He turns to his staff. "Come, gentlemen. The day is looking brighter."

Garesché cannot comprehend Rosecrans's returning optimism. Everywhere he looks, the chaos seems greater than ever, the flood of refugees unabated. Regiments and brigades still in formation collide, become entangled in the flotsam, begin washing away. And all the time the Confederate shot and shell falling, killing and mangling men, horses, and mules. Twenty yards to his left, a cannonball rips through the knapsack and torso of a very tall soldier, spraying possessions out his chest as if they were bizarre internal organs. The ball decapitates the next man in line, takes the hats off two shorter soldiers, and decapitates the two men in front of them. The two short soldiers—mere boys, he sees—look at their four comrades, dead in a split second, and begin to sob.

It is only one of a hundred horrible things he witnesses. Yet he functions, scribbles orders, dispatches couriers and staff officers, offers advice to his general, cautions him again and again not to expose himself unnecessarily. Rosecrans only repeats what he has been saying for two hours: "Never mind. This battle must be won."

What is wrong with me? Garesché thinks. This is appalling. An abomination to all I hold sacred. I should throw down my sword, strip away my rank, march out between the armies, my arms wide to mine enemies, and beg all these men with guns to lay them down, to stop firing their cannon. Last night we sang together, today we can make peace, no matter what governments say.

But he goes on writing the orders, dispatching the messengers, offering advice and caution to the general. My God, he thinks, I am enjoying myself! I am a soldier and I have always wanted this; that is the truth, all the rest a fiction, a flattery to a sensitivity of soul I neither possess nor deserve. God forgive me, but I love this.

Rosecrans is pushing men into line, personally leading regiments and even companies into position. It is simpler to lead than to risk a misinterpretation of orders or to wrestle with the stutter that comes on him when he is greatly excited. He knows that he is violating the sacred chain of command in bypassing, sometimes even countermanding, brigade and division commanders. But the dispersal of units has made it almost impossible for the chain to work efficiently, and he cannot help giving orders that he knows need giving.

He has heard that Grant repeatedly refused to violate the chain at Shiloh, had allowed regiments and brigades to fall back or to go in the wrong direction because they were following orders given by commanders intermediate in the chain. Grant had run the battle through his division commanders in blind devotion to the principles instilled at West Point. But Rosecrans cannot function this way. Not now. To hell with all traditions, principles, textbooks: This battle must be won!

He dashes along the line, ignoring the swarming buzz of minié balls and the whoosh of passing shells. He cannot worry about his own death, for his life is in God's hands—has been in God's hands since he accepted the true Church. He positions the Chicago Board of Trade Battery, perhaps the army's finest with its matched teams and fourteen-pounder James rifles, on a height near army headquarters where it can sweep the half mile of open ground to the south. Next he leads Harker's brigade of Wood's division up the pike, puts it in at the far end of the new line cobbled together from many pieces of the center and left. He slaps smiling, handsome, lucky Charlie Harker on the shoulder. "You've got the flank, Colonel. Hold it for dear life. I'll be back in a while, and we'll see about doing some attacking of our own."

He needs to check on Sheridan. He gallops down the pike, his staff gamely following, Garesché close at his side. A splash of blood spatters his uniform. He glances over, sees blood on Garesché's chest and face. "Hit, Julius?"

"No, General. But I'm afraid my poor horse just had his nose stung by a ball."

Rosecrans laughs, rides on toward the cedars where Sheridan is fighting for the army's life.

CHAPTER 4

Wednesday, 7:00 A.M.–11:00 A.M.
December 31, 1862
The Confederate Left Center below the Wilkinson Turnpike

While Wharton's Confederate cavalry rampages across the Federal rear, the Confederate infantry presses forward against Sheridan's division south of the Wilkinson Pike. But coordination of the Confederate attack proves difficult. McCown's division has drifted to the west, leaving Cleburne's division to execute the right wheel called for in Bragg's plan. Major General Benjamin F. Cheatham's division is supposed to advance in echelon on Cleburne's right, but Cheatham, unsure of his tactics, delays.

ON A RISE behind the Confederate left center, Braxton Bragg can hear his plan going wrong. The firing on the left has widened far beyond what should be the extremity of his flank, and he concludes correctly that McCown has drifted left instead of wheeling right. He is about to dictate a stern message to Hardee when a staff captain on a steaming chestnut mare climbs the rise to hand a message to Brent.

"What is it, Colonel?" Bragg asks.

"From Hardee, General: 'We are driving the enemy but Cleburne's right is exposed. Where is Cheatham?'"

Bragg contains his anger with difficulty. "Take a message: 'General Hardee, McCown appears to have directed his advance too far to the west. Immediately correct his elliptical path and restore him to the front line with

Cleburne in reserve. If you cannot execute this maneuver, place McCown in reserve behind Cleburne.'"

It is a peevish message and one almost impossible to obey now that both McCown and Cleburne are in action. But how dare Hardee—the supposed master of maneuver—deviate from the plan at the very opening of the battle? Is it carelessness or treachery? Well, Professor Hardee should know that Bragg is alert to his every move.

Colonel Brent waits patiently while his chief frowns at the misty cedars to the west, his eyebrows twitching. At last Brent speaks: "Do you wish to say any more, General? Regarding Cheatham, that is."

"General Cheatham's division is not part of General Hardee's command and is not his concern."

"Yes, sir. Shall I include that?"

"Oh, for God's sake, Colonel! You don't remind a lieutenant general of what is obvious in the table of organization. General Hardee is not a fool! Send the message I gave you."

"Yes, sir."

Bragg stands with hands clasped behind his back, scowling at the battle smoke rising from the forest. What a preposterous war! A boy like Brent wearing the insignia of a colonel! My God, he barely knows enough to be a lieutenant. He shakes his head, concentrates on what to do about Cheatham. Polk should have ordered Cheatham's division forward as soon as McCown engaged. But from the sound of things, Cheatham has yet to move an inch. More evidence of treachery? Or another example of the Bishop's perpetual incompetence? Whatever the reason, Cheatham must move. Bragg knows he should send the order through Polk, maintaining the chain of command, but time is slipping away. "Colonel Brent," he snaps.

"Sir?"

"A message to General Cheatham, copy to General Polk. . . ." Bragg dictates, scowling all the time at the smoking cedars.

If he would permit himself the display of temper, Professor Bill Hardee would wad Bragg's message into a ball and hurl it from him. Leave it to Bragg to complain about a small deviation from a paper plan while ignoring the crucial question entirely! No plan survives unaltered once battle is joined. Yes, McCown has drifted too far to the west, but he has smashed the end of the Yankee line. And, yes, Cleburne is engaged before the plan anticipated, but he is driving in hard. If Bragg had read Clausewitz's *On War,* he might understand something of the relationship of chance, uncertainty, and luck in battle. The plan is evolving according to the Clausewitzian principle

of friction, and working the better for it. Just make Cheatham move, goddamn it, and we'll roll up the entire Yankee line!

Hardee takes a breath, looks at the staff captain waiting to carry a reply.
"Tell General Bragg that I understand and will endeavor to carry out the
plan as formulated, adjusting to circumstances only as absolutely necessary."
There, let Bragg chew on that.

General Benjamin Franklin Cheatham is confused. He is also moderately
drunk, but this contributes rather less to his confusion than might be
expected, since he has been intoxicated most of his adult life. As a farmer,
volunteer officer in Mexico, Gold Rusher, Tennessee militia general, and
now Confederate major general, he has found whiskey a wonderful companion. He starts each morning by consuming a pint of good whiskey and
reinforcing the dose as necessary throughout the day until evening gives
him the opportunity for serious drinking.

It is not drink that confuses Cheatham, but the orders sent to him by
Bishop Polk the night before. Is he to attack with the entire division at once?
Or is he to attack in echelon, one brigade after another, left to right? He has
expected Polk to arrive before this to clarify the matter. But Polk, prince of
the Church and God's fucking gift to the Army of Tennessee, has yet to
show his sorry ass.

As the sky lightens, Cheatham paces, swigging from his pint of whiskey
and cussing steadily. McCown and Cleburne are driving the Yankee flank.
He can hear the shift in the firing, the roar moving steadily from northwest
to due north as the wheel begins coming his way. But when should he join
the attack? And with how much, how soon? If Polk or Hardee or Bragg or
someone would just tell him! "Kolstad, get your lead ass over here, goddamn it!" he shouts.

His assistant adjutant hurries to him. "General?"

"Go ask that swine-fucker Polk whether he wants me to attack all at
once, or by frigging echelon. And is Withers coming in with me directly, or
is he supposed to play with himself until I've got the Yanks running? Don't
write it down! Just move your ass and get me a goddamn answer."

Kolstad goes, hiding a smile. The officers and, particularly, the men like
Cheatham all the better for his reputation as the most inventively profane
commander in the Army of Tennessee. Moreover, Cheatham is a fighter:
never asks a soldier to go where he himself is afraid to lead. They call him
"Curls" after the wild ringlets that insist on standing in a thick fringe above
his ears despite the load of pomade Cheatham regularly applies to his hair.

Cheatham snarls, kicks at a rock, misses. Everything in him wants to throw his division into the fight all at once and immediately. He has yet to see subtlety produce much in war. No, go in swinging, pounding, kicking, gouging—the same absence of rules as a barroom brawl. But he hesitates. Ben Cheatham likes being a general and would like to remain one. He knows that Bragg detests him and would take pleasure in ordering his court-martial. He will wait a few more minutes for someone to tell him what to do.

Though he has spoken to Hardee of putting other than their best into this fight, Bishop Polk has no intention of letting the Yankees off easy. Yankees are, after all, something less than human in Bishop Polk's primitive cosmography. Not an experiment gone wrong, for that would imply that the Almighty needed experiential experience in the development of the human phylum. Nor are they a corruption of the original perfection, since that would imply a flaw in the creation of the God-image. No, Yankees are what God intended them to be: pale simulacra of the chosen people of the South. Polk has suspected it always, has known it for certain since first seeing the weak flightless souls of the Yankees fluttering vainly among the dead on the battlefield at Shiloh. In his dreams, he has crushed their souls with lupine jaws and tasted a brief escharotic saltiness like fried skin—not unpleasant, but pallid compared to the rich meatiness of a Southern soul.

When the firing on the left flank begins shortly after first light, Polk expects it to spread quickly to Cheatham's front. When it doesn't, he sets down his knife and fork to listen carefully. Is Cheatham drunk? Has Bragg countermanded the order to attack? He shakes his head, returns to his breakfast and week-old Nashville paper. After twenty minutes, he sighs and gets up to investigate the delay.

Cheatham is blushing to the roots of his curls when Polk rides up. "General," he stammers, "I request immediate relief from my command so that I can go and challenge that pompous son of a bitch to a duel."

Polk smiles. "And good morning to you, General Cheatham. I perceive that you have received a message from the commanding general."

"You're goddamn right I have. Just read this goddamn—"

"Benjamin, please. Remember that I am ordained by my vows to abhor such language."

Cheatham looks confused again. "Oh, yes. Certainly. Pardon me, Bishop. But just look at this goddamn message he sent me."

Polk sighs. Benjamin, Benjamin, you are incorrigible. He takes the dispatch, reads, eyebrows lifting.

General Cheatham, you are late in advancing your division. Attack imme-
diately, conforming to Cleburne on your left while wheeling to the right in
accordance with the plan forwarded by this headquarters. If you are unable
or unfit to execute this order immediately, forthwith relinquish command to
your senior subordinate.

"Well, it would seem that the commanding general is rather on edge. I think, Benjamin, that we should forgive—"

"Forgive, hell! I'm going to resign and go wring his chicken neck. There isn't a goddamn military court in the South that's going to convict me."

"If you are going to depend on an acquittal by a military court, then you should retain your commission."

"All right, I'll keep my goddamn commission. But I'm going to throttle the son of a bitch. I've never been unfit and I've never been unable to fight anybody, anywhere, any time!" As if to emphasize the truth of this remark, Cheatham removes the pint bottle from his coat pocket, uncorks it with his teeth, and drains the last inch. He glares defiantly at Polk.

The Bishop smiles placidly at him. "Then I suppose we should get an attack underway. Kill a few Yankees, and worry about the commanding general's impolitize later."

"I'll im-poli-tease him, that's for goddamn sure. But first I'm going to show him how a real man fights, how a Tennessean fights."

"Go to it, General."

Cheatham starts for his horse, hesitates. "General, shall I send in my division all at once, or by brigade?"

"By brigade, General. Otherwise you risk being stretched too thin in some places, while in others you will have a needless superfluity of men. Strike successively by brigade, find where the Yankee line is vulnerable, and concentrate there."

Cheatham frowns. "By brigade then."

"Yes, by brigade."

☆ ☆ ☆

When Private Joe Zein, Company A, 1st Louisiana Regular Infantry, feels the need to defecate, he defecates where he wants to, when he wants to, and in whatever company he wants to. Several nights in jail before the war and twice carrying a rail in this army have done nothing to alter his opinion of his rights.

Nor does Zein compromise in the gratification of his other needs. He takes what he wants. Oh, they can stop him sometimes, gang up and keep him from taking. But not for long, not forever. And oddly, though his needs are insistent, he is a patient young man, can grin, shrug, and wait. One of these days he'll catch that boy Dickie Krall off by himself. And Dickie's gonna crawl all right, gonna beg to suck the big hammer. And the big hammer is gonna try Dickie's little pink ass, too, make him squeal like the pig Zein stuck with a bayonet on the march up to Perryville. He laughs at the memory. God, what a look the boy had on his face that day! All the boys. Couldn't goddamn believe what he'd done.

Waiting for the brigade to go forward, Private Dickie Krall also remembers the pig. It had been a small pig, a shoat of the pink, nearly hairless variety. It must have been someone's pet, for it had stood unafraid just inside the fence, nose stuck through the rails, as they'd marched past. A friendly, curious little pig. And Dickie would have eaten it. Sure. They all would have, for army rations are bad and frequently lacking. But marching into Kentucky, they'd been under strict orders not to forage. And they understood, for it would be hard to convince Kentuckians to join the banner after watching their cellars, smokehouses, gardens, coops, and pens emptied by Bragg's army.

But Joe Zein heeded no such niceties of diplomacy and discipline. He fixed the bayonet to the muzzle of his Enfield, stepped to the fence, and expertly skewered the pig over the top rail. The pig let our a squall of pain and disbelief. Zein laughed and, with a heave of his powerful arms, swung the shoat over the fence. He shook the Enfield, delighted with the squeals and convulsions this produced in the creature. "Got me a live one, boys! Makin' a hell of a fight, but he's comin' along for supper." He swung the musket across his chest in a parody of the manual of arms. "Bacon brigade. Port, arms! Left shoulder, arms! Forward, march!" He stepped out, swinging his free arm, the pig writhing and crying on the bayonet as Joe Zein broke into one of his obscene ditties:

> Oh, I wish I could screw, Dixie.
> Hooray! Hooray!
> In Dixie's twat, I'd stick my cock.
> And make her yelp, by cracky.
> Hooray! Hooray!
> I wish I could screw, Dixie.

It is a tenet of folklore, and an assurance given by every father attempting to teach a bruised and humiliated son self-defense, that bullies reveal themselves as physical cowards when sternly and expertly confronted. Mothers and children know that this is nearly always false. Private Joe Zein of the 1st Louisiana Regulars is a warrior as brave as a Viking berserker. Going into battle, he sings for the sheer joy of the slaughter to come. The tunes are familiar—*Dixie, The Bonny Blue Flag, Rose of Alabamy, Yellow Rose of Texas*—but each comes with Zein's original lyrics: filthy, perverse, and bloody. Fate seems to protect him in battle, and he is never so much as scratched while all around him men die. This never surprises him, for his mother told him that he'd come home safe to the farm when the war is over. And she's never wrong. She's his ma, after all.

While the rest of the 1st Louisiana stands waiting for the order to go forward against the Yankee line, Zein sits cross-legged in the center of the front rank, honing his bayonet on a brogan. The officers and sergeants ignore him, know that to get Zein to obey is more trouble than it's worth. Not that Zein would attack one of them. No, to think of Zein as a powder keg is to misunderstand the man completely. Zein does not hate anyone. In truth, he's a rather good-humored young man who simply enjoys food, drink, carnal pleasures, blood, and battle to extraordinary excess. Particularly battle, for which he has an inexhaustible appetite.

"First Louisiana!" the colonel shouts. "Attention!"

Zein climbs languidly to his feet, looks at Private Dickie Krall to his right. "Hey, Dickie-boy. You take care out there. After the fightin', you and me gotta get more neighborly. You, me, and the Hammer." He laughs.

Krall ignores him, though his beardless cheeks pinken to the same color as the shoat on the march to Perryville.

Despite Ben Cheatham's determination to prove himself to Bragg before he personally and severely beats the man, there is still more confusion getting the advance underway. As written by Bragg, the order of battle calls for Major General Jones M. Withers's division of four brigades to form the first line in the attack on the Federal right center, with Cheatham's four brigades forming a second line following in support. This is not one of the better aspects of Bragg's plan, since Withers and Cheatham will have to control lines nearly a mile long in an advance over broken terrain. To resolve the problem, Polk has split the line down the middle, giving Cheatham the left four brigades, Withers the right four.

For the men of the 1st Louisiana Regulars and the five Alabama regiments of Second Brigade, Withers's division, the result is more waiting. At the left end of the front line, the brigade is now part of Cheatham's command.

And since Cheatham knows the brigade's temporary commander, Colonel J. Q. Loomis, only slightly, he decides to relay his instructions in person.

The men of the 1st Louisiana stand easy as Cheatham and Loomis consult. Joe Zein wanders from the ranks, casting about for an agreeable place to defecate, finally squatting beside a smoldering fire where he will enjoy a bit of warmth on his bare backside. A few of the men are still amused enough by Zein's outrageousness to hoot. Private Dickie Krall wonders if he could shoot Zein during the attack without getting caught.

Shortly after 7:00 A.M., the brigade steps out at the regulation quick-time of Hardee's *Tactics,* muskets at left-shoulder shift, bayonets glittering dully in the drizzle. The regiments have to cross three hundred yards of cornfield, the last hundred yards uphill, to reach the Yankee line. Whatever element of surprise might have been enjoyed half an hour ago has dissipated like the thinning mist in the cedars three hundred long yards away.

Loomis's attack will overlap the crease between Colonel William E. Woodruff's Federal brigade (the last intact brigade of Davis's division) and Brigadier General Joshua Sill's brigade of Sheridan's division. Promoted only the week before, Woodruff commands the smallest brigade in the Army of the Cumberland, but he has prepared his three regiments well, positioning his men behind a rail fence on the edge of thick cedars with the 8th Wisconsin Battery on his left. Shortly before the Rebels advance, he rides over to consult with Sill.

Sill is glad to see him. He has felt melancholy since his midnight conversation with Sheridan. "I think you have done perfectly, Colonel," he tells Woodruff. "We have an excellent field of fire and should, I think, inflict heavy casualties on the Rebels before they can fire effectively. We may drive them back with artillery alone."

Woodruff seems reassured, spends a minute finishing the cup of coffee provided by one of Sill's aides. My God, he is a handsome man, Sill thinks. He imagines running his fingers through Woodruff's thick brown hair. He shakes off the thought, smiles slightly.

Woodruff tosses the cup to the aide. "Thanks, General. Good luck."

"And to you, Colonel."

Colonel Frederick Schaefer, commanding Sheridan's reserve brigade to the rear of Sill, is by nature high-strung. It is not a temper he admires in others, and he has trained himself to maintain strict control over expression, gesture, and speech. Fortunately—and paradoxically—he finds that battle eases the task, makes him calmer, more precise. After his first battle in this country—a meaningless skirmish in Kentucky—he overheard one of his soldiers call him "stone-cold." Schaefer liked the phrase, has held on to it since.

Sheridan is the opposite. Reticent, almost remote, at other times he is transformed by battle. Yet the fury that comes over Sheridan does not deflect his judgment, but rather confirms its unerring purpose. Schaefer has known certain genius only twice in his life: the first time in 1839 in Leipzig, when he'd heard Mendelssohn conduct Schubert's Symphony in C Major; the second time in October 1862 in the chaos at Perryville, when he'd watched Phil Sheridan play his guns against Hardee's flank, saving McCook's corps and Buell's army.

Schaefer smokes his pipe, watches Sheridan pace in explosive bursts of his short legs, pausing frequently to listen to the firing on the right. Sheridan pauses in his pacing, glares at Schaefer. "Hear that firing, Schaefer? That's Hardee's boys going after Post's brigade and Johnson's reserve. Baldwin, I think. It's just about our turn now. They should have hit us before, but something must have held them up. But they'll come soon. Ten minutes at most."

Schaefer nods. "Yes, General. We are ready here."

Sheridan strides to where an orderly is holding his big brown gelding. "We'd damned well better be. From what Sill's boys heard on the picket line, Ben Cheatham's across from us. You can bet he remembers what our guns did to him at Perryville, and he'll be looking to give us some back. Sure as hell."

★ ★ ★

Private Joe Zein breaks into one of his obscene ditties when the 1st Louisiana Regulars advance on the Federal line. The cornfield is soft, the mud clinging to the brogans, boots, rags, and bare feet of the soldiers. The Yankee cannons fire shell, the explosions throwing up geysers of mud and shrapnel. Zein whoops with laughter when a shell explodes fifty feet down the line, hurling men and body parts into the sky. "Good luck, boys! See you in hell!" he shouts. Another shell, this one apparently a dud, comes skidding across the field and through the line, tearing off the leg of a private named Meis. "No more dancin' till dawn for you, Billy!" Zein shouts. He laughs, tears of mirth running down his cheeks. I am going to kill him, Dickie Krall thinks. I swear I will.

At two hundred yards, the Union guns shift to canister and the Yankee infantry opens fire. The fire is stupendous. The butternut infantry leans into the storm, pushes grimly ahead. In theory, it should take them two minutes to cover one hundred yards at the quick time, half that at the double-quick, but under fire every foot takes an eternity. A private named Handrick, two men to the right of Krall, gives a wet cry, stumbles forward clutching desperately at his throat. "That one looks bad, Jim," Zein shouts. "Better lie down. There you go."

Dickie Krall is crying, can't help it. He won't run, hasn't before; but God, he is afraid of dying. Jesus, spare me. Oh, Mary, mother of God, spare me. Make them run. Make them—

The head of the sergeant carrying the regimental flag explodes. Zein slaps Krall on the shoulder. "Why, I believe the boy lost his head. Now ain't that a shame. And him so handsome and proud of waving that rag."

"Just shut up, Zein! For Christ's sake, shut up," Krall screams over the bedlam.

Zein laughs, drops a thick arm over Krall's shoulder, pulls the boy to him, and laps a thick red tongue over the boy's cheek and across his eyes. He laughs again, gives Krall the buck-up, cheer-up hug an older brother might give a younger after a lost game of base-ball. A private named DeJarlis takes a bullet in the abdomen, sits down staring disbelievingly at the wound. Zein waves. "Bye bye, Dave."

Loomis's brigade splits, three Alabama regiments on the left advancing against Woodruff's brigade, the 1st Louisiana and two Alabama regiments on the right pushing toward Sill's line. Woodruff's infantry is firing furiously, but the Alabamans are coming hard now, firing a volley every twenty paces. The 25th Illinois and the 81st Indiana shudder and then break for the trees to the rear. Colonel Thomas Williams of the 25th grabs the regimental colors, rams the staff into the earth: "Rally, boys! We'll plant it right here and rally the old 25th around it. Not another foot, boys, we'll die right here if we have to!"

No sooner have the stirring phrases left the colonel's mouth when he is drilled through the heart by a minié ball. Unlike most credited with expiring between upright and prone, Williams is truly dead before he hits the ground. Loomis's regiments storm over the position, whooping and yelling. Unable to get their guns away, the artillerymen of the 8th Wisconsin Battery fight with pistols, rammers, and fists until their captain is shot down and they are overwhelmed.

The veteran 35th Illinois is positioned at a slight angle to the right of the sudden gap in the Federal line, its own right flank holding to the 38th Illinois and the 15th Wisconsin, the last regiments of Carlin's battered brigade still holding against Cleburne's assaults. Until now, the 35th has directed most of its attention to that fight, but now it shifts fronts coolly and fires a raking volley into Loomis's flank. The execution done by five hundred rifle-muskets from an unexpected direction throws Loomis's line into chaos. Moments later, the 25th Illinois and the 81st Indiana, rallied by their officers and embarrassed by their brief loss of nerve, come storming back through the woods. Assaulted from front and flank, the three Alabama regiments break and run, not pausing until they reach the trees on the far side of the cornfield.

To the right of the seam between Woodruff's and Sill's brigades, the 1st Louisiana and the 19th and 22nd Alabama charge up the rise toward the Federal line. Private Dickie Krall feels his throat spasm with the Rebel yell. It is an unearthly sound, terrifying even to those who make it, for it bespeaks of something bestial and grisly in the soul. Krall can make the high ululating howl because the others in the ranks make it, can together with them put aside humanity in the terrified, ecstatic rush into combat. But loping along beside Krall, Private Joe Zein yells not in communal desperation but in simple wild joy. It seems that he could catch bullets in his teeth and spit them back, sweep an arm and level a score of Yankees. He is in this moment indistinguishable save for his clothing from some ancient, bronze-helmed warrior so dread that even Bishop Polk's dybbuk wolf would give way growling amid the heaps of the soul-fluttering dead.

The 1st Louisiana hits the 24th Wisconsin, a green regiment that disintegrates almost before it is touched. One youngster throws down his Springfield, tries to surrender, but Zein slams his bayonet into the center of the boy's chest. He shakes the boy, perhaps hoping that he will squeal and convulse like the pig, but the boy is already dead, and Zein wrenches the bayonet free. He bounds on into the cedars after the retreating bluecoats. Led by Sergeant Simon Buck, the rest of the squad follows behind, most of the boys hoping, in the fragmentary way they can think of anything in these moments, that some Yankee will kill Zein.

To the left of the gap abandoned by the 24th Wisconsin, the veteran 36th Illinois, with a record dating from the savage fighting at Pea Ridge in Arkansas, waits until the 19th and 22nd Alabama are nearly to the trees, then rises up and delivers a volley that stops the Rebels cold. But the Alabamans are veterans too, and the lines hold facing each other, blazing away at fifty paces. From the woods across the cornfield the Rebel cannons cannot fire for fear of hitting their own men, but the 4th Indiana battery on the left of the 36th Illinois has no such problem and rakes the Rebel line with load after load of canister.

Meanwhile in the cedars, the 1st Louisiana hunts the boys of the 24th Wisconsin. Zein loves the game, stalks through the thickets like a tiger, leaping into little knots of Yankees to kill at pointblank range. No one ever seems to think to fire at him. Dickie Krall sees Zein disappear into the shade of a thicket, realizes how easy it would be to shoot at the next glimpse of his broad back. A mistake, an accident of war. Others will share the relief, ask few questions.

A thousand yards to the rear of Sill's line, Captain Henry Hescock, commanding the 1st Missouri Battery and Sheridan's artillery, studies the struggle between the 36th Illinois and the two Alabama regiments though his field glasses. Captain Charles Houghtaling of Battery C, 1st Illinois Artillery, stands at his side, doing the same. "There goes the reserve in," Houghtaling comments.

Hescock shifts his view, watches the 15th Missouri and the 44th Illinois of Schaefer's Brigade, the slender erect German leading them, going into the woods to plug the gap left by the 24th Wisconsin. "It would be nice if we could give those boys on the line a little help until Herr Schaefer gets in position."

Houghtaling purses his lips. "Range is a bit tricky. Figure too short and we'll hit our boys instead of the Rebs."

"Well, I think my Napoleons can drop a few rounds in all right."

"Oh, and my Parrotts, too. No doubt about it. I just thought I'd point out the dangers."

It is a routine for Hescock and Houghtaling to chaff each other. They are perhaps the two best artillerists in the army, and that alone would be enough to stimulate a rivalry. That their batteries are also equipped with cannons of rival qualities has produced a custom of rigorous scorekeeping and hot debate between the batteries. Hescock is suddenly serious. "No case shot, though. That really would be tricky."

Two minutes later Hescock's battery opens fire, joined a minute later by Houghtaling's. They range with shell, then shift to a mix of shell and solid shot. Under the fire of three batteries, the Alabama regiments begin to leak men to the rear. Colonel Loomis looks desperately behind him, hoping to see another brigade coming to his support. But Cheatham is still holding the other brigades back. Loomis pushes to the front of his line, where the 19th Alabama has just managed to reach the woods, tries to urge his men forward in a final, desperate push. But just then one of Houghtaling's Parrotts sends a solid bolt slicing through the branches of an oak, severing a limb that strikes Loomis on the crown of the head. He drops as if poleaxed. Colonel J. G. Coltart takes command, orders the remaining regiments to fall back. In the cedars on the left, the 1st Louisiana is late getting the order. The men turn and run for the open, knowing that if they cannot catch up to the Alabamans, they will become the sole target of half a dozen Yankee regiments and batteries. Private Joe Zein has gone far ahead of the rest in pursuit of the Yankee boys of the 24th Wisconsin. No one wastes the time to go after him.

Brigadier General Joshua Sill rides along his line smiling, giving commands in a cheerful voice. There are few to give really: his job is mainly to be seen. It is love that enables Sill to control his fear, love for the men whose fear he understands. He rides exposed to the Rebel fire to assure them that someone is taking greater risks, is surviving, is looking out for them.

When Sill sees the Rebel line breaking, he touches spurs to his black mare, canters to where the 4th Indiana Battery is blazing away with double canister at the Rebel flank. Sill knows the tendency of gunners to ease up when they see the enemy flee, knows their fear of running short of ammunition and their even greater fear of continuing to ram powder charges down barrels so hot that they can hardly be touched. But they cannot give in to fear now, must keep double-shotting their guns, must keep firing until the Rebs are swept from the field. He swings into the rear of the battery, spotting the battery commander amid his gunners. "Captain Bush," he shouts. "A word."

Private Joe Zein comes running from the woods and, for reasons fathomable only to himself, goes bounding across the cornfield at an angle to the Yankee line. Dozens of minié balls fly about him, but he is invulnerable. They cannot hurt him; his ma told him so and it is so, will always be so. He sees the handsome, bearded officer on the black horse leaning down to speak to a captain of artillery. A colonel at least, maybe a general. Zein drops to a knee, cocks the hammer of his Enfield, and squints along the barrel. The officer looks up, and across the distance of a hundred yards, their eyes meet. The puff of smoke from the muzzle of Zein's Enfield interrupts and then he is up, bounding joyously across the field.

The minié ball enters Sill's head through the upper lip, carrying away his front teeth, passing through the oral cavity, severing the brain stem, and exiting the back of his skull. He has no time to react, has only the briefest picture of a boy kneeling in a harvested field—a handsome boy with shaggy black hair and laughing blue eyes sighting along a rifle barrel. The blue of those eyes is the last light to fade, contracting until the eyes are only pinpoints of pure blue far off in the darkness.

Captain Bush catches Sill, eases him to the ground. After a moment, he stands, looks after Zein's bounding form. "Well, you son of a bitch," he mutters. "You just killed the best man I ever hope to know."

★   ★   ★

Told of Sill's death, Sheridan reacts with a grimace and a nod. He rides forward to speak to Colonel Nicholas Greusel of the 36th Illinois, the senior regimental colonel.

Sheridan finds Greusel afoot, straightening the line of First Brigade. The carnage all about is tremendous, the blue dead lying in the shadow of the cedars, the gray dead scattered across the field to the front, the positions taken for volley firing marked by irregular rows of fallen men. The lucky dying are unconscious, while the severely wounded and likely to die clutch themselves, cry and rock, as if seeking the comfort of the cradle or the long sea-roll of a primordial memory. Sheridan ignores it all, tells Greusel to take command of the brigade. They cover the critical questions quickly: ammunition, casualties, what the Rebs are likely to do next.

"Who will command your regiment, Colonel?" Sheridan asks.

"Major Miller. He's a good officer."

"I know him. We're rounding up the Wisconsin boys who didn't hold. We'll put them in reserve behind him."

Sheridan is about to wheel his horse when Greusel speaks. "They're green, but it's odd just the same; Wisconsin troops usually hold better than that."

Sheridan frowns, for the comment seems out of place. Conversational. "Yes, well—"

"I sent General Sill's body back to the hospital near the pike. I think they're calling it the Gresham house."

"I know of it."

"Do you know what he said to me once, when I said that it was unfair how he'd been replaced by an officer as weak as Bandbox Johnson? He said that I should be charitable, that General Johnson had four years of seniority and much more field service than he did. Then he apologized for taking my place in command of the brigade, said he never would have requested assignment to this division had he known that that would be the result."

Greusel's voice has become thick and he avoids Sheridan's eyes. Sheridan sits his horse for a long moment then climbs down. This is delicate and Sheridan is rarely a man of delicacy. He steps to Greusel, places both hands on the taller man's shoulders. "General Sill was my roommate at West Point. I never would have graduated without his help. But I can't think of him now. And you can't either, Colonel. We can't think of anything except holding this position and killing as many Rebs as we can."

"Yes, General. I'm sorry. I—"

"Never mind, Colonel. Don't mind anything except the work."

Sheridan mounts, looks out over the field. Wounded Rebels are tottering back toward the cedars. A few of the closest stumble into the Union lines, collapse beside grievously wounded Yankees. Before long we won't fight this way, Sheridan thinks. We won't let their wounded walk away; we'll shoot them down. "They'll be coming soon, Colonel," he calls to Greusel. "I'll give you what help I can."

The 1st Louisiana and the five Alabama regiments of Loomis's brigade lie exhausted under the trees on the south side of the field. Colonel Alfred J. Vaughan's brigade of five Tennessee regiments and the 9th Texas comes forward in line of battle to the edge of the cornfield. There is a good deal of jeering and chaffing of Loomis's brigade by Vaughan's men, the Texans in particular. "So you yellowhammers couldn't get 'er done, huh?" one of the Texans shouts at a dozen of the Louisiana soldiers, Privates Dickie Krall and Joe Zein among them.

Sergeant Simon Buck levels a bloodshot gaze at the Texan. "We ain't no yellowhammers. We're Louisiana tigers, the 1st Regulars. And let me tell you something, son. Over there you'll find about the hottest place you ever struck. We left a lot of good boys dead over there, and it ain't fittin' that you treat them with anything but respect."

The Texan bites his lip. "Sorry, coz. Didn't mean no harm. Just funnin'."

"Well, you go have your fun over there and good luck to you."

Joe Zein nudges Dickie Krall. "I got me a tiger hammer. Wanta see?"

Krall gets up, walks a dozen paces, and slumps down next to Sergeant Buck. Zein chuckles.

Shortly before 8:00 A.M., Ben Cheatham sends forward Vaughan's brigade and the Alabama and South Carolina brigade of Colonel Arthur M. Manigault. Together, the brigades have the power to break through Woodruff and Greusel's line, but the confusion occasioned by Polk's revised order of battle delays the delivery of the message to Manigault by five minutes and the brigades go forward too far apart to support each other. Vaughan's five Tennessee regiments strike the 25th Illinois and 81st Indiana of Woodruff's brigade, driving them back from the same fence they'd abandoned in the fight with Loomis's brigade. But again the Yankee regiments rally and charge back into the fight. Unsupported by Manigault and taking fire from front and both flanks, Vaughan's Tennesseans retreat.

The 9th Texas, the adopted "foreign regiment" of Vaughan's brigade, does not get the order to retire. Advancing to the left of the Tennessee regiments, the Texans have the odd experience of finding no one to fight. They push into the cedars, making jokes about how the Yankees have run at the first sight of a Texan. Colonel William H. Young, only twenty-four and as filled with braggadocio as his men, is determined to find an opponent. He obliques the regiment to the right and stumbles into the right flank of the 35th Illinois. Enthusiastically and without orders, the Texans open fire at two hundred yards, doing little but pelt the trees about the surprised Illini. Young shouts at them to cease fire and leads them forward another hundred yards. But again the Texans can do little damage while Illinois bullets snick through the trees, dropping Texans in steadily increasing numbers.

Raging, Young leads a charge over a rail fence to within fifty yards of the 35th's line. Now, goddamn it, they should be able to hit something! But before the Texans can improve the score, the 38th Illinois of Carlin's brigade, withdrawing under the continual pounding of Wood's brigade of Cleburne's division, chances by the rear of the 9th Texas. The 38th, which along with Hans Heg's 15th Wisconsin has been holding the stub of the Yankee line for the better part of an hour, is in a thoroughly awful mood and takes great pleasure in laying several volleys into the backsides of Young's Texans.

For five minutes the Texans are caught in a ferocious crossfire. Young dashes about, trying to shout orders over the din, until his horse is shot from under him. He scrambles up, runs from company to company ordering a charge, then grabs the regimental colors and leads his men forward against the 35th Illinois.

After all the frustration and wasted Longhorn blood, Young's timing is perfect. Vaughan's Tennessee regiments come rolling across the field to strike Woodruff's line a second time. Battered and short of ammunition, Woodruff's three regiments fall back through the cedars to a new position near the Harding house, seven hundred yards south of the Wilkinson Pike. Vaughan's regiments pause for breath and to assess the cost of breaking the Yankee line. It is staggering, the 12th Tennessee alone losing more than half its men dead or wounded.

By 8:30 A.M., it would seem that no place along the entire length of Woodruff and Greusel's line could have escaped some form of human trespass by boot, wagon wheel, or shell blast. But until Vaughan's 154th Tennessee charges the 81st Indiana, nothing has penetrated one particular thicket that is home to a spectacularly fecund colony of rabbits. Suddenly, rabbits are everywhere, "hopping across the field like so many toads." It is then that a curious thing happens. As if by a common consent that would do lemmings proud, the rabbits take cover with the men of Greusel's line, snuggling against them, crawling into pockets and haversacks, taking shelter under arms and legs.

A few of the men are amused, attempt to pet the rabbits. More are disconcerted, swat at them, fearing that they carry disease or perhaps belong to some venomous southern species of lagomorphs. Colonel Francis T. Sherman of the 88th Illinois, a practical man who manufactured brick in Chicago before the war, is among the amused. "And what dastardly tactic do you suppose the Rebs will try next?" he asks his adjutant.

His adjutant, a bespectacled, bookish young man, frowns. "I have no idea, Colonel. Do you suppose that they were domesticated once?"

"The Rebs? I doubt it."

"No, I meant the rabbits."

"Hell of a lot of them for that."

The adjutant, who has read Darwin, persists. "But suppose a pair of them had been family pets and escaped. Then—"

Sherman, who is gazing into the smoke that now eddies across the cornfield, feels a sudden sting on his cheek. He raises a hand, feels a shard of glass protruding from the skin. What in hell? He turns to the adjutant for an explanation, sees the boy lying on his back, a red hole where his right eye should be, shattered spectacles askew on his nose. "Here they come, boys!" Sherman shouts.

Sheridan has told Captain Hescock, his artillery chief, to damn the ammunition supply and to hurl as much iron as he can into the advancing Rebs. The batteries of Hescock, Houghtaling, and Bush blaze away. On the line, Bush can fire canister, but Hescock and Houghtaling are too far away. Hescock takes a chance, loads his Napoleons with grape—the awkward stands of small roundshot that have fallen out of favor in preference to canister since old General Taylor made Braxton Bragg a hero at Buena Vista with his famous request. Twice the size of canister balls, Hescock calculates that the grapeshot will clear the Federal line. He is right, and the grape hits Manigault's brigade with frightful effect.

Under the fire of the Yankee batteries, Manigault's regiments advance coughing, eyes streaming, through the breeze-blown smoke from Vaughan and Woodruff's fight. Manigault, a sharp-featured thirty-nine-year-old Charleston businessman, rails at the negligible support from the Southern batteries. If private business ran like the goddamn army, every business would fail, there would be no jobs, and the country would go belly-up!

When the Rebel line is fifty yards short of the 88th Illinois, Colonel Sherman gives the order and the Illini stand, scattering rabbits, and slam a volley into the face of Manigault's two South Carolina regiments. Rocked back, the "sand lappers" try to steady, only to be hit by a second devastating volley. They retreat, soon joined by Manigault's Alabama regiments, which have likewise run up hard against Sheridan's line.

It is time to pull back. Phil Sheridan knows it, though his inclination is, as always, to stand and slug it out. But the eternally rational part of his mind, the part that refuses to rage even in battle, speaks now in a voice very like Sill's: "Your choice may determine whether you become a great general or die a foolish one."

Sheridan orders Greusel to fall back on Schaefer's reserve while Roberts's brigade—as yet nearly unengaged—draws in from the left. Sheridan gallops back to the Harding house, finds Woodruff's brigade and Carlin's two regiments refilling their cartridge boxes. To Carlin's right are a ragtag collection of companies, squads, and barely organized soldiers too stubborn to abandon the battlefield. "Who are those men beyond Carlin, Colonel?" Sheridan asks Woodruff.

Woodruff, who is concentrating on loading his Navy Colt, glances where Sheridan is pointing. "What's left of Post's brigade and a few men from Baldwin's brigade, I think. Davis is over there somewhere."

Sheridan would like to talk to General Jefferson C. Davis, whom he dislikes as a man but respects as a fighter. But time is too short. He turns to his adjutant. "Find General Davis. Tell him I will conform to his left."

The 36th Illinois, Colonel Greusel's regiment until he succeeded Sill, loses its second commander of the day when Major Miller is severely wounded. Captain Porter C. Olson takes command, requesting permission for the regiment to leave the line to refill cartridge boxes. As the rest of Greusel's brigade falls back on the Harding house, the 36th Illinois reaches the Wilkinson Pike. They find half a dozen ammunition wagons of Thomas's corps and beg for cartridges. The ordnance sergeant glances at the regiment's Model 1842 rifle-muskets. "I don't think I can help you boys."

Captain Olson, red-haired and quick-tempered, takes this to mean a refusal based on corps membership. "The hell you can't," he growls, starting to unholster his Colt.

The ordnance sergeant throws up his hands. "Hold on, Captain. I would if I could, but you need sixty-nine caliber and all I got is fifty-eight. You're welcome to see for yourself."

A dozen soldiers of the 36th take the invitation, dig frantically through the wagons. Incredibly, there isn't a .69-caliber cartridge anywhere. Cursing, Captain Olson turns, nearly colliding with a tall horse that seems to have appeared from nowhere. Olson looks up at the rider: a pasty-faced youngish man, clean-shaven except for a heavy mustache that doesn't quite mask a large mole on the upper lip. For a moment Olson hardly recognizes Major General Alexander McDowell McCook, who has about him the look of a revenant—some formerly prominent personage lost at sea or kidnapped or fugitive for debt, who has reappeared at this moment to upset the family that no longer misses him, has nearly forgotten that he ever existed.

Olson salutes. "General! I'm sorry, I—"

"Do you command here?"

"Yes, sir. Our colonel had to—"

"Pull your regiment back to the Nashville Pike. We will try to hold there."

Olson would protest, nearly does. But they have no .69-caliber cartridges here and he must go looking for some anyway. "Yes, sir."

McCook rides on. He has received orders from Rosecrans to reorganize his wing north of the Nashville Pike. But Sheridan's division still fights, and he should see to it. Brooding on choices, McCook rides slowly along the Wilkinson Pike.

★　★　★

Braxton Bragg has often heard of generals with a feel for battle, generals who know intuitively how to maneuver, when to attack, where to send reinforcements. Bragg has no such talent, must labor to fit every report, every fact seen or heard, into an overall picture of the battle. He is horseback now, a fine if rather stiff equestrian, riding from one elevation to another, trying to get a better sense of the battle. He does not approach the line and the actual fighting, for that would risk losing his grasp on the whole. He communicates with his generals by courier, feels no need to show his physical presence to the soldiers doing the fighting.

Bragg and his field staff pause atop a slight rise to the rear of Hardee's headquarters. Colonel Brent interrupts Bragg's inspection of the smoke drifting from the most recent clash between Cheatham and Sheridan. "General, there's another message from Hardee requesting reinforcements. He says that two or three fresh brigades can make the difference now."

"Tell him that Wheeler is due on the field shortly. I will send him against the Yankee flank. Beyond Wheeler, I can provide nothing at present."

Sending the message eases Bragg's mind. He will not upset his plan. There is far more risk in making an impetuous change than in sticking with a plan made in the cool, unemotional rationality before battle. Let Hardee push on with what he has while Polk smashes in the Union center. Breckinridge is best used where he is. The plan is working; just give it time.

About 8:40 A.M., the four brigades of Pat Cleburne's division and McNair's brigade of McCown's division approach the shaky Union line held by Baldwin, Post, and Carlin south of the Wilkinson Pike. Cleburne dashes from brigade to brigade, trying to keep the line together in the rough terrain. It is a nearly impossible task, and Cleburne fears a Yankee ambush; but Hardee has told him to press the enemy hard, and Cleburne keeps driving ahead.

The ragtag Federal line holds in the fields below the Gresham house for only a few minutes. Baldwin is still deploying when a cavalry sergeant brings orders to fall back. The sergeant isn't sure which general gave the order—McCook or the equally revenant Richard Johnson—but swears that the man was indeed a general. Baldwin is tempted to disobey, but he can see a heavy line of Rebel infantry stretching across his entire front to well beyond his flank. He gives the order.

With Baldwin pulling back, Post and Carlin must retreat or be enveloped. Carlin tries to get Davis's attention. But Brigadier General Jefferson C. Davis is behaving more like a first sergeant than a division commander as he drives men back into ranks with oaths, threats, and the flat of his saber. Carlin pulls a staff officer aside, shouts over the din, "Go to Colonel Woodruff. Tell him that we can't hold more than a few minutes and that he should prepare to pull back." When the staff officer is gone, Carlin lights his pipe, wincing involuntarily as a minié ball flicks by his ear. Then he walks, hands behind his back, down the rear of his line, puffing thoughtfully.

Cheatham again throws the brigades of Vaughan and Manigault against Woodruff and Greusel of Sheridan's division. Cheatham rides back and forth behind Manigault's line, yelling: "Give 'em hell, boys!"

It fancies Bishop Polk to fall into his prelatic identity, though his thoughts are bloody. "Give them what General Cheatham says, men! Give them what he says." He stifles a smile. How wonderfully preposterous! He who cares nothing any longer for little sins, for little indulgences, to adopt a decorous tone while sending men to their deaths. It is almost too absurd, would make him laugh out loud if he were not enjoying the joke so hugely. He, the eater of souls.

Behind Sheridan's line, Bush and Houghtaling shift their guns from supporting Carlin's line to ripping up Manigault's attack. Colonel George Roberts, commanding Third Brigade, hurries to Sheridan. "Phil, let me charge," he pleads. "We can drive them back, knock the pegs clear out from under them."

Sheridan stares at Roberts. Phil Sheridan long ago got over any regret for his own lack of size and good looks. But Roberts is all that an adolescent Phil Sheridan, his knuckles scabbed and his jaw swollen from his latest fight, might have hoped to be: a man who truly looks like a warrior. "Go ahead, Colonel. But don't go too far. I don't fancy having to advance the rest of the division to rescue you."

Roberts leaves one regiment behind to hold his part of the line and leads his other three forward. His adjutant gallops ahead to clear the way. He finds the 88th Illinois hotly engaged behind a rail fence, the shells of Houghtaling's and Bush's batteries howling overhead to explode out front in Manigault's line. He screams to make himself heard, but Colonel Sherman cannot understand. The adjutant runs forward and by gesture shows the men at the fence that they must tear it down to make a passage for Roberts' regiments. Sherman and his men turn to look, see the precise blue ranks coming as if on parade, battle flags flying, officers on horseback following. Hastily, they tear down the fence and scuttle out of the way.

The gap in the fence is too small for more than one regiment to pass at a time. The 42nd Illinois squeezes through, halts out front. Roberts—tall, powerful, curly black hair and beard glistening with the mist—rides bareheaded the length of the ranks, sword uplifted, grinning. He does not have to speak and could not be heard if he did over the cheering of his men. He sweeps his sword forward, and the 42nd charges. And even those veterans so horrified by war that in later years they will never speak of it, save to decry its tragedy, will secretly recall the aching glory of this charge.

The 42nd hurtles forward in a true bayonet charge: a tactic that, though often praised, is becoming a practical rarity. Manigault's men see the long rows of steel coming at them and, ignoring their officers' shouts, fall back in a rush more than equaling the speed of the 42nd's advance. From his position behind Greusel's line, Sheridan watches what he had feared start to happen: The 42nd will plunge into the maw of the Confederate line, the 51st Illinois and the 22nd Illinois hastening after, all to be swallowed entire. He shouts to his chief of staff: "Go out there and reel them in! They are not to pursue beyond support!"

Sheridan knows that he has made a mistake. Under George Roberts's spell he has given way to a romantic inclination that no commander can long afford. There is no place for the glorious charge in this war. That is the stuff of generations gone. War fought with rifled muskets and rifled cannon must be logical. That is how Phil Sheridan would wage war, with a rationality molten-hot, inevitable—as he and his kind are inevitable and George Roberts, Pat Cleburne, and theirs inevitably doomed. Again Sheridan hears Sill's voice whispering that he has overstayed his time. He orders the triumphant Roberts into a new position just south of the Wilkinson Pike, then begins pulling back the other brigades, placing Schaefer to the right of Roberts and Greusel to the right of Schaefer. Hescock's battery sets up on a knoll to protect Roberts's right, while Houghtaling's and Bush's batteries keep blazing away at the Rebels to the front.

Colonel Arthur Manigault supposes that he cannot blame every reverse on the inefficiency of army professionals. His men have run like sheep before Roberts's bayonet charge. But, goddamn it, they would have held if it hadn't been for the pounding they'd already taken from the infernal Yankee artillery. And the lack of battery counterfire he *can* blame on the unbusinesslike behavior of the professionals.

Manigault is leading his shame-faced men back to the far side of the valley, the Union cannon fire still raining down, when he meets Brigadier General George Maney bringing his Tennessee brigade up in support. "You're late, General!" Manigault snaps.

"No, Colonel, I'm not. I just received orders from General Cheatham to advance to your support."

Manigault grumbles, waves a hand as if to erase his impoliteness. "I'm sorry, George. We just took a drubbing and didn't look good taking it. It's the damned Yankee cannon. We won't break that line until we either get some decent artillery support or take those batteries ourselves."

One of Houghtaling's shells explodes fifty yards to the right, just short of Manigault's ranks. "Yes," Maney says. "I noticed that they don't seem short of ammunition."

"No, they're not. Nor are they short of skill. Now I say we forget about support from our artillery and try taking those guns ourselves. If you. . . ."

For the next twenty minutes, Colonel Arthur Manigault sketches his plan, interspersing its steps with diatribes against military inefficiency. All the while, the Yankee batteries rain shells on Manigault's and Maney's men, exposed on the field, the earth jarring beneath them. But despite the absurd vulnerability of their position, the soldiers do not break ranks and run, but hold, compelled by something more than bravado and less than insanity, something inexplicable in the custom of heedless Southern valor.

A plan agreed to, Manigault and Maney start their brigades forward a few minutes before 9:00 A.M. Maney has chosen as his objective Bush's battery, which is still firing from its forward position just south of the Harding house. Simultaneously, Manigault will sweep wide of the brick kiln southeast of the house to capture Houghtaling's battery.

Released from their long wait under the fire of the Yankee guns, Maney's men go forward almost jauntily. Ahead, Bush's battery ceases fire and limbers up, the two regiments in support falling back over a low ridge. Maney's men cheer, break into a run. Cresting the ridge, they are greeted by a barrage from Houghtaling's reinforced battery of eight guns.

The Yankee gunners have had a long minute to refine their aim while Bush's battery and infantry support are getting clear, and the eight rounds of rifled case explode from eighteen to twenty-four feet above the heads of the Rebels silhouetted atop the ridge. The hundreds of lead balls and the even more numerous splinters of casing tear through Maney's ranks. Still, the momentum of the Rebel rush is sufficient to propel the survivors over the top of the hill. They manage to re-form at the bottom as Houghtaling's guns shift to solid shot and canister. "You're shooting at your own men!" a Rebel colonel shouts and the cry is taken up by the men in the ranks. They believe it, too, for shouldn't Manigault's brigade have gobbled up the Yankee battery in rear of the ridge? This must be a Secesh battery, rushed forward in the wake of Manigault's charge, and turned now, by terrible accident, on its friends.

The Yankee gunners hear a faint wail from the butternut lines, glance at each other, shrug, keep firing. They are all nearly deaf by now anyway, and would not believe if they could hear.

Despite all evidence of deadly intent on the part of Houghtaling's battery and its two regiments of infantry support, Maney's men are in the grip of a fundamental derangement of reality so intense as to border on mass psychosis. Colonel H. R. Field, commanding the 1st–27th Tennessee, is one of the few skeptics. "Lieutenant James," he shouts. "Go find out who owns those guns."

James kicks his mount into a gallop toward the guns, only to take a canister ball through the chest before he can make a determination. He falls from his horse, dying in the back yard of the Harding house, the dwelling of his maternal grandparents until war drove them away. A second officer immediately rides out to complete the mission, coming within forty yards of the battery and returning unharmed through a cloud of canister and minié balls to tell Colonel Field that the guns are decidedly Yankee. But even when Field's men open fire, Maney's other regimental commanders remain unconvinced. The color sergeant of the 4th Tennessee marches ten paces to the front of the line, waving the unit's colors. For ten minutes he stands there, minié balls pocking the ground about him. Still the colonels are unconvinced. The color sergeant of the 6th–9th Tennessee mounts a feed crib, waves the regimental colors. A shell from one of Houghtaling's Parrotts blows the crib from under him. And at last the colonels are convinced. Yet Maney does not charge. Instead, he brings up Smith's Mississippi Battery to duel with Houghtaling, and the men must hug the earth under the fire of the guns.

Phil Sheridan is streaming with sweat, the rivulets stinging the abrasions below his armpits caused by the too-tight fit of Sill's uniform blouse. He shrugs it off, tears out the offending seams, pulls it back on, all the while gauging the firing left and right. His own line is holding, but pressure is building beyond his right flank, where the brigades of Bushrod Johnson, Lucius Polk, and S.A.M. Wood of Cleburne's division are wheeling in on Woodruff, Carlin, and the few other survivors of Davis's and Johnson's divisions.

Again the dead Sill's voice whispers of discretion, of falling back. But Sheridan is not ready. He kicks his horse into a gallop, rides to see for certain the situation to his right. He finds only a thin screen remaining to oppose Cleburne's division. Baldwin's brigade is gone, Post's nearly so. Of Carlin's brigade, only Hans Heg's stalwart 15th Wisconsin remains largely intact. Heg's Norwegians and Swedes turn when the short, stumpy officer on the big horse explodes from the cedars to survey their thin line with fierce, protuberant eyes. Sheridan swears mightily, spins his horse, and gallops back the way he came. Heg's men turn back to watching the approaching butternut line in the fields to their front. They have Hans Heg, are unimpressed by anyone else.

Riding behind Woodruff's line, Sheridan has to push through a steady stream of exhausted men—cartridge boxes empty and muskets fouled—trudging to the rear. Woodruff himself is sitting on a stump watching them go. He looks up at Sheridan. "They're finished up, General. No force on earth can turn them around."

I could turn them if they were mine, Sheridan thinks, but he does not disdain Woodruff for not being Phil Sheridan. "Never mind, Colonel. Once they have cartridges they will feel more like fighting. You should go find General Davis."

Colonel Nicholas Greusel, commanding Sill's brigade, has his men searching the cartridge boxes and pockets of the dead and wounded for ammunition when he feels a tug on his sleeve. He turns to find an ashen-faced corporal holding out a Springfield to him. "Colonel, I come to return my gun to you, for I suppose that I shall go on furlough now."

Greusel looks down, is horrified to see that the boy is hugging a blue-white mass of intestines to his midriff. He fights down the urge to vomit, accepts the musket. "Very good, Corporal. Report to the nearest hospital. They will treat your wound and give you furlough papers."

"Thank you, Colonel." The corporal gives a shaky salute. Greusel returns it, watches as the boy shuffles off toward the rear.

Greusel is still watching when Sheridan rides up. "Don't carry a musket, Colonel. Your men will interpret it as a sign of extremis. Don't even draw your pistol unless the quarters are very close."

Greusel looks at the Springfield. "Yes, of course. That boy just gave it to me and I'd forgotten I was holding it."

Sheridan turns to look at the corporal, who has stopped now, stands leaning against a tree, a double rope of intestines falling to his knees. Sheridan makes a small sound, for he is not without sympathy, then turns to Greusel. "The line's just about gone to our right. Begin falling back into the cedars north of the pike. We'll make our stand there."

When Sheridan is gone, Greusel leans the Springfield against a tree. The wounded corporal has laboriously gathered up his intestines and stumbled on into the trees.

★ ★ ★

By 9:30 A.M., Bragg's attack has folded the Union line into the shape of a jackknife with the blade two-thirds closed and at the point of snapping into the handle. Sheridan's three brigades form the acute angle at the hinge: Houghtaling's battery at the apex, Schaefer's and Greusel's brigades along the blade to the right, Roberts's brigade along the handle to the left. Holding the line beyond Roberts is Negley's division of Thomas's corps, still largely unengaged but much depleted by the shifting of regiments elsewhere. On Sheridan's right, beyond Greusel's brigade, Rousseau's division of Thomas's corps is moving up, but the going is slow through the wreckage of McCook's right wing.

Fortunately for Rosecrans's army, the Rebels give Sheridan and Rousseau nearly half an hour to redeploy. The brigades of Vaughan, Maney, Manigault, and Loomis stand stalled in the fields and woods to the front of Sheridan, waiting for guidance from Bishop Polk and Ben Cheatham. This inactivity forces Cleburne to halt his division at the Wilkinson Pike, his right flank dangerously uncovered. Hardee, who might get Polk to move, is nowhere in evidence, probably off to the left trying to regain control of McCown's wandering division. And Braxton Bragg stands aloof, somewhere behind the lines, lost in his own counsel and the laborious process of trying to grasp the battle in its every detail.

Sheridan takes his fourth position of the morning in cedars so thick that men have to use their bayonets to slash emplacements for the guns. If the confounded Pioneers didn't have most of the tools and most of the experienced swampers, the task would be easier, but the men manage. They gouge rifle pits from the thin soil, find firing positions among the immense slabs of limestone rock scattered about like the fallen walls of an ancient castle. Sheridan dismounts, strides among the slabs. Here I will make my stand, he thinks. Here we will win or die.

The Rebel attacks resume a few minutes later. What happens in the cedars of Sheridan's position over the next hour and a half becomes blurred even in the minds of the most objective survivors. The assaults fall on Sheridan's salient like hammerblows struck by half a dozen different blacksmiths, all elbowing in to swing at the anvil. Brigadier General S.A.M. Wood, least favored and least able of Cleburne's brigade commanders, is the first, charging across the pike and the open field fronting Schaefer's line. Houghtaling's gunners manhandle their Parrotts around to fire on Wood's right flank while Greusel's infantry enfilades its left. Caught in a converging fire from the front and both flanks, Wood's men go to ground, empty their cartridge boxes bullet by bullet. Cleburne pushes through the ranks, orders Wood to fall back before he loses more good men to no purpose.

Irish Pat Cleburne is angry with Wood for staying too long, furious with Cheatham for failing to support the attack. He vents his frustration with a half dozen of the epithets he has eschewed since the day he and the mare bogged in the swamp at Shiloh and made pathetic fools of themselves. He orders Bushrod Johnson and Lucius Polk forward, covering their advance with Darden's and Calvert's batteries.

With Houghtaling's guns locked in a duel with the Rebel batteries, Johnson and Polk should be able to drive home the attack against Greusel and Schaefer. But Johnson wanders off course, losing contact with Polk's flank. Suddenly his skirmishers open fire on shadowy forms ahead in the cedars. Of all the things that plague the night rest of Brigadier General Bushrod Johnson, Southerner by choice not birth, the most disturbing is the thought of firing on friends. He orders the skirmishers to cease fire and goes in person to investigate.

Ahead the woods are quiet. Has he missed Polk's flank entirely and come into his rear? He rides forward with Major J. T. McReynolds, who commands the 37th Tennessee. There is a sudden ripple of fire, no more than a dozen muskets. McReynolds lurches in his saddle, stares for a moment bug-eyed at Johnson, then spits out his tongue in a mouthful of blood before pitching forward over his horse's neck. Johnson spins his mount, canters back to the line, gesturing the skirmishers forward to kill Yankees.

But the attack is late and half-hearted. A few minutes later, Johnson countermands his order and withdraws the brigade without attacking in line of battle. In the cedars, Greusel's infantry, their ammunition almost exhausted, watch them go. In the middle of the field, Major McReynolds vomits blood a final time and dies.

Expecting Johnson's brigade to come in on his flank at any moment, Lucius Polk drives in hard against Schaefer. Colonel Schaefer walks his line, the battle-calm on him, speaking in clearly enunciated English: "Fire low, soldiers. Fire low. Mind your targets." Rebels fall by the score, while others keep coming, their yells raspy in dry, smoke-scorched throats. Schaefer positions himself behind his center, hands clasped behind his back, watches them come on until they break. "Save your cartridges, soldiers. They will come again."

Schaefer goes to sit on a boulder for a few minutes and, when no one is looking, counts the bullet holes in his clothes. Four. Out in front of the lines there are scenes too horrible to watch: men heaving, bucking, writhing, trying to crawl away from the reality of their wounding. One youngster in butternut screams and screams for his mother. There is the wet slap of a bullet striking flesh, a lone report from somewhere down the line, and the boy stops screaming. A murder of mercy or more likely irritation, Schaefer supposes.

Colonel Arthur Manigault is a little insane by now. Inefficiency—it is worse than cowardice, amounts to murder when practiced in battle. Cheatham has ordered him to support Lucius Polk and Bushrod Johnson with an attack against Roberts's stronghold on the opposite side of the salient from Schaefer. But the order is late arriving, and Manigault goes forward after Johnson has withdrawn and Polk is already falling back. Manigault's brigade does not get far before Hescock's and Bush's guns, positioned on the knoll overlooking the juncture of the Wilkinson Pike and McFadden's Lane, have the range and start gouging huge holes in the Rebel ranks. The ranks close up, press on almost to the cedars and Roberts's line. Hidden in the thickets, the 22nd and 42nd Illinois wait until they can make out the glint of the Rebel bayonets only a few feet away, then stand and deliver a volley that seems to rip the atmosphere itself in two, leaving a long gash of gray smoke and a sigh as of air escaping, though one supposes it is actually only some equalization of pressure within the ear, a phenomenon of vacuum as natural as the ignition of gunpowder by a spark.

Manigault's regiments stampede from the field, trampling the dead and wounded into the mud. Raging, Manigault goes to Brigadier General J. Patton Anderson, commanding the brigade to his right. "Lend me two regiments, Anderson, and I'll break that line and flank those goddamn guns."

Anderson, former doctor, U.S. marshal, Florida legislator, Mexican war colonel, and—until recently—a division commander, eyes Manigault coolly. "And why should I give you two of my regiments, Arthur?" (If the man is going to be familiar, Anderson will be doubly so.)

"Because I can take those goddamn guns with them! And we are getting nowhere until we do that!"

It takes no military genius to see that Manigault is correct. Anderson tightens his lips. "All right, you can have the 45th Alabama and the 24th Mississippi. Use them well."

But Manigault cannot get any further with six regiments than he did with four, as Houghtaling's guns join Bush's and Hescock's to eviscerate the attack before it can reach the cedars. Cursing himself for a fool, Anderson rides to find his superior, Major General Jones M. Withers. In an army of powerful personalities, Withers is an exception: a soft-spoken, gentlemanly Mobile merchant, lawyer, and West Point graduate who has been in poor health much of the war. "Manigault's shot his bolt," Anderson tells Withers. "Worse, he's half killed two of my regiments along with his own. We aren't taking those guns by the flank; we're going to have to go straight in."

Withers gazes at his field map for a long moment and then at the blue smoke against the cedars. In Professor Mahan's class, tactics had seemed so simple, but he suspects no one—not even Bragg or Hardee—has a clear idea of what is happening now. He looks again at the map. "I sometimes think that the battle maps we see in books are a fiction, an attempt to introduce order into chaos after the fact."

Anderson grunts, scratches a louse and a fragment of charred wadding out of his elaborate muttonchops. I should shave before battle, he thinks. Maybe everyone should.

Withers looks again at the forest. "I think you're right. No one's going to take those guns by the flank; you're going to have to rush them."

"Yes, General."

Withers glances at him. "Come, Patton. We don't need formality now. Do you have the men to do it?"

Anderson hesitates. He would like more, wishes he had not squandered so many in Manigault's attack. "I'd rather go forward with what I've got than wait for more."

"All right then. Godspeed."

Anderson sends forward his three remaining regiments, the 27th, 29th, and 30th Mississippi. There is to be some subtlety to this assault. Oh, certainly not subtlety to elicit the admiration of a Sun Tzu or Frontinus, the great ancient admirers of stratagem and style; but not the straight-ahead pounding that has been failing for the better part of an hour. The regiments will take advantage of cover, maneuvering into position before making the desperate 200-yard rush across the open to strike the guns. Or at least that is how it is supposed to be.

Captain Henry Hescock wishes he had some chain shot for the eight Union guns on the knoll. He has read of chain shot whirling like a medieval war-flail through the rigging of sailing ships. How splendidly chain shot would work against the Rebel infantry coming now through the woods on the far side of the cornfield. When this is over, he must suggest to Sheridan that they experiment with chain shot. He lets his field glasses fall to his chest, thanking again his foresight in ordering from Amsterdam the finest field glasses made. He turns to his gunners. "Boys, we're going to cut some boughs. Celebrate Christmas a little late with our Rebel friends."

The first shell dropping through the cedars into the midst of the 30th Mississippi explodes within a dozen feet of Colonel W. F. Brantly, killing three men and knocking the colonel senseless with its concussion. Lieutenant Colonel J. J. Scales takes command, pushes the regiment forward. A cyclone of shell, case shot, and canister lashes through the trees, felling men by the dozen. Scales tries to form a battle line at the edge of the wood. Better to go forward across the open than to stay longer here. The men know better, gaze in horror at the impossible distance. A scarecrow old man runs out in front of the color detail, shakes his musket at the blazing Yankee cannons. The 30th Mississippi steps into the open to follow Private Com McGregor.

Com McGregor has lived half a hundred years and more, will not tell how many more for fear he will be sent home. He has married and buried three wives, raised fourteen children, all but three still living, and farmed the same forty acres of Mississippi bottomland all his life. He knows no Yankees, has never wanted to. He owns no slaves, and counts three or four free niggers of his acquaintance as better men than most white men he knows. Though he has never advanced the opinion to any man, black or white, Com McGregor considers slavery a moral evil that should be abolished lest the Almighty punish the South for its sin. Perhaps God is doing that now, scourging the land with war and famine. If so, so be it. Com McGregor will accept his part, will go forward to take his punishment along with the rest. And if the war is not God's wrath come upon his People, if God has instead sided with them despite all their wickedness, than Com McGregor will fight as a Christian soldier to drive the Yankees back to their frigid north of dirty, sinful cities and lonely hardscrabble farms. Either way, he is a soldier in a holy cause.

The Mississippians have advanced a bare dozen paces when two of Roberts's regiments and three regiments from Colonel Timothy Stanley's brigade of Negley's division open fire. The sheer number of minié balls loosed gives the volley a brief visibility to the naked eye like cloud shadow, Raven's wing, or the blade of a giant scythe sweeping across the cornfield. Lieutenant Colonel Scales stumbles, regains his footing, looks to either side, expecting to find that he alone is left alive. But the 30th Mississippi is still there, thinner but still advancing.

The Yankee fusillade comes in a continuous blast. Nothing should live, ultimately can live, in the open. Seventy-five yards from the cedars, the Mississippians can go no farther, drop down into the muddy furrows. Scales tries to rally them but cannot make himself heard. Com McGregor rushes out front again, gesturing wildly at the Yankee line. He runs from group to group, trying to pull men to their feet. But the men refuse to rise, and McGregor turns, marches alone toward the trees. Shamed, half a dozen men climb to their feet to follow, but a Yankee Napoleon fires a double load of canister, and in a puff Com McGregor is gone as if he had never been.

No hope at all remains of advancing across that last hideous distance. Scales orders a retreat, the word passing from man to man down the line. The men are only too happy to make use of their legs, run back the way they've come, leaving nearly half their number dead or wounded, while the small, absurd recollection of Com McGregor floats away like tattered smoke over the cornfield.

The rest of Patton Anderson's assault fails just as certainly. The 29th Mississippi takes shelling every step of the way to the Yankee line, where it receives a single tremendous volley that sends it flying. The 27th Mississippi makes it into the open, only to see its colonel shot through the brain. It falls back to regroup as command is passed, then retreats.

☆ ☆ ☆

It is 10:30 A.M. Sheridan's division has absorbed assaults by eight Rebel brigades. Casualties are huge, ammunition and energy nearly exhausted. The men fight without water or food, many of them wounded, holding on with a grimness beyond simple courage or stubbornness. The fight itself has become something immeasurably precious: a struggle in which they have invested all but life and will do that as well, rather than give way.

More order is coming to the Rebel attack as the ring tightens around the Yankee salient. No overall commander engineers it. Rather, it is the outgrowth of individual brigade and regimental commanders recognizing the need for concerted action after so much ill-spent time and blood.

The new Rebel discipline brings an increase in the accuracy and volume of musket and cannon fire. In the cedars, Sheridan's men cling to their shallow rifle pits, limestone caves, and low breastworks of rocks, logs, and bodies. Though most of the Rebel musketry is aimed blindly from two or three hundred yards, chance shots take a steady toll. The cannon fire is worse. Case and canister rounds spray clouds of iron and lead balls through the brush. Shells bounce across the forest floor to explode at wildly random heights. Most unnerving are the solid cannonballs that tear through the trees and ricochet off the limestone slabs in clouds of whirring splinters.

Major General Lovell Rousseau is pushing his division in on Sheridan's right. He gallops into the cedars to speak to Sheridan, finds him striding across the limestone slabs, sword in one hand, crushed black hat in the other. Before Rousseau can speak, a sergeant bending to sight a Napoleon stumbles back, a splinter the size and shape of an ax head embedded between his eyes. "Get a man in there," Sheridan snarls. "Keep that gun firing." He turns to Rousseau. "Get down from there, Rousseau, before they blow your goddamn head off!"

Rousseau dismounts, finds himself almost amused at Sheridan's pugnacity. He will fight them hand to hand, he thinks, go down kicking and gouging like a drunken Mick in a barroom fight. "I have contact with Greusel's flank," he shouts. "How long can you hold?"

Sheridan seems surprised by the question, frowns for a moment. "An hour if we die right here without resupply, half the afternoon if I can get the goddamn cartridges."

"I'll send you what I can find," Rousseau yells, begins to mount.

Sheridan shakes his head. "Go back on foot a hundred yards. Then ride."

Rousseau complies—for it is not cowardice, but survival. And, like Phil Sheridan, he intends to survive long enough to kill many Rebels.

Brigadier General Alexander P. Stewart refuses Patton Anderson's request for regiments to renew the attacks on Roberts. He sends a note to Withers: *General, I shortly intend to assault the Yankee salient to my left front. Having trained my brigade and sharing with my soldiers what I believe is a mutual confidence, I trust that I may be accorded the privilege of leading them personally.* It is vintage Stewart: cool, correct, befitting a commander his men have dubbed "Old Straight."

Withers replies: *General, I trust completely in your success.*

Stewart prepares carefully as he might for a lecture in mathematics or natural and experimental philosophy, the disciplines he has followed since leaving the army in 1845. His four regimental commanders are fully briefed, his artillery in place, the brigade carefully aligned when he orders it forward against Roberts.

In the Federal line, men count the last few cartridges in their boxes, shout for ammunition. Roberts, who has refused to dismount all morning, rides along his line, calling on the men to hold position with the bayonet. They can do it, these splendid men. He knows it, feels that he can lend them each and all the strength he feels welling up inside. We can do this, he thinks, stand against the charge, break it like a headland before a hurricane.

Stewart's brigade looses a volley. Three bullets strike Roberts and he pitches forward from his horse. "Get me up. Get me up," he gasps. Aides boost him into the saddle but he goes limp and they must ease him down. He convulses once, as if trying to shake off a chill, and dies. In armor, he might have ridden lifeless like El Cid down the cheering ranks of his men; but that, like George Roberts, is a romance out of time.

Colonel Fazilo Harrington of the 27th Illinois takes command of the brigade. Within minutes a shell tears away his lower jaw, killing him. Colonel Luther Bradley of the 51st Illinois assumes command, readies the men as well as he can to hold with bayonets and clubbed muskets. Then Sheridan is suddenly there, leaning down from his tall horse. The noise is too great for either to be heard. Sheridan shakes his head, points toward the rear. "We are to retreat?" Bradley screams. Sheridan nods, points again toward the rear.

The brigade backs out of the fight. The men try to bring the guns off but it is too late. Several cannons are dismounted, nearly all the artillery horses dead, the gun crews decimated. Houghtaling is carried to the rear, a fearful wound in his thigh splashing the limestone with blood. Stewart's men are close now, maintaining ranks, coming hard, straight in.

Watching Sheridan's line at last begin to give, Major General Ben Cheatham can no longer hold himself back. "Come on, boys, follow me!" he shouts to Maney's brigade. But the men are unprepared, and Cheatham has to turn and gallop back. "Follow me, boys! Follow me!" he keeps yelling. Private Sam Watkins, Company H, 1st Tennessee Infantry, has been lying patiently in the field in front of the line since taking two wounds in the left arm in Maney's first assault. He sighs, pulls himself to his feet. "Well, General, if you're so determined to die, I'll die with you."

McCook meets Rousseau riding out of the cedars to the rear of Sheridan's salient. "Alex, you should see Sheridan!" Rousseau shouts. "It's hell in there, but he's fighting like the devil incarnate! He'll have to pull back soon, but if he can hold just a little longer, I'll be in position to reach across the gap to Negley." Rousseau kicks his horse, gallops toward his guns.

Alex McCook is immensely relieved. Rousseau is here to take the weight. Now he can pull Sheridan back. He'll reorganize his corps north of the Nashville Pike. By late afternoon, perhaps he can counterattack like Grant did at Shiloh, regain ground and reputation. Tonight he will write to his father, tell Old Dan how the Rebs had done their worst but that he had stood it, taken the blows and, when the time was right, had attacked, driven them, won for the Union and the family.

He hurries forward, finds a thin brigade holding the right end of Sheridan's line. A handsome, clean-shaven colonel turns inquiringly to him. "Whose brigade is this?" McCook shouts.

"Sill's, General. But General Sill is dead. I'm Greusel. I'm in command."

"Fall back to the far side of the Nashville Pike! I'll send a staff officer to guide you. We'll re-form and resupply and then come back to give them a whipping."

Greusel stares for a moment at McCook. Well, certainly Sheridan must know of this. McCook is, after all, the corps commander. "Yes, sir," he shouts.

By this time Greusel has only the 88th Illinois and the 24th Wisconsin under his direct command, but their disappearance from the line produces a dangerous gap. Schaefer is astounded when the news reaches him. He sidesteps his already thin line, filling the hole with the 15th Missouri, and then sends to Sheridan for orders. Swearing, Sheridan dashes to Schaefer's position. He sees at a glance that it is too late to save the line. "Schaefer, charge that brigade coming in on Roberts!" (Roberts is dead, he remembers. Does not take time to correct himself.) "Stop them and then fall back."

Schaefer has little left in the way of men or ammunition, but he manages to stretch the 15th Missouri and the 24th Illinois along the length of the line while the 73rd Illinois and 2nd Missouri charge Stewart's left flank. The charge is both brief and costly, but it gains the ten minutes needed for Bradley to lead Roberts's brigade out of the fight. Schaefer watches calmly as his men fall back, many of them clicking empty muskets at the Rebels, as if the mere threat of a shot could momentarily slow the onslaught. A minié ball drills Schaefer's forehead neatly, blows off the back of his skull. Without expression, he topples backward off his horse.

★   ★   ★

Of his 6,500 men, Sheridan has lost 1,796 enlisted men and 72 officers dead or seriously wounded, including all three of his brigade commanders, four regimental commanders, and the captain of one of his batteries. Eight of his eighteen guns have been left behind, captured or too seriously damaged to pull off.

Rosecrans and Garesché watch Sheridan's men emerge from the cedars: exhausted, bloody, panting, faces black, angry. That anger is the universal, unreasoning emotion among them as they troop by. Rosecrans understands, takes off his hat solemnly, his staff following suit. Sheridan rides up on his tall gelding. "Here we are, General. All that's left of us. . . . General, if we'd just had some goddamn cartridges, we could have held off the whole goddamn bunch of them!"

Rosecrans, who can and has been swearing like a trooper all morning, says mildly: "Mind your language, General. The next bullet may send you to eternity."

Sheridan looks away. "I can't help it," he says gruffly. "Unless I swear like hell, the men won't take me seriously."

Watching Sheridan blink back tears, Garesché suddenly understands this man who has always been a puzzle to him. My God, he thinks, Sheridan loves those men, swears so terribly because he can barely stand to see them suffer.

Private Sam Watkins of the 1st Tennessee is a veteran of Shiloh, Corinth, Perryville, and a dozen smaller fights. But he has never seen anything like the carnage in the cedars. The Yankee dead lie on all sides, strewn across the rocks and lying in heaps on the forest floor. He cannot even begin to count them, counts instead the dead battery horses. At eighty, he quits, starts for the rear to have his arm tended.

He passes the body of a dead Yankee colonel, shot several times in the chest. He is a large, handsome man with a curly black beard and the finest uniform Watkins has ever seen. The boots attract Watkins in particular— knee-high black boots, polished to a mirror finish. They would not, Watkins supposes, be very good for marching in, but he can certainly trade them for something better than his own sad brogans. He kneels, lifts one of the colonel's feet and tries to work the boot free with his uninjured arm. He feels an odd tickling at the nape of his neck, turns quickly, and then jumps back with a cry. The colonel is staring at him, blue eyes hard. And dead. Watkins nudges the body. "Colonel?" No, the man is dead, unbreathing. Still, Watkins edges backward a dozen paces before turning away from the body of Colonel George Roberts.

Private Joe Zein of the 1st Louisiana Regulars has fought all morning, first with one regiment and then with another. He needs no orders, simply goes where the fighting is hottest and kills every Yankee he can find. He cannot recall ever having a grander day: a day filled with everything a man could want. Or nearly.

When he returns to his company, he has half a dozen Yankee haver-sacks thrown over a shoulder. He swings them off, tosses them in a mound in the middle of his friends. And aren't they his friends? Why, certainly.

He opens one of the haversacks, digs about in it, pulls out a handful of hardtack. He likes hardtack, has strong teeth to crush the iron-hard crackers. He notes that several of them are stained with Yankee blood. Other men have found the same. But they are desperately hungry, break off the soiled pieces and chew the rest. Zein grins, bites off a soaked, red corner, chews with utter satisfaction. Other men see, protest. Zein goes on chewing, showing for everyone his strong, white teeth turning the hardtack to a blood-tinged paste.

Private Dickie Krall is urinating into a clump of brown ferns when he feels strong arms go around him from behind. A foot trips him and he sprawls in the ferns. Zein is laughing quietly, mouth next to Dickie's ear. He grabs the waist of Dickie's trousers, pulls them down, tears away the frayed, threadbare underdrawers. Dickie tries to pull free, to run on all fours, but Zein is on top of him, and suddenly there is a pain like nothing he can imagine. He tries to buck away from it, but Zein is expecting this, thrusts to meet him, drives his engorged member deep into Dickie's rectum so that the boy screams, would collapse except that Zein grips his thighs, lunges into him hard over and over, whooping and laughing until he climaxes with a howl of utter pleasure. Now the day has all that a man could want.

Zein comes back into the clearing where his messmates are making coffee. He squats by one of the fires, helps himself to a cup. Sergeant Simon Buck makes the connection that both Zein and Krall have been gone at the same time. He curses silently. "Did you hurt that boy, Joe?"

Zein looks up with an expression of innocence, cannot hold it, laughs, shakes his head at the humor of the question. Buck gestures to Corporal Tom Binder and they go to look for Dickie Krall. They find him curled up, sobbing, pants drawn up but the blood soaking through the seat. "You stay with him," Buck says to Binder and starts back for the clearing, then changes his mind. "No, we'll bring him. He should be there." Together, they lift Dickie between them, help him stumble through the brush.

At the edge of the clearing, they pause. Everyone watches them. Zein turns from his squat beside the fire, smiles with his white teeth, eyes dancing merrily beneath black curls. Sergeant Simon Buck lets Dickie Krall's arm fall from his shoulder, walks deliberately to Zein and bayonets him, high up, between the heart and the clavicle. He holds Zein down, pinning him to the ground. The other men rise, come one at a time with their bayoneted Enfields. Zein laughs at them. They cannot kill him; his ma said he would come home safe.

After Binder has used his bayonet, Buck hands a musket to Dickie Krall. "You got to do it, Dickie. We're all in this together. They don't hang one unless they hang us all."

Sam Watkins falls in beside a wounded lieutenant with a dispatch rider's pouch flapping against his side. The lieutenant is young, more boy than man, with a mustache so blond and sparse to be all but invisible against his pale skin. Watkins, tired from fighting and the seepage of blood from the wounds in his arm, does not at first scrutinize the lieutenant. But when he turns to say something neighborly, he sucks in his breath. The lieutenant's left arm is entirely gone, the frayed sleeve seemingly sucked into the wound. Through shattered ribs, Watkins can see the boy's exposed heart beating. "My God, Lieutenant!" Watkins manages. The boy does not turn his head, but walks another dozen paces before falling dead without a word or a groan.

CHAPTER 5

Wednesday, 10:30 A.M.–Noon
December 31, 1862
The Confederate Left
North of the Wilkinson Turnpike

With Sheridan forced back from the cedars north of the Wilkinson Pike, Major General Lovell Rousseau's division fights a holding action. Meanwhile, Hardee regroups his forces for the push that will break through to the Nashville Pike, effectively surrounding Rosecrans's army.

IEUTENANT GENERAL BILL HARDEE feels the great chance coming. For the last hour, while Pat Cleburne has been smashing in the right side of Sheridan's stronghold, Hardee has been pulling McCown's division together for a drive on the Nashville Pike. If he only had three fresh brigades—even one or two—he could be certain of success. But Bragg has refused to see the grand opportunity of enveloping the Yankee right, insists on blindly following the original plan of the giant wheel. Yet with Sheridan in retreat at last and Cleburne sidestepping to join his left to McCown's right, Bill Hardee has a rush of optimism. Even without reinforcements, he may do it, may break through to the pike and confound Rosecrans and Bragg both. He sends an outline of his plan to Cleburne: *The moment of glory is upon us, Patrick.*

With Sheridan pulling back on his left, Major General Lovell Rousseau is planning his withdrawal to the Nashville Pike. He does this with surprising coolness for a political general of little experience. Another Kentucky lawyer-politician promoted by the Lincoln administration in hopes of keeping the wavering state in the Union, Rousseau has taken to the job as if born to wear a general's stars.

He is a big man, well over six feet, with a rugged, pockmarked face. Comparisons to Lincoln are inevitable, for Rousseau, too, is rough-hewn, self-educated, humorous, and wily. Even George Thomas, who has little patience for political generals, likes Rousseau. They are nearly the same age and—off the political platform—Rousseau has an easy, mildly sardonic way about him. With the congenial Negley, the three generals make a comfortable trio of large, assured men: a solid center for the army.

When Bill Hardee crushes the Union right at first light, Rousseau's three brigades are camped in reserve beside the Nashville Pike near Rosecrans's headquarters, some two miles from Carlin's brigade at the center of McCook's line. Listening to the sound of heavy fighting to the south, Thomas orders Rousseau to prepare to reinforce the right. Shortly after 8:00 A.M., a courier from Rosecrans brings a message confirming Thomas's expectation.

Thomas reads the order, hands it to Rousseau, gives him a moment to absorb it. "Is it clear to you, General?"

"Yes, sir. I am to support Sheridan's right, refusing my right flank as necessary."

"It will be. My guess is that you won't find much of Johnson's division, or Davis's either, out beyond Sheridan."

"It's a debacle, General."

"No, not yet. But it may fall to you to see that it doesn't become one. How do you intend to deploy your brigades?"

"I thought Jack Beatty behind and to the right of Sheridan's right flank. Shepherd's regulars next to him, and Scribner in support."

"Is that the best marching order?"

"Yes, otherwise I would put the regulars in reserve."

Thomas nods. "So would I. Carry on, then."

Rousseau tosses a salute and rides off. Thomas stretches his spine, settles back in the saddle. He thinks of Mexico, of Bragg, Hardee, Cheatham, and the others. I know these men, can predict them, he thinks. I wish I knew Cleburne, who's a lethal pup from all I hear. Not that it makes that much difference; I know who commands him.

Thomas has never liked Bill Hardee. Most Academy graduates drop at least some of their strut as junior officers. But Hardee was a popinjay throughout his time in the Old Army. Hardee with his imperial, his French tastes, his enthusiasm for lancers and élan. Thomas considers it all a lot of nonsense for making comely females swoon into the arms of bedecked, courtly, randy Bill Hardee.

Rousseau's three brigades plow through the torrent of refugees from McCook's rout. Rousseau orders his line into the cedars to Sheridan's right and then rides forward for his brief interview with Sheridan and his even briefer encounter with McCook. Returning, he posts Beatty's brigade in a thick brake with open woods to the front. He places a broad hand on the younger man's shoulder. "John, Sheridan's fighting like the devil and we'll need to do the same. I want you to hold this position until hell freezes over."

Beatty, a thirty-four-year-old banker who writes fiction in his spare time, cannot help wondering why so talented an orator as Rousseau cannot produce in this moment of desperate drama a more original figure of speech. "We'll do our best, General."

"I know you will. I'm off to see Shepherd."

Beatty turns to the task of getting his regiments into line. The drizzle continues to fall, gray and icy, the men chattering as the sweat of the hard march freezes beneath their wool tunics. Now just what, Beatty wonders, will constitute frozen hell? I think I might actually prefer it to this damned rain.

If there is a man in the Army of the Cumberland molded on the archetype of a regular-army colonel, it is Lieutenant Colonel Oliver L. Shepherd. A classmate of Thomas, McCown, and Bushrod Johnson, Shepherd was dour and inflexible even as a youth. Twenty years of regular service have encrusted his reputation until he is a legend even among his contemporaries. Offered a general's commission in the volunteer army, he refuses, growling that his only ambition is to become a full colonel of regulars. His friends are relieved.

Thanks to the newspapers, many civilians hold a romantic view of the regulars, imagining that every private could assume the stripes of a first sergeant in a volunteer regiment and every junior officer the epaulets of a colonel. But the common opinion among the volunteers is that the regulars are a coarse lot, mostly Irish, who have joined the army one step ahead of the law or starvation. The truth is only a little more complicated: Many of the regulars are actually recent recruits with nothing except unit tradition to link them to the Old Army. But like the true old soldiers, they are in the main tough, unlettered, unmarried, *and* disproportionately Irish. They are also believers: not in grand causes, but in their units. They stand together, do not shirk, do not flinch, do not straggle, and never run. Fuck the sneering dandies and mama's boys of volunteer regiments; the regulars need only their self-respect. They don't have to like their officers, don't like Shepherd, who is a mean son of a bitch if there ever was one. But they will follow him, go where he says to go, not for him or cause or country, but because they are regulars and will hold to that pride unto death.

When Rousseau finds Shepherd, the five battalions of regulars are advancing into the cedars to the right of Beatty's line. Here the forest is more open, and the sixteen hundred regulars manage a compact line, their distinctive field blouses and crossbelts still looking dressy despite the rain and the hard marching of the last few days. Rousseau pulls alongside Shepherd and, though he is rarely intimidated by any man, feels a quiver in his stomach when Shepherd turns his lowering gaze on him. "General Rousseau."

"Good morning, Colonel. Your men look well."

Shepherd turns to look at the ranks. "Yes, well enough. Do you have additional orders, General?"

"No, push forward until your skirmishers make contact and then hold your position. When it becomes untenable, fall back on the pike. I will send word when I'm ready to receive you."

Shepherd stares at him, as if waiting for something inside his massive head to grind the word "untenable" into manageable syllables. "Then I am not to hold position at all hazards." It is a statement, not a question.

"No, Colonel. Sheridan is taking a pounding and he'll have to fall back. We'll cover his retreat and then fall back alongside Negley's division to the Nashville Pike. Under no circumstances can we allow ourselves to be enveloped."

Shepherd nods. "Yes, General. If that's all, I need to position my guns."
"By all means."

Rousseau watches him go, feels the discomfort he always feels on meeting men of inflexibility. Shepherd is certainly to be trusted, but trusted only to be what he is and nothing more.

George Thomas is little given to metaphor, yet it seems to him that he has been asked to play the role of Helios astride the harbor at Rhodes: colossal, cast of a defeated foe's engines of war, but unable to move, unable to strike. And he would strike, drive a great bronze fist into the onrushing Rebels, but he cannot, must instead stand and let them break upon him.

Thomas trots his big, smooth-gaited mare along the Nashville Pike, checking and adjusting the posting of his artillery. If the guns do serious execution among the Rebels, the infantry will see and hold. Of this he is sure, for above all else Thomas is an artilleryman of unequaled skill. To judge from the poor performance of the Rebel guns so far this morning, Bragg has lost some of what once made him a premier artilleryman, but Thomas has never been more certain in his trade.

☆   ☆   ☆

Lieutenant Jack Dulin of the 6th–7th Arkansas has hemorrhoids so swollen that riding the jouncing seat of the ordnance wagon is a nearly intolerable agony. Worse, he is lost. Brigadier General St. John Liddell has personally dispatched him to bring up two wagon loads of cartridges, but now Dulin cannot find the brigade. He needs a horse, damn it! With a horse he could ride ahead, stand in the stirrups, spot the brigade, and save his ass both literally and figuratively.

South of the Wilkinson Pike, Yankee prisoners and stragglers wander across the fields, waiting to be told which direction to go or where to muster. Many of them are still armed, their rifle-muskets reversed in sign of submission. But their mood could change, and Dulin rides with a cocked pistol in his lap. The teamster glances over. "I wish you'd let down the hammer on that Colt, Lootenant. We hit a bump and you might shoot yourself, me, or one of my mules."

"It's not a Colt, it's a Rigdon," Dulin grits. "And I'd happily shoot you or one of your damned mules if I didn't have to get this ammunition to General Liddell."

The teamster shrugs, decides not to press his point. At the edge of a cornfield, Dulin spots a lone rider coming toward them. "Stop," he snaps. "I'm getting that horse." The teamster complies, and Dulin hops down onto the soggy ground and runs, pistol drawn and piles stinging, toward the rider. "Get down from there, soldier. I'm taking that mount."

The man stops, abashed. He is dressed in butternut, the chevrons of a corporal stitched to one sleeve. "I'm sorry, Lieutenant. I can't—"

"Are you a courier?"

"No, sir. But—"

"Then get the hell off that horse or I'll shoot you off it!"

The corporal stares at Dulin's leveled pistol, then slides off the far side.

Dulin leads the nag roughly toward the wagon. He is a short, very round man, barely five feet tall but weighing close to two hundred pounds, and he finds it necessary to use whatever step he can find to get aboard a horse. A humiliation.

"Uh, Lootenant," the teamster says.

"What?" Dulin clambers onto the wagon step and prepares to mount the horse.

"That man." The teamster points.

Dulin looks, sees for the first time that the corporal has lost his left leg ten inches below the knee, the bloody stump already blackening under the pressure of a tourniquet. The soldier stands balanced on his one foot, staring in perplexity at the wound. "General Liddell needs this ammunition and I need this horse," Dulin snaps, though he feels he might vomit. "There are discarded muskets aplenty around here. He can use one as a crutch. Now go!"

The teamster snaps his whip and they roll on, the second wagon following, a rear wheel splashing mud on the shoe of the one-legged corporal. He looks up, mournful, as if expecting further insult.

A mile away, Private Ezra Brown supposes he has been dealt a mortal wound when the impact of a bullet spins him out of the saddle and stretches him amid the thundering hooves of Company G, 3rd Indiana Cavalry, in headlong retreat. He waits for death, too stunned to review his life, sins, or now unattainable dreams. The 14th Alabama Battalion of Wharton's brigade comes instead of death, thundering over Brown in wild pursuit of the Hoosiers. A mare named Netty steps firmly on Ezra's midriff, squashing the wind out of him and leaving behind a livid hoof print whose trace he will carry the rest of his life.

It takes Ezra the better part of an hour to decide he isn't going to die. He stumbles up and makes his way to the Gresham house, where a field hospital is operating in the wake of McCook's rout. He slumps down in the long line of wounded to wait his turn. He has always supposed that a field hospital would be somehow exempt from the tumult of battle: a place of muffled sounds, of suffering and tragedy, but also of dignity and calm. But except for the suffering, Gresham house resembles nothing in his imagining. The noise from the fight on all sides is beyond tumult, belongs to that order of pandemonium shared only by deluge, earthquake, volcanic eruption, and hell. Nor are the house and yard immune to the missiles of the combat. Ezra watches a howitzer shell fall into the shallow declivity of an old cellar, missing by incredible luck every appendage of the five stragglers crowded within before burying itself two feet into the soft earth beneath their feet. There is a pause—no more than three or four heartbeats—then a soggy *foomp* and a brief spout of mud and body parts. After a few minutes, a hospital orderly scuttles to the side of the hole, stares in, and comes back, face pale though he has already seen much of horror this morning.

An orderly sergeant squats before Ezra. "Show me your wound, trooper." Ezra pushes the blouse off his shoulder, revealing a ridge of purple flesh across his left breast above the nipple. The sergeant pokes at the lump at the terminal end. "Pistol ball. Want it out of there?"

"Well, yes. I guess."

"Come on. We'll get it out and then put you to work." He leads Ezra to the end of the porch. "Sit down. Pug, give me a hand." He starts digging into a wooden box of dressings.

Another orderly pushes in beside the sergeant, pulls Ezra's blouse off his shoulder and swabs the blood away with a wet, grimy rag. The sergeant leans in over Ezra's chest, scalpel in hand. "But don't I get to see a surgeon?" Ezra asks.

"You don't need one. Besides, you're safer with us," the sergeant says. He makes a quick cut, pinches, and drops a ball of lead into Ezra's palm. "Souvenir. Thirty-six caliber. Must have been nearly spent when it hit you."

"You're a lucky son of a bitch," Pug growls. "Sit up." He expertly wraps a broad bandage around Ezra's chest, knotting it in the back.

"Now make yourself useful," the sergeant says. "Go tear down some of that fence over yonder and make a fire for the boys. Them that can't move are going to freeze to death unless we get them a fire."

Lieutenant Jack Dulin has still not found Liddell's brigade when he reaches the Wilkinson Pike. He hesitates, doubting if the brigade has come so far so fast. But where else to look? The wagons bump up and over the shoulder of the turnpike, the teamsters flailing at the mules. Riding alongside, Dulin feels himself focused in clear silhouette against the gray skyline and shivers with the sense of Yankee rifles coming to bear on his chest. Then the wagons are across, off the pike, and bumping across the furrows of another cornfield. Dulin lets out his breath. Now where the hell is the bri—

Suddenly, Yankees are everywhere, an entire line up and running across the field ahead of the wagons. The teamster of the lead wagon hauls back on the reins, shouts, "I think we come too far, Lootenant!"

Dulin watches the running Yankees with bug-eyed astonishment. Christ, there must be two hundred of them! "Turn around," he yells. "We've gone too far."

I just told you that, you dumb son of a bitch, the teamster thinks. He hauls the mules around in a slewing turn, follows Dulin back toward the pike.

Brigadier General St. John Liddell rides into the yard of the Gresham house past a slightly wounded Yankee private prying boards from a fence. Liddell surveys the yard, picking out the skulkers hiding among the Yankee wounded. If I live, I will come back tonight and take one of them, he thinks. I'll take him out into the fields and strangle him with my bare hands. Then I will come back for another and another, until my hands are too tired to grasp another Yankee throat, to twist another Yankee neck. Then I will weep.

Lieutenant Willie Liddell, only sixteen and the darling of his father's staff, is dead. Bullock, one of the staff sergeants, has seen his body crumpled in a field beside the Gresham Road, goes to find his commander, weeping as he goes, for Willie in life had shone upon them all: blond, laughing; oblivious to danger, death, or the cares that weigh down any man much beyond the age of sixteen.

Surgeon John Doolittle looks up from the operating table to see a hard-faced general in gray step through the door. He turns back to his work, ripping a capital saw through a femur and then slicing through the muscles and fat on the other side with an eight-inch amputating knife. The patient, only lightly anaesthetized to save on chloroform, gives a shudder, tries to kick the leg that an orderly has just tossed through an open window onto a heap of severed limbs. "Sew him up," Doolittle tells his assistant, wipes his hands on his bloody apron, and goes to welcome the general.

Liddell stares at the lithe, mustachioed man coming toward him, takes a dislike to him before he even hears the man's flat Ohio accent. "General, I'm glad you're here," the doctor begins without preamble. "There are hundreds of wounded along the fences near the pike. Men who can't get here because of their wounds or for fear of getting shot a second time. With a cease-fire of an hour and your help, I can get them into the yard. We're already swamped and we won't be able to save all of them, but we'll save a damned sight more than we can now. Then if you could tell your gunners—"

"I would rather die than give you so much as a minute."

The doctor's mouth drops open. He recovers, stammers, "But, General! There are Southern boys out there too. We don't play favorites here. A wounded man is a wounded man to us."

"And aren't you a pretty little fellow, coming down here to tell us what to do, trying to chain us to your accursed Union. You assault our homes and our women, try to take our niggers, and would weld us in shackles for a thousand years!"

Doolittle rubs at his mustache, leaving fragments of dried blood amid the carefully trimmed whiskers. "General, this is not the time for politics. I only want a cease-fire for an hour so I can save as many boys as—"

"It's all politics, sir! War is political. Death is political! The maiming of every poor stupid farm lad out there is political! And it is your politics that are the cause of all this suffering and death. You ask for a cease-fire? For what? To give your army time to regroup so it can kill and maim more of us? Well, you are not going to get one, sir! Because we are going to cut through your army and kill it like a snake. Hack it into a thousand pieces so that it can never come crawling through this land again!"

Liddell storms out. Doolittle finds himself pressed back against a wall. "Jesus Christ," he says. "Who was that?"

"General St. John Liddell," a young Rebel officer says. "He just heard that his son is killed." He touches the doctor kindly on the shoulder, follows his general out the door.

Liddell finds his men filling their cartridge boxes from two muddy ordnance wagons. He looks at the short, fat lieutenant officiously supervising. Dooley. Dulin. Something like that. "Good job, Lieutenant."

The man beams, salutes. "Thank you, General."

By the time Liddell's brigade has crossed the Wilkinson Pike and disappeared from sight, Private Ezra Brown has a good pile of boards torn from the old fence. He carries an armload, his chest hurting ferociously, to a spot near a long line of the severely wounded. By propping a board at an angle on several others and jumping on it, he is able to break up some kindling. He borrows a barlow knife to make some shavings and then stacks a neat teepee of kindling over them. Two lucifers and he has a thin flame in the shavings, and soon a crackle and some sparks from the kindling. He is crouching on hands and knees, blowing gently on the fire, when someone hits him across the backside with a board, throwing him forward, upsetting the teepee and nearly setting his beard on fire. "Hey, goddamn it!" he yells, twisting about and slapping at the sparks on his uniform. But there is no one behind him and his right leg is a sudden dead weight.

Ezra is staring dumbly at the bubbling wound in his thigh when the orderly sergeant saunters over. The sergeant shakes his head sadly. "Well, now you do have something to worry about. Now you've got to see one of the docs."

As much as his hemorrhoids will allow, Jack Dulin is a happy man as Liddell's brigade advances across the muddy cornfield north of the Wilkinson Pike. Like most lieutenants, he has marched on foot with the men until now. The horse—sorry plug that it is—elevates him above the throng, makes him feel a true officer. Moreover, the general told him that he'd done a good job. If he can manage to come to Liddell's attention a time or two more, perhaps the general will remember him when the next captaincy opens. Jim Slusser, who was a lieutenant only a month ago and is now a captain, points to the skid marks made an hour before by Dulin's slewing ordnance wagons. "Looks like those boys decided to change directions in a hell of a hurry. Must've decided they were going the wrong way."

Dulin, who is a young man almost completely without a sense of humor, laughs out loud, wonders if Slusser or anyone would believe him if he told them how he'd routed half a Yankee regiment with a pair of ordnance wagons.

For all his desire to kill Yankees in Willie's memory, St. John Liddell is too good a commander to push too far beyond support. North of the pike, he finds himself alone with his brigade in thick woods. He halts, sends an aide back to find Cleburne or Hardee to ask for orders.

He sits on a log, closes his eyes, tries to ease the thudding pain in his temples. "General, he's not dead!"

Liddell opens his eyes, stares at his aide-de-camp, Captain June Bostick. "Who's not dead?"

"Willie, sir. Weren't you told that he was dead?"

"Yes."

"Well, he's not, sir. I put him in an ambulance myself. He got knocked off his horse by a shell burst and stunned. One of the gunners found him and called me. I imagine he'll be back with us tonight or tomorrow."

Liddell stares at Bostick for a long moment. "My son is alive?"

"Yes, sir. He's going to be fine."

Liddell runs his tongue over his lips, frowns, can hardly think of anything to say or feel. Willie not dead. Amazing. I had already buried my boy and set about plotting to avenge him. "Thank you, Bostick. I am greatly relieved."

★ ★ ★

At twenty-nine, Brigadier General James Earl Rains is the youngest general in the Army of Tennessee, Joe Wheeler excepted. He is tall and slender, with striking gray eyes and a clump of thick chinwhiskers that only accentuate his youth. A Yale-educated attorney and editor in Nashville before the war, he is neither a romantic nor a gloryhunter. Still, he has the sense this morning of not contributing his share to the Confederate triumph. True, his brigade helped rout Willich's at the far end of the Union line in the first attack, but even that had been mostly Matt Ector's doing. Since then, Rains and Ector have led their brigades north along Overall Creek, collecting Yankee prisoners and mopping up the few scattered spots of resistance bypassed by Wharton's cavalry.

Rains is uneasy with their separation from the rest of the division, suggests to Ector that they should oblique to the right. But Ector, who is senior and a decade older, refuses: McCown knows where they are, will redirect them when he thinks best. So they move along at a measured pace, protecting their flanks, eschewing audacity in the absence of orders. Finally, to Rains's great relief, McCown arrives to lead them back to the rest of the division.

Hardee is waiting impatiently with McNair's brigade near the Gresham house when McCown brings Rains's and Ector's brigades into view. Hardee is tempted to relieve McCown for the inexcusable tardiness. Instead, he takes him aside, noting the ashen face of his fellow Academy graduate and Old Army friend. "John, are you ill?"

"No, Bill. I'm—"

"Because if you are, there's no disgrace in asking to be relieved. I've already sent McNair back and put Harper in command of his brigade."

"McNair's been sick for a month."

"I'm aware of that. Now, do you want to go back, or can you carry on?"

McCown stares for a moment at his trembling hands. How can this have happened, he wonders, this faintness under fire? He's been a professional soldier for a quarter century. He'd gone to Mexico, winning a brevet at Cerro Gordo. He never thought he'd be a general, but in his secret imaginings he thought he would be a good one: that a general's stars would bring an apotheosis, make of him the decisive agent of grand designs. But the rank has done none of that, has revealed instead a fear that makes his heart race every time he faces a decision. He lifts his eyes to Hardee's. "I'm fine, General. A mild indisposition that will pass in a moment."

This is plausible enough. Half the army is afflicted with some indisposition or another, most of them dysenteric. The sight of soldiers, from privates to generals, emptying watery bowels along a line of march is so common as to excite no notice at all. So Hardee nods; he will spare McCown the humiliation of being relieved under fire. But when this business is concluded, he will tell him that he should seek a transfer to a quiet post. "All right, John. As soon as the men are resupplied with cartridges, we're going to make a push for the Nashville Pike. If we succeed, we'll have won the day. Send Rains forward on your right, Ector in the center, Harper on the left. Cleburne will come in to the right of Rains once you're engaged."

Half an hour later, Rains's skirmishers advance cautiously into the misty woods northeast of the Wilkinson Pike. They wear the blue overcoats issued them on enlisting in the 3rd Georgia. The blue is not quite Union blue; but soaked by rain it is very close to the same color as the uniforms of the two battalions of Union regulars of Shepherd's brigade, Rousseau's division, advancing in the opposite direction. Momentarily confused by the strange cut of the regulars' blouses, the Georgians fall back, holding their fire. The regulars are not confused but altogether mistaken, pulling in their own skirmishers and following in the certainty that they are now under the cover of another Federal formation.

Major Adam J. Slemmer, commanding 1st Battalion, 16th U.S. Infantry, rides behind his ranks, ducking to keep branches from plucking the spectacles from his face. Slemmer is an awesomely talented soldier. At the Academy, his classmates assumed that he would rise to the top echelons of the army staff. Yet Slemmer refused a staff commission, chose the artillery instead, for staff officers are rarely made generals and Slemmer intends to be a general. He could, like his contemporaries Sheridan, McCook, Stanley, and Sill, be one already. But a volunteer commission, even with stars attached, does not suit his purposes. Not yet.

Of those four, only Sill and possibly Stanley have ever heard of Machiavelli, but Slemmer can recite long passages from *The Prince*. He does so only to himself, reveals nothing to others. He is thinking beyond this war to the great conquest that will add Mexico, Cuba, Central America, and perhaps even Canada to the American empire. He has analyzed his probable rivals for command in that war, and only John Schofield, Jim McPherson, and now—surprisingly—Phil Sheridan concern him. But he has formulated a careful plan, expects that it will best McPherson, who is too nice by half, and Schofield, who is too abrasive by an even larger margin. Sheridan? Well, the man is a ditch-digger's son, cannot survive both that and this war.

In accordance with his timetable, Slemmer is already well on his way to a solid combat reputation. By spring, he will be able to afford a transfer to the staff. He expects Garesché will ask for a field command, and no one will be better qualified to take his place than Adam Slemmer. Then to play politics for a year: make Rosecrans his patron and, through him, Secretary of the Treasury Salmon Chase. By a year from this spring, Slemmer will have reputation, powerful connections, a general's stars, and a division. Perhaps an independent command. (He would love the chance to go raiding like Forrest, or to hunt down the man himself.) Then, when the press and public tire of all the old, battle-worn generals, they will find a new hero in Adam Slemmer.

As the regulars push ahead into open forest, Slemmer glances to his right, makes out the line of 1st Battalion, 15th U.S. Infantry, commanded by Major John H. King, a regular almost as crusty as Shepherd. But King is smart, despite his lack of education: a good ally to have among the regulars. Slemmer ducks to avoid another limb, guides his horse between a pair of trees, and stares out from the vantage of height at a long butternut line of infantry, Enfields at the ready, while a skirmish line in blue overcoats, but with butternut pants showing below, scuttles out of the way. Slemmer has a quick, decisive mind, but even he does not fully comprehend the ambush before the Rebel volley explodes into his ranks. Slemmer feels a blow to his left shoulder, reels in the saddle, hears vertebrae pop as he tries to recover his balance. Another ball cuts through a stirrup strap, shatters his right ankle. Half a dozen bullets strike his horse in the chest and neck. The beast stumbles backward, pitching Slemmer onto the stony ground.

King is also down, his battalion falling back, firing by the rear rank. Captain Robert Crofton takes command of Slemmer's battalion, orders it into the cover of a limestone outcropping. For fifteen minutes, Slemmer's men deliver a cool, disciplined fire against the 29th North Carolina. Half a dozen of the blue-clad Georgia skirmishers have been caught between the lines and taken prisoner. They huddle under cover not far from Slemmer. One offers to tend Slemmer's wounds, receives a glare in reply.

Slemmer knows that he will lose the arm and probably the foot. Alone, the foot would not be so bad. An officer less a foot can still command an army. But Congress does not make one-armed officers commanding generals. It goes against the sense that even generals must be able to personally throttle their opponents. Even gouty old Scott possessed a great, imperturbable might, gave the impression that, if he chose, he could rise and advance, wheezing and grunting like an ancient grizzly, to crush any opponent of the Republic. No, Adam Slemmer will never be commanding general now. Not even a hero. If he lives at all beyond this day, it will be to die obscure.

Crofton gives the order for the battalion to fall back by companies. Four soldiers tumble Slemmer into a makeshift litter. The corporal in charge gestures at the blue-clad Georgians. "What about them, sir?"

Eyes swimming with myopia and pain, Slemmer cannot at first focus on the object of the corporal's gesture. "Shoot them," he grits.

Major General Lovell Rousseau is preparing his second line along the Nashville Pike. He positions Lieutenant George W. Van Pelt's Battery A,

1st Michigan Artillery on a low hill where it can sweep the four hundred yards of cottonfield lying between the cedars and the pike. He goes forward again, pulls back two regiments of Scribner's reserve brigade to protect the guns, and then dashes over to Shepherd's brigade. King's battalion is just coming out, badly cut up. Shepherd is fuming. "Colonel," Rousseau says, "send your battery back and then bring your men out and form on the pike."

"I would prefer not to ask my regulars to retreat, General."

Goddamn it! Rousseau thinks. Spare me the bullcock. "We are not retreating, Colonel. We are taking a better position—one I intend to hold to the last extremity. Now, pull your brigade back, please."

Shepherd grumps, obeys.

Rousseau would like to go to Beatty's brigade, but there is no time. He rides back to the pike to make sure Shepherd's battery gets into position beside Van Pelt's. Satisfied, he sends a courier to Beatty.

Scribner's three remaining regiments have passed a nervous twenty minutes. Receiving the order to fall back, they forget their parade-ground training and stream across the cottonfield in a mob. Scribner, on the pike consulting with Rousseau, is humiliated. He dashes down the pike, intending to angle into the field to restore some order, but comes face to face with Major General George Thomas sitting his horse on a low rise, watching the spectacle. Thomas may be "Pap" to the men, but he scares the bejesus out of nearly every officer in the army, Scribner included. "General! I'm sorry, General, it looks like hell. But we didn't—I didn't—want the men concentrated in case some Rebel battery got the range on us. This isn't a rout, General, no matter how bad it looks."

Thomas turns his great head to study Scribner for a moment, then turns his gaze back to the field. To Scribner's infinite relief, his soldiers begin falling into ranks on reaching the pike. "See, General, they're forming now. Do you have any additional orders?"

"No, re-form on the pike," Thomas says solemnly.

Scribner salutes uneasily, rides back to hurry the re-forming. Thomas sighs, lights a cigar. I suppose the wonder is, he thinks, that we manage to resemble an army at all.

Riding through the cedars to deliver the withdrawal order to Beatty, Lieutenant Arthur J. Billup, a former schoolteacher attached to Rousseau's staff, represents one of the lesser vector forces within a problem of projectile geometry. Or so he comes to see it during the lengthy period of retrospection resulting from his participation in the problem. As near as he can determine, a Rebel cannon of unknown caliber has fired a solid shot from somewhere in the rear of the Rebel line advancing on Beatty. The vector represented by the cannonball is briefly interrupted by its convergence with a static cylinder (a tree trunk), the point of convergence occurring about thirty feet above the intersection of the x–y axes at the foot of the tree. Converted from static to vector force by the impact of the cannonball, the severed treetop gains velocity while traveling in a negative direction through the upper left-hand quadrant until it reaches the x axis (the ground) at a point of intersection with the vector represented by Billup and his horse. The result is a considerable amount of noise and confusion, little of which Billup appreciates since he has been rendered unconscious by the impact of a limb against the back of his skull. All this happens very quickly.

He wakes to find himself spread-eagled on his stomach, a limb across his buttocks, a second across his shoulders. He has no idea what has become of his horse or how he is going to extricate himself. After a few minutes of struggle, he is pretty damned sure that he isn't going to find the answer to either question any time soon, much less get the message to Beatty. Still, though he's incredibly uncomfortable, he doesn't seem to be much hurt. Someone will find him sooner or later. Until then, he might as well meditate on how best to describe his accident in terms of geometry. Should he ever be fortunate enough to return to the classroom, his students may find the example enlivening to an otherwise dreary subject. Then and now, it will help to pass the time.

$$\star \quad \star \quad \star$$

Pat Cleburne reads the last line of the message from Hardee again: *The moment of glory is upon us, Patrick.* Cleburne would like to believe, but he doubts. If we could just see what lies between us and the pike, he thinks. But first we have to plow through more of this damned forest, and my men are already as exhausted as I've ever seen them.

Cleburne's casualties have been brutal, exceeding forty percent in some regiments. North of the Wilkinson Pike, he halts his line to reorganize, and then sends Lucius Polk's brigade forward to probe for the Yankee line.

Posted in the thick cedars halfway between the Wilkinson and Nashville pikes, Colonel John Beatty knows nothing of the withdrawal of Scribner's and Shepherd's brigades. As Lucius Polk's skirmish line approaches through the open forest to the front, Beatty's men crouch low, hold their fire. The Johnnies come on cautiously, breath steaming, eyes searching for movement. They are men of all sizes, ages, and descriptions. Yet what remains in the memory is an impression of lean wolfishness, as if in another manifestation these men had been of that lupine clan found in dark tales of sleighs, winter steppes, and bawling infants torn from mothers' arms.

Beatty's men rise up, deliver a volley that seems in a thunderclap to sweep the woods bare of living men. In reality, most of Polk's skirmishers survive, disappearing to the rear under cover of the smoke or going doggo in brush or behind trees. Beatty's men tear cartridges in their teeth, ram powder and ball, steel rods rasping in barrels. Above the clatter of reloading they hear the Rebel battle line coming at the double quick, the pulsation accompanied by a rising gasp, hoarse at first, then breaking out in the high wail of the terrible Rebel yell that is enough to freeze the blood, the hand, halt a musket on the way to the shoulder, or to set a leveled barrel shaking so violently that the front sight blurs. Beatty's men fire, hurrah, reload, and fire again. The Rebels give way, fall back. Beatty rides down the line, yelling for his men to cease fire, to save their ammunition. The men comply, squint through the smoke to make out the effect of their volleys. Yet the butternut fallen blend in so perfectly with the forest floor that, save for the cries and thrashing of a few of the wounded, the woods might once again be empty, untouched, primeval.

Beatty sends couriers to ask Shepherd and Scribner for reinforcements, sends a third to petition Rousseau for a battery. The Rebels come on again, striking at the right flank held by the Union 15th Kentucky and its boy colonel, James B. Forman. Only twenty-one, Forman strides down his line, sword in hand, careless of the fire. His men, the greenest in a veteran brigade, hold among the rocks and trees until Forman suddenly staggers, sits down hard on the ground, and then tilts slowly over on his left side, his arms and legs curling up as if he had decided to nap amid the battle. The Union 15th Kentucky begins to tremble and, though the Johnnies are falling back, comes apart.

The slight hesitation of the Kentuckians before flight gives Beatty time to swing back the 88th Indiana to protect his flank. The Rebels charge again; but, decoyed by the flight of the Union 15th Kentucky, they present their right flank at an oblique angle to the 88th. The Union volley tears apart Polk's line, sends the remnants fleeing.

Men on both sides slump to the ground panting, rocking, trying to regroup senses shredded by nearly an hour of fighting. Beatty's couriers return, report that they have found no one right or left or immediately behind. As far as they can tell, Beatty's brigade is standing alone against the

Rebel advance. Beatty sucks meditatively at a tooth that has been bothering him since the day after the army marched from Nashville, then turns to his adjutant. "It would appear, Major, that the contingency of which General Rousseau spoke has come to pass: Hell has frozen over. Issue orders to withdraw in reverse line of battle. We'll try to hold together across the field."

Pat Cleburne has caught up with Lucius Polk. He reinforces Polk's assault on Beatty with S.A.M. Wood's brigade on the left and Vaughan's brigade (lent him by Cheatham) on the right. The three brigades strike before Beatty can get his withdrawal well underway. The Yankees break and run. Beatty tries to rally them, but his horse is shot from under him and he can only scramble up, grab his sword, and join the footrace across the cotton-field while Van Pelt's battery opens fire from the pike to cover the retreat.

In the wake of the latest Rebel victory, a pair of Alabamans from S.A.M. Wood's brigade pause by a shattered spruce to take a few minutes of ease. For more than a year, Jim Bundy and Jim Graffunder have shared their kits, their first names, the occasional whore, and a desire to avoid as much work and risk as possible without shirking beyond the limits of dignity. Pursuing Yankees across an open cottonfield is both work and risk: a task best left to greener boys.

They have just gotten their pipes lit when a distinctly Yankee voice speaks from the depths of the foliage behind them. "Say, could you fellows give me a hand here? I suppose it means I'll be a prisoner, but I'm too damned miserable to care."

Bundy and Graffunder have not lived this long without knowing when to move quickly and when to sit still. They sit still. After a moment, Bundy removes his pipe from his mouth. "What seems to be the problem, friend?"

"I'm trapped."

"Under this here treetop?"

"Yes, under this here treetop!"

"Hmmm. . . . Got a gun in there with you?"

"I've got a revolver, but I can't reach it."

"Then you ain't got a gun on us?"

"No."

"You sure?"

"Positive."

Bundy considers this, glances at Graffunder, who shrugs. They climb to their feet. Bundy spreads the branches while Graffunder trains his Enfield. Bundy squints into the shadows, makes out a spread-eagled form pinned to the ground by a pair of thick limbs. "Say, son, seems you're in a bit of a 'dicament."

"Yes, and it isn't getting any better as time passes."

"How'd you get under there in the first place?"

"It more got on top of me than me under it."

"Figures up the same."

"Are you gonna get me out, or not?"

Bundy looks at Graffunder, who shrugs again. "You an officer?" Bundy asks.

The Yank hesitates. "Yes."

"Cap'n?"

"Just a lieutenant."

"Well, that ain't so bad. We might not help you if you was a cap'n, but lootenants generally don't know no better."

Graffunder sets down his musket, and they begin wrestling with the treetop. "So what's your name?" Bundy asks.

"Art Billup."

"Not Lootenant-Arthur-call-me-goddamn-sir-Billup?"

"Not in present company."

Bundy laughs. "Got any whiskey?"

"No. Sorry."

"Any money?"

"A few dollars. You're welcome to it."

"Well, we could use a small loan."

They have torn their way through to Billup, together get hands under the large limb across his buttocks, and, with a grunt, lift the treetop. "Crawl out fast, Lootenant. We ain't gonna hold this all day."

Billup drags himself from under the treetop, manages to stand. He wobbles a few steps, unbuttons his fly, and urinates a long yellow stream. He shivers. "God, that feels good."

"Any blood in it?" Bundy asks.

Billup looks. "No."

"That's good. Way you was pinned, I was afraid you might've gotten ruptured."

"I seem to be all right," Billup says, flexing arms and legs. He buttons up, digs through his pockets, finds half a dozen soiled bills held by a clip.

"Don't you officers usually carry pocketbooks?" Bundy asks.

"Sorry. I left mine with the chaplain back in camp."

Bundy sighs, starts counting the money.

"So, where shall I go?" Billup asks.

Bundy looks at him curiously. "Go where you want, Lootenant. We're even."

"But I'm your prisoner."

Bundy glances at Graffunder, who doesn't even bother to shrug. "Not ours, Lootenant. Try to stay alive best you can. That's what we're planning to do."

"Call me Art." Billup extends a hand.

"Jim. Both of us. You be careful, now. Try not to shoot us and we'll try not to shoot you."

"Fair enough," Billup says, glances at the sky to verify his direction, and starts for the Federal line on the Nashville Pike. When he's ten yards away, Graffunder shoots him through the back of the head.

Bundy sucks on his pipe as Graffunder reloads. "Never knew what hit him. Way I'd want to go."

Graffunder shrugs. "Dead's dead."

CHAPTER 6

Wednesday, 8:00 A.M.–Noon
December 31, 1862
The Federal Center between the Wilkinson and Nashville Turnpikes

As Sheridan and Rousseau fight desperately to hold back the Rebel tide, pressure begins building on Negley's and Palmer's divisions between the Wilkinson Pike and Stones River. By late morning, Hazen's brigade of Palmer's division will hold the critical hinge of the Federal line in a modest grove of oak and cedar known locally as the Round Forest but dubbed Hell's Half Acre by Federal troops.

AZEN AND BIERCE squat beneath a gutta-percha blanket held by four orderlies, a map open between them. While Bierce orients the map with his compass, Hazen cocks his head to listen to the sound of heavy fighting to the south. He lays a finger on a small rectangle denoting a farm not far below the Wilkinson Pike. "Our flank must be here or a little to the west, which means Johnson's division has broken and Davis is giving back fast. What's this farm called?"

"Grisham or Gresham," Bierce says. "It's a hospital now. Johnson's reserve was posted near it last night. Also McCook's ammunition train. I spoke to his ordnance officer, a Captain Thruston."

"Well, he'd better be agile. Reb cavalry will be coming around the flank." Hazen studies the map. "Bragg is wheeling to his right by echelon of brigades. But from the sound of things, Sheridan's stuck an ax handle in the spokes. Until Bragg breaks Sheridan, our side will have a little time to set things right." He traces a finger along the line of the Wilkinson Pike. "I suspect General Rosecrans is already deploying Rousseau's division to Sheridan's right, here, behind the pike."

"Do you think Sheridan can hold long enough?"

"If it can be done, Phil Sheridan will do it."

"I thought you didn't like him."

"I don't, but he's a fighter."

They stand, the orderlies stepping back hastily with the blanket. Bierce rolls the map, slips it into a case while Hazen stares at the battle smoke rising above the cedars marking Sheridan's position a mile to the south. "Sheridan will give them all the trouble they can handle. He'll slip, he'll slide, keep them from hitting him solidly as long as he can. People think Sheridan's a brawler, a little Mick who doesn't know when to quit. But the truth is he's a devious bastard. And he's surpassingly ambitious, which people don't understand either."

"Is that why you don't like him?"

"It's why he doesn't like me. He knows I know him."

Hazen mounts his horse. A sharpshooter's bullet fired at a half mile or more sings by him. He ignores it, studies the surrounding fields. Unlike most of the Federal line, Hazen's position lies in open ground, its left abutting the Nashville Pike a half mile northwest of the intersection of the pike with the Nashville and Chattanooga Railroad. To the left of the pike, Wagner's brigade of Wood's division extends the line through a grove called the Round Forest, over the railroad, and into the fields fronting Stones River.

In the cedars to Hazen's right, Cruft's brigade occupies the remainder of the ground assigned to Crittenden's left wing. Beyond lies Negley's small division of Thomas's corps: Miller's brigade holding on to Cruft's right and Stanley's brigade holding on to Sheridan's left.

On Wayne's Hill, a Rebel cannon plumes white smoke and a shell howls overhead to explode in the cedars to the rear of Hazen's brigade. Bierce ducks but Hazen only glances irritably at the hill. "You must learn not to flinch, Bierce. On a battlefield you are largely as safe or as endangered from artillery fire one place as another. If you are unlucky enough to be in the wrong place, ducking won't save you."

"Yes, sir."

"There's still a chance we may advance this morning, and I'm concerned about maintaining the integrity of our line through that farmstead." Hazen points at the scorched remains of the Cowan house some four hundred yards to their front. "Go have a closer look at the layout. Find me the best way through. Better take a squad with you. Last night, some of Cruft's boys had a scrap with some Rebs over the farmhouse."

"I'll go alone if it's all right, Colonel. There's not much cover."

"As you wish."

Bierce rides across the pike, climbing the slight elevation into the Round Forest. He tethers his horse in the rear of Wagner's line and finds the adjutant. The man hesitates. "I'm not sure I can accept responsibility for your safety in Colonel Wagner's area."

"I'm not asking you to, Captain. Just pass word to your pickets that I'm going to scout down the railroad and then across to the Cowan farm." The man looks uncertain. "Look, I need to hurry," Bierce says. "Can I speak to your colonel?"

"No, no. I'd prefer not to bother him. I guess it's all right. But, remember, I haven't taken any responsibility for your safety."

"I'll be sure to keep that in mind if I'm shot, Captain."

Bierce works his way along the railroad embankment, taking advantage of the small cover. Half a dozen times bullets slap into the clay on the opposite side or strike rock and whir away overhead, but there is no way to know if he is the actual target. Abreast of the Cowan house, he scuttles across the turnpike to the edge of an unpicked cottonfield. He lies panting in a shallow ditch for several minutes before starting to crawl through the cotton toward the farm. Across the river there are hundreds of cold, wet infantrymen on the slopes of Wayne's Hill, every one looking for an excuse to take revenge on a Yankee. There may even be an artillery sergeant sufficiently resentful that he will risk his lieutenant's ire for wasting a round of shell or case on a lone Yankee slithering through the cotton.

If Bierce could change one law of physics, he would treble the speed of sound, for he fears not so much dying as dying unawares, that he will not hear the bullet or shell that kills him, will have at most only a vague sense of a disturbance of the air in the instant before death. He remembers watching a snake coiling through the wet grass of the yard back home in Ohio, himself on the porch with a broken leg, immobile for all the demands of his sixteen-year-old body to move, to hunt, to crave, as the snake must have craved in its ophidic alertness to scent, heat, and vibration in the moment before Bierce's father took three long strides, his hoe already descending to sever the serpent's head, though it was only a bullsnake and harmless except to moles and field mice.

Bierce is halfway across the two hundred yards to the farm when he feels through his belly—as the snake might have felt—the vibration of footfalls. He pauses, listening to the rap of drummed cadence, and then peeks over the top of the cotton to see the long blue ranks of Hazen's brigade advancing toward the farm. Cruft's brigade emerges from the cedars to the left, falling in alongside. Both brigades have skirmishers deployed a hundred yards to the front and it is these nervous men who frighten Bierce. He crawls forward as fast as he can, reaches the cover of the outbuildings with his palms and knees raw and his lungs gasping. He stands shakily, rests his back against warped, sun-bleached boards. He will wait here for the line, take no chance on being shot by accident.

At first, the singing is almost too low to hear, the words coming three or four at a time, as if the old hymn wandered in an eddy of disheartened fragments about the desolate farm. But it is the whining accompaniment that raises the hair on Bierce's nape, for though the singing is explicable enough—the easily imagined crooning of a wounded man trying to comfort himself—the accompaniment hints at nothing human in its anguished discordance. Bierce has vowed to understand horror in all its manifestations, but he is in this moment terrified almost to the point of flight. He huddles shivering against the wall until the panic recedes, then unfastens the holster of his Colt and slides the weapon free. Rising, he takes a step toward the corner of the shed. For a moment the voice seems to hesitate and then continues its song, the whining accompaniment uninterrupted. Bierce recognizes *'Tis So Sweet to Trust in Jesus* in the instant he steps around the corner and points the Colt at the two men leaning against each other in the dank, fetid passage between the sheds.

Both men are grievously wounded, though Bierce cannot at first make out the exact nature of their injuries in the dim light. The taller of the two— the one who is humming the whining accompaniment—nudges the other with an elbow. The singer raises a face black with powder burns, the blisters oozing blood. One eye is swollen shut, the other shot away, leaving a pulpy mass where it should be. Or that is the impression Bierce has until the soldier lifts a hand to push a dangling flap of skin back onto his forehead, the revealed eye shockingly blue in the burned face. The mouth opens, its red equally disturbing, smiles. "Well, howdy, Lieutenant. Gloomy day, ain't it. Private John Polinex, Union Second Kentucky, at your service."

"From Cruft's brigade."

"Right you are, Lieutenant." The other figure makes a sound like gurgled laughter. Polinex glances at him. "And this here is Willie or Billy or Arty or something. God knows what his last name is. He's a Reb but not a bad fellow."

Bierce peers at the Rebel and makes out in the shadows what he has missed before and what explains the man's inability to make more than gurgles and whines. "Christ!" he hears himself say.

"Nope, pretty sure it ain't him," Polinex says, "though I suspect getting crucified might be a damned sight more comfortable than what ails him." He moves obligingly out of the way, talking on while Bierce squats to examine the Reb's wound. "But though he ain't no Jesus, I think you might fairly call me Polyphemus after that Cyclops in the story about Ulysses and his wanderings. My pa read it to me when I was a kid and I recall liking 'specially the part where Ulysses and his boys drove that heated stake straight into ol' Polyphemus's eye. But now I think I'd side with the Cyclops, advise him to eat up those Greek sailors afore they got to thinkin' too much."

At another time, Bierce might have found Polinex's blather amusing, but he ignores it now. The Reb opens his mouth wide for Bierce to see. The ramrod has entered the man's mouth at a slightly downward angle, skewering the tongue, passing through the pharynx, and exiting through the posterior musculature of the spine, leaving some nine inches of exposed rod outside the mouth, the remaining two and a half feet protruding from the back of the neck.

"I seen them ramrods shot before," Polinex says. "Specially by raw regiments, almost like a shower of arrows ol' Ulysses might've seen in his time. At first, he was asking me to pull it out, but I was afraid it'd kill him. So we've been singing songs and waiting for a little help. Figure it had to come sooner or later from one side or t'other."

"How'd you men come to be here?"

"We was out here last night with skirmish parties, poking around the old place, when we ran into each other. Far as I know, we was the only two got hurt 'cept for a couple boys that got killed over by the corncrib. I was carrying a howitzer charge wrapped up in my slicker. It was the captain's idea that we'd mine one of the sheds to give the Rebs a surprise. When the firing started, I set it down by my feet to do a little work with my Springfield. I don't know what happened next. Maybe I set it off with my own gun. Maybe the damned charge got hit by a bullet somebody shot at me. Anyway, it went off with me standing almost on top of it."

"A wonder it didn't kill you."

"Well, it didn't exactly explode, Lieutenant, more flashed up, if you get my meaning. I was just about to fire my rifle, and the hammer cut my forehead. Did a pretty good job from what I can tell. I went and rolled in a puddle till my pants stopped burning and, when the fightin' was over, I went over to the corncrib and took the trousers off one of those dead boys. It was there I found Arty or whatever his name is."

Bierce, who distrusts sympathy almost as much as he distrusts heroism, places a hand on Arty's shoulder. The man makes his gurgling laugh, tries to smile. Bierce looks away, embarrassed, rises and goes to the corner of the passage to check on the progress of the brigade. The battle line has halted, the skirmishers kneeling while a pair of Union batteries duel with the Rebel guns on Wayne's hill. Behind the line, Bierce can make out General John Palmer cantering toward Hazen. He turns to the men. "I've got to make a few notes for my colonel. Then I'll see if I can help you back to our lines."

Polinex has apparently run out of talk, sits with head hanging, the flap of skin fallen over his good eye. The Reb has leaned his cheek to the wall, attempting to rest despite the protruding ramrod. He looks oddly peaceful. "Sure, Lieutenant," Polinex says. "Take your time."

Despite the roar of heavy fighting on the right, Brigadier General John Palmer has received no order canceling Rosecrans's original plan. Shortly after 8:00 A.M., he orders Hazen's and Cruft's brigades forward, Grose's brigade following in support, with the intention of crossing Stones River below McFadden's Ford to support Van Cleve's attack on Bragg's right flank. But when Negley's brigades do not appear on his right, Palmer calls a halt to wait for further instructions. He rides to Hazen's position, finds him studying the Cowan farm through his field glasses.

"What are you looking for, Bill?"

Hazen lowers the glasses. "I sent my topographical officer to have a look at the farmstead. He's a rather irritating youngster, but I'd prefer not to have him shot by my own skirmishers. Have you heard anything from General Crittenden?"

"No, but Negley's holding back and Sheridan's catching hell. I'm going to hold the line here until my adjutant gets back with a clarification."

Hazen nods. He is a professional, dislikes halting a maneuver in mid-sequence; but Palmer is a good man, has made the cautious decision.

Ten minutes later, Palmer's adjutant gallops up. "General, we're to fall back to our original position, extending our left across the pike and the railroad. General Rosecrans is pulling Van Cleve back and sending him along with Harker's and Hascall's brigades to shore up McCook."

Palmer is incredulous. "The general is sending *five* brigades to the right?"

"Four, General. He's leaving Price at the ford."

"Who'd you get this from?"

"General Wood."

Palmer compresses his lips. "McCook's gotten into shit up to his neck again. All right, Bill," he says to Hazen, "deploy on the far side of the pike. It'll be you and Wagner between there and the river, apparently. Entirely too little for too much ground, but do your best. I'll go see to Cruft."

As Palmer rides off, there is a roar to the south in front of Sheridan's position, a fresh Rebel attack going in.

Bierce, Polinex, and Arty—if that is truly his name—hear the sudden surge of firing to the south. Bierce makes rapid sketches of the layout of sheds and fences about the ruins of the Cowan house, then steps back into the cover of the passage. He flips through his sketches, decides he has enough, and then glances toward the brigade. The skirmishers are falling back on the main line, which itself seems poised to withdraw, though it is impossible to say exactly what it is in the posture of the ranks that indicates a retrograde movement. Involuntarily, Bierce feels himself tense, afraid to be left behind.

"Don't even think about it, Lieutenant." Bierce turns to Polinex, sees the pistol dangling from the wounded man's hand. It is an unusual weapon to see in these days when soldiers have discarded all but the bare necessities from their kits: a pocket pistol of the sort often called a bulldog, a lethal weapon for alleys, sailors' dens, and the sleeves of gamblers but an absurd weapon on the battlefield. Yet its menace is perhaps all the greater for the incongruity of its appearance in Polinex's hand. Polinex makes an almost apologetic gesture with the pistol. "We ain't gonna be left behind, Lieutenant. You're gonna get us across that field somehow. Elsewise, we're gonna die here and we ain't partial to that outcome."

Arty gives his gurgling laugh around the ramrod, a long string of bloody saliva sliding from his mouth to the dirt between his splayed legs.

"I wasn't going to leave you," Bierce says.

"Well, that's good, Lieutenant, though it'd be natural enough, what with the things you're suppose ta be doin' out here for your colonel. So you can't blame us for being suspicious, us not knowing you real well and all."

Bierce weighs a half dozen ironic responses, rejects them all. "We have to go. My brigade is falling back."

Polinex nods, struggles to his feet, and reaches down to help Arty up.

"You can put away the pistol," Bierce says. "I'm not going to run."

"Oh, I'm sure you're not, Lieutenant, but I'll keep it handy all the same."

Bierce ties his handkerchief to a stick, and together the three step from the cover of the passage. "Wave that flag a little," Polinex instructs. "Let them see our flowing white banner of submission."

Arty laughs, gurgles.

"Of course," Polinex says, "could be a flowing banner of truce, even of cease-fire. That'd be better. You see, Arty and me kinda worked things out last night. We figure if all the boys North and South were just to go home, leaving you officers to settle things among yourselves, this war might actually accomplish something. You'd have a fine time killing each other, and we'd have a fine time never taking orders from the likes of you again, in or out of uniform. Which'd be a good thing. No offense meant."

"None taken."

"See, as officers go, you don't seem a bad fellow. Just all us boys are kinda sick of this war. It weren't so bad at first, but it's gotten damned uncomfortable of late. So we figure it's time to leave it to them that gives a damn how it turns out. Which pretty much means officers, from all we can tell. So Arty and me are fixin' on going home, figuring most of the other boys will follow us pretty soon."

Polinex ceases his wheezing monologue. Bierce glances back, sees him walking head down, the flap of skin and flesh dangling over his good eye. Arty, his mouth wide, the ramrod protruding like a half-swallowed arrow, has taken his arm, guides him across the furrows. Arty seems almost cheerful, as if his wound is familiar: painful but expected. He might, Bierce supposes, have been a medieval foot soldier in some former life, skewered by a crossbow bolt while storming castle walls. Perhaps he fought at Châlus-Chabrol where Richard Coeur de Lion was struck down by an arrow through the eye; Richard the sodomite, insane with drink, venereal pox, and lost reputation. In his desperation, Richard would have been ten times dangerous, for it is wild romantics gone mad who get the likes of Arty and Polinex killed in any age.

Above them, there is the howl of a plunging shell, and though Hazen has told him never to duck, Bierce cringes.

"What the devil?"

Hazen turns at the exclamation from his adjutant, looks out past the retreating picket line. Three figures move haltingly across the unharvested field, the geyser of an exploding shell raining them with mud and white bolls of cotton. He lifts his field glasses, sees Bierce holding aloft a white rag on a stick, behind him two wounded men, one in blue, one in butternut, moving like a single beast, so joined are they at hip and shoulder. A second shell explodes near them. Bierce is frantically waving the pitiful banner, first in the direction of Wayne's Hill and the Rebel batteries and then toward the Federal batteries under the cedars behind Palmer's division.

"For God's sake, run, man!" the adjutant growls.

Hazen says nothing, continues to watch. The two wounded men are dancing now, or at least that is the impression they give as they wheel over the furrows, the cotton hiding them from thigh down, so that they seem to wobble legless across a froth of white. Hazen can see Bierce screaming at them, then another shell falls and another and another and the dancers—for that is how Hazen will remember them always—are lost in the successive explosions. The smoke eddies away, and Hazen can make out Bierce on his knees in the cotton, gazing at the vacancy of blasted mud, his mouth wide though it is impossible at this distance to tell if he is laughing or crying.

"I'll go get him," the adjutant says quietly.

Hazen lowers his field glasses. "Send an orderly; you've got more important work." He turns away to start redeploying his line north of the Nashville Pike in the Round Forest.

☆ ☆ ☆

While Cheatham and Cleburne bash away at Sheridan, Major General Jones Withers, commanding the Confederate division to the right of Cheatham, sits his horse on a low rise southeast of the Cowan farm. With him is Brigadier General James Chalmers, a fractious thirty-one-year-old Mississippi prosecutor with a natural bent for war. He makes Withers, who is nearly fifty, feel old.

They watch Hazen and Cruft's line advance toward the Cowan farm and then draw up, as if offering battle in the open. Chalmers fidgets. "Shall we attack, General?"

"No, not yet."

"General, my men have been lying in muddy rifle pits for the better part of two days without fires or hot food. I would like to give them some action."

"Shortly, James. Shortly. Let the Yanks come a little closer."

"But they may fall back. Then it will be us who have to cross the open."

Withers does not reply. All these young men so eager to fight, so eager to risk death. Was he like that, an eternity ago in Mexico? He supposes he must have been, though it was but a brief affliction of the spirit.

To the south, the sound of fighting swells: Manigault and Maney going in hard against Sheridan. Chalmers can hardly contain himself. "General, please, if I can't attack, may I at least—"

"Watch for a moment, James. I think you may have been right about the Yankees withdrawing."

In the field to their front, Hazen's skirmishers have begun falling back.

Chalmers rises up in his saddle, as if he might shout at the Yankees to hold their position until he has had time to convince this stubborn old man to let him attack. He settles back. "Yellowbellies. Can't stand to fight in the open."

Withers does not comment, spends a long moment studying his watch. Overhead, shells howl back and forth between Wayne's Hill and the cedars cloaking the Federal batteries. At last, he sighs. "I'd hoped Cheatham would make better headway by now, but we can't wait any longer. Prepare to attack. Perhaps we can relieve the pressure long enough for Cheatham to break through."

"Yes, sir! By your leave, then."

Withers nods, watches as Chalmers canters down the rise to his brigade. Where the hell is Bragg? Or Polk? Someone else to make the decision sending so many young men to their deaths. Well, by echelon then. Chalmers first, then Donelson as soon as the line in front of Chalmers begins to give.

Major Joseph O. Thompson, acting commanding officer of the 44th Mississippi, Chalmers's Brigade, could weep while inspecting his men. They are good men, fine men, veterans. Then why in hell are they being expected to fight with flintlock muskets little better than clubs? It is insulting, humiliating, mad. He clenches his jaw, stalks down the line.

Three weeks ago, when Colonel Blythe was carried deathly ill to the hospital, the division chief surgeon put the regiment under quarantine. The men accepted their lot, busied themselves with the innumerable small tasks that keep soldiers from lassitude or outright insanity in the endless tedium of camp life. They played cards, read, sewed buttons, stitched seams, wrote home, threw dice, told the same old stories again, and cleaned their new Enfield rifle-muskets, of which they were inordinately proud. So it was an extraordinary agony when the brigade ordnance officer arrived to gather up the Enfields for distribution elsewhere. The men cast hard looks Thompson's way, grumbled that Colonel Blythe would never have let this happen to his boys.

The regiment was released from quarantine the day after Christmas. Thompson sent a detail to the ordnance officer for weapons and waited in his tent with an anticipation he hadn't felt since Christmases as a child. But when the detail returned, the men were stricken, stunned with humiliation. Wordlessly, the sergeant threw back the canvas atop one of the wagons to reveal a jumble of rusted, dented, and bent muskets, some of them awkward percussion-cap conversions, many still with their original flint locks. Thompson picked up an 1816 Harpers Ferry musket with a cracked stock, a missing hammer, and no ramrod.

"The ramrods are in the other wagon," the sergeant said. "They just gave us a bunch and told us to match them up the best we could. Half of 'em are bent."

"How about bayonets?"

"They spared us one for the entire regiment, Major. Ain't much of one neither."

Thompson started to drop the musket on the pile, thought better of it. "I must go see the general. In the meantime, do your best to salvage something from this . . . this refuse."

"Yes, sir," the sergeant said.

But there were no better weapons. General Chalmers would like to say otherwise, but he cannot: 44th Mississippi must do the best it can to requisition arms on the field of battle. Thompson tried to argue, held up the battered, hammerless Model 1816, but Chalmers cut him short: "Major, we are a small nation fighting a large nation that is far superior in manufacturing capacity, including the means to produce firearms. Therefore, we must take from their soldiers what we need to maintain our independence. That should not be too difficult as long as we remember that Southern manhood excels theirs by a far larger margin than their manufacturing capacity exceeds ours."

Thompson, who until a few months ago had taught French, classics, and introductory logic in a boys' school in Biloxi, blinked several times. "But if we are to win our independence—"

"We do not need to win it, sir! It is ours by natural right. We have declared it, now we must defend it."

"But, General, my men—"

"Tell your men to be manful! Tell them to go forward with a bold front and whatever weapons come to hand. Defeating the Yankees will provide them with more than enough to choose from in the way of arms."

The men of the 44th Mississippi stand downcast, only loosely at attention, as Thompson inspects the line a final time before the attack. Many have refused to carry the rusted flintlocks at all, have chosen hefty clubs or staffs instead. A few have spades with sharpened edges. Still others have axes and old swords. My God, Thompson thinks, give us a few pitchforks and scythes and we shall look like the Paris mob storming the Bastille.

He returns to the center of the line, sets himself as if he actually had the confidence he means to assume. "All right, boys. We've got more to fight for than just victory. Today I'd see us become a legend: the regiment that thrashed the Yankees with clubs and fouled flintlocks. After this fight, we shall be the best-equipped regiment in the army. And no one—mark you, no one—will ever take our rifles again."

For a long moment, there is silence, then someone starts to cheer and then the entire regiment is whooping its agreement. Thompson is startled, has to blink back tears. Please, God, he prays, let it come true. Don't let these boys down.

Bierce stands a few yards from Hazen, watching the quiet woods beyond the Cowan house. Except to give his report, he has not spoken to his colonel since returning. Hazen pauses in his pacing, stares at Bierce with his usual mix of irritation and irony. "You are quiet, Lieutenant. No philosophical observations?"

"No, Colonel."

"Did you see something out there that shocked even you?"

Bierce hesitates. "No, Colonel. I'm afraid I saw nothing that didn't confirm my opinions."

"And the confirmation?"

"Just two wounded men caught between the lines, Colonel. Nothing exceptional."

Shortly after 9:00 A.M., with the bizarrely armed 44th Mississippi on the right flank, Chalmers's brigade steps out to the rap of drums and the playing of *The Bonny Blue Flag*. The latter is a rather dismal effort, the band having difficulty concentrating on the music in the cold, the damp, and the slippery footing. The distance to the Yankee line is wide, eight hundred yards, and all of it under a rain of case, shell, and solid shot.

Halfway across the open, when the advance should be gaining momentum for a charge, the line becomes entangled in the sheds and fences of the Cowan farm. It emerges into the cottonfield in two parts. Led by Chalmers himself, the 7th, 10th, and 41st Mississippi sweep ahead against Cruft's line, while the 9th and 44th Mississippi angle to the right to strike Hazen's position in the Round Forest.

The 31st Indiana and the Union 2nd Kentucky of Cruft's brigade wait behind fences, boulders, and hastily erected breastworks until the Rebels are within easy range, then lay down sheet after sheet of volley fire until the field to their front is hidden in acrid smoke. Chalmers's line stumbles back, regains its footing, and plunges forward with a yell. But Cruft's men are veterans, too, answer the high-pitched yelling with a growling cheer of their own, and stand to the work. Fifty yards short of the Yankee line, Chalmers can take his men no farther. They hold there, blazing into the smoking

woods while the Yankees blaze back. It is hellish, indescribable, the smoke
so thick that no one on either side can make out a clear target to the front
or a friend a half dozen paces to left or right. Many of Chalmers's men strip
bolls of cotton from the plants to shove in their ears against the din. Yankee
gunners ram double canister, cut fuses short so that shells explode only feet
above the Rebel line. It is dangerous, but the Yankee gunners are surpassingly confident while, as usual, the Rebels are given nothing in the way of
support from their own batteries.

Chalmers, riding his third horse of the morning, gallops behind the line,
shouting for a bayonet charge. A shell fragment that has already decapitated
one private and torn the arm off another expends most of its remaining
velocity ricocheting off Chalmers's skull. He drops senseless into the cotton.
The line gives way, the staff officers too confused and deafened to assume
direction of the line. Command should devolve on Colonel T. W. White of
the 9th Mississippi, but no one knows where to find him.

Colonel White is leading the 9th and the ill-armed 44th Mississippi against
the Round Forest. At first the advance seems strangely easy despite the
artillery fire, but then the 41st Ohio rises up from cover to open a tremendous fire on the Mississippians. The Rebel line goes to ground to return fire.
Among the men of the 44th, soldiers struggle with their ancient weapons,
trying to prime locks and coax sparks from wet flints. Men armed only with
clubs, staffs, spades, axes, and broken muskets can do nothing except
scrabble in the earth for rocks to hurl at the Yankee line. Several of the flintlocks explode, iron fragments injuring a dozen men. Private Absalom
McMurra's musket lets off a sputter of escaping gas, more a fart than an
explosion. He lowers it in disgust only to have it kick violently in his hands.
To his horror, he sees the slouch hat of the private lying in front of him go
cartwheeling across the field. The private feels about his scalp for blood or
perhaps flame, finds none, and goes back to wrestling with his own flintlock. McMurra is shaking too hard to risk reloading, lies down to survive or
not survive as God wills.

Amazingly, the Rebel line holds for an hour under the Yankee fire until
the 41st Ohio, its ammunition exhausted, gives way to the 9th Indiana. The
disciplined fire of the Hoosiers is too much. The Mississippi line falls back.
Most of the 9th Mississippi streams back to the abandoned rifle pits. The
majority of the 44th Mississippi takes cover in a hollow behind the Cowan
house, where the men will become spectators to the carnage for the rest of
the day. To augment their flintlocks and improvised weapons, the regiment
has gathered a total of eight abandoned rifle-muskets, none of them Federal.

In the shelter of the hollow, Private McMurra hands his hat to the private whose head he nearly shot off. The man nods, inspects the inside for lice, then pulls it down over his forehead, nearly to his eyes, folds his arms, and falls asleep.

☆ ☆ ☆

Watching from the low ridge southeast of the Cowan farm, it seems to Major General Jones Withers that Chalmers's brigade is pushing the Yankees slowly but steadily into the cedars. He trots forward to the rifle pits, where Brigadier General Daniel Smith Donelson has mustered his big Tennessee brigade.

"General," Withers calls. "You can make ready to go forward momentarily."

Donelson turns, a ferocious old man with rumpled hair, the burning eyes of a zealot, and a mouth set hard by unabashed certainty. "About damned time! We should have gone in half an hour ago."

Withers ignores this, begins delivering careful instructions. Old Dan nods impatiently, mutters: "Yes, yes, of course."

A sudden ripple of consternation runs down the ranks. Withers looks up, is stunned to see Chalmers's brigade streaming across the field through the raining fire of the Yankee guns. "Goddamn it!" old Dan snarls. He kicks his horse forward, bringing his sword up to order the charge.

"General!" Withers shouts.

Donelson wheels his horse. "What, goddamn it?"

"You can't go forward and maintain your ranks. Not against that flood."

"We'll push them aside with bayonets or drive them before us!"

Withers stares steadily at the old man until Donelson lets his sword arm drop limp to his side. "I am disappointed, too, General," Withers says. "I may have erred in not sending you forward sooner. But now we will have to wait another chance. Open your ranks, let Chalmers's men through, and then join me. We'll plan what to do next."

Shortly after 10:00 A.M., the firing all along the line eases for perhaps twenty minutes. Sheridan holds on, amid the cedars and limestone outcroppings north of the Wilkinson Pike. Davis has given way under Cleburne's pounding, but Rousseau has managed to bring in the brigades of Beatty, Shepherd, and Grose in to cover Sheridan's right.

Shortly after halting Donelson, Withers receives Brigadier General Alexander Stewart's cool note announcing his intention of leading his brigade against Sheridan's stronghold. Withers supposes it is inevitable:

Cheatham has squandered his brigades and Patton Anderson's brigade, too, and now Withers and Stewart must throw weight in his direction rather than minding their own responsibilities. Well, Stewart will get the job done. If there is a man in this army serving far below his capacities, it is Stewart. If asked, Withers would cede command to him in a moment and go home to raise troops. Or, better still, let Stewart take Polk's place. Send the Bishop off to raise money and recruits; Withers would happily take orders from Stewart.

He takes a dispatch book, writes: *General, I trust completely in your success. I will order Donelson forward when I hear your attack.*

While Stewart sites his batteries and briefs his colonels, Donelson's Tennessee brigade waits behind the flimsy breastworks constructed by Chalmers's men in their two-day wait in the rain. The 8th Tennessee doesn't enjoy even that much protection, must wait behind the slender cover of a rail fence. The range from the Yankee line is eight hundred yards, but a Springfield or an Enfield can kill at a thousand yards and more. Minié balls sing across the field, slapping into the fence, the ground, and occasionally a man. By the end of fifteen minutes, the 8th has suffered twenty dead and wounded. But though this sacrifice is hard, harder than any made when the feet are moving forward, the 8th stands firm with the rest of the brigade. All Donelson's Tennesseans have something to prove: a question of manhood to the general they hate to a man, General Braxton Horse's-Ass Bragg, who despises Tennesseans almost as much as he hates (with solid reason, the Tennesseans believe) the Kentucks.

Considering the amount of their blood Bragg had squandered at Shiloh and Perryville, the Tennesseans have long guessed his animosity. But in the last month they've had documentary evidence: a letter written by none other than the general's whore-witch wife, Elise. How exactly a copy of the letter came to be passed around the brigade staff and eventually—in a dozen copies—through the ranks, no one knows or is willing to admit. But few doubt its authenticity: *Dear husband, please do not trust the Tennessee troops. Put the Tennesseans where your batteries can fire upon them if they attempt to run. Lead them into action yourself and shame them into fighting.*

All right, we're waiting, General. Lead us yourself. And when we're done whupping those Yankee boys, we'll invite you to count our wounds, invite you to count how many prisoners and guns we've taken, invite you to count all the dead and wounded—theirs and ours—we've strewn across the landscape; and then you can tell us why you and your whore don't trust Tennesseans.

Oddly, the one man in the entire brigade who may not have seen the letter is Brigadier General Dan Smith Donelson. Not that it matters greatly; he already despises Bragg with every fiber of his sixty-two-year-old body. Others may call him "Old Dan," but Dan Donelson doesn't feel old. Age has only burned away the foolishness of youth, the glut—the veritable hyperemia—of desire for food, drink, and women. He feels purged, supple, immeasurably alive. He has no more desires, save to show them all how sixty-two is not old, but rather transcendent with power. He could be a shaman, already looks the part, can feel the power roaring into him from the ground, the trees, the very air. Give him the order, goddamn it, it is time for Dan Donelson to kill Yankees.

Shortly before 10:30 A.M., as Alex Stewart's batteries open a devastating fire on Roberts's portion of Sheridan's line, Withers orders Donelson's brigade forward. Watching from behind Cruft's batteries, Brigadier General John Palmer is deeply moved, will later write his wife: *They came toward our position in solid lines and moving in admirable order. It was not easy to witness that magnificent array of Americans without emotion.*

But the Cowan farm still stands in the way. Like Chalmers's brigade before them, Donelson's regiments lose their careful order in the warren of sheds and fences. The brigade straggles into the cottonfield as the Yankee guns open from the cedars ahead and the Round Forest on the right. Grimly, Donelson prods the line into order. A battery of Federal Napoleons deploys in front of the Round Forest, trying to enfilade Donelson's line at an angle that will make every solid shot a dozen times lethal. Donelson splits off the 16th and half of the 51st Tennessee to drive the guns back under the cover of the trees while he pushes ahead against Cruft's smoking line.

Captain Drury Spurlock, whose parents came to Murfreesboro the day before to tell him of his brother's death, leads Company C, 16th Tennessee, along the railroad embankment toward the Round Forest. His brother died of a wound gotten fighting for the Confederacy's hold on Kentucky, a state too gutless to fight for its own rights. What does Spurlock fight for? He had answers once, could add revenge for his brother's death, but he can't imagine any reasons now. He is terrified. God, they are all terrified, go forward because others go forward, drive ahead shooting, screaming, sobbing. The first bullet strikes him to the left of the navel, puncturing his spleen, the second tears through his left lung, the third enters just below the left nostril, passing through the oral cavity to lodge in the hard muscle right of the spinal cord. The succession of impacts is so rapid that he cannot for a moment absorb the reality that he has been hit at all. He stumbles, curious why his legs have suddenly gone wooden, then pitches onto the hard-packed cinders. He lies there, feet passing over him, other men falling nearby, wonders at the oddity of the cinders, their burned-out desolation. I'll roll onto my back, he thinks, let my eyes clear, then pick one up and look at it carefully. He has the sudden realization that he is wounded, is probably dying. Poor mother, he wants to think. Poor father. But he cannot keep his mind from wandering. I'll roll over in a moment. That will make everything clearer. But the moment stretches out, becomes immaterial.

Colonel John H. Savage, commanding the 16th Tennessee, sees Spurlock go down. A moment later, Savage's brother and second in command, Lieutenant Colonel L. N. Savage, pitches from his horse. Major James Womack swings a leg over his saddle to go to the lieutenant colonel's aid, but a Yankee minié ball tears through his shoulder before he can dismount. The major yells, tries to regain his seat, but loses it. He lands next to the lieutenant colonel, lies writhing in pain.

Colonel Savage curses, kicks his horse off the embankment in a shower of black cinders. Donelson is a hundred yards away, pushing his line toward Cruft. "Donelson, you goddamned fool!" Savage screams. "You're going to get us all killed!"

Donelson turns in his saddle, eyes glittering like an ancient cockatrice that might at any moment rise winged from the slough of the man. "Return to your men, Colonel, or I shall shoot you myself!"

"Murderer!" Savage snarls.

In the middle of Donelson's line, Colonel William L. Moore feels his horse shudder beneath him. A half dozen years ago, Moore might have been agile enough to jump free; but his second wife has proven a far better cook than the first, and Moore's girth has expanded by a belt notch with each passing year. The mare goes down on her knees, as if giving him another moment to get free, but he is too slow, and she rolls onto her side, pinning Moore's leg beneath her. The line pushes forward without them, losing definition in the battle smoke and the fountains of earth, cotton, and flesh thrown up by the exploding shells of the Yankee cannons. Moore curses his slowness of body, his even more unforgivable slowness of mind. He grabs his knee with both hands, tries to wrench his ankle free. Come on, girl, rise up a little.

The mare tries, slumps back. So does the colonel. Damn. Double and triple damn. He grits his teeth against the pain of her weight, manages to free his saber. God, he hates to do this. Damned good horse. Hit in the chest but went down like a camel to give him time to jump free. And he'd been too damned slow. He prods her with the point of the saber. Come on, girl. You can rest in a minute. Just rise up now. That's it, that's it.

Moore hobbles to his feet as the mare lays her head down again. He would like to dispatch her with his revolver, but it is gone, perhaps lying beneath her, and he has no time to find another. He limps forward as fast as he can to overtake his line. Damned good horse. He'll miss her.

Brigadier General Charles Cruft cannot imagine what ferocity drives the Rebels forward through the cannon blasts. He orders his reserve regiment, 1st Kentucky Union Volunteers, into the cottonfield to blunt the charge. Briefly, Cruft's tactic seems to work. Colonel David Enyart deploys the 1st Kentucky smartly, first rank kneeling, second and third ranks standing, in the classic formation for volley firing since the time of Marlborough. Colonel John Carter of the 38th Tennessee responds exactly as Cruft hoped, halting his regiment to the front left of the Cowan house and returning fire by volleys.

Carter's halt uncovers the flank of the 8th Tennessee to a murderous fire from the 31st Indiana and Captain William Standart's Battery B, 1st Ohio Artillery. The 8th Tennessee shudders to a halt. Lieutenant Colonel John H. Anderson, commanding the 8th in place of Colonel Moore, is trying to mount a charge when the colonel reappears, limping but otherwise seemingly uninjured. "How is it we're stalled, Anderson?" he shouts.

Anderson stares at him. "Colonel! I thought—"

"Yes, so did I for a moment. Come on, the men can't stay here."

Moore pushes through the line, sword uplifted. Color Sergeant J. M. Rice sees him, shouts "Come on, boys. The colonel's back."

But before the word can spread far enough to stimulate a cheer or a lunge toward the Yankee line, both Moore and Rice are felled by Hoosier bullets. Shot through the heart, Moore is killed instantly. Rice tries to struggle ahead on his knees but slumps forward, the banner going down into the smoke.

To the left, the slugging match between the Union 1st Kentucky and Carter's 38th Tennessee has taken on a more modern look, every soldier firing as fast as he can while maintaining as low a profile as possible short of digging a hole. Satisfied that he's done his job in stalling the Rebel charge, Enyart begins withdrawing the 1st. But rather than finding Cruft's main line shored up in the minutes won in the open field, the Union 1st Kentucky stumbles into a scene of inexplicable chaos, courtesy of Brigadier General Alexander P. Stewart, C.S.A.

✯ ✯ ✯

It has always puzzled Alex Stewart that his men call him "Old Straight." He has never viewed himself as particularly stern or strict. He likes his boys, enjoys a joke, will sit up late with his young officers trying to untangle a philosophical conundrum. When he sits for a photograph, he smiles. But he does believe in rigor—in order, method, accuracy, and preparation, whatever the task. After fifteen years of teaching these principles as professor of mathematics and natural philosophy at Cumberland University in Nashville, he sees no reason to abandon them now that he has once again donned a uniform.

The attacks on Sheridan have failed because they were made piecemeal without effective artillery support. Stewart doesn't intend to make the same mistakes, even if his lengthy preparations cause other commanders some personal distress. Their comfort is not his concern. At 10:25 A.M., he sends his infantry forward behind the first effective Rebel bombardment of the day. The infantry breaches the east side of Sheridan's stronghold, ending nearly three hours of furious Yankee resistance.

By 11:00 A.M., Stewart has ripped a gaping hole in the center of the Federal line. The brigades of Patton Anderson, Manigault, and Maney come in on his left, widening the breakthrough as Stewart wheels to charge Colonel Timothy R. Stanley's brigade of Negley's division.

Colonel William B. Cassilly, commanding the 69th Ohio Volunteers of Stanley's brigade, hates the cold. After all, Bill B. Cassilly isn't a young man anymore. Not old, mind you, but old enough to worry about the cold penetrating the joints and triggering the rheumatism. And that worry justifies a certain amount of medicinal brandy. So it is that the colonel is taking a counteractant dram when Stewart hits Stanley's line. By now, five Rebel batteries have coordinated their fire. The result is not a rain of shot on Cassilly's position, but an absolute deluge. The colonel tries to ride through it to bolster the confidence of his men, but his damned horse won't cooperate, insists on bolting for the rear. "I have to see the general," Cassilly shouts at Major Eli J. Hickcox as his steed carries him out of sight.

Hickcox does not exactly know what the colonel has shouted, but gathers that he is now in command. "Hold on, boys, hold on!" he yells. "Take the best cover you can." This is, of course, not only a superfluous command but a rather silly one. Yet, Hickcox feels it is important to say something. Dozens of men are blown apart by the cannon fire. The air is full of shell fragments, treetops, and body parts. Hickcox is knocked off his feet by a blow to his right side, cannot rise. It is the strangest sensation, his legs entirely unaccountable, as if they had ceased to be. He feels his side, cannot at first identify the rough object protruding from the anterior of his right kidney. He cranes his neck, stares in horror at a wooden splinter as thick as his forearm and twice as long. For a moment of desperate disbelief, even hope, he searches for the opposite end, only to find it three inches to the left of his navel, its point piercing the wool of his uniform blouse. His viscera has turned liquid and he has the sense that he's soiled himself. God, not that, he thinks. Not that, too.

Captain David Putnam takes command from Hickcox but is shot within minutes through the left palm. He tries to carry on, but the wreckage of bone and muscle is too complete, the pain too excruciating. Captain Joseph H. Brigham assumes command, but by then the 69th Ohio is in full flight and he can do nothing but run to catch up.

Outflanked by Manigault and Maney and hit straight on by Stewart, Stanley's brigade breaks for the rear. Its collapse uncovers the right flank of Negley's other brigade, commanded by Colonel John F. Miller. Miller is caught off balance, an unusual circumstance for a man who has, at thirty-one, achieved remarkable success in law, politics, and most recently the army. The approbation of Jack Miller is not quite universal. Phil Sheridan likes but distrusts him, Bill Hazen despises him, and George Thomas has cautioned Negley against reposing too much confidence in him. Their reservations are based on the same perception, that Miller, although a man of great enthusiasm and charm, is careless of the details of soldiering, simply does not know enough to command a brigade in a crisis.

Seeing Stanley's line buckle, Miller rushes to realign his regiments to meet Stewart's attack. But refusing a flank under fire is a movement requiring no small precision and proves beyond him. Stewart's brigade rolls around Miller's right flank into his rear, while Patton Anderson's brigade plows headlong into Miller's east-facing line.

Fortunately for the Army of the Cumberland, the soldiers of the 78th Pennsylvania have snugged themselves into a limestone outcropping on Miller's right flank. In relative misery, they are about as comfortable as any soldiers in the army. The rocks provide a degree of protection from the weather and the opportunity to boil coffee over small fires. The limestone also provides a first-class fortress, and the Pennsylvanians blaze away on three sides as Stewart and Anderson envelop Miller's line.

Whatever his deficiencies as a tactician, Miller is an exceedingly resolute man. If his men must fight back to back like the Texans at the Alamo or Herkimer's militia at Oriskany, so be it. He rides among them, showing not the least fear, though the air is filled with the twitter-buzz of minié balls. The men respond, fire until their cartridge boxes are empty. The 37th Indiana runs short first. Miller pulls it back, sends it to resupply from the brigade ammunition wagons.

Lieutenant Colonel William D. Ward leads the 37th back into the fight a few minutes later. "The wagons are gone, Colonel!" he shouts. "Must have pulled out with the first shot."

Miller looks at him with what seems to Ward an oddly detached curiosity. "Where's Colonel Hull?"

"Shot, Colonel. Wounded, dead, I don't know. I took command."

Miller nods. "Very well. Search the pockets of the dead and wounded."

It is a fearful thing, this searching of the pockets of dead and maimed men. Private Jimmy Reid crawls to the body of Private Horst Mueller, a man he has never liked but with whom he has shared many a cooking fire and chill night when a soldier would snuggle up to the devil himself for a little warmth. Mueller is dead, must be, from the look of the terrible wound in his chest. But as Reid reaches across the body to search the far coat pocket, Mueller's big hand closes on his forearm. "Vhat for you doing? My vatch is mine, you little shit."

Before Reid can respond, Mueller has rolled atop him, other hand clawing for his throat. "Jesus, Mueller, stop! I need bullets. I thought—"

A kick tumbles Mueller off him. Sergeant Elehazer Prust points a bayoneted rifle at Mueller. "Fight Rebs if you can still fight, Mueller."

But Mueller comes up with a rock in a big hand and Prust whips the rifle butt across his head. The big man sprawls, the chest wound that seemed only to ooze a moment before whining as it sucks air. Prust rips open Mueller's pockets, scoops up a handful of cartridges. "Take these and get in line, Jimmy. Make 'em count." Prust's hand hesitates over Mueller's watch at the same moment Mueller takes a final, croaking breath, convulses, and lies still. Prust jams the watch into the gaping mouth. "Here, take it to hell if it means that much to you!"

The Rebel infantry is moving too fast for the Rebel gunners to cover the advance. They cease fire to shift their guns forward. The fight between Miller and Patton Anderson becomes a slugging match between lines of infantry. The Pennsylvanians are driven from their rocks. Miller intercepts them, leads them back into line. The 37th Indiana gives way for want of ammunition. The 74th Ohio follows. Miller lets them go, orders the 21st Ohio to cover the retreat with their Colt Revolving Rifles. Colonel James Niebling shouts, "Give 'em hell by the acre, boys!" The Buckeyes, particularly those without their gloves, grit their teeth and obey.

The five-shot, .56 caliber Colt Revolving Rifle is a spectacularly bad weapon. Heavy, awkward, and temperamental, its cylinder throws off a shrapnel of lead, brass, and burned powder with every shot. The Buckeyes have learned to wear heavy gloves to reduce the hours spent picking fragments out of their hands. But for all the defects of design, the Colts can lay down an impressive volume of fire, and the 21st manages to hold back the Rebels long enough for the brigade's three other regiments to cut their way through to the Nashville Pike. The Buckeyes launch a forlorn bayonet attack to gain a few more minutes and then try to follow. But they are now almost surrounded and most have to surrender, the bargain slightly improved by the opportunity to part with their revolving rifles.

Miller leaves behind half a dozen guns. Riding forward through the carnage, Stewart spots a Yankee gunner trying to haul away a twelve-pounder field howitzer with a single horse. One of the howitzer's wheels has jammed between two rocks, and the soldier is working feverishly to pry it loose with a rail. "No one harm that man!" Stewart shouts. He rides forward, reins up beside the man. "Give it up, son. Your horse isn't strong enough, and there's only one of you."

The soldier looks up, tears streaming down his cheeks. "I drug this gun all the way from Ohio, General."

"I know, I know. You've done a good job. Give over now. We'll see to things."

The man drops the rail, stumbles away sobbing toward the Rebel rear. The butternut soldiers part, a few of the men reaching out to pat him on the back.

Funneled by Anderson's line on one side and Stewart's encircling line on the other, the refugees from Stanley's and Miller's brigades flee northward through Cruft's position. Colonel Enyart's Union 1st Kentucky, falling back from its standup fight with the 38th Tennessee in the cottonfield, is flabbergasted by the resulting chaos. On every side, fleeing men are shouting of disaster; of Sheridan and all his men captured; of Stanley's brigade pulverized; of Miller, his entire staff, and a good half the men gobbled up by the butternut horde.

Enyart fights his way through to Cruft. "My God, General. What's happening?"

"Panic is what's happening! Form your men facing south and hold them steady. I won't be stampeded!"

For an hour now General Dan Smith Donelson has held his men to the fight against Cruft. Donelson's line strains, writhes, would give way, but he holds it, rides along behind it, sword hacking the air, shouting at the men to keep firing. The Yankees are killing them, maiming them—two, three, perhaps ten to one—but he will not give way, will not retreat, will never take his Tennesseans back so that Braxton Bragg can accuse them of cowardice. "Return with your shield or upon it," he screams at one point, quoting the Spartan mother, but his words are lost in the racket of cannon and musket fire. One aide hears, looks at the general strangely, but is killed before he can suggest to any of his fellows that the general is mad.

There is chaos in the woods behind Cruft's line and the Yankee fire becomes disjointed. Donelson cranes, trying to make out what is happening. "The Yankees are retreating, General!" his adjutant shouts. "Stewart's gotten in behind them."

Stewart! An over-educated twit, but a Tennessean. Well, good for him and his boys. "Charge!" Donelson shrieks. "Charge, you sons of Tennessee!"

Only minutes after he announces his determination not to be stampeded, Cruft has little choice but to retreat. Captain William Standart's Battery B, 1st Ohio Artillery, manages to hold off Stewart briefly, but Donelson's line charges then, rolling over Cruft's position. Half a thousand Yankees, not counting the wounded lying on the field, are forced to surrender. Donelson would kill them all, sends them to the rear instead.

☆ ☆ ☆

Rosecrans has another sudden memory of the ball of fire, incredibly lovely within its cloud of glass splinters, rolling across the laboratory table to envelop him, swallow him, take his breath and replace it with flame. He'd burned then within the fire, watched himself reflected in the beakers, the crucibles, the windows, a torch from waist to hair, dancing with flaming arms thrown wide.

Now, as then, the roaring about him seems subdued, though clear in its every detail. He gallops down the Nashville Pike toward the Round Forest, past where George Thomas is siting a battery of Parrott rifles in support of Rousseau. "General Thomas," he shouts. "Deal with that situation in the woods yonder. I'll look to the fight ahead."

Thomas raises a hand in acknowledgment, kicks his mare a bit too hard so that the horse jerks forward with a start that must wrench Thomas's agonized back. Rosecrans notes this, as he notes everything, his brain aflame with consciousness as it was on the night he breathed the living fire and knew for a few wild moments the divine horror that must have visited the disciples in their Pentecostal ecstasy.

George Thomas eases the mare into a smooth trot, rides up the pike to find Shepherd and the regulars. Since the war's beginning, generals have debated whether to break up the regular units, distributing the veterans of the Old Army among the new volunteer regiments to supply a leavening of experience. But old Scott—and Thomas agrees—favored keeping them together for moments like this. Thomas cannot see the fighting in the cedars, but he can hear it, can guess from the survivors streaming from the woods that Stanley, Miller, and now Cruft have given way. Yet he does not hurry up the pike, both for his back's sake and because to do so, when he is famous for deliberate speed, would be to communicate undue alarm, might even be interpreted as panic.

All the time shells and bullets scream and buzz about him. Staff officers and orderlies fall, men whom Thomas knows, will later regret losing should he himself survive. But for the moment their loss is irrelevant to the task. He must not show fear, worry, or sorrow, must devote himself utterly to constancy, to restoring the line.

Lieutenant Colonel Oliver Shepherd watches Thomas coming up the pike, guesses what the orders will be, can even guess how they will be stated. He turns to his adjutant. "Get the men ready."

The regulars are beat up, three hundred out of sixteen hundred men lost when they'd been ambushed by Rains's brigade in the woods to the right of John Beatty's position. Now, from the look of things, they're about to be asked to plug another hole. But that's all right; they know who they are, know what they're made of.

Thomas points toward the cedars where Cruft's line is coming apart. "Shepherd, take your brigade in there and stop the Rebels."

"Yes, sir," Shepherd answers.

Thomas turns his mare, trots back the way he's come. Nothing more is necessary; Shepherd and the regulars know their trade.

First Sergeant Delford Sullivan, Company B, 16th United States Infantry, lifts the dead boy's right ankle, places it over the left, and rolls the corpse over with a deft twist. He begins going through the boy's pockets. Behind him, Lieutenant Gilbert Winston snaps, "For God's sake, Sullivan! Leave the poor bastard in peace."

Sullivan finds the boy's tobacco, settles back to fill his pipe. "That boy's not minding, Lieutenant. He's at peace sure enough."

Winston shakes his head in disgust.

Sullivan lets his brogue thicken. "Now, now, Lieutenant, darlin'. 'Tis truth he don't mind. Besides, from the look of things, a good many of us will be joining him presently."

Winston turns to follow Sullivan's gaze. Shepherd is issuing orders as Thomas's staff trots after their boss. "They're sending us in again," Winston says.

Sullivan draws deeply on his pipe, savoring. The lieutenant is all right, is learning quickly. In a moment, First Sergeant Sullivan will rise, get the boys ready for the lieutenant to lead forward. A hard fight, but a squarer one this time. Maybe they'll live through it, maybe not. There's no telling, and no point wasting this little time with good tobacco worrying about it.

Stewart knows history too well to let his ranks become disorganized during a pursuit, and his regiments are still moving in good order when the regulars hit them straight on.

The regulars come into the woods in tight formation, the entire brigade line extending only a quarter mile. They will be flanked, that is a certainty, but there is no other way to stop a foe advancing with the speed and confidence of Stewart's brigade. So the regulars go forward shoulder to shoulder. They might be a Macedonian phalanx or one of Caesar's legions or a line of Wellington's Miserables, for they are truly at home only in ranks, only in moments like this, when all the feuds, all the bitching, all the drudgery of soldiering is forgotten, and they share the gut certainty in each other. In the end, there is no other reason for doing what they do, but it is enough and more.

The two lines bore in on each other until they are no more than seventy yards apart, blasting each other with torrents of musketry. The Rebels fight as individuals, loading and shooting as fast as their skills and temperament dictate. Some abandon aiming altogether in the thick smoke, simply point their Enfields toward the enemy and let fly, then reload as quickly as hands can manage.

The regulars fire by volleys, the men loading, capping, presenting, and firing according to the metronomic repetition of commands by officers and sergeants. But as casualties mount, they too are overwhelmed by the desire to fire absolutely as fast as possible. When the volley fire starts becoming uneven, the order is passed to fire at will. The regulars cheer, pour it into the Rebels.

Lieutenant Winston walks coolly behind Company B's line. Sullivan glances at him with pride. Yes, the lad's come a long way, hasn't even drawn his revolver yet. At seventy yards, an Army Colt is a decidedly ineffective weapon. Experienced officers carry theirs mostly as symbols of authority, drawing them only when the work is very close, the addition of a few rapid shots of some possible value. Otherwise, best to leave a Colt holstered and rely on the men to do the shooting.

The Rebel line is pressing in from the left, Patton Anderson's brigade catching up with Stewart's and joining the fight. Shepherd has anticipated this, swings back Major Stephen Carpenter's battalion to meet the assault. Maney's brigade is coming in on Stewart's left, and Shepherd prepares to swing back King's battalion, now commanded by Captain Jesse Fulmer. But there is a cheer from that direction and a crash of musketry. Two of Stanley's re-formed regiments, the 18th Ohio and the 11th Michigan, come charging through the woods, led personally by General Lovell Rousseau, who looks as fearsome as one of Napoleon's guard officers, though his mustache is a bit too ragged and his form a little too heavy. Shepherd, who takes a pride in Rousseau something similar to that felt by Sullivan for Winston, nods in approval: Rousseau is coming along.

Lieutenant Winston's Company B holds the hinge of the regulars' line at the point where the left flank has been refused to meet Anderson's envelopment. The work is grim now, dozens of men down, the survivors rifling the cartridge boxes and pockets of the dead and wounded for more bullets. Sullivan shakes blood off his nose, guesses that he must have a splinter lodged at the hairline. Ahead in the smoke, the Rebel line is closer, edging forward as numbers begin to tell. In the midst of reloading, Sullivan shouts to Winston, "You might want to get that Colt out now, Lieutenant. Looks to be some close work ahead."

Winston looks at his right hand, seems surprised to find it empty. "I'd forgotten about it. Thank you, First Sergeant."

For all his vaunted stubbornness, Lieutenant Colonel Oliver Shepherd has no intention of letting his brigade die in the cedars. If he has lost hundreds, he must have inflicted even greater losses on the Rebels. They won't pursue, will need time to recover before going forward again. "Send word to Major Carpenter to start pulling back on the left," he tells his adjutant. "Go yourself to tell those formations on our right that we're going to fall back. General Rousseau if he's there, whoever's in charge if he's not."

In the smoke and confusion of the withdrawal, Company B becomes separated from the rest of the battalion. Winston takes it back, counting out twenty-four paces, ordering the men to turn and fire, and then counting out twenty-four more. Sullivan shouts to him, "Lieutenant, darlin', could you make those paces a mite longer?"

Winston is about to reply when a minié ball smashes into the bridge of his nose, shattering the center of his face and killing him instantly. Sullivan staggers, chokes back the animal howl that rises in his throat. "All right, lads," he shouts. "By the numbers, twenty-four paces, turn and fire." Only when Company B reaches the edge of the cedars, sees the rest of the battalion double-timing for the pike, does Sullivan release the boys from the cadence.

At the pike, Shepherd has the roll taken. Four hundred men lost in a bare twenty minutes in the cedars, including Major Carpenter, shot six times withdrawing his battalion. So far this morning, three of four majors lost, half the captains and lieutenants, and seven hundred of sixteen hundred men. Shepherd could work out the percentages, but the day isn't over. For a moment an image of his three young sons flashes in his mind. I will kill anyone, he thinks, who tries to make one of my boys a soldier.

✵ ✵ ✵

For more than an hour, Stewart's brigade has led the Rebel charge. Now it sags like a pummeled fighter between the brigades of Anderson and Maney. Stewart reorders his line and takes it forward through the cedars to the edge of the fields fronting the Nashville Pike. For the first time, he has a clear view of the compressed Union line. For two miles west from the line's apex in the Round Forest, Yankee batteries are firing over the fields into the woods. Masses of blue troops, some of them disorganized but rallying, others marching under streaming battle flags, cover the ground from the near side of the pike to the far side of the railroad.

Stewart dismounts, slumps on a log. His adjutant is alarmed. "General?"

Stewart waves a hand at the Yankee line. "We're finished. All we've done is force the Yankees to concentrate. We can't cross that field; they'll butcher us."

General Dan Smith Donelson isn't finished. Not by a long goddamn shot. He swings his brigade around the right of Anderson and Stewart, leaves the brawl with the Yankee regulars to them. He is going to plow over that damned little grove of trees and take the pike and the railroad. Then let Bragg call Tennesseans cowards.

Donelson's line emerges from the cedars three hundred yards southwest of the pike and the Round Forest. A thin butternut line wavers at the

southeastern edge of the trees. Donelson laughs aloud. Savage and the 16th
Tennessee. Why, the craven bastard hasn't taken his boys back after all!
"Come on, men," he shouts. "Just that far to Glory."

Men look curiously at him, shake their heads in failed understanding,
for Dan Smith Donelson has lost his upper plate and no longer makes the
least sense. They lean into the Yankee fire, plunge ahead across the field.

If he had a respite as short as a minute, Colonel John Savage might consider
surrendering. He has brought his men to within fifty yards of the Round
Forest. It is impossible to go farther, equally suicidal to fall back. The 16th
Tennessee and the three companies from the 51st Tennessee can only slug
it out with the Yankees until they are ground up.

"Colonel! Colonel!" one of the men shouts. Savage looks to the left
where the man is pointing, sees the 8th, 38th, 84th, and the rest of the
51st Tennessee whooping out of the woods, with Donelson, sword flailing at air or perhaps at giants and windmills, driving them toward the
Round Forest. The line is thinner than when Savage saw it last, yet still
hugely impressive in its bulk. My God, Savage thinks, the crazy old fool
is going to do it.

The screaming of the blinded cannoneer reminds Bierce of the wailing of an
old woman he'd seen dragged behind a horsecar on a Cincinnati street in
the winter the war began. The similarity lies not so much in volume or tone
as in the sudden ending. A fragment of case shot slices through the cannoneer's windpipe, ending his screaming with the same abruptness as the
old woman's had when her skidding body struck the curb, her head cracking with the clear audibility of a breaking bowl.

Hazen steps his horse around the man's body and continues walking it
behind the battery of Napoleons answering the Rebel cannons on Wayne's
Hill. Bierce follows. In the racket of musketry and cannon, it is odd how
some sounds penetrate. I must ask the colonel's opinion of the phenomenon, he thinks. Hazen is an engineer, must have some understanding of the
science involved. On the other hand, perhaps we perceive more with our
imagination than we actually hear with our ears. We see the rain evaporat-
ing off the cannon barrel, see the steam when a gunner swabs the bore, and
imagine we hear hissing, like water squeezed from a sodden dish cloth onto
a hot stove. But we don't actually hear it.

The *thuck* of the bullet penetrating the forehead of Hazen's horse
requires no imagination to apprehend. The creature shudders, collapses on
its right side. Hazen drops nimbly to the left, steps clear of the kicking legs.

"Your horse, Lieutenant." Bierce is already dismounting. Hazen takes the reins, swings up. "Take an orderly's. I want you on horseback."

"Yes, sir."

Before Bierce can look around for another horse, there is a shout from the line facing southwest. Hazen rises in his stirrups. "There's the rest of them! I knew this bunch wasn't all of them." He wheels the horse, gallops to the colonel of the 110th Illinois, as Donelson's line charges across the field.

Donelson's line officers are screaming: "Charge bayonet!" But it is a hopeless command. For all the times the command is given in this war, few charges succeed in locking men in hand-to-hand combat. The accuracy and stopping power of the rifled musket are simply too great, the volume of fire of a line of infantry too intense for any body of troops of similar size to endure in the last few score yards. Despite their general's raving to press ahead, Donelson's Tennesseans stumble to a halt eighty yards short of Hazen's line.

Bierce fires his Colt over the heads of the infantry. Amid the stink of powder smoke he detects another smell, wonders at it for a moment before putting a name to it: cedar. Little wonder since the air rains with green twigs clipped by Rebel minié balls. A Christmas smell, a smell of being home, of not dying in the rain and the mud. He breaks down the Colt, drops out the spent cylinder, snaps another in its place. He'd brought three loaded cylinders, has only this one left. He should hold off until the Rebels make a rush.

Nearby a young officer lies moaning, head against a tree, a bubbling wound in his chest. Bierce steps to him, picks up the revolver beside the boy. He takes deliberate aim at the Rebel line, correcting as well as he can for the Colt's poor ballistics that will make the ball drop precipitously beyond fifty yards.

Bierce is a rational young man, alert to the possibilities of accident, and deliberate in their avoidance. When he loads a cylinder, he greases the balls to seal the chambers and prevent a spark from one igniting the charge in another. Not so the young lieutenant dying against the tree. The flash of the first shot from the Colt ignites all the charges, blowing apart the revolver and spraying the nearby infantry with its parts. Bierce stares at the pistol handle, lets it fall beside the dying lieutenant. He cannot feel his hand, rubs at it. Amazingly, none of the infantrymen seem to have been wounded. Or at least not so far as he can tell in the torrent of fire engulfing the lines. He turns away, goes to find a horse and Hazen.

Along the Federal line, generals wade into the fight like junior officers. Brigadier General Tom Wood, already lamed by stepping on the nail the night before, is re-forming a regiment of Illinois troops when a shell explodes a dozen yards away, chopping two privates into barely recognizable pieces and spraying Wood's legs with splinters. He is momentarily stunned by the explosion, thinks he has been hit in the chest, but realizes that he has only had the wind knocked out of him by the clap of the concussion. He manages an agonized breath, then another. His pants are shredded and he is bleeding from a score of lacerations, but his testicles and his femoral artery seem intact. He tries to rise, but blood squirts from his legs and the pain is like fire. He slumps back, slams a fist into the earth. His chief of staff is leaning over him, a gash in his cheek but otherwise uninjured. "Tell General Hascall that he has command of the division," Wood grates. "I'll send word when I am able to resume. Tell him to support Hazen at all hazards."

Since capturing the turnpike bridge over Stewart's Creek, Brigadier General Milo Hascall has felt a peculiar possessiveness about the battle his small victory made possible. Hazen's position in the Round Forest has become the crucial point in the Federal line, and Hascall is determined to see it held even if it costs every man he has or can find. He puts his own brigade into line to Hazen's right, leaving its immediate management to the senior colonel. He rides back into the center of the salient to help structure a defense in depth. To his surprise, he finds that no one has taken charge of this task. Confused colonels welcome the sight of Hascall's star, present themselves for his orders. He pushes more regiments into line to the right of Hazen, then forms a reserve to counterattack any Rebel breakthrough.

The reserve is hardly safer than the front line. The Rebel artillery, managing one of its rare instances of common purpose, pours fire from three sides into the salient. Firing from the elevation of Wayne's Hill, two of the Rebel batteries consistently overshoot Hazen's position, their shellfire seeming to wall off the Round Forest from the rest of Hascall's line. Brigadier General John Palmer plunges through the wall of fire and iron to reach Hazen. He is appalled by what he finds. The grove is a shambles of shattered trees and shot-plowed earth. The ground itself jumps with the explosion of shells and the answering crash of cannons. Case shot bursts in the treetops, sending balls and splinters screaming among the men. Not a single horse, artillery or staff, is upright, although Palmer spots two apparently unwounded horses being kept down by orderlies. Another orderly dashes to Palmer's side. "Get down, General!" he shouts. "I'll see to your horse."

"Where's Colonel Hazen?"

"Over there, sir. Him and his aide. He's told everybody else to stay down."

It's true. No officers are standing behind their men, making a show of courage and coolness. Instead they are kneeling behind the ranks, revolvers in hand. Palmer cannot at first make out Hazen, sees him then, striding through the smoke, a single aide following. Palmer recognizes the brigade topographical officer. Pierce. Bierce. Something of the sort.

All around men are shouting for cartridges. "Fix bayonets," Hazen shouts.

"We have none, sir," a plaintive voice calls from the smoke.

"Then club your rifles!"

A minié ball clips Palmer's hat brim. Another jerks at his coattail so that he momentarily turns, expecting to find a recumbent figure—or perhaps a child—trying to attract his attention. He hurries to Hazen. "Bill, you're going to have to fall back!"

Hazen glares at him, eyes blazing. For a moment he doesn't seem to recognize Palmer. "I'd like to know where the hell I'm supposed to fall back to, General!"

Palmer clamps his jaw, stares at the man. "Can you hold?"

"We are holding."

"How long?"

"Till they kill us, General. And I'll take the gravedigger with me to hell!"

"Very well, then. I'll get you cartridges if I have to bring them myself."

Rosecrans gallops into the reserve behind the Round Forest, spots Milo Hascall. "Give me a report, General!"

Hascall summarizes what he's done.

"Excellent, General. This line must hold. Everything else depends on it."

"Yes, sir. I know."

Rosecrans leans across his saddle, grips Hascall by the shoulder. "This battle must be won, Hascall! And we are going to win it." He turns to Garesché. "Colonel, get in there and talk to your friend Hazen. Tell him we're bringing everything we can to his aid."

"I should be with you, General."

"I'll be back presently. Go."

Battery F, 1st Ohio Artillery, Captain Daniel T. Cockerill commanding, holds the center of Hazen's line, blazing away with canister at Colonel John Savage's 16th Tennessee a bare 150 feet down the railroad. A shell from Cobb's battery on Wayne's hill explodes beside the right-hand Napoleon of the battery, killing half a dozen gunners. Hazen points to it. "Get that gun in action!"

Bierce springs forward, helps wrestle bodies away from the cannon. An infantryman grabs up the rammer, pauses to inspect it as he might a new and unfamiliar farm implement, and then steps to the muzzle. "Come on, boys. Let's shoot this thing. Lieutenant, do you know how to aim it?"

Before Bierce can reply in the negative, an artillery sergeant comes running up. "I've got it, sir."

Bierce steps back, watches the gun go into action. He turns to see Garesché on a bloody-nosed gelding. For a moment he almost doesn't recognize the man, for Garesché is transformed, seems harder of feature somehow, the gentleness burned away.

Hazen looks around. "Julius! For the love of God, what are you doing here?"

"Fighting Rebs, Bill, same as you."

"This is no place for you. The general needs—"

"The general wants you to know that we're sending all the help we can. Just hold this position, and we'll beat them back along the rest of the line."

"We'll hold, Julius. Bierce, get the chief of staff out of here!"

Garesché laughs, begins turning his horse, but then pauses to look down at Bierce. My God, Bierce thinks. He's more than transformed, he's gone mad. Garesché sweeps an arm toward the enemy line. "Do you see, Lieutenant? *The hope of the ungodly is like dust that is blown away with the wind!*" He leans down, grins. "It's *The Wisdom of Solomon.* Do you believe, or are you still the skeptic?"

Bierce would speak, cannot. Can only shake his head.

Garesché rears up in his saddle. "*Like dust,* Bierce! Believe!"

Savage's 16th Tennessee clings to the railroad embankment, trying to hold through the blasts of Cockerill's battery until Donelson can force the Yankee line from the left. Privates Junior and Hugh Ottlein, a pair of raw-boned farm boys, lie near Savage, firing their Enfields carefully.

"I got one of them gunners, I think," Junior says.

Hugh snorts. "If yer talkin' 'bout that boy with the ram stick at that gun on the left, I got him two, three minutes ago. Just took him a while to fall down."

Junior is about to reply to this barb when a solid shot fired from somewhere to the left carries away both his legs below the knee. He looks down at the stumps and then turns to say something to his brother. But Hugh has slumped forward onto his musket, the top of his head exploded by a canister ball. Junior stares, then reaches beneath him to extract a pistol from his belt, puts the barrel to his temple, and pulls the trigger. All this before the horrified Savage can scream.

Brigadier General Phil Sheridan has just found water and cartridges for Schaefer's brigade when Rosecrans comes hurtling down on him. "Sheridan, take your men in there and support Hazen!"

Sheridan, who has never avoided a fight in his life, stares open-mouthed at Rosecrans. His three brigades have been wrecked in four hours of intense combat. And now Rosecrans wants him to take perhaps the most battered of the three back into battle? He clamps his mouth shut, turns, starts shouting orders. In ten minutes, the men are jogging—many of them stumbling—down the pike toward the Round Forest.

Whatever hesitancy Sheridan feels disappears on entering the Federal salient. He knows Hascall from Academy days, counts him a friend if not an intimate. "Milo! How shall I deploy?" he shouts.

Hascall shouts back over the tumult, still managing to sound calm, cultured. "How many regiments do you have?"

"Four."

"Leave two with me in reserve. Put the other two in between my boys and Hazen." He points to the southeast corner of the salient.

Bierce supposes it is his way of not going mad, but part of his mind seems to hover entirely outside himself, observing the slaughter. The two lines have achieved a frightful equilibrium in the trading of death—an exchange that, if left undisturbed, might eventually lead to the last two men in the world killing each other.

Sheridan upsets the balance, pushing the 2nd and 15th Missouri in between Hascall's and Hazen's brigade. It is bloody ground, the forest floor strewn with the bodies of dead Ohio and Illinois boys. The Missourians clear space by rolling the bodies from the firing line. Riding with Hazen to find Sheridan, Bierce sees a macabre breastwork of tangled bodies four deep filling the gap between two limestone boulders. Perhaps it is only the earth trembling with the discharge of Cockerill's battery, but the breastwork seems to heave as if transformed into a living creature. An arm extends, lifts a hand. "Colonel," he shouts. "Those bodies—" At that moment, he sees with horrifying clarity a round of spherical case, fired with an inadequate or damp charge, bouncing across the field. It bursts twenty yards short of the Federal line, its load of iron balls ripping into the breastwork of bodies. The pile seems to rise a foot, a sad creature of many arms, heads, and legs making a final effort to crawl off to some more private place to die. It collapses, and through the din, Bierce hears a long sigh, perhaps of the bodies settling against each other as gases escape punctured stomachs and intestines—perhaps of something even he dare not imagine.

He looks to Hazen, sees the man's face unmoved. The part of Bierce's mind that hovers detached begins muttering ancient words, as if trying to decide among them—*rakshasa, shedu, barghest, fiend.*

The added fire of the 2nd Missouri crumples Donelson's line. As it gives way, Sheridan sends the 15th Missouri forward in a heavy skirmish line to push Savage's line off the railroad. Savage gives way, his men rolling down the side of the embankment to take what cover they can among the cornstalks in the field north of the tracks.

Among the guns of Battery F, 1st Ohio Artillery, a minié ball creases the leather pouch of one of the gunners, igniting the friction primers inside. The primers explode like a string of fire crackers, the cannoneer leaping and capering as hundreds of copper shards flay his legs and crotch. Thinking the jig is a victory dance, one of Donelson's retreating men turns in a rage, sights carefully along the barrel of his Enfield, and shoots the gunner down. It is perhaps just as well.

Donelson rides back to the woods in a fury. He is as unharmed as if he had ridden to Sunday service, though his horse bleeds from half a dozen wounds that will, by evening, kill it. A little decent artillery support, another regiment, a rush by Stewart or Maney at the right moment, and Donelson would have smashed through the Yankee line. But others have done nothing, and Dan Smith Donelson will suffer the blame.

The brigade has suffered staggering losses. Of the 440 men of the 8th Tennessee, 41 are dead, including Colonel Moore, and 260 wounded. When Colonel Savage at last manages to lead the 16th Tennessee to safety, it will muster only 150 of its original 377 men.

Passing a fresh column marching to renew the attack on the Round Forest, one of Donelson's men calls, "What regiment?"

"Fourth Florida," comes the reply.

The soldier lifts the bloody stump of an arm. "Do it up right, Gators. Pay them back for my arm."

CHAPTER 7

Wednesday, Noon–3:00 P.M.
December 31, 1862
The Federal Right on the Nashville Turnpike

Hazen's defense of the Round Forest has temporarily stymied the Confederate assault on the Federal center. Behind the Round Forest and northwest along the Nashville Pike, Rosecrans has cobbled together a strong line of infantry and artillery. Meanwhile, Hardee prepares to renew his attack on the Federal right.

BOUT NOON A silence falls on the field. The hush cannot be absolute, of course—not with some eighty thousand men fighting inside a square not a mile and a half on a side—but after a tumult Colonel John Beatty likens to the beating of a thousand anvils, the diminished volume is as profound as utter stillness.

On the Nashville Pike, Lieutenant Alfred Pirtle, Rousseau's ordnance officer, watches the woods from the vantage of Van Pelt's battery. Between the pike and the cedars lies a long, irregular field, some of it in cotton, some in corn, some in pasture. The ground has been trampled by the retreat of Rousseau's division to the pike. Shepherd's remaining regulars have been detached to back up Hazen and Hascall's position in the Round Forest. John Beatty's and Scribner's brigades have joined the Pioneer Brigade and the brigades of Sam Beatty, Fyffe, and Harker in support of the batteries emplaced along the pike. Without clear targets, the guns have ceased firing.

Now and then a gun will drop a round of shell into the quiet woods, but mainly they are waiting, saving their ammunition.

Pirtle massages his midriff. A dread like nothing he has ever felt seems centered just to the right and slightly above his stomach. He presses the spot with fingertips, detects a hard lump, wonders if it is an organ undiscovered in all the centuries of human dissection. Perhaps it is microscopic except in battle, when it expands to the size of a pomegranate, ventricose with a thousand fears that may any moment burst the exocarp, blowing apart his abdominal cavity like a load of canister fired from within.

A Rebel officer leaps from the woods with a shout, brandishing his sword toward the pike, and a Rebel brigade seethes out of the trees. The regimental color guards race each other across the cottonfield, the ranks surging after. Pirtle turns, searching desperately for Rousseau or someone else of sufficient authority to give the command to fire. He can spot no one, screams: "Fire!"

Eighteen Union guns and their four supporting regiments open fire with a roar that cracks windows in Murfreesboro three and a half miles to the southeast. Brigadier General James E. Rains, leading the Rebel brigade, is killed in the first volley by a bullet through the heart, nearly his entire staff swept away with him. For ten minutes, the Rebel line tries to push forward against the barrage of shells, canister, and minié balls, but it is impossible. The lines dissolve, flow back into the woods.

Rains's charge is a blunder: ill-prepared, ill-timed, and unsupported. Coming to the edge of the trees in advance of Lucius Polk's brigade, Major General Pat Cleburne shakes his head at the litter of butternut dead in the cottonfield. How impossibly foolish. Where was McCown when Rains—a good man but an amateur—conceived the charge? Where is McCown now?

A quarter mile separates Hardee's corps from the Nashville Pike and victory. But it is an unspannable crevasse. Cleburne holds Bill Hardee in an esteem bordering on adoration, but no matter what Hardee thinks, the path to glory does not lie in charging down the throats of the Union cannon. If they are to win at all, they must get around the Yankee flank. He halts his line and rides back to find Hardee.

Cleburne has the brigades of Bushrod Johnson, A. J. Vaughan, and Lucius Polk in line left to right, but St. John Liddell's brigade has slipped from his hand. Liddell is a troublesome man, forever going off on his own hook, and Cleburne guesses that he may already be maneuvering to get behind the Yankee flank. Well, in this case he may have stumbled on exactly the right tactic.

Cleburne finds Hardee with Harper's brigade, until recently under McNair. Hardee is expansive. "So, Patrick, are you ready to deliver the *coup de maître* to the Yankees?"

"Not just yet, General."

Hardee frowns slightly at Cleburne's tone, rides off with him a few paces so they can talk privately. "What's the matter, Pat?"

"Rains took a drubbing, General. He attacked without support and suffered the consequences of inexperience. I'm told that he paid for it with his life."

"I'm sorry, I had not heard."

Cleburne hesitates, knowing that he presumes much on Hardee's friendship in gainsaying his plans. "The Yankees have set up several batteries on the pike, all of them well supported with infantry. You know that I am not opposed to frontal assaults when they have a good chance of success. You have even accused me of something less than subtlety on a few occasions. But I don't think we can gain much this time without suffering great loss."

Hardee, who though courtly is never stiff, wishes Cleburne could relax the formality of their relationship. He listens, absently massaging his left hand, which, after all the years he's spent holding reins, has begun to cramp with arthritis. "What do you suggest?"

"Let me try to get my division around the Yankees' flank nearer the creek. At the least, I can distract their attention long enough for General McCown to launch an attack with better hope of success."

"How long will it take you to get in position?"

"An hour, perhaps a little more."

"And all that time Rosy Rosecrans will be reinforcing his line against us."

Cleburne feels himself slipping away. It is a sensation familiar since childhood. He has given his best opinion, must submit now to those of greater authority. He will carry through Hardee's order as he had his stepmother's at home or his sergeant's in the 41st Regiment of Foot. The slipping away is the relinquishing of self to duty, a subsuming of will in the will of others. Necessary for a soldier, perhaps, and easy enough to accept once the habit is formed, but enervating to the soul.

Hardee gazes morosely at his gloved hand, works the fingers individually. "If we just had a fresh division, even a brigade or two, we could carry the pike now. But Bragg ignores my pleas."

"Perhaps you should go see him."

"No, I won't leave here. McCown needs my guidance. . . . All right, Patrick, move your division to the left. But hurry. The rest of this day will go quickly."

★ ★ ★

Private Wayne Hodges, the orderly sent by Garesché to summon General Stanley and his cavalry from Stewart's Creek, has always been a thief. Even his name is a theft, taken from a farm boy decapitated trying to hop a freight when they were traveling together to Cincinnati to enlist. Hodges, who was then the thief Eli Smith, searched the dead boy's pockets. He'd only known the boy a day, but he'd seemed an innocent rube, unlikely to have done anything to attract the notice of the law. So Eli Smith, who has felt the eyes of the law upon him most of his life, slipped the boy's birth certificate into his pocket and walked away a different if not a new man.

Though Garesché still senses the vulpine in Hodges, a good deal of the furtiveness has disappeared from his face in the months since he joined the army, the reflection of an odd reality: Hodges no longer steals. The change comes from no moral awakening, nor from any absence of need, since he is, like all soldiers in the Army of the Cumberland, frequently hungry and bereft of comforts. Hodges himself has no clear idea why he no longer steals. The approximate answer is that he, unlike many soldiers, is a true believer. He cannot discuss Constitution or Union, but he senses with absolute certainty that in their failure will fail all hope for him and all like him, that kings and priests and rich men will then tyrannize them always, will grind them down, hang them and torture them and shit on them forever.

Within a half hour of leaving Rosecrans's headquarters, Hodges is captured by a patrol of Wharton's cavalry. It is not a great concern to him. He has already discarded his dispatch pouch, carbine, and hat, muddied his face and uniform, and assumed the desperate look of thousands of other stragglers from the Union right. Relieved of his horse, he stands for a while in a crowd of prisoners and then approaches a guard. "I gotta go visit the bushes, Sarge."

"You don't need no bushes."

"Sarge, I ain't gonna run. It's safer here than anywhere. I'm gonna stick here till I get my parole and then go home. Never should've come in the first place."

"Well, at least you've got that figured out. Go on. I don't want to see your skinny ass anyway."

Hodges saunters into the brush and keeps going. He doesn't hurry, doesn't even have to tell himself to be casual, for seeming innocence is for him a craft of long practice. He is captured again near Overall Creek and again wanders away. But escape takes time, and it is noon before he is across the creek and well up the Wilkinson Pike in the direction he was told he would find Stanley. Like Garesché and the commanding general himself, Hodges cannot understand why Stanley has not come galloping down the road to join the fray. Even at this distance, the sound of battle can't be mistaken. Yet Stanley has not come. So Private Wayne Hodges must go fetch him.

General Braxton Bragg is sitting hatless in the rain, his tall black gelding pawing nervously under him. Brigadier General Joe Wheeler is shocked by the old man's visage. It might be a death's-head, the sunken cheeks riveted with rain, drops hanging from the eyebrows, the eyes themselves hollow save for a deep flicker. "You are tardy, General," Bragg rasps.

Wheeler salutes. "We made the best time we could, General."

"You told me that you could deploy by late morning. It is afternoon."

The rain, the mud, the broken-down mounts, the men fainting with exhaustion. . . . How can he explain it all? "I'm sorry, General. We'll be ready to move in an hour."

"You must move now. The battle is reaching a crisis; no one has the luxury of ease."

"But I must have remounts for at least half my men. And the men themselves must have a little time to rest. We have been—"

"And I have been fighting a battle in anticipation that you would be here to help me win it! Deploy what men you can immediately. Let the others catch up or fight on foot."

"Yes, sir. Where shall I take them?"

Bragg waves vaguely to the northwest. "Support Hardee. He's been crying for reinforcements all morning, but I've had nothing to give him. And, as usual, Professor Hardee has no conception of what may be required of this army beyond his own quarter, while I must contend with that!" He points angrily at a low forested elevation crowned with smoke. Stretching out to either side in an acute angle, Wheeler can make out the battle lines.

"Rosecrans and Thomas have piled infantry into that angle," Bragg continues, "and backed it heavily with artillery. Rosecrans may know nothing beyond what he learned at the Academy about artillery, but Thomas is a master. You can be assured that those guns are well placed."

Then why are you attempting the assault? Wheeler wonders. He glances sidelong at Bragg, considers if he dare speak. No, it is not his place. "I should be about supporting Hardee, General."

"Yes, go. Send me a report of his dispositions."

Wheeler salutes, rides back to the staff huddled beneath a low awning on the reverse of the hill. He sees Brent, beckons him over. "Colonel, why is the general set on assaulting the strongest point of the Yankee defenses?"

The chief of staff shrugs helplessly. "It's the plan. We must drive the Yankees from that point to complete the wheel and pin their army against the river. Hardee has had great success on his part of the field, but General Bragg says the main effort must be made against the apex of the angle. Only if we carry it will we carry the day."

My God, Wheeler thinks, even Brent sees the error, and Brent is nothing more than an accomplished clerk without a speck of military training. He looks back over his shoulder at Bragg sitting his horse in the rain. Even at this short distance, man and horse seem molded of one piece: a cenotaph of bronze against a gray sky.

Brigadier General John Wharton can manage the feat that has eluded Hardee, Cleburne, McCown, and all the rest: He can reach the Nashville Pike and cut Rosecrans's lifeline. Could, that is, if he only had the men. But he doesn't.

The morning of fighting and hard riding has cost Wharton over a hundred casualties. Several hundred more men have been detailed to guard prisoners and to drive captured wagons toward the rear. With the pike only a short gallop away, he has perhaps thirteen hundred men, enough to get astride it but not enough to hold it against a counterattack by Yankee infantry.

His other concern is the Yankee cavalry. He has seen nothing of them since the old colonel on the small brown horse spirited the ammunition train from his grasp. Who the hell was he? Not Stanley, who is a man his own age. Not Zahm, whom he'd met a few weeks ago under a flag of truce. But whoever the old colonel is, John Wharton intends to have his revenge, would have it now if he just had the troops for a dash at the pike. That would bring the old bastard out of hiding to learn the penalty for insulting Lone Star honor with devious tricks and ironic salutes.

Judge John Kennett, the very man who has so nettled the usually sensible John Wharton, is enjoying the best pot of coffee he's had in months. Not that the actual coffee is better. Christ, it's as vile as all the sludge served in this army. But he drinks it with a satisfaction he has not known since. . . . Well, he cannot recall since when. Thruston's ammunition train is safe behind the Nashville Pike, Zahm has established a straggler line at the extremity of the army's right flank, and several additional companies of cavalry have re-formed and joined Kennett. It is about time to take another ride to see what the Reb cavalry is up to. Yes, another cup of coffee and he will do that.

Brigadier General David Stanley has waited all morning for some word from Rosecrans. Assuredly, there is fighting to the east—a good deal of cannon fire, some sparring between the infantry—but he has no sense that it is a pitched battle. Still, he should be at hand if needed, not out here guarding a wagon park.

He has just about made up his mind to take a detachment and have a look at the extent of the action when Colonel Burke of the infantry guard and his chaplain arrive bearing three tankards of the hot punch from breakfast, freshened with eggs and an additional lacing of brandy. Stanley examines his pocket watch, noting with relief that it is past noon—an acceptable time for bracing body and spirit against the cold and what other rigors may lie ahead.

Private Wayne Hodges is surprised to find no traffic on the Wilkinson Pike. He had expected to join a stream of refugees that would long since have given notice of the severity of the battle to Stanley. But, incredibly, he is alone by the time he is a mile west of Overall Creek. He trudges on, keeping a wary eye out for Reb or Union cavalry. Both have guns, both may shoot before asking questions.

He covers the four miles from Overall Creek to Stewart's Creek by 1:30 P.M. A half mile out, he is challenged by a pair of vedettes. He explains himself and is passed to the officer in charge of the picket line—a spectacularly dim lieutenant who actually asks him to recite the words to *John Brown's Body*. This asshole doesn't know there's a battle going on, Hodges thinks. He repeats enough of the song to satisfy the lieutenant that he is not a Southern spy and is passed to a captain. The captain is a decent sort, gives him a cup of coffee and a chaw from his plug, and then takes him to a major, who can't be bothered, and then to a colonel, who is in the sinks with the runs but who listens politely enough before telling the captain to take Hodges to the general.

General Stanley is drunk. Not terribly drunk—not nearly as drunk as the colonel with him or the chaplain snoring in the corner of the tent—but drunk. Private Wayne Hodges, who as the thief Eli Smith might have laughed at the absurdity of it all, is incensed. He pulls a brogan off a blistered foot, fishes out the folded message written in Garesché's fine hand, shoves it at Stanley without a word.

Stanley unfolds it, squints to read, his face going pale. "That will be all,

Captain. I'll deal with this man." When the officer is gone, he looks at Hodges. "When did you get this?"

"'Bout eight."

"What took you so long?"

"There's a barrel of trouble down there. I was captured twice, lost my horse, had to stick to the woods."

"Say 'sir,' damn it!"

Hodges spits tobacco juice out the fly of the tent. "Sir."

Stanley reads the message again. "Can I get through on this road?"

"Well, there's about fifty thousand Rebs over east, but maybe they wouldn't mind. Sir."

Stanley glares at him. "Go get a horse. You're going to lead us back."

"Yes, sir," Hodges drawls. He goes to look for the captain who lent him the tobacco—the one fucking officer in the brigade who seems to know what he's doing.

★ ★ ★

Captain James H. Stokes suspects that he is the oldest captain in the Army of the Cumberland. He is certainly the oldest Academy graduate below the rank of brigadier general. Probably major general. He could wear stars if he chose, may even let the War Department make him a general one of these days. But, for the moment, he values his battery more than rank.

The Chicago Board of Trade Battery is Stokes's creation, a hard-muscled representative of the brawling city that Jim Stokes has helped build in the twenty years since his resignation from the regular army. In the fevered summer of 1861, he'd raised a generous subscription from his friends on the Board of Trade to buy the best guns, mounts, and equipment available. Hundreds of young men clamored to join. He took the best, frequently passing over the sons of the rich to sign a mechanic or a carpenter who understood the working of machines or had an eye for line and angle. Through long hours of drill, he has made them splendid artillerymen.

The guns are good, though not quite matching the men. Stokes wanted to equip the battery with the best, but not even the Board of Trade's money could secure three-inch Ordnance rifles or twelve-pounder Napoleons in that summer. He could buy the new ten-pounder Parrott rifles, but distrusted the strength of the wrought-iron barrels. He settled on fourteen-pounder James rifles for their bronze tubes and heavier projectiles, though their design is not particularly to his liking.

The polished bronze guns shine even in the rain and smoke as the

Chicago Board of Trade Battery waits on a rise near army headquarters between the Nashville Pike and the railroad. The wait is irksome for Stokes, but the commanding general himself positioned him on the rise not long after McCook's wing broke.

Rosecrans's normally red face had been mottled with pale splotches and streaming with perspiration as he'd leaned down from his horse to speak confidentially. "It's not going well, Jim. Someone's got to hold the flank until I can shift some of Crittenden's corps. So I'm leaving the best: your battery and Morton's Pioneers. I'm expecting you two to do the job."

Stokes had been flattered. "We'll do our best, General."

"It's not my practice to order men to hold to the last extremity. Any plan requiring such measures is innately flawed. But this battle must be won, Jim. If we lose here, I fear for the country. Burnside and Grant have put us in a position where we absolutely must win. Otherwise, I think the cause may be lost."

"I understand, General. We'll die here before we give way."

Rosecrans had nodded, set spurs to Boney's flanks.

Stokes and his cannoneers wait through the rest of the morning. They have perhaps the best view of the battlefield of anyone except the Rebels holding Wayne's Hill on the east side of the river. For hours, Hardee's juggernaut appears unstoppable as it grinds up one Union brigade after another. But, if nothing else, Rosecrans is a brilliant engineer. If the machine fails in one configuration, he will rebuild it in another. He shifts Rousseau's division to Sheridan's right, pulls the brigades of Sam Beatty, Fyffe, and Harker from Crittenden's corps, sends them out beyond Rousseau. No longer alone on the flank, the Pioneers and Stokes's battery are left unengaged and seemingly forgotten in rear of this new line.

Captain James St. Clair Morton joins Stokes behind the guns to watch Rousseau's batteries beat back Rains's assault on the pike. Morton fidgets. He is a restless man, content only in motion. When Rosecrans had decided to form the Pioneer Brigade, he'd chosen the brilliant West Point engineer to put the innovation into practice. But the brigade is unpopular with the many officers who begrudge the loss of their best craftsmen and mechanics. The infantrymen have an even lower opinion of the Pioneers, viewing them as slackers avoiding the dangers of combat.

Stokes is one of the few who does not agree with the criticisms. He has seen Morton's Pioneers accomplish prodigies of work, and expects that all the Union armies will soon field pioneer brigades. He has grown fond of Morton, who for all his intelligence seems to doubt his own judgment and needs it frequently validated by the older man. He pats Morton on the shoulder. "Don't fidget, James. We'll have our chance soon enough."

Morton brushes back his shoulder-length hair, a nervous gesture repeated a dozen times an hour. "I just hope my men haven't forgotten how to fight. We've concentrated on quite other things lately. They're a good deal more familiar with axes and shovels than rifle-muskets these days."

"I wouldn't fear. They have pride in their brigade. That's what men fight for. All the rest is forgotten in battle."

The smoke drifts away from Rousseau's line. Morton lifts his field glasses. "I wish we weren't in reserve again; it makes the waiting worse." He stiffens. "That brigade to our front is gone. No, wait. There it is over to the right in that cedar brake. But they've left a hole."

Stokes studies the scene through his field glasses. "I guess you've got your wish; we're no longer the second line." He turns, finds he is talking to no one, sees Morton hurrying to his small staff to give orders. Stokes runs fingers through his rich, gray beard, lifts his field glasses to study the wide cottonfield beyond the pike. Below the hill, Battery B, Pennsylvania Light Artillery clatters off the turnpike and up the rise to unlimber to his left. Good, he thinks. We're not the only ones to notice that the devil is about to demand his wages.

The approaching Confederate line is made up of the 10th, 11th, 14th, and 15th Texas, unmounted cavalry regiments fighting as an infantry brigade under Brigadier General Matthew Ector. Their lack of horses has been an extreme irritant to the Texans. Ah, if they only had horses. Then they could make a proper charge, cross the fields with all the grandeur, glory, and poetry befitting the Texas character, which is not—goddamn it—a foot-slogging, toe-blistered, earth-bound spirit but a horse-mounted, hoof-thundering, come-heaven-or-hell spirit!

But they don't have horses, and the Texans have barely cleared the trees when two Yankee batteries open on them from a rise on the far side of the pike. Case shot howls overhead, exploding in white puffs and a rain of lead balls and iron fragments. The Texans hunch their shoulders, stride ahead.

In the absence of instructions from McCown, Ector has repeated Rains's mistake, ordering his assault before Harper's brigade can move up on the right and Cleburne's division can deploy on his left. At an oblique angle to the Texans' advance, Brigadier General Sam Beatty's Union brigade lies hidden in the grove of cedars surveyed a few moments before by Morton and Stokes. Beatty is related by neither blood nor temperament to the erudite, accomplished Colonel John Beatty. Sam Beatty is an Ohio farmer and county sheriff: phlegmatic, unpretentious, and quietly commanding. So far, he is concentrating on receiving the brigade he is sure will follow to Ector's left. When it does not come, he frowns, shifts his chaw to the other cheek, and says to his adjutant: "Push out skirmishers. Tell them to whittle on the left of that advancing Reb line."

Five minutes later, a sharp volley from Beatty's skirmishers hits the flank of Colonel Julius A. Andrews's 15th Texas Cavalry on the left end of Ector's line. Ector responds by wheeling the 15th and the 14th Texas toward Beatty, while the 10th and 11th Texas continue toward the pike. The 15th and 14th drive in Beatty's skirmishers, pursuing them three hundred yards toward the trees, where Beatty's main line waits. For years after, Beatty's adjutant will shiver any time he hears a door latch click, recalling the sound made by twelve hundred musket hammers drawn back in the instant before the command *Present!* is given on Beatty's line. Some of the men of the 15th and 14th Texas also hear the sibilance of the hammers cocking, but few can identify it before a sheet of flame, smoke, and lead lashes from the trees ahead.

The volley stops the Texans in their tracks, but they are solid if unwilling infantry, do not break but stand and return fire. Colonel Andrews knows his men cannot hold for long in the open with a full Yankee brigade to their front and two Yankee batteries on their flank. He gallops down the line to find his brigade commander. Ector is behind the 14th Texas, encouraging the men in a duel with the 19th Ohio. "General, where's the rest of the brigade?" Andrews shouts.

Ector stares at him. "Well, I'm not quite sure, Colonel."

"We need support! We can't carry that line with two regiments against a full brigade."

Ector considers this, the bullets *whicking* by him. "I suppose you're right, Colonel. Take your men back. I'll bring these."

Morton need not have worried about his Pioneers' readiness for a fight. When Ector's 10th and 11th Texas reach killing range, the Pioneers give a shout and pour a volley into the Rebel ranks. It is all Morton can do to keep his men from charging with the bayonet, but he holds them. When the Rebels begin giving way, he takes the Pioneers across the pike. The Texans are falling back in haste and Morton is tempted to pursue. But he stifles the notion, recalls Professor Mahan and his preachments that discretion, more than valor, determines the success of a commander. The line along the pike must hold, and this is no time for gambles by mere captains.

Brigadier General Sam Beatty reaches the opposite conclusion and drives hard after the 14th and 15th Texas. As a sheriff, he knows two invariable rules for winning a brawl: sobriety is a far better weapon than whiskey; and never let a stumbling opponent regain his balance. Beatty's brigade pursues the fleeing Texans back across the field and into the woods.

   Beatty is about to pull back when Major General Lovell Rousseau comes dashing from the rear. "Well done, General! Keep pushing them." Beatty hesitates, for his brigade is from Van Cleve's division, not Rousseau's. "It's all right, General!" Rousseau shouts. "Old Rosy's coming with the rest!"

   Exactly who the hell the rest are is lost on Beatty, but he has what seems to be an order. He passes his first-line regiments to the rear, advances his second line to the front, and continues the pursuit.

☆   ☆   ☆

The referent dropped by Rousseau in his excitement incorporates the brigades of colonels James Fyffe and Charlie Harker. Rosecrans leads them out into the field to Beatty's right. For the first time since daybreak, the Army of the Cumberland is launching a significant counterattack. Rosecrans is ecstatic. He sweeps sweat-limp hair from his forehead, gestures excitedly, gives commands almost too fast to follow. It falls to Garesché to translate when the general's agitation overcomes his syntax and he begins to stutter.

   Garesché is likewise excited almost to the point of mania, and it takes all his self-discipline to appear calm. Please, God, he prays, don't let this day end without seeing us triumphant. Deliver up the Rebels to us as you did the Amorites to the children of Israel when Joshua called on the sun to stand still upon Gideon.

Major General George Thomas frowns at the sight of Rosecrans leading Fyffe and Harker's brigades into the cottonfield. This is too early, he thinks. If the Rebel attack has spent its fury at this end of the field, good. But a counterattack should come only when the fight is going our way at all points. Then, when we have our feet under us, hit them hard.

   But Rosecrans is commander, and it is too late to advise him to hold position. Thomas rides at his customary slow trot up the pike, checking the batteries and their infantry supports. He pauses at the rise to the left of the pike where Stokes has positioned the Chicago Board of Trade Battery with Morton's Pioneers protecting to either side. Stokes salutes. "General."

Thomas smiles. "How are you, Jim?"

"Exceedingly well. And you, George?"

"Passable. What do you think of this advance?"

Stokes stares across the field, runs a hand absently through his beard. "It would seem that the general is risking a great deal."

"Yes, a great deal. Be ready to support him if he loses the bet."

In most senses, Rosecrans has done a brilliant job in constructing the new line along the Nashville Pike. But in his rush to get brigades into line, he has seriously jumbled the chain of command, rendering Crittenden, McCook, and several division commanders supernumerary. Brigadier General Horatio Van Cleve, commanding Third Division, Crittenden's wing, knows less about the counterattack than Sam Beatty or James Fyffe, whose brigades ostensibly belong to his division. Nor can he depend on Crittenden to inform him. Riding at the rear of Rosecrans's staff, Van Cleve watches with disapproval as Crittenden takes another surreptitious nip from a flask. The man shouldn't be here, he thinks. Utterly incompetent, and a sot besides.

I shouldn't be here either, he reminds himself. I'm an old Michigan farmer who graduated from the Academy when most of these generals and colonels were children. My God, McCook, Sheridan, and that lad Harker are young enough to be my sons. And Sill, poor boy. Van Cleve shakes his head, drops behind, signals his own small staff to follow him. Enough of this tagtailing. He will go with Beatty and Fyffe, see if he can be of any assistance.

Van Cleve is surprised to find Beatty, Fyffe, and Harker nearly to the trees on the far side of the field. Good God, Rosecrans can't mean to push beyond the cover of the artillery, can he? Not with so much undecided elsewhere. Surely we shouldn't risk another crisis here. Van Cleve sets spurs to his horse, gallops forward to stop the advance. He will send back to Rosecrans for instructions, take it on his own head if he errs on the side of caution now.

On the right end of the line, Colonel Charlie Harker is appalled when Van Cleve halts the line sixty yards short of the trees. He does not come directly under Van Cleve's authority, could push on. But Charlie Harker, lucky though he is, won't press his luck that far. The old farmer has a sternness about him, an edge like an old scythe forgotten in the rain behind a shed but still dangerously sharp beneath the rust.

Harker prances his horse back and forth behind his line. Let's go, damn it. Let's get around the Reb flank and give them back a little of their own medicine.

Major General Alexander McDowell McCook sits his horse on the pike, watching the line waiting a few score yards from the trees as a pair of couriers dash back toward the pike. He has managed to cobble together a few regiments from his shattered wing and has them coming now to fall in on the position vacated by Harker. McCook frowns. Where the hell is the cavalry to protect Harker's flank? He's hanging entirely in the air, exposed to anything. McCook bites his lip against a sudden stinging in his eyes. God must be a cavalryman, never around when you need him.

Brigadier General Sam Beatty spits tobacco juice. "Well, Tanner," he says to his adjutant, "we chased the Rebs in there. I wonder if they've stopped to regroup, or if they're still running."

Before the adjutant can reply, there is a stirring in the trees, branches moving, as if by something casually, confidently powerful. The adjutant has the absurd recollection of an afternoon when he'd paddled a skiff through a narrow, reedy channel in search of ducks, only to come face to face with a bear. The bear had come as whatever is coming now, pushing slowly through the reeds and brush of a low island to emerge on the muddy bank within a paw's swipe of skiff and boy. The bear's small, red eyes stared disdainfully at him, almost dared him to reach for the shotgun. And when he didn't, the bear had made a noise almost like a *harrumph,* had turned his broad behind and shambled back into the brush. And so it is with an almost eidetic horror that Major Tanner watches the disturbance in the cedar branches resolve itself into a long line of butternut skirmishers.

Beside him, Sam Beatty pauses in his chewing. "Well, son of a whore," he mutters.

The clash at the edge of the trees midway between the Wilkinson and Nashville pikes sets Lucius Polk's brigade against Sam Beatty's; S.A.M. Wood's against Fyffe's; Vaughan's brigade, lent Cleburne by Cheatham, against Harker's left; and Bushrod Johnson's brigade against Harker's right. With his flank dangling in the air and two brigades coming at him hard, Charlie Harker, who has never doubted that the stars work in his favor, loses his composure. Forgetting Fyffe's flank, he retreats to the Burris house ridge, six hundred yards to his right rear. Fyffe sends three messengers, one after another, with pleas for Harker to cover his flank. But Harker, his men flat on the ground either side of the Widow Burris's house, refuses to budge.

A Union surgeon bursts from the Burris house, heads for Harker. "For God's sake, man! We've got wounded here. Take your fight down into the field."

Charlie Harker cannot stop trembling, although when he looks at his hands they seem steady enough. He wonders if he can speak in a normal tone, tries: "This is your fight, too, Doctor. All of ours."

The surgeon sweeps a hand at the long rows of wounded. "These men have done their fighting! Now it's the job of my surgeons to save as many as we can. And they can't do it if we're in the middle of a battle."

Harker turns his back on the man. "We can't leave here, Doctor. Now do your work and I'll do mine."

The surgeon stands tight-lipped for a moment, then looks where Harker is looking. Slowly, his mouth falls open in amazement. "Colonel, you've abandoned the flank! That brigade can't hold!"

"Neither could we. There are too many Rebs."

"But Christ, man! You've got to do something!"

"We can't leave this hill, Doctor. Now, please, I have things I must do."

Abandoned by Harker, Fyffe swings back the 86th Indiana to form a crochet. Before the Hoosiers can get in position, Vaughan envelops Fyffe's flank, enfilading the entire length of the Yankee line. Fyffe's and Sam Beatty's brigades buckle, the men fleeing for the safety of the pike. Liddell joins Bushrod Johnson's assault on the Burris house ridge. Under fire, Harker withdraws from the yard of the hospital, leaving dozens of the waiting wounded with second and even third wounds.

Brigadier General St. John Liddell steps into the Burris house to visit with the Yankee surgeons. He regrets having spoken so brutally to the doctor at the Gresham house in the hour he thought his son killed. Not that he would grant a truce if asked again, for it is impossible in the midst of this tumult, but he would at least refuse with a courtesy befitting a Southern gentleman.

Liddell is hardly a squeamish man, but the stench of chloroform, vomit, blood, and excrement almost overwhelms him. In the parlor and dining room on either side of the hall, surgeons and orderlies bend over makeshift operating tables. The floors are slick with blood, the men on the tables moaning, the doctors panting and perspiring with the effort of sawing off limbs. The chief surgeon approaches from the kitchen in the rear, wiping his hands on a bloody rag.

Liddell extends a hand. "Liddell, commanding Second Brigade, Cleburne's division."

"Burns, General. Ninety-third Ohio." He gestures at the surroundings. "I apologize for the conditions. This wasn't supposed to be a hospital, and we don't have what we should. But we're doing what we can."

An orderly pushes between them with a tub of severed arms and legs. Liddell is struck with the paleness of the skin, the dead whiteness that comes so soon after the amputation of a living limb. I must leave here, he thinks. I need to fight yet today.

A shriek from the kitchen makes Liddell wince in spite of himself. Burns turns a casual glance in that direction. "We're nearly out of chloroform, and the pain is too much for some of the lads. And there's the horror of losing an arm or a leg. I suppose it might be the same with any of us. If they protest too much, we have to put them outside without doing the work that might save their lives. It's a pity, but we can't waste much time on any one man. But some additional chloroform would help if you have some to spare."

"I'm sorry, Doctor, but my surgeons are far behind by now, treating our wounded in equally poor circumstances."

"Yes, I suppose so. . . . Well, General, I should see to my patients. There's a bottle of acceptable claret somewhere around here if you'd care for a drink."

"Thank you, but no. Is there anything else I can do for you, Doctor?"

"Well, we've had some trouble with stragglers going among the wounded, demanding money."

"No one from my command!"

"No, sir. They were from our side. But there will be Southern boys straggling and more of our Northern toughs about. If you could post a guard. . . ."

"I don't have any men to spare, Doctor. But if you can find some whitewash, paint on the outside of the house that you are under the protection of General St. John Liddell. That will give at least those who know me pause."

★   ★   ★

Garesché has never seen Rosecrans more in command. In a day which should have stretched every fiber of the man's physical and mental strength to breaking, the rout of Sam Beatty, Fyffe, and Harker seems only to stimulate Rosecrans to greater exertions. He rallies the retreating regiments, re-forms them along the pike. "It's all right, boys. They got the better of us that time. Next time it's our turn." And so he turns them: regiment, company, squad, and soldier.

Rosecrans is foremost but not alone in rallying the troops. Van Cleve, snow-white beard identifying him from a great distance, rides calmly among the retreating men. Even Crittenden, buoyed no doubt by alcohol, has Harker's men in surprisingly good order. Down the road, Garesché can make out Thomas walking his smooth-gaited mare along the pike, pointing soldiers to positions. We are not whipped yet, Garesché thinks. My God of Battles, stand by us, we are not whipped yet.

For hours now, Rosecrans has been in a state of such extraordinary con-centration that the capacity for fear or wonder has been blotted entirely from his consciousness. The army is terribly battered: cracked and riven in a hundred places so that one more blow may shatter it entirely. The coun-terattack on Hardee was a mistake, an impulsive gamble to regain the offen-sive. Impatience, always his worst enemy. Now, he thinks, we may have given them one more success than we can stand. But I don't think so. I still have the pieces of this army in my hands, know where every regiment is. I can pull this line together one more time. And sooner or later Hardee must stop and rest his men. They have fought now for nearly nine hours and not even they can fight forever—not even that Irish boy Cleburne who would attack hell itself if Hardee told him to.

Rosecrans spurs Boney up the pike again, pushing yet more men into position, anchoring the line on Morton's Pioneers and Stokes's battery. "Rally, boys," he shouts. "We're going to give them a taste of real hell this time."

He spots two begrimed, exhausted regiments limping across the pike. An officer bareback on an artillery horse rides forward, salutes. "Bradley, sir. Fifty-first Illinois."

"I know you, Colonel."

"Colonel Roberts is dead, sir. I've taken command of his brigade. Two of our regiments are back with General Sheridan. I'm taking these two to resupply at the ordnance train."

"There's no time for that. Re-form and fill that gap a hundred yards up the pike."

"But, General, we don't have a cartridge among us!"

"Then you must fight with bayonets, Colonel. Go on now. The Rebs will break this time. I know it for certain."

★　★　★

It is not the sort of attack Pat Cleburne likes. For all his aggressiveness, he is never reckless. But he has the order in Hardee's own hand: *Push them, Patrick! Now, before we lose the light!*

Cleburne orders his five brigades forward against the pike and Rosecrans's shaky line of infantry. But the Union guns are solid. Anchored by the Chicago Board of Trade Battery and the Pennsylvania battery on Stokes's hill, the Federal batteries pour a converging fire on the butternut line. Encouraged by the guns and the disciplined fire of Morton's Pioneers, the Union infantry steadies.

For the rest of the day and the rest of the war, Cleburne's colonels and brigadiers will dispute which unit broke first. The majority of opinion will blame a regiment of Vaughan's brigade, but this may be simple prejudice against a brigade only temporarily attached to the division. When Colonel Bradley leads Sheridan's exhausted veterans in a bayonet charge that should be at best a forlorn hope, the blue soldiers are astonished to see the Rebels turn tail.

Son of a bitch if Rosy wasn't right! Bradley thinks. "Remember Roberts, boys!" he shouts. "Remember Roberts!" He glances back over his shoulder, catches sight of Rosecrans waving his hat wildly.

Brigadier General St. John Liddell is still on the Burris house ridge when he sees Secesh soldiers running. He mounts, dashes down the hill, saber drawn. He menaces the soldiers with his blade, recognizing them as Bushrod Johnson's men, and manages to halt the retreat near the base of the hill. He gallops on, finds Johnson. "What is the meaning of this disgrace, sir?" he shouts, for in his rage he is no more a respecter of Johnson's seniority than he was, at the Gresham house, of gentle Doctor Doolittle's petition of mercy.

Johnson turns a mild look on Liddell, then points to the west. Liddell looks, feels color drain from his face at the sight of his own brigade, ranks broken and colors at the trail, fleeing for the cover of a copse of trees. My God, Liddell thinks, we are undone. He turns to Johnson, "General, I beg your pardon."

"Never mind, John. It is a disgrace, and I have no explanation for it."

★　★　★

The great clash of cavalry fated in the convergence of the forces of Stanley, Wharton, Kennett, and Wheeler never takes place. Wharton withdraws from his forward position near the pike to make a sweep to the southeast to pick up a few more Yankee prisoners and wagons. In so doing, he narrowly misses Kennett who is swinging to the west with Zahm, Otis, and a section of mountain howitzers.

Coming along the country road just east of Overall Creek to find Wharton, Wheeler is within sight of the Ashbury church when cannon and carbine fire erupt from the woods ahead. Instead of shifting smoothly into attack formation as they would if fresh, Wheeler's lead squadrons give way. Wheeler rides forward, trying to get an idea of what he faces. There are only two guns—mountain howitzers, judging from their bark—but he has none, his own guns back in the rear, teams broken down. And like his friend Charlie Harker, Joe Wheeler loses his nerve, decides nothing of commensurate value can be gained by pressing an attack in the face of such odds.

Watching Wheeler retreat, Judge John Kennett is not foolish enough to press his luck. Except for the howitzers, the odds are entirely on the other side and the hour itself dictates caution. The judge looks at the pale outline of the sun low above the trees, feels his belly grumble. He'll ask around, see if anyone on the staff has a cracker or two. Another hour or so and maybe they'll have a chance for something hot. Coffee, at least.

Stanley leaves the Wilkinson Pike west of Overall Creek, following a narrow lane north until it intersects with the east–west road that crosses the creek a few hundred yards west of the Ashbury church. He finds Kennett waiting for him at the crossroads, munching a piece of hardtack. "Judge! I'm glad to see you."

Kennett smiles with the sort of grim forbearance he might direct at a young lawyer rushing into court fifteen minutes late. "Stanley. We'd begun to wonder what happened to you. We've been busy."

"So this man told me." Stanley gestures to a wiry private, who stares at him with obvious loathing. "I can't understand why General Rosecrans didn't send for me sooner. It wasn't until this man came with a message from Garesché that we even knew there was a battle."

Kennett lets this pass without comment. "This flank is secure, General. I think you can safely leave it while you seek instructions from the commanding general. Minty's brigade can take the front here while Zahm's boys cook some supper. They've had a long day."

"Yes. Yes, of course." Stanley puts spurs to his horse, rides off with his staff to find Rosecrans, leaving Judge Kennett to carry out the tactical deployment of the cavalry division, as is his right and responsibility as division commander.

Kennett takes a bite of his second cracker, chews with huge satisfaction.

Lieutenant Otis brings him a metal cup. "Coffee, Colonel? It's a bit on the weak side, but it's hot."

"Thank you, Otis. At this moment it could be made from boiled mule piss and I'd relish it."

Rosecrans and Garesché watch as the Rebel assault on the army's right streams back across the fields into the darkening cedars. Rosecrans slaps Garesché on the shoulder. "We've sent them running here, Julius. Come, we must look to the center. It sounds like Bragg is making another try at breaking Hazen."

Garesché feels his face stretched to an unfamiliar tightness, realizes he is grinning in a way he hasn't grinned since he was a boy wandering through a street carnival in Havana. And though he has known much happiness in his children, Mariquitta, and the embrace of his church, he has never, between that day and this, felt such joy.

Pat Cleburne can see the exhaustion in their stumbling, leaden walks, in the eyes gone deep and glassy in haggard faces. These are brave men, but they have nothing left of the store of courage they brought into the fight. He will not order them to attack again, though he could fight on forever. There is something in Cleburne that hungers, will hunger eternally, even if he is killed. He imagines that he will then become part of the hunger itself, will go with it in search of another soul. He has never met Robert E. Lee, but he has seen the man's picture, suspects that he is haunted by the same hunger for battle. Someday he should like to meet Sheridan, for he suspects that he too has it, but that unlike Lee he is not merely haunted but possessed by it in entire acceptance, as Pat Cleburne is. Yes, Cleburne could fight on forever, but not these men, not now when the hour is too late to bring up cannon or to petition Bragg again for reinforcements.

Hardee comes riding through the dripping cedars, his head bowed, shoulders slumped, the soldiers parting to either side of him without looking up. He stops before Cleburne, raises red-rimmed eyes. "Bragg is unfit, Patrick," he whispers. "Unfit to be a general, unfit to command men such as these."

CHAPTER 8

Wednesday, 1:00–4:00 P.M.
December 31, 1862
The Confederate Right Center

Bragg has ordered brigades from Breckinridge's division across the river to reinforce Hardee's attack on the Union right. But confusion thwarts that plan and, with the failure of Hardee's final assault, the Round Forest again becomes the focus of the Confederate attack.

THE PLEAS RAIN on him, bombard him like hail: for more troops, more artillery, for a diversion here, a thrust there. And Bragg can do nothing but sit his tall gelding in the drizzle, waiting for others to obey orders. Last night he gave them a plan and assigned them the means to carry it out. But they have failed to execute the great wheel, have squandered their forces. Now they act as if he is being selfish, as if he is withholding vast reserves. Hardee's messages in particular have become shrill to the point of insubordination. He has sent him Wheeler, though the cavalry is badly broken down by its raid through Rosecrans's rear. Beyond that he has nothing to give, must concentrate what he can muster to break the Yankees' hold on that miserable grove at the apex of their line.

If only people understood how little he'd wanted to be a general. Oh, he'd wanted the rank as a reward for his ability, for his striving after merit. But he has never enjoyed generalship. No, he would rather command a flying battery, hurl himself into battle, questing for the particular moment, the particular point, where his beautiful guns would make all the difference.

Buena Vista. He could live that day a thousand times, ten thousand, and never grow tired of it.

But that was another war, another time, when a lowly captain and a single battery could change all. Such things happen rarely, if ever, in this war of great armies bludgeoning each other until both must fall back to rest. In Mexico, there were clear victories, accomplished with style. Not in this war. His critics accuse him of lacking subtlety, of ordering massed attacks with little room for maneuver or the exploitation of a sudden opportunity. But what else can he do with this ill-trained multitude of country boys? Name one time in this war where subtlety has triumphed. Is Lee subtle? Hell, Bob Lee is a pounder, more reckless of his men's lives than Bragg has ever been. Look at Malvern Hill. My God, Lee had thrown five divisions straight into the teeth of two hundred and fifty Federal guns. And, oh, we may scoff at much about Yankee soldiery, but they understand machines, understand artillery, work their guns with immense skill. Lee's doomed assaults cost the Army of Northern Virginia five thousand men, yet Lee emerged a hero, a master tactician, while Bragg is called a bumbler after nearly defeating a Yankee army four times his number at Perryville at a cost of only three thousand.

Beneath him, the black gelding shifts. Bragg pats the big animal's neck absently. If he had his way, he'd mount his staff now, lead them down into the battle, dash about placing batteries, instructing colonels on tactics, shouting encouragement to the men. And would any of that do any good? Momentarily it might, but in the course of things such a frenzy would disturb the chain of command, confuse the picture until no one understood the whole, even the half of it.

Elise believes she sees everything entire, badgers him constantly with advice. In grand strategy she is not a bad novice. Really quite good. But strategy is easy, a matter of pointing to a map and announcing an Anaconda Plan or the like. Even tactics, though more difficult, are easy compared to the daily management of an army. In this Bragg excels, is better even than Lee or Joe Johnston. Yet Elise still has her advice on all things connected with the army. He almost smiles. That silly note about not trusting the Tennesseans, about putting the artillery behind them to shoot those who would flee. The Tennesseans are good enough troops, no better and no worse than most, and much preferable to the Kentuckians, who truly are unreliable. But Elise will have her say.

He loves her with an intensity almost beyond bearing. Shakespeare or Milton might have managed some sense of his love, but no lesser poet. Elise is, he believes, God's reward for his suffering, his forbearance, his striving after excellence. For her he can go on being a general, though it is using him up, making of him an old man before his time.

Brent approaches. "General, we have word that Adams's brigade is across the river."

"What's the time?"

"Nearly half past one, General."

Bragg shakes his head. Three and a half hours for Breckinridge to obey an order. Well, one thing is for certain. No matter how this battle turns out, he shall go straight to the president with the charge that Major General John C. Breckinridge is a traitor.

Bragg has been trying to get reinforcements across the river since mid-morning. Shortly before 10:00 A.M., with the Yankees in flight everywhere to the left of Sheridan's salient, Hardee appealed to him for *a fresh division if possible, two brigades if you can supply no more.*

Whatever his generals may think, Bragg is not absolutely dedicated to the great wheel. He fully recognizes the chance handed him by Hardee's triumph on the left. If Hardee can get across the Yankee rear to the Nashville Pike, they will have Rosecrans cut off from Nashville and nearly surrounded. He instructs Major Clare, his assistant inspector general: "Go to Breckinridge. Tell him to shift two brigades to this side of the river. They are to march as rapidly as possible to General Hardee's support."

Fifteen minutes later, Clare is back. "General Breckinridge respectfully declines to transfer any troops to this side of the river. He says he's about to be attacked by a heavy Yankee battle line."

Bragg thinks rapidly. How can Rosecrans have found enough men to launch a flanking attack while fighting for his life everywhere else? It seems improbable if not impossible. More likely it is some pathetic feint to hold Breckinridge in place. Still. . . . "Very well, I withdraw the order. Tell General Breckinridge to attack unless he is certain that the enemy is upon him in force."

Clare rides off. A few minutes later, Brent brings a muddy cavalry lieutenant from Brigadier General John Pegram, commander of the small cavalry brigade east of the river. The lieutenant salutes. "General Pegram sends his regards, sir. He would like to know if you have been informed of the Yankee battle line advancing east of the river on General Breckinridge's position."

Bragg is not an intuitive general, but he senses something amiss here. "Yes, I've been told of it. But, tell me, Lieutenant, when did General Pegram observe this Yankee battle line?"

"About eight, General. We let General Breckinridge know and then went on a scout up the Lebanon Road in case the Yanks had a column coming down on his flank."

"Then the sighting of the Yankee battle line is more than two hours old?"

"Well, yes, sir. I mean our first sighting. I got only the one, but I think General Pegram must have left someone to watch the Yanks."

Bragg frowns. Pegram is a West Pointer and, though a bit of a dilettante, a soldier of good judgment. All right, there is a Yankee battle line east of the river, but it cannot be in great force with Rosecrans's need for men to hold off Hardee. Nor can it be advancing vigorously if it has yet to make contact with Breckinridge's line. The sooner it is broken up, the better. "Colonel," he says to Brent, "send Major Johnson to repeat my order: Breckinridge is to advance, capturing or destroying all Yankee formations east of the river."

Time edges past. Cheatham, Cleburne, and finally Stewart hammer at Sheridan's salient, finally break it. A message comes from Polk asking for reinforcements. Bragg shakes his head angrily. Do they think I have a pocket full of dragon's teeth that I can sow every time they need soldiers?

At 11:45 A.M., Major Clare returns with a message from Breckinridge: *I am obeying your order with reluctance since advancing will take me away from the Lebanon Road and expose my right to a heavy force of the enemy advancing from Black's bridge.*

Bragg is stunned. What heavy force? He has had no report of any force on the Lebanon Road, although he has worried about an attack from that direction for days. He sends the panting Clare back to Breckinridge with an order to halt his advance in place and protect his right. He dispatches a second courier to Pegram with instructions to determine the size and, if possible, the intentions of the force coming down the Lebanon Road. He sends a third officer pelting off to ask Polk if he can send two brigades to reinforce Breckinridge.

For the better part of an hour, Bragg paces. Finally, the mud-splattered and rather dazed Major Clare returns. He hands Bragg a note from Breckinridge: *It is not certain that the enemy is advancing on me.*

Bragg explodes. "Which enemy? From which direction? What does the man mean?" He glares at Clare.

"I think he means that there is no enemy between his line and the river."

"And where is his line?"

"About a half mile forward of his original position."

"And his right? Is it threatened?"

"Not so far as I know, General. No one seemed concerned about it."

"But there was supposed to be a heavy force coming down the Lebanon Road! Breckinridge said so himself."

"I didn't hear of any such, General. All I heard was some speculation that if a force appeared from that direction, it would be behind their right flank."

Bragg is astounded. "It was a *speculation?*"

"As far as I heard."

A rider arrives from Pegram. The colonel has found no force approaching by way of the Lebanon Road. Some Yankee sharpshooters have occupied the east bank of Stones River near McFadden's Ford, but the remainder of the battle line observed earlier in the day seems to have withdrawn across the river.

Bragg stares at Pegram's scrawled report. He should be furious, towering in his wrath, but he is simply too astonished. Pegram is a West Pointer, a professional. Breckinridge held the second highest office in the land prior to the war. How in God's name could they have made such a botch of things? He sighs, feeling very old, very inadequate. "Colonel Brent, tell General Breckinridge to bring four of his brigades across the river and report to General Polk. Tell him to leave Hanson's Kentucky Brigade to hold Wayne's Hill and to protect the flank."

He mounts his black gelding, rides to the top of the low rise to see what he can of the battle. Too late to send infantry to Hardee. He will revert to the original plan, put the great wheel in motion again. But first he must smash that miserable grove of trees at the apex of the Yankee line.

Bragg refuses lunch, munches a cracker instead. Brent brings him reports of the fighting. He acknowledges them with a nod or a few words. Finally Brent brings news that Adams's brigade is across the river. Good, Bragg thinks. Three more to come over and then we can smash the Yankee salient in those trees, perhaps draw off enough troops from the Yankee right flank for Hardee to break through to the pike. All may work out yet.

✶ ✶ ✶

Breckinridge is profoundly humiliated by the morning's blunders. He can trace exactly how things went wrong. Pegram had come to his tent at first light to share coffee, bacon, and cornbread by the fire. He is an exceptionally handsome young man, intelligent and cultured despite a West Point education, which—from what Breckinridge has observed—does nothing to refine a young man save to give him a passing fluency in French.

They have shared breakfast on many mornings, talking of literature, history, art, and—most fascinating of all—what manner of civilization the South can build once it is free of Yankee tyranny. They agree that something must be done about slavery, perhaps a gradual emancipation followed by a benign peonage binding the coloreds to the land as an eternally subservient race. Then let the arts, the manners, the culture of the South flourish in a pastorale without end.

But this morning Pegram was edgy, talked not of the future but of the day. "Rosecrans is their great secret, their best general by far. They've brought him along slowly, given him a chance to succeed. Now they're giving him his first great opportunity."

Breckinridge yawned. Though he is a politician—one of the most successful of his generation—he is slightly bored by talk of the plotting in the Federal capital. "By *they,* I assume you mean Lincoln and Stanton."

"And Halleck."

"And you contend they have been grooming Rosecrans?"

"Absolutely. Grant is a nobody. He won't last the winter. Burnside is as good as gone now. If Rosecrans wins today, they'll order him east to take command of the Army of the Potomac."

"And his present army?"

"They'll give it to Thomas, the traitor."

Breckinridge nodded, blew on his coffee. "So what's your point, John?"

"I'm saying, General, that I don't think anyone in this army appreciates how subtle, how devious Rosecrans is. I saw it at Rich Mountain, where he got a column over an impossible road into our rear. We barely got out with our lives and would have been destroyed completely if McClellan had attacked from the front at the right time."

"Yes, but that was fighting on a rather small scale."

"True, but Rosecrans won at Corinth and there wasn't anything small about that battle. Van Dorn and Price had him outnumbered and he still gave them a thrashing. Now he's taken Buell's sorry lot and made them into a first-rate army. He'll use it well. He's got something up his sleeve, some stratagem, and I suspect he intends it for us on this end of the line."

Pegram had his full attention. "Do have any guess as to the nature of this stratagem?"

"I think he's going to loop something wide, something to get into our rear to distract us at the critical moment."

"Cavalry?"

"No, I doubt if he has enough. More likely an infantry division, at least a brigade or two."

Breckinridge was skeptical, but then Pegram was the professional. "Well, keep on the lookout and keep me informed. For the time being, it seems that the commanding general has little planned for this flank of the army."

Breckinridge does not recall thinking overmuch on this conversation as Hardee opened the battle on the opposite flank. But when Pegram sent him the first reports of Yankee infantry crossing McFadden's Ford, he somehow fell into assuming that Pegram's predictions must be right in every detail, including the eventual arrival on the division's right flank of a Yankee column from the north. He sent word of the crossing to Bragg and braced for the onslaught. For two hours nothing happened, but then this was not an undue amount of time if Rosecrans was bringing two or three divisions across the river. He received no further word from Pegram, but assumed only that the cavalry must be scouting the edges of the Yankee lodgment.

At 10:00 A.M., Breckinridge was thunderstruck to receive the order from Bragg transferring two brigades to Hardee. My God, Breckinridge himself was about to be struck front and flank! He demurred, sending the dutiful Major Clare back with a polite message to Bragg. Clare returned with orders for Breckinridge to advance against the enemy battle line forming on the east side of the ford. Again, Breckinridge was astonished. A forward movement would leave his right flank open to the Yankee column coming down the Lebanon Road. (That no such column had actually been detected seemed immaterial, what with the accuracy of Pegram's other prediction.) Again, he demurred, and again Clare galloped off for Bragg's headquarters.

Clare returned with a second order to advance, an order which was repeated soon after by Major Johnson. After expressing his concern for his flank in a note to Bragg, Breckinridge advanced a half mile in line of battle. There he halted and sent a pair of staff officers to reconnoiter. The bedraggled Clare returned yet again, this time with an order for Breckinridge to halt in place—an action on which Breckinridge and the commanding general could at last agree.

An oddly long time passed before the two staff officers returned from their scout. They had found not a single Yankee on this side of the river, no great battle line, not so much as a cavalry patrol. Breckinridge had the sensation of trying to swallow a peach pit, identified it as dread. He sent his chief of staff for a look. The colonel returned shortly. "They must have gone back over, General."

"Did you see anything of Colonel Pegram and our cavalry?"

The chief of staff looked exceedingly unhappy. "No, sir. Perhaps they've gone up the Lebanon Road on a scout."

"Has anyone heard shooting from that direction? Any indication that the Yankees are up that way in force?" His staff officers shuffled, avoided his eyes. After a pause poignant with collective embarrassment, Breckinridge took a dispatch book, wrote the dispiriting message to Bragg: *It is not certain the enemy is advancing on me.* He signed it, ashamed for having been misled by his own fears and the fears of a not overly bright young man who once had the stuffing knocked out of him by Rosecrans in western Virginia. He handed the message to Major Clare. "Major, if you would be so kind."

Now, with the time approaching 2:00 P.M., Breckinridge has sent Adams's and Jackson's brigades across the river, is about to follow with Palmer's and Preston's. He will lead his four brigades to the attack himself, win a triumph that will blot out the morning's farce. That or die in the attempt, for he would rather lay down his life on this field than face Braxton Bragg without first regaining some measure of self-respect.

☆ ☆ ☆

Brigadier General Milo Hascall continues to engineer the defense of the Round Forest while more senior generals muster artillery and reorganize shattered brigades. He replaces jaded regiments, orders in ammunition and water, evacuates what wounded he can when more important work is done. Wagons cannot get through to Hazen's line, and soldiers manhandle the heavy cases of cartridges and cannon rounds over the downed trees, shattered artillery carriages, and bodies of the dead. The wounded struggle out of the forest, leaving evidence of their passage in bloody splashes and drips almost as distinct in pattern and volume as the variety of their wounds.

Hascall picks his way forward. Hazen is using the pause between attacks to build a rough breastwork along his line, his voice cracking as he shouts directions. Hascall dismounts, nods to Bierce, and hands Hazen a canteen. "Keep it, Bill. As soon as we get the ammunition in, I'll be sending water."

"Milo, we have to hold this position."

"I know it, Bill. Thomas has fifty guns in place to support you." He produces a handkerchief. "Wash your face. You look like a coal miner."

They talk for ten minutes, though there is surprisingly little to say. Yet it is not time wasted. They are more rivals than friends, but they are both West Pointers, can in that identity share for a few minutes a camaraderie more profound than blood.

Fighting flares again on the army's right flank: the Rebels driving in, making their last attempt to breach the Federal line along the Nashville Pike. Hascall looks in that direction. "Rosy is over there. I think Hardee's the one trying to break through."

"And Cleburne," Hazen says.

"Yes. He's apparently quite remarkable. I'd like to meet him."

"I'd like to see him dead."

Hascall nods. "I suppose that would be better. A pity we don't have him with us. . . . Well, I'll look to the water and the ammunition, then."

"Thank you, Milo."

★ ★ ★

Bishop Polk recalls the feeling from adolescence, the stickiness on the belly, in the fine pubic hair of youth, on the thighs and the sweaty sheets. Shocking, embarrassing, for night clothes and bedding must then be washed on a different day than usual. The nigger washerwoman grinned at him, made a pouting of her great lips, darted a tongue like a snake's head between them. She laughed uproariously at his blush. Ashamed of his own desire, he went to the woods, masturbated, letting his seed fall on the oak leaves. That summer, her daughter went with him to the woods. When he left for West Point a year later, there was a new mulatto baby in the slave quarters. He saw it a time or two, never thought much about it, went on to become a cadet, a convert, a minister, a husband, and a bishop.

Before Shiloh, before he became the eater of souls, Polk would have been shocked to find his drawers sticky with drying semen in the midst of a battle. He was an honorable man before Shiloh, a servant of his church, his state, and his race; a husband, the father of half a dozen children, and the possessor of a sexual history numbering one decent woman (his wife), three whores, four or five more or less willing colored women, and one other experience that he preferred not to count, although sometimes he dreamed of it, waking with his member painfully swollen and requiring immediate relief.

In August 1831, only sixteen months ordained and yet without an assignment, Polk had found himself suffering from a "general disability." Advised that he should seek foreign climes, he left his wife of fifteen months and his child of five months to sail for Europe. He found the South of France agreeable, and in a few months felt strong enough to preach to the sailors of Nice on a blustery night that tasted of Africa. For the rest of his life, he will remember the ill-lit seaman's refuge, the harsh smell of the French tobacco, the odor of the sailors themselves. Every port—at least every port in Christendom—has such a hall serving sermons and soup. He preached on an obvious text from the Psalms: *They that go down to the sea in ships, that do business in great waters. These see the works of the Lord, and his wonders in the Deep.*

He had labored on his own translation, hoping to preserve the charm of the King James Bible while rendering the verses understandable to these illiterate seafarers. His French was halting at first, but he seemed to have their attention, gained in confidence and fluidity as the Spirit came into him. When he finished, there were gruff murmurs of approval, a smattering of applause, although he was unsure if these expressions praised his sermon or the uncovering of the soup cauldrons.

During supper, he circulated among them. At one table, he was invited to sit, got on famously, and, when the meal was over, went with these rough men to a tavern on the waterfront. The risks would have been apparent to a more worldly man, but Polk was yet very young and very innocent. He was not a drinker, suspected nothing in the odd bitterness of the wine, made no connection when the faces of the sailors became blurry, their laughter oddly muted around him.

They buggered him for hours in a tiny room above the tavern, pressed in laughing around him, each waiting his turn at the pale buttocks and the bleeding rectum of this arrogant landlubber who would dare preach to them of God's wonders manifest upon the Deep.

Major General Jones Withers is appalled by the damage to his division. Patton Anderson and Alex Stewart have suffered frightful casualties in breaking Sheridan's salient and driving Shepherd's regulars from the cedars below the Nashville Pike. Worse are the losses in Chalmers's brigade, and worse yet those in Donelson's from their assaults on Cruft's line and the Round Forest. My God, what can justify this? We must give over this battle, fall back, beg our men to forgive us. He stands aside, shaken, nearly in tears.

Bishop Leonidas Polk has no doubts, knows that the shedding of blood must beget more of the same. The dybbuk wolf must be fed, lest it turn, devour the souls of the living, become even more monstrous in its ravening. He doesn't wait for Breckinridge to get his four brigades across the river, orders Adams's Louisiana brigade forward into the fields against the Round Forest.

Adams's brigade advances in line of battle about 2:15 P.M. Once again the outbuildings of the Cowan farm play hob with the Rebel line. Adams feeds his regiments through one at a time, eventually bringing the line back together on either side of the pike. All this is done under terrible fire from the batteries on Hazen's line and the line of guns assembled by Thomas to the rear of the forest. At three hundred yards, Hazen's sharpshooters open fire. At two hundred yards the infantry commences firing by volleys, the entire front rippling with muzzle flashes.

On Hazen's left flank, Colonel George Wagner grabs his chance to join the battle. His guns have done good execution against the earlier Rebel attacks, and he has sent two regiments to Hazen to shore up the Round Forest line. He, however, has had little personally to do. Only when he sees the right flank of the 13th–20th Louisiana exposed to his front does he have the satisfaction of leading an attack.

Wagner's Hoosiers hit the Louisiana flank at charge bayonet. For once the tactic works, and seventy-eight Tigers surrender in the face of cold steel. The Hoosiers push ahead, become caught in a desperate exchange at fifty paces as Adams rallies his line. The Reverend John Whitehead of the 15th Indiana carries Captain Roger Templeton to the rear, lays him down, copies his final words, mutters a short prayer, returns to the regiment. He's not back five minutes when he sees a single minié ball kill two privates and mortally wound Captain J. N. Foster. He catches the falling Foster, eases him down, holds him while he dies. Nearby, Lieutenant Colonel Isaac Suman of the 9th Indiana is shot from his horse, lies hemorrhaging from a severed artery in his arm. Whitehead goes to him and binds the wound. "There's a goddamn ball between my ribs," Suman grates. "I can feel it, but I can't get my fingers on it." Whitehead rolls the colonel on his side, hesitantly probes the wound with a finger, feels the base of the conical minié ball an inch below the skin. "Get it out, man!" Suman snaps. Whitehead forces his thumb and forefinger into the wound, manages to pinch the ball. On the third attempt he draws it out. Suman rips a pocket out of his coat, crams the fabric into the wound. "Help me up."

"Colonel, you should go to the rear," Whitehead pleads.

"I've got boys fighting. I'm not going to any goddamn rear. Help me up!"

Whitehead manages to get Suman on his feet, and then boosts him into the saddle with both hands under the colonel's buttocks. Suman kicks the horse, dashes back into the fight.

A stray Federal cannonball bounces through the 15th Indiana, shattering the leg of Private John Long. Long contemplates the wound for a moment, and then deliberately takes out his barlow knife, strops the blade on a brogan, and cuts off the dangling appendage. He loops his belt around the stump to staunch the bleeding and, using his Springfield as a crutch, manages to hobble a dozen yards. When he falters, Whitehead sweeps him up, carries him to the rear. He sets him down behind a tree. "I'll be all right, preacher," Long says. "Go help the boys that needs you." Whitehead leaves him studying the stump of his missing leg.

The Rebel brigade tries to push ahead on the axis of the pike while holding off the Hoosiers on its right. Finally it breaks, the soldiers streaming back across the fields. Whitehead looks about him, aghast at the carnage. "Reverend," a small voice speaks from near at hand.

Whitehead searches, spots Private Calvin Zenner. "Calvin! Are you badly hurt, son?"

The boy manages to smile. "Looks like. Can you carry me back? I'd like to die with some of the boys around me."

Whitehead carries him. His own eyes overflow, for the boy is warm against him, peaceful. He sets him down near Long and a half dozen other wounded. Zenner opens his eyes. "Reverend, can we have a song? I'd like to hear *O, Sing me to Heaven* a last time." Without waiting for an answer, he starts singing. Whitehead and the others join in. When the hymn is over, Zenner smiles. "Good-bye, boys, I'm going home. I'm mustered out." Within a minute, he is dead.

Whitehead closes his eyes. They are preposterous, these brave boys in their deaths. Too much courage, too little doubt of heaven. He takes a deep breath and goes to comfort the maimed and the dying.

Fleeing under the rain of the Federal artillery, Adams's men upset the careful order of Brigadier General John King Jackson's brigade advancing in column up the pike toward the Round Forest. More than physical collision is involved, for among these retreating are men without hands, without arms, men trailing ropes of intestines, men hobbling on the stumps of legs. Blood seems to fly from them, splattering everything in their way. It is obscene, this flight of the maimed, for most will die anyway, needn't confound the chances of others to carry out an attack and perhaps survive.

The Federal cannons blaze, the Yankee gunners ramming shot, shell, and case, stepping to the side, snapping the lanyards, the guns bucking back. The gunners, many of them stripped to the waist even in the cold, grasp the wheels, throw the guns back into position, swab, load, ram, fire.

Jackson's men struggle through the wave of their own countrymen, emerge, straighten their ranks, go forward at the double-quick, poised for the order to charge bayonet.

✯ ✯ ✯

Galloping down the pike from the right flank, Rosecrans and his staff arrive at Thomas's gun line in time to see the repulse of Adams's brigade. Rosecrans reins up beside Thomas. "Well, George, we seem to have held on the right. Will we hold here?"

Thomas nods. "I have no doubt of it, General." Thomas gives a rapid explanation of the fight before the Round Forest.

"I suppose it must be the very reverend Bishop Polk across from us," Rosecrans says.

"Yes, I believe it is."

"Did you ever know him?"

"No, never."

"I met him once. He didn't impress me as a theologian of any depth."

Thomas lets this pass, watches the fall of shot among the fleeing survivors of Adams's brigade.

McCook and his staff have drawn up a few dozen yards behind Thomas. McCook edges forward, like a whipped dog unsure if he yet dares to share the company of his harsh but adored master. Rosecrans and Thomas ignore him. For all his other flaws, McCook is neither a physical coward nor entirely without judgment. We are too closely grouped, he thinks, and in plain view of the Rebel guns on that hill on the far side of the river. My God, a single shot could kill the two senior officers in this army, leave me in command. He clears his throat. "Gentlemen, this is a nice mark for shells. Can't we thin out? Perhaps one of you should move to the other side of the pike."

Thomas and Rosecrans exchange glances. "It's about as safe one side as the other," Thomas growls.

Rosecrans smiles. "He's right, George. The army can't stand to lose both of us to one lucky shot. The men would be unnerved."

Thomas, always loath to give way, nevertheless nods. "I'll go to the other side of the pike." He rides off. McCook hesitates, watching Rosecrans, and then follows Thomas.

Garesché moves up beside Rosecrans, waits for orders. But for the first time all morning, Rosecrans seems relaxed, content to watch the battle without exercising his personal intervention.

To the left of the fight between Wagner and Adams, a lone oak stands by the road, its crown and branches shot away so that it stands a rampike against the background of river and rolling land. Though the fighting is ferocious, Garesché's attention keeps wandering to the shattered tree, as if in search of some hidden yet ineluctable truth. I wonder if it will sprout new branches come spring, he thinks, and where we will be by then.

Adams's brigade shudders, breaks, goes streaming down the pike. The staff cheers. Corporal Willie Porter approaches Garesché and Rosecrans. "General, Colonel, I've got your lunch with me. Major Goddard told me to bring it to you."

Rosecrans seems not to hear. "In a moment, Corporal," Garesché says. "That's very thoughtful of both you and Major Goddard."

"Look at that, Julius!" Rosecrans exclaims. "Some damned fool has sent another brigade forward in column right behind the first. My God, why didn't they send them both in at once? Concentration is everything in this business. That must be Polk over there; that's an amateur's mistake if I ever saw it."

"Let us remember that Bishop Polk is a graduate of the same institution that educated us, General."

"Yes, but he was never a soldier. Jack Magruder once told me that Polk spent his entire monthly allowance fornicating with a nigger kitchen maid down the road and the rest of his free time in the chapel praying for forgiveness."

Garesché laughs. "Yes, I'd heard something of the same."

Rosecrans warms to the subject. "According to Magruder, the saying was that Polk had the phallus of a donkey and the encephalon of a mule. He told me that one night he and some of the other fellows tied Polk to his bed and made a plaster cast of his extraordinary member. Supposedly, it's still somewhere in the natural sciences department."

"Little Willie" Porter has no idea what the two officers are talking about, readjusts the haversack holding the lunch sent by Major Goddard, and stares at the tumult on the pike.

Adams's retreating brigade has become entangled with Jackson's brigade trying to move in column up the pike. The Federal guns blaze away with any round that comes to hand, saving only the canister for close work. Jackson's ranks wrestle free, come up the pike at the double quick. Rosecrans rises in his stirrups, studies the approach. "Come on, Julius, we'd better go down and brace up the men. That Reb brigade is coming hard."

"General, you shouldn't expose—" Garesché begins, but Rosecrans is off, ignoring the protest which has become almost pro forma anyway. Garesché plunges after him, heart elated.

The sense that they are winning has begun to spread through the Federal ranks. Men cheer, wave hats at the sight of Rosecrans aboard his big, gray horse. Passing through Colonel William Grose's brigade, drawn up to go forward in support of Hazen, Rosecrans pauses. "Men, do you know how to be safe? Shoot low! Give them a blizzard at their shins! But to be safest of all, give them a blizzard and then charge with cold steel! Forward now!"

He charges on, the staff galloping behind. They are suddenly within the barrage of the Rebel guns on Wayne's Hill. An exploding shell kills Sergeant David Richmond and unhorses two orderlies. A fragment rips through Willie Porter's haversack, scattering the lunch he's carrying for his general and his colonel. He wails, "Now the dinner's ruined!" The staff laughs, Gareshé with them. A shell explodes in a harmless flash against a limestone outcropping and for an instant Gareshé stares at the image of a young woman—a girl really—smiling gently, perhaps a little sadly. There is a black mote in the corner of his vision—a tiny fragment of burned powder, he supposes—floating on the eye, waiting for a single tear to wash it away.

The cannonball explodes the head of Lieutenant Colonel Julius Gareshé in an instant too small to calculate. Nearest him, Little Willie Porter is drenched by a plume of blood and brains. Gareshé's body rides on, keeping pace for another twenty yards. Rosecrans turns in his saddle to say something, winces at the sight. On the general's uniform blouse, a splash of Gareshé's blood seems unnaturally red and a strand of brain tissue hangs thick and translucent from Rosecrans's beard. Rosecrans clamps his jaw, flicks away the strand of brains, and gallops on, as Gareshé's hands loosen on the reins and his body rolls slowly forward, leading with its left shoulder so that the right foot disengages smoothly from the stirrup, and Julius Gareshé makes a last graceful dismount.

Jackson's regiments come forward against Hazen's line at charge bayonet. The Rebel gunners on Wayne's Hill fire as fast as they can load, trying to clear a path for the infantry. Down the line from Hazen and Bierce's position behind the 9th Indiana, an artillery caisson explodes with a *whump*. Bierce stares at the rising pillar of smoke, sees it crowned by the caisson's slowly revolving spare wheel. And though Lieutenant Ambrose Bierce is a skeptic, a believer in reason and science, he has the absurd recollection of a verse from Ezekiel: *And when the living creatures went, the wheels went by them: and when the living creatures were lifted up from the earth, the wheels were lifted up.*

Rosecrans is among them, blouse streaked with blood though he seems uninjured. "Shoot low, men! Shoot low! Give them a blizzard at the shins!"

The musketry becomes an uninterrupted roar, drowning out even the artillery. The Rebel column tries to deploy in line of battle, folds back on itself, explodes in a thousand fleeing human fragments. A cheer wavers above the Federal line.

★   ★   ★

Breckinridge arrives with Palmer's and Preston's brigades in time to see the shattering of Jackson's brigade. He goes storming to Polk. "Bishop! What is the meaning of this? All four of my brigades should have gone forward together under my command!"

Polk gazes down at John C. Breckinridge, wonders why he ever took such dwarfs seriously. "I had my orders, sir. Now let me give you yours." He points to the Round Forest. "Take that grove of trees."

Breckinridge would press his complaint, but Polk turns away, stands staring at the litter of dead strewn across the fields either side of the pike, as if in deep spiritual contemplation on the folly of man. Breckinridge stalks off.

Milo Hascall is again shifting regiments between Hazen's line and the reserve. Rosecrans, having ridden the line and braced the men, goes off to check Colonel Price's hold on McFadden's Ford. Thomas resumes his previous position behind his gun line, lights one of the cigars Grant prefers.

Shortly before 4:00 P.M., a long line of butternut infantry emerges from the trees beyond the Cowan house. At the same moment, the sun bursts through the clouds for the first time in days, illuminating the fields and woods in warm, long-shadowed light. Watching the Rebel battle line, Hazen is moved by the "dreadful splendor" of three thousand bayonets glittering so that briefly they seem to form a single undulating cord of silver above the Rebel ranks.

On the rise to the rear of the Round Forest, Thomas takes the cigar from his mouth, studies the worried end, then turns to his chief of artillery. "You may commence firing, Major."

The muzzle flashes roll down the gun line, the shells and solid shot arcing briefly from the howitzers and Napoleons, traveling almost flat from the Parrott rifles. Case shot explodes over the Rebel ranks. Flags go down, the line itself beginning to crease and ripple, jagged holes appearing as the batteries in the Round Forest open with canister. Watching from Wagner's line, the Reverend Whitehead murmurs to no one in particular—perhaps to his God—"The fall of Lucifer in brimstone and hellfire. I understand it now."

Colonel Joseph Palmer, a former mayor of Murfreesboro, can see the hopelessness of advancing into the fury of the Federal guns. He breaks off the attack, hurries his brigade into the woods near Alexander Stewart's line.

Brigadier General William Preston pushes his brigade into the grounds of the Cowan farm where he, too, is presented with the reality that further advance will lead only to pointless slaughter. He pulls Sergeant David Gallagher, color bearer of the 4th Florida, up behind him, gallops toward the cover of the friendly woods. His men cheer, race after him. Only the 20th Tennessee, separated from the rest amid the burning buildings of the Cowan farm, pushes ahead.

Bill Hazen lets the Rebels struggle to within a hundred yards of the Round Forest and then orders his men to stand and fire. A single volley tears apart the butternut line with a sound like the ripping of a great banner. The 20th Tennessee fragments, leaving behind half its number dead, dying, or crawling forward under the smoke, begging to surrender.

Hardee arrives at Alexander Stewart's position in time to watch Palmer leading his men into the woods. He turns to Stewart. "For God's sakes, Alex, who ordered this assault?"

Stewart shrugs helplessly. "I assume the commanding general through his vicar, Bishop Polk."

"Well, it's madness! That position couldn't be taken by three times the number! My God, George Thomas is over there, and nobody carries a position by frontal assault against him."

"I know. That's why I didn't take my men across that field."

Hardee takes a ragged breath. "Don't let Palmer go on from here. Tell him it's an order from the commanding general." Stewart looks at him gravely. "Well, damn it, Alex! If Bragg won't come down here and command, I must."

Stewart nods, raises his field glasses again to study the field. "Preston's falling back to the woods. I think he's carrying the flag himself."

"At least he has good sense. I'm going to see the Bishop, stop this disaster here and now."

At dusk, Brigadier General Dan Smith Donelson, still raging for Yankee blood, finds Brigadier General William Preston. "Why did you give over the assault, sir?"

Preston glares at him. "Because, sir, I have the honor to command men of great courage and of great value to their country! I will not squander their lives. As it is, I lost a tenth of my brigade. If I'd hammered away like Adams, I would have lost half."

"I, sir, lost more than half!" Donelson snarls.

"Then, sir, may God have mercy on your soul!"

Southern manhood is such that this exchange, if taken any further, will inevitably lead to a duel. Staff officers intervene, pry the generals apart.

No one seems to know the whereabouts of Bishop Polk in the failing light. Bill Hardee gives up trying to find him, rides slowly through the shadows toward Braxton Bragg's headquarters.

Milo Hascall rides forward a final time to Hazen's line. "Orders from the commanding general, Bill. As soon as it's dark, pull back to Thomas's guns. We're going to straighten the line. Tomorrow morning, the Rebs can have this position if they want it."

Hazen nods, leans an arm against Hascall's horse for support. "Yes, that's a good decision. We held it when we needed to."

Hascall hesitates. "Bill, Julius Garesché is dead."

Hazen goes rigid, causing Hascall's horse to shift nervously under his hand. After a long moment, Hazen lets his arm drop. "Poor Julius. He always worried how he would behave in combat."

"He behaved well."

"Yes, I know. I saw him."

Lieutenant Ambrose Bierce stands a little apart, listening, overwhelmed with grief.

CHAPTER 9

New Year's Eve
Wednesday, December 31, 1862
Along Stones River, Tennessee

The repulse of Preston's and Palmer's brigades in front of the Round Forest in the hour before dusk ends the day's fighting. The night is cold, the drizzle occasionally turning to sleet and snow.

FTER SIX HOURS waiting for death, Private Eben Hannaford, 6th Ohio Volunteers, is still alive. This is surprising, almost embarrassing. God knows, the wound he'd taken shortly before noon should have killed him. Like all veterans, Hannaford is an expert on wounds, and he has yet to see anyone shot through the neck and shoulder survive more than an hour or two. But here he is, still alive half a day after crawling into some brush to bleed out his life in privacy.

It takes Hannaford some time to reconcile himself to continued existence among the quick. He has, after all, said his good-byes, shed a few tears, prayed a sincere few minutes, and pretty much resigned himself to eternity. To reverse direction now seems like a hell of a chore, particularly since he is not uncomfortable lying on his belly in the brush. Movement will mean pain, almost certainly a hemorrhage, and probably the death he has so far—somehow—avoided. He should wait for the litter-bearers to find him. Not that they are medical people in any real sense, but they may be able to get him into an ambulance and to a hospital without his wound hemorrhaging.

There is, however, the problem of the cold. Since Hannaford last

opened his eyes, the light and the battle have faded. Meanwhile, the pool
of blood beneath his right shoulder has turned slushy, the crystals around
the edge freezing like shore ice. Yet he has no sensation of cold, feels surprisingly warm. He closes his eyes again, trying to get his mind around this
paradox, dozes, wakes horrified. I'm freezing to death, he thinks.

He feels beneath himself for his right wrist, grasps it tightly, and tries to
roll over. He makes it on the third attempt, the pain so intense that he is
afraid for a moment that he will faint. He lies breathing deeply, clutching his
wrist to his stomach. The sky is gray, though he has a recollection of brief
sunshine two or three hours past. Or perhaps that was only a fever dream.
He feels his forehead, is shocked by the coldness of his hand. I must get
help, he thinks. He takes the knit cap from his head, waves it feebly. No
good. He feels about his left side, finds a stick. He perches the cap atop the
stick, waves it overhead. The stick breaks, the cap falling out of reach in the
brush. For a few minutes he lies shivering, his earlier warmth fled like sleep
and resignation. He must rise now, hope that he does not bleed too awfully.

Colonel Hans Heg of the 15th Wisconsin supposes that his Norwegians and
Swedes should endure the cold better than most men, yet walking among
them he finds little evidence that generations of exposure to northern climes
have imbued them with any particular hardihood. They look as cold, miserable, and sad as any men might under the circumstances. Yet none ask him if
they can break the prohibition against building fires. Heg tastes snow on the
air, puts up his collar. By morning it will freeze hard. "All right, boys," he says
quietly. "You can build your fires. But only small ones and well hidden. Boil
your coffee and step back. Everyone gets a turn to get warm."

Corporal Jeremy Andrews, late of the Queen's 19th Regiment of Foot and
now of McCook's ammunition train, has the old soldier's habit of routine
whatever the weather. He straightens his kit, passes a packet of coffee to
Sergeant Barnes, who is tending their small fire, and then looks to his feet.
He cleans them with a dampened rag, scrapes at a corn with his pock-
etknife, and then pulls on marginally drier socks. Chores done, he accepts
coffee and a couple of crackers from Barnes. From his haversack he produces a thick slice of sowbelly. He scrapes away a bit of greenish mold and
then saws it into three pieces. As is custom, he takes his choice and passes
the other two to Barnes and Captain Thruston. While Barnes and Thruston
fry their portions, Andrews chews his raw to make it last longer. Besides,
frying wastes valuable fat and who knows when they will get more rations.

Amid the darkening cedars, the firing has diminished to a spattering of musketry and the occasional boom of a field gun. Yet there is little reassuring about the comparative quiet. The Yanks—and Andrews thinks of Northerners and Southerners alike as Yanks—don't have the sense of civilized races to give over fighting at a decent hour. Bunch of bloody savages capable of anything, including a night attack.

Andrews supposes he's known as much fear as most men who've spent their lives soldiering. It's not something a man gets over, just a reality the professional learns to ignore. But dusk spooks even old soldiers, and Andrews recalls the charm taught him by a Cornish private long ago as they'd lain watching a blue dusk in the Hindu Kush—a land where a man might wake in the night to find his throat cut by one the tribesmen whose forefathers had cut the throats of Alexander's sleeping men twenty-odd centuries before. Now, in the near darkness a mile northwest of Stones River, Tennessee, Andrews repeats the charm, whispering it once, twice, three times, crossing himself each time as he'd been taught: *From ghoulies and ghosties and long-leggety beasties, and things that go bump in the night, Good Lord, deliver us.*

"Barnes tells me you were a soldier of the Queen," Thruston says.

Andrews is instantly wary, for he is always on guard with officers, even these democratic Yanks. "Aye, sir. That I was."

"For how long?"

"Nigh twenty years, sir."

"So you must have seen a great many battles."

"My share, sir."

"And how does our fighting compare to what you've seen?"

Andrews hesitates. How can he tell these men? He'd been with Raglan in the Crimea, scaled the heights at Alma to drive the Russians into Sevastopol. And God, what a ghastly business that had been. But this . . . this tremendous brawl in the cedars overwhelms his understanding. "If you'll pardon the language, sir, you bleedin' Yanks don't know when to quit. Just fuck-all and keep charging. And that's a barbarous sort of fighting. Wasteful and to little purpose, it seems to me."

Andrews is surprised at himself for saying so much, is even more surprised that he has so firm an opinion. That lad this morning, the one crushed in the wagon box when the gun carriage had ridden up over the rear axle. He hadn't known the boy's name, and a soldier should know the names of the men he serves beside, the lads he must bury if their luck runs ill. "Begging your pardon, Captain, but it doesn't seem there's much plan in this war except to bash the other fellows around until one side or the other quits."

"Isn't that what it comes down to in all wars?"

Does it? Andrews is not sure. Is that what it's been about every time, all through the last twenty years? It hadn't seemed so. He stares again into the dusk creeping on toward darkness. *From long-leggety beasties. . . .* "I wouldn't know, sir. Perhaps it is."

Private Dickie Krall, 1st Louisiana Regular Infantry, would sit apart from the others, but they don't let him, force him to sit close with them around the small fire. A little while ago, Sergeant Simon Buck helped him clean his backside again, tore a piece from his own fresh drawers for a pad to absorb the seeping blood from his anus. Like a woman with her monthly, Dickie thinks, fighting back the shame of it again. But no one speaks of it or treats him any differently. He wonders what they have done with Zein's body. All the bayonet wounds would be something to attract the notice of an officer, so they must have hidden it somewhere, perhaps even buried it, though everyone is exhausted and the ground is hard.

Someone has procured a canteen of whiskey and it passes around the fire. Dickie doesn't take his swallow. "Go on, boy," Sergeant Buck says.

"I can't, Sarge. I told Ma I wouldn't."

No one laughs. "I think she'd understand, son. It's cold, and it'll be a lot colder by morning."

"I can't, Sarge."

Buck nods, takes his swallow, and passes on the canteen.

Dickie Krall watches the dusk falling in the cedars. He supposes the boys over there in the Yankee lines are not that much different than he is, but he cannot quite imagine it. They seem a race, almost a species, apart. He recalls the long-unused verse from the Litany that his father so liked to mutter under his breath in the midst of the service: *From the scourge of the Northmen, dear Lord, deliver us.*

All day, James Foster has limped up and down the yard of his plantation house, listening to the sound of battle a few miles to the northwest. His five boys, ranging in age from seventeen to twenty-five, are over there, fighting for Tennessee and the Confederacy in that order. Around the house, Bob, the nigger groom, has gone about his work. It was Mrs. Foster, of late and sacred memory, who first called Bob a groom. But he is more the all-purpose factotum of his master: handyman, driver, emissary to the field niggers, frequent drinking companion, and occasional confidant.

When the firing begins to ebb and dusk comes on, Foster at last halts his pacing. "Bob, hitch a wagon. Go bring home my dead and wounded boys."

"Yessir," Bob drawls.

Bob is atop the wagon seat behind the two mules when Foster approaches him. "You ain't gonna run off on me, are you, Bob?"

Bob spits. "Do you suppose I'd'a waited this long if I'd wanted to go live with Yankees?"

Foster stares into the lined black face, the expressionless eyes. What are we, after all these years? he wonders. Certainly not friends. Yet I've told this man more of my soul than I've ever whispered to another living creature. "Because if you want to be free, Bob, do this and I'll give you your papers."

Bob stares away from him into the dusk. "I'd best be goin'."

"Do you want your freedom, Bob?"

Bob looks down at him. "Twenty years ago, I would have taken freedom from you. Now you don't have it no more to give. You're old like me. We neither of us got a chance of freedom now. . . . I'm gonna go get those boys." He releases the brake, slaps the reins, rolls off into the gloaming behind the two mules.

Lieutenant General Bill Hardee dismounts in the yard of the modest frame house that Bragg has taken as his field headquarters. He limps toward the door, working his cold, arthritic fingers in their doeskin gloves. God, he feels a thousand years old.

Bragg looks up from his desk. "General Hardee. Good. I have just this minute finished a wire to the president. Here, sit. Do you want coffee?"

"If you please, General."

An aide gives Hardee a cup of coffee, but rather than warming him, it sets him shivering. He huddles over it, hands shaking, trying not to spill any on his uniform. Bragg is correcting a word or two on the telegram, frowning through the reading glasses perched on his nose beneath the ferocious eyebrows. He sets down his pen. "Here's what I've written: 'We assailed the enemy at first light and after ten hours hard fighting have driven him from every position except the extreme left. With the exception of this point, we occupy the entire field. At dusk, the enemy began falling back. We will follow. God has granted us a happy New Year.'" Bragg looks up. "Well, Professor, what do you think?"

Hardee stares dumbfounded at the unwonted satisfaction on Bragg's face. My sweet Lord, he thinks; he actually believes that rubbish! Hardee looks about for the aide who supplied the coffee. "Lieutenant, if you would be so kind. Thank you." Having delayed long enough to gather his thoughts, he sips from the fresh cup. "I think, General, that the battle today was a nearer thing than you imply. We did drive the Yankees, but the cost was very heavy; and their latest line, even if awkwardly formed, seems to me one of great strength. I saw no sign that they plan to withdraw from it."

Bragg has stiffened. "I am not one to mislead my superiors, sir!"

"I don't suggest that you are, General. I simply point out that you are more sanguine in your interpretation of events than—"

"You dispute that this army fought magnificently today?"

"Not at all, General. I am exceedingly proud of our men."

"And did we not drive the Yankees from every position save their extreme left?"

"I've always considered the ford in front of Breckinridge's line as the extreme left of their line."

Bragg dismisses this with a disgusted wave of his hand. "An outpost not contiguous with the rest of the Yankee line and not among our objectives."

"Then your phrase is accurate. Nevertheless, General, I saw no evidence on my way here that the Yankees plan to retreat. As long as George Thomas is among them, I think—"

"George Thomas is a traitor!"

"Yes, but he is also a splendid soldier. I know no other I would trust to hold a position with greater determination."

"A man who cannot stand firm with his country will not hold his ground with any greater conviction." Bragg snatches up his pen, begins writing furiously.

Hardee is not sure if he is dismissed or not. He leans back, remembers his coffee, and drinks. No, it was not George Thomas who failed to stand with his country. We were the ones who abandoned it. And though I believe we were entirely justified, that the election of the Original Gorilla represented an overthrow of the republic established by the Constitution, I cannot call George Thomas a traitor. But whatever he is, he is a soldier. He will not let Rosecrans retreat.

Bragg slaps his pen down, glares at Hardee. "In the morning, General, we shall pursue the Yankees. I have already sent Wheeler and Wharton to obstruct their withdrawal. We shall catch General Rosecrans's army on the roads and destroy it utterly. I will send you orders before first light."

"Yes, General."

"And since you've made George Thomas your personal bugbear, I will tell you that I have reports he was killed this afternoon riding beside Rosecrans."

Hardee starts. "How definite are the reports?"

"Not certain, but I have them from two sources."

George dead, Hardee thinks in wonder. He'd never particularly liked the man, found him rigid, uncommunicative, and suspected that he was secretly censorious of those of a more social disposition, particularly regarding the ladies. Yet he supposes that Thomas was ultimately his friend, must have been, for he feels his eyes stinging. He clears his throat, rises, straightening his tunic in the unconscious habit of decades. "I will await your orders. Good evening, General."

Hunger comes with the dark and the cold. For all his failings, Bragg is a good quartermaster, and most of the Confederate regiments receive rations. Several colonels in the Confederate lines order whiskey barrels opened for their men. Leaning in to fill canteens, men become drunk on the fumes alone, stagger back to their comrades, giggling with the absurdity of inhaled inebriation.

On the Union side, the situation is considerably grimmer. (Joe Wheeler has seen to that.) In the Federal rear, some of McCook's re-formed regiments plunder the remaining supply wagons. On the front lines, few of the soldiers have anything to eat. They paw through the haversacks of the dead, check their own pockets a hundred times for overlooked crumbs of hardtack or shreds of sowbelly. Enough dead horses and mules lie about to give every man in the army a decent steak; but the American taboo against the eating of equine flesh persists, and only a few take advantage of this abundance. One Ohio battery almost comes to blows with a company of Indiana infantry desecrating the battery's fallen horses for a meal.

Perhaps no other beast in the army is more coveted than George Thomas's waddling, arrogant, ill-tempered goose. But Thomas is very much among the living, and no one is foolish enough to risk his wrath in the assassination of the fowl.

Private Eben Hannaford stumbles across corn and cottonfields, clutching his right arm to his stomach. He ignores the pleas of wounded men for aid, though the cries twist his heart. There are arguments aplenty for lying down among them: the torment of his wound, the fear of sharpshooters, the instant death embodied in the occasional artillery shell screaming across the field. Most of all there is the loneliness of being upright and walking—no matter how clumsily—among the dead and maimed. It seems somehow traitorous, an abandonment of comrades, a running away.

At roughly the same time as Hannaford spots a low log building with red rags hanging from its eaves to denote a field hospital, Private James Ellis of the 4th Arkansas, McNair's Brigade, manages to reach a hospital in a cotton warehouse on the outskirts of Murfreesboro. A minié ball has gone through

Ellis's left arm just above the elbow, shattering the humerus. A bad wound but survivable, particularly since he has lost less blood than he might have if not for the prompt application of a tourniquet.

He pauses inside the door, trying to perceive some order in the seeming chaos. A boy lying on a table nearby catches at his sleeve. "Oh, sir, if you have a sharp knife, please cut this ball out of my hand. It's nearly killing me, and the surgeon says there ain't nothing there. Please, sir, if you love your mother, please." The boy starts crying.

Ellis, only twenty-two and unaccustomed to being called "sir," is touched by the plea. He feels the boy's hand, can at first detect nothing. "Press down, right there," the boy begs.

Ellis presses, feels the ball—a small one, perhaps a piece of buckshot or a bullet from a small-caliber revolver. "I feel it. But I don't have a knife and I only got one good arm, coz." The boy starts sobbing, and Ellis looks about desperately. Nearby, a civilian is looking after several wounded, gently giving them sips of water and wiping their faces. "Sir, could you do something for this man?"

The civilian comes over, a bald cadaverous man but kindly, though he looks like Death itself. He feels the hand as instructed. "I'm no doctor, but I can find one."

Ellis stays with the boy until the civilian returns with a doctor, also a civilian and, from the evidence of his thick spectacles, all but blind. But he is expert, cuts the ball out of the boy's hand with a quick stroke and a pinch. The boy gasps, lies still on the table, tears running down his cheeks. Ellis is about to show the doctor his arm when there is a sudden commotion in a corner, a desperately wounded soldier thrashing about, tearing at his bandages. The kindly civilian and the doctor hurry away.

An orderly intercepts Ellis's wandering. "Sit over here by this colonel, coz. He ain't gonna live till morning and could use some company."

"But I need a surgeon to look at my arm."

"You ain't bleeding bad. I'll come get you when one of the surgeons has time to look at it."

Ellis looks uncertainly at the mortally wounded colonel. "Who is he?"

"Colonel Bratton of the 24th Tennessee. A cannonball took off his right leg, went clean through his horse, and smashed up his left leg so bad that the surgeons took it off to make him more comfortable. Come on, now. He's a good man and sitting with him will take your mind off that arm. . . . Colonel, here's a man to sit with you. He's got a pretty nasty wound in one arm but the other's all right. He can get you anything you need." The orderly bustles off.

Ellis sits beside the colonel. His own pain is terrible, but he can hardly imagine the agony of losing both legs. Yet Bratton lies unmoving and uncomplaining, staring at the slow drip from a crack in the roof high above. "Is there anything I can do for you, Colonel?" Ellis asks.

The colonel turns his head slowly, inspects Ellis. "No, but thank you, son. The orderly took a note to my wife and there's nothing more to do but wait." He returns his gaze to the ceiling.

Ellis feels that he should offer comfort. "You have been a brave man, Colonel. I'm sure your men will miss you."

"Yes, I suppose they will. Those who have survived me."

"And our cause is just, Colonel. I truly believe that."

Bratton smiles slightly. "As just as any, I suppose. God knows, many better men than I have died for it." He turns again to Ellis. "You should have that arm looked to."

"The orderly told me to wait with you. He said he'd come get me when a surgeon had time to look at it."

"What's your regiment?"

"Fourth Arkansas, McNair's brigade. We were off on the left."

"Yes. You did well, I'm told."

"We drove 'em, Colonel. Drove 'em across one pike and all the way to the next. Couldn't take it any farther, though. We were powerful tired and beat up by that time."

"Yes, even brave men get tired." The colonel is again staring at the ceiling and the drip that appears, drop by slow drop, out of the shadows among the beams. *"Il faut cultiver notre jardin,"* he murmurs.

"Colonel?"

"It's a French phrase I have been trying to recall. 'We must cultivate our garden.' Lying here, it seems very sound advice."

"I don't understand."

"I've been meditating on bravery, and it occurs to me that it is not so much the meek who inherit the earth as the sensible, the ones who repudiate bravery as civilization's posturing and remain at home. Yesterday I would have called such men cowardly, now I see them as sensible. If we were all like them and had stayed home cultivating our own gardens, none of this slaughter would have happened."

"But, Colonel, the Yankees—"

"I am assuming a like good sense among the Yankees. Let everyone stay home and tend their own fields." Suddenly the colonel's face contorts and he chokes back a sob. After a moment, he regains his composure. "I'm sorry. I forget myself."

"It's all right, Colonel."

"I was thinking of my rose garden. I will miss my flowers."

For several minutes, they do not speak. "Are you sure there's nothing I can get for you, Colonel?" Ellis asks.

The colonel sighs. "Nothing. I asked them to put me outside so that someone with a chance to live could have my place. But they said there was room enough for me yet. Still, I would like to see the stars a final time."

"It's still raining, Colonel. There are no stars."

"I know, but I had hope."

The orderly is suddenly beside Ellis. "Your turn, coz. Come along quick. The surgeons are busy and kinda touchy."

Ellis follows the orderly to the far end of the warehouse where several surgeons are operating on rough tables made from sawhorses and doors. One of them finishes amputating a leg, tosses his saw and knife into a bloody basin. "Let me see what you've got," he snaps at the orderly.

The orderly pushes Ellis forward. The doctor tears away the dressing, peers at the wound. "He won't die tonight. Don't fool with him now and we'll take that arm off in the morning."

The orderly leads Ellis to the end of a rank of men slumped against the wall, quickly rebandages the arm. "It don't look that bad to me," Ellis pleads, although in truth the wound is gruesome. "And I can't farm with one arm."

"Gonna have to figure out a way, coz. They don't change their minds. Try to rest." He hurries off.

Ellis waits in the line of wounded men, listening to the groans, the low swearing around him, the shrieks from the end of the room where the surgeons are probing for bullets and sawing off limbs. He could go sit by the colonel again, but though he plans to protest the loss of his arm to the last, he is afraid of losing his place in line.

Private Eben Hannaford is waiting by a smoky fire for his turn in the low log building with the red rags hanging from the eaves. A familiar voice says, "Eben?"

He turns to find John Marsh, a former member of his company, assigned now to the Pioneer Brigade. "John! Are you wounded?"

"No. A couple of us are fixing ambulance axles." Marsh squats by him, peers at the wound through Hannaford's neck and shoulder, whistles. He's immediately all business. "Here, let me get you a place closer to the fire. You men, give this fellow a little room." Men clear a space closer to the fire. Marsh strips off his overcoat, drapes it around Hannaford's shoulders.

"John, you shouldn't."

"Ah, no matter. Workin' keeps me warm. Let me go find you a place in an ambulance. You don't want the quacks here carvin' on you."

Hannaford dozes despite his pain. Then Marsh is again at his side. "Come on. I got you a place." He helps Hannaford to his feet, gets an arm around him. The ambulance is one of the antiquated two-wheeled models with a leaky canvas top and no springs. Half a dozen men are jammed inside, the floor slick with blood. Marsh helps Hannaford in.

"Jesus Christ," one of the men mutters. "There's no fucking room." Nevertheless, he makes enough space for Hannaford to sit.

Marsh pushes his overcoat into Hannaford's lap. "Here, stay warm."

"No, John. You need it."

"Not as much as you're likely to. I'll come see you. You can give it back to me then."

☆ ☆ ☆

Rosecrans has again taken headquarters in the exposed cabin close by the Nashville Pike. George Thomas tosses his cigar into some weeds before going inside. Three orderlies scramble for the butt. Tobacco, like food and optimism, has grown scarce in the army.

Rosecrans sits in his shirtsleeves on a low stool before the fire, feet bare, his uniform coat drying over the back of a chair. He seems unaware of Thomas until the other has dropped into a chair and removed his hat. "Garesché was killed this afternoon," Rosecrans says, his attention fixed on the socks he is holding to the fire.

"Yes, I heard," Thomas says. "A good man."

"Brave men must die in battle, but that doesn't make their loss the easier on their friends."

Thomas does not respond, for there is no point in agreeing with the obvious, though he might point out in the interests of logic that not only the brave but the cowardly, the inconstant, and the merely ordinary also die in battle, if in somewhat lower ratios than the brave.

Rosecrans sighs. "When the others get here, we'll decide what to do about tomorrow."

Thomas does not respond to this either, for that, too, is obvious. He lets his chin drop to his chest, dozes while Rosecrans dries his socks.

Hazen and Bierce take a small squad of men in search of Garesché's body. Litter-bearers are bringing the wounded to a clearing in rear of the Round Forest and loading them into ambulances for the trip back along the pike to the hospitals. Bierce and the squad sergeant question several of the bearers until one leads them a little way off to the body of a headless colonel. Hazen kneels by the corpse, shines his lantern on it. Only a piece of the lower jaw and the chin whiskers of a thick brown beard remain of the head. Yet it is definitely Garesché, the uniform somehow a little crisper, a little more stylish than the ordinary, even soaked as it is with blood and rain. Hazen reaches out, lifts the right hand. A tremor passes through the arm and the hand clutches at Hazen's.

"God Jesus," the sergeant breathes, crossing himself, as the other enlisted men step back. Bierce, the most rational of young men, holds his ground, for he—unlike most of these men—does not believe in ghosts or the other manifestations of the unquiet dead.

"It is only the rigor," Hazen says calmly. He works the West Point ring off Garesché's hand. He lays the hand gently on the ground, reaches for the other and removes the wedding band. He puts these, clinking faintly, into the watch pocket of his vest. He stands, looks about. "Over there, a little out of the way. That will do for now."

The men start digging a grave. Beside Bierce, Hazen is shivering. My God, Bierce thinks, I didn't know he was human enough to feel the cold. A Rebel prisoner with a leg wound limps toward a waiting ambulance. He stops by Hazen, holds out a blanket. "Take my blanket, Colonel. It's soiled some but not too bad. I ain't bled as much as I might've."

Hazen inclines his head. "Thank you, soldier. I'm grateful."

"My pleasure, Colonel. I'm grieved for your friend."

"Thank you."

Despite the Rebel's assurance to the contrary, the blanket is stiff with dried blood and dirt. Hazen pulls it around his shoulders, continues to shiver. At length, he says, "It seems that you will have the last sally in your battle of quotations, Bierce. I assume you have the appropriate words for the occasion."

"I had not thought on it, Colonel."

"Well, be about it, man. I don't know poetry, the Bible, or the Catholic burial service, so I must depend on you."

"Yes, sir," Bierce says, tries to think. "I know something from *Pilgrim's Progress.*"

"Is it appropriate?"

"I think so."

"Well, keep it handy then."

The digging is hard in the rocky earth, and Hazen calls a halt when the men have a hole waist deep. They clamber out. Hazen hands the bloodstained blanket to the sergeant. "Wrap him in this. It's a gift from one of our foemen. I think Colonel Garesché might find that appropriate."

The sergeant and two of the other men wrap the body in the blanket, lower it as gently as possible into the grave. "Well, Lieutenant?" Hazen says.

Bierce has to clear his throat of an unexpected aching. "'My sword I give to him that shall succeed me in my pilgrimage, and my courage and skill to him that can get it. My marks and scars I carry with me, to be a witness for me, that I have fought His battles who now will be my rewarder.'" Again he has to clear his throat. "'So he passed over, and all the trumpets sounded for him on the other side.'"

"Amen," says the sergeant, and the other enlisted men chorus agreement.

"Thank you, Lieutenant," Hazen says. "Go ahead, Sergeant. Fill it in."

Bill Hardee prowls his line, trailed by a small staff. Twice his adjutant cautions him about the danger from pickets, blue and gray alike, who may be quick to shoot at any horseman. Hardee is too angry to heed, and the adjutant drops back.

Brigadier General St. John Liddell, peacetime planter and sometimes confidant of Bragg, greets Hardee near the far left end of the Rebel line. "I hope you've come to order a night attack, General."

Hardee dismounts, pats Liddell on the shoulder in passing, and squats by the small fire to take a cup of coffee. "We have a little brandy, General," Liddell's adjutant offers.

"Thank you, please," Hardee answers, holding out his cup. Returning to Liddell, he sips at the cup, still making no reply.

"So, General, are we going to attack or not?"

"Why would you attack, John?"

"Well, hell's bells, Bill! The pike and the railroad are right over there. Reach out and take them! Then we'll have Rosy Rosecrans and his whole damned army bagged!"

"Night attacks are always costly. Too many men get shot by their fellows."

"But the Yankees will entrench tonight, and we'll take twice as many casualties in the morning."

"True. So with what do you intend to make this assault?"

For the first time Liddell is caught without a ready answer. "Well, with my brigade."

"And that alone?"

"No. I assumed that the whole division would be used. And McCown's too."

"With no reinforcements?"

Liddell is becoming heated with Hardee's seeming obtuseness. "With reinforcements if they are at hand. Otherwise, we'll do the job ourselves."

"If that is your plan, then I suggest you take it to the commanding general."

Liddell gapes. "Good Christ! Then you're not here to order a night attack?"

"I'm afraid not."

"Why not?"

"Because it is unnecessary. The commanding general has declared victory."

"What?"

"Victory. We have won, John. The Yankees are withdrawing. We will catch them on the roads and destroy them tomorrow."

"Like hell they're withdrawing! I've been here since dusk, and there's no traffic on the pike except some ambulances. More likely they will be reinforced."

"No, they'll withdraw. If not now, soon."

"You don't believe that."

"No, but General Bragg does."

For a long moment, Liddell cannot speak. Hardee sips from his cup, returns Liddell's gaze levelly. "Bill, you must go to him," Liddell says. "Tell him that we are within a stone's throw of winning."

"I'm too tired to make the ride, John. Too tired and too disgusted. If you believe in your plan, take it to the commanding general yourself. Tell him that I consider it worthy of examination."

"You approve it?"

"No, I approve of nothing at the present." He hands the empty cup to Liddell, walks to his horse and mounts. "Go ahead, John. I've heard that General Bragg welcomes ideas from many sources, though he rarely welcomes them from me."

Left standing, Liddell considers going to see Bragg. But bigger plans must be afoot for the commanding general to pursue another course. Better to get his men ready and then try to sleep for a few hours.

The ride in the ambulance is a torment, the men moaning and crying out with each bump. Hannaford tries to brace himself, every moment expecting his wound to hemorrhage. But it does not, and at last the driver draws rein next to a jumble of tents. An orderly helps Hannaford out of the ambulance. "Where should I go?" Hannaford asks.

"Every regiment is supposed to have a tent, every tent a surgeon. Do your best to find yours, or you'll have to wait with them that's so bad off they can't tell us where they're supposed to go."

Hannaford wanders among the tents but cannot find the 6th Ohio's. He leans against a tree, horrified to hear himself weeping. A black-bearded teamster with a patch over one eye pauses by him. In contrast to his ferocious appearance, the man's voice is gentle. "Now, now, lad. Where do you need to get to?"

"I need a surgeon. I need a surgeon or I'm going to die," Hannaford wails.

The man makes a sympathetic noise. "I know how you feel, son. I lost an eye and half a hand at Shiloh and I cried. Let me help you to the ninetieth Ohio's hospital. Got a couple of fine surgeons there. They'll do their best for you."

Inside a clean and surprisingly well-lit tent, the teamster helps Hannaford to sit, lays a palm on his head as if in blessing, and departs without another word. Hannaford has the odd thought that Peter the Fisherman might have been such a man. A surgeon finishes bandaging a gruesome wound in a corporal's arm, helps the man to lie down in a corner. He kneels by Hannaford, begins examining his wound. "A very narrow escape, young man. The ball went right through the base of the neck and behind the left clavicle, which it evidently struck and fractured, and then glanced upward to shatter the acromius before exiting. How the trachea escaped without serious injury, I can't understand."

Hannaford summons his dignity. He has wept once tonight, wailing like a baby afraid of the dark. "I know it's a bad wound, doctor. But if I do well, very well, is it possible for me to get through?"

The doctor compresses his lips. "If you were at home, I wouldn't hesitate to say yes. But here in an army hospital. . . . Well, the case is different with so many wounded and so few nurses. But we'll do the best we can for you."

Hannaford takes this like a man, though he feels like crying again. "Thank you, doctor."

The surgeon cleans and dresses the wound, whistling softly through his teeth all the while. "There. I'll come by and check on you in a while. Try to rest."

Despite the pain and the frightful parade of wounded, Hannaford finds himself slipping into an odd contentment. An orderly brings him a cup of coffee and a biscuit. He eats and then dozes, right arm cradled in his lap.

George Thomas rouses when the conference of division and corps commanders begins. As is traditional, the generals speak in reverse order of seniority, the most junior beginning. Every man present has the look of fatigue, even discouragement, but Thomas reads no panic in their faces. He lowers chin to chest again, closes his eyes.

The generals report their positions and their losses. Many regiments have suffered twenty, thirty, even forty percent casualties, but the Rebels have suffered at least as heavily. Thomas takes in all with the small, wakeful part of his mind that is always posted against the unexpected.

When it is the corps commanders' turn to speak, Crittenden confirms what his division commanders have said of casualties and positions, and then gives way to McCook. For once in his life, Alex McCook has rehearsed. "I wish I could report that the right wing held against the Rebel attack. But we were driven and driven hard by overwhelming numbers. Still, we killed and wounded thousands, never broke, and always fell back in the best order possible under the circumstances." He glances warily at Sheridan. "General Sheridan's division and much of General Davis's held until forced to withdraw for lack of ammunition." He waits for anyone to dispute his claims. The others avoid looking at him. Thomas closes his eyes again. Damned fool boy. Well, Rosecrans will have to relieve him when this fight is over.

Rosecrans stares into the fire, listening absently; he already knows the disposition of every unit in the army better than anyone else present. For the moment, his mind is absorbed with other things. I believe, he thinks, with all my soul in the Resurrection and the Life, in the eventual rising of all souls, even those lost in the deepest deeps; but if it were up to me, I should choose to lie a long while beneath a quilt of coals before rising for the eternity of praising Him. . . . He gathers himself, lets the eternal fade, interrupts McCook. "So what would you do about tomorrow, General?"

The question is out of the customary order, since Thomas has yet to present his summary of the day's fighting on his portion of the line. But McCook stumbles only briefly before beginning the response he's prepared to this inevitable question. "I think, General, that we are the only army protecting Nashville, Louisville, and Cincinnati. We have temporarily lost the initiative, but we're not grievously hurt. We can retire safely and with honor on Nashville, fortify strongly, and defy the enemy's efforts to dislodge us until we have the reinforcements to retake the offensive."

"General Crittenden?"

Crittenden looks unhappy. He rises, although this is unnecessary and only a politician's unthinking reaction to the opportunity to speak to an audience. "My men fought exceedingly hard to hold against the Rebels today. I think they will be loath to abandon ground paid for with so much blood. But my own military experience is so small that I am unable to advise what course makes the best strategic sense. Therefore, I have to pass on the question."

Rosecrans turns to Thomas. Thomas's eyes are lidded, his look furious. "General Thomas?"

"This army does not retreat." Thomas growls. He rises, surveys the room. "Gentlemen, I know of no better place to die than right here!" He picks up his hat, swings his coat over his shoulders, and lumbers toward the door, jaw set hard against the pain in his lower back and the inconstancy of other men.

Rosecrans watches him go. "Major Goddard, please ask General Thomas to remain a moment so that I can have a word with him." He turns to the generals.

Phil Sheridan is on his feet. "General! I request the honor of leading tomorrow's attack."

"Your request is noted, General Sheridan. Gentlemen, General Thomas is right. We have come to fight and win this battle, and we shall do it. Our supplies may run short, but will keep right in and eat corn for a week. *We will win this battle!*"

There is a chorus of assent. Rosecrans stands. "There is, however, the question of whether or not it would be advantageous to fall back beyond Overall Creek where we could straighten our line. I am going to examine that possibility presently. I beg you to remain here until I return. General McCook, join me."

Outside, Rosecrans leaves McCook by the horses, goes to speak to Thomas. "George, I'm going to examine our right flank to see if it's feasible to pull back beyond Overall Creek."

"The line we have is strong, General. I would not want to pull back from it."

"Yes, but it's subject to flanking, and the concentration of our forces makes their artillery all the more effective."

Thomas is silent a moment. "It would be very difficult to pull back in the dark. We couldn't possibly have the army over the creek by dawn and a single thrust might rout us entirely if we are disordered. Bill Hardee would see the chance, even if Bragg and Polk didn't."

"Nevertheless, I need to gauge the feasibility of the maneuver even if the chances are small that we can undertake it."

Thomas nods. "Very good, General. I will see to our center in the meantime."

Following Rosecrans toward Overall Creek, McCook is not quite sure what to make of the general's invitation. Is he not so disgraced as he'd imagined? Sheridan's division is, after all, part of his corps, and he deserves at least some credit for its stand in the cedars. He begins humming to himself while out in the fields the cries, the shrieks, the begging, and—beneath all—the low, incessant moaning of the wounded eddy in a miasma of human suffering that McCook manages not to hear.

Ahead, Rosecrans pulls up, watching specks of fire moving along the course of Overall Creek. McCook draws rein at his side. "What do you make of that, General?" Rosecrans asks.

"I'm . . . I'm not entirely sure. Cavalry carrying torches, perhaps."

"And why would they be doing that?"

"I have no idea, General."

Rosecrans is suddenly angry. "Use your head, man! If you have become incapable of reasoned opinion in small matters, then I will have to consider you incompetent to judge larger matters. And then there will be nothing for me to do but relieve you of your command!"

McCook stumbles, desperately trying to form an opinion. But, really, he has no idea what the cavalry are doing by torchlight. "I suppose they might be looking for wounded."

"You have no other thought?"

"No, sir," McCook says miserably.

Rosecrans sighs with the same impatience McCook heard in the voices of so many West Point instructors, including Professor William J. Hardee, who has this day delivered a lesson of lessons to his erstwhile student. McCook's good mood collapses in a despond so deep that he hears Rosecrans' voice as if from afar. "Does it not occur to you that it might be *Rebel* cavalry? That they might be lighting a battle line of infantry into position to close off our line of escape?"

"No, General."

Rosecrans snorts, lapses into silence, watching the torches bobbing along the line of the creek.

McCook has a thought. "But, General, wouldn't you consider it improbable for Bragg to deploy infantry at such a distance from his main line?"

"Then what explanation do you have?"

"None beyond our cavalry looking for wounded or perhaps helping our boys start a few fires."

"Fires are forbidden."

McCook looks curiously at Rosecrans. On their ride, they have passed scores of small fires flickering in rocks, ravines, and hollows. Whatever the orders, the men must have some warmth, at least enough fire for a cup of coffee in the cold drizzle that changes every few minutes to sleet or snow. McCook is suddenly aware of the night about him. He takes a deep breath of the damp air, tries to fix the lucidity of the moment in his memory. "General, many are ignoring your orders."

"Perhaps. But those riders are not Good Samaritans of the torch. That's Reb cavalry. Probably young Wheeler. And they'll have infantry with them to block any movement on our part. Tomorrow we will have to fight where we are now."

Rosecrans swings his horse in a tight circle, starts back to army headquarters. I suppose he must be right, McCook thinks. But from what I overheard of his conversation with Thomas, Pap thinks it's a poor idea to fall back anyway.

Inside the cramped cabin again, Rosecrans drops cape and gloves on a chair, braces his hands on its back, staring at his generals, many of whom were a moment before slumped in a dozen attitudes of exhausted slumber. "Gentlemen, they have gotten around our right flank and are forming a line of battle by torchlight. We will fight and, if needs be, die where we are. But in the end, this army will prevail!"

Major General George Thomas watches the bobbing torches from his headquarters in rear of the artillery supporting the Union center. His two dogs snuff about in the grass, keeping a wary eye on the goose, which has settled itself possessively on the general's boots. Thomas lifts a toe, forcing the goose to readjust its position. Thomas repeats the movement and the goose lashes out at the offending boot. "So, what do you think of those lights, goose?" The goose doesn't respond except to settle itself more comfortably. Thomas watches the torches for a few moments more. Probably our cavalry poking about, he thinks, maybe getting a few fires going for the boys.

He listens to the night. Like McCook, but for entirely different reasons, he is able to ignore the sounds made by the wounded. What can be done is being done, and other things must concern a general. Now and then a nervous picket discharges his musket, but the cannons have been silent since nightfall. Thomas does not expect this to continue. By early morning the cannoneers will be getting fidgety, will start taking potshots at any fire allowed to grow too large. A complete prohibition on fires is impossible, and everyone on both sides accepts this, but an informal truce holds only so long as neither party pushes the limits too far. Thomas turns to an aide waiting respectfully a dozen feet away. "Captain, send a squad from the headquarters escort to have a look at those horsemen carrying torches. I doubt if they represent any threat, but I want to be sure."

The aide hurries off. Thomas lights a cigar, careful not to drop the match on the goose.

Rosecrans issues orders in minute detail, mindful that young Major Goddard, for all his competence, is no Julius Garesché. He reconfirms the order to abandon the Round Forest salient; issues directions that will straighten and strengthen the line; and dictates a message relieving Van Cleve of command of his division and appointing Brigadier General Sam Beatty, the unflappable farmer and sheriff, in his place. "Is General Wood still here?"

"Yes, sir. Outside having his legs treated."

"Good. Send him in as soon as convenient."

Goddard bustles away. Rosecrans stares into the fire. In a few minutes he will ride out to have another look at the lines but now he needs to be close to the fire. The back of his throat feels grainy, the old scar tissue irritated by too many cigars, too much shouting. He closes his eyes, lets his mind fix on the memory of the beautiful plume of fire reaching out for him from the shattered crucible.

"General, you sent for me?"

Rosecrans opens his eyes to see Tom Wood balanced on crutches. "Sit, Tom. How are the legs?"

"I'll be all right, General."

"Good. I'm temporarily relieving you of command of your division and sending you back to Nashville with every wagon we can spare. You'll have an escort of a thousand infantry and cavalry and a section of guns. Once you're in the city, instruct General Fry in my name that he is to load the wagons with victuals and ammunition and have them back on the road by nightfall under strong escort. I'm also sending General Van Cleve. Nominally, he'll command the train while you command the escort. However, he's much troubled by his foot, so I wouldn't count on him for much."

"General, I'd much prefer to remain with my division. There must be any number of colonels who could command the escort."

Rosecrans leans back in his chair, reminded that he has never liked Tom Wood with his imperial, his airs, his sardonic superiority. "This is an assignment of surpassing importance, General Wood. For the moment, we have adequate ammunition, but young Wheeler has burned most of our food. We can fight for a day, perhaps two, but after that we will need rations."

"But General Crittenden depends on me—"

"General Crittenden will be all right. I will look after him."

"General, I must protest! I have earned—"

Rosecrans explodes. "No, General, you have not! No one in this army has earned special indemnity from immediate obedience to orders! Now be about executing yours or I shall relieve you of duty entirely."

The room is still, the orderlies and staff officers turning from their tasks to stare. Wood flushes a deep crimson. "Very good, General." He salutes crisply despite the awkwardness of his crutches, stumps toward the door.

★　★　★

Irish Pat Cleburne sits with Bill Hardee before a fire in the lee of a low mound of boulders and stumps cleared from a nearby field. In the firelight, Hardee seems to have aged ten years. He sips from a cup of coffee laced with whiskey. "We were that close, Patrick. If the moronic bastard had given us a single fresh brigade, we could have broken through to the Nashville Pike. And they would have collapsed. No army can fight surrounded. We had them. Just one more brigade. . . ."

They sit in silence for a time. Hardee listens to the crying of the wounded. "Poor devils. I hope we're doing the best we can for them."

"We are, General. I've seen to it."

Hardee sips from his cup, stares moodily in the direction of the Federal line. "Bragg had a report that George Thomas was killed this afternoon. But I have a report that he was seen alive at dusk behind that concentration of Yankee cannon. It could have been someone else, I suppose, but the man who gave me the report was one of his students at West Point. I'll have to confess that I was relieved, even though I suppose George's death would be a great gain for this army. But, personally, I would miss him."

"I've heard him called a traitor."

"No, George Thomas is no traitor. It would have surprised me if he'd thrown in with us. He's not a man who changes his mind."

"You liked him?"

"Liked him? . . . Yes, I suppose I did. We always got along well enough in Mexico and when we were majors in the Second Cavalry. He was closer to Bob Lee. They both enjoyed eating and would plan their dinners together weeks in advance. Odd how Lee has lately gotten the reputation of being an ascetic. He's not. He and Thomas are Virginia gentlemen who enjoy their china, silver, wine, and food."

"As do you, General."

Hardee looks sharply at Cleburne. "Why, I believe you have just chaffed me, Patrick!"

Cleburne is embarrassed. "I only meant a small joke, General. If I—"

"No, no, Patrick. You're right. I love all those things. The difference is that I am a Georgian, not a son of the Old Dominion. We Georgians tend to be a bit less ritualistic in our pleasures. I've heard tell of Virginia officers, their nether members engorged to near bursting, pausing to bow and ask 'May I?' before mounting a four-bit whore."

"I'm shocked, General. From what I've heard of Lee and Thomas, I can't imagine the situation occurring."

Hardee snorts. "Pardon me for being cynical on the subject, Patrick. Every man has his needs, though I will grant you that I never witnessed either of them in the company of a strumpet. More's the pity. A little wanton diversion would have done them both good." He glances at Cleburne. Nor do I think it would do you any harm, lad.

Cleburne doesn't seem disposed to comment and, after a moment, Hardee goes on. "I've always thought them lonely men. Lee because I suspect he's a profound fatalist, that he doubts that men have any control of events. It's an odd posture for a general, particularly for one as aggressive as Lee, but it's what I have always sensed in the man."

"And Thomas?"

"With George I don't think it's anything philosophical. He is simply a very reticent man. He never permitted himself any closeness to his staff, was never at ease with his messmates. Even when we were young and at the academy together, I never saw him truly enjoy the company of others."

"Yet he's married, I believe."

Hardee smiles. "Oh, yes. His courtship was a great surprise to us all. He was teaching artillery tactics at the Academy, thirty-five or thirty-six and still a bachelor, when a visiting widow and her spinster daughter ambushed him. He surrendered without a great fuss and the esteemed Miss Frances Kellogg became Mrs. George H. Thomas. I believe every mess in the army toasted the union for no other reason than its improbability. And I think George has thoroughly enjoyed being married. Frances is of . . . well, let us say statuesque proportions, within an inch or two of being as tall as he is. But she's not at all bad to look at and she's got merry eyes. She's the only person I've ever seen make George laugh."

"So there's hope for me, too?"

Hardee has forgotten Cleburne's sensitivity on the issue of marriage, looks at him with sympathy. "Of course, Patrick. What we did here today will make you a hero. The young women will pursue you by the bevy. You may have your pick."

"I should be better satisfied with a more restrained onslaught."

"I doubt that you'll have a choice."

Cleburne lets this pass, closes off as he always does when the discussion becomes personal. Hardee does not press him, but goes on recollecting. "When we served together in Texas, I think George kept himself busier than any officer in the regiment. He studied the geology and the flora, learned to speak Comanche, and read everything in the post library, even the Walter Scott and the silly romances, though he's the least romantic soul I know. He likes animals and always had two or three scrawny dogs hanging around his quarters. He'd feed them up, try to make them presentable and obedient. But they were usually beyond reform and would go sneaking about the camp, grabbing and gobbling anything they could find. Buck Van Dorn used to shout, 'Cry Havoc! and let slip the dogs of George!'

"I think those dogs produced the only friction I ever had with George. What I'd seen in Mexico made me despise all dogs, convinced me that they were the kin of hyenas and jackals rather than anything noble. After a battle or a skirmish, we'd bury the Mexican dead and the Mexican dogs would dig them up. Them and the hogs, working side by side, as if they had some infernal compact. And all the time the ravens, the cats, and anything else with a taste for human flesh would look on, waiting to join the feast. Christ, it was terrible. I remember marching through a deserted village where the dogs and the pigs had dug up a trench of Mexican dead. Everywhere you looked there were arms, legs, heads, and torsos of human beings, while everything that walked, flew, crawled, or slithered was feeding on them. Did you know that even rabbits will eat human flesh? Well, the Mexican ones did in that season. And after that day, I would never own a dog. I even refused my daughters when they begged me for a spaniel. And I never ate pork again. Not until this war and now only because there is so often nothing else to eat. . . . Can you guess what we did to that village?"

"I should imagine you burned it."

"Yes. But more than that. First, we put a cordon of men around it with clubs, sticks, shovels, axes, pitchforks, anything we could find. Then we slaughtered everything that fled the flames, right down to the beetles and the scorpions. I had the men throw the carcasses into the crypt of the village church to burn."

"You'd burned the church?"

"It was defiled, Patrick! Everything in that place was desecrated beyond anything you can conceive of. Sometimes I dream that even the horses and the cows were eating the dead, their muzzles red with gore and their eyes all aflame with hatred for us. But that, at least, wasn't true. . . . A night or two later, when the shock had begun wearing off, one of my volunteer officers opined that the dead had only been Mexicans, after all. I cursed the man, would have struck him had I not been restrained. I challenged him to meet me at dawn outside the camp where we could settle matters with pistols. But later that night my adjutant assigned him to carry a message to General Scott. We never saw him again. I understand that he was assigned to the general's staff and killed by a shell at Churubusco."

Hardee lapses again into silence, gazing at the fire. When next he starts to say something, he sees that Cleburne has fallen asleep. Hardee watches him, feeling something akin to love. What a clear conscience you must have, lad, he thinks. You are the most thorough killer I have ever known, yet you sleep as if untroubled by any dreams at all.

When Bierce shifts his position for the third time in five minutes, the captain lying beside him throws an elbow into his ribs. "Bierce, if you can't lie still, get the hell out of here and let the rest of us sleep."

Hazen speaks from the other side of their circle. "Go take the names of the wounded, Lieutenant. I'm unhappy that we don't have a better count."

Bierce leaves willingly. He has never felt more alive, as if any moment he might glow luminous, give off sparks if touched. He goes among the wounded waiting for the ambulances, recording the names of those from the brigade. Many of the men ask him for something that will identify their bodies should they die of their wounds. Bierce writes their names and regiments on corners torn from his dispatch book, leaves the men clutching these shards as if they held some runic power.

Night, cold, and pain have reduced faith to the primitive: a clutching at talismans in the form of photographs, letters, medallions, crosses, wedding rings, and trinkets of every description. There are those men who find in battle and even in their wounds confirmation of elaborate systems of faith. There are even those—particularly among the politically sophisticated Forty-Eighters—who find in the day's savagery a larger earthly purpose: another step in the bloody forging of the universal rights of man. But those who perceive either temporal or eternal purpose number very few compared to the multitude who put faith in atavistic charms against evil. For it is a night when anyone might imagine encountering demons, ghouls, or even Old Scratch himself.

Two litter-bearers lower a gravely wounded man to the ground nearby, take seats on a log to light their pipes. Bierce steps to the litter. The soldier is young and blond, quite beautiful despite the face smeared with blood and powder smoke and the dark sputum trailing from his gasping mouth. "Did anyone ask this man his name and regiment?"

The litter-bearers look up, surprised. "Well, it ain't exactly our job, Lieutenant," the older one says. "We just carry 'em off."

"You didn't do anything else for this man?"

"What's to do? He's shot through the lungs. He weren't hardly conscious when we found him, and didn't stay that much for long. He's gonna die before morning no matter what anybody does for him."

"How do you know that? You're not a surgeon."

The litter-bearer sighs. "Lieutenant, two things I can tell you: a deck of cards has just as much chance of stopping a bullet as a Bible, and nobody shot through the lungs survives till morning."

The other litter-bearer laughs. "From what we seen, those little books with the dirty pictures got the best chance of stoppin' a bullet. Some good thick covers on them naughty books."

"And you couldn't find the common decency to ask this man his name?" Bierce asks.

The older man is suddenly very angry. "Common decency, my ass! There ain't nothin' decent about what went on here today. You don't believe that, you come out with us next time. Come see those boys all shot to hell. And then you tell me about decency!"

"Now see here—"

"No, you see here, Lieutenant! Right goddamn here!" The litter-bearer tears the blanket from the wounded man, revealing a sucking chest wound. "You think we had to carry this boy back here? He's gonna be dead by morning! Probably won't even wake up again. But we carried him back so he could die among friends. That's what we did! Now you can shut the hell up about decency or you can take off that pistol so I can kick your ass!"

The other litter-bearer lays a hand on his arm. "Easy, Rodge." He looks at Bierce. "Lieutenant, we seen some terrible things. You likely has, too. Maybe it's best you just leave us alone."

In the Smith house behind the Rebel left flank, Surgeon Solon Marks has been operating since the first attack overwhelmed Bandbox Johnson's line sixteen hours before. The stream of wounded never abates, the endless individuality of their injuries resolving into several fairly distinct categories.

Severe wounds to the head are simply ignored by the surgeons, who cannot waste time on fatal injuries. Serious wounds to the abdomen or torso are considered nearly as fatal. If the ball or fragment can be removed easily, the surgeon does so before binding the wound and sending the victim out to the yard where he may or may not survive long enough to make the trip to the hospital in Nashville. If he does make it to the hospital, he may recover, although it is more likely that he will simply linger for a few days before dying of suppuration.

The lightly wounded are dealt with almost as perfunctorily. Simple flesh wounds where the projectile has passed through the offended area without causing hemorrhage are relegated to the orderlies' ministrations. Grazes are similarly treated, with the surgeon—if he looks at them at all—usually delivering a stern word to the victim about abandoning the fight when other men have continued with far worse. There are a surprising number of simple fractures, mostly caused by falling tree limbs. The doctors set these quickly and ruthlessly, anesthetic withheld in punishment for not being more agile.

Amputation of arms and legs take up the majority of the surgeons' time. Some involve completing the work done by grape, canister, shell, or cannonball. In these cases, the limb is simply sliced away, the protuberance trimmed back, and the resulting flap of skin sutured over the wound. Amputation of a limb damaged by a minié ball requires only slightly more skill. A one-ounce minié ball propelled by sixty grains of black powder is a fearsomely effective projectile, shattering bone and so mangling muscles, nerves, tendons, and arteries that most damaged extremities are beyond repair.

Solon Marks takes his calling with great seriousness, tries to save as many arms, legs, hands, feet, and ears as he can. But the longer he operates, the easier it is for him to give into the probability that he cannot save an appendage devastated by one of Captain Minié's ingenious slugs. He is acutely conscious that every chance taken, every additional minute spent on a patient, means that another will spend that much longer waiting and bleeding. Yet to know that, if given time, he might do so much more is a sorrow almost beyond the strength of a will sagging under so much fatigue, so much suffering. God forgive us our butchery, he prays. I, for one, cannot, will stand appalled at the memory of this night all the rest of my life.

Outside in the darkness, some of the Federal wounded cannot bear both their injuries and the thought of remaining prisoners of the Rebels. So far in this war, most of the captured have been paroled within a day or two of battle. But tonight a rumor sweeps the grounds of the Smith house that all paroles have been discontinued. "They're selling the niggers to the Mexicans for gold. We're going to take their place."

"I didn't think the Mexicans had slaves."

"Well, they do now. People are even sayin' the Rebs and the Mexicans are gonna unite, make one country and invade the North. Old John Bull's going to lend his fleet and send an army down from Canada. The Frenchies is gonna help too. All of 'em are comin' in on the side of the Secesh. And meantime, there ain't gonna be no more paroles for us."

In the cold and the dark, the rumor gains many adherents. An hour after midnight, a hundred ambulatory wounded form and march toward the Federal lines. The Rebel sentries watch uninterested, let them go. Behind a single torch, the Yankees hobble across the open fields east of Overall Creek. They cry out like lepers, like those carrying plague. Watching from horseback in the gloom, St. John Liddell recalls the story of the 14,000 Bulgar prisoners blinded by the Byzantine emperor and sent home across the mountains, a single one-eyed guide for every hundred sightless men. So do these one hundred follow a single eye through the night.

From the forward slope of Wayne's Hill, Corporal Johnny Green of the 9th Kentucky watches the winking fires along the Federal line. It is not his turn to stand picket, but he has volunteered rather than sleep through what may be his last night on earth. Alone of all the Confederate infantry formations, Kentucky Brigade has seen no action today. Tomorrow, General Braxton Bragg, who hates all Kentuckians, will no doubt correct this error by sending them into the hottest of the fighting, where they will need to stand to the slaughter for honor, if nothing more.

On the crest behind Green, Cobb's battery stands silent, only a single gun lobbing an occasional shell across the river. The Yankee fires are too small to make decent targets, and the purpose is more harassment than destruction anyway. Larger fires burn in the hospital areas beyond Overall Creek, but the Rebel artillerymen have marked these sites for what they are and leave them alone. Green watches a single torch creep across the upper left of his view, curious in its fitful progress. The gunners must find it strange, too, for Green hears low commands and the grating rasp of a shell being rammed. A moment later, the gun fires, the shell's fuse pinwheeling sparks over the dark field. The shell explodes short of the mark, revealing nothing of the target.

This first shot sets off a brief cannonade. Half a dozen Confederate guns elsewhere in the line fire in quick succession. The Rebel shells arc, plunge, explode in distant winks of yellow, the sound coming only faintly. The Rebel gunners cease firing, take cover, as the Yankee batteries return fire. Green squints, trying to make out the torch, cannot find it.

Behind him, a deep voice murmurs, "Are you awake, picket?"

"Yes, sir, General!" Green looks up at the mountainous bulk of Brigadier General Roger Hanson.

"Any guesses what that torch was?"

"None, General."

"I came down to let my eyes adjust to the dark but now the damned gunners have made me blind as a bat."

After a minute, Green chances a question. "Have you heard plans for tomorrow, General?"

"Not a one. I'll let you boys know as soon as I hear anything. Sing out if you see anything I should have a look at." He lumbers up the hill, the limp from a pre-war dueling wound throwing his gait askew.

Three miles behind the Rebel lines, lights shine in all the streets of Murfreesboro. Every church and public building, nearly every private residence, holds at least some wounded. Bob, the Negro groom sent in search of the five Foster boys, pokes in at every one. Several times he is told to do this or that, but he refuses respectfully. "Mah massa's Mr. James Foster, and ah needs be about what he done told me to do."

The hat-in-hand, shuffling-nigger act is, of course, a sheer hoodwink. Bob no more respects these white folk than he does old man Foster, his sons, or the memory of the departed Mrs. Foster. His own long-dead wife told him daily that he ought to be grateful that the Fosters were owners who worked beside their slaves, understood their toil, and expected no more of them than they expected of themselves. But Bob has never given a possum's balls for the lot of other niggers. As far as he is concerned, it is the Fosters who have enslaved him and it is the Fosters he intends to see brought low, crawling like so many spine-shot curs. If the death of any or all of the Foster boys will hurry this personal Jubilee by so much as a minute, Bob will shed no tears.

At a brick home on a corner, he sees a tall white woman handing out journey cakes to a crowd of hat-tipping Secesh soldiers. He catches the eye of the black maid at her elbow. The girl makes an almost imperceptible gesture with her chin toward the side alley. He waits there by a low window. A few minutes later, she slides it up, hands him two journey cakes and a thick slice of ham. "Here's a bottle. Drink your fill and then give it back. They's more like to miss the bottle than the liquor."

Bob takes the decanter, tilts it back, tastes good whiskey. He swallows three times quickly, hands it back. "Girl, ain't you takin' an awful chance?"

"Nah. Secesh officers is in and out. Missus'll just think one of them drunk it. I gotta get back."

"First tell me who won this battle."

"Thought it was the Secesh at first. Now I hear them Yankees held their own. Everyone's mad at Gen'rl Bragg."

"Let me have 'nother swallow from that jug if you sure it's all right."

She hands it back, and Bob takes a long, delicious swallow, running his tongue around the lip of the decanter, a kiss for the Rebel officer who pours from it next.

He goes on up the street, checking each house for the Foster boys or anybody from their company. He sees a familiar figure stretched on a counter in McKinty's Dry Goods, steps close. Abner Crosthwait stares up at him, eyes as dead as a salted fish. Well, isn't that a wonderment, Bob thinks, pretty Abner Crosthwait stretched out dead. Some girls be a-cryin' now.

Most of the wounded in McKinty's Dry Goods appear to be among those who will live, though probably crippled. Bob approaches a lanky Reb who is staring morosely at the bloody dressing binding his right foot. "Beg pardon, sir. Have you see'd any of the boys from Company A, Eighteenth Tennessee, Colonel Joseph Palmer's brigade?"

The Reb lifts bloodshot eyes. "No, we're South Carolina here. Were some Tennessee boys, but they left. All 'cept that lieutenant over there." He points to Crosthwait. "They forgot to take his boots. Go bring 'em here, nigger."

"Oh, no, boss. I dasn't." Bob rolls his eyes, showing the whites. "His spook it'd get me. And then Massa Foster, I's his slave, he'd beat me sure if'n I got messin' with dead white folks and their spooks 'stead of hurryin' on his errand. So I dasn't mess with no boots, boss. I dasn't." Bob delivers all this while backing away until he can duck out the door.

Behind him, the Sand Lapper shouts, "Hey, you, nigger! Get back here!" Bob keeps going.

For another hour he pokes about. He hears whispers about a Murfreesboro woman who has lost all four sons in the battle. We could do her a son better, Bob reflects. On the edge of town, he finds the brigade's wounded in a three-room frame house. Thanks to Colonel Palmer's refusal to dash his brigade to pieces against the Round Forest, the hospital contains only twenty casualties. Bob sees two or three familiar faces, none of them Fosters. He asks an orderly if there are more wounded.

"Not so far as I know. We lugged 'em all in."

"Dead, boss? Many dead?"

"Only three. Those two over there in the corner and Lieutenant Crosthwait. We left him up at the dry goods store."

Bob approaches the two corpses lying wrapped in thin blankets. Suddenly his hands are trembling. He lifts a corner of one of the blankets, does not know the man. He exhales, reaching for the blanket of the other.

"What you up to, boy?"

He turns to the speaker, a young man with a wounded arm. "Lookin' for any of the Foster boys, boss. I was sent by their daddy."

"Well, that man's name was Richards. Last I saw of them Fosters, they was all fine."

"Thank you, sir."

The man studies Bob, not unkindly. "That's all right. You're probably pretty close to those boys, huh?"

Bob stares down at his hands, cannot understand their trembling. "Yes, sir. I guess I am."

"Well, tell their daddy he raised a good bunch of boys, and that they've been lucky so far. But there's a piece of fightin' to do yet, and he oughta keep prayin'. Now you get going, or someone'll set you to work and you'll be a week gettin' home."

Bob slips out of the house. He must ponder on his trembling, on his accountable hatred, his unaccountable love.

Preston's brigade of Breckinridge's corps has shifted to the south to cover the ground fought over by Cheatham and Sheridan. First Sergeant William J. MacMurray, 20th Tennessee, goes out as officer of the guard in charge of forty pickets. The detail follows a staff officer along the edge of the woods, dropping off men every fifty feet. Half the men have been disposed when the officer pulls MacMurray down beside him. "This is your closest point. The Yankee picket line is about a hundred yards in front of you."

MacMurray peers into the darkness. "How can you tell?"

"I can tell. See that line of trees over there?"

MacMurray peers, thinks he can detect slightly darker shapes. "Yes, sir."

"That's where they are."

"What's in between?"

"Nothing. Few rocks and bushes. My guess is it'll be quiet, but keep the boys alert."

MacMurray posts his men and then takes his own position fifty yards to the rear of the center. He sits shivering in the dark, counting minutes. He does not look forward to inspecting his line. Give a man a gun and enough time to let his imagination work, and he's very likely to shoot at anything, including his sergeant.

Even with the artillery quiet, the battlefield is hardly still. Picket shots ring out every minute or two, sometimes single, sometimes in small clusters. About one in the morning, there is general firing half a mile up the line. MacMurray tenses, expecting the deep-throated hurrah of Federal troops and the high-pitched yelping of the Rebels. But the firing dwindles off, ceases altogether. MacMurray sighs, starts forward to inspect his men.

The overcast has broken since midnight, clouds scudding east beneath a waxing moon. The wind has freshened and the grass crackles beneath his brogans. Crossing a glade, he glances behind him, feels a jolt of fear at the sight of his own footsteps tracking him across the moonlit frost.

"Johnny?"

The voice is close at hand. MacMurray crouches, thumb on the hammer of his Enfield. "I hear you, Yank. What d'ya want?"

"I'm cold and hurt bad, Johnny. If you've got a canteen, I'd be obliged."

"Where are you?"

"Down a little hollow to your left."

"Can you see me?"

"No, just hear you."

"How do I know you ain't gonna slit my throat if come over there?"

The voice has a sudden catch in it, almost a sob. "On my mother's life, Johnny, I couldn't hurt you if I tried."

MacMurray compresses his lips, wishes he had the sense of his pa or grandpa. "All right, Yank. But I can't give you much 'cept a drink of water."

He finds the man in the bottom of narrow, rocky ravine, chest shot and nearly frozen. The Yank reaches out, grasps him by the forearm, holds tight, sobbing. "Hey, son," MacMurray says. "Ain't as bad as all that. Morning 'll come, and we'll get you out of here. Hell, you'll get to go home. Now let me prop you up and give you that drink."

He manages to make the man a bit more comfortable, gives him a drink from his canteen. The man is beset by a paroxysm of shivering. "Build me a fire, Johnny. I'm begging you."

"Ain't supposed to have no fires out here, Yank. One of your own guns might take an aim on it."

"I don't care. I'll die of the cold if I don't have a fire."

MacMurray considers. The ravine is deep, six or eight feet, and the man will probably die if he can't move or have a fire. "All right. But you got to promise to keep it small."

"I will."

MacMurray quickly gathers a small pile of sticks from the brush close at hand. He strikes a lucifer, gets the tinder going, and adds a few twigs. "What's your unit, Yank?"

"Eighteenth Regulars."

MacMurray takes a closer look at him in the light of the small fire, expecting to see a weathered face, a hint of gray in the hair. But the man is young and slight, barely out of his teens and hardly one of the fearsome regulars of legend. "How'd you get suckered into the damned regulars, son?"

The boy smiles wistfully. "My brother went and got hisself shot at Shiloh. I was told regulars killed more of you Rebs than volunteers, so I went and joined up with the Eighteenth. Now I wish't I'd stayed to home and not made the same mistake he did."

"Getting shot ain't no fun."

"No, it ain't."

"I gotta go see to some boys I got on picket. I'll come back and visit you around first light. We'll get you out of here."

"Thanks, Johnny, but I don't expect I'll make it to morning. I'm bleeding way down inside. I can feel it."

"Don't talk that way. It's bad luck. Just hold on and keep that fire small."

MacMurray climbs out of the ravine, moves carefully from tree to tree until he is behind the midpoint of his line. He crouches, hisses, "Novak."

"Come ahead, Will."

He creeps up beside Corporal Ben Novak, who is his friend and long-time messmate. He is about to tell him to report, only to lose all thought of military propriety at the view of the narrow field to their front. At first he tries to tell himself that the dark forms on its surface are only the rocks and bushes mentioned by the staff officer. But many of them creep, wave arms, moan, weep, mutter insanities of delirium. "Jesus Christ," he hears himself say. "How many are there?"

"I dunno. Gotta be two, three hundred. You look up this way or down that way, and there are more of 'em as far as you can see. Must've been some hellacious charges across this field. The crawlers don't get nowheres. Just go in circles."

"Can you tell if they're mostly our boys or theirs?"

"Can't tell. Sometimes I think one way, sometimes t'other. What we gonna do, Will?"

"Hell, I don't know. Nobody told us to do nothing 'cept stand here and watch for the damned bluebellies."

"Was you talkin' to one of 'em back there?"

"Yeah. You could hear that?"

Novak snorts. "Whenever the wind dies down, you could hear a squirrel fart out here. What we gonna do about those men, Will?"

"I told you, I don't know. We gotta check on the rest of the line before we do anything. You go up to the right, I'll go down to the left. Next hour, we'll switch."

"Oh, so I got to risk my neck, too, do I? You was the one who got elected first sergeant."

"Yeah, and you nominated me. Lucky I don't make you inspect the whole damned line."

Twenty minutes later, they meet again at the center of the line. "Everything's fine," Novak says, "except all the boys want to know what we're gonna do about those wounded. Gives 'em the spooks seein' 'em creepin' around like that."

MacMurray sighs. "All right. Stay low." He takes a breath and shouts, "Hey, over yonder! Let me talk to your sergeant."

Novak has thrown himself on the ground. "Jesus Christ, Will! Give a man some warning, huh?"

"I told you to stay low."

They wait, expecting a sudden volley from the Yankee line. When nothing happens, MacMurray shouts again: "Hey, Yank!"

A voice comes back out of the gloom. "Pipe down. We heard you. We're gettin' an officer."

MacMurray swears under his breath. He doesn't want to talk to any goddamn officer. Another voice comes out of the darkness. "This is Captain Beltrain. What do you want?"

"We want to go out and get our wounded, Captain. You're welcome to come out and get yours."

There is a muffled conversation and then the sound of voices raised. Finally, the first voice calls again. "Captain's gone back to camp. Says we can do anything we goddamn want."

"Who're you?"

"MacCaffrey, first sergeant."

"I'm MacMurray, also first sergeant."

"You a Scot or a Mick?"

"Scot."

"Me, too. All right, we got a couple of things to work with. Now let's go easy. Don't want to get the damned gunners riled, seein' they don't give a shit who they're shooting at."

"Agreed. I'll bring out ten men, you bring out ten. I'll meet you in the middle."

"All right. No weapons."

"Right, no weapons."

MacMurray passes the word for volunteers, gets the ten easily. They crawl out into the field, wary of accident or treachery. The two sergeants meet at a boulder in the center. McCaffrey reaches a hand over and they shake. "Christ, what a night," the Yank says. "Got a plug?"

"Sure." MacMurray works his plug out of a pocket, hands it over.

He sees a flash of moonlight on a blade. The Yank cuts a chunk from the plug, snaps the knife shut, chews with satisfaction. "Good tobacco. Thanks, brother. Here." He hands MacMurray a flask.

MacMurray opens it, smells raw whiskey, drinks, coughs. "Jesus, I wish I could say the same about the whiskey."

"It's mule piss, ain't it? Least it'll warm you some."

MacMurray takes a second swallow, hands it back. "Thanks. Think we can bring out another ten men now?"

"Suits me." They send word doubling the size of the detail, then sit, propped against opposite sides of the boulder, companionable. "Who would you say won today?" the Yank asks.

MacMurray answers cautiously. "I'd say we did. Drove you boys quite a ways."

"Yeah. Didn't do it easy, but you're probably right."

"What do you think'll happen tomorrow?"

"Likes be we'll try killing each other again."

"Don't think your general's gonna hightail it then?"

"If he ain't so far, he ain't gonna. Not unless he's fixin' to go alone and that ain't like Rosy."

"You like him?"

"For a general? Yeah. He's on the boys' side. All over the officers sometimes, but no harm in that as far as I can see. How do you like your General Bragg?"

In daylight, MacMurray might have said otherwise, but it is the dead watch of the night and no time to lie. "He's a son of a bitch."

"Heard tell as much. Sure ain't bashful about chargin', that's for sure. God, you boys took a pounding when you was trying to take that little grove of trees this afternoon."

"That we did."

"You know, men are just goddamn brave. Not all of them but more'n I would have thought before this war. Just goddamn brave. Funny thing, ain't it?"

"Yes," MacMurray says. "A damned funny thing."

The youngest is ten, the oldest sixteen. They call themselves the Seed Corn Contingent, swagger about with captured rifle-muskets, pistols, and sabers.

In the course of the evening, they've rounded up thirty Yankee stragglers, forcing them into a ragged circle around a smoky fire. The boys assigned guard duty insist on no talking, threaten severe punishment for breaking the rule. The Yanks are too tired and too disheartened to protest.

Earlier, the contingent's first leader, a rough but imaginative fifteen-year-old named Riggins, had been determined to make the Yanks reveal secrets. It is Riggins's belief that several of the prisoners must be couriers carrying vital messages. Doesn't everyone know that Rosy Rosecrans is the most devious, the most diabolically clever of all the Yankee generals? This night he will be sending orders to hidden formations of infantry, to long columns of blue cavalry, all waiting to fall on Bragg's flank and rear. The contingent must intercept and decode these messages; the outcome of the battle, perhaps of the entire Confederate cause, may depend on it.

Coercion is, of course, a complicated and delicate topic. The boys are too imbued with Walter Scott and Fenimore Cooper to sacrifice virtue and heroic ambition by resorting to actual torture. (They are, after all, white men.) They could issue challenges to single combat, but this seems impractical considering the weapons at hand and the physical size of their captives. After much debate, they decide to make the prisoners run in a circle, flapping their arms like crows, until exhaustion forces the couriers into confessing. The prisoners, however, cannot be induced to follow this program, only gaze glassy-eyed at the boys and then fall asleep again. After a few frustrating minutes, the entire experiment is declared a failure and Riggins voted out of office.

The tenure of the second leader, an intellectual fourteen-year-old named Titsworth, is even shorter. Titsworth decides to introduce himself to the prisoners with a few short sentences regarding the rules of captivity before demanding they render up couriers and dispatches. All the boys have long since exhausted the possibilities of making plays on Titsworth's unfortunate name. Not so the Yankee prisoners, who despite their fatigue and pessimism find it extraordinarily amusing. The redoubtable Titsworth makes it no further than "I'm Captain Benjamin Titsworth, and I command the Seed Corn Contingent of the irregular forces of—" before he is discomposed by a swell of snickers, guffaws, and (yes) titters.

The contingent's third leader of the night is Timothy Schuyler, a sixteen-year-old Murfreesboro boy. Schuyler would be off with the Army of Tennessee if not for his dwarfed left arm, which is not only unsightly but too short and weak to support a musket. This is decidedly his country's loss, since Schuyler possesses both a grasp of tactics and considerable leadership ability. He has relieved a Yankee cavalryman of an immense Savage revolver, the most fearsome and unusual weapon the boys have ever seen. Fourteen inches long, the Savage weighs three pounds, seven ounces, almost more that Schuyler can steady with his good hand. The oversized trigger guard houses a conventional trigger and a ringed lever operated by the middle finger. Pulling back on the lever rotates the cylinder and draws the hammer, an innovation that supposedly guarantees a better grip and a higher rate of fire than the usual single-action design.

In reality, the Savage is a poorly balanced and troublesome weapon, but young Schuyler recognizes that its striking appearance will serve admirably to symbolize authority. "Look here, boys," he says. "Let's make the Savage our Excalibur. If I die, the man next in line takes it. And so on down. Even if we all die, let's pledge that the Yankees will never take the Savage. The last man must throw it in a lake first."

Riggins frowns. "Ain't no lake around here."

"Come on, Rigs. You know what I mean."

"I think it's a great idea," Titsworth says, ignoring a glare from Riggins. The other boys voice like approval, and the Savage is duly sanctified.

Schuyler points to the prisoners. "Now, these bluebellies are just a bunch of stragglers who run at the first shot. I don't think they got any secret messages and I don't think they know anything we want to know. We've got to go scouting."

Riggins scowls. "I ain't doin' no damned skulkin' around unless we're gonna kill some Yankees."

Titsworth nimbly shifts to supporting his rival. "Yeah, we got the guns now for a good ambush. What do you say, Schuyler?"

Schuyler looks about the circle of boys, sees eagerness on every face. "Sure, we can have an ambush, but first we got to find the enemy, scout his strength, and make a plan."

"The enemy's right over there on the pike, asshole," Riggins says.

"But they're all stragglers, Rigs. No point in shootin' a bunch of men who are already running away."

Riggins, who would like to do exactly that, shrugs morosely.

"But a couple of the boys said they heard wagons, too," Titsworth offers.

Schuyler resists the inclination to shorten Titsworth's name to Tits. "Yes, but they're likely only ambulances. We can't shoot at ambulances."

"Well, what the hell can we do?" Riggins demands.

"Go scouting. Like I said."

Brigadier General Tom Wood would prefer to ride alongside the wagons, but the shrapnel wounds in his legs force him to sit beside an exceedingly odoriferous teamster on the swaying seat of an ammunition wagon. At least the man is not loquacious, which allows Wood time to brood on his humiliation by Rosecrans. Goddamn the ill luck that cost the army Julius Garesché! He would have stepped in, cooled Rosecrans's temper, won for Wood the right to stay with his division.

Wood shifts on the hard seat, notes sourly that the teamster has padded his ample buttocks with a folded blanket. Should he ask the man if there is another blanket? Or perhaps he should set aside his pride and lie down in the wagon box. His legs burn with his wounds. His staff surgeon had spent an hour probing for iron splinters that afternoon, and Wood suspects that the doctors in Nashville will need several times as long to finish the job. Damn the luck.

The Seed Corn Contingent has watched the Yankee wagon train passing for half an hour when Tim Schuyler orders a withdrawal. "Why don't we ambush 'em?" Riggins hisses.

"Rigs, don't be a fool. There's hundreds of bluebellies over there. How many are there of us?"

"You're the damned captain. You ought to know."

"Well, last time I counted, there was eighteen and a few of them looked plenty scared. You like the odds?"

"Screw the odds! We bushwhack a few Yankees and then run like hell. Down the road a mile we do it again. Two or three times and they'll stampede sure."

Lieutenant Titsworth, conciliator and politician, decides to side with Schuyler and sweet reason. "Come on, Rigs. Let's go find a better spot for an ambush. Maybe wait till first light when we can see better."

The contingent starts pulling back, Schuyler, Titsworth, and Riggins bringing up the rear. It is then that Riggins decides to satisfy honor and bloodlust. He aims his revolver in the general direction of the Yankee guard and empties all six cylinders as fast as he can cock and fire.

The response surpasses in alacrity and ferocity anything the boys can imagine. The road blazes with return fire, the Yankee infantry outlined in the continuous muzzle flashes. An incredible swarm of minié balls buzz through the woods, whining off rocks and trees. The boys run, some screaming, some sobbing, most just running.

About half the contingent rallies in the clearing. Titsworth notes that all the guards and prisoners have departed. Riggins doesn't seem to notice. "Where the hell is Schuyler?"

"He got hit," one of the other boys says. "I saw him go down."

They sit in the dark beside the embers of the fire. "Well," Titsworth says cautiously, "I suppose one of us has to take command."

Riggins ignores him. "Goddamn it, where is he?"

"Right here. I'm right here."

Tim Schuyler, captain, Tennessee irregulars, stumbles out of the woods, the left side of his shirt soaked with blood. He slumps beside them, tries to laugh. "All these years I wished I didn't have it. Now I ain't, and I want it back more'n anything." He puts his head between his knees, sobs.

Wood has to go among the men, clubbing a few with his crutch before they will cease firing. He orders half a dozen bull's eye lanterns lit and sends a company forward to probe the woods. He clumps along behind on a crutch. They haven't gone thirty paces when one of the men jumps back with a yelp. Wood pushes through to his side. A severed arm lies in the brush, so small that its owner must have been no more than four or five.

A sergeant steps forward, picks up the arm, turns it over in the light of a lantern. "This ain't no kid's arm. Look at the hair. It's a cripple's."

Another soldier holds up an oddly designed revolver. "Looka here. Never seen anything like it."

Wood takes the Savage, recalls hearing something of the design. He hefts it, isn't impressed. He turns to the company captain. "Take your men back to the road. We need to catch up with the train." He glares at the sergeant holding the dwarfed arm. "Bury that monstrosity!"

Brigadier General Joe Wheeler is waiting to spring his own ambush when he is startled by the eruption of firing down the road. He curses. "Withdraw the men!" he snaps. "Send someone to find out who's responsible for that blunder."

Twenty minutes later, a staff sergeant and a pair of privates discover the boys of the Seed Corn Contingent. "You cause that ruckus yonder?" the sergeant growls.

Presented at last with an opportunity for exercising command, Acting Captain Ben Titsworth stands to attention. "Yes, sir. We ambushed the Yankee train."

"Who the hell are 'we'?"

"We're the Seed Corn Contingent, Tennessee irregulars."

The sergeant snorts. "Get your ass up behind that man. The general wants to talk to you."

With Titsworth holding on for dear life to the waist of one of the troopers, the sergeant leads the way back along the path. They find Wheeler and his staff mounted. The private lets Titsworth down. "That one's the general," the sergeant says. "Tell him how you fucked up our ambush."

Titsworth manages a salute. "Captain Benjamin Titsworth, commanding the Seed Corn—"

"What did you say your name was?" Wheeler asks.

"Titsworth, sir. I command—"

"That is, I assume, an alias?"

"No, sir. It's my real—"

"Oh, for Christ's sake," Fighting Joe Wheeler mutters. "Major, get *Captain* Titsworth's report. Tell me later." He rides off. *Titsworth!* About all the goddamn night's been worth.

About 2:00 A.M., Bragg reads Wheeler's report from north of Stewart's Creek. As he suspected all along, the Yankees are withdrawing, their wagon trains already moving up the Nashville Pike under heavy guard. Yet Bragg feels no satisfaction in being right. A pursuit will mean giving even greater latitude to the Professor and the Bishop. (And Wheeler, of course; but at least he is loyal, will not try to claim undue credit.) He leans back, feeling an odd lethargy. Perhaps it is simply exhaustion, the cry of an aging body for a few hours sleep. Best to wait until dawn to issue orders. The men need their rest, and the Yankee retreat will be slow, hampered by the wounded and Wheeler's sniping. Besides, Rosecrans is still dangerous, yet capable of devising some trap along the road. Yes, best to wait until daylight. Wheeler's message slips from his fingers, floats on the warm current of air from the fire on the hearth, settles to the floor feather-soft, nearly weightless.

The temperature plummets with the clearing skies. Litter-bearers find many of the wounded frozen to the ground in pools of their own blood. Despite orders to stay in camp, many soldiers go forward to look for wounded and dead comrades. Half a dozen men of Company C, 16th Tennessee Confederate Infantry, creep up the railroad embankment toward the Round Forest to recover the body of Captain Drury Spurlock. Even in the dark, they can sense the emptiness of the woods ahead. An infantry brigade, no matter how quiet, has a definite mass, alters the air about it as certainly as a ship displaces water. Leaving the others to carry the captain back, a sergeant crawls forward to the woods, finds it empty except for the dead.

Passed up the chain of command to army headquarters, the report of the evacuation of the Round Forest seems to confirm Bragg's earlier judgment that the Yankees are in retreat. He waves away Colonel Brent's query about orders for Hardee and Polk. "Has it stopped raining?" Bragg asks.

"Yes, sir. The skies are clear and the thermometer's down eight degrees since midnight."

"Excellent. We'll have good marching weather. Wake me at first light."

In some Federal regiments, discomfort overwhelms caution, and the men build up the fires until sparks flutter among the cedars. Two dozen men of the 21st Ohio, Miller's Brigade, are startled by the sudden appearance of a horseman at their fire. Rosecrans clears his throat, speaks hoarsely. "You are my men and I don't like to see any of you hurt. Where the enemy see a fire like this, they know twenty-five or thirty men are gathered about it and they are sure to shoot at it. I advise you to put it out."

As if by the virtue of some power invested only in generals, a shell shrieks overhead exactly on cue, exploding in the cedars beyond. The Buckeyes start feverishly extinguishing their fire. Rosecrans wishes them good night, rides on.

He has determined by this time that there is no significant Rebel force beyond his right flank. Thomas's scouts have reported only Union cavalry searching by torchlight for wounded and setting fires for freezing men. The report lifts Rosecrans's spirits, lets him concentrate on what he knows for certain of the Rebels' dispositions. Bragg will attack in the morning, but where? He has failed against the right, failed against the center. Does it then follow that he will try the left? Above all things, Bragg is an artilleryman, an advocate of force over maneuver. He will fight closed up, eschewing any looping swings at flank or rear. That is why he failed today. If he'd doubled his cavalry or sent one or two brigades of infantry wide. . . .

Rosecrans checks this line of speculation. Later he can reconstruct the battle, analyze how it might have been fought differently on both sides. But for now it is a pointless exercise, as wasteful of time as mourning for poor Garesché and all the thousands dead. Now he must concentrate, make ready to fight Braxton Bragg in the morning. He is beginning to feel how it will be. Bragg will feint against a flank, probably the left, and then come in hard, like the body puncher he is, against the army's center and Thomas's guns. Rosecrans feels a sudden, triumphant confidence. Let him come.

The night crawls on. In the hospital tent of the 19th Ohio, Private Eben Hannaford feels his lungs filling with blood. He cannot breathe except sitting up and then only in thick irregular gasps. I'm dying with the old year, he thinks, won't see the first dawn of the new. Earlier in the day, before all his struggle to stay alive, it might have seemed a poetic thought. Now it is maddening. He leans forward, rolling his shoulders inward, trying to get another breath. He feels an overwhelming sense of suffocation, loses consciousness to a darkness so sudden and complete that he has no time for panic.

At the Confederate hospital in Murfreesboro, Private James Ellis, 4th Arkansas Infantry, has pilfered several rolls of gauze. He makes a tight cylinder of one, stuffs it in the hole in his left biceps. He wraps two rolls around the wound, tucking in the torn flesh as he goes. He takes a deep breath, for the pain will come now, worse than ever, and loosens the tourniquet. The wounded soldier to his left watches. "What you about, coz? Leave that cord in place and it'll make the doc's cutting that much easier on you. That arm must be half dead already."

"I'm keepin' this arm," Ellis grits as the blood and pain pulse down his arm.

"The hell you are. They'll have it off before you can open your mouth."

"I ain't letting 'em. It's my arm and I'm keepin' it."

The other soldier snorts. "What makes you think you're so different? You think those boys screamin' their heads off tonight wanted to lose an arm or a leg? They all said the same thing: 'Save my arm, doc. Save my leg. Don't send me home a cripple.' Lot of goddamn good it did them."

"So I suppose you're gonna let 'em take your leg without a whimper?"

The soldier shrugs. "I expect I might do a little bellyachin', but it's not like I expect it to do any good. I don't figure I got much choice in the matter."

"Well, I figure I do. We'll be seein' you."

The soldier raises his eyebrows. "You're headin' out?"

"Headin' out and headin' south. Gonna go home and get fixed up. Enough war for me."

"Well, good luck, coz. I'd go with you if I could walk. But mind those sentries. Ain't nobody supposed to be wandering around without a pass."

Returning from the midnight conference at Rosecrans's headquarters, Major General Tom Crittenden drinks off two-thirds of a bottle of brandy before falling face down on what may be the only field cot available in the entire Army of the Cumberland. About 3:00 A.M., his bladder rouses him. He stumbles out the tent door and starts unsteadily toward the brush. A blow to the forehead knocks him flat on his backside. He tries to rise, only to flop on his back, the sky whirling. In what seems only a moment but is actually several, a young captain is leaning over him, a shielded lantern in hand. "General, are you all right?"

Crittenden struggles to a sitting position, glares at the man. "Officer of the guard!" he shouts. "Arrest this man for assault!"

"Uh, pardon, General, but I am the officer of the guard and you walked into a tree."

"Sergeant of the guard!" Crittenden shouts.

"Here, sir."

"Arrest this man! He's going to be court-martialed and shot for striking a senior officer. Well, go ahead, man. Arrest him!"

The sergeant looks at the captain, the captain at the sergeant. Several enlisted men of the guard take wary steps backward, sensing the seriously fucked up. Fortunately, the sergeant is a man of uncommon good sense. "Yes, sir, General. But we need to look to that head of yours, too. I think there's some whiskey in the medical chest we can use to clean it up."

"Waste decent whiskey on cleaning a wound? Nonsense, man! Help me up and we'll have a drink together. Captain, consider yourself under arrest. You men, see he doesn't sneak off."

Halfway to the tent, Crittenden folds up like a jointed doll. The sergeant catches him, hoists him over a shoulder in a fireman's carry. "Come along, General," he mutters.

One of the braver privates looks at the captain. "Captain, do you want us to go ahead and shoot you now? I hear them court-martials are a powerful lot of trouble."

"We'll see what the general determines in the morning," the captain says sourly.

The soldiers laugh, return to their posts.

Bierce wanders through the Union camp. He is bemused by his exchange with the litter-bearers, amazed by his callow citing of decency in the midst of hideous carnage. If he is to understand war, he must reassert rationalism in its brutal simplicity. Yet this is difficult for one who feels his viscera charged with fire, lightning crawling beneath his very skin.

He walks rearward through Thomas's silent guns supporting the Federal center, descends an abrupt and unexpected slope into a wooded hollow. The Yankee batteries have taken advantage of the cover to make a park for caissons and auxiliary wagons. Coal fires burn in several forge wagons, the ring of hammers on iron reverberating through the hollow. He goes to the closest one to get warm.

The blacksmith is an immense man, his face ruddy with the fire, his beard singed to the skin in several places. He is shirtless, a leather apron protecting his chest. Scars pepper his arms, some white with age, others livid and oozing. He turns over a long bar hooked at either end, studies it a moment, and then goes back to hammering, all the while muttering in a low, angry argot that Bierce cannot identify.

Though the man is of terrifying appearance, something in his tone amuses Bierce. "What are you swearing at? The metal or the hour?" he asks.

The smith looks up, neither surprised nor resentful. "No, not at the metal; it does what I want it to do. And I like the night. The fire is calmer at night."

"What makes you so angry, then?"

The smith studies the hooked bar again, shoves an end into the fire, banks coals over it. Bierce hears a sibilant muttering, sees the bellows inflate, worked by some unseen hand. He looks about.

"He's under the cart. He likes it there."

"Your apprentice?"

The smith frowns. "No, I wouldn't call him that. A gilley, perhaps, imp, acolythist, something of the sort."

Bierce is trying to place the smith's accent, which is distinct, yet somehow indefinite. "What were you speaking?"

The man shrugs. "A little Italian, a few words of French, a little German. I was Swiss once, speak them all. Romansch, Polish, and some Slav, too. I find them all more expressive than English."

"You are no longer Swiss?"

"I am no longer anything. I curse all nations."

"You are an anarchist then?"

"No, I am nothing."

The sibilant chatter beneath the wagon increases, almost resolves itself into words. Bierce takes a step back. "What is he?"

The smith raps on the side of the wagon. "Show yourself, *Singe*. Officer, here."

A tiny Negro pokes his head from beneath the wagon. He grins horribly at Bierce, the glow of the forge gleaming on his bald scalp, his narrow, simian torso. "Kil-dem-al," he hisses.

"I call him 'monkey,'" the smith says. "He doesn't seem to mind."

"Who's he want to kill?"

"Ask him. He isn't deaf or stupid."

The little man chortles. "Kil all de white folk. Kil dem all."

"Why do you let him say that?"

"Why not? He's just cheering the abattoir we've arranged here. Besides, I happen to agree with him. The white race is a curse and a plague on this poor world. We should be exterminated." He shrugs. "And he says I can be the last one to die."

Bierce feels a tug on his trouser leg, looks down. Singe leers, eyes wide as half dollars. "You wan' be second last? We kil you easy quick."

Lieutenant General Leonidas Polk rests against a tree trunk, sheltered by an awning, a small fire at his feet. As always, his aides fuss about his health and comfort. Different members of the staff approach him, suggest that he ride back to town where he can get a decent supper and dry clothes. But Polk intones: "No. My men, dead and alive, sleep on this field, and I shall, too." Eventually they desist.

Through the night there is the occasional question, report, or request from lower down the chain of command. Polk's responses are calm, measured, for the most part sound. Between times, his staff believes him asleep, but the Bishop is awake, his visions as exquisite as a painting by Heironymus Bosch, the Eater of Souls no longer the dybbuk wolf but a great-beaked, stilt-legged crane feeding among the fluttering souls of the dead.

☆ ☆ ☆

An hour before first light, Colonel Brent wakes Bragg with a message from Wheeler. Two, perhaps three, brigades of infantry have reinforced the Yankees, apparently causing Rosecrans to cancel the retreat, although the heavily escorted wagon train continues north on the Nashville Pike.

Bragg steps to the window, studies the night. It is foggy and much can be imagined on such a night. Dawn will find the Yankees retreating, the supposed reinforcements melted away like mist. He returns to his bed without issuing orders.

The Yankee brigades—there are two—belong to colonels John C. Starkweather and Moses B. Walker of Thomas's corps. Starkweather's men, marching from Jefferson where they had their brush with Wheeler the day before the battle, come in closed up, wary. Walker's brigade is equally alert, its skirmishers flushing two ambushes and chasing off Wheeler's horsemen before they can do any harm. The Rebel troopers seem confused, wearied, hardly the same men of a day or two before.

Since leaving the line of wounded waiting for amputations, Private James Ellis has hidden in a dark alley. At first light, he picks up a bucket and strides confidently past a pair of sentries toward the pump at the end of the street. "What regiment?" one of the sentries calls. But his tone is not challenging but conversational.

"Fourth Arkansas," Ellis shouts over his shoulder, keeps going.

Private Eben Hannaford gives a single choking cough and wakes with a start. His pain is extraordinary but his lungs fill and deflate as easily as if he had woken in perfect health. He waits for the gasping to return, but his lungs continue to work untroubled. My God, he thinks, I'm going to live. I'm going home.

First Sergeant William J. MacMurray, 20th Tennessee, leaves his picket line to check on the young Yankee regular he left by the fire in the ravine. The youngster has passed over, his limbs stiff, his eyes frosted with rime. MacMurray returns to his line. He counts twenty-two dead Yankees within fifty feet of his tree.

Not long after dawn, the parents of Captain Drury Spurlock start home from Murfreesboro with his body. Mr. Spurlock's brother has a farm a few miles from town where they can stop to let the women clean and dress the body.

Mrs. Spurlock turns in her seat to gaze at the covered body. "Did you look at him?"

"Yes. He ain't bad."

"His face? They said a bullet hit him in the face."

"His face is all right, mother. His mustache hides the wound."

For a quarter hour, they ride without speaking. "He'll have bled a good deal on his uniform," she says.

"Yes."

"It will have to be cut off him."

"John will have a suit for him."

"I wish he could be buried in his uniform."

There are many things Mr. Spurlock could say about uniforms and armies. But after consideration, he only says, "Yes, I suppose he would have liked that."

Ahead, a lone soldier struggles along the road, a crudely bandaged arm cradled in a sling against his stomach. "Whoa there," Mr. Spurlock says to his mule, pulls up beside the man. "Need a ride, son?"

Private James Ellis turns on them a face pale but triumphant. "Thank you, neighbor. I wouldn't mind. I'm told they're coaling and watering the locomotives a couple of miles down the line. I'll take the cars from there. Goin' home to get fixed up." He sees the blanket-wrapped corpse of Drury Spurlock in the back of the wagon, hesitates. "This'n be one of your own, I'm guessing."

"A son," Mr. Spurlock says.

"I'm sorry for your loss, sir." He touches his good hand to his slouch hat. "Ma'am."

"Thank you," Mr. Spurlock says. "Do you need a hand climbing in?"

"No, sir. I'll just perch here on the back." Ellis manages to get himself seated, feet dangling over the end. Mr. Spurlock reaches out with his whip, flicks the mule expertly on the ear.

Bob, the nigger groom, climbs down from the wagon, stretches his back. Old man Foster glares at him. "Where you been, Bob? Believe I told you to do something."

"Weren't none of the boys needed bringin' home, boss. All alive, all kickin'. Saw 'em myself. And believe me, they's lucky, cause I saw a lot that weren't."

Foster sits down hard on the porch step. "I was sure at least one or two. . . ."

After waiting a moment, Bob says. "Well, if it's all right with you, boss, I'll unhitch these mules and go get some breakfast. Didn't have much since I left." Except the best damned ham and whiskey I ever tasted, he thinks. Delivered by a pretty hand, too.

"I'll unhitch 'em, Bob. You go find your breakfast. And thank you for going, Bob. I didn't have the courage."

Bob hesitates. "Just don't stop prayin', boss. I 'spect there's a lot of fightin' yet to come."

Private Dickie Krall falls in with the rest of the 1st Louisiana Regular Infantry, dresses ranks. "You know," one of the privates drawls. "When I get through this war, I'm gonna get me a couple a pups and name 'em Fall In and Close Up. Then when they're growed up enuf to answer to their names, I'm gonna shoot 'em both. And that'll put an end sure to Fall In and Close Up."

The other men chuckle, hands busy from long practice, checking canteens, bayonets, cartridge boxes, cap pouches, and muskets.

Swaying on the back of the Spurlocks' wagon, James Ellis has nearly fallen asleep when he hears a train whistle ahead. He turns, sees a dozen box cars waiting behind a chuffing locomotive, the whole shrouded in steam and morning mist.

I'm going to live, Ellis thinks. Gonna get home, by God.

CHAPTER 10

New Year's Day
Thursday, January 1, 1863
Along Stones River, Tennessee

Hazen has withdrawn from the Round Forest in the night, falling back to a new line of breastworks behind McFadden's Lane. Rosecrans has likewise drawn in other exposed elements so that the army holds a compact semicircle. Bragg's army has remained in about the same alignment as the previous evening, with all but Kentucky Brigade west of the river.

THE EARLY LIGHT turns the scattered hills west of Stones River into islands afloat on an ocean of mist. The sensation is unnerving, as if the world had reverted in the night to some earlier age where a scylla might rise to snatch a man or horse from the shore or where gorgons, brass-clawed and snake-browed, might sweep down with fell intent on wings of gold. Or so it seems to Lieutenant Ambrose Bierce as he stares into the mist, trying to distinguish the details of reality.

He is not alone in the task. Staff officers from various commands ride to the top of the hill behind Hazen's line, lift field glasses to study the mist, and then gallop off to report that they can see nothing of the Rebels. Thomas and his staff take position on the crest. The general rests both hands on the saddle pommel to ease his back, puffs on a cigar. Crittenden and his larger staff clatter to the top, set up nearby, orderlies hastily building a fire to brew coffee. Crittenden trots his mount to Thomas's side, calling out a cheery "Good morning, George" that must cost him dearly considering his foul hangover.

Thomas turns a cool gaze on him. "Good morning, General. Slept well, I trust?"

"Excellently. My boys are brewing coffee. Would you care for a cup?"

"I've had mine, thank you." Thomas turns back to watching the mist.

Crittenden does not recognize the dismissal. "So, did you sleep well, General?"

"Passably in what time there was."

Crittenden gestures toward the fog. "So, what do you think we'll see once the mist clears?"

Thomas removes his cigar, studies the chewed end. "I think, General, we will see something between thirty and forty thousand of the finest infantry in the world advancing with the intent of destroying this army. I am confident that my line will hold against them. I hope you and General McCook are similarly prepared."

Crittenden hesitates. "Well, I can't speak for General McCook, but I think my line is in good condition. I suppose there are some things I could look to."

"I understand General Rosecrans sent Tom Wood and Van Cleve back to Nashville. Who commands their divisions?"

"Hascall has taken Wood's. Sam Beatty has Van Cleve's."

Thomas nods. "Good men. Depend on them."

The audience—for audience it has become—is over. "Good day, then, General. Good luck."

Thomas nods.

Stones River smokes with the cold. Coming down the bank at McFadden's Ford, the skirmishers of the 38th Indiana break through glass-thin ice, let out involuntary yelps and curses as the water floods over the tops of their brogans. They wade across, holding Springfields and cartridge boxes aloft, scramble up the opposite shore. So far they haven't taken a shot or a casualty. They push ahead, bayonets leveled, expecting any moment to come face to face with the Johnnies who must certainly be there.

The rest of the regiment crosses quickly, followed by the 8th and 21st Kentucky Union Volunteers. Some of the Kentucky boys would stop to take off their shoes, but Colonel Samuel Price, the brigade commander, yells at them to keep going. It's a hard order, means the men will have to fight all day in wet shoes, but speed is necessary now.

General Sam Beatty watches from the low bluff west of the ford. Fifteen years as a county sheriff have given him an understanding of human nature that any number of philosophers might envy. Most of his staff officers are surprised by the absence of Rebel fire, but Beatty isn't. Few soldiers at this hour of a cold morning are going to be dutiful about standing picket. No, the Rebs will have gathered back from the river, huddling around small fires to brew coffee. They have, after all, been the victors in the battle so far and must be thinking that they damned well deserve a hot cup of field coffee. If his own men would just stifle their yelping and cursing, they might catch the Rebs totally unawares. But that, too, is against human nature and, hence, beyond Beatty's control. He cuts a chaw from his plug, works it meditatively between strong teeth.

At the river, one of the Kentucky boys shouts, "Hey, Gen'rl, this water'd freeze the tits off a sow pig. Cain't the fuckin' Pioneers build us a bridge?" The question gets a good laugh. Beatty allows himself a smile.

A sudden flurry of skirmish fire crackles in the fog, followed by a solid volley and a hurrah as the 38th Indiana drives the surprised Johnnies. A few minutes later, a staff officer dashes across the ford, splashing the infantry and getting roundly cursed. "We've driven them, General. We have full control of the high ground."

"Excellent. Tell Colonel Price to hold his position. I'll come up there in a few minutes." The staff officer salutes, gallops off. Beatty turns to his adjutant. "Tell Colonels Fyffe and Grider that their boys can stop long enough to take off their brogans before crossing." He touches spurs to his horse, trots toward the ford.

The Confederate pickets interrupted at their coffee belong to Brigadier General John Pegram's brigade of Wheeler's cavalry. The skirmishers of the 38th Indiana come at them out of the fog, looking seven feet tall and of an altogether non-hominid species. Better men than Pegram's troopers have fled for less cause. By the time Pegram can rally them a mile to the rear, the low ridge southeast of the ford is crawling with an industrious brigade of Yankee infantry felling trees for a breastwork.

Pegram is humiliated. He rides back to explain to Breckinridge, who is still responsible for the Confederate right, why he has yielded the ford without inflicting a single casualty.

Major General John Cabell Breckinridge feels he has lived a providential life. How else to explain so many accomplishments for a man just past forty? But listening to Pegram, Breckinridge has the horrifying feeling that Providence has deserted him. Only yesterday he'd spent hours resisting Bragg's orders on the false impression that the Yankees were across the river in force to his front. Now it has actually happened, and Pegram is again to blame. When the man is finally done reciting his excuses, Breckinridge fixes him with a long, bitter stare. "I think, General, that you should report this matter directly and immediately to General Bragg."

"John, I wish—"

"Please pay a bit more attention to military formality, General. If you please."

Pegram stares at the man he has considered his friend, colleague, and—in matters of tactics—his pupil. He straightens, assuming the position of attention. "As you wish, General. Should I tell General Bragg anything for you?"

"I will attend to any messages from this command. You need not act as a courier on my behalf."

When Pegram is gone, Breckinridge slumps. Damn the man. Just what did he think he was supposed to be doing at the ford? Now the Yankees are across and without a price paid. He takes a deep breath, turns to his chief of staff. "Tell General Hanson of the developments. He is to hold Wayne's Hill to the last extremity. As soon as General Bragg gives me permission, I will send reinforcements to his support."

As the fog lifts, the Confederate pickets on Wayne's Hill can make out a heavy column of Yankee infantry crossing the ford a mile to the north. The sergeant of the guard sends Johnny Green to inform General Hanson, but Hanson and his chief of staff are already gazing through field glasses at the ford. Hanson lowers his glasses to his large stomach. "Goddamn it! What the hell was Pegram doing up there? Give me two companies, and I'd hold the Yankees for half a day and turn the river red."

"West Pointer, sir," the chief of staff replies.

Hanson snorts. "Damn the lot of them! Lee and two or three others excepted, they're all drones, imbeciles, or charlatans!" He glares at Green. "I suppose you've come to tell me that the Yankees are crossing the river?"

"Yes, sir."

For a moment, it seems that Hanson will say something sarcastic. Instead, he sighs. "Thank you, son. We observed the same, but I appreciate your vigilance. Don't worry overmuch. We've got a good position here. We can hold until General Breckinridge brings us help."

☆ ☆ ☆

Braxton Bragg does not believe the reports of a threat to the army's right. It is a trick, another of Rosecrans's nefarious strategems. The Yankees are withdrawing, trying to cover their trains with a show of aggressiveness. Soon they will be in headlong retreat, and then Bragg will pounce.

When Pegram comes to report the Yankee capture of McFadden's Ford, Bragg gives the young man only a mild reproof. The Yankees should have been made to pay for their prize, but the loss of the ford is no great matter. Rosecrans is only securing his flank while trying to make Bragg uneasy about his, but the move is without real significance.

Pegram leaves Bragg's presence immensely relieved and with a wholly revised opinion of his chief's judgment and charity. He will redeem himself by harassing the Yankees without letup. And he will never trust John Breckinridge again. By God, no. The next time the man speaks to him as he did this morning, he will offer to resolve differences on the field of honor. By Christ, he will.

For hours Bragg waits. Breckinridge sends repeated pleas for a shift of some of his brigades back across Stones River to support Hanson's position on Wayne's Hill. Finally, Bragg has to admit that the Yankees may be holding position after all. He sends a message to Hardee: *General, please probe the enemy line to determine what strength he has remaining in position.*

Hardee reads the message, muses a few moments, and then writes a brief note to Cleburne: *Patrick, unless I am sorely mistaken, our Yankee brethren are strengthening their position and have no intention of withdrawing. The commanding general directs that we probe their line. Do so cautiously, taking care not to bring on a general engagement.* He underlines the concluding phrase and hands the message to an aide.

Pat Cleburne's latest plowhorse has proved more spirited than its appearance warrants. Cleburne wishes he could ride a mule, but knows that no officer could possibly demean himself so far and maintain his soldiers' respect. Not in this army, at least.

The horse's behavior makes Cleburne irritable, the prating of his chief of staff about personal safety even more so. So much so, in fact, that he kicks the horse into an awkward canter, leaving his astounded staff behind. By the time they catch up, Cleburne has detoured into a field and dismounted to inspect an overturned cannon in full view of a dozen surprised Yankee pickets. Horrified, the chief of staff yells, "Wait here!" to the staff, and dashes to the gun. The Yankee pickets are blazing away, their minié balls whicking around Cleburne, who is intent on his study of the gun. "General, come back with me!" the chief of staff shouts. "This place is much too dangerous for you."

"This is an interesting piece. Have it salvaged. I'd like to put it back in service."

"When we can, General. But I must insist, I must *implore* you to come away from here!"

Cleburne glances darkly at him and then at the Yankee pickets, as if they, too, were no more than another irritation. But he mounts and follows, though not in any hurry; he has had his one canter for the day.

Watching the two officers coming under the cover of the trees, Dr. John M. Johnson, the division medical officer, turns to another member of Cleburne's staff. "I'm reminded of the goat that tried to knock the locomotive off the track. You could admire his spunk and still have a very low opinion of his judgment."

Cleburne welcomes Hardee's instruction to probe the Yankee line. He orders St. John Liddell's brigade forward, but Liddell runs into heavy artillery fire before he can sufficiently develop the strength and disposition of the Yankee infantry. Cleburne sends S.A.M. Wood's brigade to cover Liddell's flank, but Liddell is already falling back and Wood has to give way precipitously, losing a hundred prisoners to a quick Yankee thrust. The loss is needless, and Cleburne resolves to censure Wood in his battle report.

Cleburne's probe sets off a series of sharp skirmishes. Bishop Polk orders a test of the Yankee line. "Send a message to Cheatham and Withers to probe all points on the line to their front," he tells his adjutant. "We shan't let the Yankees have any rest this frosty morning, and our own men could use the warming."

Despite the long, cold night under the awning, the Bishop is positively bumptious this morning. He teases his staff, exchanges jibes with the men as they pass to the front. A blast of musket and cannon fire greets the skirmish line. The line wavers, men dropping by the dozen, finally falls back. The Bishop watches, humming a few bars of one of the Church's livelier hymns.

For the rest of the morning, artillery duels and infantry skirmishes ripple along the front. Finally convinced that Rosecrans has no intention of withdrawing before nightfall, Bragg allows Breckinridge to shift Colonel Joseph Palmer's brigade to the other side of the river to counter Beatty's threat to Wayne's Hill. Bragg is distracted from further consideration of the situation by the arrival of an entirely undesired addition to the army: Brigadier General Gideon J. Pillow, fifty-six, grand sachem of Tennessee politics, former major general of volunteers in the Mexican War, and one-time law partner of the late President James K. Polk.

Barging into the office without waiting to be announced, Pillow sticks a hand across Bragg's desk. "How are you, Bragg?"

Like every artilleryman of any meaningful length of service, Bragg is a little deaf. He has not heard Pillow's entrance and is unaware of his presence until the thin grayish hand inserts itself between his gaze and the report he is carefully composing. He looks up, sees Pillow, and leans back from the hand in alarm.

Colonel Brent, who has hastily followed Pillow into the room, sees Bragg's eyebrows twitch furiously. At last Bragg manages, "General Pillow. I confess surprise."

Pillow drops his untaken hand without concern. "Hear you had a hell of a scrap yesterday. Didn't quite whip 'em, eh?"

For the first time in Brent's recollection, Bragg looks to him in supplication. Brent bustles forward. "Coffee, generals? Or something stronger perhaps?"

"Coffee," Bragg croaks.

"I'll have the something stronger. With a dollop of water. Not much, mind you," Pillow says. He plops himself comfortably in a chair. "So, tell me, Bragg. What happened here yesterday?"

"Do you come from General Johnston? Or from the president?"

"No, no, I'm not here as anyone's spy. Regular transfer. I haven't had much to do since that business at Donelson where Floyd made such a jackass of himself. Man would have done us all a favor if he'd surrendered along with Buckner and the boys. Me, I had to get out. I wasn't going to let Floyd hand me a sack of dung and then scuttle off like the yellow dog he is. No, sir. I needed to get out and fight for the cause. . . . Thank you, Colonel. Most appreciated." He takes a swallow of the whiskey and water, smacks his lips.

Bragg accepts a cup from Brent with shaking fingers, coffee sloshing into the saucer. Brent is embarrassed. Why should Pillow so unnerve Bragg? Pillow is a buffoon, a coward, and quite possibly a lunatic. Everyone knows the story of how Grant had invested Fort Donelson on the Cumberland River the previous February. Fearing trial and execution, former Secretary of War Floyd handed over command to Pillow, who immediately passed it to Brigadier General Simon Bolivar Buckner. So it fell to Buckner to ask his old friend Grant for terms while Floyd fled by steamboat and Pillow sneaked away in a leaking two-man scow.

Bragg seems to remember his authority, asks in a cool tone, "What is it I can do for you, General?"

Pillow looks surprised. "Well, as I said, I'm transferred here. I'm part of your command. At least for the present. I assume it may shortly be my command, once the president has gotten rid of Joe Johnston and called on you to take his place."

"The president is getting rid of General Johnston?"

"Of course he is. Don't be thick, Bragg. Jeff Davis hates Joe Johnston. Has ever since they fought over a girl when they were at the Academy together. Everybody knows that."

Or at least knows the story, Brent thinks.

Pillow rises, handing his empty glass to Brent and then stepping to a mirror on the wall. He straightens his uniform blouse, smoothes his sideburns, runs fingers through his ample white goatee. "I was a major general in Mexico, you know. Rank everybody in this army now that old Twiggs is dead. Hell, most of you boys were only captains when I was already a general." Satisfied with his appearance—and he is a handsome man—he accepts his refilled glass from Brent and sits again. "But I won't argue seniority at the moment. I need to fight. So give me a corps or a division, and I'll be happy until this scuffle is over."

"I don't know that I can replace any of my current commanders in the middle of—"

"Oh, poppycock, Bragg! You can replace anybody any goddamn time you please. You're not putting me on your staff where I have to consort with a bunch of paper-soiling puppies. No offense, Colonel. I need the company of fighting men."

Bragg's eyebrows resume their convulsive twitching. Send him somewhere he'll be shot, Brent thinks. If any man in this army deserves shooting, it's Pillow.

"So what do you say, Bragg?" Pillow demands. "If you want me to suggest who you might replace, I—"

"No. No, General. I believe I have the solution. Colonel Palmer was wounded yesterday afternoon. He's been in command of one of General Breckinridge's brigades. You can take it temporarily. Colonel Brent will draw the orders."

"So a brigade's all you can spare, eh?" Pillow slaps his empty glass on Bragg's desk. "Well, all right. I'll do the best I can with it. But tell that whelp Breckinridge not to get in my way. Former vice president of the United States, indeed! Proof of just how far the Republic had fallen by the time the sisters of the South quit the damned Union. All right, Colonel, point the way. I don't need to carry any goddamn written orders. Send 'em after me."

When Pillow has gone, Brent steps back into Bragg's office. He is thinking of risking a joke, something along the lines of ordering Pillow shot before rather than after the next fight. To his surprise, he finds Bragg smiling grimly. "So, Colonel, do you think Generals Breckinridge and Pillow will get along?"

"I rather doubt it, sir."

"So do I. So do I."

Hazen joins Bierce atop the hill in rear of the brigade's line. "Let me see your map again, Lieutenant," he says. Bierce unrolls the map he's been constructing for the last three days. Hazen studies it and then gazes across McFadden's Ford to the low ridge where Sam Beatty's division has deployed. "That ridge is the prize we'll fight for next. If we load it with artillery, we can blast Bragg's flank and center. If he takes it back, he can do the same to us."

"Why aren't we getting more guns on it now?"

Hazen smoothes his imperial. "My guess is that General Rosecrans ordered the movement as a demonstration. But once he has the rest of the line consolidated, he'll start reinforcing Beatty and developing the offensive possibilities. The advantage is coming our way."

Joe Wheeler has gone raiding again, but the pickings are much slimmer this time. Beyond Lavergne he encounters a southbound wagon train escorted by a full brigade of Yankee infantry. The strength of the escort can only mean a cargo of ammunition, but Wheeler's men are too few and too exhausted to attack. He rides on, the afternoon turning blustery, the temperature dropping toward freezing again. Twice in four days he has ridden around the Yankee army, an act that when done once on the Peninsula made Jeb Stuart into the beau ideal of the Southern cavalier. But Joe Wheeler, small and bedraggled, looks more the sneak thief, the cutpurse, the low highwayman. 'Tis pity, but true.

Rosecrans spends most of the day in the saddle, riding Boney and Tobey alternately. It seems that sending Sam Beatty's division across the river to threaten Bragg's right has produced the desired effect. The Rebels seem hesitant, almost passive. Meanwhile, every hour makes his line stronger. By dusk, it may be unassailable.

The skirmishing dies down in the early afternoon. The armies turn to necessary chores while watching each other warily. Litter-bearers remove the remaining wounded while surgeons, dizzy with exhaustion, continue their rough medicine. Burial parties dig long trenches, bury the fallen en masse. Along Overall Creek, Colonel Parkhurst's provost guards flush hundreds of Union stragglers out of the thickets, herd them back to their regiments.

Rosecrans's headquarters staff tabulates the dead, wounded, and missing. When Rosecrans pauses in his peregrinations for a late lunch, Major Goddard hands him the estimate. Of just over 43,000 men, the Army of the Cumberland has suffered some 2,000 dead, 8,000 wounded, and 4,000 missing. Even given that the final figures will be the usual ten to twenty percent less than initial battlefield estimates, the army has taken a terrific pounding.

Rosecrans studies the list of unit losses, his frown deepening. At last he sighs, looks at Goddard. "I think, Major, that we'd best keep this to ourselves for the time being. It is very serious, worse than I'd imagined."

"Yes, sir. There's only the single copy I made. I'll keep it safe."

"Good. So do you think we can fight another day?"

Goddard is nonplussed. He has always thought of himself as a clerk, has not considered that Garesché's death might elevate him to the position of advising the commanding general. He licks his lips. "General, if you fight, the men will fight with you."

Rosecrans nods, faintly amused by the young major's obvious distress. "Yes, I believe they will. This is a fine army, Major. Fine men."

Lieutenant Colonel George Brent, who has undertaken the tabulation of the Southern dead, wounded, and missing, finds the Confederate commanders maddeningly casual in their reports. How is it, he muses, that we can keep track of four million coloreds and every boll of cotton and leaf of tobacco they produce for us, and not be able to count our own dead and wounded? It is a contrariety, one of many in the Southern character: a seeming refusal to do anything that might stink of clerkishness, of the tight-fisted avarice of the Yankee shopkeeper. Does this reluctance exacerbate the Confederacy's difficulty with logistics? Explain why so many soldiers are poorly fed, shod, and clothed? Why Bragg, as skilled a quartermaster as any soldier in the South, is reviled for lacking imagination and dash? Brent, who would himself prefer to command a regiment to serving as chief of staff, rather supposes so.

Despite the difficulties, Brent produces a surprisingly accurate estimate. Out of just under 38,000 men at the beginning of the battle, the Army of Tennessee has lost 1,300 dead, 7,900 wounded, and 1,000 missing. When he presents his report to Bragg in early afternoon, the general sets it aside until he finishes the letter he is composing to General Johnston regarding the unexpected and unwelcome arrival of Pillow. Only when he has read the letter over and signed it does he pick up Brent's report. He studies the report without expression, his huge eyebrows drawn together behind his spectacles. He sets it down and gazes out the window at a snow flurry eddying in the cedars. At length, he looks at Brent. "Thank you, Colonel. These are heavy losses but not fearful ones. They fall within acceptable limits, and we have done great damage to our enemies. Tonight they will retreat. Tomorrow we will follow and finish the work."

Whatever his critics may think of him, Bragg is not without human feelings. When Brent has left the room, Bragg again reads the casualty figures, this time allowing himself a sad shake of the head. They could have been so much lower if men had just done what he'd told them to. The main fault lies with Breckinridge and Polk: Breckinridge for delaying in the face of a phantom advance until his brigades could no longer be sent to reinforce Hardee; Polk for squandering those same brigades in piecemeal attacks against the Round Forest.

Despite the failure to take that miserable grove of trees, Bragg still views yesterday as a triumph. Hence his great surprise that Rosecrans has not retreated. He shares with most Old Army professionals the opinion that Rosecrans is brilliant but erratic, likely to come apart under pressure. Perhaps he has underestimated the man. Or perhaps Hardee is right in crediting George Thomas. Yet the more Bragg considers Rosecrans's refusal to retreat, the more it seems a blunder. The Yankees have been marching and fighting for nearly a week. Wheeler has devastated their supply trains, and tonight they will again go cold, hungry, and shelterless. Meanwhile, Rosecrans the engineer will have them awake chopping and digging. By morning, they will be exhausted, even less capable of defending themselves than this morning. True, Bragg's own men will also spend the night in the open, but they will at least have something in their bellies and as much sleep as they can manage.

During the afternoon lull, Confederate details scavenge the field for abandoned Yankee weapons. They retrieve thousands of small arms, including a large number of new Springfield rifle-muskets. Even more satisfying is the tally of thirty-one cannons salvaged and presented to the army's artillerymen. In several regiments, color guards set about adding crossed cannons to their battle flags. It is an award supposedly granted only by army headquarters, but generals have their priorities and timetables, enlisted men theirs.

Oddly, the Rebel cannoneers are slow to integrate the Union guns into their batteries. Part of the problem is ammunition, another part their suspicion—not entirely unfounded—of the Parrott rifles, which have a reputation for exploding. A third part is their distrust of any gun that would allow itself to be captured. The Rebel cannoneers are an exceedingly superstitious lot, endowing their guns with names and suprarational personalities. To part with a trusted gun in favor of a treacherous Yankee piece—although it may fire a heavier load a longer distance—is more than they can be persuaded to do on short notice. So the majority of the captured guns go into the army's reserve artillery of old, tired, obsolete cannons.

Thousands of Confederate soldiers scour the battlefield on their own or in small groups, motivated by curiosity, the love of missing comrades, or simple greed. A squad of Cheatham's men comes on the body of Colonel George Roberts. They bury him in the rocks, laboriously etching his name in the limestone. They know a hero when they see one, whatever his uniform.

All but the most heartless men obey an unwritten set of rules when looting the dead. Clothing, shoes, coins and shinplasters (the fractional bills issued by both governments), pocketknives, sewing kits, and the innumerable small, useful items of the soldier's life are considered expedient items of plunder. The scrupulous turn the watches and wedding rings of fallen comrades over to their officers. The same items taken from a foe become part of the barter currency within the armies.

Earlier in the war, most soldiers considered it unseemly to read a dead man's letters or diary. But by now curiosity, boredom, and a general want of reading material have made these almost as valuable as cash. Men pass them about, for the most part respectfully. There is, of course, something titillating in reading these letters. Photographs pass from hand to hand, the images becoming the object of late-night onanism by many men: a small and momentary pleasure that inevitably leads to sleepless ponderings on the possible faithlessness of wife or sweetheart, oaths of revenge, and—finally—small heartsick whimpering.

Private Dickie Krall, Company A, 1st Louisiana Regular Infantry, finds a carefully folded and much-read letter in the inside blouse pocket of a red-haired Yankee private with a bullet hole through the forehead. He reads:

Dear Husbend Charly,

You no i said in my last leter that i culdnt go on bein fathful to you les you culd com hom and act lik a fathar to yur kids and a husbend to me. I aint got no mony atall and fathful dont pay for nothin. But you didnt com hom and you didnt send no mony so i tok up with homer pike from ovr in wadsworth. I am sory for this but i aint got no chois since you didnt com hom to be a good fathar and husbend and didnt send no mony. Homers a good man and had enuf mony to by hisself a substut and not go messin rond with a lot a things that wernt non of his concrn and mite hav got him

kiled anywy. But i hop tht aint hapened to you and tht yur wel. Gues this
means you can go west lik you alwys sad you wnted to. Ifn it dont go rit with
homer me and the kids i mite go long ifn youll hav us. Tho nowin you I dont
supos youd hav us back even tho what i don wer only cuz you wodnt com
hom and be a good husbend and fathar or send no mony.

Yur wife Eleanor Bonnard

Dickie Krall reads the letter a second time, feeling infinitely sad, before slipping it into a pocket. Later, when no one is looking, he'll drop it in the fire. Why, he wonders, had the Yank kept such a hateful thing, folding it carefully after each reading? This seems to him entirely incomprehensible in the aftermath of his own shame. He thinks of Joe Zein dying of a dozen bayonet wounds, but whose face had still been beautiful in death, even sublime, as if waiting for whatever resurrection may yet come at the behest of a Mercy not only beyond knowing but inconceivable.

With the afternoon fading, the scavengers and working parties abandon the field. Amid the cedars and the death, the dusk brings on atavistic fears even in the most rational. Colonel John Beatty, banker and writer, recalls the French phrase for twilight: *Entre chien et loup*—between the dog and the wolf—and shivers for no good reason.

At sundown, a heavy exchange of fire blazes up at the center of the facing lines, but it withers quickly, curling away toward the flanks. Men settle down to making themselves as comfortable as possible. The Confederates receive their rations, but, forbidden fires, must eat their sowbelly raw. On the Union side of the line, the fare is much poorer. Even coffee, more treasured even than tobacco, is in short supply. John Beatty sups on a slice of raw pork and a few crackers, recording in his journal that *no food ever tasted sweeter.*

At army headquarters, Magee, the ubiquitous orderly, brings Rosecrans a fresh uniform jacket. Rosecrans removes the old one reluctantly, touching the wide stain on the right sleeve and breast where Julius Garesché's blood has dried a dirty brown. He cuts the buttons off, drops them in an envelope, writes on the outside: *The buttons I wore the day poor Garesché was killed.*

The snakes are torporous with the cold. Their handlers rub them, blow on them, stick them inside their shirts to warm, but the snakes refuse to rattle or hiss with any enthusiasm. But the two snake-handlers are zealous for Jesus. They dance, contort, speak in tongues. The older one, a skeletal hill man with a scraggly gray beard, offers his tongue to a big timber rattler before taking the snake's wedge-shaped head entirely into his mouth. This is more than some of the watching soldiers can take, but Bierce is transfixed by the sight. The man withdraws the snake's head, dances around the fire, rattling the coins in a tin pan. "For the work of Jesus, brothers! Come, give a penny, a hay-dime, a dime. All for the work of Jesus! To let these two poor disciples wander the land, showing the power, showing the glory, showing the blessed grace of Jesus! Come brothers, a penny, a hay-dime, a dime."

Colonel John Parkhurst, former disciple of the philosopher Descartes and ongoing provost marshal of Thomas's corps, pushes through the crowd, followed by two grim privates with bayoneted Springfields. "Who the hell authorized this? Get these men out of here. This is an army, for Christ's sake, not a goddamned circus!"

The older of the handlers croons, "Would you deny the power of Jesus, Colonel? He protects from the serpent's sting, the arrow of the enemy, the jibe of the unbeliever."

"He is not, sir, going to protect you from my boot landing on your backside!"

The younger snake-handler, a low-browed boy with a widow's peak, reaches a snake over the older man's shoulder. Bierce can see that the boy's eyes are rolled up into his skull, wonders if this is trance or show. "Take the snake, Colonel," the older man says. "If you believe in Jesus, it will not harm you. Not a snake has bitten me in forty years 'cept when my faith was weak. But even then Jesus forgave my sin, allowed not the venom to reach my heart."

Parkhurst does not flinch from the snake. He draws his pistol. "You are threatening an officer of the United States volunteers, Army of the Cumberland. I will defend myself with deadly force unless you withdraw forthwith."

For the first time the old man seems unsure. "Colonel, we ain't threatenin'. We're offering you a test of—"

Parkhurst levels the pistol, cocks it. Either side of him, his privates bring down their Springfields into the position of charge bayonet. Behind the handlers, the crowd parts quickly. Bierce cannot help but smile. "I am going to count to ten," Parkhurst growls. "At the end of that time, I expect to see you and your pets on the way out of this camp."

The snake-handlers do not dally, but toss their snakes into gunnysacks and scuttle from the circle to the catcalls of the men. Parkhurst turns on Bierce. "What's your name, Lieutenant?"

"Bierce, sir."

"Why didn't you stop this travesty?"

"They're not my men, Colonel. I'm a staff officer, Colonel Hazen's—"

"You're an officer, damn it! If you're going to wear the rank, then behave like one!"

"I'm sorry, sir. I didn't see that much harm in it."

Parkhurst glares at him, mouth tight. "Hazen's staff, you say?"

"Yes, sir."

"I'll speak to him. A certain lieutenant needs instruction in his duties as an officer. Good order and discipline, Lieutenant. That, more than anything else, is our responsibility!"

There is a sudden commotion among the men and the younger of the snake handlers stumbles shrieking into the circle of firelight. "Behold the fate of unbelievers and all that dwell with Evil!" He hurls the snake in his left hand, not at Parkhurst but at the fire. The snake lands in the flames, writhes, flows down a blazing log, coils circinate, burns. For the briefest of moments, it seems to Bierce that its body glows entirely translucent, fragile as blown glass.

Night falls. Men lie hungry, shivering, fearful. Some pray, some die of wounds; a few remember a cause, still believe.

Colonel John Beatty takes out his pocket Bible, reads from the Ninety-first Psalm:

> *I will say of the Lord, He is my refuge and my fortress: my God; in him will*
> *   I trust.*
> *Surely he shall deliver thee from the snare of the fowler, and from the noi-*
> *   some pestilence.*
> *He shall cover thee with his feathers, and under his wings shalt thou trust:*
> *   his truth shall be thy shield and buckler.*
> *Thou shalt not be afraid for the terror by night; nor for the arrow that flieth*
> *   by day;*
> *Nor for the pestilence that walketh in darkness; nor for the destruction that*
> *   wasteth at noonday.*
> *A thousand shall fall at thy side, and ten thousand at thy right hand; but it*
> *   shall not come nigh thee.*

CHAPTER 11

Friday, January 2, 1863
McFadden's Ford, Tennessee

By the morning of the third day of the battle, breastworks cover the Union right and center west of Stones River. East of the river, however, Brigadier General Sam Beatty's division is largely unprotected on the ridge southeast of McFadden's Ford. On the Confederate left, Hardee has withdrawn his line a half mile to the cover of a broad band of woods. Polk has remained in place in the center, except for some minor straightening of his line. East of the river, Kentucky Brigade continues to hold Wayne's Hill, with Brigadier General Gideon Pillow's brigade (formerly under Colonel Joseph Palmer) in support.

J T IS A day of early risings, the ground too cold, the air too damp for the body to sleep longer than exhaustion demands. Those who have coffee or a lump of sowbelly build small fires, the smoke mixing with the mist off the cold waters of Stones River to lie in the cedars and the hollows with the bodies of the dead.

The smoky fog burns the throat, makes eyes already red with fatigue sting all the worse so that men welcome the first gusting of a morning breeze. At least the dead do not stink too horribly yet, putrefaction arrested by the chill, though it is not cold enough to freeze the smell of blood and emptied bowels. It is here that the analogy of slaughterhouse and battlefield goes awry, for herbivores, bawling in their death agonies, discharge only an excreta of vegetable matter, while human death stinks of the digested flesh of other mammals. So it is that the burial parties go about with bandannas over their mouths even in the cold: hollow-eyed, nauseous with the horror of their duty.

At first light, Captain W. P. Bramblett and Lieutenant Lot C. Young of Company H, 4th Kentucky Confederate Infantry, Hanson's brigade, edge forward from the picket line for a view of the Yankee dispositions on the east side of McFadden's Ford. Most of the land between Wayne's Hill and the ford has been cleared of trees but then left to grow up in sassafras, briars, and brush. Thickets and the rolling ground provide some cover until the land opens into a cornfield 150 yards short of the Yankee line.

Bramblett and Young take cover in a gully carved by an ancient stream. Peering over the edge, they can make out the rough line of the Yankee bivouac on the low ridge southeast of the ford. They count cooking fires, search for regimental flags. "I'm guessing four regiments," Bramblett murmurs.

"I thought four with maybe one or two more over to the right. Looks to be a couple more back on the ridge," Young says.

Young is skilled at this sort of thing, his eyes sharper. "I only see the one battery. Do you see any more?" Bramblett asks.

Young hesitates. "No. And that's odd, ain't it? If I had that ground, I'd load it with guns."

Bramblett nods. They are very junior officers but veterans, can sense the odd disposition, the missed chance. They slide along the gully to the river, mindful of the possibility of Yankee scouts taking advantage of the same cover. Nearby, Harker's brigade waded the river three days and a night ago to attack Kentucky Brigade on Wayne's Hill. That crazy, almost blind fight seems an incalculable time ago, part of a past ridiculous in its innocence.

Bramblett studies the cold, fast water. "I'd as soon keep my feet dry, but we ought to get a look at what's going on down by the ford."

"Let me climb a tree. Maybe I can see."

"Some Yank will pick you right out of it."

"Nah, they haven't had their coffee yet. Won't notice."

Bramblett shrugs. "Your ass, coz."

Young scrambles up a slender oak barely thick enough to support his weight, manages to fix his field glasses on the Yankee line on the west side of the downstream bend. After a minute, he says, "Well, if that ain't strange."

"What?"

"Guns on the high ground west of the ford. Three batteries at least. Mostly smoothbores, all trained on the ford."

"What are they doing on the west side of the river? Why not have them up with the infantry?"

"Maybe it's a trap. Maybe the infantry on this side is just bait."

Young scrambles down, and they hurry to report to General Hanson on Wayne's Hill.

Captain John Mendenhall, chief of artillery, Crittenden's corps, rides slowly along his gun line overlooking McFadden's Ford. He has probably overdone the defense of a position not likely to be attacked anyway. But the Mendenhalls believe in being prepared. Family tradition has it that his great-grandfather so nearly starved on Benedict Arnold's invasion of Canada in 1775 that, once back home in Maine, he never again left the house—even to go to church—without three days' rations. It is a principle adhered to by the Mendenhalls ever since. At West Point, young John was always the best prepared for inspection or recitation. Since his commissioning in 1856, he has received excellent if unenthusiastic evaluations from his superiors. Now, as Crittenden's chief artillerist, he commands the most thoroughly supplied artillery command in the Army of the Cumberland. He also has enough to smoke, a warm coat, and dry socks: three items almost entirely unknown in the rest of the army.

Satisfied with his inspection, Mendenhall rides a few dozen paces back from the guns, reaches beneath his rain cape for a cigar. By necessity, artillery officers spend a great deal of time around vast amounts of gunpowder. Perhaps that is why a good cigar is a particular satisfaction for Mendenhall; reward for a preparedness so complete that he can absent himself for a few minutes from the close company of his guns and the danger of accident.

Braxton Bragg has been awake since before dawn, expecting news that Rosecrans is retreating at last. But the reports gathered by Colonel Brent and the headquarters staff seem to indicate the opposite. Still disbelieving, Bragg orders Polk and Hardee to probe the Yankee line again. For once, the Bishop and the Professor are prompt in executing orders. Within a half hour, skirmish fire crackles along the line. It dies away quickly; the skirmishers having paid with another dozen lives to prove that the Yankees are still very much in place.

Bragg paces furiously. If he cannot budge Rosecrans in the next twenty-four hours, it is he who will have to consider retreating. He pulls a map from the pile at the corner of his desk, studies it, his artilleryman's eye attracted to the low ridge southeast of McFadden's Ford. The tally of rations, ammunition, fodder, and casualties slip from his consciousness, replaced by the calculation of ranges, elevations, and angles. He runs fingers through his beard. Good high ground, he muses. Give me good high ground and I will win this battle.

"Colonel Brent," he calls.

Brent, ever alert, is there in a moment. "General?"

"What is the latest from Pegram on the Yankee dispositions east of McFadden's Ford?"

"He hasn't sent anything this morning. As of sunset, he reported two, perhaps three, brigades across the river but no sign that they intended any forward movement."

"How many batteries?"

"Uh, I believe only one, sir."

"I need better than your belief, Colonel. Send a message. Tell Pegram. . . . No, wait, go yourself. Find out what the Yankees have over the ford. We may be able to do something yet to push neighbor Rosecrans into retreat."

Brent cannot help lifting an eyebrow at the characterization of Rosecrans—a flourish entirely out of character for Bragg. "Yes, General. I'll leave at once."

"Take Robertson with you. I want an artilleryman's opinion, too."

Brent dislikes Captain Felix Robertson, a young man of such fawning sycophancy that he has become something of a joke around army head-quarters. Some two weeks past, Brent—who labors mightily to be a hail fellow—was stung to overhear one of the captains refer to Robertson as "Brent's ass-kisser."

"And an ample target it is," one of the other officers added, to the collective merriment.

Brent was mortified by the reference to his unfortunately large and womanly posterior. Immediately, he drew up papers transferring Robertson to command of a battery in Withers's division. Bragg signed them without comment.

Robertson objected strenuously: "See here, Brent. I'm no field officer. My temperament's for staff work. And I do it damned well. Since when has this army had better records of its ordnance?"

Brent fixed him with a cool stare. "You have discharged the duties assigned you. Now the general feels that you would benefit from some practical experience in command of a battery. I agree."

"But you haven't had field command. Yet you're chief—"

"I hope the commanding general will entrust me with a field command in the near future. It is my fondest wish. Good day, Captain."

But Robertson is not a young man easily diverted from his chosen course. Within days he managed to get his battery transferred to the army reserve for refitting, a position that again gives him access to army headquarters.

Leaving Bragg's office, Brent spots Robertson lounging among the staff officers in the hall. "Come along, Robertson," he snaps. "We have an errand to perform for the general." Painfully aware of the breadth of his posterior, he strides toward the front door.

Many generals are abroad in the early light. Breckinridge encounters Hardee and Polk riding together along the river. The three pause to discuss the tactical situation. Breckinridge, the comparative neophyte, asks if he should begin erecting breastworks east of the river.

Hardee and Polk exchange glances. Breckinridge's political prestige and influence have always complicated his status as a subordinate. Moreover, his division, though officially part of Hardee's corps, has functioned independently since being assigned to protect the army's right. On Wednesday, Polk had exercised tactical control; but has his authority lapsed in the day since the assault on the Round Forest? If so, has it passed back to Hardee? Or does Breckinridge answer only to Bragg?

Hardee flexes his arthritic right hand. "I would suppose, John, that you should seek the commanding general's direction on that point. Given the Yankees' move across the ford yesterday, I think General Bragg may be preparing to shift the rest of your division in that direction."

"I've requested such a redisposition half a dozen times since yesterday. So far he has only let me move Palmer's brigade."

The Bishop chuckles. "You mean General Pillow's brigade."

Breckinridge winces. "Yes, General Pillow's. I had forgotten that unfortunate change of command."

"I think, John," Hardee says, "that you should reconnoiter the position the Yankees have taken east of the ford. If this battle is resumed, it will be on that front."

Polk, whose attention has wandered to the possibility of an early lunch if the day is quiet, frowns. "I wonder why we haven't heard more from them. A few batteries on that ridge southeast of the ford could discomfort my line."

"Hanson still has two batteries on Wayne's Hill," Breckinridge says. "I believe they could suppress a bombardment of your flank. Still, I'd better have a look at the Yankees' dispositions."

"Perhaps I'll come with you," Hardee says. "Bishop, would you care to join us?"

Before Polk can answer, his chief of staff interrupts. "General, there's a courier here with a message from the commanding general."

Polk accepts the dispatch, frowns at it, and then dips into his ample vest for his watch. "The commanding general directs that I open a bombardment to test the Yankee center, firing to commence twenty minutes from now at eight o'clock precisely. So I must wish you good morning, gentlemen." He wheels his much-belabored mare, switches at her rump until she breaks into a trot.

Hardee sighs. "And I suppose I should look to my line, much as I'd prefer to go with you, John. I'll send Major Pickett as my representative. You'll find him good company."

Breckinridge hesitates. "Bill, you don't think the commanding general will order another attack, do you? My men need a period of recuperation. We suffered very heavily in General Polk's assault."

"I know. Even Cleburne is telling me that his men can do little more for the moment, and I've never met a man with a greater taste for a fight. Still, I no longer pretend to predict General Bragg. He is betimes aggressive and timid. I don't know what his mood is today."

Breckinridge dispatches his chief of staff, Lieutenant Colonel John Buckner, to test the left end of the Yankee line with artillery and, if necessary, a regiment of infantry. While the Yankees are thus distracted, he and Pickett will try to get a better idea of their dispositions closer to the river.

Shortly after Breckinridge and Pickett set out, Colonel Brent and Captain Robertson arrive from Bragg's headquarters. They don't bother consulting with Breckinridge's headquarters but go directly to the picket line. They quiz some of the pickets, and are about to go forward themselves when Buckner opens fire on the Yankee line with eight guns. The fire is returned by the six guns of the 3rd Wisconsin Battery. Brent and Robertson retreat to the lower slopes of Wayne's Hill to watch the duel.

On the Federal side of the line, the skirmish comes at an awkward time for Brigadier General Sam Beatty. He has four brigades on the east side of the river: Price on the ridge southeast of the ford, Grider in reserve behind it, Fyffe on Price's left, and Grose behind McFadden's Lane. He has, however, only the single battery and seems unlikely to get more, since Crittenden and Mendenhall (or perhaps it is only Mendenhall if Crittenden is drunk again) have ignored his requests in favor of building up the gun line on the west side of the ford. He breaks off the artillery duel and, over Colonel Price's objections, orders the battery withdrawn behind the safety of Grose's line.

Beatty is dissatisfied with the state of his other defenses as well. Weeks ago the division was stripped of most of its tools to equip the despised Pioneer Brigade. If he just had the axes, spades, cant hooks, blocks, pulleys, and ropes in his own barn back in Ohio, he could treble what he has at hand. But without adequate tools, he has been able to build only a few breastworks at the weakest points of his line.

By midmorning, Breckinridge has a good sense of the Yankee presence. It is strong, alert, and unaggressive—a blocking force probably designed to protect the Yankee left flank during a withdrawal. Leave it alone and it poses no danger. Satisfied, he returns to his headquarters for a late breakfast and a change of clothes.

Colonel Brent, however, has reached an entirely different conclusion. Robertson has focused on the danger of Yankee artillery on the ridge southeast of the ford enfilading Polk's line in the Round Forest. Brent, much as he dislikes Robertson, is impressed by the argument. Again bypassing Breckinridge's headquarters, they return to Bragg.

★ ★ ★

While Breckinridge, Pickett, Buckner, Brent, and Robertson investigate the ground already—and more effectively—scouted by Bramblett and Young, Bishop Polk opens his bombardment of the Yankee center. Despite the short notice, his chief of artillery has managed to concentrate twenty-two guns. The unexpected fire falls on the brigade of Colonel Charlie Harker and the 8th Indiana Battery commanded by Lieutenant George Estep. Harker's men throw themselves to the ground and suffer only a handful of casualties, but shell and case rip through Estep's battery, splintering carriages and caissons and killing or wounding a third of the battery's men and nearly all the horses. Returning fire is impossible, and Estep withdraws, leaving two disabled guns behind.

Captain Cullen Bradley, commanding the 6th Ohio Battery, opens fire to cover Estep's retreat. But his gunners have no sooner gotten the range when a blast of canister sweeps the rear of his battery, killing or maiming fifteen horses and wounding half a dozen teamsters. Bradley spies the telltale puffs of smoke on the slope to his rear. He jams spurs into his horse's flanks, pounds through the wreckage of caissons and the screaming of wounded horses, rockets up the slope waving his hat frantically. A second salvo roars, his horse grunts, pitches forward, head down, as if seeking to examine the wound made in its chest by the canister. Bradley somersaults over his steed's head, lands hard on his left shoulder, feels something crack. But he has no time to investigate, leaps to his feet, sprints up the slope, screaming: "Cease fire, you idiots! Cease fire!"

Captain James Stokes, the oldest West Point captain in the United States Army, sees Bradley coming, shouts for his gunners to cease fire even before he can make out Bradley's words. The young officer stumbles the last few paces, chest heaving. "Goddamn it, Stokes, you just shot up my battery!"

Stokes suddenly feels immensely old, is for a minute incapable of action or apology. "My God. I'm—" He can't go on, simply stares at Bradley.

"Well, elevate your guns, damn it! Get firing. The Rebs aren't stopping. Then get me a goddamn horse. You killed mine!"

This war has two nearly invariable rules: Southern cavalry always makes fools of Northern cavalry; and Northern artillery always beats the absolute bejesus out of Southern artillery. The latter rule holds now. Within minutes, over forty Federal guns are blasting Polk's twenty-two. By 8:30 A.M., a short half hour after opening fire, Polk's gunners give way, pulling back to avoid annihilation.

George Thomas watches the end of the duel from behind Morton's Pioneer Brigade and Stokes's Chicago Board of Trade Battery. Thomas expects Stokes to be triumphant, but he is pale, almost staggering when he approaches. Morton follows a few paces behind, looking worried. Thomas removes the cigar from his mouth. "Are you wounded, Jim?"

Stokes shakes his head, puts a hand on Thomas's horse for support. "We fired into Bradley's battery. Killed some of his horses and wounded six of his men. A couple of them will probably die."

George Thomas stares toward the cedars hiding the Confederate line. Thomas is an extraordinary soldier, one of the best of his generation. Moreover, he is a decent and kind man. Yet in the giving of sympathy he has little skill, cannot shrive this man who is among his oldest friends. "Battle is at best chaotic, Jim. We do our best to make it otherwise, but mathematical inevitability dictates that sometimes we will wound or kill our friends. We do their memory no credit by allowing that ill-chance to keep us from the further performance of our duty." He looks down at Stokes, wishes he could think of something more comforting to say.

"And you, George? Have you made such an error?"

Thomas frowns. "I don't recall. I suppose I must have. We will talk of it another time. But look to your guns, now, Captain."

Bragg listens to Brent and Robertson, the habitual scowl drawing his heavy eyebrows together. An hour ago he would have dismissed the danger Brent and Robertson describe, confident that Polk's artillery in the center and Hanson's batteries on Wayne's Hill could out-duel any Yankee guns positioned on the ridge southeast of the ford. But since then, the Yankee gunners have pounded Polk's artillery, turning what Bragg had intended as a reconnaissance by fire into an ugly and embarrassing withdrawal.

He dismisses the two young men and again studies the map that has been close to his hand all morning. He will take his own counsel this time. He has been too generous with the Bishop and the Professor, given them more opportunity to speak their minds than either has earned. He summons Brent, tells him to send for Major General John C. Breckinridge, who needs to learn the importance of exact and prompt obedience to orders.

Near noon the cold drizzle turns to sleet. Between Sam Beatty's and Breckinridge's lines, skirmishers dispute ownership of half a dozen farm buildings. The Buckeyes of the 51st Ohio retreat, receive reinforcements, and push back into the farmstead. The soldiers of the 18th Tennessee give way grudgingly. The Buckeyes fire the buildings, fall back through the sleet. Three of them pause long enough to investigate a root cellar, leap back at the sight of an old man standing just inside the door, a rusty hatchet upraised. "Hold on there, grandpa," one of the Buckeyes says. "There ain't no cause to go chopping people."

The old man drops the hatchet, walks past them into the yard, stands staring at his burning home. Two of the boys duck into the root cellar while the third keeps a rifle-musket trained uncertainly on the old man. His companions come out, their arms loaded with hams and slabs of bacon. "Come on, Buster," one of them calls.

"Ain't right leavin' him like this."

"There's plenty left in the cellar, and he'll be dry. Now come on before the Johnnies catch us."

They run. Looking back, the soldier called Buster sees the upstairs windows explode, enveloping the old man in a cloud of splinters that might, if judged by appearances alone, be mistaken for a gust of sleet.

Breckinridge is with Hanson on the crest of Wayne's Hill, watching the farm buildings burn, when the courier arrives to summon him to Bragg's headquarters. Hanson is immediately suspicious. "I hope that damned fool isn't thinking of attacking at this end of the line. The Yanks have had plenty of time to make that ford tighter than a nun's twat."

The courier obviously enjoys this metaphor from Hanson's famous collection. Breckinridge smiles slightly. "Tut, General, as we discussed not long ago, we should be mindful of our choice of words around the men."

Hanson grumbles. "Yes, General. I apologize."

"Tell the commanding general that I will be with him shortly," Breckinridge tells the courier. He slides his field glasses into their case, draws up his collar. "Thank Captain Bramblett and Lieutenant Young for me. Their report and what I observed should be enough to convince the general that an attack in this quarter would be exceedingly wasteful."

Hanson, the last man to speak to Private Asa Lewis before the firing squad murdered him on that rainy noon a week ago, has ample reason both to hate Braxton Bragg and to doubt Breckinridge's ability to dissuade the general from any action, no matter how heinous. "I hope to God you're right, General. Rosecrans is not such a fool as to leave his flank open a second time."

"No. Not such a fool. Did I ever tell you I met him once? He was running a Sunday school for little colored children in Washington. Had hundreds of pickaninnies reciting their prayers and singing their hymns like God's own African choir. Quite a pleasure to see it."

Hanson grunts. "I had not heard he was a brimstone abolitionist."

"Oh, I don't think he is. He's a fellow Democrat, I believe. Or was when we had a party. But he's an intensely religious man. Has a priest on his staff, I'm told. And it's only religious duty to look to the spiritual welfare of our Negroes."

Hanson, who assumes that Breckinridge is simply clearing his rhetorical pipes in preparation for his meeting with Bragg, doesn't bother to comment. Of Rosecrans's ministry to the pickaninnies he has no opinion. Hanson is a Kentuckian and a white man, sees his responsibilities entirely within those definitions. The rest of the states and the rest of the species can rise, fall, or maintain according to their collective or individual efforts. He has Kentucky Brigade to look after, and that is quite enough.

Despite the ugliness of the day, Bragg needs fresh air. He walks briskly around the headquarters camp and then settles to work again at a field desk beneath an awning and a towering sycamore. He concentrates on the minutiae of running the army, a small part of his mind ticking off the time since he sent for Breckinridge, ready to add tardiness to the complaints he has already recorded against the man.

Breckinridge arrives almost exactly at noon, swings down from his splendid black stallion. Bragg looks up from his work, decides to stand, taking advantage of his height over the smaller man. "Good day, General," he says in response to Breckinridge's greeting. "I have a task for you." He describes the danger represented by the Yankee control of the ridge southeast of the ford. "I desire that you lead your division forward at four o'clock to take that high ground. General Polk's guns will support your advance. In addition, I will send Captain Robertson with two more batteries to augment your artillery. Once you have occupied the hill, emplace his guns on it and commence firing on the Federal line. I believe that demonstration of enfilade fire will cause our enemies to think better of holding their position longer. However, if they are foolish enough to remain, recommence firing at first light and be prepared to cooperate with a renewed assault by Bishop Polk's corps on the Yankee center."

Breckinridge stands aghast. There are so many flaws in this plan—and he has no high opinion of his own military sagacity—that he hardly knows where to begin. He attempts to summon every skill of persuasion gained during all his years in politics, but he remains tongue-tied. Bragg watches him coolly and then continues. "You will have Wharton and Pegram to extend your right. Consider them directly under your command until otherwise notified."

"General, I believe this plan is unwise," Breckinridge blurts. "The Yankee position is altogether too formidable." My God, this is blunderous, seems to accuse Bragg of a lack of wisdom while at the same time sounding craven.

Surprisingly, Bragg responds mildly. "How so, General?"

Breckinridge tries to calm himself, describes his reconnaissance and the reports of Colonel Buckner and the two young officers of Hanson's brigade. He illustrates by tracing the Federal positions in the soft earth with a stick. Bragg watches, his face hardening. At last he interrupts. "Your principal fear seems to be the threat of the Yankee guns on the other side of the ford. But I do not desire you to carry the ford. You are required only to take the ridge, emplace your guns, and commence fire."

"But, General, the hill is heavily defended by Yankee infantry. Even if we are initially successful, they will quickly mount a counterattack."

"Then you do think you can take the ridge?"

Breckinridge hesitates, mousetrapped. "Only at great cost."

"And I think your casualties will be within acceptable limits. He draws a boot heel savagely across Breckinridge's sketch, obliterating Beatty's right. "*My* information is that your approach can be made well under cover until you are within easy assault distance. On the other end of your line . . ." He makes a second gouge. ". . . Pegram and Wharton's troopers will overlap the Yankee left, enabling you to turn his flank."

"But a counterattack—"

"It will be too dark for a counterattack by the time the Yankees can rally."

"But the Yankee artillery on the other side of the ford will cut our flank to ribbons while we advance, and then make the ridge itself untenable for artillery or men."

"Nonsense! If your guns are properly handled, they will put the Union guns to rout long before your infantry comes under canister fire. Polk's gunners had considerable success against the Yankee batteries this morning. If they'd held position a little longer, they would have triumphed."

Standing nearby, staff officers exchange glances of disbelief. Major Pickett of Hardee's staff, thinks: My God, this is insanity! That, or he's trying to get Breckinridge killed. I must get word to Hardee.

Breckinridge draws himself up a little taller. "General, it is my opinion that this attack is doomed."

Bragg loses his temper. "Sir, I did not call you here to seek your opinion! I called you here to give you the instructions which it is now your duty to execute. Your division has suffered little in this battle, and it is time for you and your men to do their share!"

"My God, sir! I lost fifteen hundred men on Wednesday! A full quarter of my division. You cannot say that we have not bled our share!"

"I do say it, sir! I do say it because I do not believe you suffered nearly such losses. Subtract those who ran and those who used slight wounds to excuse themselves, and you have suffered but slightly in comparison to the other divisions." Breckinridge is shaking with rage, his face crimson. Bragg only bores in harder. "And your Kentuckians, sir, have fought not at all! While the rest of the army has engaged in mortal combat, they have basked in safety on your little mountain."

"Your orders kept them on Wayne's Hill, General!"

"Nevertheless, it is time for them to take their part. You will ensure that they do. And may I also remind you, General, that the losses you suffered on Wednesday were caused in large measure by your tardiness. Had you proceeded in a timely fashion in the forenoon, I could have sent you to reinforce Hardee on the flank where the battle was all but won. But you did not move in that timely fashion, and I was forced to order you to General Polk's assistance in a task far more difficult. Even then you might have led a successful attack, but your brigades went forward piecemeal instead of using mass to carry their objectives."

"General Polk determined the order of attack!"

Bragg stares at Breckinridge with contempt. "You may seek to avoid responsibility, sir, but I do not release you from it."

For a long moment, the two men stand almost chest to chest, eyes locked. About them, the staff officers are frozen in place, for this is one of those moments swollen with all the ritual and danger of Southern custom. My God, we are violent men, Pickett thinks. No wonder our generals risk such headlong attacks and our men carry them out with such utter disregard for life. The Yankees must think us madmen, as crazed as dervishes.

Staring into Bragg's eyes, Breckinridge sees the man truly for the first time. He knows the reputation Bragg gained at Monterey and Buena Vista, saw him in action at Shiloh, knows only too intimately his merciless treatment of malefactors within this army. Nevertheless, he has always thought Bragg a martinet: a deeply insecure man hiding behind a uniform and a reputation gained long ago. But now he sees his error, recognizes Bragg for the stone killer he truly is. And though Breckinridge cares little for his own safety or reputation in this moment, others will die if he allows passion to govern the next minute of his life. He steps back, bows formally. "I beg your pardon, General. I spoke with more vehemence than I intended."

It is now Bragg who must respond with grace or violate the code. The staff officers watch, critical. Bragg bows stiffly. "Very good, General. Please execute your orders."

Breckinridge takes a shallow breath, chooses his words with great care. "General Bragg, I must plead with you a final time to consider the difficulty of the terrain and the strong disposition of the enemy's infantry and particularly his artillery. I cannot in good conscience carry out this attack without again stating that I consider these factors exceedingly disadvantageous to its success."

Bragg glares at him, for Breckinridge has taken a dangerous step beyond propriety. "Sir, my information is different! The orders are peremptory. Carry them out immediately or turn over command to your senior brigadier and place yourself under arrest."

Breckinridge bows. "I will carry out your orders to the best of my ability. Good day, General." He turns, strides off.

"General Breckinridge," Bragg calls after him. "The signal to advance will be four closely spaced cannon shots from General Polk's line. I will give the order myself."

★   ★   ★

Rosecrans rides his line. He has risen early, much refreshed from two hours' sleep before the fire in the rough cabin that remains his headquarters despite its vulnerability to Rebel artillery. His mood is further improved by what he sees along his line. The soldiers are dirty, wet, hungry, but resolute to a man. They cheer him, wave their hats. He responds grinning, joshing with them. The men like him, recall over and over his disregard for danger during the fighting on Wednesday. Rosecrans's friendship with Garesché is well known; the colonel himself remembered fondly for his great kindness. "Don't worry, General," one soldier shouts. "We'll pay back the Rebs for the colonel."

Rosecrans smiles sadly. "No, boys. Fight the Rebs for your own sakes and the sake of your country. Colonel Garesché is in paradise and beyond worrying about earthly matters."

The onset of Bishop Polk's bombardment startles Rosecrans, nearly sends him dashing to the point of attack. But he is aware that his frenetic movements on Wednesday, though encouraging to the men, have been criticized by some of the officers. In truth, he'd given too many orders, muddled the chain of command, become so excited at times that Garesché had been needed to interpret his stammerings. He must be calmer today, less impulsive.

As the Federal guns force Polk's batteries to withdraw, Rosecrans joins Thomas on the slope behind the Chicago Board of Trade Battery. White-bearded Captain Jim Stokes is walking, head down, back to his guns. Rosecrans looks after him. "Jim looks in poor fettle."

Thomas removes his cigar. "An accident with the guns. They fired into a friendly battery. Killed a dozen horses, wounded a few men. Unfortunate."

Rosecrans nods. "Well, have it looked into when we have the leisure. Most times these things are best forgotten. Misfortunes of war."

Thomas resumes smoking. After a moment, he asks, "Have you been to the left? I suspect Bragg may test us there."

"I have the same feeling. We don't exactly have a position that Professor Mahan would approve, but it will hold. Our right and center are strong now, and Bragg must know it. That leaves only our left. I told Crittenden to send Cruft's brigade to the ford to reinforce Van Cleve's division. Sam Beatty has command of it now."

"I think you might consider assigning him permanently to the command. Van Cleve is an old man, might do better commanding a post."

"I'm afraid I have less say in such matters than I would like. We'll see. Could you spare Negley if I needed him on the left?"

Thomas ponders this. "Yes, take him now. He has only two brigades, but they're good ones."

They talk on, smoking in the drizzle and watching the cannons exchange desultory fire.

Waiting below on the Nashville Pike with the main part of Rosecrans's staff, Father Treacy sees a terrible thing. The Rebel guns on Wayne's Hill aim a solid shot down the pike every few minutes to harass formations trying to use it. The twelve-pound balls scatter chunks from the macadam surface, bounce down the road in long, lazy arcs. The balls are small, barely more than four and a half inches in diameter, hardly deserving the name cannonball if one thinks only of the massive projectiles of siege and naval cannons. It is this almost harmless appearance that fools a youngster recently arrived with the brigade of Colonel John Starkweather. Laughing, the boy dashes onto the pike, makes to catch one of the solid shot as if it were a grounder hit to a fielder in the newly popular game of base-ball. The shot explodes his hands and forearms, punches through the boy's body at the sternum, and bounces on down the pike, leaving the boy disjointed as an unstrung puppet.

"Jesus Christ, would you look at that?" a young staff officer breathes.

Treacy sighs, gets off his horse, goes to administer last rites to the boy, though he is certainly, emphatically killed.

Breckinridge rides south to retrieve Preston's brigade, which is still west of the river, supporting Polk's center. He explains Bragg's plan to his friend, concluding formally, as if for the record: "General Preston, this attack is made against my judgment and by the peremptory orders of General Bragg. Of course, we all must do our duty and fight the best we can. But if it should result in disaster and I be among the slain, I want you to do justice to my memory and tell people that I believed this attack to be very unwise and tried to prevent it."

Preston nods, also formal, for the moment seems to call for it. "If I survive and you do not, I will take that message to the president."

"Thank you," Breckinridge says, starts for Wayne's Hill and Kentucky Brigade.

"I'll kill the son of a bitch!" Hanson roars. He unbuckles his sword belt, shoves sword, scabbard, and belt at Breckinridge. "General, I herewith resign. I am going to headquarters to challenge General Bragg to a duel."

"Put your sword back on, General. He will not fight you, only put you under arrest."

"Like hell he will! If he won't fight me like a man, I'll shoot him like a dog!"

Breckinridge leads the raging Hanson out of easy earshot of the officers and common soldiers. "General Hanson, you must not do this thing. I need you to command this brigade. We will do our best, carry that ridge if we can. But even if we die to the very last man and fail in the attempt, no one will be able to say that this division and particularly Kentucky Brigade didn't do its utmost."

"General, I can't—"

"No, let me finish. I cannot permit you to go to headquarters to challenge General Bragg to a duel. If you insist on resigning, I will put you under arrest myself. To do less would be to condone mutiny. And once we start having mutiny among us, this army is doomed and our cause is doomed."

Hanson stands fuming, refusing to meet Breckinridge's eyes. At last he rebuckles the sword around his thick waist. "Very well, General. I will get my brigade ready."

"Thank you, General. God watch over you."

Corporal Johnny Green of the 9th Kentucky does not know any man who considers himself a hero. Yet the men of 9th Kentucky protest vehemently when word is passed that the regiment will remain on Wayne's Hill in support of Cobb's battery. Colonel Hunt carries their complaints to General Hanson.

"Do you know, Colonel, that half your men or more could die in this ill-omened attack?" Hanson asks.

"I know it, General. But it is a matter of honor with them. They don't want to be members of the only regiment not to fight in this battle."

"You did fight. You had your scrap the night the Yankees waded the river and charged this hill."

"General, that was barely a skirmish."

"A little more than a skirmish, if I recall. But, all right, Colonel. You may select four companies by lot. Send them forward with the Second Kentucky."

"I will lead them myself, General."

For a moment, Hanson considers telling Hunt he must stay behind. But he nods. "Very well. Good luck."

Breckinridge and Colonel Buckner, his chief of staff, discuss the order of battle. Hanson's brigade will lead on the left, Pillow's on the right. Colonel Randall Gibson of the 13th–20th Louisiana, now commanding Adams's brigade, will follow Hanson with two regiments, leaving his other two in reserve. Preston's brigade will follow Pillow's line. To the right of Pillow,

Wharton and Pegram's dismounted troopers will extend the line to overlap the Union left. In all, 4,500 infantry and 2,000 cavalry will storm the Yankee positions.

Breckinridge has been assigned thirty-two guns to support the attack. But here the preparations become fouled. After sending Colonel Buckner to write the orders coordinating the attack, Breckinridge explains to Robertson that he wants the captain's ten guns to go forward between the two waves of infantry.

Robertson demurs. "I have specific orders from General Bragg to keep my guns well back until you occupy the ridge."

Breckinridge looks confused. "But we are making this attack to secure you a position for your guns."

"I understand that, and once you have it, I will bring my batteries forward."

"But, damn it, man! I'll need the support of your fire to help drive the Yankees off the ridge."

"I'm sorry, General, I was told to keep my guns at a safe distance and to conserve my ammunition."

"Captain, I am in command here. I order you to deploy your batteries between the infantry lines."

"And I, General, must respectfully refuse on the grounds that I am obeying the directions of high authority. You must appeal to General Bragg if you wish me to deploy as you suggest."

They wrangle, the argument becoming heated. Breckinridge revises his order, asking Robertson to go forward immediately behind the second wave. Again, Robertson demurs. Finally, Breckinridge throws up his hands. "Then come forward when I send for you."

"I will come forward when you have taken the objective, General."

Breckinridge turns away defeated, for there is no budge in Robertson and little hope that Bragg will intervene. He directs Colonel Buckner to send the division's three batteries forward in rear of the second line and then steps apart to rage in private.

Shortly before 3:00 P.M., Bragg rides to Polk's headquarters behind the Confederate center. The Bishop is in a good mood, having enjoyed a heavy lunch and an afternoon doze in the shelter of his rain fly with a quilt wrapped about him by a member of his devoted staff. On seeing Bragg, he frees himself from the quilt but does not rise. "Good afternoon, General. Forgive me for not rising, but the damp seems to have exacerbated the gout in my foot."

Bragg dismounts, comes forward. "That's quite all right, Bishop, though in a few minutes I think you will want to be on horseback."

Polk frowns. "Why? Are we expecting an attack?"

"No, we are preparing to make one. I am sending Breckinridge to take the high ground this side of the ford."

"I hadn't heard. I discussed the Yankee incursion with Generals Hardee and Breckinridge this morning, but I didn't know any decision had been made to drive them back across the river."

"It was my decision, General. I need no councils of war to make elementary tactical decisions. Yankee possession of that ground threatens any advance by our center. If General Rosecrans continues to hold position tonight, I intend to renew the attack on his center tomorrow. When your line goes forward, Captain Robertson's guns on that ridge will enfilade his line."

"The Robertson who commands a battery in Withers's division?"

"Yes. I ordered him to take his battery and a battery from Cleburne to support Breckinridge."

"I did not know that either."

"I'm sorry to hear it. In your place, I would look to the efficiency of my staff. They were informed."

For a long moment, Polk ponders. "From my understanding of the ground, I don't think this attack is necessary. I would rather have Breckinridge's division deployed as part of my attack tomorrow than see it cut up taking that ridge today."

"I disagree, Bishop. The attack has been ordered and will go forward promptly at four o'clock. I will give the signal myself. In the meantime, please deploy your artillery to support Breckinridge's left."

Polk looks at his pocket watch, sees that it is already past 3:00 P.M. He considers arguing further, but there is little time to get ready and Bragg seems unmovable. "Yes, General, I will see to it immediately." He rises, the swollen foot sharply painful, limps toward his staff. The dybbuk wolf is silent within him, sated for once, leaving Bishop Leonidas Polk a heavy, gimpy old man, trying desperately to remember all that he'd learned so long ago about the proper siting of artillery.

Since midmorning Hardee has expected Bragg to summon him for a discussion of tactics. He knows that Bragg intends some advance on the right. A Captain Robertson had presented himself at Cleburne's headquarters with an order detaching a battery to Breckinridge's support. Cleburne had been miffed at receiving an order outside the normal chain of command, refused to comply without Hardee's consent. Robertson arrives at Hardee's head-quarters much out of temper. He presents Hardee with the order from Bragg. "I must say that General Cleburne was most uncooperative. I think you might instruct him on the courtesy and cooperation expected of an offi-cer in an American army."

Hardee, only three years past commandant of cadets at West Point, remembers Robertson as a youngster with no particular talent but eager to please. My, haven't we put on airs, Hardee thinks. "General Cleburne makes no particular pretense of being a gentleman, Captain. He's a fighting man, perhaps the best in this army. He's also a stickler for protocol, and this order should have come through me."

"I'm sorry, General. I didn't mean to criticize General Cleburne. I sim-ply meant to suggest—"

"Yes, yes." Hardee waves a hand. "But you're in a hurry."

"I'm sure that a copy of the order was sent to you, General. It's proba-bly just late in arriving."

"No doubt," Hardee says dryly, endorses the order detaching Semple's battery.

Hardee waits through noon and on into the afternoon. He inspects his lines in the company of Cleburne, happy to see the breastworks nearly com-plete. St. John Liddell approaches, again opines that they can reach the pike, cut the Union line of retreat. "No, General Liddell," Hardee replies. "We could have on Wednesday afternoon if we'd had a fresh brigade or two, but the chance is past now."

Liddell grumbles. "If the president hadn't sent Stevenson's division to Pemberton at Vicksburg, we'd be marching for the Ohio right now."

Hardee glances at Cleburne. They have discussed the same possibil-ity, but it is quite another thing to hear the argument from Liddell, who is considered friendly to Bragg and Davis both. Hardee decides not to com-ment, redirects the discussion to the completion of the breastworks. It is getting late, and Bragg must have abandoned any thought of attacking on the right today. Tonight he will probably summon Hardee and Polk to dis-cuss what can be done if Rosecrans continues to hold position. Hardee wonders what he should say.

Brigadier General Gideon Pillow ignores Colonel Buckner's protests, stomps up the rise to where Breckinridge is staring sourly at the broken ground his division must cross to engage the Yankee line. "Breckinridge, did you send orders to the cavalry telling them to extend my line?"

Breckinridge gives Pillow a withering look that has no effect on the man. "Yes, General, of course."

"Well, they're not there. My skirmishers are already pulling down fences, my infantry is in line ready to go forward, and the goddamn cavalry is nowhere to be seen!"

Breckinridge feels his stomach lurch. "Thank you for informing me, General. There is no doubt some slight delay. I'll check on it. Now, you'd better return to your brigade."

"See that you do more than *check* on it. Otherwise I'm flanked on my right the second I step out. Flanked and buggered!" He stomps off.

Breckinridge beckons Buckner. "Andy, did you send the order of battle to Wharton and Pegram?"

"Yes, sir."

"Better send it again. Something's gone wrong if they're not in position by now." He glances at his watch. Christ, only twenty minutes to go, and he's spent the better part of an hour reviewing his grievances against Bragg. He calls for his horse. Dear God, he prays, protect my boys. Please don't take too heavily of them.

★ ★ ★

Corporal Billy Erb, Company C, 19th Ohio Volunteers, is famed throughout his brigade for never missing a meal. His messmates, all senior sergeants, look the other way when Erb disappears for long periods, allowing him to keep his stripes despite his disregard for all duties beyond keeping the mess pot full. But in the last day, even Erb's formidable skills have failed. He takes this as an insult to his professional pride. With only a cracker and a cup of weak coffee on his stomach, he goes scavenging. And, because he is also phenomenally lucky, he strikes victual gold.

Beyond the northern extremity of Grose's line, Erb ducks when a Rebel shell from Wayne's Hill explodes in the yard of an abandoned shanty. It is a poor place and no doubt already well investigated, but Erb's sharp ears detect an unexpected cackling in the aftermath of the explosion. He creeps forward to peek through a crack in the shanty wall. And sure as shit, there she is: a fat laying hen just settling back on her nest. Erb enters, lets the hen eye him long enough to lose interest, and then whisks her expertly off the nest. He tucks her head in his armpit and wraps an arm firmly around her body. After a half dozen squawks and thwarted flaps, she grows still.

Erb scoops up the nine eggs in the nest, lodging them carefully in his voluminous haversack. He hesitates with the last in his hand. Nine divided by four leaves an extra left over. It should by all rights go to him, but dealing with sergeants—hungry or otherwise—is never easy. He cracks the egg, lets it run into his upturned mouth, the yolk plopping satisfyingly on the tongue. He sucks it down, eyes closed, licks his lips. God, that was good. He's tempted to eat another, but then he'll be confronted with an even more complicated mathematical conundrum. Besides, there is the matter of reputation, and eight eggs are a more impressive haul than seven, six, five, or four.

Returning to camp, Erb keeps the chicken hidden beneath his overcoat. No one stops him. He has a businesslike air, corporal's stripes, and his fine leather haversack is easily mistaken for a dispatch pouch. Only when he crosses into the camp of the Union 9th Kentucky does he grasp the chicken by the legs and swing her from under his coat. The hen squawks at the indignity, keeps squawking, as Erb dogtrots through the camp. Kentucks shout: "Drop that chicken!"; "Hey, son, five dollars silver, ten scrip for that hen!"; "Thief, thief! He stole our chicken!"; "Come here, soldier. That's an order!" Grinning, Erb crosses the regimental boundary, trots into the safety of C Company's camp.

One of the sergeants takes charge of killing, plucking, and cleaning the hen, a second goes to commandeer a pot and tripod, and the third gets the fire built up. Erb rests in his glory, putting off questions on the origin of the chicken until he can tell the story over supper. Men drift in from other messes, ask forlornly if any more chickens are to be had. "Sorry, ain't none but this one, boys," Erb says. "Why, hell, don't you think I'd've brought more if they'd been available? Yessir. I'd've brought 'nough to feed the entire company. But there weren't but this one and she's going to this mess. The rest of you boys can inhale the aroma of chicken stew. Should be some sustenance in that."

The camp settles down, the men preparing as well as they can to survive another cold night with no shelter and little food. Everyone knows that the Rebels have been moving men and guns, but with little more than an hour of daylight left, no one thinks that an attack will come this afternoon. Even General Sam Beatty, who knows man to be a beast predictable only in his foolhardiness, has relaxed, riding down to the ford to consult with Colonel Grider on night dispositions.

At 3:50 P.M., Brigadier General Roger Hanson rides to the front of Kentucky Brigade, unleashes his stentorian voice. "The order is to load, fix bayonets, and march through this brushwood. Then we will charge at the double-quick to within one hundred yards, deliver fire, and go at them with the bayonet. Maintain ranks, mind your officers, fire low. Remember that you are men of Kentucky Brigade. Carry this line, win this battle, and I promise you we shall see Kentucky again before the leaves turn green on the trees!"

Kentucky Brigade roars its approval. Officers and sergeants bark orders. Ramrods clatter in musket barrels. On command, companies and regiments fix bayonets, the rattle of steel on steel cold, chilling to the blood. Hanson rides down the line to speak for a minute to the men of the 41st Alabama, adopted sons of Kentucky Brigade. Back in front, he waits. At precisely 4:00 P.M., Stanford's Mississippi Battery of Stewart's brigade fires four quick shots from the vicinity of the Round Forest. Hanson sidesteps his horse, brings the pommel of his sword to his lips in salute to his flag and his men, turns his horse about, and swings the sword forward. Kentucky Brigade roars, lunges forward.

Behind the signal guns, Braxton Bragg steadies his horse with the same unthinking authority that he uses on all dumb creatures, waits for the smoke from the guns to clear. He half hopes there is a delay, perhaps a last-minute appeal from Breckinridge. He doesn't suppose that he can actually have a former vice president shot. But he can sure as hell relieve him.

Brigadier General Sam Beatty is cutting a chaw of tobacco while listening to Colonel Grider report that, except for one chicken, the brigade is down to a dozen boxes of hardtack and a few pounds of coffee.

"A chicken, you say?" Beatty asks.

"Yes, sir. Our Corporal Erb has been foraging again."

"I've heard of the corporal's talent. I should assign him to my staff."

"I'm afraid you'd have to separate him from three very possessive sergeants."

Beatty smiles. "Well, I suppose there are some things even a general daren't risk." He is about to offer sympathy on the hardtack situation—for he has nothing more to offer—when four rapidly spaced reports roll down the river. "Look to the ford, Colonel," he snaps. "It appears we still have some work to do today." He jams the chaw into his mouth, kicks his horse toward the front line.

Captain Mendenhall and General Crittenden are returning from army headquarters when Polk's guns give the signal. Since his early morning eye-opener, Crittenden has abstained from alcohol the entire day. With Tom Wood no longer at his side, it is his intention to continue doing so as long as the army is in the immediate proximity of the Rebels. But with less than an hour of daylight remaining, he feels his resolve weakening. As soon as it is dark, he will take a restorative dram and then lie down for a nap. Rosecrans will no doubt call another of his midnight councils of war. He wonders if the commanding general might treat the assembled generals to a hot punch as he had back in Nashville on Christmas night. That had been exceedingly good punch, and though one can hardly expect the same ingredients under the present circumstances, a hot punch would nevertheless send all off to bed in a good humor.

Lost in this contemplation, Crittenden does not immediately recognize the significance of the four successive reports until Mendenhall shouts, "General! I think the Rebels are attacking!"

Crittenden frowns. "An attack? On whom?"

"On our line on the far side of the ford. I think we should ride forward quickly."

"Very well. Lead the way."

They gallop along the lane toward the low bluff west of the ford where Mendenhall has established his formidable line of twenty-four guns. Coming over the top of a brief rise, they can see a seemingly endless line of Rebel banners advancing across the brushy land on the far side of the river. "My God, Mendenhall!" Crittenden shouts. "Can you do anything to help my poor men?"

Mendenhall is already wheeling his mount to dash back along the lane to where Lieutenant George Estep's 8th Indiana Battery is repairing its guns beside the road. Mendenhall feels a sudden, unexpected ebullience. I know where every battery is, he thinks, know where to site every gun. I am prepared for this. God, let me get all my guns in line, and then you can kill me. I ask nothing more than to do this once, triumphantly, precisely.

On a low hill to the right and rear of the Rebel line, Pegram and Wharton have no orders to join Breckinridge's attack. "Well, Wharton, what do you suppose we should do?" Pegram asks.

Wharton shrugs helplessly. "What *can* we do? We have no orders. Breckinridge knows we're here. General Bragg knows we're here. Sooner or later someone is bound to send orders. Until then, I guess we wait."

"We could send Huwald's battery forward to enfilade the Yankee left. That would be something."

"Yes, but suppose they're going to send us wide to try for the pike again. We don't want to go with our artillery ammunition expended."

Pegram, who hasn't been given a battery of his own, glowers. "Well, it's your battery. I guess you can handle it as you like."

Hardee is still prowling his line in the company of Pat Cleburne when the guns signal Breckinridge's advance. Hardee stares to the east. "I didn't think he'd do it, but I guess General Bragg feels this army must participate in one more hecatomb before it retreats."

Cleburne, who is used to both Hardee's erudition and his bitterness, waits a moment and then says, "I'm sorry, General. The word is not one I know."

"Hecatomb. The sacrifice of a hundred oxen, a ritual enjoyed by our bloody minded ancestors, the Romans."

Not my ancestors, Cleburne thinks. I'm a Celt, and we have our own sacrifices.

"Intellectual ancestors, that is," Hardee says, as if divining Cleburne's objection. "Lovers of gladiatorial contests, war, and blood sacrifices. Do you know they used to illuminate the Colosseum with living human torches? Coated prisoners in tar and set them afire. Puts rather a different light on the grandeur that was Rome, wouldn't you say?"

"I suppose so, General. Do you think General Bragg intends to push across the ford?"

"I don't know his intentions, but I know Breckinridge will never make it that far. Poor John; he's about to take a pasting. The Yankees will do what they do best: kill with artillery. If their infantry and cavalry ever get half as good, we'll be in for a very hard time of it."

Cleburne gives Hardee another minute with his dark thoughts, lights his short pipe, keeping the flame of the lucifer cupped against the drizzle. He knows the general's pedantry is not intentionally condescending but more a bleak wondering at the mysteries of history and war. When the pipe is going well, he asks, "What if Breckinridge succeeds in driving the Yankee left?"

"He won't."

"All right. If he doesn't, then what?"

Hardee turns to stare at him in the settling dusk as the roar of cannon fire increases on the right. "Then what, Patrick? Why, then we have more blood, amputation, death, burial, and the weeping of women. The normal course of civilization. You know the problem with you Irish? You're irretrievable optimists. I suppose it's an endearing trait, but it's a terribly mistaken one. Preposterous, really."

After considerable discussion, Corporal Erb and the three sergeants decide to soft-boil the eggs in the pot with the stewing chicken. They have just added the eggs when the four signal guns fire. The sergeants are up and moving before the echoes come shuddering back along the river from the bluff west of the ford. Erb grabs his Springfield, kicks dirt over the fire, and runs to catch up. He may not be much of a soldier for routine, but no one has ever found him malingering when the brigade is under fire. But, damn, to lose a chicken dinner for duty. . . . It is almost more than a man can bear.

✩ ✩ ✩

From a distance, the Rebel lines appear splendidly ordered, the ranks moving forward in precise step, Enfields at right shoulder shift, the endless rows of bayonets undulating with the flow of the ground underfoot. Up close, there is little precise about the Confederate advance. Johnny Green and the other soldiers of the front rank thrash through brush, brambles, and thickets, the weight of the lines pushing them while thorns and branches snag their uniforms, carry away their hats, slash at their eyes. The second rank has it little better, the green branches and brush bent by the first rebounding to switch them hard enough to leave welts through their uniforms. Trying to break a wrist-thick sapling, a soldier two over from Green bends it down with his entire weight. But the sapling refuses to break, lashes out from beneath his brogan to strike the soldier following directly between the legs. The man yells, pitches forward. The soldier behind him grabs at his belt, but trips, his bayoneted musket flying from his shoulder and nearly impaling Green, who in dodging upsets two more files of marching men. The order of the entire company disintegrates in seconds, and the captain, with Colonel Hunt all the while yelling at him like the bloody devil, has to call a halt to re-form. The men regain their places, push forward, only the soldier with the lambasted genitals lagging behind, nauseous and swearing revenge.

The Yankee guns on the far side of the river puff smoke, the black dots of the projectiles visible for an infinitesimal instant against the white. Solid shot tears through the undergrowth, goes bouncing and skidding through the ranks, knocking down men by the dozen. Case shot shrieks overhead, exploding in downbursts of grape and shrapnel. Shells explode at various heights from high above, to torso level, to a foot or two deep in the soft ground. A plunging shell buries itself a dozen paces ahead of Green's squad, exploding in a geyser that drenches them in mud but leaves them otherwise uninjured. Similar miracles abound, allow the men to march on through what appears certain death.

Watching Hanson riding calmly out front of the first line, Breckinridge yells to his staff: "Look at old Hanson! Come along, gentlemen, or we shall seem mere jackals in the lion's wake." He leads them forward, his blood up, for Breckinridge is a fighting man, can believe even in forlorn hopes once battle begins.

Polk's guns and Cobb's battery on Wayne's Hill respond to the Yankee fire. But there is no matching Yankee artillery, and the weight of Federal fire increases as batteries closer to the ford begin lobbing shells over the trees. The river serves as an organ pipe, sustaining the concussions until the roar of the guns overwhelms the ear's ability to distinguish between reports. The butternut lines fight through the brush, absorbing the fire, the men no longer erect but hunched forward as if struggling up a steep slope, though the actual ridge they have been sent to take is still seven hundred long yards ahead.

Gideon Pillow is an old man, nearly sixty, believes more in probability than Providence. He has known accident, disease, and riot; has fought duels and battles; has survived to an age when he deserves some consideration. Besides, he is a general, the value of his life multiplied manyfold by his responsibilities. If he is foolishly killed, others will suffer heavily in his absence. My God, how can they replace him on this field? The goddamn cavalry still isn't in position, Breckinridge obviously too incompetent to muster a third of his assault force. Pillow cannot risk dying out front, no matter how glorious the death. He is a general, must forget such temptations in order to save as many of his men as he can from what promises to be the buggering of all buggerings. "Dismount!" he shouts. "Take cover behind those trees."

Pillow's staff dismounts, scurries to the cover of a low hillock crowned with a few stubbly trees. Pillow himself takes shelter behind the largest trunk and, after a couple of minutes to catch his breath, calls for map and magnifying glass. The two dozen officers and orderlies of his staff crouch in the brush, praying that the Yankee artillery won't spot the sudden accumulation of horses and men in this entirely too visible spot.

Pillow squints through the magnifying glass. "Damn it! Hold the map steady," he snaps at his adjutant, though it is Pillow's hands that shake. To calm himself, to seem in command, he complains of the missing cavalry, of being buggered on the right by the longer Yankee line, of the need to halt the infantry until the cavalry comes up. It is all meaningless, mere show to cover the terror sluicing hot in his bowels. Dear God, he thinks, don't let me shit myself.

"General Pillow! Why aren't you advancing with your men?"

Pillow looks up to see Breckinridge, features flushed a dark crimson so that he looks more than ever like some Sicilian bandit and not at all like the former vice president of a pale-skinned nation. Pillow straightens, shoots back: "I am trying to figure a way clear of the goddamn mess you've made! Where's the goddamned cavalry? Without it we're buggered! Or have you been too busy shifting blame to me or General Bragg to notice that our flank's in the air?"

Breckinridge points his quirt at Pillow. "One more word, General, and I shall have you arrested! Go forward this instant and lead your men into battle."

Pillow hurls the magnifying glass to the ground, where it explodes against a rock, stalks to his horse. Major Pickett of Hardee's staff knows of a sudden that nothing but the raw courage of the men can save this day. But is it not always so when generals behave like squabbling brats? Pickett feels a sudden, untoward sympathy for Bragg.

Breckinridge has done everything possible to bring the cavalry onto the field to extend Pillow's right. He has sent three times to Wharton and Pegram; but though the two haven't moved in the last hour, none of Breckinridge's staff officers manage to find them.

When the infantry is halfway across the thousand yards to the Yankee line, Breckinridge makes a desperate decision. He halts the lines under fire, orders the 20th Tennessee forward from Preston's brigade to lengthen Pillow's right and then sends two batteries galloping forward to cover the extended flank. All the while, the men stand under arms, sweating and shaking under the rain of Yankee iron. Courage is commonplace in this army but not universal, and some men drop out of ranks, scurry for the rear. Those who can stand the gaff wait with jaws clenched, silent, or seemingly so. But Colonel R. P. Trabue of the 4th Kentucky notes a low, continuous moan as he rides along his line: a discouraged, deeply frightened sound— unconscious, no doubt, but there nonetheless.

With the new dispositions complete, Breckinridge orders the infantry forward in a slow left wheel to bring the advance face-on to the Yankee line. The movement fails to take account of the outward swing of the river which simultaneously forces Hanson's line to the right. Hanson's right and Pillow's left begin to overlap, the lines becoming entangled. It is a cor-rectable situation, requiring only a quick decision by the division com-mander, but Breckinridge is distracted, fails in this moment because he is a far better friend than he is a general.

The shell explodes directly under Hanson's horse, gutting the beast and pro-pelling a fragment through the rib cage and saddle into Hanson's thigh, severing the femoral artery. By the time Johnny Green reaches him, the wound is gouting blood. Greens slaps a hand over the wound, but the blood only squirts through his fingers. "Go on, son," Hanson breathes. "I'm killed sure enough."

"I can't, General. I'll stay with you."

"No. You know the orders."

Orders there are, straight from Bragg: *No man is to drop out of ranks to tend a wounded comrade.* The penalty for disobedience is death by firing squad, a punishment also invoked in the East, where Stonewall Jackson is a particularly rigid adherent to the principle. And it is an expedient rule, for without it every attack would dissolve in real or feigned pity. But, God, it is hard. Johnny Green feels a hand on his shoulder, drawing him away, and Major General John C. Breckinridge kneels by his friend, covers the wound with both hands, unmindful of the blood staining his uniform.

Hanson is in great pain. Dr. John Scott of the 2nd Kentucky pushes in beside Breckinridge to apply a tourniquet. "Is the wound fatal, Doctor?" Hanson asks.

"It is grievous, General, but we will do our best. I've sent for an ambulance."

"Do what you can do for me here and then go look to my wounded. I would rather die than have them deprived of your ministrations."

A moment later a two-wheeled ambulance rattles up, guided by Captain Richard Helm, Hanson's brother-in-law and the brigade commissary. Tears stream down Helm's face. "There, there, Dick," Hanson says. "I die in a just cause, having done my duty." He looks at Breckinridge. "And you need to look to yours, John."

Major Pickett is deeply moved, knows he will always remember: *The dying hero, his distinguished friend and commander kneeling by his side holding back the lifeblood, all this under the fiercest fire of artillery that can be conceived. A portrait as glorious as the death of Wolfe on the Plains of Abraham.*

But all the while Pillow's and Hanson's lines tangle, ranks stumbling into each other, officers cursing, the center sagging as the flanks push forward.

Sobbing, Johnny Green runs to catch up with his company, falls into the third rank as the line breaks free from the brush and into a field of dry cornstalks. An eerie silence falls, the guns on both sides holding fire for fear of hitting friends as the distance between butternut line and blue narrows. Atop the ridge, Price's brigade watches the Rebels coming through the corn, the brown stalks falling in a long sibilant wave before them.

On the extreme right of the Yankee line, Lieutenant Colonel Richard W. McClain of the 51st Ohio walks calmly along his line. "Don't stand until you see their hats come over the hill, boys. Then rise and give them hell." Sure every man has the word, he kneels near the center of the line, pistol in his right hand, sword in his left. The men wait, listening to the crackle of dry corn, the tramp of boots. The crown of a slouch hat bobs into view, then the forehead and hazel eyes of an extraordinarily tall Reb. His eyes widen at the sight of the long line of prone Yankees. "There they are, boys!" the Reb screams.

At the same moment Colonel McClain shouts, "Rise up, Fifty-first!"

At twenty yards the front lines fire simultaneously. Forty-two Yankees and nearly sixty Rebels are killed or mortally wounded in an instant. The Rebel line shivers like a stricken animal, regains its footing, charges. Johnny Green leaps over the body of the man who'd taken his place in the first rank, rushes forward, bayonet leveled. He cocks the hammer of his Enfield, fires on the run. The shot hits a thick-chested Yankee private in the side. The man throws up his hands, as if suddenly taken by the Spirit and intent on crying hallelujah. Green drives his bayonet at a young lieutenant who flinches aside so that Green misses the chest, hitting the man in the trapezius muscle between shoulder and neck. The officer chops at Green with the sword in his left hand. Green dodges, holding the man off on his bayonet. Jesus Christ, nobody is killed in this war with a sword! Green has never even heard of a sword wound! "Give it up, Lieutenant. Drop the. . . . Goddamn it." He dodges another slash. "Just drop the goddamn—"

Running full tilt, Private Harry Graebel hits the officer square in the middle of the chest with his bayonet, driving him off Green's and laying him down amid the bluecoat dead and dying. The Yanks retreat across the top of the hill. Green and Graebel ram cartridges, push new percussion caps on the cones of their Enfields. "Thanks, Harry," Green manages.

"Sure 'nough. For a second, I thought he was gonna get you with that toadstabber."

The Yanks are coming back. The Rebel line steadies, makes them pay with a volley, and then charges. The lines collide in a melee of bayonets, clubbed muskets, pistol shots, and swinging fists. Green thrusts at a rangy Yank, misses, clouts the man with the barrel of his Enfield. The man goes down at his feet, dead or unconscious. The Yankees fall back again, keep going this time. Green kneels, steadies rifle on elbow and knee, fires, reloads, fires again. The pole-axed Yank raises dazed eyes, blinks at Green, looks around, makes a face, and puts his head back down, lying very still. No fool, that boy, Green thinks. When the company is called to re-form,

Green gives the man a neighborly clap on the shoulder before running to fall into line.

Private Sam Mullet of the 51st Ohio has taken a minié ball through the lower right leg. He drags himself to a tree where his friend Nathan Shannon lies wounded, shirtfront soaked with blood. Mullet cradles Shannon's head in his lap, waits. He can hear the second Rebel line coming up the slope at the double-quick. He pokes gingerly at his leg, trying to detect damage to the bone. Apparently, he has been lucky. In a minute, he will put a tourniquet above the wound. Perhaps one of the Rebs will pause long enough to help.

The second Rebel line crests the ridge. To Mullet's horror, the first man to see him throws up his gun and fires. The range is no more than a dozen feet and Mullet feels the muzzle blast, sees the flame of exploding powder. The slug strikes the bark an inch from his ear. "Christ!" he screams. "Do you want to shoot a dead man?"

The Reb looks horrified, hurries on. Before Mullet can ponder the meaning of his odd protest, half a dozen men in butternut gather around, grinning, asking questions, offering their canteens. Where's he from? What's his unit? Has he got any kin fighting for the South? One of the men kneels by Shannon. "Might as well lay this boy down, coz. He's about done for."

Another man binds a rag above Mullet's wound. "Keep that tight and you should be all right. Don't look like it broke no bone, so don't let 'em take yer leg off."

A sergeant is yelling for the men to hurry. The man who tied the tourniquet scrambles up. "What regiment did you say?"

"Fifty-first Ohio."

"Well, bully for the Buckeyes! Looks like you put up a hell of a fight." They jog away, leaving Mullet amazed. A second later, a dog—some sort of beagle mix—leaps his legs, makes a skidding turn, and rushes back, tail wagging, to nose his face.

"Come on, Frank!" one of the Rebs yells. The dog dashes away, hurdling the bodies of the dead and wounded. A rabbit breaks from a thicket, streaking across the brown grass. Frank cuts in a tight turn, yelping with joy. The Rebels hoot. "Run, cottontail, run!" one of them shouts. "If I didn't have no reputation to sustain, I'd run too."

With the 51st Ohio and the Union 8th Kentucky gone from its right, the 35th Indiana occupies a nearly untenable position. Colonel Bernard Mullen orders his men to fall back, but the Buckeye blood is up, the roar of the battle drowning commands. Mullen drags the men back by company, but much of his regiment is overwhelmed, shot down or captured.

The retreat of Price's first line becomes a rout. The 99th Ohio and the Union 21st Kentucky try to hold, but their field of fire is obstructed by fleeing survivors, and Hanson's Kentuckians are coming hard. The second line breaks, streams back with the first. Hanson's men pause to fire volley after volley, littering the reverse slope of the ridge with hundreds of Federal bodies.

Kentucky Brigade has taken the elevation that Hanson and Breckinridge thought unassailable. But not all is going well. Farther to the right, where the ridge descends to almost level ground, the 18th Tennessee of Pillow's brigade hits two fresh Indiana regiments, the 79th and the 44th. The 79th is a new three-year regiment, blooded for the first time only two days before but already infused with the calm of its commander, Colonel Frederick Knefler, a former Hungarian officer and another of the 1848 revolutionaries in this army. Knefler sits his horse in front of the Hoosier ranks, watching the Rebels come yipping and howling across the open ground. When he judges the range close enough, he turns, rides back through the ranks. There is altogether too much noise for speeches, but he smiles at his boys, nods his head. On command of the company officers, the Hoosiers raise their Springfields, take careful aim at the pumping legs of the onrushing Rebs, as Knefler has taught them, and fire.

The volley rips through the 18th Tennessee with horrifying effect. The natural inclination of every rifleman, no matter how expert, is to jerk the muzzle of his rifle up when pulling the trigger. So a shot aimed at the torso will too often fly high while a shot aimed at the legs strikes groin, belly, or chest. War is brutal business, cannot be made otherwise. Like the wolf, the professional goes for the belly, knowing that the most painful wound is the best, that a shrieking, pitching victim disconcerts its herd-mates, panics them. And though Knefler is a kind man who bears no man ill will, he is a professional.

The 79th Indiana fires a second volley, and a third. The 44th Indiana joins in, pouring fire into the right flank of the 18th Tennessee, before shifting smoothly to meet the charge of the 20th Tennessee with an equally withering fire. The confusion in the Rebel line becomes general. Pressing forward, Preston's line stumbles into Pillow's. Nearly hysterical with excitement and apparently unable to recognize the difference between a line's front and back, Colonel William Bowen of the 4th Florida orders a volley that rips through the 20th Tennessee from the rear. Screaming curses and imprecations, the men of the 20th throw themselves to the ground.

The 13th Ohio jogs forward to join the Federal front line to the left of the 79th and 44th Indiana. For a few minutes it appears that the Federal line may hold. But as Pillow and Preston start blaming each other for the failure of the attack, Captain E. E. Wright's Tennessee Battery trundles up on the right of the 20th Tennessee, opens fire with shell and canister on the 13th Ohio. The 20th charges again, manages to reach a rail fence, starts doing terrible execution in the 44th Indiana at a range of forty yards.

Colonel Fyffe, the Union brigade commander, tries to bring the 59th and 86th Ohio forward to outflank Wright's battery. But his horse spooks amid the exploding shells. Fyffe lands on a sharp rock, breaking his hip and cracking his pelvis, and is carried screaming from the field. The 13th Ohio falls back, tries to stand, and then gives up, streaming with the 59th and the 86th Ohio toward Grose's line behind McFadden's Lane. Seeing the Buckeyes giving way, the 20th Tennessee leaps to its feet, crashes through the rail fence in a body, and drives the 44th Indiana toward the lane.

In the midst of the chaos, the 79th Indiana stands firm. Colonel Knefler rides along behind the line smiling, winking, occasionally shaking a finger at a weakening man. When he sees the 44th Indiana break on his left, he knows his regiment can do no more. But good boys these, will make soldiers in time. He spreads his arms wide, draws his hands together, turns to point with both index fingers toward the rear. The company officers understand, start withdrawing their men exactly as taught. The flanks fall back, the center withdrawing slowly, until in a column—albeit a rather rough one— the 79th Indiana falls back to Grose's line.

In the space of less than fifteen minutes, the 20th Tennessee has lost every member of its color guard except for Private Frank Battle, a slender fifteen-year-old whose father was the regiment's first colonel. Yankee bullets have twice broken the flag's staff, and Battle is not strong enough to carry the colors by the stub remaining. So he drapes the flag over his shoulders, wrapping it around his narrow chest, and marches out in front of the line so that all can see and follow.

The compression of the Confederate line by the inward wheel of the right and the outward swing of the river has forced several companies of the 6th and 2nd Kentucky out of line on the left. Intent on getting into the fight somehow, the men splash across Stones River. In the trees on the far side, they encounter a thin line of Yankee pickets, many of whom are ignoring their principal duty of defending the riverbank to take potshots at the flank of the Rebel line storming the hill. Private Gervis Grainger of the 6th Kentucky sees a flimsy cabin bristling at door and window with musket barrels, all blazing at the boys across the river. Grainger lies down behind a sycamore tree, positions cartridge box in easy reach, lays his ramrod next to it, and opens fire, sending five bullets into the cabin as fast as he can reload. He hears a scream, shouts of consternation. He rolls behind the tree, reloads again.

In the rain, sleet, and failing light, General Sam Beatty cannot at first find Colonel Benjamin Grider, commanding the three-regiment reserve brigade between the ridge and the ford. When he picks Grider's squat figure out of a knot of mounted officers, he shouts, "Grider! Take your brigade forward and retake that hill! Help's coming!"

Beatty is surprised how easily the lie comes to his lips. He has no word from the far side of the ford, has no idea if the brigade will be reinforced or sacrificed. I suppose this means I have truly become a general, he thinks.

Grider takes his regiments forward. The 19th Ohio, closest to the river, makes contact first, smashing into the Confederate 4th Kentucky and parts of three other Rebel regiments. For the second time in twenty minutes in a war that rarely sees hand-to-hand combat, Corporal Johnny Green finds himself trying to skewer another human being with a bayonet. The Yank, a big, unshaven sergeant, knocks aside his bayonet, swings at Green's head with a clubbed Springfield, but is shot through the left eye before he can bring the rifle butt through to its target. Green loses his Enfield in the melee. He grabs up the sergeant's Springfield, clubs it, and lurches ahead. He swings at a private who is simultaneously swinging at him. The rifle butts meet with a crack, splinter. Both men go down, grabbing hands and forearms that must, it seems, be likewise shattered. Green stumbles up, afraid of being trampled, manages to fall back a dozen paces. "No retreat, there!" a lieutenant yells. "Get back in line, Corporal." Green ignores him, bends over, hands between his knees. Christ, it's like someone had simultaneously lalloped both his funny bones.

Grider brings forward the Union 9th and 11th Kentucky. The compact blue lines clear their fronts with heavy volleys at less than fifty paces. The Rebels fall back across the top of the hill. Grider dispatches a message to Beatty: *We have them checked! Give us artillery and we'll whip them.*

But it is already too late. An officer of the 19th Ohio shouts to its commander, Major Charles Manderson, points to the trees across the river. Manderson squints through his fogged spectacles. "How many do you make them to be?"

"I don't know, sir. A lot of 'em. And they're Rebs sure."

Manderson, a courageous but pessimistic man, concludes that he is flanked when in actuality the Rebels number fewer than a hundred men of the Confederate 2nd and 6th Kentucky, intent only on finding a better position in their fight with the Yankee pickets on the west bank of the river. Manderson refuses his right and sends word to Grider that a Rebel formation has gotten on the brigade's flank. With no artillery and heavily outnumbered, Grider orders his three regiments back to the ford. The withdrawal is barely underway when the Rebs come storming back. They seem in the dusk twice as tall as when they retreated. They yell, yip, howl, bay, seem transfigured, spectral, their long beards and tattered uniforms cloaking not flesh and blood but only bone: a thousand reincarnations of the Reaper. The assault is too much for Grider's men. They break, run headlong for the ford, each man seeking the center of the crowd, hoping to put as many living, racing bodies as he can between himself and death.

The sun is well down, the sky lowering so that the ground between the ridge and the ford lies in shadow. The fleeing soldiers lose individuality, become an undulant blue mass. The soldiers of Kentucky Brigade fire volley on volley into the mob, their vision dazzled by the flash of their own muskets. My God, if they just had some artillery, they could slaughter them all. But there is no time to worry about guns; it is late and they must hurry. They reload, check cartridge and cap boxes, re-form their line. They have taken the ridge as ordered, but every man can see the wink of Federal cannon fire from higher ground beyond the ford. It is not only artillerymen who covet high ground, and though a few of the officers hesitate to go on without orders, the men know they must. Their certainty is voiced in the urgency they dress the line, their expectation a powerful thing, rendering officers all but irrelevant except to give the single command to go forward.

Breckinridge is desperately trying to get Robertson to bring his guns forward. He writes a third message, hands it to a staff officer. "Tell him the order is peremptory."

"Yes, sir."

Breckinridge turns to Major Pickett. "It has cost Hanson's life and the lives of too many of our boys, but if we can get guns on that ridge, we may have accomplished the impossible."

"Yes, General. I would not have believed it. General Bragg was right to trust in the gallantry of your men."

Breckinridge snorts. "I doubt if it was that, Major. I doubt if it was that."

In the near dark and without orders from Breckinridge, the Confederate line goes forward again, still wheeling to the left, approaching McFadden's Lane on a front six hundred yards wide. Beyond the lane, a low bluff rises just high enough to cloak the slightly higher bluff on the west bank of the

river. There are two or three batteries of Yankee guns on that coveted
ground, but they are poorly handled, firing at irregular intervals and almost
always too high. A few of the Southern officers wonder if the division may
not be on the point of outflanking the entire Federal line. A pity there is not
more daylight.

The enlisted men don't worry about grand tactics, go forward at the
double-quick, covetous only of the high ground.

Sergeant Sam Welch of the 51st Ohio runs for McFadden's Ford with scores
of other men from Price's brigade. They are not quite panicked, still have
their rifle-muskets, but, oh, they are beaten as surely as the Army of the
Cumberland is passing out of existence on this winter eve, collapsing upon
itself, streaming in a great, dark torrent of men and beasts up the roads
toward Nashville. Welch and the others tumble down the bank to the ford,
splash across—the river a mere two feet deep and twenty yards wide—claw
their way up the far bank either side of the lane already jammed with horses
and ambulances, break through the scrub into an open field, and halt
amazed.

Negley's division lies in the field, four thousand prone men, their ranks
rising and dipping with the roll of the land. Left and right and along the lane
where it runs north toward the high ground in the crook of the river,
columns hurry at the double-quick. On the high ground itself, guns. God,
how many? A tremendous line of guns, only a few firing, their muzzle
flashes illuminating their silent brothers and the crews at attention, waiting.

Officers and troopers appear in the gloom, shepherd the men onto the
lane. "Up this way, up this way. Follow that man on the brown horse. Re-
form to the right of the guns."

A big man in a cloak on a tall, rangy horse, rides beside them, his voice
raspy from overuse, but gentle, friendly, consoling. "Well done, boys. Well
done. Chins up now. Re-form over right of the guns. We're about to give the
Johnnies a hell of a greeting."

A youngster pleads, his voice tearful. "General, I'm sorry, but I ain't
got my gun. I dropped it back over there. Didn't think there was no more
army left."

"That's all right, son. Never mind. You can pick up another in a little
while."

Rosecrans cuts away from the lane, canters along the slope of the bluff
below the guns to guide a regiment into position by the river. Above him,
a cannon fires, looping a shell over the facing bluff toward the unseen line

of Secesh infantry coming to take the ford and the high ground. Seeing Rosecrans's face silhouetted by the flash, one of his staff officers fancies that he rides in the presence of a great captain, a hero as implacable as Alexander, Caesar, Napoleon, or the great Khan.

★　★　★

For the past hour Rosecrans has been pushing infantry into place in support of Mendenhall's line of guns. Negley brings Stanley and Miller's brigades into position in front of the gun line, orders the men to lie down. Rosecrans himself posts the Pioneer Brigade and Cruft's brigade of Palmer's division behind the guns. He finds Carlin's brigade of Davis's division a quarter mile back. He speaks loud enough for the men to hear. "Colonel Carlin, I beg you for the sake of the country and for my own sake to go at them with all your might. Get in position quietly and at the command, go at them with a whoop and a yell!"

Rosecrans expects the men to cheer, but they only stare at him impassively. An officer makes a quick translation into Norwegian, and then there are nods, many a thoughtful "Ya." Rosecrans peers at them more closely, recognizes Colonel Hans Heg's imperturbable 15th Wisconsin. The massive Heg says something in an undertone and the men are silent. Rosecrans salutes them, gives Carlin, who is sucking on his unlit pipe, a nod and gallops off, embarrassed.

Carlin gets his pipe lit, gazes at the sky. "Well, Colonel," he says to Heg. "I suppose we should go forward to do the general's bidding while there is still a little light."

"Ya," Heg says, in his fatigue nearly lapsing into his native tongue. "I suppose ve should."

Hazen has been swearing under his breath almost continuously since orders came to take the brigade to the ford. "This is a goddamn disaster, Bierce. You and I, we saw this coming yesterday, but nothing was done. And now we'll have to fight tooth and claw to hold a flank that should have been impregnable! General Rosecrans must have lost his wits entirely. Thomas should take command before it's too late."

The brigade forms, hurries overland toward the ford. Rosecrans intercepts it a quarter mile short of the gun line. "Colonel Hazen, keep your men in column. I want you in formation to cross the river as quickly as possible. General Beatty has Price's and Grider's brigades re-forming behind the right flank of the guns."

Hazen frowns. "But surely, General, I should deploy for the defense before considering going over to the attack."

"No need. I have infantry enough in place."

Still Hazen frowns. "May I ask how much?"

Rosecrans takes only an instant to calculate. "Counting yours and Gibson's brigade in easy supporting distance and not counting Price's brigade, which is pretty cut up, twenty-three regiments and three battalions of Pioneers. Across the river Grose has his brigade and what's re-forming of Fyffe's. They've got a good position, can hold off the Rebels' right flank."

For the only time in Bierce's experience, Hazen is discomposed. Finally, he manages, "My God, General, you have laid an extraordinary trap. I had not appreciated it till now."

Rosecrans chuckles. "Yes, it appears that we have. I wish I could claim to have planned it a day or two ago, but the circumstances and the pieces seem to have fallen together rather nicely. But hurry, Colonel, your brigade is a piece not quite in place."

"General, if I may ask, how many guns are in—" But Rosecrans is cantering away.

A staff captain pauses before following, grins. "At last count, forty-two."

"Holy God," Hazen whispers, surprising Bierce a second time, for he had never imagined hearing either awe or the invocation of the deity from Hazen.

The staff captain's count is low. By the time Hazen orders his men to lie down two hundred yards south of the right end of Negley's line, Captain Mendenhall has forty-five guns of various types and calibers standing hub to hub from the northern edge of the high ground to the field south of the lane. Another dozen guns are in place six hundred yards to the south, their muzzles trained on the ford's right flank.

Rosecrans is betting everything on the Rebels' aggressiveness. He orders Mendenhall to fire only enough pieces to lure them on. Mendenhall passes on the order, instructing the remaining gun crews to double-shot their guns with canister.

Mendenhall lights a cigar, either forgetting or choosing to ignore for once his rule about smoking close to the caissons and limbers with their loads of powder and explosive shells. He studies the gun line. It is perfect: forty-five guns to fire straight on with canister, twelve more to throw solid shot, case, and shell from the flank. Thank you, God, he thinks, I am fulfilled.

The Confederate infantry plunges on through the early dark. Ahead, a gentle slope rises to the top of the narrow bluff on the east side of the river.

Beyond it they will find the Yankees, a milling herd, pathetic as sheep pan-icked by wolves. They will tear through them, scattering them across the landscape, cross the river, never-minding the cold, climb the far slope, shooting the battery horses, bayoneting the cannoneers, then manhandling the guns around to fire on the fleeing bluecoats. Then and only then will they have the high ground—high ground and rest.

Riding behind an Ohio regiment of Stanley's brigade, Rosecrans unsheathes his saber for the first time in three days. But the sword is heavy in his hand: a trinket, symbol of an era passed long, long ago. He sheathes it again. I'll send it home, he thinks. Let my sons hang it on the wall.

He should go back up behind the guns now, get the best view he can. Some of the men prone in front of him turn, look up, faces pale with fear. He smiles. "Boys, do you see that little ridge beyond the river?"

There is murmured assent.

"Well, in about five minutes, the Rebs will pour over it and come right at you, yelling that infernal yelping of theirs. Don't pay it any mind. Lie still until you can see the buttons on their coats and then fire low. Drive them back. Do you understand?"

Again, murmured assent. He laughs softly. "There, boys. You see, it's as easy as rolling off a log."

Later, Corporal Johnny Green will hear another man muse: "It was like we kicked in the door of hell and the devil was there to greet us." Cresting the slope and flooding down the far side, all of them yelling like lunatics, Kentucky Brigade is hit with a blast beyond human imagining. The concus-sion of so many guns—and there are not six or eight or ten, as they'd expected, but dozens, scores—blasts everything in front of the gun line, lays the brown grass flat, stupefies the prone ranks of Federal infantry, leaving hundreds of men bleeding from nose and ears, levels the riverside brush, combers the river, and slams into the far slope with a crash that shivers the ground itself.

Mendenhall will make a rough calculation later that night: Each double-loaded piece on the gun line fires between 48 and 66 lead or iron balls per discharge. Using as an average figure the 54 fired by a twelve-pounder Napoleon, multiplied by 4 rounds per minute, times 45 guns, and roughly 9,720 canister balls hit the charging Rebel line in the first minute.

Johnny Green remembers the plucking fingers, the snatching at his clothing, the invisible hand that slaps the slouch hat from his head, tugs repeatedly at his long hair, and all the while the whispering—unheard, for nothing can be heard in the roar of the guns—yet detected by the skin itself: the whispered breath of the bullets in their passing. That he remembers; that and the sensation of being illuminated, as he supposes someone might be by footlights on a stage, exposed to an immense audience beyond the lights, unable for the moment to move in the glare, stage-struck, without line or cue. But it is only a momentary sensation, for to hesitate is to die, and no one except those instantly killed really stops moving. Those in the front ranks plunge on toward the river bottom, no longer charging, only seeking the deepest, darkest cover. The middle ranks die, a very few men managing to scramble back up the slope. The following ranks turn, flee, scores of men dropping in the seconds they are silhouetted against the sky. Green, stumbling back through the screaming wounded, the mangled dead, sees a shell from the flank drop into a mass of men. The explosion flings body parts high as the trees, kills a dozen men in less time than the flare of a match. Green throws himself into the gap created by the explosion, rolls down the reverse slope, scrambles to his feet, and runs.

On the west bank of the river, the Yankee soldiers cheer wildly. The 78th Pennsylvania rises up, splashes into the river, firing at the backs of the Rebels. Colonel Joseph Scott of the 19th Illinois sees the Pennsylvanians going forward, will be damned if he'll watch a bunch of Easterners stealing a Western victory. He draws his sword, screams "Follow me!" and plunges into the river. Colonel John Miller is caught only momentarily off guard before ordering his other three regiments forward. He is not a professional, doesn't give a damn what the professionals think; the chance is here and he will take it.

On the far slope, a Rebel color sergeant marches stiff-backed toward the crest, refusing to run. At the top he turns, his face gaunt with anger and despair, shakes a fist at the Yankee line. It is an act of such surpassing bravado that many of the Federal infantrymen cheer.

Hurrying toward the river with Hazen's brigade, Bierce witnesses the scene, thinks: We will never beat such men unless we destroy them utterly. We will have to burn our way clear across the South to do it.

Private Gervis Grainger is tardy again. All his life, people have yelled at him for being late: his mother, his father, the priest, his teachers, in the last year corporals and sergeants. With a few dozen others of the Confederate 6th Kentucky, he has worked his way through the trees west of the river to within sight of the ford. Crouching behind a tree, he adjusts the sights on his Enfield, squints down the barrel, trying to pick out the sergeant among the crew of a silent Napoleon near the end of the Yankee gun line. Shouted commands drift across the quiet field, remind him of the shouts of men at harvest time, bidding goodnight in the gloaming.

Before he can choose his target, a tremendous flash blinds him. He drops flat, holds onto the pitching earth. How long this goes on he cannot calculate. Five minutes? Ten? Then cheering from downstream, the crash of musketry, the sound of men whooping as they go over to the attack. A band begins playing *The Girl I Left Behind Me*. He can see the shine of brass instruments as it crosses the ford, leading a heavy column of infantry. It is an outrage this music. He looks about to see if the other boys are likewise incensed. But they are gone, and he knows suddenly that he is tardy again, as if abandoned daydreaming by a brook while the rest of the class ran to lessons at the ringing of the schoolhouse bell.

He jumps up, sprints for the river. Downstream he hears shouts, sees men in blue. "You, Reb, halt!" He fires at them, sees the bullet skip on the water, flying through the band. He jumps as far as he can, lands in the water, bullets shivering the surface around him like trout rising to feed. He tries to save his Enfield, cannot, drops it, and scrambles up the opposite bank, the bullets whirring about him.

The field beyond is chaos, thousands of men running for their lives. Two or three intact regiments are trying to cover the retreat, firing by the rear rank at the long dark line of blue infantry rising out of the river bottom. A riderless gray horse gallops past, dragging the body of an officer. Grainger lunges for a trailing rein, just manages to grab it. At that instant a solid bolt from a Parrott rifle decapitates the beast. Blood erupts from its neck, thick and powerful as a fire hose, drenching Grainger to the waist. He runs on, wiping at his eyes. He comes abreast of four men struggling under the weight of a litter bearing a grievously wounded colonel. Another solid shot, this a round one fired from a smoothbore, strikes the party at an angle, killing the man at the front right, the colonel, and the bearer at the opposite corner. The surviving men stand unhurt, dumbstruck, the splintered poles in their hands. "Come on!" Grainger yells. "Run!"

Bierce cannot recall hearing a single note of music since the last measure of *Home Sweet Home* echoed on the river the night before the battle. This is entirely different music, the blare of the Irish tune in hard cadence, warlike. Hazen's brigade double-times across the rear of two of Cruft's regiments thrown out in a long line and sweeping down to drive the pesky Rebels of the 2nd and 6th Kentucky back across the river. General Palmer is leading them personally, shouts to Hazen: "Go after them hard, Bill! God, for another hour of daylight!"

Rosecrans meets them at the ford. "Colonel, leave three of your regiments in reserve on the other side of the river."

"General, I must protest—"

"Colonel, for the love of God, be still! Take your lead regiment over to the left, pick up three of Grose's regiments, and drive hard for the Rebel flank. Turn them if you can. Now go, man!"

Hazen slaps his horse with the reins, gallops across the ford, shouting orders.

All the hours of seemingly pointless drill are paying off. The Yankee regiments wade the river, sweep in parade-ground order, bands playing, up the slope covered with the Confederate dead and wounded. Hundreds of Rebs taken prisoner in the river bottom trudge in the opposite direction under a provost marshal's guard.

In the fields beyond the bluff, Miller's brigade forms on the right, Stanley's brigade in the center, and Grider's brigade under General Sam Beatty on the left. Brigadier General Negley, the affable botanist, takes command, orders the line forward into the gloom. Hazen's column circles behind, reaches Grose's breastworks. Grose is blazing away at the Rebel flank with musket fire and two freshly arrived batteries. "Colonel!" Hazen shouts. "I'm to take three of your regiments, form a column, and try to get round the Rebel flank."

Grose turns, and Bierce is impressed, as he always is, at the kindness in the old man's face. "Take them, Bill! Godspeed."

In minutes, the 36th Indiana, Union 23rd Kentucky, and the 24th Ohio fall into column behind Hazen's 41st Ohio. All three of Grose's regiments have been roughly handled in the last hour. The 24th has had four commanding officers since 3:00 P.M., fighting first under Colonel Frederick C. Jones, then Major Henry Terry, then Captain Enoch Weiler, and now Captain A. T. Cockerill. Yet the men cheer as they come out from behind their breastworks to chase the Rebs.

Color Sergeant George Lowe tries to rally the 18th Tennessee. He plants the Confederate colors, shouts, "Rally here, boys! Come—" At that, he grunts, throws out his arms. Corporal William McKay catches at the staff as Lowe half turns and pitches on his face. A minié ball drills McKay through the thigh, felling him within an arm's length of Lowe. Captain Nat Gooch shouts at Private Logue Nelson, "Pick up those colors, soldier!"

"Pick up the fucking things yourself. I got a wife and kids," Nelson snaps.

Gooch does, is immediately shot down.

Nelson swears, grabs the colors. "Come on, boys. This ain't no place for reasonable men."

Left behind, Corporal McKay lies in the brown grass, feeling the blood running warm down his leg. He manages to get his belt off, cinches it above the wound. He hears a clatter of horses, curls up to avoid being trampled. A four-gun Confederate battery swings into position atop the rise. "Down here," McKay shouts. "Give me a hand, boys."

No one responds, and a moment later, the first of the guns fires directly over him. The muzzle flash sizzles McKay's hair, scorches his skin, leaves him deafened. He shouts, screams, curses, barely able to make out the faint sound of his own voice. No one pays the least mind. Fleeing men rush up the hill, throwing themselves flat each time the gun captains shout: "Ready!" The mob becomes so thick that the gunners of Wright's Tennessee Battery have to cease fire. They start to limber up but Major Rice Graves, chief of division artillery, shouts, "Wright, you've got to hold them back! Double-shot your guns and fire as soon as our boys get clear!"

McKay tries to crawl, but his leg won't hold under him. He tries pulling himself out of the way with his hands, cannot. He screams again, sees a cannoneer glance his way and then back at the approaching enemy. McKay burrows his head against Gooch's corpse, pulls a flap of the captain's tunic over his head. A Yankee battery gets the range, starts firing at Wright's guns. McKay sees a shell come bouncing up the hill, trailing fuse sparks. It bursts a dozen feet over his head, fragments raking his legs, the concussion breaking his left arm and rendering him blessedly unconscious.

Federal infantry rushes the hill, so close behind the fleeing Rebels that Wright gives the order to fire too late, most of the canister flying high. The Yankees shoot down the horses, overwhelm the cannoneers, kill Wright. Only one gun gets away.

Privates Mike McClarey and Pat Reilly run for Wayne's Hill, the brush whipping around their legs, the shouts, cheers, and fire of the Yankees urging them on. Reilly stumbles, rolls over clutching a leg drilled by a minié ball. McClarey sweeps him up in a fireman's carry, manages to reach down for his own musket, and stumbles on toward the hill, the bullets whicking around them.

Brigadier General Gideon Pillow passes Colonel William Preston at the gallop. "We're buggered, Preston! Run for your life!"

Preston has no intention of running. He grabs the banner of the 45th Tennessee, begins laying about him with the flat of his saber. Joined by the regiment's colonel and a corporal's guard of stubborn veterans, they begin forming a line, fall back step by step before the Yankee tide.

The Confederate cavalry finally moves to aid the infantry. Pegram leads his small brigade forward against Grider's brigade on the Yankee left flank. But he mistakes the 20th Tennessee for Yankees and fires on them instead. The 20th has had about all it's going to take for one day, immediately returns fire. But Private Logue Nelson, the most unwilling of color bearers, runs out in the field, waving the regiment's banner and screaming profanities at both sides. Pegram's cavalry joins the retreat.

Wharton has better luck. He deploys Huwald's battery of horse artillery and a double line of dismounted troopers to block Hazen's flanking column. It is enough. In a cold fury, Hazen has to waste most of the remaining light deploying in line of battle.

Negley's advance drives all before it. Many of the men who fled an hour earlier join the advance, scooping up muskets and cartridge boxes, attaching themselves to the nearest company. The line recaptures the lost ridge, pushes on into the field past Beatty's original line and toward Wayne's Hill. But there is no light to go farther, and Negley has no choice but to order the line to halt.

Corporal Johnny Green is nearly to the shaky Confederate line forming on the lower slope of Wayne's Hill when he hears a strangled voice behind him: "Johnny. Give me a hand, son." Green turns, sees Private Mike McClarey struggling along under the weight of Private Pat Reilly. "Take my gun, Johnny," McClarey gasps. Green does, and they struggle the last few rods to the line.

Green helps McClarey ease Reilly down and they collapse beside him. After a minute of panting, McClarey reaches out a hand to nudge Reilly. "So how are you, boyo?" Reilly's head rolls to the side, revealing a bullet hole through the temple. McClarey groans. "Oh, for pity's sake, Pat! I thought it was your *leg* you said you was shot through."

Corporal McKay of the 18th Tennessee regains consciousness in the darkness below the ruin of Wright's battery. A column of Yankee infantry climbs the hill. "Look out," one of the officers calls. "There's a wounded man here."

Most of the Yankees step carefully over McKay, but a few kick him, call him "a damned Rebel."

Finally, much later, two Wisconsin boys looking for a missing friend stumble on him. "Boys, help a fellow Christian, won't you?" McKay begs.

The boys kneel beside him, examine his wounds. "Damn," one of them says. "Looks like you was run over by a damned herd of buffalo."

"How would you know?" the other says. "You never seen a buffalo."

"Well, I can imagine. I heard enough about 'em. You wait with him, Carl. I'll go find a litter."

Company C, 19th Ohio Volunteers, straggles back into its camp in the late evening. Plodding disconsolately to the fire where they'd cooked the hen, Corporal Billy Erb stops dead, then advances foot by careful foot, as if approaching a wary prize. He lifts the lid off the pot. "Well, I'll be a son of bitch," he breathes. "Must've been a thousand men fought through this camp going one way or the other, and not one of 'em stopped to eat our chicken."

The four messmates kneel around the pot, worshipful. Erb stirs the stew of chicken and eggs, lifts out a leg, the meat falling from bone. He takes a morsel in his mouth, lets the meat dissolve on his tongue. "Perfect," he murmurs. "Just goddamn perfect."

Bragg sends Patton Anderson's brigade to cover the withdrawal of Breckinridge's division. Breckinridge rides among the survivors, raging like a wounded lion. When he sees the remnants of Kentucky Brigade, he breaks down in tears. "Oh, my poor orphans! My poor orphans!" he sobs.

They cannot comfort him.

EPILOGUE

*O*N THE EVENING of January 2, Breckinridge reports that the failed assault on the Yankee left has cost his division 1,700 men. Bragg is unmoved. After announcing that the Army of Tennessee will hold position at all hazards, he goes to bed. In the night, he reconsiders. The next morning, he seeks the opinions of Hardee and Polk. The Professor and the Bishop report that nearly every division and brigade commander believes that the army must retreat.

Brigadier General St. John Liddell arrives late in the morning to argue vehemently against any retreat. Bragg responds, "I know that you would fight it out, Liddell, but others will not."

"Give the order, General, and every man will obey you!"

But Bragg shakes his head. "No, it has now become a matter of imperative necessity to withdraw."

All Saturday, January 3, the armies wait in the rain for the other to attack. The Rebel retreat begins at 10:00 that night. Kentucky Brigade, rechristened the Orphan Brigade, leads the march down the Nashville Pike through ankle-deep mud. Bragg and his staff leave Murfreesboro shortly before midnight. Behind the last infantry regiment, Joe Wheeler deploys his cavalry to fight off pursuit.

Rosecrans does not pursue, but waits cautiously in position through January 4 as his Pioneers rebuild the bridges over Stones River. Late that afternoon, Colonel Zahm leads a regiment of cavalry south, sweeps up a few stragglers, tangles briefly with Wheeler, and withdraws to Murfreesboro.

Riding past burial parties dragging Union and Confederate dead into mass graves, Colonel John Beatty comes upon Rousseau, McCook, and Crittenden imbibing from a jug of corn whiskey. When the last swallow has been drained, Crittenden—apparently the host—hurls the jug as high as he can, unmindful of the half dozen enlisted men who must dive out of the way of the falling pottery. Crittenden rides off toward his headquarters singing *Mary Had a Little Lamb.* Rousseau and McCook follow, laughing so hard they can barely keep their saddles. That night, Beatty writes of Crittenden in his journal: *Evidently the lion had left the chieftain's heart, and the lamb had entered and taken possession.*

A party of Nashville citizens arrives to petition Rosecrans for the release of Brigadier General James E. Rains's body. Rosecrans growls, "You may have it, sirs, but you'll make no damned Secesh demonstration over it. Not in the face of my bleeding army. My own officers are here, dead and unburied, and the bodies of my brave soldiers are yet on the field, among the rocks and cedars. You may have the corpse, sirs, but I warn you, there best be no infernal pow-wow over it in Nashville!"

On the road to Tullahoma, Bragg and his staff overtake a straggler marching grim-faced through the mud. Bragg inquires as to his regiment.

"Ain't got none," the man snaps.

"You are a member of the Army of Tennessee, are you not? You must be assigned to a regiment."

The man snorts. "Bragg's army? Hell, he ain't got none. He shot half of it in Kentucky, the other half got killed up at Murfreesboro."

The Army of the Cumberland crosses Stones River to occupy Murfreesboro on January 5, 1863. That afternoon, Father Treacy holds an open-air mass of thanksgiving for the army's victory. Rosecrans stands at the front, head bowed, red face sagging with fatigue. Lieutenant Ambrose Bierce stands off to the side with Hazen, whose name has this day been forwarded to the War Department for promotion to brigadier general. Hazen watches the service without expression, turning Julius Garesché's class ring over and over in his palm. Bierce would ask to hold it for a moment, to wonder at its weight.

Father Treacy turns from the altar, stares out over the congregants, gray eyes thoughtful. "Let us take for our text today, in humble thanksgiving for the Word of God, chapter two, verse eighteen, from the Gospel according to St. Matthew: 'In Ramah was there a voice heard, lamentation, and weeping, and great mourning—Rachel weeping for her children, and would not be comforted because they are not.'"

✮ ✮ ✮

Official casualty figures for the Battle of Stones River (called the Battle of Murfreesboro in the South) placed the losses for the Army of the Cumberland at 1,730 killed, 7,802 wounded, and 3,717 missing or captured; for the Army of Tennessee at 1,294 killed, 7,945 wounded, 1,027 missing or captured. A third to a half of the wounded die. Both sides called it a victory.

Two Federal officers received the Medal of Honor: Captain Milton T. Russel, Company A, 51st Indiana Volunteer Infantry, for leading Harker's attack across Stones River on the evening of December 29; and the Reverend John M. Whitehead, chaplain of the 15th Indiana Infantry, for succoring the wounded and the dying on December 31, 1862, and January 2, 1863.

AUTHOR'S NOTE

*T*HE CHARACTERS IN the list that follows are historical, the biographical facts as accurate and complete as I have been able to make them. I have included state of birth and (if different) the state in which the individual resided at the time the war began. I have also included principal pre-war professions.

For West Point graduates, I have included year of graduation and class standing. The latter is particularly interesting for what it reveals or more often does not reveal about ability to command. Class standing was determined by a combination of academic performance and military deportment. Hence, a poor student like Alexander McDowell McCook might, through careful attention to military bearing, finish near the middle of his class, while a first-rate student like Bushrod Johnson might finish far from the top because of a careless attitude concerning dress and drill. Some superb commanders, including William B. Hazen and the Army of Northern Virginia's James Longstreet finished near or at the bottom of their classes.

Any reader in the literature of the Civil War is constantly bedeviled by the similarity in name of several armies, North and South, and the seeming discrepancy in the ranks of Confederate and Federal generals.

Federal armies were named in most cases after rivers flowing through their operating areas. Confederate armies were named after regions. Hence, Grant's Federal army in December 1862 was the Army of *the* Tennessee, while Bragg's army was the Army *of* Tennessee. There are exceptions, however. In the spring and summer of 1862, the main Confederate army in the West was the Army of *the* Mississippi, which became the Army of Tennessee in November of that year. Simultaneously, the relatively minor Federal Army of *the* Mississippi existed from February 1862 until it was incorporated into the Federal Army of *the* Tennessee that October. Since no amount of explanation can ease the confusion completely, I have occasionally referred to an army by its subsequent and more famous name prior to the actual change in title.

The problem of rank is similarly complicated. In the history of the United States Army prior to the Civil War, only George Washington held the full three-star rank of lieutenant general. Winfield Scott, general-in-chief in 1861, held it by brevet. Congress finally revived the rank of lieutenant general in 1864, awarding it to Ulysses S. Grant when he became general-in-chief.

Throughout the war, Federal major generals (two stars) commanded everything from divisions to corps, regional armies, military departments, and the army itself. Date of appointment determined seniority and was often the source of heated argument and competition.

Brigadier generals wore one star and commanded brigades and occasionally divisions and even corps and armies. (In the summer of 1862, before becoming commander of the Army of the Cumberland as a major general, William S. Rosecrans commanded the five-division Army of the Mississippi as a brigadier general.)

Numerous brevet promotions at all ranks in the Federal army further complicated matters. Brevet promotions were given for outstanding performance in the field (at least in theory), and granted the holder the insignia, privileges, and responsibilities of the higher rank. Eventually, the system became so widely abused that Congress passed a law forbidding those holding a brevet from exercising the authority of the higher rank until confirmed in the full rank by the Senate. In the field, however, many generals continued to function according to their brevet ranks.

By the end of the war, 583 Union officers were confirmed by the Senate in the ranks of brigadier or major general. In addition, a staggering 1,367 officers held brevets to brigadier or major general.

The Confederate system was simpler. Army commanders were usually full generals, entitled to wear four stars within an oak wreath. Among these were Robert E. Lee, Joseph E. Johnston, P. G. T. Beauregard, and Braxton Bragg. Corps commanders were commissioned lieutenant generals; division commanders major generals; and brigade commanders brigadier generals (although often colonels commanded brigades). In all, 425 officers held one of the four ranks of general in the Confederate army. The Confederate army did not indulge in brevets to the rank of general, although a small number of officers held "acting rank," unconfirmed by the Confederate Senate.

OFFICERS ATTACHED TO THE
ARMIES AT STONES RIVER

Brigadier General Daniel W. Adams, C.S.A., commanding First Brigade, Breckinridge's First Division, Hardee's Corps, Army of Tennessee. Age 41. Kentucky/Louisiana. Lawyer, politician.

Brigadier General J. Patton Anderson, C.S.A., commanding Third Brigade, Withers's Second Division, Polk's Corps, Army of Tennessee. Age 40. Tennessee/Florida. Physician, politician. Mexican War service.

Colonel Philemon P. Baldwin, U.S.A. (volunteers), commanding Third Brigade, Johnson's Second Division, McCook's Right Wing, Army of the Cumberland.

Colonel John Beatty, U.S.A. (volunteers), commanding Second Brigade, Rousseau's First Division, Thomas's Center, Army of the Cumberland. Age 34. Ohio. Banker, poet.

Brigadier General Samuel Beatty, U.S.A. (volunteers), commanding First Brigade, Van Cleve's Third Division, Crittenden's Left Wing, Army of the Cumberland. (Commands the division on January 2, 1863.) Age 42. Pennsylvania/Ohio. Farmer, sheriff. Mexican War service.

First Lieutenant Ambrose Bierce, U.S.A. (volunteers), topographical engineer, Hazen's Brigade, Army of the Cumberland. Age 20. Ohio. Writer.

Colonel Luther P. Bradley, U.S.A. (volunteers), commanding 51st Illinois Infantry, Roberts's Third Brigade, Sheridan's Third Division, Crittenden's Left Wing, Army of the Cumberland. (Commands the brigade after mid-morning December 31, 1862.) Age 40. Connecticut/Illinois. Bookkeeper, militia officer.

General Braxton Bragg, C.S.A., commanding the Army of Tennessee. Age 45. West Point 1837, 5/50. North Carolina/Louisiana. Soldier, planter. Mexican War service.

Major General John C. Breckinridge, C.S.A., commanding First Division, Hardee's Corps, Army of Tennessee. Age 41. Kentucky. Former senator and vice president of the United States. Mexican War service.

Lt. Colonel George Brent, C.S.A., acting chief of staff, Army of Tennessee.

Lt. Colonel John A. Buckner, C.S.A., chief of staff, Breckinridge's First Division, Hardee's Corps, Army of Tennessee.

Colonel William P. Carlin, U.S.A. (volunteers), commanding Second Brigade, Davis's First Division, McCook's Right Wing, Army of the Cumberland. Age 32. West Point 1850, 20/44. Illinois. Soldier.

Brigadier General James R. Chalmers, C.S.A., commanding Second Brigade, Withers's Second Division, Polk's Corps, Army of Tennessee. Age 31. Virginia/Mississippi. Lawyer, politician.

Major General Benjamin Franklin Cheatham, C.S.A., commanding First Division, Polk's Corps, Army of Tennessee. Age 42. Tennessee. Farmer, militia general. Mexican War service.

Major General Patrick R. Cleburne, C.S.A., commanding Second Division, Hardee's Corps, Army of Tennessee. Age 34. Ireland/Arkansas. Druggist, lawyer.

Major General Thomas Leonidas Crittenden, U.S.A. (volunteers), commanding Left Wing, Army of the Cumberland. Age 43. Kentucky. Lawyer, diplomat. Mexican War service.

Brigadier General Charles Cruft, U.S.A. (volunteers), commanding First Brigade, Palmer's Second Division, Crittenden's Left Wing, Army of the Cumberland. Age 36. Indiana. Lawyer, railroad executive.

Brigadier General Jefferson C. Davis, U.S.A. (volunteers), commanding First Division, McCook's Right Wing, Army of the Cumberland. Age 34. Indiana. Soldier. Mexican War service.

Brigadier General Daniel Smith Donelson, C.S.A., commanding First Brigade, Cheatham's First Division, Polk's Corps, Army of Tennessee. Age 61. West Point 1825, 5/37. Tennessee. Planter, militia general, speaker of the Tennessee House of Representatives.

Brigadier General Matthew D. Ector, C.S.A., commanding First Brigade, McCown's Division, Hardee's Corps, Army of Tennessee. Age 40. Georgia/Texas. Lawyer, politician.

Colonel James P. Fyffe, U.S.A. (volunteers), commanding Second Brigade, Van Cleve's Third Division, Crittenden's Left Wing, Army of the Cumberland.

Lt. Colonel Julius P. Garesché, U.S.A., chief of staff, Army of the Cumberland. Age 41. West Point 1842, 9/56. Cuba/Missouri. Soldier.

Colonel William H. Gibson, U.S.A. (volunteers), commanding 49th Ohio, Willich's First Brigade, Johnson's Second Division, McCook's Right Wing, Army of the Cumberland. Ohio. Lawyer, state treasurer.

Major C. Goddard, U.S.A. (volunteers), assistant chief of staff, Army of the Cumberland.

Colonel William Grose, U.S.A. (volunteers), commanding Third Brigade, Palmer's Second Division, Crittenden's Left Wing, Army of the Cumberland. Age 50. Ohio/Indiana. Lawyer, politician.

Colonel Nicholas Greusel, U.S.A. (volunteers), commanding 36th Illinois Infantry, Sill's First Brigade, Sheridan's First Division, McCook's Right Wing, Army of the Cumberland. (Commands the brigade after midmorning December 31, 1862.)

Colonel Benjamin Grider, U.S.A. (volunteers), commanding 9th Kentucky Infantry (Union), Samuel Beatty's First Brigade, Van Cleve's Third Division, Crittenden's Left Wing, Army of the Cumberland.

Brigadier General Roger W. Hanson, C.S.A., commanding Fourth Brigade, Breckinridge's First Division, Hardee's Corps, Army of Tennessee. Age 35. Kentucky. Lawyer, politician, militia colonel. Mexican War service.

Lt. General William J. Hardee, C.S.A., commanding Hardee's Corps, Army of Tennessee. Age 47. West Point 1838, 26/45. Georgia. Soldier. Mexican War service.

Colonel Charles G. Harker, U.S.A. (volunteers), commanding Third Brigade, Wood's First Division, Crittenden's Left Wing, Army of the Cumberland. Age 27. West Point 1856, 16/27. New Jersey. Soldier.

Colonel R. W. Harper, C.S.A., commanding 1st Arkansas Mounted Rifles (dismounted), McNair's Third Brigade, McCown's Division, Hardee's Corps, Army of Tennessee. (Commands the brigade after midmorning December 31, 1862.)

Brigadier General Milo S. Hascall, U.S.A. (volunteers), commanding First Brigade, Wood's First Division, Crittenden's Left Wing, Army of the Cumberland. (Commands the division on January 2, 1863.) Age 33. West Point 1852, 14/43. New York/Indiana. Engineer, lawyer, politician.

Colonel William B. Hazen, U.S.A. (volunteers), commanding Second Brigade, Palmer's Second Division, Crittenden's Left Wing, Army of the Cumberland. Age 32. West Point 1855, 28/34. Vermont/Ohio. Soldier.

Colonel Hans C. Heg, U.S.A. (volunteers), commanding 15th Wisconsin, Carlin's Second Brigade, Davis's First Division, McCook's Right Wing, Army of the Cumberland. Age 33. Norway/Wisconsin. Farmer, politician.

Captain Henry Hescock, U.S.A. (volunteers), commanding division artillery and Battery G, 1st Missouri Artillery, Sheridan's First Division, McCook's Right Wing, Army of the Cumberland.

Captain Charles Houghtaling, U.S.A. (volunteers), commanding Battery C, 1st Illinois Artillery, Sheridan's First Division, McCook's Right Wing, Army of the Cumberland. New York.

Brigadier General John K. Jackson, C.S.A., commanding Jackson's Brigade, Breckinridge's First Division, Hardee's Corps, Army of Tennessee. Age 34. Georgia. Lawyer.

Brigadier General Bushrod R. Johnson, C.S.A., commanding Third Brigade, Cleburne's Second Division, Hardee's Corps, Army of Tennessee. Age 45. West Point 1840, 23/42. Ohio/Tennessee. Educator, militia colonel. Mexican War service.

Brigadier General Richard W. Johnson, U.S.A. (volunteers), commanding Second Division, McCook's Right Wing, Army of the Cumberland. Age 35. West Point 1849, 30/43. Kentucky. Soldier.

Colonel John "Judge" Kennett, U.S.A. (volunteers), commanding Cavalry Division, Army of the Cumberland. (Note: Kennett is an elusive figure and I have largely invented his persona.)

Brigadier General Edward N. Kirk, U.S.A. (volunteers), commanding Second Brigade, Johnson's Second Division, McCook's Right Wing, Army of the Cumberland. Age 34. Ohio/Illinois. Lawyer.

Brigadier General St. John R. Liddell, C.S.A., commanding Second Brigade, Cleburne's Second Division, Hardee's Corps, Army of Tennessee. Age 47. (Attended West Point 1833-1834.) Mississippi/Louisiana. Planter.

Colonel J. Q. Loomis, C.S.A., commanding First Brigade, Withers's Second Division, Polk's Corps, Army of Tennessee.

Major General Alexander McDowell McCook, U.S.A. (volunteers), commanding Right Wing, Army of the Cumberland. Age 31. West Point 1852, 30/47. Ohio. Soldier.

Major General John Porter McCown, C.S.A., commanding McCown's Division, Hardee's Corps, Army of Tennessee. Age 47. West Point 1840, 10/42. Tennessee. Soldier. Mexican War service.

Brigadier General Evander McNair, C.S.A., commanding Third Brigade, McCown's Division, Hardee's Corps, Army of Tennessee. Age 42. North Carolina/Arkansas. Merchant. Mexican War service.

Brigadier General George E. Maney, C.S.A., commanding Third Brigade, Cheatham's First Division, Polk's Corps, Army of Tennessee. Age 36. Lawyer. Mexican War service.

Colonel Arthur M. Manigault, C.S.A., commanding Fourth Brigade, Withers's Second Division, Polk's Corps, Army of Tennessee. Age 38. South Carolina. Businessman. Mexican War service.

Lt. Colonel Solon Marks, U.S.A. (volunteers), chief surgeon, Richard Johnson's Second Division, McCook's Right Wing, Army of the Cumberland. Ohio. Physician.

Captain John Mendenhall, commanding Artillery, Crittenden's Left Wing, Army of the Cumberland. West Point 1856.

Colonel John F. Miller, U.S.A. (volunteers), commanding Third Brigade, Negley's Second Division, Thomas's Center, Army of the Cumberland. Age 31. Indiana. Lawyer, politician.

Captain James St. Charles Morton, U.S.A., commanding Pioneer Brigade, Army of the Cumberland. Age 33. West Point 1851, 2/42. Pennsylvania. Soldier.

Brigadier General James S. Negley, U.S.A. (volunteers), commanding Second Division, Thomas's Center, Army of the Cumberland. Age 36. Pennsylvania. Botanist, militia general. Mexican War service.

Captain Elmer Otis, U.S.A., commanding 4th U.S. Cavalry, attached to headquarters, Army of the Cumberland.

Brigadier General John M. Palmer, U.S.A. (volunteers), commanding Second Division, Crittenden's Left Wing, Army of the Cumberland. Age 45. Kentucky/Illinois. Lawyer, politician.

Colonel Joseph B. Palmer, C.S.A., commanding Second Brigade, Breckinridge's First Division, Hardee's Corps, Army of Tennessee (Dec. 31, 1862). Age 37. Tennessee. Lawyer, former mayor of Murfreesboro.

Colonel John G. Parkhurst, U.S.A. (volunteers), commanding 9th Michigan Infantry (assigned as provost guard), Thomas's Center, Army of the Cumberland. New York/Michigan.

Brigadier General John Pegram, C.S.A., commanding Pegram's Brigade, Wheeler's Cavalry Division, Army of Tennessee. Age 29. West Point 1854, 10/46. Virginia. Soldier.

Major W. D. Pickett, aide, Hardee's Staff, Army of Tennessee.

Brigadier General Gideon Pillow, commanding Second Brigade, Breckinridge's First Division, Hardee's Corps, Army of Tennessee (January 2, 1863). Age 56. Tennessee. Lawyer, politician. Mexican War service.

Lt. General Leonidas Polk, C.S.A., commanding Polk's Corps, Army of Tennessee. Age 56. West Point 1827, 8/38. North Carolina/Tennessee/Louisiana. Episcopal Bishop of Louisiana.

Brigadier General Lucius E. Polk, C.S.A., commanding First Brigade, Cleburne's Second Division, Hardee's Corps, Army of Tennessee. Age 29. North Carolina/Arkansas. Planter.

Colonel P. Sidney Post, U.S.A. (volunteers), commanding First Brigade, Davis's First Division, McCook's Right Wing, Army of the Cumberland. Age 29. New York/Illinois. Lawyer, editor.

Brigadier General William Preston, C.S.A., commanding Third Brigade, Breckinridge's First Division, Hardee's Corps, Army of Tennessee. Age 46. Kentucky. Lawyer, politician, diplomat. Mexican War service.

Colonel Samuel W. Price, U.S.A. (volunteers), commanding Third Brigade, Van Cleve's Third Division, Crittenden's Left Wing, Army of the Cumberland. Kentucky.

Brigadier General James E. Rains, C.S.A., commanding Second Brigade, McCown's Division, Hardee's Corps, Army of Tennessee. Age 29. Tennessee. Lawyer, editor, politician.

Colonel George W. Roberts, U.S.A. (volunteers), commanding Third Brigade, Sheridan's Third Division, McCook's Right Wing, Army of the Cumberland (Dec. 31, 1862). Age about 30. Illinois. Lawyer, militia officer.

Captain Felix H. Robertson, C.S.A., commanding Florida (Robertson's) Battery, Loomis's First Brigade, Withers's Second Division, Polk's Corps, Army of Tennessee. Age 23. West Point 1861 (ungraduated). Texas. Cadet.

Major General William S. Rosecrans, U.S.A. (volunteers), commanding the Army of the Cumberland. Age 43. West Point 1842, 5/56. Ohio. Soldier, industrialist.

Major General Lovell H. Rousseau, U.S.A. (volunteers), commanding First Division, Thomas's Center, Army of the Cumberland. Age 44. Kentucky/Indiana. Lawyer, politician. Mexican War service.

Colonel John H. Savage, C.S.A., commanding 16th Tennessee Infantry, Donelson's First Brigade, Cheatham's First Division, Polk's Corps, Army of Tennessee.

Colonel Frederick Schaefer, U.S.A. (volunteers), commanding Second Brigade, Sheridan's Third Division, McCook's Right Wing, Army of the Cumberland (Dec. 31, 1862). Age about 35. Germany/Illinois. Soldier, revolutionary, teacher.

Colonel Benjamin F. Scribner, U.S.A. (volunteers), commanding First Brigade, Rousseau's First Division, Thomas's Center, Army of the Cumberland. Indiana.

Lt. Colonel Oliver L. Shepherd, U.S.A., commanding 4th Brigade, United States Regular Infantry, Rousseau's 1st Division, Thomas's Center, Army of the Cumberland. Age 47. West Point 1840, 33/42. Soldier. Mexican War service.

Brigadier General Philip H. Sheridan, U.S.A. (volunteers), commanding Third Division, McCook's Right Wing, Army of the Cumberland. Age 31. West Point 1853, 34/52. New York?/Ohio. Soldier.

Brigadier General Joshua W. Sill, U.S.A. (volunteers), commanding First Brigade, Sheridan's Third Division, McCook's Right Wing, Army of the Cumberland (Dec. 31, 1862). Age 31. West Point 1853, 3/52. Ohio/New York. Soldier, professor.

Major Adam J. Slemmer, U.S.A., commanding 1st Battalion and Company B 2nd Battalion, 16th U.S. Infantry, Shepherd's Fourth Brigade, Rousseau's First Division, Thomas's Center. Age 34. West Point 1850, 12/44. Pennsylvania. Soldier.

Captain Drury C. Spurlock, C.S.A., commanding Company C, 16th Tennessee, Donelson's First Brigade, Cheatham's First Division, Polk's Corps, Army of Tennessee. Age 30. Merchant.

Brigadier General David S. Stanley, U.S.A. (volunteers), commanding Cavalry, Army of the Cumberland. Age 34. West Point 1852, 9/43. Ohio. Soldier.

Colonel Timothy R. Stanley, U.S.A. (volunteers), commanding Second Brigade, Negley's Second Division, Thomas's Center, Army of the Cumberland. Connecticut/Ohio. Lawyer, politician.

Colonel John C. Starkweather, U.S.A. (volunteers), commanding Third Brigade, Rousseau's First Division, Thomas's Center, Army of the Cumberland. Age 32. New York/Wisconsin. Lawyer.

Brigadier General Alexander P. Stewart, C.S.A., commanding Second Brigade, Cheatham's First Division, Polk's Corps, Army of Tennessee. Age 41. West Point 1842, 12/56. Tennessee. Educator.

Captain James H. Stokes, U.S.A. (volunteers), commanding Chicago Board of Trade Battery, Morton's Pioneer Brigade, Army of the Cumberland. Age 48. West Point 1835, 17/56. Maryland/Illinois. Industrialist.

Major General George H. Thomas, U.S.A. (volunteers), commanding the Center, Army of the Cumberland. Age 46. West Point 1840, 12/42. Virginia. Soldier.

Captain Gates Thruston, U.S.A. (volunteers), chief ordnance officer (commanding the ammunition train), McCook's Right Wing, Army of the Cumberland. Ohio.

Father Patrick Treacy, confessor and confidant of General Rosecrans. Ireland/Ohio. Age, about 45.

Brigadier General Horatio P. Van Cleve, U.S.A. (volunteers), commanding Third Division, Crittenden's Left Wing, Army of the Cumberland (Dec. 31, 1862). Age 53. West Point 1831, 24/33. New Jersey/Michigan/ Minnesota. Farmer, engineer.

Colonel Alfred J. Vaughan, C.S.A., commanding Fourth Brigade, Cheatham's First Division, Polk's Corps, Army of Tennessee. Age 32. Virginia/ Mississippi. Engineer.

Colonel George D. Wagner, U.S.A. (volunteers), commanding Second Brigade, Wood's First Division, Crittenden's Left Wing, Army of the Cumberland. Age 33. Ohio/Indiana. Politician.

Brigadier General John A. Wharton, C.S.A., commanding Wharton's Brigade, Wheeler's cavalry division, Army of Tennessee. Age 34. Tennessee/ Texas. Lawyer, Texas Ranger.

Brigadier General Joseph Wheeler, C.S.A., commanding Cavalry and Wheeler's Brigade, Army of Tennessee. Age 26. West Point 1859, 19/22. Georgia/New York. Soldier.

Brigadier General August Willich, U.S.A. (volunteers), commanding First Brigade, Johnson's Second Division, McCook's Right Wing, Army of the Cumberland. Age 52. Germany/Ohio. Soldier, revolutionary, carpenter, newspaper owner.

Major General Jones M. Withers, commanding Second Division, Polk's Corps, Army of Tennessee. Age 48. West Point 1835, 44/56. Alabama. Lawyer, merchant, politician, militia officer. Mexican War service.

Brigadier General S.A.M. Wood, C.S.A., commanding Fourth Brigade, Cleburne's Second Division, Hardee's Corps, Army of Tennessee. Age 39. Alabama. Lawyer, politician, editor.

Brigadier General Thomas J. Wood, U.S.A. (volunteers), commanding First Division, Crittenden's Left Wing, Army of the Cumberland (Dec. 31, 1862). Age 39. West Point 1845, 5/41. Kentucky. Soldier. Mexican War service.

Colonel William E. Woodruff, U.S.A. (volunteers), commanding Third Brigade, Davis's First Division, McCook's Right Wing, Army of the Cumberland.

Colonel Lewis Zahm, U.S.A. (volunteers), commanding Second Brigade, Stanley/Kennett's Cavalry Division, Army of the Cumberland. Age about 35. Germany/Ohio.

NOT ASSIGNED TO THE
ARMIES AT STONES RIVER

General Pierre G. T. Beauregard, C.S.A., former commander Army of Tennessee. Age 44. West Point 1838, 2/45.

Major General Don Carlos Buell, U.S.A. (volunteers), former commander Army of the Ohio (Cumberland). Age 44. West Point 1841, 32/52.

Major General Ambrose E. Burnside, U.S.A. (volunteers), commanding the Army of the Potomac. Age 38. West Point 1847, 18/38.

Major General George B. Crittenden, C.S.A., commander of Confederate forces at the Battle of Mill Springs, Kentucky, on January 19, 1862. Age 50. West Point 1832, 26/45.

Brigadier General Thomas Turpin Crittenden, U.S.A. (volunteers), commander of Union forces at Confederate capture of Murfreesboro on July 13, 1862. Age 37.

Brigadier General Nathan Bedford Forrest, C.S.A., commanding Forrest's Cavalry Brigade (detached), Wheeler's Cavalry Division, Army of Tennessee. Age 41.

Major General John C. Frémont, U.S.A. (volunteers), former commander of the Western Department.

Major General Ulysses S. Grant, U.S.A. (volunteers), commanding Federal Army of the Tennessee. Age 40. West Point 1843, 21/39.

Major General Henry W. Halleck, general-in-chief, U.S.A. Age 47. West Point 1839, 3/31.

General Albert Sidney Johnston, C.S.A., late commander of Confederate forces in the West. Age 59. West Point 1826, 8/41. Killed at Shiloh, April 6, 1862.

General Joseph E. Johnston, C.S.A., commanding Department of the West. Age 55. West Point 1829, 13/46. Though technically Bragg's superior, President Davis and Bragg usually bypass Johnston.

Major General George B. McClellan, U.S.A., former general-in-chief and former commander of the Army of the Potomac. Age 36. West Point 1846, 2/59.

Colonel John H. Morgan, C.S.A., commanding 2nd Kentucky Cavalry (detached), Wheeler's Cavalry Division, Army of Tennessee. Age 37.

Major General William "Bull" Nelson, U.S.A. (volunteers), late division commander in Buell's Army of the Ohio (Cumberland). Killed in an argument, September 29, 1862. Age 36.

Lt. General John C. Pemberton, C.S.A., commanding Confederate forces at Vicksburg. Age 48. West Point 1837, 27/50.

Brevet Lt. General Winfield Scott, former general-in-chief, U.S.A. Age 76.

Edwin M. Stanton, secretary of war. Age 48.

Major General Zachary Taylor, commander of forces in Northern Mexico during the Mexican War, 12th president of the United States. Died 1850.

Major General Earl Van Dorn, C.S.A., commanding Confederate cavalry in Mississippi. Age 42. West Point 1842, 52/56.

Major General John E. Wool, U.S.A., commanding Middle Department with headquarters at Fort Monroe, Virginia. Deputy to General Taylor and Bragg's commander during invasion of northern Mexico in 1846–1847.